FORGED IN BLOOD

The Golden One Trilogy: Book Three

NOELLE EDWARDS

For my mama in heaven –

Like Aurelia, the heart and soul of our family.

Forged

in

Blood

Prologue

1973 Post Creation

"Tell me the story again, daughter."

The twelve-year-old girl, onyx-haired and dark-eyed, took a long, deep breath. "Several centuries ago, a boy named Aratus Pharos left an orphanage when he came of age. He survived for a few years by working as a gravedigger in exchange for food and clothing. One day, he was attacked by thieves who wanted his clothing. They stripped him, blindfolded him, and tied him up. Then they took him all the way to the east coast and left him there because they thought it was funny. He managed to free his legs because the rope on his ankles wasn't tight enough, but he still couldn't see or use his arms."

"What happened next?"

"He started walking. He knew the cliffs were nearby because he could hear the ocean roaring, but he kept walking, anyway. He didn't fall into the ocean, though. He started to hear his footsteps echoing, so he assumed he walked into a cave. Then he heard something rumbling, and he thought the cave was going to collapse. He fell when he tried to turn around and run, and then he cut his hands on a sharp rock. He used the rock to cut the rope on his wrists, then freed his arms and removed the blindfold. He was in a cave, like he thought, but he wasn't alone."

"Who was with him?"

She shifted on the horse's saddle, giddy. "Aratus wanted to see where the cave led to once he realized it wasn't collapsing. He couldn't see anything, so he stepped on something crunchy and gooey by accident. He heard the rumbling again, but it sounded more like growling now, and then he saw a giant, glowing golden eye in the shadows. He didn't know what the beast was, but he realized he'd stepped on its egg, and it was angry at him. Instead of running away like prey, he fell to his knees and started singing an ancient lullaby he learned at the orphanage. He waited for the beast to devour him, but it didn't. He saw the beast's eyes get lower to the ground like it was laying down, so he laid down, too. When he woke up the next morning, the sun showed him what the beast was."

Though she couldn't see him, Raebo raised an eyebrow at his daughter. "And?"

"It was a dragon." She giggled. "A violet vipertail. Aratus saw lots of eggs around her, but they were all petrified, so he hadn't actually killed one of her babies. He tried to leave while she was sleeping, but the thieves came back to see what became of him. They tried to beat him and leave him for dead, but the dragon poked her head out of the cave and roared at them. Her roar produced a shockwave that sent them all flying through the air, and they died when they hit the ground. Aratus realized the dragon had bonded with him, so he went back to the cave once every week to check on her."

"How did she survive in the cave all those years since the persecution?"

"A mage cast a spell on the dragon during the persecution. The spell froze her body in hibernation. She processed the last meal she ate slowly, over many years, and trained her body to survive on little sustenance. She woke up when Aratus found her because it was destined to happen—her soul felt him coming and told her body to wake. She ate the corpses of the thieves, and she was able to survive on them for many years, too."

"And what became of Aratus?"

"He taught himself to read and spent most of his life learning about the dragon. He named her *Rieza* after the ancient word for *survivor*, and their bond grew stronger. He introduced his only son to Rieza before he died, and made the boy promise to protect her—and to keep her a secret. When Aratus died, Rieza bonded with his son, and then his grandson, and then his great-grandson, and so on."

Raebo didn't reply as he watched the dark path ahead. He could already hear the roaring of the ocean—slightly muffled by the rocky cliffs towering over it—and smell the salty air as it lifted his daughter's hair from her shoulders. She sat in front of her father on his horse's saddle, her small hands wrapped around the horn as he clutched the reins, and was starting to lean forward in anticipation as they inched closer to their destination.

"There's one part of the story you haven't yet told." Raebo set a gentle hand on her arm. "What is it?"

She hesitated for a moment. "Aratus wanted Rieza to leave the cave with him. People at the orphanage told him that his parents were nobles who lost everything to the king's greed, and he thought he could rebuild his family name if he had a dragon by his side. But Rieza wouldn't do it. Aratus thought she was scared of what might happen to her after what happened to the other dragons during the persecution. Aratus knew she would reveal herself on her terms, eventually, but keeping the secret of his incredible power drained him. He died young because of it."

"That's right. He wanted the Pharos name to become legendary once more, but he failed. That's why today, hundreds of years later, our family continues to live in squalor. Aratus couldn't lift us from the ashes, but he succeeded in giving us a power nobody else in the realm can dream of—even if we can't use it."

When they reached their destination, Raebo climbed down from the horse and tied the reins to a nearby tree with no leaves. After lifting his daughter from the saddle, he set a hand on her shoulder and said, "You know what to do. Exactly as we practiced."

Nodding, she walked over to the horse's rear, where the steed had been pulling a small wooden cart. She removed a tattered quilt from the cart to reveal the corpse of a plump fox, which her father had found and killed in the Violet Forest. She took the fox by the rope tying its paws together, while Raebo created a torch out of a length of wood, flint and steel, and a piece of cloth soaked in whale fat.

When the torch was lit, father and daughter joined hands and slowly trekked over to the mouth of a dark, damp cave. As Raebo began to hum the same ancient melody that their ancestor, Aratus Pharos II, had sung in this very same spot long ago, his daughter mimicked him, never taking her eyes from the cave.

At the cave's entrance, Raebo tossed the torch inside, casting an orange glow over the stone walls. He smiled down at his daughter, encouraging her, as she took a deep breath and threw the fox with all her might. The fox didn't make it as far as the torch, but that didn't matter—the torch was only to help the little girl see the wonder of the Pharos family more clearly.

But that's not all the torch revealed. For yards and yards, the bones of those who'd ventured into the cave, both human and animal, stretched on. Dozens of poor souls had sought shelter in the cave over the decades, unaware of what lurked within, and only one of them—Aratus—lived to tell the tale.

After a moment or two, a deep rumbling sound echoed throughout the cave. Raebo glanced down at his daughter in search of any signs of fear, but he found none. Just as he turned his gaze back to the depths of the cave, the structure began to shake, and something appeared on the ground just inches from the torch: a dark purple, reptilian foot with silver claws.

"Keep your composure," Raebo advised. "She'll know if you're afraid of her. You don't want to hurt her feelings, do you?"

Before she could answer, Rieza's foot snapped forward, extinguishing the fire as she swiped the fox in her direction. She hadn't bothered chewing it, but she belched after it slid down her gullet, and her head inched forward as she sniffed the air—either in search of more food, or to make sense of her young visitor.

Raebo took a few steps closer to Rieza, hand extended, until her snout came in contact with his palm. He closed his eyes, smiling, as she chuffed and released a hot breath of air against his face. He looked over his shoulder at his daughter and beckoned her by holding out his free hand. She accepted it without hesitation, and she didn't so much as flinch when he pressed her hand to the dragon's snout.

"Rieza," he murmured, "this is my daughter, Diantha. She knows all about you." Even in the darkness, he saw Rieza's glowing golden eyes blink slowly, as if she was saying hello. "She'll be responsible for you, one day, and she'll care for you as she'd care for her own children. Won't you?"

Diantha nodded. "I will."

"Death is unpredictable. I may leave you tomorrow, or a year from now, or ten years from now. Whenever my time comes, you must be prepared to look after her." Raebo removed his hand, leaving Diantha's still pressed against Rieza's snout, and took a knee before her. "Remember the story. Don't ask her to leave the safety of this cave under the guise of vengeance. You wouldn't be the first of our line to think that way, but it's foolish, not to mention, dangerous. The realm destroys what it fears and what it can't control. If the world were to see you and Rieza as a threat rather than as a miracle, they'd kill you both. She didn't bond with our family only to be slaughtered because someone thinks they can become a hero. She'll leave when she's ready—even if you're not alive to see it."

Diantha nodded as Rieza's breath lifted her hair from her shoulders. "I understand, Father."

"Good." Smiling, he touched his palm to her cheek, prompting her to tilt her face against his touch. "You'll have to learn more about her—and other dragons, of course—if you wish to be worthy of her. I'll teach you everything I know, but eventually, you alone will be responsible for this pursuit of knowledge."

"Yes, Father."

He sighed as he rose to his feet and touched Rieza's snout again. "It's time for us to go home, old girl. Your future mistress has lessons to attend to."

As they lingered in the cave for a moment longer, Rieza eyed Diantha with a distant, omniscient shimmer in her golden eyes. Of the three souls in the cave that night, only Rieza knew that the twelve-year-old girl *would* become the hero her father warned her about—the future Queen of Dofell.

In that moment, the ancient creature knew that her time in the cave was almost up.

BOOK ONE: CURSES

1992 Post Creation

H e can't have that, Lena."

"Why?"

"Because he could choke on it."

"Why?"

"Because babes put things in their mouths when they aren't supposed to."

"But *why?*"

Halle sighed exasperatedly. "Because—"

Jack's chest rumbled with laughter. "All right, all right. Listen to your sister, Halyna, and don't be a nuisance with your questions."

Three-year-old Halyna huffed at him. Obeying her elder sister, she refrained from handing a gold-plated knucklebone to her one-year-old brother, Harlen. She moved like she wanted to hand it to Harlen's twin sister, Holly, but thought better of it when she saw the scolding look in Halle's eyes.

Jack grinned from ear to ear when Halle met his gaze and offered him a small, shy smile. The look of her eyes—a swirling combination of blue, green, and gray, like the sea during a storm—was identical to his, but the look *in* her eyes—authoritative, confident, and demanding respect—was a perfect match for her mother's.

Jack turned to his wife and chuckled when he saw her suppressing a smile. He knew they were thinking the same thing: Halle, Crown Princess of Akkinor, was already well on her way to becoming an exceptional queen.

She's learning from the best, after all, Jack thought to himself. He must've been giving Aurelia some sort of look while he thought it, because her pale cheeks quickly turned pink.

"Give it here, darling." Aurelia held out her hand, prompting Halyna to set the knucklebone on her mother's palm. Aurelia returned the piece to a linen bag with the others, then tossed a glance over her shoulder at the piano in the corner of the parlor. "That sounds lovely, Sisi. You're getting better every day."

Hyacinth turned and opened her mouth to respond, but Henry— perched on the bench alongside her—beat her to it: "I'm helping, Mama!"

"No, you're not." Hyacinth, eight years old like Halle, gave her brother a slight push. "Go play over there."

Jack snorted into a laugh as the five-year-old prince dragged his feet over to the floor, where Jack was sitting with the other four Brentwood children. Across from where they sat on the carpet, Aurelia was curled up on the couch watching Hyacinth play the pianoforte. Jack knew exactly what his wife was thinking: Hyacinth may not have inherited much from her biological father—Aurelia's brother, the late Prince Archie—but she'd certainly inherited his musical talent.

Ser Rayan Haze, Hand of the Queen, hummed along to the tune from his seat beside Aurelia. His position—head tilted back against the couch cushions, shoeless feet propped up on the tea table, and hands splayed over his stomach—made Jack envious while he strained his back on the floor. As if he could sense Jack watching him, Rayan cracked an eye open and stifled laughter when he met Jack's eyes.

"Would you like to trade seats?" Rayan teased.

Jack grunted and lay flat on his back, trying to find comfort on the hard floor. "I fear we've allowed you to grow too comfortable here, my Lord Hand."

Rayan guffawed, making both Jack and Aurelia grin, as Henry dashed over to Rayan. He set his small hands on Rayan's thigh, putting his entire body weight on his hands, as Rayan tousled the young prince's auburn hair—the same color as his.

"Uncle Rayan," Henry started, "would you like to play with me?"

"I would love to," the Hand replied, "but I feel I must remind you— again—that I'm not your uncle."

Jack's gaze snapped over to Aurelia's. Her smile faded a bit, the light in her eyes dimming, as she sighed and turned back to Hyacinth. Over three years had passed since Aurelia met Rayan Haze, and she still hadn't told him that they were born to the same father. It'd been a coincidence—or fate, Jack couldn't decide—when their paths crossed, but still, she didn't feel it was right to place such a burden on his shoulders. After all, learning the truth meant acknowledging that Aurelia wasn't the trueborn daughter of the last king, and such a secret was a damning one for Rayan to keep.

Halle sighed. "He thinks we have to call you *uncle* because of Uncle Arian."

"How so?" Rayan slid from the couch to sit on the floor with Henry, who immediately handed him a wooden ship to play with.

"Because Arian is a Hand of the Queen, too, and we call him *uncle*."

"That's not how it works, Henry," Hyacinth said from the piano, not bothering to look over her shoulder.

The prince huffed and folded his arms over his chest. Before he could argue with his sisters, little Holly began to shriek, her twin brother following her lead. Then Halyna covered her ears and whined, inching away from the twins while Jack swept them into his arms. At the same time, Halle and Henry began bickering over something, shouting so loudly that Hyacinth stopped playing so she could holler at them for interrupting her.

Jack met Aurelia's eyes as the pair struggled to contain their amusement. As frustrating—and, oftentimes, *annoying*—as their children were, it was entertaining to watch such tiny people express such fierce emotions.

The children quieted when Aurelia scolded them. As soon as they calmed down, she looked at Jack again, smirking, and said, "I don't recall there being so many of them. When did *that* happen?"

He laughed while Rayan chimed in, "Well, Omarans *are* known for being terrible breeders."

"Your sarcasm is less than appreciated," Jack teased, as they all knew that natives of Omara—Jack's home kingdom—tended to produce the largest broods in Akkinor.

As the adults laughed, a knock came at the door, and a servant entered shortly after. The messenger boy bowed as Aurelia rose to meet him by the door. She accepted a scroll and thanked him, then held the parchment between her fingers while she poured herself a glass of wine from a nearby table.

Jack turned his attention to the twins as they climbed on his legs until he heard something shatter on the floor. Everyone silenced, alarmed, and looked up at Aurelia while she stood beside the piano. Her goblet had fallen from her grasp, staining the beige carpet with burgundy liquid, and the unraveled scroll shook like a leaf in her trembling hands.

"Aurelia? What's happened?" Jack asked, climbing to his feet. "Is everything all right?"

Hyacinth gasped from her seat on the piano bench. "Oh, no."

Aurelia met Hyacinth's gaze and held it for a moment, then turned to Jack, an answer to his inquiry brewing on her lips. She didn't get the chance to speak, though: at that exact moment, her dragon, Halvor, shrieked from somewhere on the grounds. She bolted out of the parlor faster than a lightning strike, letting the scroll flutter to the ground as she did so.

"Follow her." Jack had given the command to Rayan before he knew what he was doing. As the Lord Hand scurried out of the parlor, Jack's eyes landed on Halle, who was holding a whimpering Halyna on her lap. "Irina and Celesse are in their quarters. Bring them here to mind your siblings. Quickly, now."

Halle set Halyna down, scampered to her feet, and dashed into the hallway to fetch the governesses. Jack was on his way out of the parlor, too—trusting Hyacinth to watch her younger siblings—when he spotted the fallen scroll and plucked it from the ground.

For the Queen of Akkinor -
You are not alone. Either of you.

Jack sucked in a sharp breath through his teeth, unintentionally meeting Hyacinth's eyes, exactly as Aurelia had just moments before. Hyacinth may not have known that her power to see glimpses of the past, present, and future meant that she was a mage, but she *did* understand that she had a special gift.

Jack's voice was nothing short of a whisper: "Sisi? What do you know?"

His daughter gulped, her hands trembling on the keys of the pianoforte. "There's more than one now."

His eyes widened, but before he could reply, he heard Halvor shriek again, louder and fiercer than before. Crumpling the message in his fist, he left the children in the parlor—passing Halle and the governesses as he ran through the halls—and followed the sound of Halvor's roars. He could hear his own heartbeat rattling his eardrums as he bolted toward the rear of the palace, where the doors to the gardens had been left wide open.

Aurelia was standing in the center of the gardens, the wind lifting her wild golden curls from her back, with her neck craned backward as she stared at the sky. Rayan stood a few feet behind her, mimicking her, with his hand resting on the hilt of his sword at his side.

Jack rushed to Aurelia's side, barely able to skid to a stop when his own momentum betrayed him, and stared at her face—whiter than a sheet, like she'd just seen the dead rise from the catacombs—before following her gaze.

Halvor was perched atop the stone walls surrounding the palace grounds, his long neck extended as high as it could go, roaring at something lost amongst the clouds. Jack spotted a tiny, faint golden glow on the very top of Halvor's head—Aurelia's sprite, Edom. He was opening his mouth to call for Edom, hoping the creature could explain the situation, but he didn't get the chance.

A shadow about the size of a small writing desk became visible from beyond the clouds. As the shadow descended, Jack saw a silhouette of wings, four limbs, and a reptile-like head attached to a long neck. Then the clouds parted, and Jack's heart plummeted to his knees when an emerald dragon swerved through the air while releasing a weak, somewhat juvenile screech.

The dragon wasn't large enough to bear a rider, but it was certainly large enough to pose a threat. And based on the contents of the message, it had a master or a mistress. What mattered more, though, was that another dragon of old existed in the realm, and Halvor was no longer the only one of his kind.

There's more than one now.

Jack snapped his gaze over to his wife again. Her jaw was clenched and her lips were pressed in a thin, taut line. When she turned her head ever-so-slightly to follow the intruder's path, the moonlight illuminated the thick, silver scar along her cheekbone, making her look as menacing as the dragon whose soul she shared.

"Aurelia—" he started, unsure of what he was going to say.

Halvor shook the entire garden, interrupting Jack, when he released a bellowing shriek as the intruder flew just a bit too close for comfort. He must've succeeded in spooking the green dragon, because his tiny counterpart released one last screech before disappearing beyond the clouds again. Halvor growled and chuffed at the sky for a few moments longer, then roared one last time—telling the little one to stay far, far away.

Rayan appeared at Jack's side, gray and clammy. "W-Was that an innocent exploration of the Folly, or...was it a warning?"

Aurelia hadn't looked away from the sky since Jack found her outside. "I believe we'll be finding out soon enough. We need to send word to—"

Halvor interrupted her with another shriek, but this one was different. Before, he'd been warning an unexpected visitor to keep its distance, but he hadn't been violent. Now, the sound he emitted was the same one he'd made in the past while threatening—or devouring—enemy soldiers during wartime.

A battle cry.

Aurelia gasped when Halvor lifted off from the wall and soared into the clouds, his roars so terrifying that even she winced at the sound. Jack reached for her hand instinctively, squeezing, and started to speak—but he didn't get the chance to utter a single syllable before another shadow, much larger than the first, joined Halvor's behind the clouds.

The wind picked up, causing the trees in the gardens to sway and the birds to fly away in terror. Aurelia tightened her grip on Jack's hand, while setting her free hand on Rayan's forearm. The three of them stared up at the sky, having lost the shadows to the darkness, while the only sounds to be heard—for just a moment—were their pounding heartbeats.

A strangled scream escaped Aurelia's throat when Halvor plummeted through the clouds, just barely catching himself before he collided with the wall. He managed to land atop the wall, Edom now clinging to a spike on his back. Halvor's claws scraped the stone while he struggled to gain traction, then he craned his neck to release an enormous ball of fire from his throat. The flames didn't reach their destination, though—an unseen force, like the strongest gust of wind man had ever known, met the flames halfway, threatening to force the fire back against Halvor's face.

Just as the flames and the strange force subsided, another shriek echoed throughout the grounds. It was just as loud and terrifying as Halvor's, but it hadn't come from Aurelia's dragon. Jack caught a faint glimpse of the source—a purplish, scaly wing—before it disappeared even higher into the dark sky, camouflaging itself above the clouds.

Halvor shifted like he was prepared to follow it. Aurelia, trembling beside Jack, merely shook her head. Halvor hadn't even been looking at her, but the connection between their souls allowed him to receive and obey her command to stay put. He bellowed into the sky again, rattling the gardens, and growled as he turned to face the west, where the third dragon had disappeared into the night.

"Aur-Aurelia..." Jack sounded more like his five-year-old son than Henry did, unable to form the words. "That's—"

"Impossible." He barely heard her when she spoke, as the winds were still dying down and Halvor was still growling into the sky. "I..."

Just then, a flash of golden light appeared on her shoulder. Jack tried to listen to what Edom was whispering in her ear, but he couldn't make it out. He and Rayan merely watched as her face blanched and her lips parted. She muttered something to the sprite, making it nod, before the creature zipped off toward Halvor again.

Aurelia cleared her throat when she saw Jack and Rayan eyeing her. "Edom says the little one appears to be young—a few years old, at most—but the bigger one..." Her eyes fluttered shut. "The bigger one is ancient."

"Like Halvor," Rayan murmured.

For the first time in years, Aurelia looked at Jack with pure fear glistening in her pale blue eyes. He tried to reach for her, to bring her into his arms, but she took a step backward, clearly too shaken.

"Summon the Assembly," she croaked, flicking her gaze back to Halvor. "It would appear that we've made an enemy or two."

I

The Queen of Akkinor held her breath, her heart pounding against her ribcage, and stared at the darkness above. Careful not to make a sound as impatient footsteps shook the floorboards, Aurelia turned her head to the side, her cheek now pressed against the floor. Her eyes landed on her husband beside her, and she had to try her hardest to keep from laughing at the mischief in his eyes.

He reached for her hand and squeezed before turning his head to the empty space to his right. Aurelia's heart leapt to her throat when a pair of loafers appeared just a foot from his head. He turned back to her, eyes widening, as a grin spread over his lips. She covered her mouth with her free hand, fighting another urge to laugh, while he brought a finger to his lips and winked.

The woman wearing the loafers muttered something under her breath, released a frustrated exhale, and walked away. Only after the sound of receding footsteps faded, accompanied by the clicking of a closing door, did the couple finally release the chuckles in their throats.

"That was close." Jack Ashford, King Consort of Akkinor, grinned even wider as he turned to face his wife. "I thought we were done for."

Aurelia laughed. "Where do you suppose she went?"

"I have no idea, but we'd better lock the door before she comes back."

"Really?" She smiled as he brought their conjoined hands to his mouth so he could kiss her knuckles. "You don't think she spoiled the mood?"

"I'm married to the most beautiful woman in the realm. Nothing could spoil the mood for me."

Careful not to bump her head on the frame of their bed above, Aurelia turned on her side, tossed a leg over his thighs, and set her fingers against his cheek. He leaned up to kiss her while planting his hands on her hip, but she pulled away as much as she could—their bed was quite tall, but not tall enough for such shenanigans. When he grunted and narrowed his eyes at her, she grinned from ear to ear, then gave in and pressed her lips to his.

"Mmm." He rubbed his lips together when they parted as he brushed a stray curl from her eyes. "You put me in a trance, Aurelia Brentwood."

She kissed him again. "I'm sorry to disappoint, but I'll have to break the spell today. Anna's still looking for me, and—"

"She can wait. Everything can wait."

"No, it can't." Aurelia grinned and pecked him one last time. "Come on. We have things to do today."

Jack groaned as she crawled out from under their bed. She gently bumped her head on the frame in the process, making him chuckle. As he emerged across from her, his midnight black hair tousled, his amused eyes landed on their bed. It was made, but the comforter was rumpled and wrinkled, and a few of the throw pillows had lost their shape. Aurelia was sure that Anna—her lady-in-waiting—would be gossiping to the rest of the palace staff about what she'd almost walked into.

Aurelia snorted when she saw her reflection in the floor-length mirror. The front of her gown was completely unbuttoned, and the skirt was wrinkled from crawling along the floor. Jack didn't look much better: his tunic was bunched up in his grasp, the front of his trousers were unlaced, and he was only wearing one boot.

"You'd think we'd be better at hiding this after eight years," Aurelia remarked.

"We can't help it when duty calls, my love."

She rolled her eyes and ignored the footsteps in the hallway outside. "You need to learn to keep your hands off of me, Jack Ashford."

"*You* were the one who jumped *me*, remember?"

He had her there.

"It wasn't my fault," she argued, smoothing out her skirt while he redressed. "You were giving me *the look*, Jack, and you know what that look—"

A knock came at the door, making both of them freeze. "I can hear you in there, and honestly, I haven't the patience for your shenanigans today." Anna's voice rang out, making Aurelia cover her mouth with her hand as she suppressed a giggle. "A raven just arrived. I'll slide it under the door so you can keep doing...whatever it is you're doing."

A folded piece of parchment appeared on the floor, closely followed by the sound of Anna's shoes clicking against the wood.

Anna had been a quiet, timid little thing when she was first hired at the palace, but nowadays, she had no trouble talking to Aurelia like the two were old friends—exactly how Aurelia liked it.

Jack collected the parchment while Aurelia sat at her vanity to fix her smudged lipstick and messy hair. She took the pins out of her hair, letting her golden curls spring free to cover her bruised neck, all while scolding Jack for being so careless about where he put his mouth.

When he refused to answer, she looked at his reflection in the mirror. "Are you listening to me?" she demanded. No reply. "If the message is so interesting, do you care to tell me what it says?"

"She's dead."

Aurelia turned and draped her arm over the backrest of her chair. "Who?"

"Lady Swann. Arian wrote to let us know."

Her heart sank. She hadn't seen Odeya Swann, Lady of Runeia in the kingdom of Krotis, since the two forged their alliance over eight years ago. Lady Swann had been one of four Carthinian rulers who'd helped Aurelia reclaim her throne from her brother and usurper, Archie; and while they'd never been particularly close, Aurelia had a soft spot for the old woman. Lady Swann had been difficult at times, but she was a spitfire, and as clever and loyal as they came.

Jack sighed as he set the letter on the writing desk. "What do you suppose happened?"

"She was an old woman, Jack. I assume she died of natural causes."

"Her heir will be wanting to meet with you soon enough," her husband continued. She nodded. "It's not her son, though, is it?"

"No. Her grandson. He's about twenty now, if memory serves. His father died two years ago. I imagine he'll be inviting us to his coronation, so we can form our opinions of him then."

Jack donned that innocent, yet wicked grin she loved so much. "Will we gossip like schoolgirls the moment he turns his back on us?"

"Of course we will."

He boomed with laughter, making her mirror his grin. "Wonderful. Say—where on earth is Edom? Talking about Carthe just made me realize that I haven't seen that pesky creature in days."

Aurelia's grin faded as quickly as it'd formed. "I've sent it out on a mission to gather intel on...well, you know."

Jack's face went slack when he saw the worry undoubtedly gleaming in her light eyes. That look had accompanied her gaze more often than not, as of late.

It'd been just over a season since she received a mysterious letter from an unknown sender. At the very least, she hadn't been forced to wonder about the cryptic message. Almost immediately after it arrived, two unexpected visitors took a trip to the Palace of Akkinor: a small emerald dragon, approximately two or three years old; and a larger violet one, estimated to be almost as old as Aurelia's own dragon, Halvor.

Until that night, every soul in the realm believed Halvor was the only dragon of his kind left in the world. Other dragons from the old days had been slaughtered during the magical persecution over a thousand years ago, and those that'd survived—hatchlings—were fed manmade concoctions meant to stunt their growth and turn them into slaves. They were smaller, less formidable versions of their ancestors: no larger than a cattle dog, unable to fly, and only capable of emitting tiny flames. They'd become as domesticated as the average housecat, and while they still had lifespans of hundreds and hundreds of years, a hatchling hadn't been born in centuries.

Jack cleared his throat. "Edom won't have much luck here in Akkinor, but it's worth trying. Has your uncle found anything in Carthe, by chance? Or your allies?"

Aurelia shook her head. "Nothing. Both dragons have been spotted once or twice, but nobody knows where they came from or where they've been hiding. Nobody has claimed them or claimed to know anything about them, either."

"Someone will come forward, eventually," Jack offered. Aurelia only sighed as she turned to glance out the window beside her, as if the dragons would reappear on cue. "Would you like some fresh air? Whatever Anna needs can wait a few moments longer."

"Please."

Aurelia stood from her vanity and accepted Jack's arm as they left their bedchamber. Fortunately, thoughts of the dragons almost disappeared entirely when they descended the grand staircase and found themselves in the palace foyer. Servants were bustling through the halls, hollering at one another, while rushing to prepare for an upcoming event: a celebration to mark Aurelia's twelve years as Queen of Akkinor—twelve being the holiest and most important number in the realm, as the world was created by twelve deities.

But that wasn't *entirely* accurate. This was technically her thirteenth year as queen, but the celebration had been delayed by a year because of Aurelia's last pregnancy. She'd delivered the twins, Holly and Harlen, about five weeks before the day of the celebration. It'd nearly killed her, forcing her to take a full season to recover, and she'd gotten so caught up in her duties after her recovery that it was only logical to delay the celebration until the following year.

At least the traumatic birth had solidified Aurelia's decision that she was done having children. She'd wanted another child about two years after giving birth to her daughter, Halyna, but she certainly hadn't expected to have another *two*. After looking death in the eye, she'd grabbed Jack by the scruff of the neck and told him that if he ever impregnated her again, she'd let Halvor eat him for lunch.

She'd only been *partially* serious.

As they strolled to the rear doors of the palace to visit the gardens, Jack said, "I wonder if the nobles of Krotis will come to the ball. We invited all of them, didn't we?"

"We did, but I never expected any of them to show up—except for Lady Swann, of course. The others have no connection to Akkinor. I doubt her heir will come now that she's gone, though. He'll have enough to worry about. Did Arian mention anything about when the coronation will take place?"

"No. The new lord has already assumed his role, of course, but it seems they're delaying the official coronation for now. Things have been messy enough in Krotis since Lord Selle's death."

Aurelia grimaced. "I'd almost forgotten about that."

"How? Bruila is experiencing the same thing Akkinor did thirteen years ago, after all."

She knew he was teasing her, but the grimace didn't fade from her lips. Bruila, one of the five Kroti provinces, had buried its liege lord, Amarion Selle, last season. His only heir was his seventeen-year-old daughter: she was barely of age, unmarried, and, well, a girl.

It'd been difficult even for the formidable Lady Swann to secure her position in a kingdom dominated by men, and she'd been much older and more experienced when she took the throne. Shasta Selle would face one of two fates: either her counterparts would be convinced to accept her as Lady of Bruila; or they'd deem her unfit, and Selle rule in Bruila would come to an end—as would Shasta's young life.

Aurelia had faced the same predicament when she took the throne. Her reign hadn't been contested for five years, and then her own brother usurped her. She'd managed to take it back, albeit at the expense of Archie's life, but she hadn't forgotten what it felt like to be cast aside and wanted dead by her own people.

As soon as they stepped foot into the gardens, peace washed over Aurelia—a feeling she attributed only to being closer to Halvor, her most loyal and devoted ally, in her favorite place on the grounds. He was resting on the opposite side of the gardens, his body curled up like a cat's with his head resting on his arms, and every snore he emitted blew a strong gust of hot air toward the trees and flower fields surrounding him.

One of Halvor's golden, reptilian eyes cracked open as Aurelia and Jack inched closer to him. He didn't bother lifting his head or moving to greet them, though. He only repositioned his head, still intent on napping, while they brushed by him to visit the young woman cleaning scorched animal bones from the lawn.

"Good morning, Lucyra," Aurelia mused. "I see he hasn't yet grown tired of Bozari sheep."

Lucyra Belreos, Halvor's Carthinian caretaker, snorted as she tossed a blackened ribcage into a wheelbarrow. "Their blood must be sweeter than other animals, because he devours them like children devour cakes. It's sickening to watch."

That made the queen laugh. "Oh, Lucyra. I do love you."

She grunted. "Yeah, yeah."

Aurelia laughed again as she observed Lucyra. The heavyset, brown-skinned woman wasn't just a random person Aurelia had tasked with minding the dragon—she was family. Aurelia first met her three years earlier after the Battle for Dofell when Lucyra, a mage, helped save Jack's life on the battlefield. Arian Cristos, Aurelia's uncle through her biological mother, later explained that Lucyra was the granddaughter of his paternal aunt.

When Lucyra expressed interest in leaving Taundosa after the battle, Aurelia had invited her to live in Akkinor at the palace. In exchange, Lucyra offered to serve as Halvor's caretaker. She'd dedicated her life to studying dragonkind, so she'd offered to help Aurelia learn more about the creatures, too.

Jack coughed into his fist, pulling Aurelia from her thoughts. "You know, Lu, you don't have to do this. There are plenty of—"

"—big, strong men capable of doing this for me?" Lucyra scoffed as Aurelia stifled laughter. "I'd rather saw off my own arm and feed it to the pigs than watch incompetent men do my job. They'd make a mess of things, like men always do."

Jack held up his hands, surrendering. "All right, all right. I was only trying to help. This isn't exactly a fun task."

"No," she replied, blowing a lock of curly brown hair from her eyes, "but it keeps my mind busy, and I know the job isn't done right unless I do it."

He snorted and nudged Aurelia in the side with his elbow. "If I ever doubted that you two share blood..."

"Quiet, you." Aurelia took a few steps toward Lucyra and playfully wiggled her eyebrows. "Someone asked about you last night, you know."

Lucyra dropped a few bones into the wheelbarrow. "Who? That nosy footman with the lazy eye and the bad breath? Tell him not to bother. He has a brain the size of a walnut."

"I think he's rather nice," Jack chimed in. He clamped his jaw shut when both women shot annoyed looks in his direction. "Sorry."

"Not him," Aurelia said, turning back to her cousin. "Rayan."

Lucyra nearly stumbled over a sheep's skull. "Really?"

"Really."

"Oh, for gods' sakes." Jack's voice interrupted them again. Aurelia could practically *hear* him rolling his eyes. "I'm going to find the children. I can't bear to listen to another word of—"

"Go on, then." Aurelia shooed him with her hand, making him grunt at her, before donning a grin as she met Lucyra's excited gaze. "He was watching you pull a thorn from Halvor's foot while we were having an evening drink. He had this look on his face...I haven't seen it since Keera died."

"Oh." Lucyra's lips parted for a moment, but she shook her head and quickly resumed her task. "I...I don't think it meant anything, Aurelia. He's probably just lonely now that Keera's gone."

The queen frowned. "If that were the case, he'd be at a brothel instead of making eyes at you whenever you're nearby."

"He can't be seen at a brothel. He's a knight, remember?"

Aurelia winced. With all the freedoms—albeit *secret* freedoms—she'd granted Rayan Haze, Hand of the Queen, she often forgot about the oath he'd taken. Knights weren't allowed to marry, sire children, or have any sort of sexual relationship. Rayan had broken the oath years before he met Aurelia when he fell in love with a Follian barmaid, Keera, and sired three children with her. Aurelia had invited Keera and the children to live in the palace under the guise that Keera was a new handmaiden, but nobody other than the royal family and Lucyra knew the truth.

Keera died two years ago when she caught scarlet fever, and while Rayan mourned privately, he just wasn't the same after she died. Something changed when he started seeing more of Lucyra, but the pair of them were as stubborn as mules. Rayan didn't want to break his oath again, and Lucyra didn't want to be the reason he broke it.

"Either way, I think—"

Aurelia's words died on her lips when a familiar golden glow appeared on Halvor's back. Halvor didn't so much as open an eye as the glow faded to reveal Edom. Lucyra rolled her eyes and muttered something about a *wretched creature,* but Aurelia grinned and held her hand out, prompting the sprite to zip over and perch on her palm.

"Hello, my friend," she said. "How were your travels?"

Edom grimaced. "Not good."

"You didn't find anything?" Her heart sank as it shook its massive head. "All right. Did you learn anything else while you were spying on our subjects?"

That made the sprite grin, revealing a mouthful of razor-sharp teeth. "She's dead."

"Lady Swann? I know. Arian sent—"

"No." Edom shook its head again. "The empress."

"The Empress of Quapebet?" Aurelia frowned as she thought of Akkinor's neighbors to the south. "That's nothing to grin about, Edom. The emperor must be in shambles."

"No. He celebrates."

She scowled while Lucyra scoffed beside her. "Why?"

"He will remarry. He wants a son." Edom poked her palm with its long, wiry finger. "If he succeeds, he wants his son to marry your daughter. Unite the continents."

Aurelia's heart leapt to her throat. She knew Emperor Timman Kaplo, Sixth of His Name, had a daughter already, but she knew nothing about the girl. It was rumored that the emperor didn't allow her to leave their palace, as he was ashamed to have sired a daughter. He had no other heirs, and another rumor suggested he'd forced his wife to conceive again and again, despite her poor health, to no avail. If he couldn't sire a son, he'd bring shame to his family line (in his eyes, of course) by naming his daughter as his heir.

"I'm not in the business of betrothing my children without their consent," Aurelia started, "particularly when such an arrangement would leave them under untrustworthy leadership. They'll be free to choose their own partners, exactly as I was."

Edom hissed disapprovingly. "But an alliance—"

"We don't need another alliance. We're strong enough as it is. I'm sure the emperor will understand if and when he writes to me about this." She frowned. "How did you find out?"

"I went to the border at Vilgh-Azhor. Imperial soldiers were gossiping."

"Of course they were. Did you learn anything else while you were there?"

The sprite nodded. "The emperor is coming to your ball."

"Really?" She couldn't hide her surprise. She'd sent him an invitation, of course, but he hadn't responded. He'd never responded to any of her invitations before. "If that's true, then this will be the first time a Quenosi emperor visits Akkinor. He may not come back if I offend him by refusing his offer, but that's a risk I'll have to take."

Lucyra snorted like a bull. "I'm sure little Holly will thank you when she comes of age in fifteen years."

Aurelia laughed. "Or she'll resent me for failing to make her an empress."

"Oh, please." Lucyra waved a dismissive hand. "Life as a boring empress in Quapebet, or life in Akkinor as the daughter of a queen who commands a dragon. The choice is a simple one."

Aurelia turned her gaze to Halvor. He sensed her watching him, as he peeled an eye open and chuffed affectionately. She allowed herself a small, smug smile as he blinked at her, like he was trying to tell her something.

Lucyra, as usual, was right.

II

The following morning, Aurelia hardly had the chance to say her prayers before her lady's maids arrived to ready her for a busy day. Jack's footmen weren't far behind, and when they eventually succeeded at pulling him out of bed, he followed them out of the room to get ready elsewhere—but not before kissing his wife on the cheek and laughing when she recoiled at the smell of his morning breath.

When her maids finished painting her face and styling her hair, they helped her into a gown—cornflower blue with white, lacy flowers sewn into the skirt—and set a pair of matching slippers on the floor for her to step into.

Before sending her off, a maid called Geena secured Aurelia's crown atop her head. "I must say," Geena mused, "I like the new crown much better."

Aurelia beamed as she observed her reflection in the floor-length mirror. "I do, too."

Years ago, after changing the official Akkinorian and Brentwood sigils to a blue-and-gold dragon, Aurelia asked the palace blacksmiths to make a new crown. She'd spent the first ten years of her reign wearing various tiaras, which had all belonged to former Queen Consorts—never a reigning queen. The crown her father and his predecessors had worn was too big for her head, too, so it'd never been an option for her. Her new crown was a daintier, simpler version of her father's: Akkinorian bronze with six peaks to symbolize the six kingdoms, and the sigils of each reigning family engraved along the base of the crown.

She was the first Akkinorian queen to wear it, but she knew she wouldn't be the last.

After leaving her bedchamber, Aurelia met two people at the bottom of the grand staircase in the foyer: Jack and Rayan. She ignored the sharp hunger pains in her stomach while she greeted them—she hadn't had enough time for breakfast—and looped either of her arms through theirs while they trekked through the front doors and onto the bailey.

Their carriage awaited them just a few feet from the front steps of the palace. This wasn't anything like the carriages everyone in the realm was accustomed to, though. Instead of being pulled by two horses and directed by a coachman, it was pulled by two centaurs.

Not long after the Battle for Dofell three years earlier, Edom had surprised everyone by awakening its fellow magical creatures in the Folly—all of whom had been hibernating, hidden from humanity, since the persecution. At first, there were only a handful of them: a few nymphs, fairies, a lone Cyclops, and even a few gnomes. They went on to awaken others across the kingdoms of Akkinor, and soon enough, there were as many magical creatures roaming the country as there were highborn people.

The centaurs, among other large creatures, had been hibernating underground in tunnel systems that nobody—even Aurelia, the queen, and her priests, the most knowledgeable people in Akkinor—had known about. Those who'd protested the persecution had created the tunnels in secret to protect the creatures. These tunnels hadn't been discovered until chunks of land caved into the earth like collapsed drawbridges, instigated by the centaurs when they decided to emerge.

Aurelia had assured every magical creature on her soil that they were free to live as they pleased. Most of the centaurs, however, opted to stay in the Folly to serve Aurelia and her family. They claimed they sought purpose and duty, and as long as Aurelia treated them with respect, they'd continue to serve her—not as slaves or vessels, but as volunteers.

The two centaurs bowed—one arm bent over their midriffs, their upper bodies lowered, and their heads tilted—when the trio approached them. Aurelia held out her hand to Cheol, the larger of the two, but instead of shaking it, he kissed her knuckles and held her hand between both of his.

"My queen." His voice, gruff and gravelly, didn't match the kindness etched onto his face. "It's lovely to see you again. You're as radiant as ever. We were delighted to hear that you require transportation today, as always. We came as soon as Fiora found us—I couldn't wait to gaze upon your beauty once more."

Aurelia blushed and chuckled. Fiora was a wind nymph: yet another creature who'd opted to stay close to Aurelia, serving as a volunteer messenger for the royal family.

Jack grunted and gave the centaur a look of warning. "I've told you a dozen times now, Cheol—stop flirting with my wife."

"I can't help it, Your Highness."

Jack shook hands with Cheol's brother, Geon. "I've always liked you better."

"Many do." Geon winked at Aurelia. "A pleasure to see you, Your Grace."

She beamed. "And you, my friend."

The trio climbed into the carriage and took a moment to settle before calling for the centaurs to proceed. The carriage lurched forward as it inched closer to the gates, with Cheol and Geon making pleasant, seamless conversation like they weren't tugging over five hundred pounds behind them.

As they rode through the Folly, Aurelia glanced through the window and smiled at the many friendly faces waving from the streets. It'd been shocking when the people of Akkinor didn't protest the creatures' return. Given Akkinor's distaste for mages, Aurelia expected them to riot in the streets. Instead, the creatures' return (and, of course, the moon goddess's brief visit to the realm) seemed to change Akkinor's perspective on magic. The people just couldn't get enough of the things they'd only ever read about in fairytales and folk stories.

Until three years ago, Carthe was considered to be the magical capital of the world, as it was the only place where magic was still common in the modern day. But even then, the number of magical creatures in Carthe was slimmer than anyone truly knew. Nowadays, Akkinor was home to more magical creatures than anywhere else in the world, all because the ancient beings had chosen to hibernate rather than take their chances in an unpredictable land.

It was ironic: Akkinor had been responsible for the near erasure of magic, and now, one couldn't walk a mile down the street without spotting a magical creature.

Soon enough, they reached their destination: the Follian town of Casirren. A small crowd had already gathered around the perimeter of a vast estate called Briarwood. The castle, recently renovated, hadn't been lived in since Aurelia's grandmother died. It was meant to serve as home to the widows of kings, but since Aurelia's parents died together, it hadn't been touched in thirty years.

The golden gates of Briarwood were closed, with three people standing in front of them flanked on either side by Follian soldiers. Two of the individuals were lowborn in charge of minding the estate, as they had back when the late Queen Charlotte lived there. The third woman, Odessa Linderli, was Aurelia's paternal aunt and the new resident of Briarwood Manor.

Cheol and Geon stopped a few feet from the gates before moving off to the side. Both kept their hands nestled on the hilts of the swords strapped to their waists. That was another wonderful thing about the centaurs—they were rarely bested in battle by mortals, so while they were nearby, there was no need for soldiers to follow Aurelia on her every endeavor.

"Aunt Odessa." Aurelia, with Jack and Rayan trailing behind her, approached Odessa and kissed her on either cheek. "It's lovely to see you. I hope you're as excited as I am."

Odessa forced a smile. "I'm a bit nervous, in truth."

"I'd be concerned if you weren't."

Aurelia winked at her aunt before turning to face the crowd—a combination of lowborn and highborn Follians—and clearing her throat.

"Welcome, all! It's an exciting day here in the Folly. With the reopening of Briarwood Manor, I will officially step down as Lady of the Folly and pass the torch to my aunt, Lady Odessa Linderli. Never before has the Folly responded to a leader other than the monarch, and while it pains me to break so many centuries of tradition, I feel it's only right that this kingdom be given the same direct leadership as the others. I can't be the ruler you deserve while I have five other kingdoms to mind, and that isn't fair to you. Lady Odessa will be a just, capable leader for all of you—just like her father and her brother, your former kings."

The crowd erupted in jubilant cheers, thrilled to have another Brentwood ruling in Akkinor.

Aurelia waited for the cheering to die down before she continued. "This decision, as you may know, isn't the only change to the Folly I've implemented. I've done a bit of thinking, and I feel it's unfair to the rest of Akkinor that an entire kingdom serves as our country's capital. To restore equality amongst the kingdoms, I've decided to establish a capital city instead. The city will be composed of the territories within close proximity to the palace, including Casirren, and it will be given a new name: Kalenbrar."

"'City of Light.'" An older lowborn man with one blind eye met her gaze and smiled. "That's what it means in the old tongue, isn't it?"

Aurelia mimicked his expression. "That's right. Every smaller territory within Kalenbrar will maintain their borders and their names, but the area as a whole will serve as the capital city. It's my hope that we may turn Kalenbrar into a place befitting of the Almighty Buen himself: a place that prospers to unforeseen heights, booming with wealth, joy, and inspiration. The palace may be regarded to many as the center of the capital, but the royal family knows that the true heart of the capital is you—its people."

The crowd whooped, whistled, and clapped so loudly that Aurelia's ears began to ring. Her people had been more supportive than ever in recent years, but this was different. It wasn't support they were throwing in her direction, but *love*.

On Aurelia's word, soldiers opened the golden gates, and Odessa took her first steps toward her new home. Aurelia watched from behind the gates with Jack and Rayan as a banner bearing the sigil of the Linderli family—Odessa's late husband's family—was raised up on a flagpole planted on the estate's bailey.

Jack snaked an arm around Aurelia's waist as they watched Odessa walk into the castle, the cheering voices of their people drowning out the sounds of celebratory drums and trumpets nearby.

"With everything that's happened lately," he murmured into her ear, "I think this was a wonderful idea. You've given them something to be excited about. Our people may have a funny relationship with change, but I daresay they've taken well to this one."

Aurelia smiled, but it faded as quickly as it'd formed. She sometimes forgot that more than half of the Folly had been awakened by the two dragons that'd visited the palace last season. The entire country knew about it within days, and it'd been a constant worry in the back of their minds ever since.

"My reign will be different than those of my predecessors." Her smile returned as Halvor appeared within the clouds, shrieking as he circled the towers of Briarwood Manor. "Akkinor has always been exactly the same as it was a thousand years ago. It's time for us to evolve, even if no king before me ever attempted it."

Jack chuckled as a fairy zipped through the air around the manor. "If your goal is to lead Akkinor to a new age, I'd say you've already achieved that. Look around."

She tore her eyes from Halvor to follow Jack's gaze. She saw the fairy first, encased in a transparent sphere of lavender light, and then the two centaurs, who were laughing with a trio of Follian soldiers. Then she spotted a tree nymph lounging in the branches of a tall maple tree, casually fanning her face with an orange leaf while she conversed with a group of lowborn men and women sitting below her.

All Aurelia could do was grin.

***

"It's *outrageous*." Darius Reesa, Lord of Vrurith, seethed so aggressively that Shasta expected him to start foaming at the mouth. "The one woman among us dies, and we're left with another. I'd hoped we'd find a solution to this predicament before the old woman finally returned to the heavens, but—"

"Have some respect." Lazelus Swann practically squeaked when he spoke, leading the other nobles at the table to scoff or snort at him. The new Lord of Runeia turned crimson immediately, but he stood his ground. "You may not have liked ruling beside a woman, but my grandmother was every bit as powerful as you."

"Oh, please," Lord Reesa snapped. "Your grandmother all but betrayed us three years ago. She sent those gryphons of yours to kill us, if you've forgotten. She could've helped her own kin, and instead, she chose *foreigners*. There's no greater act of disrespect."

"Speak for yourself. Mekya had no part in that battle, and still, I think Lady Swann was right to do what she did. It's what the Almighty would have wanted." Firadus Keer, Lord of Mekya, shot daggers at Lord Reesa with his amber eyes. "You chose to fight for the wrong side—all of you. Lady Swann's actions may have been alarming at the moment, but they led to a deity's return to the realm. I'll bet you're more upset that it wasn't you who took a stand against Kanibar. You needn't tarnish her memory because your pride is wounded. Accept your wrongdoing and be done with it."

Shasta held her breath. She wasn't fond of this conversation, but at the very least, they'd forgotten they were meant to be talking about *her*.

Lord Reesa's nostrils flared. "You dare—"

"Oh, *enough*." Varidos Quagg, Lord of Osanad, massaged his temples until his skin turned red. "What's done is done. There's no use in dwelling on the past when our future is at risk." Shasta's stomach turned when he looked in her direction. "What are we going to do with you, girl?"

She gulped. "I-I—"

"She can't even form a coherent sentence," Lord Reesa said with a snort. He gestured to the seventeen-year-old girl as she sat at the head of the meeting table, flanked on either side by the lords of Krotis. "Look at her. She's a child."

"She's only three years younger than me," Lord Swann muttered.

"*Quiet.* You aren't disproving my point, either."

"Lady Swann managed to keep her seat because Runeia had no other option. Her reign began while the three of us were babes." Lord Quagg gestured between himself, Lord Reesa, and Lord Keer. "There was nothing we could do about her, and I daresay there was nothing our predecessors could've done, either. But the Codex demands that all five rulers of Krotis are male. I don't believe the gods will continue to favor us if we break that law for a second time."

Lord Keer shook his head. "The gods don't favor those who murder young girls, either. Our Almighty is the goddess of virtues, and nothing about the way you've all gone about this matter is virtuous in the slightest. You'll damn the entire country if you take her head."

Shasta gasped aloud, but the men didn't pay her any heed. As much as it terrified her, at least it confirmed one thing: if the nobles refused to let her take her place as the rightful Lady of Bruila, they wouldn't just replace her and send her away—they'd kill her.

She wished her parents had sired a son. They'd managed it twice, but both boys were dead when they were born. Even after her mother died, her father—Lord Amarion Selle—had refused to remarry for the chance of having a son, claiming his orphaned nephew would succeed him. Unfortunately, his nephew died after being thrown from a horse not long before Amarion's own death. With no other options, he'd declared that Shasta, his only child, would succeed him. The other leaders of Krotis had accepted his wish, only to revoke their support the moment he died.

Lord Reesa growled in frustration before marching over to Shasta and bending over, hands on his knees, so the pair were eye-level. She tried her hardest to keep from trembling or looking away from him, as she knew how much he despised weakness.

He tugged at the woven scarf covering her hair. "You look like my daughter when I last saw her: not yet a woman, afraid of anything that breathes, and clueless about the world. You're a fool if you think Bruila will respect you as their leader." Shasta didn't answer as he folded his arms over his chest. "Have you anything to say? I'd recommend choosing your words carefully—your life may depend on it."

"For gods' sakes," Lord Keer muttered. "She's just a girl."

"Exactly. We can't have a child ruling beside us, let alone another woman, and unless she can convince us of her value..." He raised an expectant eyebrow. "Well? What do you have to say?"

Shasta opened her mouth to reply, but no sound emerged. The nobleman scoffed, shook his head at her, and marched back to his seat.

"We shall have to appoint a new noble family to rule Bruila," Lord Quagg stated. "It's regrettable that Selle rule in Bruila has come to an end after so many centuries, but we haven't another choice. Perhaps we can—"

"Wait!" Shasta didn't realize she'd sprung to her feet and cried out until every pair of eyes snapped in her direction. She gulped, suddenly feeling no larger than an ant, as she looked down at her fiddling fingers. "I...I think I have something that might sway you."

After a moment of silence, Lord Quagg snapped, "Spit it out, girl!"

Shasta felt her face turn scarlet. "I couldn't help but overhear your conversation before I joined you today. You've all been wondering about an incident that happened in Akkinor last season." When the nobles stiffened, she allowed herself a small smile. "My father gave me a gift before he died—a gift, and a letter he received from King Willem before the Battle for Dofell. I'll share the letter with you, as he wished, once my life and my throne have been assured. But I can promise that if you betray me or choose to kill me, you'll never find the letter."

"What is it?" Lord Swann's dark eyes shone with curiosity. "The gift."

She only stared at him. To her left, Lord Keer inhaled sharply and scrubbed a hand over his mouth, having put the pieces together for himself. The others still hadn't figured it out.

"I can see that you require a hint—" Shasta started.

Lord Reesa practically hissed at her. "Watch yourself."

She acted like he didn't frighten her, but he certainly did. In response, she reached into the bodice of her gown and produced an object, which she then tossed onto the meeting table. Lord Keer took one glance at it before letting his head fall into his hands, but the others inspected it more closely before turning their wild-eyed gazes to Shasta.

"It was my father who sent the message to Akkinor," she told them. "I don't know anything about the other one that made its way to the east—that was unexpected. But I know my family's part in it, and now the rest of you do, too."

For a moment, nobody spoke. Then Lord Quagg whispered, "We can't get rid of her now."

"No." A calculating look filled Lord Reesa's eyes as he stared at her. "No, we can't."

As Shasta's smug smile grew wider, she flickered her dark eyes over to the object on the table: a green piece of shell from a dragon's egg.

III

On her way to her bedchamber, Aurelia heard shouting from outside, stopping her in her tracks in front of a hallway window. A snort vibrated her nostrils when her eyes found the source of the commotion: Jack and Lucyra.

They were sparring on the lawn with nothing but the moon to light their way. They stopped yelling as they circled each other, both weighing their swords in their hands. In the time it took for her to blink, Lucyra released a ragged shout and charged, missing Jack by inches. Aurelia's husband only grinned, wiped sweat from his forehead with the back of his hand, and returned the favor like it was as easy to him as breathing—because it was.

That was something else she loved about having her cousin at the palace: Lucyra and Jack, for all of their squabbling, had become the best of friends. They reminded Aurelia of her relationship with Linden Elliot, her best friend and her first Lord Hand. They bickered like siblings, but they shared many similar qualities, and they brought out the best in one another.

It was late in the evening by then, and most of the Folly was fast asleep, but she knew Jack and Lucyra would be out there until one of them drew blood. They never harmed one another beyond a small scratch, but neither seemed satisfied until they'd actually nicked the other.

Aurelia went on her way to her bedchamber, yawning, and greeted her lady's maids as they assisted with her evening routine. They helped her out of her gown and into a nightdress, washed her face, and took the pins out of her hair before tying her golden curls in a loose braid. When they were dismissed, she stayed seated at her vanity while massaging a hand cream onto her skin.

A few moments later, someone knocked at her door. She quickly threw a dressing robe over her shoulders before calling for the knocker to enter. A smile graced her lips when Rayan entered, also dressed in his nightclothes with a dressing robe pulled over his garments.

"Apologies for the lateness of the hour," he said, taking a few steps toward her. She waved a dismissive hand. "This just arrived for you. I've already read it. Normally, I wouldn't bring a message to you so late in the evening, but..."

When he trailed off, she frowned and accepted the scroll clutched in his fist. Her frown didn't fade as she inspected the broken wax seal: silver and stamped with the image of an arctic wolf, symbolic of the Styrmodr royal family.

"Glacier Bay." She raised an eyebrow at him. "They haven't written to accept our invitation to the ball, have they?"

Rayan grimaced. "Not exactly."

Mirroring his expression, Aurelia unraveled the scroll and proceeded to read the longest message she'd ever received from the northernmost continent:

For the Vasira of Akkinor:

I write to you bearing grim news. As you may have heard, a blight of the Silent Death recently struck Glacier Bay. The plague has done tremendous damage to our people, and now it has affected the crown directly. This past week, the royal family suffered two tragic losses: both the Vasira and the Vasirel have been taken by the plague, not a week after the latter's nineteenth name day.

This may come as a surprise to you, but the Vasir had given permission for both his son and daughter to attend your celebration this year. It was his hope that you might betroth his son to your daughter Hyacinth. As you can imagine, he intends to keep the Vasirella here on the continent—if she happens to be a carrier of the plague, we do not wish to bring it to your shores. However, he would now like you to consider a union between his daughter and your eldest son instead. If you accept, we shall organize an audience between our two great nations as soon as the matter here has been dealt with.

Please keep Glacier Bay and every Isalder man, woman, and child in your prayers. We hope to see an end to this tragedy in the near future, and until then, we have placed the continent on lockdown. You needn't worry for any Isalders arriving on your land and infecting your people.

Sincerely,
Ragnar Purcell, Agadr Ova of Glacier Bay.

"My gods." Aurelia swallowed the lump in her throat. "This poor family..."

"Both Queen Margrete and Crown Prince Tomas have perished." Rayan sat on the edge of her bed and ran his hands through his hair as she swiveled to face him. "The prince's twin sister still lives, but she'll never see the throne."

"King Viggo's Hand didn't say a word about the succession," Aurelia added. "I know the king has many nephews—he'll probably pass the throne to *their* side of the family. The princess is the only daughter ever born to an Isalder king, and everyone knows how much Isalders despise answering to women. There isn't a single one in power in Glacier Bay. If the king decides to name his daughter as his heir, she won't survive. The people will kill her the moment her father dies."

Rayan nodded and grimaced again. "King Viggo proposes a union between his daughter and your son—but didn't he propose a similar union when you were a child?"

Aurelia's lips parted. He was right, but she'd completely forgotten about that. "Yes, he did. I was almost fifteen at the time, and the king's twins were seven. Those numbers don't add up, though, if the twins *just* turned nineteen. King Viggo must've lied to my father in a desperate effort to unite our continents." She took a moment to do the math in her head before scoffing. "There are fourteen years between me and the twins. That would've made them about a year old, if not younger, when the king expressed interest in marrying me to his son."

"His lie would've been revealed if your father gave the proposal even an ounce of thought. King Viggo probably didn't think anything of it—most highborn Isalders are betrothed as infants and children. They may not marry until they come of age, but for many of them, they're still promised to people old enough to be their parents. It's sickening."

Aurelia chewed on her lower lip as she scanned the message again. "We'll send a response tomorrow, along with a gift to express our sympathies, and we'll claim to be considering the proposed union between Henry and the princess. I won't arrange marriages for my children, and I certainly won't betroth my five-year-old boy to a grown woman, but the Isalders are going through enough as it is—I don't think the king would take kindly to my refusal while he buries his heir. We'll break the news after he's had time to grieve."

Rayan nodded. "I'll write our response as soon as the sun rises."

"Thank you. Goodnight, my friend."

"Goodnight, Aurelia."

When he was gone, Aurelia lifted the scroll again and sighed. In a matter of two days, she'd received word of four deaths around the realm: Lady Swann of Runeia, Empress Ithra of Quapebet, and now, Queen Consort Margrete and Crown Prince Tomas of Glacier Bay. Was there a reason the realm's highborn were dropping like flies, or was it all a matter of coincidence?

***

In the blink of an eye, the eve of Aurelia's celebratory ball had arrived.

Highborn from across Akkinor trickled into the Folly in the days leading up to the party, all invited to stay in the palace like they did during the seasonal Changling Celebrations. Guests from around the realm were expected to arrive in the morning on the day of the ball, but one particular set of attendees had shown up the night before: the Taundosans.

Other than their protection detail, only two people arrived from the City of Gold: Reyna Caltheos, Queen of Taundosa, and Arian Cristos, Lord Hand of Taundosa. Reyna knew better than to expect Arian to stay at home while she visited Akkinor, so she'd left her husband and her heir behind to rule on her behalf—and Arian's, for that matter.

Aurelia saw their carriage roll into the bailey from a balcony on the second story of the palace. As soon as she spotted the Taundosan banners flying high alongside the carriage, she bolted downstairs and raced through the foyer to the door, propriety and bare feet be damned. Arian was just stepping out of the carriage, violently scratching his arms, when he saw her dashing toward him. Luckily, he managed to open his arms just in time for her to collide with his chest.

Her uncle made an *oomph* sound and staggered back a bit, but quickly steadied himself as he wrapped her in an embrace. He chuckled, making his chest rumble against her cheek, as he pressed a kiss to the top of her head. She knew she must've looked like a little girl to anyone observing them, but she didn't care—it'd been over a year since the last time she saw him.

"My darling Aurelia." He released her and set his hands on either side of her face, beaming as his dark eyes studied her light ones. "You look very well, especially compared to when I saw you last—practically at death's door after delivering the twins. Are you feeling well, too?"

She nodded. "Very well, uncle, thank you. And yourself?"

"Better than ever, now that I'm here." He tucked a lock of gray hair behind his ear, scratching the side of his neck as he did so, and looked over her to marvel at the palace. His eyes squinted a bit as a childlike grin formed on his lips. "Either I'm shrinking with age, or this place has gotten bigger."

"I believe you must be shrinking," came a voice to their left. Aurelia smiled and took a few steps forward to join hands with Reyna. While Arian huffed at his queen, Reyna squeezed Aurelia's hands and beamed. "Hello again, Your Grace. It's been quite a while since we last saw one another."

"Three years. Hard to believe, isn't it?"

"It feels like yesterday, but also like it was decades ago." The Golden Queen raised a dark eyebrow. "Are we the first to arrive from Carthe?"

"You're the first to arrive from anywhere outside of Akkinor." Aurelia looped her arm through Reyna's and led her toward the front steps. Arian strolled on Aurelia's other side, hands clasped behind his back, as servants transported their belongings from the carriage to the palace. "You didn't happen to hear anything about the new Lord of Runeia, did you? I sent invitations to every Kroti leader, but I haven't heard back from any of them. I only expected to hear from Runeia, but..."

Reyna sighed. "I've heard nothing. Lord Cristos wrote to him three times in hopes of arranging an audience—we must ensure that Lazelus Swann is as diligent about maintaining our alliance as his grandmother was, rest her soul. I fear he's gotten too distracted by learning the way of things, though. He'll be putting his alliances aside until he establishes himself in Krotis."

"I assumed as much," she admitted. "What about Diantha? Or Bozar?"

"Lords Zhaaran and Zhoqa are on their way," Arian told her, "but the queen has opted to remain in Dofell. I expect you'll be receiving a raven from her at some point today. I saw her briefly before we departed for our voyage—just to check on her—and while she appears to be doing very well, it's obvious she has far too much on her plate."

"I suppose that's why I haven't heard from her regarding an alliance between Akkinor and Dofell." Inside the palace, Aurelia escorted her guests to the nearest parlor, and asked a servant to bring a tray of refreshments while the old friends conversed. "I'm in no rush to form the alliance, though. She promised to pay back the coin I loaned her for Dofell's reparations, and until the kingdom is secure enough to do that, I can't be certain that Dofell would hold up their end of the bargain if we became allies. The day will come when she's ready for it."

"Taundosa and Bozar share your sentiment." Reyna perched in an armchair by the hearth while Aurelia and Arian shared a couch across from her. "Speaking of alliances, though...I have a proposal for you, while I'm here."

Aurelia raised an eyebrow. "What is it?"

Reyna's azurite eyes flickered over to Arian before settling on Aurelia again. "The number of magical creatures roaming free in Akkinor is...remarkable, to say the least. When word spread that thousands of them spent all these centuries hibernating in secret, it was startling for all of us. Akkinor, of all places, has centaurs galloping across the country. Carthe has always been a place of refuge for magic, yet we haven't seen a centaur on our continent since the persecution. It's baffling, Your Grace, truly. But..."

When she trailed off, Arian cleared his throat, scratched at his arm, and finished for her: "You see, most magical creatures in Carthe are under the protection of humans, so they rarely stray from where they live. Others, like those poor, mutated dragons, are kept as slaves. It grows harder and harder by the day to find a magical creature out in the wild. The few who survived all these years have been killed off and nearly eradicated by travelers. We'd like to bring magic back to Carthe again, but we can't do that without you."

Aurelia sighed. "You wish to take some of Akkinor's creatures back to Carthe."

He nodded. "We'd only take those who volunteer, and we'd do everything in our power to ensure their protection. But we understand if you'd rather keep them here, too."

She chewed on her lower lip. "I don't know. It's not up to me. If they wish to go and explore the realm, then so be it. I won't break the promise of freedom I made to them by forcing them to stay here. We'll have to ask them."

Reyna nodded. "Of course. And please, don't think we're proposing this because we want Taundosa to have some sort of advantage over our neighbors. We have no intention of forcing them to stay in Taundosa. It's just...well..."

"I understand." Aurelia smiled. "Akkinor and Carthe were established by the gods to be the two dominant forces in the realm—each claiming one half of our world, and each serving as birthplaces to the First Mortals. But they were meant to be equals, too, even if that much has changed over the years. If we wish to bring harmony to the realm, what better way to start than by restoring balance between our two continents?"

Reyna grinned from ear to ear. "I'd hoped you might say that. Now, about this ball of yours..."

As the trio conversed, two servants arrived, each holding a tray complete with tea, biscuits, and finger sandwiches. Aurelia tried to serve her guests like a proper host, but Arian wouldn't allow it. After politely instructing her to relax, he poured each of them a cup of tea, and Aurelia couldn't help but notice the way his hands tremored as he did so.

A fleeting feeling of worry bubbled up in her gut, but she pushed it aside as quickly as she could. She often forgot that Arian wasn't some sort of divine figure sent to earth as a guiding star—that he was human, and he aged just like everyone else. He was over sixty years old now, and as much as Aurelia tried to ignore the signs of him aging, they were becoming too obvious for her to miss.

It was one of many reasons she wished she'd had the chance to grow up with him. They'd never have as much time together as they wanted since they'd met as adults. But it was better to know him for just a decade or so than to never know him at all; especially when she'd never get the chance to meet her mother, his sister.

Besides—he was Arian Cristos. He may have been getting older, but he was still a force to be reckoned with, and he wouldn't leave the realm anytime soon if he could help it. He was too stubborn.

It ran in the family.

IV

*y*ou're a vision, Your Grace!"

Aurelia blushed. "Oh, stop it."

Her team of lady's maids stepped aside so she could examine her reflection in the floor-length mirror. She had to admit it to herself—she *did* look beautiful. It was the first time in seasons that she felt like the youthful, fresh-faced princess she'd been once before.

Her hair was pinned back in a bun at the nape of her neck, but it was fairly loose so the style wouldn't hurt her scalp. A few wispy curls framed her face, and because the strands atop her head hadn't been slicked back, they retained their natural, somewhat frizzy pattern beneath her crown. Her makeup was light and simple: her cheeks and lips were the same shade of pink, and charcoal-colored pigment lined her eyes. Though she wasn't wearing anything to conceal the long scar across her cheek, it was slightly camouflaged by the color on her cheeks. The dark gray around her eyes drew attention to her powder-blue gaze and away from the blemish, anyway.

Her gown, made just for the occasion, was the most breathtaking part. The massive hoopskirt swished when she moved, like all of the fancier gowns in her collection, but this one was layered. The train of the bottom layer extended several feet to the left, right, and back, but the layer on top of it fell from the base of her spine to her feet—though it was only visible from the back, like a veil. The fabric was royal blue like Halvor, but with gold beads stitched in ornate patterns throughout the entire gown. The entire bodice and the long sleeves were covered completely in the gold beads, but the back was sheer and blue with buttons from her neck to her waist.

She'd have a hard time moving around, but it was worth it.

After adding the finishing touches—a pair of gold slippers and her golden locket—Aurelia bid her lady's maids farewell, then left to meet Jack at the top of the grand staircase.

She was halfway to her destination when she saw a small group loitering in the hallway. It was her children and their three governesses: Irina, Celesse, and Hannah. Each of them wore their finest clothing with their hair combed and styled, their shoes polished, and tiny crowns on their heads. They weren't meant to attend the party for very long, but as members of the royal family, it was customary for them to greet their guests before bedtime rolled around.

Irina and Celesse each held one of the twins, but the other three children—Halle, Henry, and Halyna—bolted over to their mother as soon as they saw her approaching. Hannah tried to scold them so they wouldn't wrinkle their clothing or make a mess of their hair, but the poor governess didn't stand a chance.

"You look so pretty, Mama!" Henry exclaimed.

Aurelia chuckled as she touched her palm to his cheek. "Thank you, darling. The three of you look wonderful, too. Are you excited for the party?"

"Yes, Mama!" Halyna nodded about a dozen times. "We dance?"

"You may dance, but only until it's time for bed. You know the rules."

Halle set a hand on her sister's shoulder. "We can only dance when we hear the music, Lena. We have to greet our guests first."

"But—" Halyna started.

"Your sister is right. You must listen to her." Aurelia smiled when Halyna huffed, but her smile faded when she realized one of her children was missing. "Where on earth is Sisi?"

Behind the children, the governesses exchanged looks. "She's being a bit...difficult, Your Grace," Irina replied. "We've been waiting for her, but—"

"Grandmama is scolding her." Henry giggled. "She's in *trouble.*"

"That's not nice, Henry," Halle snapped.

"No, it isn't." Aurelia gave her son a look, making him blush, before turning her gaze to the women. "Escort the children to their father, and tell him to wait for me outside of the ballroom. I'll fetch Hyacinth."

The governesses nodded and ushered the children back to them as Aurelia turned in the opposite direction. She walked by the nursery and turned at the end of the hallway, where the bedchambers occupied by her three eldest children were located. She didn't make it a foot around the corner before she spotted—and heard—Jack's mother, Isobel Ashford.

Since Isobel and her husband, Alistair, returned to Akkinor from exile a few years earlier, they'd been spending quite a bit of time at the palace to be with their grandchildren. Aurelia had no problem with that, but sometimes, Isobel liked to treat Aurelia's children as hers—often times, choosing to ignore the way Aurelia and Jack preferred to raise their children.

"Sisi!" Isobel banged on Hyacinth's door with her fist, her pale cheeks flushed with frustration. "I won't tell you again! Open the door!" She grabbed the door handle with both hands and rattled it, but it wouldn't budge. The former Lady of Omara took a step back, gritted her teeth, and banged on the door once more. "Sisi! Come out right now, you insolent child! When your mother hears about this—"

"I already have," Aurelia interrupted. Isobel sighed and stepped away from the door, looking twenty years older as she massaged her temples. "What's going on?"

"She's refusing to attend the party. She's all dressed and ready, but for whatever reason, she doesn't want to come. I don't know what's gotten into that head of hers. She needs a firm hand, that's all."

Aurelia tried her hardest to maintain her composure. "She tends to respond better to a gentle touch. Thank you for your effort, but I'll take it from here. And please, don't use me to make threats against my children. I'd rather they didn't fear me, or think I'll punish them for every wrongdoing." As Isobel huffed, Aurelia leaned her forehead against the door and wrapped her fingers around the handle. "Sisi? It's me. May I come in?"

Silence. Then, a few seconds later, Aurelia heard a clicking sound. She smiled, tossed a dismissive look in Isobel's direction, and slipped into the bedroom while Isobel grumbled and stormed off.

She closed the door behind her, frowning, as her eyes landed on her daughter. Hyacinth was sitting cross-legged on her bed, wearing a pretty lilac frock with her blonde curls hanging over her shoulders, while playing with a wooden puzzle box. She didn't look up when Aurelia walked in, nor did it seem like she'd gotten up to unlock the door.

Magic, Aurelia thought. It'd been all but confirmed over the years that Hyacinth—the illegitimate child of Archie and his unwilling mistress— was a mage, but Aurelia and Jack hadn't decided what to do about it yet. On one hand, if she was given proper training, she had the potential to become a skilled mage; though it wouldn't be long before the country realized she wasn't Aurelia's trueborn daughter, because neither Aurelia nor Jack had magic to pass onto their children. On the other hand, if she didn't receive proper training, her magic would disappear when she came of age, and she'd lose her incredible gift forever—but she'd be safe from anyone who might've targeted a traitor's child.

Careful not to wrinkle her gown, Aurelia sat on the edge of the bed. "Why are you refusing to leave your room?"

Hyacinth sighed. "I don't want to go to the ball."

"Why not?"

"Because."

"That's not an answer."

The princess sighed again. "I don't want to go, Mama. Can I stay here with Uncle Arian?"

"Uncle Arian is attending the ball, just like the rest of our family. I expect you to be there, too. And I expect you to apologize to your grandmother when we get downstairs. It's not polite to ignore those who only wish to help you."

"She wasn't helping. She was yelling."

She has you there, Aurelia thought to herself. "Fair enough. It's only for a little while, though. I know you don't wish to go, but I'd like it very much if you did. I could use your support. Can you do that for me?"

Hyacinth stilled, finally meeting her mother's gaze. There was a look in her eyes—timid, uneasy, and even a bit frightened—that Aurelia didn't understand. Hyacinth had never been fond of attention or being surrounded by people, but something about the way she looked felt different tonight. Aurelia was almost tempted to relent when Hyacinth finally responded:

"Okay. I'll go."

Aurelia smiled and brushed a stray curl from her daughter's forehead. "Thank you, Sisi. Now, let's go before your father eats all of the raspberry tarts you and I love so much."

That made her giggle. "All right."

***

"I think we've hurt Mother's feelings."

Aurelia flicked her gaze to the side, where Isobel was standing next to her husband with a sour look on her face. The rest of the attendees were watching the first dance of the night—the queen and her husband, as customary—with smiles and adoring expressions, but Jack's mother didn't seem very pleased.

"I don't think she appreciated the lecture I gave her," Aurelia admitted.

Jack snorted. "I'll speak with her later. I'm glad to have her here so much, but I can't say I approve of the way she scolds our children."

Aurelia winced and glanced at Isobel once more. It was odd—everything Jack had ever told her about his upbringing suggested Isobel had been a compassionate, patient mother. Alistair, the former Lord of Omara, had always been the firm, no-nonsense parent. It was becoming clearer as the years passed that the Ashfords' time in exile had changed them. Alistair had become softer and kinder, and Isobel had become harsher and stricter.

When the song and dance ended, the guests erupted in applause while Aurelia and Jack curtsied and bowed, respectively. The royal herald, responsible for all announcements at the palace, then invited the guests to join Aurelia and Jack on the floor as the small orchestra began playing a new song.

Rather than dancing together, Aurelia and Jack made gestures with their hands to usher their children over to the floor. The children and the governesses had been standing on the platform at the back of the ballroom where the thrones sat, having already done their part by greeting the guests when the party started. They'd be allowed one or two dances, but soon enough, the young royals would have to be sent to bed.

Aurelia danced with Henry and Jack with Halle, while two of the governesses each held one of the twins. Little Halyna was swept up by Rayan, who held her on his hip and clasped one of her hands as he waltzed around the floor. Alistair had gone straight for Hyacinth—his favorite grandchild, though he claimed he didn't have a favorite—and urged her to stand on the toes of his shoes while they danced.

They were having so much fun that Aurelia didn't realize when a new song began until she saw couples around her forming groups. The song demanded they dance a cotillion—a group dance consisting of four couples—but the children didn't know it enough to participate, so Aurelia and Jack sent them off before joining a nearby group.

The man to Aurelia's left was Lord Daniel Chilton, a mage and one of her advisors, who danced with his wife. Beside them was Lady Gemma Stone of Laynoa, Linden's sister, with her husband.

The other couple, however, weren't Akkinorians. They were perhaps the best dressed individuals at the ball, nearly drowning in embellishments and vibrant colors, with more poise and grace than every highborn in the room combined. Both had a dark complexion with deep brown eyes, and while the woman's short, coarse curls were blacker than night, the man was bald. The man was several decades older than his partner, too, with wrinkled skin and a white mustache above his lip.

Aurelia had known who they were as soon as they walked into the ballroom earlier in the evening. The symbol stitched onto the man's turquoise sash—a tiger—gave it away. He was Timman Kaplo, Sixth of His Name, Emperor of Quapebet, accompanied by his new bride, Kataya.

The dance required each couple to swap partners for a time, so before Aurelia knew it, she was twirling around with the emperor. He didn't say anything at first—only watched her—so she took it upon herself to make the first move.

"I was so sorry to hear about the late empress," she told him, "though I'm pleased you've managed to find happiness with another so quickly."

The emperor smiled at her. "Thank you. The Imperial Bride has been a blessing for all of Quapebet. It is my hope that she will bless us further by providing me with a son in the near future."

And what of your daughter? Aurelia wanted to ask. Instead, she chose cordiality, knowing this wasn't the time nor the place to bring up his neglected child.

"A healthy heir is all one can hope for" was all she said.

"Indeed." The corner of his mouth twitched as he spun her under his arm. "I do hope you've considered my proposal. A union between our countries would be—"

The conversation was brought to an abrupt halt when they were reunited with their original partners. Jack, having seen Aurelia dancing with the emperor, raised an inquisitive eyebrow.

"He started asking about the proposal," she said quietly. "What shall I say?"

Her husband grunted. "That we're not in the business of betrothing our children when they aren't even speaking yet."

"He may not be thinking of Holly. He may have Halyna in mind, or even—"

"We're not in the business of betrothing our children, period. Tell him exactly what you've always wanted for them, and exactly what your father wanted for you: our children will choose their own spouses. We won't use them as bargaining chips for alliances."

Aurelia smiled weakly. "Can you tell him for me?"

Jack laughed as he spun her under his arm. "I would, but there's the matter of the word *consort* in my title. It's not my place."

"Any other man would jump at the chance to play the part of king, even for a moment."

He leaned over to peck her on the lips, startling her, before pulling away and grinning. "You married me for that exact reason—because I have no interest in ruling. Or have you forgotten?"

"Maybe I married you simply because you're too handsome, and I couldn't stomach the idea of any other woman bringing you to bed."

That made him guffaw. "Whatever helps you sleep at night, Lily dear."

The song ended, relieving Aurelia of another interaction with the emperor—for now, anyway. She and Jack curtsied or bowed to the other dancers, mimicking them, but instead of staying on the floor for another dance, the couple returned to their thrones on the platform.

They tried sending the children to bed, but only Halyna, Henry, and the twins relented. Halle and Hyacinth wanted to stay, and despite Aurelia's better judgement, she obliged. They may have been only eight, but Halle was heir to the throne, after all, and Hyacinth...It wasn't often that Hyacinth enjoyed social settings, so Aurelia wanted her to savor it while it lasted. Plus, she'd forgotten about her previous apprehension, which had to count for something.

About halfway through the evening, the herald announced that it was time for Aurelia to make her address. She'd greeted her guests individually at the beginning of the ball, but she was still expected to give a small speech to the entire crowd. At least her duties ended here, though. After her address, she wasn't expected to do anything other than dance, chat, and drink.

As the orchestra stopped playing and the conversations faded into silence, Aurelia took a moment to observe those around her. The vast majority of her guests were Akkinorian, of course, but she easily picked out the foreign visitors in the crowd: the emperor and his bride lingered by the refreshments table, the former burning holes through Aurelia's skull; Arian and Reyna stood in the center of the room with Rayan and Lucyra; and Aurelia's allies from Bozar—elderly Lord Jalhor Zhaaran and his wife, and foul Lord Balor Zhoqa with two of his four wives—were standing off to the side, apart from the crowd.

She resisted the urge to smile. It still dumbfounded her that so many faces from around the realm were gathered in her ballroom. Until eight years ago, the only people who would've shown up to an Akkinorian party were Akkinorians themselves. Aurelia was the first ruler ever to have highborn from not one, not two, not three, but *four* nations under her roof at the same time.

"Good evening, all!" she called out, clutching a glass of bubbly liquor in her left hand. "I humbly thank each of you for coming tonight to celebrate my twelve years as Queen of Akkinor. The anniversary of my coronation is bittersweet: while I thank the gods for the role they've given me, I also remember the tragedy that resulted in my ascension. I know many of you still grieve the loss of my parents as much as I do."

A few people hung their heads and murmured prayers for the late king and queen. Others shot dirty looks at Alistair and Isobel—they still hadn't forgiven Omara's former leaders for abandoning Edmund and Cressida during the shipwreck that'd claimed their lives.

"I hope to see more years on the throne than my father did," Aurelia continued. "I wouldn't be standing here today without each of you. Your support, friendship, and guidance over the years helped me not to only reclaim my throne during the worst year of my life, but also to guide Akkinor toward a new age of promise. Because of your support, the realm has started to unite. Because of your support, a dragon roams the skies, centaurs gallop through the fields, and nymphs lounge in the trees. The last twelve years have brought more greatness to Akkinor than anyone could've imagined. Thank you, my friends and—"

The rest of Aurelia's sentence died on her lips when a strange, guttural sound echoed throughout the ballroom. As the guests started murmuring and glancing around for the source, Aurelia did the same. She scanned the crowd, frowning, until she found what she was looking for.

A strangled gasp escaped her lips as people rushed to the aid of Arian Cristos, Lord Hand of Taundosa. He was clutching his chest with one hand, the fabric of his tunic bunched in his fist, while his other arm was extended like he was trying to steady himself. His face turned crimson as the cords in his neck bulged against his flesh. His mouth was open as he emitted a horrifying choking sound, but he hadn't been eating anything that might've gotten lodged in his throat.

Aurelia took one step off the platform, and in the time it took her to do so, Arian collapsed to the floor. Reyna hollered for help and knelt at his side while the other guests gasped, shouted, and backed away from Arian's convulsing body.

Aurelia hiked up her skirts and darted for him. She fell to her knees beside him and rolled him onto his back while Reyna pleaded for a medic. Arian's arms were bent in the air like a praying mantis, white foam gurgled on his lips, and his body tremored violently. His eyes were closed, and he wasn't responding to anyone.

After a few seconds, he stopped convulsing, and his arms fell limply onto his chest. A medic had pushed through the crowd by then and was now kneeling beside him. Reyna moved so the medic had enough room, but she was still crouched on the floor, one shaking hand resting on Arian's calf.

Aurelia watched, unable to speak, as the medic pressed his ear to Arian's chest. The world seemed to move in slow motion as Aurelia looked over at the platform, where she'd left Jack and their children. Lucyra was standing at Jack's side now, and Halle had sought refuge beneath Lucyra's skirts. Hyacinth, on the other hand, stood on the platform beside Alistair, watching with a look on her face that suggested she wasn't at all surprised by what had happened.

A fist clenched around Aurelia's stomach. Just a few hours earlier, Hyacinth had refused to attend the ball, but wouldn't give a reason for it. Now, too late, Aurelia understood.

V

"How is he?"

The royal medic, a Sadian man named Bodren, sighed. He didn't say anything for a moment as he wiped his sweaty hands on a washcloth. Aurelia's heart pounded as she looked over his shoulder at where Arian lay in bed, hands folded over his stomach, while Reyna sat in a chair beside him and set her hands over his.

"He's stable, for now." Bodren grimaced as he held up a small vial of blood he'd taken from Arian's arm. "There are plenty of mages at the palace—I'll ask one of them to examine His Lordship's blood for any signs of poison or illness. He has no injuries, and his symptoms are rather atypical. It could be any number of afflictions. We'll know more once his blood has been analyzed. For now, it's just a matter of keeping an eye on him and maintaining his comfort."

Beside Aurelia in the doorway, Jack folded his arms over his chest. "That's the most you can tell us? You don't have any definitive explanations?"

"None I'd stake my life on, Your Highness. I'm sorry."

Aurelia gnawed on the inside of her cheek. "The Silent Death is currently plaguing Glacier Bay. This isn't—?"

"Heavens, no." Bodren dabbed at the beads of sweat on his forehead with the cloth. "That particular epidemic is easy to identify. His Lordship wouldn't be the only person infected at the ball, either. Whatever this is, it's contained. I don't have any reason to believe it's contagious. It may be a result of something he consumed, or of a disease that's been slowly eating away at him from the inside. Again, I'll have a more definitive explanation when his blood has been tested."

Aurelia sighed. "All right. Take that to be examined at once."

Bodren nodded and bowed. "Of course, Your Grace."

When he left, Aurelia glanced over at Arian once more. Jack and Rayan, among others, had carried Arian's limp body to his temporary bedchamber after Bodren confirmed he was still breathing. While Aurelia, Jack, and Reyna stayed with Arian as Bodren examined him, Rayan had left to announce that the party was over, and the guests were urged back to their rooms. Fortunately, most of the guests were staying in a different wing of the palace, so the halls surrounding Arian's room had been silent while Bodren worked.

She tore her eyes from Arian to meet Jack's gaze. "Where are the girls?"

"Lu took them to Sisi's room. I don't know if she's gotten them to sleep, or if she's still trying to calm them down. Sisi was rather stoic about everything, but Halle couldn't stop weeping once she started."

Aurelia winced. "We shouldn't have let them stay so long, anyway, but...I think Hyacinth knew this was going to happen. This has to be the reason she tried to stay in her room tonight."

"I'd assume so." He exhaled and bent down to peck her on the cheek. "I might as well go relieve Lucyra. I'll see you later."

When he left, she took a deep breath and strode over to Arian's bed. She knelt beside Reyna, worry creasing her brows, as the Golden Queen refused to peel her eyes from Arian. Tears stained her cheeks, creating trails through her makeup, and her chin was trembling like she couldn't will her cheeks to stop chattering.

Aurelia had never seen her ally so vulnerable before. She thought she had, but now...

"Your Majesty." Aurelia cleared her throat when her voice cracked. "You should get some rest. We both need it. I'll have Rayan or Lucyra stay with him for a few hours. We may have an answer by the time we wake in the morning."

Reyna refused to peel her eyes from Arian. "Thank you for being so calm. I don't know how you're managing it, but...but it's keeping me from losing the run of myself, so thank you."

Aurelia didn't say it aloud, but the only reason she wasn't screaming from the balcony was because she was still too shocked to fully comprehend what was happening. Her beloved uncle had collapsed in the middle of her party, seemingly for no rhyme or reason, and the Folly's best medic couldn't figure out what had happened to him. Arian was one of the most powerful people alive, and yet, he was unconscious in a sickbed, gray and burning up, while everyone around him was helpless to aid in his recovery.

"I've known him for eight-and-thirty years. I was just a girl when we met." When Reyna spoke again, fresh tears rolled down her cheeks. "Do you know why I asked him to be my Hand?"

"He told me once, but I'm betting your reason is different than what I'm thinking of."

That made her smile. "Maybe. I never understood why my father sent Arian and his father to Akkinor. It was odd, since our countries were never exactly friends. I think my father was hoping for a future with Akkinor, but your grandfather was too wary to commit to it. Edmund the Elder liked Arian and Lord Dyron tremendously, and he wanted them at his disposal, but he wasn't ready for an alliance with Taundosa. Neither was your father when he took the throne, for whatever reason. But when Arian returned home after Lord Dyron's death, and he spoke of the many great things he'd learned in Akkinor...It wasn't just that he was a strong leader with experiences that set him apart. It was because I could see in his eyes that his hopes and dreams for the future of Taundosa—and the realm—were the same as mine."

Aurelia's eyes welled with tears as she watched Arian's chest rise and fall. "He loves your country with everything in his soul."

"He loves Akkinor the same way. That's how I knew he was the best choice for my Lord Hand: he opened his heart to everyone, to every possibility, to every adventure. I knew he would help me lead Taundosa to greatness—not only in Carthe, but in the realm as a whole. That, and..."

Aurelia smiled a bit. "What is it?"

"He was the only highborn in Taundosa who spoke to me like I was his equal. Everyone else spoke to me like I was a child—because I was one, even if I was a queen, too." Reyna sighed as Aurelia nodded in understanding. Sometimes, she forgot Reyna had only been fourteen when she was crowned. "If it weren't for him, none of us would be here today. Taundosa and Akkinor never would've become allies. You might not have reclaimed your throne or released your dragon, and the realm would be exactly the same as it was a thousand years ago."

"He's the root of everything, isn't he?"

"The heart and soul of the realm." Reyna sniffled as she finally met Aurelia's eyes. "I've always known he'd go before me, but I never quite prepared myself for this. I-I thought I'd have more time with him."

Aurelia took her hands and squeezed. "He'll be all right. I know he will. Whatever this is, he'll prevail as he always has. Arian Cristos has been through more than most people can even dream of—this won't be enough to bring him down. I have to believe that."

"And if he doesn't recover?"

Aurelia flinched, and judging by the way Reyna's eyes flashed, her fellow queen had noticed that she didn't fully believe her own words.

"If he doesn't recover..." Aurelia bit the insides of her cheeks to keep from crying. "We shall work together to find a new normal. He brought us together for a reason, and that reason wasn't merely to help me reclaim my throne. Whatever happens, we'll help each other through it. We have to."

Reyna squeezed her hands before turning back to Arian. "I should like to stay with him."

Aurelia nodded as a thickness coated her throat. "Of course."

She left the queen in Arian's bedchamber, and as soon as she closed the door behind her, she released a shaky exhale that quickly transformed into a choked sob. She covered her mouth with her hand so Reyna wouldn't hear, but a part of her knew it was too late for that.

As tears clouded her vision, she leaned against the wall and tried to ease her racing thoughts. She didn't want to think about what might happen if Arian died. It was exactly as Reyna had said: he was the heart and soul of the realm, and she wasn't prepared to see what it would become without him.

***

Lucyra massaged her temples. "Tell me about the different species again."

Aurelia glowered at her. "We've been through this ten times, Lu."

"And I don't think you're getting it. Tell me again."

Aurelia gritted her teeth. In an effort to distract herself from Arian's mysterious affliction—which still hadn't been explained, even two days later—Aurelia asked Lucyra to resume her lessons on dragonkind. Nearly every guest had left the palace by then, save Reyna and the Bozari lords, after Aurelia requested privacy while Arian received care under her roof. She'd put her duties on hold, temporarily, so everyone's attention was focused on helping her uncle; unfortunately, Aurelia herself couldn't do much to help.

While she waited for an update, she and Lucyra sat at a small table in the palace library, mulling over ancient books, scrolls, and pages upon pages of notes. It was the only thing Aurelia could think of that would wrack her brain enough to serve as a decent distraction, but so far, all it had accomplished was making her bicker with her cousin.

"There are four species of dragons: the ironwing, the vipertail, the longbelly, and the steelspike," Aurelia said. "The species can mate with one another, but it's impossible for their offspring to be a combination of both species. They're born as one or another."

"You're forgetting another major detail. *Again.*"

Aurelia gave her a sharp look. "What is it?"

"Dragons are categorized by three aspects of their being: their physical characteristics, their color, and their elemental specialty. You've forgotten the latter two every time we sit down for our lessons. I know you know this, Aurelia."

It came back to her as soon as she heard the categories. "Right. Dragons come in seven colors: sapphire, violet, silver, amber, emerald, scarlet, and black. Silver, scarlet, and amber are the rarest. Sapphire, violet, and silver are the strongest. Black, emerald, and amber are the weakest."

"What's Halvor, then?"

"A sapphire steelspike."

"*And?*"

Aurelia resisted the urge to throttle her. "A fire dragon. Obviously."

"The intruders that visited the Folly last season. Do you remember what species they were?"

"The large one is a violet...vipertail?" she offered. Lucyra nodded. "We think it's an air dragon, but we're not sure. And we don't know what element the little one is, but it's an emerald ironwing."

"Try again."

"Longbelly?"

"Exactly. Why should you be worried about them?"

Aurelia pondered that for a moment. "Vipertails have poisonous spikes on their tails. There's no antidote for their poison. Violet dragons are the most easily offended, too. And while longbellies are much smaller than others—and longer than they are tall or wide—they're the fastest species. Emerald dragons are among the weakest, because they're easily spooked."

"And why should *they* be worried about *you?*"

"Steelspikes like Halvor have the strongest body armor. They're heavier and slower than the others, but three times as strong—practically invincible compared to their kin. And sapphire dragons are the most intelligent and loyal of the entire race. They're most lethal when they have someone to protect. And, of course, his element is the most dangerous one."

Lucyra pointed to an illustration on the book splayed out before them. "What about *them?*"

The illustration featured one of the modern day's tiny, mutated dragons. "Dragons common to today's world were the last to hatch during or after the persecution," Aurelia replied. "Because fire dragons are the strongest, they prevailed longer than the others. The last of them were found protecting their eggs. After they were slaughtered, humans stole the clutches of eggs and mutated the hatchlings. Every clutch belonging to dragons of other elements had already been destroyed by then. So, today, the domesticated dragons common around the realm are connected to fire magic, even if their power is exceptionally weak."

"Good. Now, let's get back to—"

"Your Grace."

Both women gasped, alarmed, when a voice rang out to Aurelia's right. She hadn't heard the door open, but Rayan was standing a few feet away from the table, hands clasped behind his back and a stoic expression etched onto his face.

Aurelia stood immediately and rushed over to him. "What news?"

Rayan grimaced. "Bodren would like to speak with you."

She nodded, her heart pounding against her ribcage, and followed him out of the library. Lucyra scampered after them, clutching her notebook, and asked question after question that Rayan didn't have the answers to.

The trio joined Bodren, Jack, Reyna, and Edom—perched on Jack's shoulder—in the hallway outside of Arian's bedchamber. When he spotted Aurelia, Bodren removed his foggy spectacles and wiped them on his tunic. Clearly, whatever news he had, he wasn't expecting her to take it well.

"Bodren." Aurelia raised an eyebrow when she stopped in front of him. "What's happened?"

"I asked three different mages—Lord Zhaaran, Lord Chilton, and one of your handmaidens—to examine His Lordship's blood sample, just to be sure." The medic looked between everyone around him while he spoke, beads of sweat dripping down the sides of his face. "It doesn't appear to be poison or an illness of any kind. In fact, all three of them found traces of dark magic in His Lordship's blood."

Lucyra, gulping, rushed to aid her mortal friends when she saw their confusion: "A mage can detect the presence of any foreign entities in human or animal blood. They can observe things that can't be seen with the naked eye—the mortal eye. Poison would look like a fog or something cloudy floating in the sample. Illnesses look like shattered glass, but the pattern is different for each individual affliction. Dark magic, on the other hand, presents itself as blackness, like splotches of spilled ink."

"It's hard to miss," Bodren added, nodding. "It would appear someone placed a curse on His Lordship. I'm just a mortal, so I can't tell you what the curse is or who cast it. You'll need a few mages to spend some time with him if you wish to know more. He's still stable, and as long as he receives proper care, he'll remain as such until the curse is broken."

Reyna's eyes fell shut. "And if it can't be broken?"

"Well..." Bodren sighed. "It doesn't appear that the curse was meant to kill him. If that were true, he'd be dead already, or I'd have found evidence of severe damage to his physical form. His suffering when he collapsed was likely a result of the curse taking hold, but I suspect that was the worst of it. If the curse isn't broken, he'll survive, but he'll have no quality of life. He'll require constant care."

Aurelia brought a hand to her throbbing forehead. This couldn't be right. Arian Cristos was perhaps the kindest, most merciful, most understanding person alive in the realm—why would anyone want to curse him? And more than that, why would anyone want him in a comatose state?

"Maybe we can convince Lord Zhaaran to stay a little while longer." Jack tilted his head to look down at Edom. "Go find him. See what he thinks about that." Edom nodded and zipped off in a stream of golden light while Jack turned to the others. "I'll send a raven to the monastery. They have plenty of mages to spare—mages who also happen to be medics. I'll ask that a few of them be temporarily reassigned to the palace to look after Arian."

"I'll send word to Taundosa, Your Majesty," Rayan said to Reyna. "Your husband and your advisors will be needing to hear about this."

She nodded. "Thank you."

When he and Jack left, Bodren cleared his throat. "I'll prepare a set of instructions regarding His Lordship's care. I have other duties to attend to, unfortunately, but you know where to find me."

"Thank you, Bodren," Aurelia said. "You've been so wonderful." He tipped his head in gratitude, bowed, and took his leave. As soon as he disappeared around the corner, Aurelia locked eyes with Reyna, who looked like she hadn't slept in weeks. "You need to rest, my friend. I'll look after him."

Lucyra coughed into her fist. "You have an audience with the Assembly in twenty minutes."

Aurelia cursed. She'd completely forgotten about that. "All right. Well—"

"I'll stay with him." Lucyra smiled weakly and gestured to her notebook. "I'll read to him for a bit. He's always loved my stories."

Aurelia took her hand and squeezed. "Thank you."

"No thanks are necessary. He's my family, too."

Reyna sighed. "He's family to everyone who knows him."

VI

Your hyacinths seem to be doing well." Rayan peered out the window over the kitchen counter at the flowers decorating the yard behind the cottage. "You still haven't told me why you love them so much."

"They were shown to me by an old friend. I've adored them ever since."

"Hmm." Rayan turned, planting his hands on either side of the counter behind him, and gestured toward his father with his chin. "Would you like some help?"

Eric smiled as he swept dust into a pile on the floor. "I'm all right, son. Thank you." He ran a hand through his short gray hair and paused while clutching the broomstick to his chest. "My neighbor looked after the cottage and the yard while I was gone, but I can't manage it by myself anymore. Ginny's only staying for another week or so before she goes back to Holos. What with you being so busy nowadays, I think I may need to hire an extra set of hands. That, or..."

Rayan raised an eyebrow. "That's your meddling voice. What is it?"

"I was wondering if you might send the children to stay with me. I know they must be enjoying life in the palace, but Elderhost is their home, and I don't get to see much of them now that—"

"Father...I may not be able to claim my children as my own in public, but at least we can live under the same roof. The queen has jumped through hoops to accommodate us at the palace. Just because their mother is dead doesn't mean I'm going to ship them off to live with someone else."

Eric's pale blue eyes hardened. "You wouldn't be shipping them off to be shoeshiners or milkmaids. They'd just be helping me with some of my chores. I'm not getting any younger, you know."

"I know that. I'll hire someone trustworthy to lend you a hand, but I'm not sending my children away." Rayan sighed. "They're getting older, too, and as much as they love you, they won't want to be cooped up here.

They've made friends with the other children living in the palace. They have routines and lessons. We can't hold them back."

Eric's shoulders slumped. "All right. It was just a thought." He paused to look over his shoulder at the grandfather clock in the corner of the room. "Ginny should be back from the market within the hour. Do you have time to wait for her? It's been too long since I had both of my children in the same room, and she's leaving in a week."

"I know. You've already told me." Rayan flicked his gaze to the clock, too. "I only have a few more minutes before I'm needed at the palace. I'll try to come back before she leaves, but I can't promise anything."

Eric's eyes flashed with displeasure, but he didn't reply. He merely exhaled, clenched his jaw, and started sweeping again. Rayan watched him for a moment, debating between conversation and silence, before choosing the latter and redirecting his attention to the flowers in the yard once more.

A part of him wondered if he was being too hard on his father. Eric was two-and-sixty now—not considered terribly old for an Akkinorian, but lately, he seemed to be having some trouble with his memory. Rayan hadn't seen the signs for himself until today when he visited his father's house in the Follian town of Elderhost. For the last three years, Eric had been living in Holos with Rayan's sister and her family, as they'd needed an extra set of hands around the house after the birth of their fourth child.

Even so, it was a bit difficult for Rayan to have sympathy for Eric. He loved his father, of course, but they'd always had something of a rocky relationship. It wasn't Rayan's fault: Eric had been a bit of a brute when his children were growing up. That, and he'd been absent from their lives for over a year when Rayan was a young boy.

But that was another issue, of course. Eric (and Rayan's late mother, Cordelia, for that matter) claimed his absence hadn't been his fault. When Rayan was four, a fire broke out in their house while Eric was working the nightshift as a guard at the Holosi bank. Both of Eric's elderly parents perished in the blaze while Rayan, Ginny, and Cordelia managed to escape—but only barely. Cordelia, carrying both children with what little strength she had left, managed to stumble over to a neighbor's house before collapsing on their doorstep. Rayan and Ginny had already fallen unconscious because of smoke inhalation.

Luckily for them, the home belonged to a pair of mages. The family awoke days after the fire to find themselves healed without so much as a burn left behind. They'd promised not to utter a word about the mages' abilities (mages were still in hiding back then) before returning home to see what was left of it—and to find Eric.

Eric was nowhere to be found for seasons, so Cordelia decided to move away and begin anew. When Eric returned over a year later, he shared his side of the story: he'd returned home to find nothing but smoldering remains and charred bones in the rubble. He'd assumed his entire family was dead, and, in his grief, fled to start a new life somewhere else. He never told his family where he went, but after finding out they'd survived the fire when an old friend sent word, he returned to Akkinor and reunited with them like nothing had happened.

Neither Cordelia nor Ginny had ever resented Eric for leaving, but Rayan did. He thought it was a great dishonor for Eric to leave so soon after the accident. If he'd made more of a fuss about losing his entire family, the neighbors who'd taken them in would've heard about it and told him they'd survived. That, and Eric hadn't so much as hosted a memorial for his family after believing they'd perished.

Rayan didn't like to say that he was ashamed of his father, but everyone knew he felt it—Eric included. They hadn't spoken of the tension between them in years; if they did, it wouldn't end well. It never did.

Ginny's voice in the back of Rayan's head, telling him to have some empathy for their poor father, prompted him to break the silence: "Father?"

"Hmm?"

"If you're interested," he said slowly, "I can speak with Her Grace about hosting you at the palace before Ginny leaves. We can have dinner together, and I'll give you a tour of the grounds."

Eric's face brightened. "I would love that."

"Good. It'll have to wait a bit, though. The Lord Hand of Taundosa collapsed at the queen's ball earlier this week, so there's a bit of disarray at the palace right now. We'll give it a few days so things can calm down, but—"

"Arian Cristos?" Eric stopped sweeping, eyes widening, as his strong grip on the broomstick made his knuckles turn white. "He's still the Lord Hand of Taundosa, isn't he?"

"That's right."

"Oh." Eric's gaze lowered to stare into nothingness. "Is he going to be all right?"

"I don't know, but he's stable, for now." Rayan furrowed his brows. "Why do you look like that?"

"Like what?"

"Worried."

"I just...well..."

Rayan folded his arms over his chest. "Spit it out."

"Mind your cheek, boy. You may be Hand of the Queen, but that doesn't give you the right to disrespect your father," Eric snapped. For some reason, that made Rayan smile. As much as his younger self resented Eric's authoritative parenting style, he was relieved to find that Eric's older age hadn't completely changed him. "I was, erm, *acquainted* with Arian Cristos many years ago. We met when I was...away."

After you abandoned us, Rayan thought. "Were you friends?"

No response to that. "I'd heard he's been spending more time in Akkinor since the alliance with Taundosa was formed, of course, but I suppose I never thought much of it. Now that you're Hand of the Queen, and you're probably spending so much time with him...It's odd, isn't it? The coincidence."

"I suppose it is."

"Well, if the opportunity ever presents itself, maybe I'll find a way to see him. It's been far—oh, look!" Having spotted something through the window behind Rayan, Eric dropped the broom to the floor and bolted across the cottage. It didn't seem like he remembered what he'd been saying not five seconds earlier. "Come on!"

Rayan exhaled and reluctantly followed his father out of the cottage. They weren't the only people gathered on the streets. Half of the townspeople had left their homes to catch a glimpse of the magnificent sight soaring overhead: the queen's blue-and-gold dragon, Halvor, who stood almost as tall as his mistress's grand palace.

Eric craned his neck back to stare at the dragon. A small, contented smile formed on his lips as his pale blue eyes followed the creature's path. He always had a certain look about him whenever he saw Halvor parting the clouds—as if he were a little boy again, finally seeing his favorite story brought to life.

"I knew someone once," Eric murmured.

He paused for so long that Rayan couldn't tell if that was the end of his statement. Eric had been speaking strangely like this all day, as if his body couldn't keep up with everything his mind wanted to say.

Rayan chuckled. "Did you?"

Eric ignored him. "She believed so strongly in the existence of dragons in the modern age that I, too, felt compelled to believe in it for the first time in my life." He laughed, eyes nearly disappearing beneath his lashes with the force of his chuckle. "I can see her now, saying *I told you so* to everyone she knows. She's gloating about it, that clever girl."

Smirking, Rayan asked, "Who was this clever girl of yours, Father? Was it Mother? Or a lover from your teenage years, perhaps?"

"No, no..." Eric's expression grew somber and distant, like he couldn't remember where—or when—he was. "She was someone I knew many years ago, back when her dreams were the closest we ever came to experiencing such wonder."

He gazed at the dragon for a moment longer before closing his eyes. He was still and silent for so long that Rayan debated setting a hand on his shoulder to make sure he was all right. Just as Rayan lifted his arm to do so, Eric erupted in a grin and chuckled before speaking again:

"Oh, yes. Wherever she is, she's enjoying this as much as I am. I can feel it."

Rayan smiled a bit. "I'm sure she'd like to share this experience with you, even if it's been years since you saw her last. Perhaps you might find her so you can admire Halvor together."

No reply. Eric merely stood there, swaying a bit, with his eyes still closed and the grin still beaming on his lips. Rayan's eyes flicked down to his father's side, where Eric's hand was slightly outstretched and his fingers were twiddling, as if attempting to grasp something that wasn't there.

"No need." Eric's grin morphed into a soft smile as he finally opened his eyes. "She's always right here with me."

***

"I'll be the first one to say it." Balor Zhoqa, the Bozari Lord of Kazamir, shook his head and scoffed as he filled a chalice with wine. "I've had enough to do with curses for a lifetime."

Aurelia sighed as he collapsed on the opposite end of the couch she was sitting on. Jack stood behind her, hands planted on the backrest, while Reyna paced across the parlor in front of the hearth. Jalhor Zhaaran, the Bozari Lord of Orestes, took up the entire couch across from Aurelia so he could elevate his aching feet.

Balor raised an eyebrow as he gulped from his chalice. "Who's with him now?"

"Our cousin. Lucyra," Aurelia replied. "Rayan will relieve her when he returns from his outing. Hopefully, the medics from the monastery will arrive within the next two days, so they can look after him instead." She turned to the other nobleman. "Could you detect anything regarding the curse when you visited him, Jalhor?"

It felt strange to refer to him by his given name, even over a year after the two lords had given her permission to do so. Apparently, they'd always secretly preferred being called by their given names—just like Aurelia—

and they felt it was high time the allies started treating each other like friends.

"Not quite," Jalhor said. "There seems to be some sort of a blockage preventing us from further examination. Think of it like a fog restricting your view of the city. Whoever did this went to great lengths to keep the curse's nature from being identified. When the mages arrive from the monastery, it'll take all of us working together to remove the blockage."

Jack sighed. "All right. He collapsed during the ball, which more than likely means that the individual responsible was here at the same time. Even if the guests stayed after the incident, there were too many of them for us to interview. Most of them would've thrown fits if they knew they were suspects, too. We've tasked some of our creatures with gathering intel, so it shouldn't be long before they return."

Aurelia winced. She didn't like the idea of spying on her own subjects—and her foreign guests, for that matter—but it had to be done. Edom, along with a handful of nymphs and other sprites, had left to acquire information immediately after Bodren confirmed that Arian had been cursed. It wasn't the most honorable thing to do, but in this situation, she didn't have much of a choice.

"I don't think we'll find anything." Reyna spoke for the first time since the allies gathered in the parlor. "I-I didn't think anything of it before, but he was acting a bit strange even before we departed Taundosa. He was awfully...*itchy.*"

Aurelia could hear the frown in Jack's voice when he said, "Itchy?"

"Yes. Itchy."

Jalhor exhaled and pinched the bridge of his nose. "Itchiness can be a side effect of magic," he told Aurelia and Jack. "Young mages in training often experience excessive itchiness while they're familiarizing themselves with their power. We don't experience it after we've come of age and connected ourselves to our abilities, though—unless we're affected somehow by strong external magic." His violet eyes focused on Aurelia. "Had you used the moon goddess's amulet three years ago, I would've known: not because I would've felt its powers of compulsion restricting my free will, but because it would've made me itch like I was crawling with scabies."

Jack, now sitting on the armrest beside Aurelia, raised an eyebrow. "So, you're saying someone cursed him before he left Carthe? How can that be? Anyone with a grudge against him probably wouldn't be able to access him in Taundosa—he's too protected. Is it possible that the curse was enacted from a distance?"

"It is," the elder nobleman replied. "A strong mage can cast a spell—and curses are considered spells, mind you—on any individual in the realm, so long as they have everything they need to do it. There are three requirements: the spell must be recited exactly as it's written; the caster must audibly state the exact moment they wish for the spell to take effect; and they must burn something that belonged to or touched the person they're cursing, both to ensure they reach the right target, and as an offering to the gods. There are no restrictions when it comes to the distance between the caster and their target, as long as those requirements are met."

"How could our caster have come to possess something that belonged to him?" Balor demanded. "Only those closest to him could manage that, and anyone who knows Arian Cristos personally would have no reason to do this."

Aurelia turned to Reyna, who was still pacing. "Is there any tension between Arian and his fellow Taundosan lords?"

The Golden Queen's eyes hardened. "If there were, I would've diffused that tension as soon as it arose. I have no patience for petty squabbling between my nobles. They know that."

"Who else could've gotten close enough to take something that belongs to him?" Jack pressed. "Other than his fellow lords, and those of us in this room, I can't—"

"A letter," Aurelia blurted. All eyes turned in her direction. "That counts, doesn't it? After all, if he wrote and sent a letter, he would've touched it more than once. Maybe someone he wrote to is responsible for this, or they intercepted a message meant for someone else."

Balor shrugged as he stood to refill his chalice. "That's the most plausible theory I can think of, too. If that's the *how*, then we just need the *who* and the *why*."

"Wait a minute." Reyna stilled as her round, vibrant eyes widened. "We left two days after he returned home from visiting Diantha in Dofell. I saw him scratch at his arms on the night he returned to the palace. He has bouts of eczema every once in a while, so I didn't think much of it or put it together until now. I should've known as soon as we started talking today—his eczema never makes him itch as much as he has been lately."

"That's not a bad theory, either," Jalhor offered. "If I cast a spell right now, that doesn't necessarily mean it'll take effect immediately. It's like I said before: the caster must state when they wish for the spell's effects to take place. The moment a mage casts a spell on another person, the spell connects to their target, but it isn't activated until the moment of the caster's choosing."

Jack's face paled. "You don't think Diantha—?"

"Gods, no." It was Reyna who spoke, nervously chewing on her bottom lip. "But she's had people from across the continent living in Dofell for over two years now. I personally sent a few hundred volunteers from Taundosa to help rebuild the kingdom. I know the two of you sent laborers, too," she said, directing her last sentence at the Bozari lords. They nodded to confirm. "Kanibar hasn't contributed—King Harryn knows the Dofelli are still suspicious of the Kanish after Willem's attempted conquest—but I'm not sure about Krotis. Arian's the only person who would know."

Aurelia sighed. She knew exactly where this conversation was going.

"Diantha might know something," Jalhor mumbled. "He was in Dofell right before he started itching. Maybe someone who holds a grudge against him saw him there. She'll know who he interacted with and where he went while he was there. If he was being watched, too, then maybe someone followed him into Dofell—her soldiers are still taking the names of everyone who enters and exits the kingdom, so if they spotted anyone suspicious trailing him, they might be able to provide us with a name."

Balor snorted. "A fake name, most likely."

"It's a start, at least."

Aurelia, gazing off into nothingness, snapped her gaze up when she felt Reyna's eyes burning holes through her skull. She resisted the urge to exhale—again, she knew exactly what was going to be suggested.

"Your Grace," Reyna murmured, "it'll take us weeks to get back to Carthe. We can't know for certain if Arian will hang on that long. We need a conversation with Diantha, not an exchange of written words, so sending ravens back and forth wouldn't do us much good. I think—"

"You want me to take Halvor to Dofell," Aurelia finished.

Reyna sighed. "Yes."

Aurelia offered her a painful smile. "We'll leave tomorrow."

VII

As promised, Aurelia met Halvor in the gardens the following night to depart for Dofell. Her allies didn't see them off, but her family did. As Halvor catapulted himself into the sky, Aurelia looked down at the gardens below and smiled when she saw Jack and their six children waving at her. It was funny: every other infant in the Folly shrieked in unison as soon as Halvor roared from the sky, but Aurelia's babies didn't make a peep.

Aurelia and Halvor weren't alone on their flight. Edom had returned earlier that day—with no news to share after spending the last few days spying on Myran nobles—and she knew she had to take it along. While she spoke with Diantha, the sprite could sneak around Dofell in search of any suspicious figures.

There was a small, uninhabited island in the middle of the Alkamura Ocean where Aurelia and Halvor normally stopped to rest during flights to and from Carthe, but she didn't bother with it this time. She needed to get back to Arian and her allies as quickly as possible; that, and she'd felt more awake than ever since her uncle collapsed. It was like her body refused to succumb to exhaustion while he was vulnerable—like she couldn't stop, even for a moment, until she found a way to help him.

She hadn't bothered sending a raven to Dofell to inform Diantha of her visit, either. Diantha would have enough of a warning as soon as she saw Halvor's silhouette among the clouds.

As they flew, Aurelia kept her eyes peeled for the two mysterious, unclaimed dragons. Neither of them had been spotted in weeks. Until she knew why they'd visited Akkinor, though, it was in her best interest to be prepared for absolutely anything—like a sneak attack while she was in the sky.

After about a day of flying, they reached the eastern coast of Carthe, soaring directly above the port province of Khaba and the kingdom of Bozar. Halvor flew lower and lower as they got closer to their destination, and soon enough, they found themselves directly above the border of Dofell and Taundosa.

During the battle three years ago, the allies had destroyed a portion of the massive stone walls separating the neighboring kingdoms. They assumed Diantha would opt to take the walls down in their entirety, but so far, she'd only demolished a few segments. It wasn't ideal, but at the very least, travelers didn't have to cross the treacherous Ngora Valley desert to reach one half of Carthe from the other anymore.

Aurelia had heard stories about Dofell's reparations since she was last here, but this was the first time she was seeing everything with her own eyes. She peered down at the kingdom below, lips parting in shock, as she observed the miracles enacted by Dofell's new Almighty deity—the moon goddess, Edea—who'd broken the curse that had turned the kingdom into a pit of despair.

What was once brown, brittle grass was now lush and green. There hadn't been a single flower in Dofell when Aurelia first visited eight years ago, and now, the terrain was practically overrun by them. The trees, formerly dead and leafless like they were trapped in an endless winter, bloomed in shades of juniper and amber. The houses and establishments—which had once been roofless, shutterless, rendered lopsided from mudslides, and composed of termite-eaten wood—were standing upright with intact roofs, shutters on the windows, and pristine planks of wood. The only paths or roads Aurelia recalled were nothing but muddy trails, and now, strips of cobblestone connected every structure and every territory.

They'd done more than enough to establish Edea as their most worshipped deity, too. Anything that once bore the symbol of Myenar— the scales of judgment—like banners and carvings on wood, had been altered to display the moon instead. The streets were quieter than Aurelia remembered, but that made sense: according to Diantha's letters, most of Dofell had turned to being more active at nighttime.

Dofell—now referred to as *the City of Refuge*—had become one of the loveliest places in Carthe in just three short years, all because of Diantha and the moon goddess.

There was nowhere for Halvor to land other than atop the walls surrounding the palace. As he situated himself and lowered his wing so Aurelia could climb down, she spotted a few individuals from the corner of her eye. They were lingering by the palace's front steps, watching, but nobody appeared surprised by the intrusion.

The only face Aurelia recognized was Diantha. The Queen of Dofell stood in front of the group, hands daintily clasped over her midriff, with the barest hint of a smile playing on her lips. She looked exactly as she had when Aurelia saw her last, but nothing like she had when the pair first met.

The Diantha Pharos who'd first walked into Reyna's palace, unaware of what her future held, had been painfully thin, sallow, covered in filth, and wearing tattered rags. She clearly hadn't bathed in weeks, and it hadn't seemed to bother her in the slightest. *This* Diantha Pharos, however, was the epitome of grace and beauty. Her sleek black hair was knotted in a tight bun on the back of her head, her tanned skin was polished and clean, and her dark brown eyes were bold against the lilac pigment on her lids. She wore a beautiful gown that matched the powder on her eyes, with billowing sleeves and a loose, flowing skirt. The blush on her cheeks hadn't been painted on, either—it was just her natural flush now that she was eating properly, sleeping enough, and, well, *happy.*

"Your Grace." Diantha's smooth voice rang out before Aurelia was halfway to the front steps. Only as she walked toward Diantha did Aurelia realize Edom had disappeared—likely already scouring the kingdom for suspicious persons. "I wasn't expecting you, but I'm pleased to have you here. It's been too long."

"Yes, it has." Aurelia smiled when she met the queen on the steps. "Forgive me for barging in unannounced. There's been a bit of an incident, and we could use your help."

"'We?'" Diantha looked around, frowning, as Halvor lifted into the sky. "I don't see anyone else."

"My allies opted to stay in Akkinor. They couldn't manage such a long flight."

Diantha chuckled. "Of course. Well, I'm glad to have you here, even if you haven't come for a more joyous reason." She cleared her throat and gestured to the people behind her. "Allow me to make a few introductions. This is Aesin Pharellos, my Lord Hand, and Erinya Phaero, my Lady Hand. I thought having two of them would make things a bit easier for me."

The two Hands either bowed or curtsied in response to Aurelia's greeting as Diantha turned to the four others. "This is my husband, Aerodos Pytheon, and our children. Princess Jethya is next in line for the throne."

"It's lovely to meet you," Aurelia mused as the royal children and their father greeted her with bows or curtsies. "I'm glad to see you're all doing so well here."

Princess Jethya, no older than ten, giggled at her. "You're very pretty."

Aurelia couldn't help but blush. "Thank you, Your Highness. As are you."

Diantha was smiling. "All right. You're dismissed. I'd like to chat with Queen Aurelia, and the lot of you aren't invited."

Aurelia laughed as the children whined. Their father—a quiet, sheepish looking man—asked them to accompany him on a walk around the grounds so they could watch Halvor. The two Hands whispered something to each other, eyeing Aurelia, but they seemed less suspicious of her and more intrigued by what she was doing in Dofell.

"You'll have to excuse Aesin and Erinya," Diantha said, as if she could read Aurelia's thoughts. She offered Aurelia her arm as they climbed the steps into the palace's foyer. "If I'm being transparent, neither of them are politicians. I worked with Aesin at the bank—he was a cleaner, too—and Erinya has been a friend of mine since childhood. There really isn't anyone left in Dofell who knows a thing about running the kingdom, so my only option was to pick a Hand I could trust with my life. I couldn't choose between them, and I needed all the help I could get, so now, my two closest advisors are former peasants like me."

Aurelia smiled. "I think that's lovely. My Lord Hand is lowborn, too, and he's one of the most admirable people I know. Status doesn't mean a thing anymore."

"It never should've meant anything, but that's the way of the world, I suppose."

Diantha brought them into a parlor, where a servant was leaving a tray of tea, biscuits, and fruits on a table. Aurelia had been right to assume that Diantha had seen her coming.

As the pair sat, Diantha poured them both a cup of tea. "What brings you here? You're ten shades paler than you were the last time I saw you, and you've been fidgeting with your fingers like a child who can't sit still during lessons."

Aurelia's face warmed. She hadn't realized she'd been doing it, but when she looked down at her lap, she saw that Diantha was right.

She took a deep breath, accepted a teacup from Diantha, and explained everything. As she spoke, Diantha watched her intently, lips pursing in shock and confusion. By the time she finished, Diantha appeared to have shrunk into her chair, and her curious smile had been replaced by solemnness.

"Edea have mercy," Diantha murmured. "That's horrible. Unfortunately, I don't know how helpful I can be. I met Lord Cristos at the border and rode with him to the palace—he didn't interact with anyone other than me, my family, and my staff, and I can tell you with full certainty that none of them are responsible for this. I do, however, have numerous people from Espos and Krotis working in Dofell. I don't know which provinces the Kroti hail from, though. I received a letter from all five Kroti leaders about a year ago, along with four hundred volunteers, and they claimed it was their way of making amends for what happened here during the battle. More than half of Krotis stood by King Willem, if you recall."

Aurelia nodded. "That helps a bit, but it still doesn't give us a heading. Anyone could be responsible—Taundosans, Kanish, Kroti. Even Akkinorians or Isalders, for that matter." She sighed in defeat. "I'm sorry to waste your time."

"Not at all. I must insist that you stay the night and leave in the morning—I can tell you flew through the night, so I can't in good conscience let you leave until you've rested. While you're here, I'll have my men do some snooping. If anyone in this kingdom utters a word about Lord Cristos, we'll hear of it."

Aurelia released the breath she hadn't realized she'd been holding. "Thank you. But I must ask: why go through the trouble? I appreciate it, of course, but—"

"—but I'm under no obligation to make such efforts while I hold no alliances. I know." Diantha chuckled a bit. "We'll get to the matter of alliances later on, but to answer your question...I suppose I have something of a soft spot for Lord Cristos. He's always been so kind to me, and he's the only one of you who visits me every now and then. I don't mean that as an insult to you—I know how busy you are—but I do appreciate his friendship and thoughtfulness. If there's anything I can do to help him, I'll try my best to oblige. He deserves that much."

"Yes, he does." Aurelia tried to bury her disappointment by indulging in tea and biscuits, but it didn't work very well. "Thank you for trying."

"Of course. Now, there's something I've been meaning to write to you about, so I'll ask while I have you here. How fares the Phyre family now that they're living under your banners?"

"I wouldn't know," Aurelia admitted. "I had them settled in Sadia when we returned to Akkinor. King Elrin sent me a letter after I left them informing me that the entire family would be moving and changing their names. He didn't want me to be able to find them and offer them any sort of charity. He was rather persistent that his family make their own way, like everyone else, without any special treatment from the crown."

"He really hasn't written a word to you since?"

"Nothing. I couldn't find them if I wanted to. I couldn't even tell you if they're all still alive."

Diantha sighed. "That's a bit sad, but I suppose it's what they asked for. Did I tell you he left a letter for me when I ascended the throne?"

"No."

"He wished to aid in my transition as best he could, so he left a few tips for me. Of course, things are different now than they were when he sat the throne, but it was a kind gesture, regardless." She sipped from her teacup and raised an arched eyebrow. "Speaking of gestures...Have you given any thought to what I told you when last we spoke?"

A shiver traced Aurelia's spine. "Of course. You got inside my head."

She cracked a smile when Diantha guffawed. It was odd: the last time she'd seen Diantha, the Queen of Dofell had been a bit...enigmatic, if not slightly bitter and condescending. She'd said some cryptic things, and she'd phrased them in a way that made Aurelia feel like an ignorant fool. That was the very reason Aurelia had asked Lucyra to teach her more about dragonkind.

Diantha set the teacup down and leaned forward, elbows digging into the table. "And what have you learned?"

As best she could, Aurelia relayed her lessons with Lucyra to Diantha. She didn't know all that much—excluding the different species of dragonkind, how they were characterized, and what had become of them in the modern day—but it was more than she'd known three years ago.

When she finished, Diantha sat back in her chair and nodded. "That's all very good. Have you learned anything about dragonriding, though? That's the most important part. You'd be surprised at what doors open for you when you know exactly what it means to be a dragonrider—and the rider of your particular dragon, too."

Aurelia's eyebrows furrowed. "I'm afraid I don't understand. We haven't gotten to any material regarding dragonriding in our lessons yet, and everything my uncle told me about Halvor suggests that our connection is enough. Halvor is loyal to me, and I'm equally loyal to him. I've always assumed that's all there is to it."

"Nothing in life is that simple," Diantha reminded her. "Your connection assures three things: Halvor's loyalty to you, his ability to understand and carry out your commands, and his protection over those closest to you. But until you know him like you know yourself, you're still at risk."

"At risk of what, exactly?"

"Don't forget that dragons are wild animals, and don't mistake their loyalty for a lack of intelligence. There may come a day when you give him a command that he refuses to carry out—you may ask something of him that doesn't align with what he wants or believes. He's an ancient creature, so he's experienced more in his lifetime than you could possibly imagine. If you place him in a situation that reminds him of a past incident, you have no way of knowing how he might react or why he'd react in a certain way."

Aurelia chewed on her lower lip, contemplating. She knew what Diantha was trying to tell her, but she didn't understand how she was meant to follow the queen's instructions. She and Halvor were connected through their souls: they communicated through feelings, not through telepathic messages. As much as she wanted to do what Diantha urged her to, it wasn't like she could sit down and ask Halvor to tell her everything about his life.

Aurelia cleared her throat. "Have you any advice for me, then?"

"I've read about a way you can communicate with him directly, but everyone who's ever accomplished that is long dead, and they didn't leave instructions or journals behind that I've found. I assume it won't be easy, especially given everything else you have going on, but I think it's worth a shot. I'd try it myself if I could."

"Why would you want to try it?"

Diantha's lips pursed as panic flickered in her gaze, but it was gone when Aurelia blinked.

"The method I'm talking about isn't exclusive to dragonriders. It's something anyone can do, but only if they have certain resources at their disposal. I think it'd be interesting to..."

Aurelia stopped listening by then. She'd gotten distracted by Diantha's odd reaction to her question, and then by something else: the Pharos family's sigil on the banners hanging on either side of the parlor door. The base of the sigil was a deep violet, nearly black, and the animal stitched onto the fabric was a silver pig—symbolic of good fortune, abundance, community, and a long era of pig farming in the Pharos family's history.

It was the sigil's colors that caught her attention. She knew every sigil of every reigning noble family in the realm, and of the three purple sigils in existence, she'd never seen one so dark that it might be mistaken for black when placed against pure silver.

In fact, she'd only ever seen one thing in her lifetime with the same contrast of the same two colors, and that *thing* wasn't supposed to exist.

That's when the realization finally struck her, making her heart drop to her knees. Diantha had always been somewhat odd when it came to Halvor, and while she claimed she'd learned so much about dragons through ancient texts, Aurelia didn't know anyone else—even Arian or Lucyra—who knew as much as Diantha did about dragonkind. She didn't know anyone else who spoke so passionately about dragons, either.

Aurelia couldn't believe she hadn't seen the signs sooner.

"...to the dead, which is partly why there's so little information on this method," Diantha was saying. "Some consider it to be a form of necromancy, which is strictly prohibited for mages. Most spells in this particular area can only be found in the Book of Hega, and any mage who—"

"Stop." Aurelia's voice was barely a whisper, but it silenced Diantha, anyway. The Queen of Dofell frowned as Aurelia's eyes fluttered shut. "I'm going to ask you something, and I need you to tell me the truth."

"Of course."

She peeled her eyes open. "The violet vipertail is yours, isn't it?"

Diantha stilled. Her lips pursed, and her eyes widened in shock—or maybe just a touch of admiration.

"What gave it away?"

VIII

My father told me the story dozens of times when I was a girl." Diantha filled her teacup, and then Aurelia's, but with rum instead of tea. "I thought it was just a tall tale, even though he insisted on teaching me everything there was to know about dragons. Then I turned twelve, and for whatever reason, he decided it was time for me to know that it was more than a legend. He brought me to the very same cave from Aratus's story, and that's when I met Rieza for the first time. My father continued to care for her on his own until he died when I was nineteen. She's been mine ever since."

While explaining herself, Diantha had begun with a story Aurelia already knew: the tragic tale of Althaia Phyre. Three years ago, while searching for King Elrin's successor, Aurelia had come across a short biography about Althaia. She'd been the daughter of Ophelos Phyre III, King of Dofell, and was renounced by him as soon as he sired a son. She was sent away to be raised by another family, and she eventually married Aratus Pharos, a nobleman. When Dofell was cursed by their original Almighty god, Myenar, during the reign of Ophelos IV, Althaia and Aratus lost everything—including their only son.

While Althaia and Aratus were lost to history after being forced into peasantry, their young son, Aratus II, was left at an orphanage. Nobody knew what became of him after he was left there—nobody except for his direct descendants, the new reigning family of Dofell.

According to Diantha, a twist of fate led an adult Aratus to a cave on the eastern border of Dofell. There, he found an ancient violet vipertail, who'd woken from centuries of magic-induced hibernation when Aratus found her. She was destined to bond with him and his family, and after she saved his life, he dedicated his existence—and the lives of his descendants—to protecting her. Now, the dragon was Diantha's charge.

"My word." Aurelia swallowed the rum in her cup, quickly poured herself another drink, and fanned her sweating face with her other hand. "So, all those centuries while Halvor was hidden away in a land between worlds, Rieza was hibernating in the cave. I shouldn't be as surprised as I am, given what's happened in Akkinor recently with *our* magical creatures, but—"

"—but sprites and nymphs can hide themselves better than a dragon can," Diantha said with a chuckle. "I suppose the cave is what made the biggest difference. Hardly anyone ever travels to that side of Dofell. Everyone knows there's nothing there except for empty land and caves, but the caves don't lead anywhere, and they don't contain any valuable resources—they never have. The few souls who wandered into the cave quickly met their deaths. It's not like any of them had the chance to tell the world about a dragon of old hiding out there."

Aurelia understood that much. Since the reign of Ophelos IV, magic had all but gone extinct in Dofell, so even if someone *had* managed to tell others about spotting Rieza, it wasn't likely that they would've been believed.

She cleared her throat. "Why haven't you claimed her yet? She's been bonded to your family for generations now. She'd be a powerful asset for you."

"My father always told me that it isn't up to us to command a dragon to leave their sanctuary. He said she'd leave when she was ready, and it wasn't my place to ask such a thing of her if she didn't feel safe in the realm." Though her eyes shimmered with pity, a smile formed on her lips. "She left on her own not long after I took the throne. I thought about claiming her publicly, but...May I be frank?"

"Of course."

"I'm frightened," she admitted. "I've only been in this role for three years, and I know there are many who'd jump at the chance to claw at my power if I show any vulnerability. A dragon may be an unstoppable strength, but claiming responsibility over one makes us vulnerable in other ways. It draws attention to us."

Aurelia furrowed her eyebrows. "So, why are you telling me? You could've lied to protect yourself and Rieza."

That made Diantha's smile grow. "Because you were in the exact same position once. You understand how terrifying it is, and you're probably the only person alive who does. That, and...you're you. I know that if I ask you to keep this secret for me, and you give me your word, you'll stay true to it."

"Of course I will." Aurelia didn't hesitate. It may have placed her in a difficult position to keep this knowledge to herself, but like Diantha had said, she'd been here once before, too. "I don't think any harm will come to you or Rieza if you claim her, nor do I think anyone would dare to use this against you. But as long as you want this to stay between us, I'll respect your wishes."

Diantha's body appeared to deflate when she exhaled. "Thank you. I fear I may be forced to claim her sooner than I'd like to, though. She's left the cave on her own more times than I can count since I took the throne. She's a bit wilder than Halvor, you see, and has ignored my commands to stay put. I think she just misses the realm."

I'm sure she does after spending centuries in a cave, Aurelia thought. "Did you send her to Akkinor, or was that all her doing?"

"I had nothing to do with that." Diantha's voice, sharp and firm, didn't match the flicker of worry and uncertainty in her dark eyes. "She was following that little emerald longbelly, to my understanding."

Aurelia straightened up in her chair. "You don't happen to know anything about that one, do you?"

"I'm afraid not. I'm as curious as you are. Have you found anything?"

"Nothing."

"Rieza managed to follow it to Akkinor, but after it left your shores, she couldn't find it. I think it was a stroke of luck when she spotted it flying to Akkinor—she must've seen it while she was exploring outside the cave."

Aurelia raised an eyebrow. "Do you think it answers to anyone?"

"It must. Young dragons—especially emerald ones—are timid and easily spooked. I don't think it would've gone all the way to Akkinor, let alone any place that poses a threat, unless it'd been ordered to do so."

As she replayed that night in her head, she remembered something odd: it'd looked like Halvor and Rieza were fighting each other. She recalled the blast of power emitted by Rieza that'd blocked Halvor's flames like a magical shield, and the way Halvor had bellowed like he was ready to fly to war. He hadn't been so defensive against the emerald dragon, youngling or not, and the little one hadn't attempted to fight him in any way.

"Rieza is an air dragon, isn't she?" Aurelia asked. Diantha nodded, her lips curling into a smile, as Aurelia's eyes hardened. "I saw her use her power against Halvor. It looked like she was attacking him."

That made Diantha laugh. "You didn't do as much research as I thought."

"How do you mean?"

"If you did," the Queen of Dofell mused, "then you'd know they were only saying hello."

***

"And this," Diantha explained, "is our new symposium. The Phyres hadn't touched it in centuries because they didn't have anyone to meet with. When they lost everything, they were forced into solitude. This room was boarded up until we managed to pry the wood from the doors. We just finished cleaning it up last week."

Aurelia poked her head into the doorway of a massive, circular meeting room. The round table already had maps and things splayed over the surface, and it was surrounded by marble pillars that reminded Aurelia of the bars of a cell. An enormous crystal chandelier hung above the table, and the wall across from the entrance was gone, creating one massive window that overlooked the courtyard.

"This next room is my personal study, but I'm afraid it's a bit of a mess," Diantha continued, gesturing to another door in the hallway. "We're in the process of appointing new nobility. We've reestablished some of the old territories that fell when the curse struck, but we've created a few new ones, too. Unfortunately, I'm solely responsible for all of them. There's nobody beneath me other than my Hands to oversee those territories. Now that the people are growing stronger and more adept, I'll be conducting interviews so I can create a new hierarchy."

Aurelia could barely keep track of everything Diantha was telling her. She'd never been inside the Palace of Dofell, so she took Diantha's offer of a tour, but she hadn't expected the new queen to be so thorough.

After their conversation about Rieza the day before, they'd quickly realized how late it'd gotten, so Diantha ushered Aurelia to a guest room for the night. Aurelia hadn't realized how exhausted she was until Diantha's personal handmaidens prepared her a bath, so instead of joining the Pharos family for dinner, she'd politely requested that her meal be brought to her bedchamber. She'd only managed a few bites before she fell asleep, still with the tray on her lap.

She was meant to depart today, but not so soon. Diantha's men were due to return in a few hours to report anything they might've overheard regarding Arian's curse. Until they returned with information, Aurelia had nothing to do but tour Diantha's palace and observe what had become of it over the last three years.

81

"I must admit," Aurelia remarked as they strolled, "I'm finding it difficult to understand how this palace functions so well with so few servants. I've only seen a handful since I arrived."

A wicked glint shone in Diantha's eyes. "There were no servants in this palace when the Phyres ruled. Everyone you see was invited to work here after I took the throne. Some were my neighbors, or old family friends, or people I worked with."

"Do you mean to say that the Phyre family spent centuries without employees minding their estate? How can that be?"

"That's a Phyre family secret," Diantha teased, making Aurelia snort into a laugh. "This palace isn't what it seems—not entirely, anyway. Follow me."

Obeying, Aurelia trailed behind as Diantha turned a corner at the end of the hallway, descended the grand staircase, and walked for a bit longer before stopping in front of an open doorway. The room ahead looked like it was some sort of display: paintings hung on every inch of the walls, and suits of armor, sculptures on pedestals, and marble statues lined either side of the carpeted path.

"I wish for my cloak," Diantha said suddenly.

Aurelia furrowed her brows, but then the coatrack beside the doorway sprung to life. The tall iron structure squeaked as it moved, extended its curled hooks like a human stretching their arms, and removed a black cloak from one of the hooks. The coatrack shook out the cloak and gently draped it over Diantha's shoulders before returning to normal.

Aurelia didn't know what to say. "I-I—"

"It's rather dim in here," Diantha continued. "Might we have a bit more light?"

On her cue, every candle or torch in the vicinity—on skinny tables or bookshelves lining the hallway, on wall sconces, and even on the chandeliers—illuminated in the blink of an eye.

"This is...This is..." Aurelia tried her hardest to think of something coherent to say, but words seemed to fail her.

Diantha chuckled. "I know. It gave me a good fright when I first moved here. Nearly everything in this palace is alive—when it wants to be, of course. The dining table sets itself. The hearths ignite on their own. The pantries used to fill themselves, so I've heard, but one of my servants is responsible for acquiring our food now. It's marvelous, isn't it?"

"That's putting it lightly," Aurelia muttered, watching as a feather duster worked on its own to clean one of the sculptures in the room ahead. "I've never seen anything like this."

"I think it all started because of the Phyre family's curse. Nobody other than the family could step foot in this palace without going mad, so they had to dismiss their staff—again, to isolate them from the rest of the world as much as possible. The palace provided them with absolutely everything they needed, so many of them found no reason to leave the estate. I don't know why the palace is still alive now that the curse is broken. My husband likes to say it's a gift from Edea."

As astonishing as it was, it made sense. The kingdom's former Almighty sought to punish the Phyres for their ancestor's greed by keeping them isolated. Part of that isolation meant they were unable to leave the kingdom. The other part meant that they were compelled to stay within the walls of their palace, far away from their civilians and the horrors of Dofelli poverty, where their plates and cups filled themselves, their hearths burned without being tended to, and their home was always kept clean and orderly.

When they walked away, Diantha soon stopped them in front of a window. They both smiled at the sight of Halvor coasting over the courtyard, delighting the Pharos children as they whooped and clapped from the lawn.

"They don't know about Rieza, do they?" Aurelia asked. "I don't think they'd be so enamored with Halvor if they knew their mother possessed a dragon, too."

Diantha grimaced. "No, they don't. I've told them the story, but like me as a girl, they think it's another fairytale. I'll tell them when they're a bit older—if I haven't claimed her by then, anyway."

Aurelia recalled something Diantha had told her the day before. "You said Rieza and Halvor were saying hello to each other when I thought they were fighting. Does that mean they know each other?"

"Of course. They're siblings."

Aurelia's jaw nearly fell to the floor. "*What?*"

Diantha laughed as she looped her arm through Aurelia's and began to walk again. "That's right. I felt it when I first found myself in close proximity to Halvor. I imagine you'll feel the same thing if and when you come close to Rieza. Their souls are bonded, just as our souls are bonded to theirs."

"How—?"

"I don't know the details, exactly. Remember what I told you: if I had the power to communicate directly with Rieza, I would. All I know is what I feel, and I feel that they've known each other since they took their first breaths. I think I confirmed their relationship during the Battle for Dofell."

Aurelia's head was spinning, but she tried to play it off. "Care to explain?"

"Their bond, remember? Much like humans, they have a unique soul bond with their relatives. Mages can merely summon and observe the soul of a loved one, but dragons can actually connect with souls within their bloodline. When Halvor fell during the battle, I used my connection with Rieza to ask her to help him. She didn't have to leave the cave to do it, either. She reached for their connection and gave him the strength she could sacrifice so he'd recover in time to save you. She empowered his soul, giving him the vitality he needed."

Aurelia knew that much about humans. She'd learned it from Arian on the day they met when he summoned her soul for her to see. Nothing could be done to the soul when it was summoned—it was only a visual aid, in a manner of speaking.

"That's what fueled the fire during the persecution." Diantha's voice lost its exciting edge, now sounding distant and forlorn. "Dragons are close to unstoppable unless enough enemies stand united against them, but when you take their soul bonds into consideration, they can help each other replenish enough that they can't be bested. That's why those who participated in the persecution tended to follow dragons back to their clutches before they were killed—to find and destroy as many of their relatives as possible."

A shiver traced Aurelia's spine as anger flushed her cheeks. "That's maniacal. Those poor creatures...."

"Yes, well...I think nowadays, the realm knows better than to ever attempt something like that again. If we can't learn from our ancestors' mistakes, then we don't deserve the magic this realm has to offer us."

"I couldn't have said it better myself.

After walking for a bit longer, the pair were stopped in the middle of the hallway by a trio of Dofelli knights. Aurelia's heart sank as soon as she saw the grim expressions on their faces. They clearly hadn't found anything of substance regarding Arian and the curse, but in truth, she hadn't expected them to. They'd need more than a day to survey the entire kingdom, and even then, it was unlikely that whoever was responsible for this—if they were even in Dofell—would talk about it aloud.

Aurelia swallowed her disappointment as they continued on their tour. She barely heard Diantha, who was saying something about ordering her men to keep looking for answers.

Suddenly, Diantha stopped them and erupted in a grin. "I have a surprise for you."

"A surprise?" Aurelia blinked at her. "What have you—"

A gasp escaped her when she spotted something behind Diantha. Standing by the front doors of the palace was a familiar face Aurelia hadn't seen in years: a short, elderly woman with braided white hair, emerald eyes, and fawny brown skin. Perched on the woman's shoulder was Edom, baring its razor-sharp teeth as it laughed. It was no wonder the sprite had been so quick to flee when they arrived—it must've known a friend was coming.

"Maysa," Aurelia whispered.

IX

"You knew I was coming, didn't you?"

"Of course I did." Maysa chuckled as a pot of tea rose from the table, filled their two teacups, and set itself down again. "I left Kanibar a few weeks ago so I could meet you here. My grandson says hello, and he hopes you don't resent the entirety of Kanibar for what his uncle did to you."

"I don't. Tell him hello for me, too." Aurelia eyed the oracle as Edom snacked from a bowl of fruit on the table. "If you knew I was coming, then you must know why I came, too. What can you tell me about the curse?"

Maysa gave her a look that Aurelia translated effortlessly: *You know I can't answer that.*

"You were right to come here," Maysa murmured, sipping from her teacup. "You needed to learn what you did from Her Majesty. This is the most I can tell you: he *was* cursed when he last visited Dofell, but not in the way you think."

"Was the person responsible working alone?"

"Not quite."

Aurelia sighed. "Is there anything else you'd like to add?"

"I've already told you more than I should've." Maysa raised an eyebrow. "You can find the answers for yourself, if you know where to look. I believe Her Majesty has already hinted at the method you can use to accomplish that."

"The only thing she hinted at was a way for me to communicate with Halvor."

"Exactly."

Aurelia shook her head. She was already tired of the prophet's cryptic ways. "I don't understand."

"Your brother does."

She blanched as she curled her fingers around her teacup. "What does Rayan understand about this that I don't? He doesn't know anything about dragons or magic or—"

"My word, child! The moment your flesh and blood enters the picture, you forget all about the one whose crib you slept beside every night as a child. I know he did horrible things to you, but you know as well as I do that you still think of him as your brother."

Aurelia glowered at her. That didn't make any sense. For one, Archie was dead. For another, he'd lived during a time when magic was scarce across the realm—and nonexistent in Akkinor. He didn't know anything about magic, and he certainly didn't know anything about dragons, either. Even if he did, he wasn't alive to ask.

She stilled when a realization struck her. Not long after the Battle for Dofell, she'd dreamt of Archie—but it'd felt less like a dream, and more like he was visiting her from the afterlife. He'd said some strange things, including a few lines that sounded like a prophecy, but what'd puzzled her most was when he'd been upset with her for failing to visit him. Was that something she could even do?

She'd written to Maysa about that dream after returning to Akkinor. She'd written to her about Rieza and the emerald longbelly, too. She'd sent dozens of letters to the Palace of Kanibar in hopes that Maysa would assist her somehow, and she hadn't received any sort of response.

"Oh, don't look at me like that," Maysa said, tearing Aurelia from her thoughts. Only then did Aurelia realize she was scowling at the old woman. "I know what you're thinking. Don't be cross with me for keeping my distance. You had questions that you weren't ready to receive the answers to back then, and I always told you we'd reunite when it was time. I was a bit distracted by my newfound freedom, anyway. Willem had me locked up in that temple for over two decades, in case you've forgotten."

"I haven't," Aurelia snapped. She softened when Maysa raised an eyebrow. "I'm sorry. I just wish I'd heard from you, that's all."

"Everything happened exactly as it was meant to. Divine timing isn't something to be trifled with."

She understood that much. "Of course. But you're implying that my method of directly communicating with Halvor is the same method I can use to find answers about Arian—and the same way I may be able to visit Archie, if I ever wanted to. What can you tell me about it?"

Maysa sighed. Instead of replying, she turned in her chair to face the empty space in the parlor. She waved her hand, and after a few seconds, a shimmering light appeared in a way that reminded Aurelia of sketching— like Maysa's magic was drawing in the air with pure light.

Aurelia watched, mesmerized. After a minute passed, a complete image had formed in the air, presenting itself in four layers. The top layer looked like a palace in the clouds, and the one below it seemed to be a mountain range with a sun and a body of water. The third layer was a set of six arched doorways, and the fourth and final layer—its light duller than the rest—depicted flickering flames.

"This is a model of the universe. It hasn't been known to humanity in centuries," Maysa murmured. "Only a handful of people alive, including Lord Zhaaran of Orestes, know what it really is. At the top, we have Hanhalla. Below it is Icareth, then Vanhylde, and then Saendah."

"Hanhalla." The realization struck Aurelia as she stared at the image of a palace in the sky. "That's the name of the heavens." Maysa's lips curled into a satisfied smile. "Icareth must be the name of our world, then. And Saendah...That's hell, isn't it? Eternal damnation for those who didn't earn a place in Hanhalla."

"That's right."

Aurelia frowned. "But what's Vanhylde? I always assumed there were only three planes of existence: heaven, hell, and the earthly realm." When Maysa's eyes, twinkling with cleverness, landed on the locket dangling from Aurelia's neck, the queen sucked in a sharp breath. "Oh, my."

"For many centuries, your dragon lived within that locket, existing in a land between worlds. That's Vanhylde. It's a purgatory of sorts: if the gods can't decide what to do with a soul after its human form dies—send it to a world of eternal bliss, or one of eternal punishment—the soul is sent to Vanhylde. It's not just for people like that, either. Vanhylde is the place we visit when we dream, the place ancient mages used as a sanctuary for some of the magical creatures they put into hiding."

"I-I—"

"Visit the monastery when you return home. Ask your Elder to take you into the archives. You'll find more information there."

Aurelia's brain was melting. "I don't understand. Vanhylde is one thing, but...Why is it that nobody knows these names? Shouldn't this be common knowledge?"

Maysa grimaced. "In the old days, everyone knew. But the gods take more than they give, child, and they have no hesitations when it comes to seizing what humanity is unworthy of. Don't forget that names hold tremendous power. Hanhalla was once a miraculous place—a destination that nearly every soul in the realm dedicated their life to finding. Today, the heavens are just an idea to most people. A possibility, a hope, a dream. The majority of humans don't know if they are fact or legend."

Aurelia exhaled and brushed a lock of hair behind her ear. She still didn't fully understand it, but she was starting to. The gods had demanded that humans rely on faith in the divine to believe these realms existed, especially after humanity scorned and mocked the divine by partially destroying the gods' most sacred gift: magic.

"Before they left us," Maysa continued, "they destroyed most references to the names of the four planes of existence, replacing those names with general terms like *'the earthly realm'* or *'purgatory.'* Only those closest to the divine, like oracles and Elders, have access to the texts that weren't rewritten by the gods. This knowledge is reserved only for those whose faith has never wavered—those who don't view the heavens as a place they *might* reach after death, but rather as a marker on a map within arm's reach."

Aurelia swallowed the lump in her throat. "So, if we apply that idea to Vanhylde, then it's possible for me to reach that realm and accomplish what we've spoken of. But I don't understand *how* I might do that. How can any living human visit purgatory?"

"I'll repeat myself only this once: you'll find the answers you seek at the monastery. You must search a room with three entrances, and only one exit."

Aurelia made a face at her. "What on earth does *that*—"

"Ah." Maysa's eyes landed on a clock on the mantel above the fireplace as she stood and smoothed her skirt. "Our time together has come to an end for today. It was a lovely visit. I'll be seeing you again soon."

As the oracle glided toward the door, Aurelia called out, "Wait!"

Maysa turned, raised an eyebrow, and exhaled. "What is it?"

Aurelia cleared her throat. "I'm just wondering—how many prophecies do you know? Other than the one about the Battle for Dofell, of course. And how many did you share with Willem before he imprisoned you?"

The corner of her mouth twitched. "I know as many prophecies as you know tales of old. Some have already come true, and others won't even begin until centuries after I'm gone. Every major event in Icareth has a prophecy attached to it, but if I spoke of each of them, there'd be no mystery or excitement left in our world." Her green eyes, so much like a cat's, shimmered again. "As for Willem...Even before he imprisoned me, I knew what he was—and what he'd become, in time. I only told him fragments of the things he wanted to know. I couldn't trust him with everything. It's a good thing I chose to be secretive with him, or neither of us would be here today." She curtsied and smiled. "Good day, Aurelia."

Then she was gone.

FORGED IN BLOOD

***

Lazelus Swann peeled his calcified fingers from the stone and took a few steps backward from the well. His three counterparts were still surrounding the circular structure, peering down into the hole, while the only woman among them watched from Lazelus's left.

Shasta Selle stood quietly with her small hands clasped behind her back, the length of her hair scarf now wrapped around her mouth, leaving only her narrow brown eyes visible. For someone whose life was on the line—and who'd just brought the people threatening her existence to observe the power she held over them—she was eerily calm.

"Im-Impossible." Lord Reesa's fingers clenched as his nails scraped against the stone. "This can't be..."

Lord Quagg scrubbed a hand down his face and stepped back. "Lord Selle never mentioned a word of this."

"Lady Swann didn't mention anything about the hoard of gryphons she was housing in her catacombs, and yet, we've all seen them with our own eyes." Lord Keer's dark gaze landed on Lazelus. "Is your family hiding anything else in Runeia that we should know about?"

The twenty-year-old Lord of Runeia only scowled. It wasn't his fault, nor his grandmother's, that ancient gryphons had sought refuge in Runeia. Though Carthe never participated in the persecution, travelers from around the realm slaughtered mages and creatures alike while visiting the western continent, urging the latter to disappear into hiding. Lazelus's ancestors had always taken care of the gryphons who'd lived in Krotis, so it was his duty to answer their plea for help when they needed him most. If his ancestors had denied them, they wouldn't have spent centuries evolving and increasing their numbers in the catacombs beneath Runeia, only to emerge stronger than ever when the realm needed them most.

Of course, the Swann family wasn't the only one keeping secrets—and magical secrets, at that. Kanibar was overpopulated with sprites and skilled mages, yet nobody had known the extent of it until three years ago. Now, Lazelus and his fellow Kroti leaders were learning that yet another noble family had been keeping a massive secret from the realm, too: possession of a dragon.

Lazelus approached the well again and peered into the hole. He swallowed the anxiety in his throat at the sight of a small, emerald dragon—about the size of a young cow—eating what appeared to be a goat's leg at the bottom. There was a hole on the left side of the well that led to tunnel systems beneath Krotis, and though the darkness prevented Lazelus from seeing within the tunnel, he could only assume that the entire length of it was littered with animal bones and carcasses.

Lord Reesa turned his angry gaze to Shasta. "Explain this."

She maintained her composure. "Years ago, my grandmother visited the Bruilan catacombs to leave offerings for our ancestors. She came across the tomb of Lady Imanah Selle, wife of the first Lord of Bruila, and noticed a loose brick on the floor just beside the tomb. She tried to stabilize the brick, and when she lifted it, she found a dragon's egg in a chest hidden in a niche below it. The egg appeared to be petrified, having been there for over a thousand years, so she left it. She told my father about it years later."

"And how did *you* come to possess it?" Lord Quagg demanded.

"My father told me about the egg when it became clear that his illness would soon kill him." Shasta's voice cracked. "He believed that only Bruila's true ruler could possess such knowledge. He...He didn't think it would ever hatch, but he wanted me to have it, nonetheless, so he had a servant collect the chest and bring it to me. That was about three years ago. Not long after, while I was keeping the egg hidden in my wardrobe, I heard it moving. A part of me always believed it would hatch, one day, so I wasn't exactly surprised when it did."

Lord Keer massaged his temples. "How have you managed to hide it?"

A flicker of worry passed over her face. "I kept her hidden in the catacombs when she was a hatchling—nobody visited except for my family, so I knew she'd be safe there. I checked on her and brought her food every day. Not long after the Battle for Dofell, though, my father received a message, and he thought it was time for us to prepare to release her. She refused to leave the catacombs until last season. She goes out for a flight every now and then, only at nighttime, and always returns here, for whatever reason. It would appear that she prefers to be as close to the earth as possible."

"Queen Aurelia—and the entire realm, for that matter—has been looking for her since she visited Akkinor," Lazelus murmured. "You're lucky nobody has seen her leave or return here. Or tried to shoot her down, either."

Shasta's eyes narrowed at him. "She may have claimed me when she was born to me, but she's still a wild creature. I can't keep her from leaving without locking her up, and I won't risk stunting her growth."

"Understandable." Lord Keer waved his hand, blue sparks emitting from his fingers, and held out his palm just in time for a squirrel—its neck broken on his magical command—to land on his skin. He tossed the squirrel into the well and observed, like the others, while the small dragon feasted. "Your father was persuaded to send her to Akkinor because of a letter he received. You've spoken of it before. What did it say?"

Shasta stiffened and held her head high. "I've shown you the gift my father gave me, as promised. I also promised to show you the letter if, and only if, you respect my father's wishes by accepting me as Lady of Bruila. If you're still hesitant to do so, I'm afraid I can't tell you anything more."

"Why, you insolent—" Lord Reesa growled.

"You have my acceptance." Lazelus eyed Lord Reesa, ignoring the fear he felt at the nobleman's ferocious gaze, and tipped his head to Shasta. "The way I see it, refusing you would be reason enough for you to unleash this creature's power on all of us. I don't know what she's capable of, but I don't wish to find out if her anger is directed at me. The only other option is for us to slaughter her, and that would go against everything we stand for as leaders of Krotis. The Almighty would scorn us."

"He's right." Lord Keer removed his heavy, gray turban just long enough to wipe the sweat from his bald head as he gazed at his counterparts. "Akkinor has risen to unprecedented heights since Queen Aurelia released her dragon. Krotis now has the chance to do the same. Queen Aurelia's dragon might be an ancient, experienced threat, but this little thing is the first creature of old to be born in the modern day. That's a blessing from the Almighty if there ever was one."

"One of the greatest powers in the realm, in the hands of a teenage girl." Lord Reesa shook his head and scoffed. "It's ridiculous."

"It's our reality," Lord Quagg admitted. "There's nothing we can do about it. Our options are to kill the creature and the girl, or to claim the both of them as our allies—our family. She may be young, and she may be a girl, but she presents us with the opportunity of unbridled power. That's more than reason enough to accept her."

"Fine." Lord Reesa sighed, finally accepting that he'd lost the fight, as Shasta grinned. He scowled at her when he saw her expression. "Don't get too excited, girl. You won't be crowned until we find you a husband—*and* until you provide us with the letter."

Her eyes flashed with misery. "I-I can live with that, I suppose."

"You haven't another choice."

Lord Keer shook his head. "Gods, Darius."

Lord Reesa, now grinning like he hadn't been forced to surrender his steadfast position a moment earlier, walked up to Shasta and splayed his large palm over her cheek. She flinched, but she didn't move away.

"I have a son who'd be perfect for you," he told her. "You'll meet him, you'll accept his hand, and you'll provide us with the letter—then you'll receive your crown."

"How can she be certain you'll keep your word?" Lazelus asked.

Lord Reesa sneered at him while Shasta glanced at him with a look in her eyes that Lazelus could only interpret as a thank-you.

"If my word is not kept," Lord Reesa hissed, "then you can feed me to the dragon. Will that suffice?"

"Undoubtedly." Shasta pulled her face from his grip to shake his hand. "I appreciate your cooperation."

He grunted at her as the nobles tossed one final glance at the well before starting on their long trek back to the capital. Lazelus looked over his shoulder once more as they left the well behind, hidden in maze-like woodlands that most Kroti avoided like the plague, before raising an eyebrow at Shasta.

"Does she have a name?" he asked.

The Lady of Bruila smiled at him. "Annera."

"The goddess of the stars." That made Lazelus smile, too. "Why name her after Annera, of all deities?"

"Because she was born on a night when the stars shined brighter than I've ever seen."

The elder three lords snorted and laughed at her childishness, but Lazelus maintained his smile. "That's very nice."

She kept smiling, ignoring the others, and glanced up at the twinkling constellations above. She looked so lovely with the starlight beaming down on her face; it made Lazelus feel ill when he remembered that she would soon be wed to the godless Kaius Reesa.

X

urelia left Dofell not with what she'd set out for, but, at the very least, with something that would point her in the right direction.

She wanted to direct Halvor to the Monastery of Dhylo in Omara as soon as they reached Akkinor, but she knew her family and her allies were waiting at the palace to hear about her findings. The monastery—and the room with three entrances, and only one exit—would have to wait for now.

After leaving Halvor in the gardens, she tilted her chin to look at Edom on her shoulder. "Did you happen to know anything about what May said?"

"No. I never knew much about Vanhylde."

"All right. I'd like you to visit a few of our magical friends while I speak with the others. Cheol, Geon, Laurel, Fiora—any creature who was alive in Akkinor before the persecution. See if they know anything."

With a nod and a burst of golden light, the sprite was gone.

Within minutes of walking into the palace, Aurelia nearly crashed into Lucyra, who'd rushed out of Arian's bedchamber when she saw Halvor descending. When she explained that she hadn't found anything that might help Arian, she felt sick to her stomach at the disappointment in Lucyra's eyes. Her cousin merely sighed, bowed her head, and muttered something about excusing herself to care for Halvor.

Rehearsing what she'd say to the others when she found them, Aurelia trudged upstairs and found her way to Arian's bedchamber. Jack and her allies were loitering in the hallway—having gathered there when they saw Halvor approaching—but Arian wasn't alone in his room. Four priests wearing royal blue robes and gold ropes around their waists stood in pairs on either side of Arian's bed. Each of them had their arms extended so their palms were facing Arian's chest, warm yellow magic emitting from their flesh, and they were sweating like they'd just tried to outrun a centaur.

"Your Grace." Reyna was the first to speak when Aurelia joined them. "Did you find anything?"

"I'm afraid not," Aurelia muttered. Reyna and the noblemen sighed as Jack snaked an arm around Aurelia's waist and kissed her temple. "But I do have a lead, so I'll investigate that tomorrow. There's something else, though, that you all need to..."

She trailed off when she saw Arian—*really* saw him. It'd been just under three days since she left, and he already looked worse than he had before. His brown skin was grayer and clammier, and he was slightly emaciated; not enough to be concerning, but enough to prove that his new diet of broth and sugar water wouldn't sustain him for much longer. Even his hair looked thinner and whiter, and his face was twisted with pain.

Jack sighed and held her closer. "The mages are working on identifying the curse. Lord Zhaaran here helped them for a bit, but—"

"—I'm not the young man I used to be, nor the young mage." The elderly nobleman grimaced. "The blockage is stronger than we thought. I only managed a few minutes before exhaustion overcame me."

"They'll find something, eventually," Reyna murmured, though the wavering of her voice wasn't exactly convincing. "They've been taking breaks every three hours. Before they start up again, they feed him, change him, bathe him—as best they can, of course. They turn him every so often, too, to avoid bedsores. He hasn't made a sound or moved at all, but I saw his eyes moving beneath his eyelids when I sat with him last night. If he's dreaming, his mental state must be intact. Right?"

Balor shrugged and picked at something in his teeth, making Aurelia scowl. "Possibly. Just because he's dreaming doesn't mean he's all there. He could wake up and think it's the 1940s again, and he's here with his father training to be Hand of the King to Edmund the Younger."

"Your pessimism isn't making this any easier," Aurelia snapped.

"It's not pessimism. It's rationality."

"Whatever you want to call it, it's not helping." Sighing, Reyna pulled the door closed, forcing Aurelia to peel her eyes from her uncle. "What were you saying, Your Grace?"

Aurelia swallowed as she replayed her time in Dofell. She'd been so prepared to tell her allies about Rieza that she'd nearly forgotten the promise she made to Diantha. As much as Aurelia trusted her allies (even that foul Balor Zhoqa), she intended on keeping that promise. She couldn't keep a secret like that from Jack, gods help her, so she'd have to tell him privately.

"I was just going to tell you that Maysa met me in Dofell," Aurelia lied. She felt Jack eyeing her, suspicious, but she ignored him. "She said Arian was cursed during his trip to Dofell, but the person responsible is long gone. She also implied that I may find the answers we're looking for— among other things—in Vanhylde."

"Vanhylde?" Reyna furrowed her eyebrows. "What on earth is that?"

Balor snorted. "Probably some uncharted island. Oracles rarely make it easy, do they?"

Aurelia paid them no heed as her pale blue eyes locked on Jalhor's violet ones. The Lord of Orestes was watching her carefully, like he was trying to figure out exactly how much she knew. She was giving him the same look, which eventually made him sigh before chuckling.

"Vanhylde is one of the four realms of our universe," Jalhor murmured. "It isn't a land for the living, but rather an in-between of sorts. That's where we go when we dream, too, because sleep is considered to be a form of death, to a certain degree. That's where Halvor lived when his former mistress confined him to the locket."

As he gestured to Aurelia's neck, Balor raised an eyebrow. "So, the necklace is a portal to Vanhylde?"

"In a way," Jalhor said quickly. "None of us can simply snap our fingers and teleport to Vanhylde through the locket. There's a ritual that's meant to be performed when a living being is transported to and from the locket— and, therefore, Vanhylde. In truth, I don't know all that much about it. Most of our records about Vanhylde have been lost in time, or they're written in ancient dialects that very few people alive can translate. Bozar is home to the wisest and keenest minds in the world, and even our people haven't managed to uncover more about it."

Aurelia wrapped her fingers around the cylindrical golden tube. "My brother came to me in a dream after the battle. He claimed I could visit him. Maysa implied that the way I might visit Archie is the same way I might learn more about what happened to Arian—Vanhylde."

She stopped herself before she could say anything more, wincing, as she debated mentioning what Diantha had said about communicating with Halvor. She ultimately decided against it—even if the chances were slim that they realized Diantha's knowledge of dragonkind was related to the mysterious violet vipertail, it wasn't worth the risk.

"Maysa told me to visit the monastery," she continued, swallowing the lump in her throat. "Like I said before, I'll go there tomorrow."

"We'll depart when you do," Jalhor told her. "We've been absent from Bozar for longer than expected. My wife is itching to return home."

"As are mine," Balor added. "We'll do what we can to help from Bozar, though. I'll send my spies out to gather any information they can find about this. Perhaps, if and when the curse has been identified, we'll have better luck learning more about it then you will here. Take no offense, but the Holy Library of Iseppa has more material on curses than the monastery does."

Aurelia waved her hand dismissively. "No offense taken. I understand." She turned to Reyna, who was staring at the floor and gnawing on her lower lip. "Your Majesty? Will you be departing tomorrow, too?"

Her azurite eyes flashed. "I don't know."

"You're welcome to stay as long as you'd like. You know that."

Reyna nodded. "I do. Thank you. But my husband has been ruling on my behalf for long enough as it is, and without my Hand to relieve him, I have to return promptly. I-I don't wish to leave Arian, but..."

"He'd understand," Jack assured her. "You have a kingdom to govern and children to dote on. We'll take excellent care of him here, and we'll update you as often as we can. I'm sure Aurelia and Halvor will fetch you if his condition changes."

"We will." Aurelia took Reyna's hands in hers and squeezed. "He'd want you here with him whether he wakes or dies."

That last part was difficult to say without bursting into tears, but somehow, seeing the emotion glistening in Reyna's eyes helped her contain them—like it was easier to fight off sobs while knowing she wasn't alone in her grief.

Reyna released a shuddering exhale. "All right, then. I'll set out for Taundosa tomorrow, too."

Aurelia nodded. "We'll reconvene at dinner tonight. The three of you should start preparing for your departure, and as for me...I stink like dragon. I'll find you after I've bathed."

With that, the group set off in two different directions: the three Carthinians to the left, and Aurelia and Jack to the right. The couple looked over their shoulders as their allies turned a corner, and as soon as they were out of sight and earshot, Jack raised a bushy black eyebrow at his wife.

"You're hiding something, Lily dear," he murmured. "What is it?"

She shook her head, eyes darting toward a trio of servants passing by, and squeezed his hand as she led him into their bedchamber. Her lady's maids were already preparing a bath, having seen her arriving on dragonback, but she dismissed them before they had the chance to embellish the bathwater with essential oils and dried flower petals—a luxury she wasn't exactly in the mood to enjoy.

As she sat on the edge of their bed and urged Jack to do the same, he said, "You're starting to frighten me."

Aurelia winced and sucked in a long, deep breath. She hesitated for only a moment, their conjoined hands nestled on her lap, before telling Jack everything she'd learned about Diantha, Rieza, and the secrets of the Pharos family.

***

"Goodbye, little prince. And goodbye to you, Princess Sisi." Balor bowed to Aurelia's two children as they giggled at him. "Say goodbye to your siblings for us, too. Where are they today?"

"Halle has a tummy ache," Henry replied, "and the others are in trouble."

Balor raised a wicked eyebrow. "What for?"

"Harlen ripped out some of Holly's hair 'cause Lena told him to."

The Lord of Kazamir guffawed as his vibrant blue eyes found Aurelia. "That Halyna of yours is a tricky one, isn't she?"

"You have no idea." Aurelia smiled at her ally—not because she was sad to see him go, but because it still shocked her that such a nauseating man could have such an innocent, gentle way with children, especially after his kingdom's old practice of marrying young girls to grown men. "It was good to see you, my lord. Safe travels, and say goodbye to your wives for me."

"Will do."

He waved goodbye to the children, gave Jack a sidelong look, and turned on his heel to meet Jalhor and Reyna on the dock. He was the last one to arrive in Seaport, having missed the carriage from the Folly, but the others weren't surprised by his tardiness; according to the allies, Balor wasn't exactly the punctual sort.

Aurelia lifted Henry in her arms as Jack sat Hyacinth on his shoulders so the children could wave at the allies while rowboats took them to their ships. Their men—and the noblemen's wives—were already on board, having rushed to the ships as soon as daybreak arrived. Apparently, the Bozari women weren't exactly fond of Akkinorian food and customs, and they were eager to return home as quickly as possible.

When the family returned to their carriage, it took them a moment to get situated, as Aurelia and Jack had to fight Henry's wish to ride home on

Cheol's back. The centaur saw no problem with it—not helping Aurelia and Jack's case in the slightest—but eventually, when he saw his sister climb into the carriage without fuss, Henry was persuaded to follow suit.

"I suppose I should set out for Omara when we get home," Aurelia said as the carriage jolted forward. "There aren't any urgent matters for me to attend to right now, so—"

Jack interrupted her by flinching. "Erm..."

"What is it?"

He grimaced and ran a hand through his hair. "It didn't feel like there was a good opportunity to tell you this after you returned from Dofell, but—"

"Uncle Rayan is bringing his family over for dinner!" Henry exclaimed. He stopped, thought about what he'd said, and tried again: "Not *uncle*. Just Rayan."

A shiver traced Aurelia's spine when Hyacinth's wide, crystalline blue eyes snapped over to hers. She'd had a feeling for some time now that Hyacinth knew Rayan really was their uncle—just as she knew that she couldn't speak of it to anyone.

When the realization sunk in, Aurelia felt the blood drain from her face. Henry wasn't referring to Rayan's three bastard children, who lived in the palace under the guise of being a servant's children. Though their mother had died, Aurelia told her staff that she didn't wish to send the children to an orphanage, so they were being brought up alongside the other children who lived in the palace. As far as she knew, nobody suspected anything untoward regarding Rayan's relationship to them; they merely thought their queen was doing a generous thing by caring for three orphans.

Henry had to be referring to Rayan's father, Eric, and younger sister, Ginny—Aurelia's father, too, and half-sister.

She could barely get the word out when she stammered, "J-Jack—"

"He asked for my permission when you were gone, and I couldn't see any reason to deny him," he said quickly. "Eric just returned home from his three-year trip to Holos. Ginny is leaving for Holos tomorrow, and Rayan isn't sure when he'll see her again. He wants to give them a tour and introduce them to us while they're both here."

Aurelia wrapped her fingers around her locket for comfort. "No, no. You were right to say yes. He deserves that much. I just wasn't expecting...."

He offered her a small, sad sort of smile. "This day was bound to come eventually."

"I know." She looked down at Hyacinth beside her as her daughter stared into nothingness. "What are you thinking about, Sisi?"

Like he knew what his daughter was going to say, Jack covered Henry's ears, ignoring the prince's protests and shushing him when he hollered.

"He's sick," Hyacinth murmured, sighing. "Your papa."

A fist clenched Aurelia's heart—why, she didn't know. "How do you mean?"

"He has a bad memory."

"Oh."

Hyacinth sat on her knees and touched Aurelia's locket. "You have to hide it, Mama, or he'll think you're *her*."

Aurelia's eyes met Jack's dumbfounded gaze. Hyacinth was right: the locket's last owner was Aurelia's biological mother, Katryna Cristos. According to Arian, his late sister had worn the necklace every day from the time she was born to the time she died. Eric would recognize it immediately.

Clearing her throat, Aurelia brushed a ringlet from her daughter's forehead. "Do you happen to know if he knows that she's dead? The person who wore this locket before me?"

Hyacinth pondered that for a moment, then shook her head. "No, Mama. I'm sorry."

"It's all right." Aurelia kissed Hyacinth's forehead. "You've been more than helpful as it is, Sisi."

With that, Jack removed his hands from Henry's ears, prompting the young prince to demand, "Tell me what you talked about!"

"Not with that attitude," Jack scolded. "It's a secret. You can know when you're older."

He pouted his lower lip. "Not fair!"

"Nothing's fair, Henry." Hyacinth sighed and peered out the carriage window. "That's how life works."

A chill ravaged Aurelia's being as she and Jack met eyes. As helpful—and intriguing—as Hyacinth's power was, Aurelia wasn't sure it was right to let her maintain her magic; she'd already seen and learned more than she should, and a little girl shouldn't need to be so jaded.

XI

Ginevra Haze—now Ginevra Clift—didn't look a thing like her brother. If Aurelia didn't know any better, she wouldn't have guessed they were related at all.

Ginny must've taken after their mother. Instead of straight auburn hair like Rayan's, her chocolate locks fell in long, loose waves. She didn't have pale blue eyes, either, but rather irises that matched her hair almost exactly. She was freckled, too, and much tanner than Rayan. She was short and curvy in contrast to Rayan's tall, athletic build, but the siblings shared the same smile—their father's smile, which Aurelia had inherited, too.

When Aurelia, Jack, and the elder three of their children arrived in the dining hall, Rayan and Ginny were already seated. Eric had gone to relieve himself, giving Aurelia plenty of time to prepare before she came face-to-face with her birth father.

The siblings stood to greet the royal family, and to Aurelia's surprise, Ginny walked toward her and took her hands instead of curtsying. Rayan muttered something, likely scolding her, as Ginny grinned from ear to ear and seemed to be desperately fighting the urge to hug the queen.

"It's so lovely to meet you, Your Grace," Ginny mused, squeezing Aurelia's hands. "You're even prettier than I thought you'd be, which isn't a surprise—everyone and their mother has heard tales of your beauty! You know, I never thought I'd find myself in this palace, let alone visiting my brother, the Hand of the Queen. It's ridiculous, isn't it? Wonderfully, poetically ridiculous! When word reached Satin Valley of Rayan's new position, I screamed so loud that I'm surprised you didn't hear it in the Folly. My brother's always been a valiant soldier and a wise man, but I never expected to find him here, ruling beside the queen. I don't know if you're positively mad or the cleverest woman alive to name him as your Hand, but either way, I'm glad you did."

Aurelia gawked at her, as did Jack and even their children. The only person who wasn't shocked by her rambling was Rayan, who merely lowered his head and tried his hardest to suppress a sheepish smile.

Never before had Aurelia been spoken to like this by someone she'd just met, let alone a commoner, but she'd be a liar if she claimed to dislike it. It was refreshing to be spoken to like a friend.

Aurelia could only laugh after she processed everything she'd heard. "It's great to meet you, Madam Clift. It's been a joy to have your brother here—we're all so much richer for it. We love him dearly. But I feel it'd be wrong of me to call myself either mad or clever; you can decide for yourself when you leave here. I'm sure your deduction will be the right one, if you're anywhere near as keen as your darling brother."

Ginny grinned, bouncing on the balls of her feet. Laughing a bit, Aurelia leaned forward and embraced her, not at all surprised when Ginny returned the hug without a second thought.

For a moment—just a moment—peace washed over Aurelia. She'd never had a sister before, and even if Ginny didn't know they were related, it felt wonderful to hug her sister for the first time.

"Call me Ginny. Please," she said when they separated, holding Aurelia at arm's length.

The queen smiled. "And you must call me Aurelia. I'm afraid I have to insist."

"Oh, really? Rayan said you were the personable sort, but I didn't believe it because why would I? Most rulers would have someone beheaded for failing to use their title, and though I know that's not your way, one can't be certain. You know, I once knew someone who—"

"Gods above, Ginevra," Rayan interrupted, fighting a laugh. "Slow down, will you?"

Ginny blushed. "Sorry."

While Aurelia took her seat at the head of the table, with Rayan on her right and Jack on her left, she introduced Ginny to her family. To her surprise, Ginny abandoned her seat on Rayan's left, instead opting to sit between Halle and Henry on Jack's side of the table. She immediately started talking to the children like she'd known them for their entire lives, going as far as to tease them by making silly faces and playing with her napkin.

Aurelia leaned in close to Rayan as servants arrived to fill their chalices. "I think I love her."

He snorted. "She's a pest."

"An endearing one."

"You haven't spent enough time with her. She'll drive you up a wall, eventually."

"Well, given how much the children already seem to adore her, we may just have to invite her back in the—"

"Father." Rayan rose from his seat and smiled. "I'm glad you found your way back."

"I got distracted for a moment—there's a beautiful statue out in the corridor that caught my eye—but I remembered my way when I heard Ginny's yammering."

Ginny scoffed. "I don't *yammer.*"

Aurelia barely heard her. She was too distracted by the sound of Eric's voice: calmer, steadier, and more musical than she expected it to be. From what Arian had told her about Eric, he was a bit rough around the edges and had a nasty temper. The gentle voice ringing out through the dining hall, however, sounded like nothing more than a kind old man.

Ignoring the way both Jack and Hyacinth were staring at her, Aurelia sucked in a deep breath and stood, just in time for Eric to appear behind Rayan's chair. She reached for her locket for comfort as soon as she saw him, forgetting she'd taken it off before dinner, and studied the man who'd helped bring her into the world.

He looked older than she thought he would, despite knowing he was over sixty years of age. His once-auburn hair was now gray, but still a bit shaggy, and though his face was clean-shaven, she could see tiny white whiskers starting to grow. His eyes were the exact color of hers and Rayan's: pure, light blue like the cloudless sky. He was tall, like his son, and still quite strong for a man of his age, but he had a slight hunch to his back. He wasn't looking at her, either, but rather at her children while they giggled at Ginny.

"Aurelia," Rayan said with a smile, "this is my father, Eric Haze."

Aurelia's heart fluttered when Eric bowed to her. "Good day, Mister Haze. It's a pleasure to make your acquaintance."

"The honor is mine, Your Grace." He held the bow for a moment too long, only rising when Rayan squeezed his shoulder. "I never..."

He trailed off, bushy gray eyebrows furrowing, as his eyes finally landed on Aurelia's face. She didn't break eye contact with him, but Rayan frowned at him as he looked between his father and his queen.

After a moment, Eric cleared his throat and blinked like he'd broken out of a trance. "Forgive me, my queen. It's just...You look like someone I used to know. Nearly identical, in fact."

A jolt traveled from the top of Aurelia's skull to the tips of her toes. She couldn't see Jack, but he hoped he didn't have a physical reaction to what

Eric had said. She didn't want anyone, least of all Rayan, to sense that something was off.

"That's all right." She pushed her uneasiness aside and sat again while Eric claimed the empty seat to Rayan's left. "May I ask who this person was?"

"A woman I met when I visited Carthe many years ago."

Aurelia couldn't stop herself from asking, "What was she like?"

"She was..." He trailed off again, and in the blink of an eye, the frail, nervous grandfather transformed into a glowing, youthful man practically oozing with life. "She was a clever girl—always knew more than she let on—and you couldn't help but smile when you were near her. Her laugh made everyone want to dance like her voice was a melody. Her smile filled every room with joy. And her wit..." He laughed. "She had a mouth on her, but she was the funniest person I've ever met. I'd wager she still is, wherever she is."

Aurelia felt Hyacinth's eyes on her. There was the answer to the question she'd asked her daughter the day before: Eric didn't know that Katryna was dead. He deserved to know, but Aurelia wasn't sure she could be the person to tell him.

"Good gods, Father," Rayan teased. "She asked you a simple question, and you responded with a novel. You wonder where Ginny gets it from."

"I heard that," his sister replied.

A pang pierced Aurelia's heart. She could see it in his eyes, hear it in his voice, and feel it radiating from his body that even now, he was as in love with Katryna Cristos as he'd been over thirty years earlier. Even if he was still a stranger to her...Well, it didn't take years of knowing someone to recognize love in their eyes.

Aurelia cleared her throat. "She sounds like a wonderful person. I'm glad to resemble her. Perhaps you'll find that I share qualities of her character, too, now that you'll be spending more time in the palace while visiting the Lord Hand. I do hope that's what you plan to do. You're always welcome here."

"Thank you." Eric brightened, pausing only for a moment as servants delivered the first course. "May I ask you something, Your Grace?"

"Of course."

His smile reached his eyes when he glanced over at Hyacinth. "Which hyacinth did you have in mind when you named your daughter?"

Her heart fluttered. "Delft blue."

"Ah." His eyes were misty with emotion. "The best kind."

She smiled. "The best kind."

And Katryna's favorite. He would've known that as well as she did.

"If you're wondering," Hyacinth piped up, "*my* favorites are the purple ones."

"I like poppies," Halle added.

Henry stuck up his nose. "I don't care much for flowers. I'm a boy."

"Boys can still like flowers," Jack told him. "I'm partial to lilies."

"You're from Omara, aren't you?" Ginny asked him. Jack nodded. "I've only ever passed through. What I've seen of the kingdom has taken my breath away, though. Your wildflower fields are unparalleled. I've never seen anything else quite like them. I keep a notebook of every new flower I come across, and I identified about five when we were traveling from Holos to the Folly a few weeks ago. Do you know about carnations? They're *stunning*. I wanted to pluck some to take home with me, but I knew they'd die before I made it back, and I couldn't stomach the thought of watching such beautiful flowers wilt and perish before my eyes."

Aurelia was barely listening. She was too distracted by the ring on Eric's right middle finger: a thick gold band with a flat, ovular plate on the center. Stamped onto the plate was the image of a hummingbird—the Cristos family sigil. Arian wore the same ring nearly every day. It was a family ring, so Aurelia could only assume that Katryna had given one to Eric.

Eric's eyes snapped over to her, startling her, before landing on the ring. A distant, painful sort of smile formed on his lips as he brought his hand to his chest and twisted the ring around his finger.

"I assumed you'd recognize this," he admitted. "It was gifted to me many years ago by...by..." He trailed off, frowning, and stared into nothingness. "It was given to me by..."

Rayan and Ginny exchanged worried looks as Aurelia cleared her throat. "By Arian Cristos, perhaps?"

Eric's eyes flashed. The name *Cristos* seemed to jog his memory, but both he and Aurelia knew Arian hadn't been the one to give it to him.

"Yes," he murmured. "I...I spent a few seasons in Taundosa decades ago. Agotia welcomed me with open arms. I served as a soldier for the Cristos family during that time, and I grew close to Arian—erm, Lord Cristos. I'd heard he was here recently. How is he?"

A lump formed in Aurelia's throat as Henry responded for her: "He's been sleeping for *days*. I want to play with him, but Mama and Papa say I can't, because he needs his rest."

"His Lordship isn't feeling well at the moment," Jack said hurriedly. "I'm sure he'll be wanting to see his old friend when he wakes, though. We'll be sure to summon you back to the palace as soon as he does."

Eric frowned. "Arian Cristos, taken ill? Why, he's never been ill a day in his life! Not that I can remember, anyway."

"Father," Rayan warned.

"It was a bit of a shock for us, too. We like to think of His Lordship as immortal," Jack said, only half-teasingly. "I suspect it's just—"

"*Mama!*"

Everyone silenced as the pitter-patter of little feet against marble echoed throughout the dining hall. In the time it took Aurelia to blink, Halyna was at her side, gripping fistfuls of Aurelia's skirt and pouting her lower lip.

"Where did you come from?" Aurelia mused, brushing hair from her daughter's face. "You're supposed to be having dinner with the twins and your governesses, little one."

Halyna sniffed and rubbed her sleepy eyes. "I ran away 'cause the babies were crying, and it made my head hurt. I..." She trailed off when she noticed Eric, distracted by him as he spun his ring around his finger. Before Aurelia could respond, Halyna zipped over to Eric and pointed to the ring. "That's very pretty."

"Thank you, Your Highness," Eric replied beaming. He took it off and held it out for her. "You can play with it, if you'd like."

Halyna grinned from ear to ear, thanked him politely, then did something nobody could've seen coming: climbed onto Eric's lap. As if she'd known him for her entire life, she perched on his thighs and leaned her elbows on the table, spinning the ring and laughing at the way it danced across the tablecloth. Eric was frozen for a moment, as startled as everyone else, but soon set a hand on her side to keep her stable while commenting on her spinning skills.

Aurelia chortled. "You shall have to forgive Halyna, Mister Haze. She's still learning about personal space."

"I don't mind." Eric snaked an arm around Halyna so he could still eat without disrupting her. Celesse appeared in the doorway at the same time, but Aurelia waved a dismissive hand, letting the governess know it was okay for Halyna to stay. "Ginny always says I have a way with children. They're drawn to me, for whatever reason."

Ginny cracked a smile. "He read to my children on our front porch when he first arrived in Satin Valley. Every child in the neighborhood stopped to listen, gathered around my property like a mob. They came back so often that we made a routine out of it. Every fourth day, the neighborhood children gathered for one of his stories, oftentimes bringing others from surrounding areas to listen, too."

"It must've been quite the story," Jack joked.

"I like stories," Halle remarked. "Can we hear it, Mister Haze?"

"I'd hate to disappoint. My brain isn't what it used to be," Eric admitted. A sad, distant sort of look appeared in his eyes, but it was gone as quickly as it'd come. "Hasn't been for a while now. I may miss a few details."

His admission made the mood turn somber, but fortunately, Henry sprung to the rescue: "I still want to hear it, Mister Haze."

Eric smiled. "Your wish is my command, Your Highness." He adjusted his position when Halyna, now curious to hear the story, leaned back against his chest, her hair dusting his cheek, and twirled his ring on her tiny fingers. "The story begins with a young soldier's first day of work—or first night, really. It was a particularly bad way to start his new job, because this wasn't any average night. The nobleman who employed the soldier was throwing an extravagant ball that evening, and the soldier was tasked with protecting the nobleman's eldest daughter from afar while she enjoyed the festivities. It was nearly impossible, though: you see, it was a masquerade ball, and the soldier hadn't met the daughter beforehand! He was shaking in his boots, trying to figure out which masked woman was the one he was supposed to be watching, because he knew he'd be fired if he was caught minding the wrong girl."

Aurelia froze. She knew Eric had been a soldier for multiple noble families—in Holos, in the Folly, and in Taundosa, of course—but she knew this particular memory was from Taundosa. The City of Gold was infamous for its masquerade parties, and according to Arian, Katryna and Eric had first met at a masquerade ball at Ardiham Castle.

"The soldier was starting to panic when a woman in a blue dress approached him." Eric paused only to say *thank you* when a servant replaced his salad plate with a bowl of tomato soup. "She was wearing a gold mask, so he could hardly see her face. She accused him of looking sour, and she told him it wouldn't hurt if he danced or had a drink, because his stiffness was ruining the mood of the party." He stifled a laugh. "He told her that much was impossible. He was a soldier, after all, and he had rules to follow."

Halle's oceanic eyes were wide with intrigue. "What happened next?"

"She asked him why he looked so nervous, so he told her about the nobleman's daughter. She claimed to know the daughter, and offered to help the soldier look for her in the crowd. She teased him while they searched, saying he should've met the daughter before the ball, and tried to convince him to wear a mask like everyone else. She hardly stopped talking long enough to breathe, and though he knew she might've been someone powerful and important, he told her she was being a nuisance, anyway."

Jack snorted and gave Aurelia a pointed look. "I've been told that before, too."

"Quiet, you." She turned her gaze back to Eric, smiling. "Please, continue."

"She told him she enjoyed being a nuisance, and she was glad to have left an impression on him already." Eric stopped to drink from his chalice, gulping like his throat was drier than sandpaper. "Then, as they kept looking, a nobleman approached them—the very same one the soldier was serving. He greeted the soldier kindly and said, 'I see you've met my daughter.'"

"Oh!" Halle gasped, sitting on her knees and leaning so far over the table that her hair nearly dipped into her bowl. "The woman was the same person the soldier was supposed to be protecting?"

"She was," Eric confirmed. The look in his eyes made Aurelia's heart sink: it was nostalgic and joyous, but at the same time, riddled with pain and longing. "Of course, the soldier was equally betrayed and horrified. When the nobleman left, his daughter merely laughed and apologized for her trickery, but the soldier was furious. He didn't like that she'd mocked him. She said that he needed to learn to relax and find some joy in life rather than being so stoic, and he knew she was right, so he apologized for being angry with her. She curtsied to him, thanked him for a wonderful evening, and told him she was looking forward to teasing him again in the future."

Even Hyacinth—who was hard to impress or surprise, nowadays—was mesmerized. "What happened next?"

"Nothing, really. The soldier kept an eye on her throughout the rest of the ball, but they didn't speak again that night. They went their separate ways when the party ended, and the next morning, the soldier received an invitation from her, asking him to join her for breakfast in the gardens. Only then did he realize he didn't know her name. The nobleman had only ever referred to her as his eldest daughter, and she hadn't introduced herself at the ball. When he met her for breakfast, the first thing he did was ask for her name."

Halle raised an eyebrow. "What was it?"

Eric's eyes dazzled with something Aurelia could only describe as devotion—a yearning, passionate kind of infatuation that only existed between two souls destined to unite as one.

"Katryna."

XII

urelia hadn't stopped thinking about Eric and his story since she heard it. They'd resumed a normal dinner after that, making polite conversation and getting to know one another, but she'd been distracted by the tale of the night her parents met.

It'd been hard for her to say goodbye to him and Ginny when dinner ended. It was a quick goodbye, as the children had started nodding off, and she wished she'd had more time with them—especially Ginny, who was returning home to Holos tomorrow. At the very least, though, Aurelia knew she'd be seeing a lot more of Eric Haze in the near future now that he was back in the Folly.

She hadn't known what to expect from him. A part of her thought he'd be distant, cold, and bitter, given that he'd abandoned a pregnant Katryna—and Rayan and Ginny, for a time—during his younger years, but she didn't know the full story, so she had to give him the benefit of the doubt. She was pleased to find that he was none of those things, but rather a normal, kindly older man with a warm heart and a welcoming smile.

After meeting him—and liking him tremendously, for that matter—she immediately wanted to see more of him. A part of her wondered if additional interactions would become difficult, what with the secret she was keeping from him and Rayan, but another part of her remembered that he was the only parent she had left. She wanted to spend more time with him while it lasted, even if the weight of the secrecy threatened to consume her.

When they retired to their bedchamber that evening, Jack had asked, "Will you ever tell them?"

Aurelia had only sighed while slipping into bed beside him. "Maybe one day."

"Why bother waiting, then? If you have any intention of telling them, it's better to do it now."

She'd winced at that. "I don't know if I *want* to tell them, Jack. I don't want to disrupt their lives or change everything they thought they knew."

"If it were me," he'd said, yawning, "I'd want to know."

"It's not you."

He'd glowered at her before blowing out the candle on his nightstand. "I'm not saying you have to tell them, but I think they have a right to know—especially Rayan. And Eric..."

He hadn't needed to finish. Telling Rayan that they were half-siblings was Aurelia's responsibility, but telling Eric that his queen was his daughter...That was Arian's responsibility. He should've been the one to tell Eric that Katryna was dead, and that she died giving birth to the future Queen of Akkinor. They'd reach the same result if Aurelia told him, but she knew it would've meant more coming from Arian—someone who'd known Katryna as well as Eric had.

But even if Aurelia decided it was time to tell the Haze family the truth, she couldn't even consider doing so until Arian recovered. That took precedent over everything.

Aurelia wasn't able to fall asleep. She rang for a servant to bring her a cup of milk and honey, and when that didn't help, she tried reading for a bit. That only excited her mind instead of calming it, though. She even tried waking Jack so she'd have someone to talk to, and he'd planted a pillow over his head to drown her out as soon as she roused him. He might've mumbled something about marrying a pest, too, but she chose to pretend she hadn't heard him.

So she wouldn't disturb him further, Aurelia threw on her dressing robe and slippers, then carefully padded out of her bedchamber while carrying a candle to light her path. She was walking aimlessly, hoping a short promenade would lull her to sleep, until she found herself outside of Hyacinth's room. To her surprise, she saw a candle flickering inside from beneath the door.

Frowning, she knocked gently before pushing the door open. She couldn't help but chuckle when she saw her daughter sitting upright in bed, reading by the candlelight.

"You're supposed to be asleep," Aurelia murmured, closing the door behind her. "It's very late."

"So are you."

"Fair enough. What are you doing awake?"

Hyacinth sighed. "Halle asked me to sleep with her. She had a nightmare. I couldn't sleep 'cause her room is hot, so I had to sneak out. I can't sleep here, either, though."

"I'm finding it hard to sleep tonight, too." Aurelia set the candle down on the nightstand and crawled into bed beside her daughter. "You know who Mister Haze's story was about, don't you?"

She nodded and pointed at Aurelia's locket. "Her."

"Mhm. And you know who she was, right?"

She nodded again.

Aurelia sighed as Hyacinth laid down next to her, sharing the same pillow. "I know we don't talk about your ability much—far less than we should, really—but I'm sorry you know as much as you do. I can't imagine the things you've seen, Sisi. It's not right."

"I don't mind, Mama."

Aurelia pulled her daughter into her embrace, resting her cheek against the top of Hyacinth's head. She couldn't help but wonder if Hyacinth knew that she wasn't her parents' trueborn daughter. That was something Aurelia and Jack never wanted her to know, at least until she was much older, but it seemed inevitable that she'd find out.

"If there's anything you've seen that you'd like to talk about," Aurelia murmured, "you can. It's all right."

She felt her daughter wince. "I'm okay, Mama, but...Can I tell you something else?"

"Of course, my love."

"I don't want to give up my magic."

Aurelia stilled. *She* does *know*, she thought. And yet, somehow, the reveal wasn't as shocking to Aurelia as it should've been.

"Sisi..."

"I know why you want me to, Mama. It's not safe. But Innoba found a way to do the same thing, and everyone believed him."

Aurelia frowned, not understanding, until she saw the title of the book Hyacinth had been reading: *The Quest of the Mighty Innoba*. The old Quenosi fairytale had been a favorite of Aurelia's as a child. It followed the story of a young man named Innoba who'd been born with incredible gifts, despite coming from a mortal family. His neighbors called him a heretic because nobody could explain how he'd acquired magic when there were no mages in his bloodline.

After embarking on a quest for answers, Innoba returned home and declared that he, an earth mage, had been chosen by the Elemental Terra as a mortal soul worthy of claiming her gifts. It was meant to be ambiguous: nobody truly knew if Terra had actually bestowed her magic upon him, or if he'd merely invented the story to save his own skin. Either way, the people in the story believed him, and they ceased threatening him and calling him a heretic. After all, nobody wanted to get involved if they thought divine intervention was afoot.

"That's just a story, Sisi," Aurelia said gently. "The real world is more...complicated."

She could hear the frown in Hyacinth's voice: "What you have to do is complicated, too, but you'll succeed. I can, too."

"What are you talking about?"

Hyacinth only sighed. "You'll see."

***

The next morning, Aurelia left thoughts of Eric and Hyacinth behind to focus on the task at hand: finding a way to save Arian.

She and Halvor arrived at the monastery right around lunchtime. She was greeted by one of her former tutors, High Priest Octavien, who knew to expect her after his superior, the Elder of Akkinor, received a raven from Rayan.

"Elder Marvion is indisposed today, I'm afraid," Octavien said as he escorted her through the halls. "He knows you wish to visit the archives, so he entrusted me with the key. Only one soul may enter the archives at a time, so I'll wait for you outside. I can't show you around, but if there's anything in particular you're searching for, I can point you in the right direction."

Aurelia smiled. "That's all right. I'll find my way."

Neither Diantha nor Maysa had given her any details about what she was looking for, but she knew to start with Vanhylde. She wasn't sure what the priest would think if he knew she was poking around for information on the land between worlds.

The monastery had always been a quiet place. Priests, students, and patrons often kept to themselves. Since more and more mages had started visiting over the years, though, it was a bit more...chaotic.

Students of all ages strolled the halls, clutching books to their chests and exchanging notes, sometimes accompanied by a priest or priestess giving them direction. They laughed, talked, sang—a stark contrast to the silence Aurelia was used to. There were even creatures lurking about, as they liked the powerful, ancient aura of the magical institution. Some creatures even assisted the priests when they delivered lessons to students, mages and mortals alike.

The estate used to be somewhat plain, bathed in shades of white and beige, with only marble statues or sculptures as decor. It'd been completely void of color and imperfection. Now, artwork of every kind was on display in every hall and corridor, hanging ivy and wisteria flowed down the walls from the ceilings, and most of the neutral colors had been replaced with Brentwood blue and gold.

Even the attire of the priests and students used to be different. They'd all worn white and beige robes, their ranks distinguished only by the color of the rope they wore around their waists to tie them. Nowadays, everyone wore ropes in the same shade of gold, and the colors of their robes had been changed to distinguish their stations: violet for Elder Marvion; royal blue for High Priests; jade green for the average priests; crimson for mages; and white for students.

Octavien led Aurelia down a hallway she'd never seen before, then through an arched doorway blocked by a gate he unlocked with one of the three keys dangling from his neck. There was a set of winding, steep stairs—uneven after years of being treaded upon—that led to a floor beneath the monastery's ground level. Torches on scones lined the walls along the staircase, and they sprang to life, bathing the path in warm orange light, as soon as Aurelia and Octavien approached them.

At the bottom of the staircase, there was another gate in an arch-shaped doorway. A strange, overwhelming feeling of pressure washed over Aurelia as she peered through the square-shaped holes in the gate. The room behind it looked like another library, with bookshelves filled with texts of all kinds, but at the same time, it reminded her of a storage space. There were crates scattered about, objects covered with sheets, and miscellaneous artifacts on every corner, seemingly placed wherever there was room for them.

"This is where I leave you." Octavien used one of the other keys to unlock the gate, then pushed it open. A whoosh charged at them, lifting Aurelia's hair from her shoulders and making her gasp. Octavien only chuckled. "Oh, yes. There's a special energy here in the archives. Don't let it frighten you, Your Grace."

She swallowed. "I'll do my best."

He tipped his head to her. "I'll wait for you at the top of the stairs. Good luck."

She listened to his shoes against the stone steps, holding her breath, and took a few steps into the archives. Another whoosh tickled her skin as soon as she crossed the threshold. When she looked back to catch a final glimpse of Octavien, the gate swung shut.

Shuddering, Aurelia surveyed the room, hugging herself for both warmth and comfort. Though it was the middle of springtime, it felt colder in the archives, and the mysterious breeze wasn't helping.

Not knowing where to start, Aurelia turned to the far left side of the room, where a desk and a chair sat against the wall. Boxes and piles of paperwork covered the surface of the desk, so she thumbed through those first. When she didn't find anything of value, she turned to a mahogany cabinet beside the desk. There were three shelves inside, and each one contained stacks of old, disintegrating scrolls. The scrolls were written in the ancient tongue, and Aurelia wasn't fluent enough to make heads or tails out of it.

While wandering around, she heard something clang behind her. She followed the direction the noise had come from, wondering if she was truly alone in the archives, and prayed to every god she could think of that she hadn't stumbled upon something she wasn't meant to.

When she investigated, she didn't find the source of the tinkering sound, but she did find something else: an arch-shaped wooden door. The door wouldn't budge when she rattled the handle, but soon after, she spotted a faded inscription on the stone wall above it: *For the secrets of the realm to be known, another must be offered in exchange.*

"So, to open the door, I have to offer up a secret." Aurelia pondered that for a moment as she thought about something she'd never told anyone before. "All right. I suppose my secret is that a part of me resents my parents for keeping my magic from me. I understand why they did it, and it doesn't change how much I love them, but sometimes I find myself angry. That's partly why I haven't made a decision about Hyacinth."

Nothing happened. She was ready to give up, to turn around and look elsewhere, until the engraved words emitted a golden glow. She took a step back, mesmerized, as the door creaked and groaned before slowly opening for her. As soon as it did, the small room inside became bathed in light.

The room was circular and no larger than a gardener's toolshed. The sandstone walls were crumbling and cracked, yet the ceiling above was perfectly intact—though it was so low that even Aurelia, a woman of average height, nearly bumped her head. Arched bookshelves lined the perimeter, clearly built to match the curvature of the walls. Other than the bookshelves and the documents they contained, there was only one other thing in the room: an iron chest.

Inhaling, Aurelia knelt by the chest and opened it, surprised yet again to find it wasn't locked. Scrolls upon scrolls filled the chest, ranging from so old they were flaking into bits, to so new that she could still smell the fresh ink.

After sifting through the scrolls—carefully, so she didn't damage any ancient documents—and finding nothing, she saw something sitting at the bottom of the chest: a thick, leatherbound book with a gold cover and no title.

She closed the chest and set the book on top of it. She was reaching for it when the book slammed open, making her gasp, as the pages turned on their own. After a moment, the book stilled once more, and the first thing she saw on the right-hand page was the bolded word VANHYLDE.

Apparently, someone—or something—wanted her to find this.

As she glanced through the chapter dedicated to the land between worlds, she found information she'd already learned, and not much else. Then, on the very last page in the section, she saw a new heading: *For Those Who Dare to Visit.* Swallowing the lump in her throat, Aurelia read the few paragraphs, her body tingling with intrigue.

Vanhylde is accessible to anyone who has a just reason for visiting. Though the dead are its only permanent inhabitants, death is not a requirement for entry. But let this be a warning: you must accept the possibility of your demise if you hope to visit Vanhylde. It is not the journey that will kill you, nor the dead, but rather the things you may find there.

Namely, you may come across something that you do not wish to live without once you've found it. More often than not, Vanhylde's visitors choose to surrender their souls to the universe rather than returning to Icareth. You may think you are strong enough to fight it, dear reader, but you are not. Everyone crosses the threshold with the intention to leave, but very few actually do so.

A common misconception is that one must have magic to visit Vanhylde. If that were true, then mortals would not have the ability to dream. In fact, it is quite easy to visit. Connections to Vanhylde exist all around us, but only a select few are lucky enough to notice them.

You must give your blood to the realm in a place closest to the divine, and you must utter these words: 'I surrender my soul to the universe at this portal between worlds. I am prepared to leave my flesh behind in the event that my soul does not return to claim it. I am but a vessel with a gods-given purpose, and I shall endeavor to find and fulfill that purpose in the realm known as Vanhylde.'

When Aurelia finished reading, she didn't hesitate. She couldn't think of anything that would convince her to stay in purgatory, particularly when her children and her husband remained in Icareth. She'd get her answers, and she'd go home to her family right after.

That's when it struck her: *a room with three entrances, but only one exit.* The gates to the archives served as both entrance and exit, and then there was the little hidden room in the back—the second entrance. The portal to Vanhylde, then, had to be the third entrance.

Using the dagger she always kept strapped to her ankle, Aurelia cut her palm, grimacing at the pinpricks of pain, and let crimson droplets fall to the stone floor. The monastery was the holiest place in Akkinor, and there she was, giving her blood to the realm while uttering those three sacred lines.

Nothing happened. Moments passed, and still, nothing. She reread the text, wondering if she'd missed something, but brought herself to a screeching halt when she spotted an oddity on the wall behind the chest: what appeared to be a rust-colored handprint, so faded that it nearly blended in with the sandstone.

Aurelia stood and approached the brick, blood still spurting from her palm. She took a deep breath and pressed her palm against the handprint, wondering who it belonged to, when they'd lived, and why they'd come. Almost immediately, a whoosh of cool air lifted her hair from her shoulders, and the breeze only grew stronger as she uttered the three sentences once more.

By the time she stopped speaking, her heart was pounding so violently that she could feel it pulsating throughout her entire body, and the mysterious breeze encapsulated her like a cyclone. She squeezed her eyes shut, preparing to feel her soul torn from her being, as echoing whispers flooded her eardrums.

When the wind stopped and the whispers faded, Aurelia refrained from opening her eyes, terrified of what she might find. Perhaps it'd all been a game of sorts, and everything she'd just experienced was just a silly parlor trick. Or, perhaps, she'd find herself transported to somewhere unimaginably horrid. That possibility frightened her even more when she realized the book hadn't said anything about how to return to Icareth.

She should've thought about that before she cut her palm.

As she built up the confidence to open her eyes, she felt a soft, gentle breeze against her face. It was different than the odd wind from the archives, and it filled her with a sense of tranquility she hadn't known in years. That compelled her to open her eyes and pull her hand from the wall. When she did, she saw her palm had stopped bleeding, and she wasn't touching a wall—instead, it was a tree trunk.

"Hello."

A male voice spoke behind her, but she wasn't quite ready to face whoever it was. She couldn't explain it, but she *knew* she recognized it, even though she'd never heard it before.

The man spoke once more: "Welcome to Vanhylde, Aurelia."

XIII

Momentarily forgetting the man behind her, Aurelia took a few steps back from the tree, still not fully comprehending that she'd just transported from one realm to another.

The secret room, the archives, the monastery—even the entirety of Akkinor—had disappeared. Now, Aurelia stood in the middle of a forest, with cloudless blue skies above her and perfect, blooming trees in front of her. She could hear a rushing stream nearby and the chirping of birds, and when she finally turned, she saw a massive green field covered in wildflowers that seemed to go on forever in either direction.

Standing a few feet away was a young man, about Aurelia's age, who stood taller than Jack—the tallest person she knew. He wore simple brown breeches and a plain, loose-fitting white tunic, and his feet were bare. His hair, like molten gold, flowed in straight locks over his shoulders and down his back. His eyes were a piercing royal blue, like a Bozari's, that twinkled with a kind of ancient wonder and wisdom Aurelia had never seen before from a human.

She had, however, seen that *exact* look in a pair of golden, reptilian eyes. Those eyes belonged to the only living thing she trusted more than she trusted herself.

"Halvor?"

As soon as the word left her lips, he erupted in a massive grin.

Awestruck, Aurelia took a few steps toward him, studying him from top to bottom. He didn't say a word, only smiled at her, while she observed him with unblinking eyes. She walked around him in a circle, and when she was facing him again, she brought a shaking hand to his cheek. He covered his hand with hers, titling his face against her touch, and made her gasp when his eyes—for just a fraction of a second—shifted from human blue, to golden reptilian, and back again.

"How is this possible?" she whispered.

Halvor kept smiling as she dropped her hand. "After spending centuries in this place, my soul became bonded to it. A piece of me—a fragment of my consciousness—will exist in Vanhylde for eternity. I chose to portray that piece of myself as a human to make this conversation easier for you."

That's why Diantha can't communicate with Rieza like this, Aurelia thought. *Rieza was never sent to Vanhylde.*

"Exactly," he said. When she gaped at him, he laughed, the sound filling her with warmth and reminding her of a crackling hearth. "Your thoughts are not your own in Vanhylde. Everything we think is heard by those around us." She kept gaping at him as he gestured to a fallen tree trunk to her left. "Shall we sit?"

Nearly paralyzed by awe and disbelief, she followed him to the trunk and sat beside him, still studying him. She never imagined him as a human before—why would she?—but if she had, he would've looked exactly like the man sitting beside her. Even so, she had to keep reminding herself that this wasn't a random soul she'd met in Vanhylde, but her dragon in human form.

"I know you have many questions for me. I'll try to answer some of them now," Halvor mused. "Vanhylde looks different to every soul who visits it. What you see now is the reality I was welcomed to when I first arrived all those centuries ago. I don't mind that a piece of me always exists here—as you can see, it's quite peaceful. And as much as I missed being close to those I've served over the years before you freed me, I understood that I was safer here. Humans sent many other magical creatures here during the persecution, and while my brethren yearn to return to Icareth, they're still afraid of what they might find there. And before you ask, yes—I will remember this conversation when you return to my physical form in Icareth."

A shiver traced her spine. She hadn't even thought of that. "Does this piece of you ever desire to reunite with the rest of your soul? With your body?"

"No. Having a part of me exist here...It grounds me, so to speak. If not, I fear I'd be a more menacing creature than the one you know. This place ensures that a piece of my soul shall always be at peace."

Diantha's voice echoed in her head. "You know about Diantha, then, and Rieza."

Halvor nodded and smiled when a monarch butterfly landed on his knee. "Diantha was right—Rieza is my sister. Our parents and our brother were slaughtered during the persecution. Rieza does not wish to harm you, I promise. We can trust her." As Aurelia nodded, he sighed and ran a hand through his hair. "I know nothing about the longbelly who visited that night. She is young and inexperienced. Three years old, I believe. I do know that she was sent to us that night, but by whom, I couldn't say. She does not wish to harm us, either, but if her human commands it, she may not be able to fight it. Young dragons, especially emerald ones, are quite malleable. In the hands of a rotten human, a young dragon can be very dangerous. Against me and Rieza, though, she's nothing to fear—for now."

That gave her a bit of solace, but not much. "Did you speak with her? The longbelly?"

"I tried. She didn't respond, exactly. She was roaring the same word, over and over—*Annera.*"

"The goddess of the stars."

"Indeed. I believe it's her name, but I don't know why she was repeating it."

That's odd, Aurelia thought, and snorted into a laugh when she saw Halvor nod in agreement. She'd already forgotten that he could hear everything she was thinking.

"Diantha has given me hell over my ignorance of you," Aurelia murmured, shamefully glancing down at her hands in her lap. Halvor took her chin and forced her to look into his eyes, his face creasing with concern. "She says I must learn more about dragonriding—that our bond is incomplete while I remain unaware of what it means to be your rider. She didn't phrase it quite like that, but..."

"Hmm." The noise he made reminded her of the way dragon Halvor chuffed at her. He looked away from her, hands on his knees, and furrowed his bushy golden brows. "She thinks that way because of the dragon she's bonded with. Rieza is volatile. Her riders have had no choice but to become as familiar with her as possible to avoid being surprised in flight or battle. They must know what frightens her, what calms her, what enrages her. I myself have a steadier temperament, particularly when you are nearby. It isn't your friend's fault for assuming that's the case for all dragons and their riders, though. That's what she was raised to believe."

Aurelia cracked a smile. "What makes you so different?"

"As a hatchling, I got separated from my family while my parents were teaching us to hunt. Poachers found me, wanting to kill me for my scales, but I was rescued by your ancestor. Her name was Maryela Cristos, the daughter of the Lord of Agotia in Taundosa. She was a fifteen-year-old fire mage who frightened those mortals out of their wits with her power. I didn't see her much after that, but when I was old enough to go off on my own, I sought her out. I'd already bonded to her, you see. I spent all of my time with her and her family, and when she left me for Hanhalla, I bonded with her eldest daughter, then her eldest granddaughter, and so on. I think spending so much time with humans taught me to understand them better than other dragons can."

"For Rieza, it's about the riders understanding the dragon. For you, it's about the dragon understanding the riders."

"Precisely. What applies to some doesn't always apply to all." He bent down to pick a dandelion from the grass, smiling as the wind immediately blew the tufts into the air. "You don't need to waste your time learning everything there is to know about me. I shall never do anything to surprise you or weaken our bond. I shall never disobey or disregard any of your commands—we're too likeminded for that. Diantha can't say the same for Rieza just yet, and assumes the same is true for us, because Rieza's bond with the Pharos family is still somewhat new. It pales in comparison to my bond with your family."

Aurelia couldn't help but smile at that. "I knew it."

"Yes, you did. The fact that you trusted our bond as it is, despite someone with greater knowledge of dragonkind telling you to look beyond it...That's proof enough that we are indestructible together."

Her eyes welled with tears as she reached over to squeeze his hand. "You know how much I love you, don't you?"

"Of course. If I didn't, I wouldn't be here." He gave her hand a squeeze, too. "That's enough about us, though. You're here for another reason. Unfortunately, I can't tell you what you need to know about Arian."

Aurelia's heart sank. "Oh."

"That, however," he continued, eyes shimmering with mischief, "doesn't mean there isn't someone else in Vanhylde who can help you."

"Archie." Her brother's name still felt sour on her lips. "I'd assumed Vanhylde is what he meant when he told me I could visit him, but I don't—"

Halvor interrupted her. "No, no. You're right about your assumption, but he's not the one who can tell you about Arian."

A sudden realization struck her. "How is he here? Surely the gods could've sent him straight to Saendah after what he did."

"Well..." Halvor grimaced and pulled his hand from hers. "The gods may be tough, but they are not beyond reason or mercy. Saendah is reserved for the worst souls to ever exist in the universe. Your brother, for all of his terrible deeds, is not among those individuals. That's why he's here: unlike that horrid Willem Trevas, his actions weren't damning enough for him to deserve eternal punishment. His soul belongs to Vanhylde for now."

"For now?" Aurelia furrowed her brows. "What does that mean?"

"Life is only the beginning, Aurelia. There are as many ways to earn salvation or damnation after death as there are in life. A soul may leave Vanhylde, but many are too lost to realize they're even here. Some mistake Vanhylde for Saendah or Hanhalla, so they have no idea they're capable of changing their fate."

It made sense to her now. When Archie visited her in a dream and accused her of failing to visit him, he'd also delivered a warning about a danger to come in the near future. She'd asked why he was delivering the message, of all people, and she'd never forget his response: *Because I'm the last person you'd expect to be here trying to save your life.*

Perhaps helping her was the key to his salvation. He was trapped in a land between the heavens and hell for now, but maybe, just maybe, helping Aurelia succeed—and fulfill her destiny—would be enough to earn him a place in Hanhalla. She still didn't think he was deserving of it, but then again, she didn't think he was deserving of eternal torment, either.

"If not Archie," she murmured, "then who might I speak with?"

Halvor's lips curled into a grin. "There's something else you must know about Vanhylde. A soul existing in Hanhalla can enter any plane of existence other than Saendah, though they aren't visible to the living in Icareth. That's how Arian can summon Katryna's soul, and how spirits can visit Icareth, if they so choose. They can visit Vanhylde, too, but only temporarily. It's exactly like the reason a part of me still exists here: when a soul spends too much time in Vanhylde, a piece of it tethers to this world. You may visit many times in small increments, but the longer you stay, the greater the odds that you will not return to your plane of existence with your entire soul intact."

"So, the person I'm supposed to speak with is visiting Vanhylde from Hanhalla?"

"Yes. They cannot stay for long, and neither can you. The conversation must be a short one, but you may return whenever you'd like. I shall always be here to guide you and ensure you return to Icareth in time."

Aurelia's smile wobbled. "Thank you."

Halvor returned the expression. "Walk through the trees to find your answers. You'll know when you've arrived at your destination. You'll leave from there, but don't worry—I have a feeling that you and I shall find ourselves here again soon."

She reached over to hug him, not at all surprised when it reminded her exactly of what it felt like to press her forehead to dragon Halvor's snout.

"I'll see you at home," he whispered.

A shiver traced her spine as she nodded, kissed him on the cheek, and stood from the trunk. She took a few steps toward the tree she'd touched when she first arrived, but she stopped and looked over her shoulder before moving another inch. Halvor was still sitting on the tree trunk, hands on his knees, and beaming at her in a way that made her feel perfectly at ease.

Aurelia turned back to the forest, sucked in a sharp breath, and began to walk until the trees disappeared, blanketing her in darkness. She imagined this was what it felt like to be lost in oblivion: she couldn't feel her feet on the ground or hear twigs snapping beneath her shoes, she couldn't see the sun or the sky above the foliage, and she could no longer feel the comfort of Halvor's presence. She was alone in a tunnel of blackness, her entire being completely untethered to the universe.

Then the darkness morphed into something she knew like the back of her hand: the gardens at the palace of Akkinor. Everything was exactly as she remembered it from Icareth—the same species of trees, the same flowerbeds, the same marble fountains. The greenhouse was there, as was the stewardess's Little House and the massive walls protecting the grounds. Even the palace stood directly behind her, as if she'd emerged from the rear doors rather than from a forest.

Aurelia walked around, confused, but didn't see any signs of life anywhere. She had no idea who she was meant to be looking for. Then, something fell at her feet with a loud thump and a clang, making her gasp and take a step back. She still didn't see anything around her, so she bent down to collect what had fallen: a leather pouch.

Frowning, she opened the pouch and poured the contents into her hand. Her frown only deepened when a set of gold-plated knucklebones clattered onto her palm. She weighed them in her hand, puzzled, until another thump—followed by a brief trembling of the ground beneath her feet—came from directly in front of her.

A moment ago, there'd only been a tree there. Now, a young man stood in front of the tree, his arms folded casually over his chest as he leaned his weight on one leg. He wore black breeches with a flowing white shirt, the sleeves rolled up to his elbows, and, like Halvor, he was shoeless. His dark skin glistened against the sunlight, and there was a stray leaf lingering atop his bald head. He was watching her with his deep brown eyes, one eyebrow raised in amusement, and when their gazes met, he offered her the kindest, widest, most beaming smile she'd ever seen in her life.

The knucklebones fell from her palm and clattered onto the grass. She kept staring at him, lips moving as she tried and failed to speak, and for a moment, she thought she'd collapse to her knees and stay there forever.

Finally, she was able to utter one word: "Linden?"

His smile widened to a grin as he gestured to the bones with his chin. "Care to play?"

XIV

urelia's arms were around Linden's neck before she knew what she was doing. She'd run into his arms and collapsed as soon as their chests collided, forcing him to hold her upright as he struggled to return her embrace. Her feet slid against the ground, unable to find traction as her knees buckled, while she held fistfuls of the back of his shirt to keep herself steady. Golden tears slid down her cheeks, burning her eyes and staining the front of his shirt where her face met his chest.

She thought she'd start weeping uncontrollably, but somehow, she didn't turn into a blubbering mess. The joy she felt at seeing him overpowered the urge to bawl her eyes out, to release eight years' worth of pent-up guilt, grief, and longing. That, and...well, she knew her best friend, and she was fairly certain he'd mock her relentlessly if she lost the run of herself.

When she finally found her stability and pulled away from him, she reached up to set her hands on either side of his face, studying him. For a split second, she wondered if it was really him, or just a figment of her imagination that Vanhylde had created for her. As he gently clasped her wrists and smiled at her, though, she knew it was him: the kindness in his eyes and the love in his smile were impossible to imagine. Even her memories of him didn't do them justice anymore.

For a moment, she didn't know what to say. She'd never been tongue-tied with Linden in the five-and-twenty years she'd known him. He was the only person she could say that about. Now, though, there was so much she wanted to say—to thank him, to apologize, to tell him how much she missed him—that she didn't know where to start.

"Look at you." Linden's voice was hardly a whisper. "Three-and-thirty years old, and still with that same look in your eye—like a child hoping to stir up trouble."

She chuckled, barely avoiding a choked sob, and replied, "I could say the same about you. You're the one who introduced me to the art of making trouble, after all."

"That's entirely false. It was always you, and I, as your valiant protector, had no choice but to follow your lead. I was only your accomplice. Willing or unwilling...That part is still up for debate."

Not knowing what else to do, she threw her arms around him again and held him close, relishing the feel of being in his embrace after missing it every day for the last eight years. She never imagined she'd feel it again.

For a split second, she remembered the warning from the book in the archives: *you may come across something that you do not wish to live without once you've found it.* She hadn't understood what it meant, at first, but she did now. If she wasn't a queen, a mother, or a wife, she might've been swayed into staying in Vanhylde simply to be with her best friend again.

Linden coaxed her into releasing him so they could sit by the tree. As Aurelia wiped stray tears from her cheeks, she chuckled again when she saw Linden produce a bottle of wine and a few raspberry tarts wrapped in cloth. He took a swig from the bottle, handed it to her, and munched on a tart as he lay on his side, propped up on his elbow.

"I always wondered if you'd ever come here," he said as she drank. "I visited for the first time right after I died, just out of curiosity. Halvor found me right away. He wanted to thank me for taking such good care of you over the years. I asked him if you knew about this place, and he said you didn't, but there was a chance you'd figure it out some day. I came back as soon as I felt your soul cross the threshold."

"Ever the dutiful Hand," she teased. He laughed, but for some reason, the sound only made her feel guilty. "Linden, I...I'm so sorry. I don't know what more I can say other than how very sorry I am for what happened. It eats me alive to this day."

"It shouldn't. I was going to die regardless of what happened that day. If you'd surrendered to save me, Archie would've killed both of us. There were only ever two options, and the pair of us together chose the lesser of two evils. We chose right."

"Still, I—"

"Oh, would you stop it already?" His tone was playful, but his eyes had become stern and stoic. "If you think I resent you for it, you're wrong, and I'm offended by the insinuation. There's no greater honor than dying to protect someone you love. I'd tell you not to choose me over and over again if given the chance. I won't listen to another word about how guilty you feel, because you shouldn't. It was my choice."

Tears welled in her eyes, but she refused to let them fall. "I know that, but it doesn't lessen the pain."

"It will. Eventually." He ate another tart in one bite, then wiped the crumbs on his fingers on his pants. "Now, as much as I wish we had more time to catch up, we have to get you out of here before a piece of your soul tethers itself to Vanhylde. I have to go soon, too. Cee's waiting for me."

"Cicely," she whispered. Her former lady-in-waiting had been not only one of her greatest friends, but the love of Linden's life, too. She'd died after the uprising when she was shot with an arrow while shielding a child with her own body. "How-How is she?"

Linden grinned. "She's very well. Hanhalla has been kind to us both. I wish I could tell you about it, but we're not supposed to share details about Hanhalla with living souls. We can't alter your interpretation of the heavens. All I can tell you is that we're happy, and we both miss you very much. Cicely says hello, but she's a bit frightened of traveling between the planes of existence, so she'll continue to miss you from afar."

"That sounds like her," Aurelia said with a chuckle. "But you're right—there's something we need to talk about before I leave. Halvor said you can tell me about what happened to Arian." He nodded. "Forgive me, my friend, but I don't understand how you of all people can tell me about it."

A warm look filled his eyes. "Who is the one person in the world whose word you'd trust no matter what, even if you suspected they might be an imposter or an illusion?"

She blinked at him. "You, of course."

"I thought so." His grin only deepened, making her roll her eyes. "Arian thought so, too. He knew he could trust that I'd get this message to you. The state he's in right now...He's asleep, so most of the time, he's dreaming. His consciousness has been drifting through Vanhylde, in and out, since he collapsed, but his soul remains tethered to Icareth. He can't control when he visits Vanhylde, but when he's here, he knows what's happening." He cleared his throat as he plucked blades of grass from the lawn. "I felt something pulling me to Vanhylde a few days ago. It was Arian. He asked for my help pointing you in the right direction."

Aurelia frowned. "How did he know I'd be coming here?"

That made him grimace. "He knew he was cursed before he collapsed. Your oracle friend sent him a warning before his trip to Dofell. She saw all of this, but she couldn't tell you. I don't know how much she told him, but I do know that he was aware that both of you—and me, for that matter—would be visiting Vanhylde."

"That doesn't make any sense. If he knew he was cursed, why wouldn't he—"

"—say anything?" Linden finished. She nodded, still frowning, as he sighed. "I suppose he didn't want to be treated like a victim before the curse overtook him."

A sharp pang pierced her heart. She understood that well enough, but she couldn't imagine how Arian must've felt in the days and weeks leading up to the ball, knowing he could've collapsed at any moment.

"There's only so much I can tell you, because there's only so much he knows," Linden continued. "He was cursed while in Dofell, but the caster wasn't in the kingdom with him. The blockage needs to be removed before you can learn more. He did, however, sense that he was being watched in Dofell. He spotted a few individuals eyeing him under the guise of volunteering to help rebuild Dofell, and he noticed their capes—amber colored—had gazelles stitched into the fabric."

Aurelia's lips parted. "Amber is the symbolic color of Krotis, and the gazelle is the sigil of the Selle family of Bruila."

He nodded. "Arian thinks that's a good place to start. It may be the entirety of Krotis working together, and the Bruilans were merely sent to spy on him, but either way, Krotis seems to be behind this. He has no enemies in Krotis, so he isn't certain why they'd do such a thing to him."

"Did he say anything about how we can wake him up?"

"Well..." He grimaced again. "Yes and no. He doesn't know the exact nature of the curse. Your mages will have to keep working on that. There might be a spell or an anecdote to wake him up, but if not, you'll have to go to the source. A curse cast by a human, as opposed to one inflicted by a deity, can almost always be broken by killing the caster."

"So, until we find out exactly who's responsible for this, we can't wake him up." She sighed and chewed on her lower lip. "All right. I don't know how to go about this, though. We only have one ally in Krotis, and I haven't even met him yet. He could've had a part in this, for all I know, so he can't be trusted. And if I accuse all of Krotis of cursing the Lord Hand of Taundosa..."

Linden waved a dismissive hand. "They'll reveal themselves somehow. Give them a reason to think you're onto them, and they'll falter. I'm certain you'll work everything out—you always do." He paused, sitting up, and turned his gaze to the knucklebones on the lawn beside them. "We don't have time for that game. If you decide to come back, though, I'll be here to yell at you for cheating."

Aurelia laughed. "I know."

126

Snorting into a laugh, Linden stood and offered his hand for her to take. She let him pull her to her feet, then looped her arm through his as he started walking toward the palace doors.

"There's one other thing Arian wanted me to tell you," he continued. "He may even be here when you visit again, if he hasn't woken by then, but there's no telling when his consciousness will drift through Vanhylde." He cleared his throat. "Though he's confident in your success, he knows there's a possibility he may not wake up. If that happens, he'd like you to deliver a message on his behalf. The tale you need to know is in a blue leatherbound journal, which you'll find hidden in the archives. It's inside of a trunk that once belonged to your grandfather—Edmund. You'll need someone else's help to fill in the missing pieces, though. You'll know where to start when you read the journal."

Aurelia furrowed her eyebrows. "Why would—"

"That's all he told me. I didn't press for details." When he stopped them in front of the palace's rear doors, Linden pulled her into his arms. She relaxed as he rested his chin atop her head and squeezed her. "We have to go. Getting to Icareth from Vanhylde is simple: you need only walk through any door."

She nodded against him, then pulled back enough to meet his eyes. "Thank you, Linden. For everything. I love you."

"I love you, too." He kissed the top of her head and released her. "I do hope you come back. If not...Tell your husband that I approve of him, and give your children a kiss from their Uncle Linden."

Her eyes burned. "I will."

He gestured to the door and grinned. "Forward, Your Grace, ever forward."

***

"Explain this again." Lord Quagg massaged his temples as he paced across the room. "Precisely."

Shasta cleared her throat. "When my father received this letter from King Willem, he knew he had to believe it. He'd always known that Willem had a trusted oracle on his court, so the prophecy the king spoke of had to be true. Willem knew that if he failed in Dofell, my father, his old friend, would step up to finish the job. This particular prophecy is meant to come to fruition in the near future, and as you saw in the letter, Willem had every reason to believe what it suggests: Queen Aurelia of Akkinor will soon lead the realm to its downfall."

Lazelus eyed her from his seat at the table to her left. She didn't sound like she believed what she was saying. In fact, it sounded like she'd rehearsed these lines over and over, likely because her father had ingrained it in her brain. Lazelus was curious to know what she really thought, but she'd never tell him. She wouldn't say anything that might give him or the others reason to distrust her.

"My father hoped that sending Annera to Akkinor would serve as a warning, letting the queen know that she isn't special anymore," Shasta continued. "He thought she'd ignore whatever destiny she thinks she's meant to fulfill in favor of focusing on her own country for once. If she thought her power was threatened, she'd back off."

Lord Reesa snorted. "I don't know much about her, but she doesn't strike me as the type to back off from anything—especially when the warning you sent would be an appetizer for her dragon."

Shasta's face reddened, but she didn't falter. "It's not about her feeling threatened by Annera. It's about her realizing that her greatest strength isn't unique to her anymore, that her power is no longer extraordinary."

"All of that aside," Lord Keer added, "we're talking about a prophecy that only King Willem and his oracle seemed to know about. Queen Aurelia probably hasn't heard of it. Whatever Willem feared she'd do to the realm, I doubt she has any intention of going through with it—because she doesn't know. She hasn't done anything to suggest she'd put herself in a position to destroy the realm, either."

"King Willem's oracle—Maysa—has since befriended the queen. If Maysa hasn't told her about the prophecy yet, she will. Soon." Shasta dipped her finger into her hair scarf, pulling it from her face like she'd begun to swelter, before letting it fall back into place. "She may not realize that whatever awaits her will lead the realm to ruin. She may believe she's doing something good. Either way, the prophecy suggests that she'll put all of us at risk. There's no shortage of ways we can prevent that."

Lazelus raised an eyebrow. "Have you heard the entire prophecy, then?"

Her eyes snapped over to him before she looked away again. "My father knew that using Annera as a warning wouldn't be enough," she said, ignoring his inquiry. "Queen Aurelia had to be weakened, to be struck someplace she'd never expect. Weakening her, he thought, was the only way to control her; and, therefore, to distract her from doing exactly what Willem had warned him about."

Shasta reached down to her feet beneath the table, then straightened up a moment later with a folded piece of parchment in her grasp. She read a passage from King Willem's letter aloud for her fellow nobles:

"'The Dragon of Akkinor will destroy your family and the realm alike if you don't stop her. But she'll be easier to disarm than you think. The Akkinorian blood running through her veins is as common as it gets, but it's only half of her. The other half is as Carthinian as you and I. Think about the only Carthinian alive who kisses the ground she walks on, and you'll know exactly how to weaken her.'"

The answer was obvious to Lazelus, and evidently the rest of the room.

"Arian Cristos." It was Lord Keer who spoke. "She's descended from his family, then?"

"That's what my father believed Willem was implying." Instead of returning the letter to her stocking, Shasta placed it on the table between her and Lazelus. "We couldn't weaken her by telling the realm she's not the daughter of Edmund Brentwood. They wouldn't believe us. But we *could* weaken her by going after the only relative she has left—the last connection to her roots. And if she had a great reaction to the curse, we'd know we were on the right track."

Lord Quagg's eyes widened. "I heard a rumor from Bozar. Two of the Four Lords are allied with Akkinor, and they wrote to their counterparts that Lord Cristos collapsed of a supposed curse at Queen Aurelia's ball about a week ago. Rumor has it that His Lordship was cursed in Carthe."

"Gods above." Lazelus's lips parted in shock as he turned to Shasta. "That was your doing, wasn't it?"

Her lips curled into a sly smile. "Not exactly. My father gave the order before he died. Queen Aurelia invited all of us to her ball, remember? He knew when it was happening, and he knew Lord Cristos would attend, so he ordered his best mage to cast the curse right before His Lordship went to Akkinor. It wasn't enough for Lord Cristos to be cursed—my father knew Queen Aurelia had to see him fall." Lord Reesa erupted in a booming fit of laughter, making Shasta frown. "What's so funny?"

He wiped tears from his eyes, still laughing. "You don't know who your father's best mage was, do you, *Lady Selle?*"

"Not exactly. I know his name is Kaius, and he was sent to ward with my father several years ago, but as you all know, we don't use surnames with our staff and advisors. I only ever knew him as Kaius. I've hardly seen him since my father died, though."

"Kaius is my second son," he told her, grinning, "and your groom."

Shasta's eyes bugged out of her head. "B-But—"

"He owes me an explanation." The nobleman shook his head, chuckling. "He returned home to Vrurith not long after your father died. I regret that I haven't seen him since he returned, so I know nothing about what your father asked of him. That insolent child—you'd think he would've told his father and liege lord about all of this!"

"My father swore him to secrecy."

"There are no secrets between a father and his son."

"Evidently not."

Lord Reesa stilled, shocked by her cheek, as Lazelus and the others tried to mask their smiles. To Lazelus's surprise, Lord Reesa's dumbfounded expression morphed into one of pure pride. It was like he'd been waiting for Shasta to sass him, to present herself as a formidable opponent.

"Point taken." He slid into a chair across from Shasta, golden eyes sparkling with intrigue. "Well, we're in this together now. Arian Cristos has been cursed, Queen Aurelia is likely driving herself mad trying to cure him, and our dragon grows stronger by the day. What we need to know now is exactly what this prophecy says."

"Willem's oracle won't be any help if she's befriended the queen," Lord Keer muttered. "We'll have to find it on our own."

As the nobles theorized and plotted, Lazelus turned his gaze to the letter. He realized then that his counterparts had seemingly forgotten Runeia's alliance with Akkinor. They probably assumed he wasn't beholden to the deal his grandmother had made with Queen Aurelia; that the alliance died with her. They weren't thinking about Runeia's alliances with Taundosa or Bozar, either, or their own alliances with Bozar. For whatever reason, this prophecy—or, more likely, Annera—had convinced all of them that Krotis was above all the promises they'd made.

Odeya had told her heir that Runeia's alliances were eternal, meant to be respected by every Swann leader unless there was an irrefutable reason to break the contracts. Lazelus had ascended the throne with every intention of keeping those promises. Now, though, he wasn't so sure if he could without being tossed aside—or killed—by his counterparts.

When the others weren't paying attention, Lazelus casually placed his hand over the letter. He wasn't the most skilled mage in the world, but he was adept at a few basic spells—like the replication spell, for example. After murmuring a few words under his breath, he looked down at his other hand, nestled on his lap, and suppressed a smile when a duplicate of the letter appeared in his grasp.

He glanced around to ensure nobody had noticed, and fortunately, they were still distracted by thoughts of the prophecy. He folded the letter under the table, then slipped it into his sock for safekeeping.

"What are you doing, boy?" Lord Reesa snapped at him as he straightened up.

Lazelus didn't bat an eye. "I had an itch."

XV

When Aurelia walked through the door, she was immediately surrounded by blackness and silence, exactly as she'd been when she left Halvor for Linden. After a moment or two, though, her eyes snapped open, and she found herself kneeling in front of the iron chest in the archives.

After returning the book to the chest, sealing it, and closing the door to the hidden room, Aurelia darted for the exit—then stopped when she remembered the last thing Linden had told her. She scoured the archives, impatient, until a stroke of luck brought her to a large wooden trunk on the floor, with four letters engraved on the lid: *EJBI*.

Edmund Jameson Brentwood, First of His Name.

She recognized the trunk from her childhood. Her father had given it to the monastery after clearing out the palace's storage room. He'd kept most of his father's belongings, but he'd chosen to donate some of it. When she found the blue journal hidden beneath miscellaneous trinkets, she didn't understand why her father would've gotten rid of it, but she knew he'd had his reasons.

After claiming the journal, Aurelia closed the trunk and bolted for the exit again. She skidded to a stop when she saw Octavien unlocking the gate. As soon as the gate swung open, he chuckled at the sight of her while unraveling a length of cloth.

"I was starting to get worried." He took her injured hand when she approached him and immediately wrapped her cut in cloth. "I see you found what you were looking for. I don't blame you for not wanting to tell me—most people are often a bit shy when it comes to sharing their hope of visiting Vanhylde. I had a feeling that's what you came for, though."

Aurelia frowned. "How many people have come here with that intention?"

"A great many, but not in several years." He tied the cloth in a knot on her palm and smiled. "I was a student here at the monastery the last time someone came here to find Vanhylde. That was—gods, almost thirty years ago!"

"Do you remember who it was?"

"I haven't a clue."

Aurelia's frown deepened as she wondered about the owner of the faded handprint on the wall in that little room, but she didn't dwell on it. She had to get home to tell Jack and Rayan what had happened—and to send word of it to Carthe, too.

Octavien escorted her out of the archives and through the monastery, where he said goodbye in the foyer. She found her own way outside, but she didn't rush to Halvor when she saw him waiting for her on the lawn. They were staring at one another, blue eyes against golden ones, in a way they'd never done before—a way that felt more intense, like their connection had deepened.

Smiling, she approached him and reached out, prompting him to nuzzle her hand with his snout. His head was lowered so the pair were eye-level, and when he blinked at her, she could've sworn she saw his eyes turn blue like his human form.

"I remember what you told me about how Diantha's concerns for us don't necessarily apply," she murmured, "but I do feel that our conversation brought us closer. Don't you?"

He chuffed at her as if to say, *You know I do.*

"I'll admit," she said as she climbed onto his back, "I think I'll miss talking with you. Now that I know you're capable of talking back, it'll be difficult to hear nothing but chuffs and groans in response to what I say." His throat rumbled, making her laugh. "My point exactly."

At home in the Folly, Aurelia found Jack and Rayan conversing in her study while mulling over paperwork. They abandoned their task to hear about her experience, and by the time she finished telling the tale, the pair of them were looking at her like she'd grown ten heads.

"That-That shouldn't be possible," Rayan stammered. His pale eyes were wider than saucers, sparkling with a combination of fear and awe. "Halvor...Linden...*Arian,* for that matter..."

She couldn't help but smile. "I know."

Jack took her hand to inspect the bloody cloth. "All you had to do was touch a wall and say a few words? How can that be?"

"I had to do it in a holy place. I don't suppose I could do it here. A part of me thinks it's meant to be simple, like it's a test: nearly anyone can visit Vanhylde, but most will be too enamored by what they find to leave." She grimaced as she remembered something from her brief stay in Kanibar. "Maysa once told me that humanity isn't what the gods intended for us to be, not anymore, so they've been studying us. Giving us the option to leave our lives behind for an eternity in purgatory...That's quite the experiment, isn't it?"

"I'll say." He released her hand and frowned. "Vanhylde doesn't sound like purgatory to me. It sounds like an extension of Hanhalla."

"It must depend on who's there," she offered, sinking into her chair. "Halvor's reality in Vanhylde was lovely because he's never done anything wrong. The same is true for Linden. Archie, however, might have a more difficult reality there: not terrible enough that it could be mistaken for hell, but not wonderful enough that he forgets he hasn't reached eternal salvation. I suppose it's like another Icareth—a world composed of good and bad—but it was intended for the dead."

"One won't experience the darkness of Vanhylde if they don't deserve it." Rayan shook his head, still baffled. "This is madness. I can't believe you're so calm about it."

"I think it's the adrenaline," she replied, only half-kidding. "But now that we know Krotis is more than likely responsible for the curse, we have to act. Reyna and the two lords have to know. We'll need them to send their spies to keep an eye on things in Krotis."

Rayan nodded. "I'll send the ravens."

When he left to write and send the letters, Jack joined Aurelia behind her desk, leaning his backside against the edge of the furniture. She set her grandfather's journal on the desk, not yet ready to search through it for whatever Linden had spoken of.

"Arian's condition hasn't changed," Jack murmured. "The priests claim they'll have more definitive answers for us tomorrow."

A sigh of relief escaped her. "Good. They can tell us if there's a counter-curse or an anecdote to wake him up. If there isn't, our only option is to kill the person who cast the curse."

"Easier said than done."

"Indeed."

He paused for a moment as amusement flooded his face. "You've been glowing since you returned, despite everything. It must've healed a part of you, seeing Linden again. I can't imagine how that felt."

Warmth filled every cavity in her body. "I couldn't describe it if I tried."

Jack smiled a bit, but something about his face looked off. "I feel I should ask because I never have, and I've always been a bit curious: was there ever anything between the two of you? Even the tiniest little spark?"

"Good gods, Jack." Aurelia gaped at him, her eyes narrowing as she realized the look on his face was jealousy, of all things. "Why would you ask such a thing after all this time?"

"I'm just curious."

She looked away from him, a pit forming in her gut. "I loved him as deeply as I love you." When she turned to him again, sniffling, he was staring at her with his eyebrows furrowed in confusion. "Just in an entirely different way. I loved Archie like that, too, once."

"Aurelia..." He sighed and knelt in front of her, holding her hands on her lap. "I'm sorry. I didn't mean...I was just wondering..."

She waved him off. "It's all right. You never knew him, so you couldn't have known what we were like together, even with my many stories. But he asked me to tell you that he approves of you."

Jack smiled like he wanted to laugh, but the mood was too somber. "I'm glad. If I understand things correctly, he was more of a brother to you than your own brother was. I would've asked his permission to marry you, had I been given the chance."

"I know you would have." Aurelia smiled when he reached up to brush tears from her cheek. "You would've loved him as I did, too."

Jack leaned up to kiss her cheek. "I know."

***

The next day, while taking a walk around the palace, Aurelia was brought to an abrupt halt by the sight of an unexpected guest in the foyer: the Lady of the Folly.

"Aunt Odessa." Aurelia raised an eyebrow. "What brings you here today? I wasn't expecting you."

Her aunt swallowed nervously. "There's a bit of a problem in the Folly. I could use your help, but if you're busy..."

"Not at all." Aurelia closed the book she'd been reading while she strolled—her grandfather's journal—and gestured for Odessa to join her. "What seems to be the problem?"

"I don't know when or how this happened, but the people have begun...dividing." Odessa swallowed again and wiped her sweaty hands on her skirt. "I've been distracted lately—I worry for Arian, as you do—so I didn't notice until it was brought to my doorstep. Apparently, some of the richer civilians have been forcing the poorer ones to move. They claim the poor have been bad for business, so they've gone ahead and established a specific area in Kalenbrar for the poor to claim."

Aurelia stared at her, bewildered. "They've divided the capital city by socioeconomic status?"

Her father's voice echoed in her head: *When a kingdom grows richer, its subjects tend to grow poorer in more ways than one.*

"Yes, Your Grace. We've had an increase in travelers through the capital lately—both Akkinorians and foreigners—looking to trade or buy and sell goods. Some visitors are off put by the sight of beggars and peasants, so they travel to other parts of the Folly to do business instead of staying in the capital. Thus, the richer civilians have been corralling the peasants into a designated section of the capital, and they're erecting signs and such to keep travelers from going there."

"Where is this area?"

"North of Limewick. The people have begun referring to it as *Amanbrar.*"

City of Decay. It was a stark contrast to the name Aurelia had given the entire capital—Kalenbrar, City of Light.

"I sent my soldiers to restore the peace, and the wealthy rioted," Odessa continued, face creased with worry. "I fear I've let you down after less than a season as Lady of the Folly."

"You couldn't have seen this coming," Aurelia assured her. "I'll send a few troops to assist you. The relocation of our citizens will come to an end, and those responsible for instigating this will be issued a warning against continuing these behaviors. I'll speak with the Lord Hand about further efforts to resolve this, too."

Odessa seemed to deflate when she exhaled. "Thank you, Your Grace. I couldn't..."

She trailed off when she finally took note of the book Aurelia was holding. Aurelia wasn't surprised that she recognized the journal: it'd belonged to her father, after all, and his initials were engraved on the front cover.

"Where did you get that?" Odessa murmured.

"The monastery. My father donated some of your father's things."

Her aunt chewed on her lower lip. "Why would Ed donate our father's journal? Was it on display, or being used for research of some kind?"

"No. It was in one of your father's trunks in the archives. I don't suppose it's seen the light of day since it arrived at the monastery." Aurelia furrowed her brows. "Is there something you know?"

"No, no..." Odessa trailed off, still gnawing on her lip. "My father didn't write much—only when he found himself in a trying position, and he didn't feel he could speak with anyone about it. Anything he wrote in that journal is probably important, if not meant to be kept secret. Ed would've known that, too. I can't imagine why he'd donate our father's secrets to the monastery."

A thought struck Aurelia. "Perhaps he knew it'd be safer in the archives than it would be here. I couldn't say."

Still, Odessa looked worried. "Either way, keep that close to you. I don't know what my father would've written about, but I do know it's not meant for the eyes of anyone who isn't a Brentwood." Her gaze flicked to the side, where Rayan was approaching. "It looks like the Hand has need of you. I'll return to Briarwood and await your troops."

Aurelia nodded. "All right. Keep me updated, and use your men and your coven to your advantage, but ensure they're as peaceful as possible."

"Of course. Thank you again, Your Grace."

Odessa curtsied, eyed the journal once more, and hurried back to the foyer to take her leave. Aurelia watched her go, frowning at her aunt's unexplained nervousness, before turning back to Rayan as he slowed to a stop in front of her.

"Any word about Arian?" she asked.

"Not yet. The priests expect to have an answer by the end of the day." He cleared his throat and held out a hand, revealing a letter. "This just arrived. I've already read it. You need to read it, too."

She furrowed her brows and glanced at the broken seal on the parchment. The amber wax suggested it came from Krotis, and the image stamped onto it—a dragonfly—confirmed it'd come from the province of Runeia.

She unfolded the letter and began to read, but stopped when she saw who it was addressed to: Amarion Selle, the late Lord of Bruila.

"What is this?" she asked.

Rayan grimaced. "I believe someone's trying to send us a message."

She gulped, her heart hammering against her ribcage, and turned her gaze back to the letter.

For the eyes of Amarion Selle, Liege Lord of Bruila:

If this message has found you, it means I'm dead, and the continent as we know it has morphed into something unrecognizable. The realm may be at peace for now, but I'm afraid it won't stay this way for much longer.

Many years ago, you shared a story with me about an object in your family's possession. I believe you know what I'm referring to. I neglected to share something with you, too, during that conversation. There's a prophecy—one I learned from my mother as a boy, which I failed to see as holding any truth or meaning until recently. Your story forced me to consider it, and after years of research, I now believe that my witch of a mother spoke of something remarkable.

This prophecy speaks of Four Pillars, and if I'm correct about what they are, then one of those pillars is already known to the realm. I believe you have a second pillar in your possession. I know naught of the other two, but I believe they shall make themselves known in the near future. However, one individual will threaten the fulfillment of the prophecy—and therefore, the bright future of our realm.

The Dragon of Akkinor will destroy your family and the realm alike if you don't stop her. But she'll be easier to disarm than you think. The Akkinorian blood running through her veins is as common as it gets, but it's only half of her. The other half is as Carthinian as you and I. Think about the only Carthinian alive who kisses the ground she walks on, and you'll know exactly how to weaken her.

The prophecy is not difficult to find if you remember who told you about it. You will understand it as I do once you've found it, and you will know what needs to be done. Even with your failing health, I trust you to bear this burden, and to leave the responsibility to others if you don't survive.

Thank you for the army you've so generously sent to my doorstep. Tonight, I drink to your health, and to our friendship. Perhaps when we speak next, it'll be with me as King of both Kanibar and Dofell.

Sincerely,

Your friend, Willem Trevas.

***

The letter, which Aurelia assumed had been sent by Lazelus Swann, revealed three damning facts: first, Willem knew of another prophecy that Aurelia didn't, which apparently pointed to her as the villain in his interpretation of it; second, he'd shared her most precious secret with a trusted friend, who then shared it—presumably—with the other nobles of Krotis; and, finally, he'd suggested the best way to bring Aurelia down was to incapacitate Arian.

If all of that combined wasn't enough to drive her mad, then having to explain herself to Rayan certainly was.

"I thought it was strange, that day three years ago when Edom woke the creatures." Rayan sat on the couch in Aurelia's study, eyes glazed over as he stared into the crackling hearth, while Aurelia sat behind her desk. "The nymph repeated a prophecy—the same prophecy we fulfilled by helping Diantha claim Dofell. It spoke of a hero of western blood. I thought it was you, but it couldn't be, because you're Akkinorian. Jack said something about it being a mistranslation, which I assume is exactly what you told our allies."

Aurelia winced. "Yes."

"So it *is* you, then? The hero of western blood?"

"Yes."

Rayan snapped his hurt gaze from the fire. "I know you don't owe me an explanation—you're my queen, after all—but as your friend, I'd really like one."

A pang pierced her heart. "Everything Willem wrote about me in that letter is true. I don't call Arian my uncle because he was my father's best friend. I call him my uncle because I'm the daughter of his late sister. After she died in childbirth, my parents visited Arian in Taundosa, and they asked his permission to adopt me."

"Willem wrote that you're half Akkinorian."

"My birth mother fell in love with an Akkinorian man."

"What do you know about him?"

"Nothing." The lie slipped from her tongue so easily that it made her stomach churn. If there was ever a time to tell him the truth, it was now, but she couldn't bring herself to do it. "I don't know enough to—"

Just then, the door to her study swung open, revealing a panting, sweating Jack. He was dressed casually, his hair sticking up in every direction, and judging by his flushed cheeks, he'd just gotten back from a ride.

"Anna said you're looking for me. I would've been here sooner, but I was out with Valor." Jack poured himself a drink from the table to the right of Aurelia's desk, took a large gulp of wine, and raised an eyebrow. "What's going on?"

Sighing, Aurelia handed him the letter, averting her gaze from Rayan as her husband read. Jack scoffed once or twice, gasped at one point, and practically growled by the time he reached the end. When he finished reading, he held it up beside his head, the look on his face murderous.

"What the hell is this?"

"It appears to have been sent from Runeia," Aurelia replied. "If Lazelus Swann had access to this, it means his fellow nobles did, too. We have to assume the whole of Krotis—save Lazelus, hopefully—has fallen for Willem's schemes." She shook her head and released a bitter laugh. "Dead for three years, and he's still torturing me."

Jack's face was nearly purple with rage. "After Dofell, you asked me why he didn't expose you when he had the chance. I imagine it's because he was planning this. He had to make a spectacle of things, as always, even if he's not here to see it." Then his face blanched as he remembered Rayan. "Does he—?"

"I've told him that Arian's late sister is my birth mother, and that my birth father was an Akkinorian man I haven't managed to identify," she said quickly. "He knows everything now."

His eyes flashed with understanding—and a bit of displeasure—but she could only hope that he refrained from saying anything else about it. The only thing keeping Rayan from putting the pieces together, especially after Eric's story about Katryna at dinner, was his trust in Aurelia, and perhaps even his father.

"We'll have to share this with the others." Rayan's voice was low and a bit distant when he spoke again. "It's not enough for us to accuse Krotis of cursing Arian, though. We need more proof. I think our best option is to try to learn more about this prophecy Willem spoke of."

Jack raised an eyebrow. "Maysa?"

"Maybe," Aurelia muttered. "She didn't tell me when I saw her in Dofell. Maybe she's waiting for the right time, or maybe I'm not supposed to know what it says. Either way, she won't make it easy."

"What about Vanhylde?" Rayan suggested. "You said that when Archie visited you in your dream, he spoke of Four Pillars. Willem said the same thing in his letter to Lord Selle. Halvor told you that Archie is in Vanhylde, and Maysa seemed to think he'd be useful."

Aurelia chewed on her lower lip. "I suppose it's worth trying."

"I'll write to our allies and to Maysa. Maybe the oracle will decide to make things easier for us." Rayan scrubbed a hand down his face and raised an eyebrow. "Is there anything else I should know before I leave?"

Aurelia's face burned. "No. That's all."

He left the study with a curt nod, and Aurelia's face only felt hotter as she met Jack's disapproving gaze.

"His reaction will only be worse the longer you wait to tell him," her husband muttered, shaking his head. "I think you need to consider—"

"I have been." A thick lump formed in her throat. "I don't wish to say anything about it until Arian wakes."

"But—"

"Jack," she started, sighing, "as much as I want Rayan to know the truth, and as much as I trust him to keep it from Eric until Arian wakes, I can't ask that of him." She hesitated when her eyes began to sting. "Coming from Arian...Eric would learn that he sired a child with the woman he loved, and he'd think of me as just that—his child—before being informed about who the babe grew up to be."

Jack softened a bit. "Coming from you, he might not think about the fact that he has a child he never knew about with Katryna. He'd just hear his queen telling him that she's his daughter." He offered her a small smile, letting her know he understood. "You're worried he wouldn't be able to hear it from you and see beyond the crown."

"Yes." She looked down at her hands in her lap. "I want him to have the chance to grieve Katryna and accept that he has a child with her while hearing it from someone who was there for it. I don't want him to feel like he needs to react in a certain way because he's hearing it from his queen. I-I think it's better if he separates his daughter from his queen, even for just a few moments, so he can mourn what could've been with Katryna."

"I get it. But what if Arian doesn't wake up? Will you really keep this from Rayan and Eric forever?"

Aurelia grimaced. "No. I'll think of another way."

"Just don't wait too long, all right?" he said, coming over to kiss her temple. "They deserve our transparency, just as the lot of you deserve the chance to be a real family while you still can."

She winced, recalling the seamless way the Haze family had interacted with hers at dinner. They'd already started acting like a family, yet they were still strangers, to a certain degree. She couldn't let it go on much longer, but for now...for now, she needed her uncle.

XVI

I t's called *ze edhas wraisa.*"

Aurelia sucked in a sharp breath. *"The Hollow Dream."*

Marvion, the Elder of Akkinor, nodded and grimaced. It was rare for the Elder to leave the monastery, but he'd been summoned to the palace by his mages after they removed the blockage placed on Arian. Apparently, they were so surprised by their findings that they needed the most skilled mage in the country to confirm what they'd discovered.

"There are sleeping spells—meant to induce temporary slumber for insomniacs, those in severe pain, or those who need to heal in an unconscious state—and then there are sleeping curses," Marvion explained. "This specific type of sleeping curse is the strongest of them, and it cannot be broken unless the caster is killed."

Aurelia's heart sank. "What *is* the Hollow Dream, exactly?"

The elderly mage removed his spectacles to clean the fog with his robes. "It's a permanent state of unconsciousness that, over time, sucks the victim's soul into the land of dreams. Over the first few weeks, the soul drifts between Icareth and Vanhylde, unable to control its movements. After a few months, pieces of the soul tether to Vanhylde—more and more as the days pass. It takes less than a year for the entirety of one's soul to become trapped in Vanhylde. When that happens, the physical form is left without a soul. And..."

Jack, standing beside Aurelia outside of Arian's door, raised an eyebrow. "And *what?*"

Marvion sighed, looking decades older than he already was. "When the entirety of the soul has been snatched by Vanhylde, it's impossible for it to return to Icareth or to move on to another plane of existence. Most souls sent to Vanhylde can earn their way to Hanhalla. On the contrary, if they are unable to find the goodness in their hearts, they're sent to Saendah. But a soul cursed with the Hollow Dream has no hope of leaving Vanhylde at all. They're trapped in purgatory for eternity, and over time, they come to forget who they are."

Aurelia reached a hand out for the wall to steady herself, barely feeling Jack's hand on her back as he attempted to comfort her. She brought her other hand to her stomach when bile rose up in her throat, and it took every ounce of strength she had to keep from vomiting onto her shoes.

Not only had Arian been cursed with one of the worst ones imaginable, but the curse came with a time limit. It'd already been a few weeks since he'd fallen ill, so time was of the essence now: if the person who cursed him wasn't killed soon, Arian would be lost to Vanhylde, and his soul would never know peace again.

It was no wonder Krotis had chosen such a terrible curse. Publicly, she couldn't acknowledge Arian as her family, which meant she'd have to be cautious about how she proceeded when it came to saving him. But how cautious could she be when his eternal existence was dangling by a thread?

"I'm sorry I couldn't give you better news." Marvion's gravelly voice drew Aurelia from her thoughts. "My mages will continue to care for His Lordship. I knew him as a boy when he studied at the monastery, and I cared for him very much—I, too, will try my utmost to find a solution to this."

"T-Thank you." Aurelia cleared her throat when she stuttered, peeled herself from the wall, and forced a grateful smile. "I'll send word if we learn anything more."

The Elder nodded, bowed, and left the couple in the hallway. As soon as he turned his back, his body seemed to deflate, like he'd been forcing himself to stand tall while in Aurelia's presence. The sight made her feel sick again, as it reminded her of just how many lives Arian had touched.

"We're going to Carthe tomorrow," Aurelia told Jack. He furrowed his eyebrows, confused. "I wish to tell Reyna the news in person. I'd like a word with Maysa, too. Send a raven to let Reyna know to expect us. I'll be here with Arian for the time being."

He nodded and reached out a hand like he wanted to comfort her, but thought better of it and dropped his arm to his side when he saw the look on her face. She must've looked worse than she realized, because she could see the pain in Jack's eyes when he gazed at her.

When he left, she slipped into Arian's room and reclaimed her seat at his bedside. She'd been sitting there earlier, reading her grandfather's journal, when Marvion arrived to confirm his mages' suspicions. She was glad she'd brought the journal; she needed something to distract her from the sight of Arian's frail body and the sound of his labored breathing.

Before reaching for the journal again, she set her hands over his and squeezed. "I'll find a way to stop this," she whispered, biting back tears. "I promise."

He didn't answer, of course, but his eyes were darting back and forth beneath his lids. That only made her heart lurch—she knew he was in Vanhylde, the land of dreams, and fragments of his soul were likely tethering themselves to that world as she spoke.

Swallowing the lump in her throat, she took the journal onto her lap and opened it to the marked page. She was on the last page of an entry regarding an incident between Edmund the Elder and the Reilly family, the former reigning nobles of Laynoa. It was from the year 1948, when Arian and Aurelia's father were about sixteen.

Edmund Brentwood, First of His Name, hadn't been known by the masses for his incredible kindness and mercy—not like his son and namesake. Aurelia's father always suggested differently when he spoke to her about her grandfather. Now that she was reading Edmund the Elder's words for herself, she knew for certain that her father had been right about the kind of man her grandfather was; to some extent, anyway.

I found myself questioning my honor today. It has been a difficult week: Lord Cristos departed for Taundosa several days ago to visit his family, leaving Arian here with us, as Ed is meeting a potential bride tomorrow and wishes to have Arian at his side. Lord Reilly sent his grandson to accompany his granddaughter, the girl in question—not to chaperone, but to convince me to consider the boy as a potential husband for my Odessa. She is all but ten, and the young Reilly boy has just celebrated his seventeenth name day.

I was summoned to the gardens this afternoon by panicked soldiers. They escorted me to a grisly scene: Arian and my sweet Odessa covered in blood, and the Reilly boy lying dead beneath a tree. I have never seen Odessa so upset, nor have I ever seen Arian so quiet. The soldiers removed the body and escorted Odessa away from the scene so I could have a private word with Arian. I knew he would be truthful with me, but he would not speak so long as the soldiers were eyeing him as if he were a barbarian.

He explained the situation in great detail. While practicing archery in the gardens, he heard a sharp cry and rushed to investigate. He found the Reilly boy attempting unspeakable things with my little girl. Arian meant to spook the Reilly boy by shooting an arrow at the tree, but instead, he pierced the boy through the gut. He tried desperately to save the boy, to no avail.

I did not believe him. I know Arian well, and he would not have shot at the Reilly boy for fear of striking Odessa by accident. I believe Arian approached calmly and attempted to intervene, and the Reilly boy drew his sword to threaten Arian into secrecy. The blood on Odessa's gown suggests that she stabbed him from behind—likely with his own dagger—to protect Arian, who took the blame for himself to protect Odessa.

I must think of something to tell Lord Reilly. I cannot tell him that it was Arian who killed his grandson; he will demand that Arian's life be taken as punishment. I cannot admit to the world that my ten-year-old daughter stabbed a boy in the back, either, regardless of what he attempted to do to her. I must protect my daughter, but I must also protect Arian.

The following entry, dated about a week later, detailed what Edmund the Elder had done in the aftermath:

The Reilly family has been informed of the boy's death. The story circulating across the country is this: the Reilly boy was sparring with a servant's son and was killed by accident. Neither Odessa's name nor Arian's is associated with the incident. Unfortunately, Lord Reilly demanded justice, and I was forced to respond. A servant's son was chosen at random and delivered to Arpton Fortress in Laynoa to stand trial. He met his death at the gallows this morning. It grieves me to know that I played a hand in an innocent child's demise, but if I had not, it would have been Arian who met his death today. The boy is as much my son as Edmund; I cannot lose him. The price was a heavy one, but I must learn to make my peace with it.

Aurelia set the journal on the bed, stunned, and glanced at Arian's sleeping face. There were so many things she wanted to ask him—things only he could answer for her—but she quickly realized that there was one other person, alive and well, who could tell her exactly what she needed to know.

Odessa Linderli, Lady of the Folly.

***

About two hours after reading the journal entry—and finishing the entire journal—Aurelia found herself sitting in a parlor at Briarwood Manor across from her aunt. Odessa had finished reading the entry for herself moments earlier, but she hadn't lifted her gaze from the pages. Her blue eyes swam with tears, and her shaking hands around her teacup made the porcelain clink and shriek.

Tired of the silence, Aurelia cleared her throat. "I won't go into detail, but Arian wished for me to find this journal in the event of his death. There's something in here that he wanted me to know. This is the only entry in the entire journal that references anything of great importance related to Arian. What I can't figure out is why this would be so relevant to him. If you know something, I'd like for you to tell me."

Odessa's eyes finally snapped up to meet Aurelia's. "Your Grace, I..."

"Odessa." The firmness in Aurelia's voice made her aunt wince. "I can see in your eyes that you know something. Tell me."

"I promised Arian—"

"Arian wanted me to know. He wouldn't have asked me to find this if that weren't true." She raised an impatient eyebrow. "Well?"

Odessa gulped and closed the journal, pushing it away like it'd make her sick if it remained close to her. She glanced away for a moment, eyes falling shut, and took a long, deep breath before facing her queen once more.

"The boy who met his death wasn't the same child my father wrote about. I don't know the name of the boy who died. The one my father chose at random...He was the son of a footman training for the same role, though he wished to be a painter. His name was Shale. When Arian and Ed found out it was Shale who'd been chosen, they followed he and the soldiers to Laynoa, and they swapped him out for a peasant boy."

Aurelia stilled. "What?"

Odessa gulped. "The peasant boy had been recently arrested in the Folly. He'd murdered an old woman and was caught trying to sell her jewelry. Apparently, he owed a great debt to a powerful man in the Folly. The man cut out the boy's tongue and said he'd take the boy's hands, and then his feet, if he didn't pay the debt. Ed and Arian took him from the dungeon so he could switch places with Shale. It was late at night when they made the exchange, and only one soldier was awake on watch duty, so Ed distracted the soldier while Arian made the switch. Both Shale and the boy had sacks over their heads, so the soldiers didn't notice. The boy couldn't tell them what'd happened, either. They wouldn't have cared, anyway, as long as they were delivering *someone* to Lord Reilly."

Aurelia didn't know what to say. She merely sat there, her jaw nearly reaching the floor, as Odessa struggled to get the words out.

That didn't sound like her father. It didn't sound like Arian, either. Regardless of their motives, they weren't the kind of people to kidnap someone—even a prisoner—and send them to the gallows to save someone else. There was no honor in that, and they were two of the most honorable people Aurelia had ever known.

"The boy would've died, anyway," Odessa insisted, wiping tears from her cheeks. "He was still on trial, but he would've been convicted for murder, and he would've hanged."

Aurelia shook her head. "If there was any possibility he might've lived..."

"Even if he did, he would've spent his life in prison." Odessa's tone was firm now, like she was growing angry with Aurelia for disapproving of what Arian and Edmund had done. "They did what needed to be done to save Shale."

"Why? What was so special about a footman's son?"

Odessa's cheeks turned pink as she averted her gaze. "I...um..."

"*Odessa.*"

She sighed and pressed her lips together. "He and Arian were...well..."

"They were *what?*"

"They loved each other." Odessa's voice had softened to a whisper, so quiet that Aurelia had to strain to hear her. "They were seeing each other for about two years by then. Ed was the only person who knew. I found out the day I killed Rowan Reilly."

Aurelia swallowed a gulp of tea to coat her parched throat. It was no wonder Arian had never married or sired children. He wasn't interested in women, and he wasn't the kind of man to trap a woman in a loveless marriage, even to further his family line.

"How did you find out?" Aurelia asked.

Odessa's cheeks burned crimson. "I-I didn't understand that Rowan touching me was wrong. I was too young to comprehend the monstrosity of it. But when Arian intervened, Rowan said something about Shale. He'd seen Arian and Shale together, and he threatened to expose them." A haunted, desperate look filled her gaze. "You know what things were like back then, Aurelia. Same sex relationships may be more common and accepted nowadays, but that wasn't the case when I was young. A person could've been lashed for participating in such activities, and society would ostracize them. Paired with Arian being Carthinian...It wouldn't have ended well for him."

Aurelia's heart rattled. "Don't tell me you killed him because he threatened Arian."

"No," she said quickly, wincing. "Arian tried to talk him down, but Rowan became violent. He brought Arian to the ground and tried to strangle him. He dropped his dagger in the process, so I took it and stabbed him. That's when Arian staged the scene, hid the weapon, and created a story to protect me. The three of us—Arian, Ed, and me, as young as I was—we knew we couldn't tell my father the entire truth. He may have loved Arian like a son, but he wouldn't have approved of his own children engaging in such relationships, either. He would've sent Shale away, and he might've convinced Lord Cristos to find a wife for Arian immediately."

As the story unfolded, Aurelia's shock and disapproval morphed into pity. The circumstances were horrible for many reasons, and while she struggled to fathom her father and her uncle sending a boy to die—destined for it or not—she knew they'd only been adolescents at the time, and they'd done what they thought was right to save the boy Arian loved.

"O-Okay." Aurelia took a moment to process before raising an eyebrow. "Why do you suppose Arian wished for me to know this, then?"

Odessa dabbed at the corners of her eyes with a handkerchief, sniffling. "Shale's still alive. I don't know if Arian still visits him when he comes to Akkinor, but they exchange letters every so often. We talked about it not long after you took the throne from your brother. It's been years since we last spoke of it, though."

Aurelia sighed as she finally put the pieces together. "If Arian doesn't wake from the curse, he wants me to tell Shale what happened to him."

Odessa's aging face crumpled. "I imagine so."

"Do you know Shale's surname?"

"No. He was a footman at the palace until Arian returned to Taundosa for good. I don't know where he moved to—he just couldn't bear to be here without Arian."

Aurelia's heart sank, and not just because it'd be difficult to locate Shale. She couldn't imagine what it must've felt like for the two of them to be separated, living an ocean apart on separate continents, unable to love each other as they deserved. If she was forced to be parted from Jack like that, she wasn't sure she'd survive without him.

Her uncle was a stronger man than she'd given him credit for.

"I'm leaving for Carthe tomorrow," Aurelia told her aunt. "Jack and I will spend a day or two in Taundosa. If Arian and Shale kept in contact, perhaps I might find a letter from Shale among Arian's belongings. I'd like for you to try to find him, too. You know who was employed at the palace back then—if they're still alive and nearby, maybe they'll tell you something about where Shale went."

Odessa nodded. "I'll do my best."

"Thank you." Aurelia stood and smoothed her skirts, but before she said farewell, a thought popped into her head. "How are things in Kalenbrar? And...What is it?"

"Amanbrar." Odessa winced. "Better. The increased patrol around the capital city has certainly deterred the civilians from forcibly relocating their neighbors, but the tensions prevail. If they don't calm down, I may need to request more coin to increase the wages for the poorer folk. They've already had two pay raises in the last five years, but with their neighbors growing so wealthy so quickly..."

"They're still falling behind," Aurelia muttered, sighing. "All right. We'll discuss this again later. Keep an eye on it, and if anything changes while I'm gone, take the matter to the Lord Hand. He and the Assembly will handle things from there." When Odessa stood, Aurelia gave her aunt a small hug. "Thank you for sharing that story with me. I'll keep Arian's secret safe."

"I know you will." Odessa tightened her grip for a moment, then pulled back and smiled. "He would've told you eventually, anyway. I think he's just been frightened of what you—and others—might think of him."

Aurelia furrowed her brows. "Because he loves a man?"

"No. Because of what love made him do—and the life it cost."

It almost ached her to force a smile. "It's not the most honorable thing in the world, but if it were Jack, I'd probably do the same thing. I can't fault him for that."

"Remember that when he wakes up." Odessa's smile wavered as she held her niece's hands. "Good luck in Carthe, Your Grace."

XVII

*Y*ou're staying here."

Edom hissed. "Not fair."

"Oh, stop it." Aurelia gave the sprite a firm look as it stood atop a stack of paperwork on her desk, wiry arms folded over its chest. "I want you to keep searching for answers while we're gone. You're my eyes and ears across the country, remember? If you happen to learn of anything important, relay the message to Fiora, and she'll bring it to us in Carthe."

The sprite glowered at her. "As you wish."

"Thank you." Aurelia turned away from the creature when Jack bounded into her study with satchels slung over either arm. "Is that everything?"

"I think so," her husband replied. "You know, I don't see why we need to bring our belongings if we're staying in Taundosa. Reyna always accommodates us."

"We're going to Kanibar to speak with May, too." She took the lighter of the two satchels from him and slung it over her shoulder. "I don't intend to stay very long, but we ought to be prepared, anyway."

Jack huffed, mimicking the sprite with his arms crossed over his chest. "We may be cordial with the new king, but I don't suppose the people of Kanibar will be pleased to see Halvor roaming their skies after he—and the two of us—slaughtered half of their troops."

She waved a dismissive hand. "Most of them saw Edea arrive in Dofell, and even if they didn't, they've heard stories about it. They know Willem was lying so he could claw at power. They know they lost for a reason. They may not like us, but they can't resent us because their king was a greedy fool who sent their brothers and sisters to die. Let's not worry about any of that." She raised an eyebrow. "Ready?"

Jack only sighed. "Ready."

Edom zipped onto Jack's shoulder as they left the room, but quickly disappeared while they were walking to the foyer. Aurelia didn't bother calling after it to ask where it was going. For one, it moved at the speed of light. For another, it was still upset at her for ordering it to stay in Akkinor, so it probably wouldn't be cooperative anyway.

As they strolled to the front doors, they passed a group of five loitering in the hallway, talking and giggling beside a marble statue of Akkinor's hero, Oleander the Great. Thea and Mycah—the younger siblings of Aurelia's late friend, Kaia, and her former, traitorous Lord Hand, Ansyl—were accompanied by Rayan's elder two children, Alexandria and Nereida.

She'd worried that Thea and Mycah would resent her for exiling their brother, but they had shown no signs of this. She knew they understood why Ansyl had been punished, especially because his actions had put Hyacinth in harm's way. They cared for Aurelia's children like the little ones were their own siblings, and though they'd never said it aloud, Aurelia had a feeling they couldn't quite forgive Ansyl for what he'd done to Hyacinth.

After passing through the front doors, Aurelia and Jack met Halvor on the bailey. Aurelia had commissioned the construction of a saddle recently, and she'd taken him out for a ride twice since he was fitted for it, with no problems whatsoever. It was large enough for three adult riders, but only two if one of them was Jack's size or bigger.

Jack climbed onto Halvor's back first, walking up the dragon's wing while using the spikes for stability, then perched on the back of the saddle as Aurelia trailed behind him. When both were settled, Aurelia used the leather straps dangling from the saddle—attached by indestructible Akkinorian bronze rings—to tether the two of them to the mechanism. Both were wearing leather girdles around their waists adorned with matching bronze rings that connected to the straps. If anything happened during their flight, it'd be nearly impossible for Aurelia and Jack to fall from Halvor's back.

Aurelia glanced over her shoulder. "Ready?"

Jack grunted, already turning gray, and muttered, "Never."

Grinning, Aurelia tapped Halvor's scales as she'd done a thousand times before, prompting the dragon to lurch forward. He stalked over to the wall and climbed, his claws tearing chunks of stone out of the structure and sending the debris plummeting to the ground, until he gained enough traction to lift off into the sky.

Aurelia erupted in a grin as they soared toward the clouds, her stomach crawling up to her throat, and laughed when the fierce winds blew her hair back.

Jack, on the other hand, only groaned and hollered something about feeling sick.

***

After a few hours of flying, Jack finally calmed down from behind Aurelia, though he occasionally complained about the saddle digging into his groin. Aurelia wasn't fond of the feeling, either, but it was better than plummeting into the ocean.

As they inched closer to Carthe, Halvor descended by a few dozen feet, now flying beneath the clouds. A delighted laugh bubbled up in Aurelia's throat when she spotted something unmistakable in the turquoise waters of the Alkamura Ocean below: fan-shaped, vibrant, tulle-like fins splashing on the surface. There were at least a dozen of them, all in different colors, and after a moment, female heads popped up from within the waves.

"It looks like the mermaids have finally migrated beyond the western Alkamura!" Aurelia called to Jack, forced to shout over the roaring of the parting winds. "They haven't left the other side of Carthe since the persecution!"

"If they find their way to Akkinor," Jack replied, "our girls will demand we take them to the coast every day!"

Aurelia laughed. Their daughters loved stories of mermaids, but it never seemed possible that they'd see the creatures in the flesh. Of course, nobody alive three years ago ever thought they'd see nymphs or centaurs, either. Things were always changing, always evolving—and for the better.

For the most part, anyway.

Halvor followed the same route he always did when traveling to Taundosa: flying over the small port province of Khaba on the southeast side of Carthe, passing through southern Bozar, and crossing eastern Taundosa to reach the palace at the heart of the kingdom. The Bozari and the Taundosans were used to seeing Halvor by now, as were most of the native Khabish, but every now and then, people visiting Khaba to trade or sell goods from afar were startled to see a dragon of old flying overhead. They'd always been more surprised than combative, though.

Not today.

As the Khabish coastline came into view, Aurelia spotted something that wasn't unusual in the slightest: about a dozen ships floating off the coast. With Khaba being the primary trading port in southern Carthe, that wasn't a shock. What made Aurelia's gut churn, however, was the flags accompanying each ship: all amber and bronze, the colors of Krotis, bearing what appeared to be the symbol of a peacock—representing the province of Vrurith.

She was opening her mouth to say something to Jack when she saw a bright yellow light emitting from one of the ships. As the sphere of light grew larger and larger, she realized it was headed straight for them. Luckily, Halvor spotted it, too, and swerved out of the way before the ball of magic could collide with his belly.

"What the hell was that?" Jack demanded, tightening his grip on Aurelia's waist.

She didn't answer. Another ball of light—blue this time—came right for them. Halvor shrieked and released a spurt of flames from his throat, but when it met the sphere in midair, the fire was extinguished, and water splashed over Aurelia and Jack's heads. She wiped the droplets from her eyes and sputtered, barely listening to Jack while he cursed and said something about mages.

It didn't stop there. More flashes of light in various colors came soaring through the air, barely missing Halvor as he dodged each attack and responded in kind. They weren't close enough to the ships for his flames to do much damage, but Aurelia didn't want to burn the ships to ashes, anyway. They might've made the first move, but it wouldn't reflect well on her—or Halvor, for that matter—if she let her dragon disintegrate twelve ships in front of everyone currently on Khabish soil.

"We have to go around them!" she shouted. "North toward—"

Before she had the chance to finish, Halvor bellowed in pain, his neck craned toward Khaba while his body remained straight and vertical. Aurelia gritted her teeth as she tried to hang on, her back now parallel to the ocean below. While Halvor shrieked and struggled, she saw what was afflicting him: some sort of golden lasso, wrapped around his neck.

Then Halvor's lower body jerked, making Aurelia and Jack grunt as they thrusted forward, and she spotted another lasso wrapped around his lower legs, binding his feet together. Halvor roared and fought the bindings, but when he tried to breathe fire, only small, dwindling flames emitted from his mouth. The lasso on his neck wasn't just to restrain him—it was to choke him and restrict his abilities.

Halvor leaned back toward the west, attempting to yank free of the bindings, but that only made the lasso around his neck tighten. Aurelia's heart fractured when she heard him whimper like a kitten whose tail had been stepped on. It was an innocent, painful sound—a stark contrast to the growl she'd expected to hear.

"Aurelia—" Jack started, gasping.

I don't know. She meant to say the words aloud, but no sound emerged from her lips. *I don't know what to do. I don't know how to help him.*

Now more than ever, she would've given anything to speak with human Halvor. He still may not have known what to do, but it was better to talk with him about it than to watch him suffer while she was helpless to stop the threat.

Just as Halvor's body weakened when the lassos pulled him toward the ships, a horrifying roar echoed throughout the skies, rattling Aurelia's eardrums. She didn't see anything at first—then a massive shadow appeared above the clouds, and in the blink of an eye, Rieza burst through the formations, casting yet another shadow directly over Halvor.

Rieza soared over Halvor, roaring, and as she flew toward the ships, Aurelia saw something on her back: a head of long, straight, inky black hair.

Diantha.

When Rieza opened her mouth, Aurelia expected her to release a powerful gust of wind or perhaps summon a cyclone—typical powers of an air dragon, as Aurelia had learned from Lucyra. Instead, rippling energy spurted from Rieza's throat. When the energy reached the ships, a chain reaction of events occurred: the sails blew backward, the ships teetered backward like they were going to fall into the ocean, large cracks formed on some of the vessels, and small figures—people—fell overboard. At the same time, the lassos binding Halvor disappeared, and he regained his strength almost immediately.

Sonic roar, Aurelia told herself. Emitting shockwaves was another ability unique to air dragons, but only the strongest of them could do it.

Rieza flew closer to the ships, now shooting gusts of wind at them to break the masts and send the sails soaring through the air. Halvor joined her, the two dragons now hovering across from each other, and released a powerful stream of flames at one ship still bearing the flag of the Reesa family of Vrurith.

Only one, Aurelia instructed, setting her palm flat against his scales. *Limit the carnage.*

A few individuals, still intent on following what Aurelia assumed were orders from their liege lord, continued sending bursts of magic and power into the sky. Halvor and Rieza, roaring in unison, were now flying side-by-side, both facing the ships. Just a second after Halvor emitted a stream of fire, Rieza released another shockwave. The shockwave carried the fire toward the ships, morphing the flames into a shape that reminded Aurelia of a magical shield. Had it not been for what Aurelia assumed were water mages aboard the vessels creating walls of seawater, most of the fleet would've been destroyed.

As soon as their last demonstration of power was complete, the two dragons roared one last time, then flew over the fleet—low, to send another message—before traveling inland. Aurelia and Jack both glanced over their shoulders, catching one last glimpse of the broken or blazing Vrurithian ships off the coast of Khaba, while Halvor and Rieza continued screeching at one another.

"Gods be good," Jack wheezed, bringing a hand to his mouth. "I'm going to be sick."

Luckily for him, the dragons were flying over a bit of rainforest in southern Bozar when he expelled the contents of his stomach, so his breakfast of eggs and black pudding didn't splatter over one of Balor's villages.

Aurelia tried to calm her racing heart as they passed through Bozar and into Taundosa. It was all but confirmed that Krotis was responsible for what happened to Arian, but they'd made no direct attacks against Aurelia thus far, and she hadn't been in contact with anyone in Krotis. On paper, Akkinor and Krotis were neutral kingdoms—so why on earth had Lord Reesa's men attacked her?

She hadn't had enough proof to make any accusations or take action against Krotis before, but now, they'd given her the perfect opportunity to strike back.

***

"So much for a peace-loving queen." Lord Reesa snorted as he crumpled a letter in his fist and dropped it onto the floor. His eyes surveyed the faces at the table around him—the other four leaders of Krotis—as his lips curled into a sneer. "King Willem was right. She's destroying the sanctity of the realm, and she's using her beast to do it. Now she has an ally, too."

Lord Keer raised a bushy eyebrow. "Do we know who the other rider was?"

"Not yet, but we'll find out soon enough." Lord Reesa scrubbed a hand down his face and made a low, growl-like sound. "Seventeen lives were lost. Two of my ships were broken beyond repair, and another five are trapped in Khaba until the necessary repairs are made. It's a miracle the entire fleet wasn't destroyed, and it's a good thing half of my sailors are mages, too. There wouldn't have been any survivors otherwise."

Shasta stared at him, not knowing what to say. One part of her—the naive part that hadn't yet been destroyed by politics—wanted to say something optimistic, to remind him that the damages and the losses could've been worse. Another part of her—the wiser part that knew how to act in front of the noblemen—simply wanted to keep her mouth shut, only speaking when spoken to.

"Are we certain Queen Aurelia attacked first?" Lord Swann's folded hands fiddled on the table before him, his dark eyes gleaming with worry. "That doesn't sound like her, from what I've heard."

"She must've learned something," Lord Quagg muttered, massaging his temples. "Maybe she found out where Lord Cristos's curse originated from, or she knows something else that puts Krotis in the line of fire. She saw an opportunity when she spotted the Vrurithian ships, and she took it to send us a message."

Shasta pressed her lips together, contemplating. She didn't know the full prophecy—neither had her father nor King Willem. The late king had shared pieces of it with Lord Selle, but the latter hadn't relayed that information to his daughter. She'd been telling herself that whatever Queen Aurelia was prophesized to do that would lead to the realm's downfall, it wouldn't be intentional—not after everything she had done to save it. But that thought didn't matter when the realm was at stake.

Again, a part of her wondered if Lord Reesa was lying. Perhaps he'd ordered his men to lie in wait for the queen and her dragon, to strike Aurelia when she least expected it, so she'd know what awaited her. Another part of her, however, knew how foolish that would've been. Queen Aurelia and her dragon were formidable opponents, and Lord Reesa would have to be the maddest person alive to anger them by attacking unprovoked.

"Regardless of why this happened, we must proceed with caution." Lord Keer snapped his fingers, waited for a nearby servant to fill his chalice with gin, and took a sip before continuing. "We can expect to hear from her in the near future. I imagine her allies will be keeping an eye on us, too. And that other dragon..."

Lord Quagg grimaced. "We'll find out who it belongs to soon enough."

"Little Annera is no match for them yet," Lord Swann added. "We must protect her and continue providing her with everything she needs to grow larger and stronger. She's getting bigger by the day, though. That well won't hold her much longer."

"We'll think of somewhere else to keep her." Lord Reesa, who'd been staring out the window across from him like he was waiting for Queen

Aurelia's dragon to appear on the horizon, snapped his gaze over to Shasta. "Are you ready for tomorrow, girl?"

She squared her shoulders. "You may call me Lady Selle. And yes, I am."

No, I'm not.

He grinned at her defiance. "Good. My Kaius will be a good husband to you, as long as you mind him. You're not nearly as proficient a mage as he is, so it'll strengthen you—and Bruila—to have him ruling by your side."

Shasta resisted the urge to shudder. Two hours after the sun rose the following morning, she'd be saying goodbye to the life she once knew. She'd be led from her estate in Bruila to the Mekyan city of Malicia, the capital of Krotis, and she'd walk the five hundred steps to the Temple of Pherena, like every noble couple did on their wedding day. She'd kneel at Pherena's altar beside Kaius Reesa, and she'd pledge her body and soul to him forever.

She hadn't even met him properly since their betrothal was confirmed.

Lord Swann set a hand on her shoulder. "It'll be a lovely day. You'll see."

"Oh, spare me the sentimentality," Lord Reesa said with a snort. "We'll be fortunate if Queen Aurelia doesn't burn the temple down with all of us inside."

Lord Swann's eyes hardened. "I don't think she's capable of that."

"We didn't think she was capable of attacking my fleet with her dragon, and look where we are."

The young nobleman pressed his lips together, silent, as Lord Quagg cleared his throat and said, "I have spies posted in Bozar. They're posing as aspiring priests at the Holy Library of Iseppa. I've tasked them with searching for information on this prophecy King Willem mentioned to Lord Selle. If they fail, they'll take on new disguises and resume the search in Kanibar."

"Very well." Lord Keer's head bobbed approvingly. "In the meantime, let's prepare our troops. Our men must be prepared to fight at any moment, given Queen Aurelia's newfound impulsivity. We'll need those gryphons of yours, too, Swann."

The elder three lords continued chatting about war preparations, ignoring the other two. Shasta cast a sidelong glance at Lord Swann, who was clenching his jaw and staring at the others like there was something more he wanted to say. Shasta wondered if he was hesitant to deploy his arsenal against one of Runeia's allies, even though he'd be putting Krotis first—and the realm, for that matter.

There was little honor in breaking the oath one's family made to another, but then again, Krotis wasn't known for being honorable.

XVIII

Halvor didn't land in Taundosa as planned. Instead, he followed Rieza into Dofell, where both dragons landed on an empty lawn just outside of the palace walls.

Aurelia climbed down first, still trembling, and helped a green-faced Jack dismount while he, too, was shaking too much to find traction. As soon as his feet hit the ground, he put his hands on his knees and hunched over like he was going to be sick again.

She set a worried hand on his back. "Are you okay?"

"F-Fine."

"Are you sure?"

He lifted his head enough to glower at her. She wanted to chuckle—he still hadn't gotten used to flying on dragonback, even after all these years—but after what they'd just gone through, she felt fairly sick to her stomach, too.

As Jack regained his composure, Aurelia crossed the distance between the dragons to meet Diantha, who was removing a pair of gloves from her hands. Diantha paused to rub Rieza's scaly side, then tossed a smile in Aurelia's direction as they met up.

"I hope you don't take this the wrong way, but the timing was impeccable." Diantha smiled when she saw the bewildered look on Aurelia's face. "Just last night, I officially claimed Rieza before the masses here in Dofell. I assume letters from your allies in the south are on their way to Akkinor right now—they would've heard through the grapevine already, if they haven't yet received my ravens. She and I were out for a flight today when she felt Halvor in distress. Had I not claimed her last night, I wouldn't have been there to see what happened for myself. I'm sure Rieza would've come to help her brother, anyway, but I'm glad I was there."

Aurelia took Diantha's hands and squeezed. "Thank you. I don't know what we would've done if the two of you hadn't intervened. That was…"

"Unexpected?"

"Mortifying." Aurelia winced. "The only banners I saw were Vrurithian. Until we have definitive proof that Runeia is involved, we can't throw accusations at the entirety of Krotis without risking our alliance. Though, it's clear by now that Bruila is involved, too. For now, though, my focus has to be Vrurith."

"We'll have to write to Lord Reesa." Jack staggered over to Aurelia's side, still green and clammy. "He can offer us an explanation after we tell him what happened—if he hasn't already heard, and if they didn't attack us on his orders. Whatever his response is, it'll give us something to go on."

"You're welcome to send the raven from Dofell," Diantha told the pair. "I'm not afraid of Krotis coming after me to get to you—not with Rieza on my side. Krotis might as well know that she belongs to me. They'll hear about it soon enough, anyway."

Aurelia offered her a small, tired smile. "Thank you."

"My pleasure." Diantha's eyes found something behind Aurelia and Jack, making her smile. "I think they're happy to see each other, don't you?"

The couple turned and chuckled when they saw what she'd been looking at. Aurelia hadn't even noticed Rieza move from behind Diantha while they were conversing, but now, the violet vipertail was curled up on the ground beside Halvor, licking the tender spots on his back feet where the lasso had restrained him. Halvor, on the other hand, was nuzzling his snout against her, small plumes of smoke spouting from his nostrils to express his contentment.

"Dragons don't have any relation to cats, do they?" Jack asked, only half-kidding.

Diantha laughed. "Not to my knowledge."

Aurelia smiled, but the red sores around Halvor's ankles and neck worried her. "Will he be all right?"

"I imagine so," Diantha replied, though her dark eyes flickered with doubt. "Dragons heal much faster than humans do. Their scales regenerate very quickly. He'll be a bit sore for a day or two, but he should be back to normal after that. It's strange, though—steelspikes have the strongest body armor of all dragons, yet the spell used to restrain him managed to penetrate his scales. The spell must be a powerful one."

Jack raised an eyebrow. "Dark magic?"

"Doubtful." Aurelia ran a hand through her golden hair, then frowned when she felt the dampness. She'd almost forgotten about the water mage. "Krotis may not be exactly honorable, but they're strict when it comes to other virtues. There's never been a known sorcerer from Krotis. I don't think any Kroti mages would resort to using dark magic, even to incapacitate a threat like Halvor."

"I hate to say it," Jack muttered, grimacing, "but it seems like Krotis's leaders have abandoned most of their virtues. Temperance? That disappeared the moment they attacked us. Humility? Gods, no. Kindness, honesty, or wisdom? None that I can see. They're brave, I'll give them that, but still—it's a wonder their Almighty hasn't rained hellfire down upon them all."

Diantha shrugged. "They may still care about charitability and chastity. That's something. And diligence, given the lengths they've gone to lately."

Jack snorted and waved a dismissive hand. "Being hard workers who don't have sex until they're married, and giving a few silver coins to beggars on the streets—that doesn't make them virtuous. They're doing the bare minimum to appease their Almighty."

"Well, either way, we mustn't—oh." Diantha frowned, her eyes trailing something behind Aurelia, and furrowed her brows. "It looks like I have a visitor."

Aurelia turned and followed her gaze. Behind the now-sleeping dragons was a cobblestone road leading from a nearby village to the palace. Traveling upon that road were six soldiers, three on either side of a wagon being pulled by a large brown horse. A seventh soldier was guiding the horse by the reins, and when he spotted the trio with the dragons on the lawn, he redirected the group onto the grass.

Jack squinted to get a better look. "What's that on their breastplates? A roach?"

A chill traced Aurelia's spine. "A bolas spider. Symbolic of the Trevas family of Kanibar."

"Oh." He swallowed. "At least it's Harryn and not Willem, right?"

"Right." She didn't want to admit it, but the sight of Kanibar's sigil—even if the kingdom was no longer being ruled by a sadistic tyrant—still made her uneasy. "I wonder what they're here for."

Diantha took a deep breath. "Let's find out."

The trio met the Kanish halfway, and as soon as the visitors stopped moving, Aurelia saw what lay in the back of the wagon: an elderly woman with braided white hair resting atop a mountain of cushions, pillows, and blankets. She was pale and somewhat wiry, like she hadn't eaten in a few days. Her hands trembled on the blanket she clutched against her chest, and her chest shuddered with each breath she took. Even her eyes struggled to stay open, as if the sunlight was too bright for her.

"May." Aurelia, abandoning all propriety, rushed over to the wagon and climbed inside, then placed her hands over Maysa's. "W-What's happened?"

The soldier leading the horse sighed. "The Dowager Queen fell ill not long after her last visit to Dofell. Our medics and mages examined her extensively and found no signs of foul play. His Majesty the King wished for her to regain her strength from the comfort of the palace, but she was insistent that we escort her to Dofell at once."

Aurelia forced a smile as she looked down at her friend. "You knew I'd be here."

"O-Of course." Maysa's voice, normally hearty and powerful, was raspy and weak. It nearly broke Aurelia's heart to hear her like that—especially when Maysa could barely keep her eyes open, and when she used what little strength she had left to squeeze Aurelia's hands. "Don't worry for me. I've been waiting for this day for many years now. I-It's my time to go home."

Behind them, Jack cleared his throat. "I think it's best if we give them a few moments alone."

"We're under orders to stay at her side," a soldier retorted.

Maysa coughed. "Leave us. Please."

"You heard her," Diantha chimed in. "Follow me and His Royal Highness, gentlemen. You've traveled a long way on foot—I'm sure you're all in need of refreshments and a place to rest."

The soldiers hesitated for a moment, then reluctantly followed Jack and Diantha into the palace. Aurelia kept her eyes trained on Maysa while the oracle's eyelids fluttered and her breathing staggered. Even with all the signs of her impending demise, though, she kept a firm grip on Aurelia's hands.

"You should've told me, May," Aurelia whispered. "If I had known this day was coming so soon..."

"It wouldn't have changed anything." Maysa smacked her lips together and asked Aurelia to help her drink from a nearby canteen. After Aurelia dribbled a small amount into her mouth, Maysa managed a weak smile. "Thank you. Now, before I...before I go, there are things I must tell you. The voices of the gods have grown stronger in the last three years, and they don't wish for me to-to leave you without the tools you need."

Aurelia covered Maysa with another blanket when she shivered. "What is it?"

"Firstly, do not fear my grandson. Though he has allies amongst your current enemies, he has no intention of responding to any calls to arms, or participating in any squabbles to come. Anything Willem was involved in, Harryn wants nothing to do with." The oracle's eyes fluttered shut. "Your-Your Hand was right about where you might find the prophecy Willem shared with Krotis. You must speak with your brother to learn about it."

"Why him?" She couldn't stop herself from asking, despite remembering what Archie had told her when she made the same inquiry in her dream. "Of all people..."

"Finding it elsewhere would be a difficult task. Enemies lurk where the prophecy lies. Only I know it from memory, and I—"

"—can't tell me. That would be too easy." Aurelia smiled when Maysa laughed, but the sound immediately led to her coughing again. "I understand. But Archie? Really?"

Even through her coughing fit, she was smiling. "You must hear it from him to understand exactly what it means for you. And...And if he does well, he has a chance at reaching Hanhalla. I cannot say for certain that he will—even the gods don't know that yet—but by allowing him to help you, you could be giving him a second chance."

Aurelia paused, gnawing on her lower lip. She wasn't so sure Archie deserved a chance at Hanhalla. She wasn't sure he deserved eternal torture in Saendah, either, though. Despite the horrible things he'd done, his reign of terror had lasted less than a year, and he could've done much worse with the power he held. There were others in the realm who'd dedicated their entire lives to unthinkable acts of evil. Archie hadn't lost sight of his goodness until the last year of his life.

"There is something else." Maysa's glassy eyes opened. She wasn't looking at Aurelia, but rather beyond her at something that wasn't there. "You already know more about your destiny than most of your kind did. Those Forged in Gold didn't always know what they were, so they were oblivious to some things."

"Things like what?"

The oracle cleared her throat. "I-In the old days, a man called Edarvo lived in Quapebet. He was Forged in Gold, too, and he knew...he knew all about his destiny. He told himself that when he died, he wouldn't go without leaving the realm with someone else who wept the gods' golden tears. He believed he was responsible for finding a successor to his role. He didn't know it, but he was right: there must always be someone Forged in Gold alive in the realm at any given time. The gods demand it. Unfortunately, hundreds of those poor souls never knew what they were.

They never understood why they wept golden tears, and for many of them, it became a burden too great to bear."

Aurelia shushed her when she heard the strain in Maysa's voice. The old woman's face had grown clammier as she spoke, too, and her lips were drier than the Ngora Valley. Aurelia tried to offer her more water, but she refused.

"Your kind are chosen before birth," she continued, "and there can only be one of you alive at a time who actively weeps golden tears. It's you for now, but when you're gone, another will take your place. Edarvo never found the person who'd become Forged in Gold after he died, and that person didn't know what they were when they first wept golden tears. It drove them mad, and eventually, to suicide. The one meant to take your place is...different. Different from you, at least. She already lives, but without proper guidance, she won't know what's become of her when her tears change, and it may kill her. You can't let this happen."

Aurelia furrowed her brows. "How can I help her if I'll be dead by the time she becomes Forged in Gold?"

"The power of the pen, my dear child." Maysa squeezed Aurelia's hands and released a long, shuddering breath. "Whether you die tomorrow or fifty years from now, the same person will live long enough to take your place. She will do great things if she accepts what she's destined to become, but if not..."

When she trailed off, Aurelia murmured, "Who is she?"

No reply. For a moment, as Maysa's eyes fell shut again, Aurelia wondered if the oracle had taken her leave from Icareth. She was opening her mouth to speak again when Maysa's eyes shot open, greener than emeralds and wider than saucers. A gasp escaped Aurelia's lips when Maysa leaned up and set her palm against the queen's cheek, their eyes boring holes into each other's skulls.

One moment, she was staring into Maysa's eyes while sitting in the back of a wagon. The next, she was locked in a vision, the reality around her having faded away completely.

The vision only lasted a few seconds, at most. When the world around her returned, she blinked a few times to adjust, unintentionally pulling her face from Maysa's grip. The oracle fell back against the heap of cushions supporting her, looking even worse than she had a moment earlier, and gasped for air.

"Did you...Did you see her?" Maysa wheezed. "Your successor?"

For just a second, the vision played in Aurelia's mind once more: a brief glimpse of a beautiful young woman with white hair and silver eyes.

"Yes," she whispered, taking Maysa's hands again. "Yes, I did."

With a smile and a long, powerful exhale, Maysa's hands drifted from Aurelia's, and her eyes fell shut for the last time.

***

When Jack, Diantha, and the Kanish soldiers finally left the palace about an hour later, they found Aurelia exactly where she'd been since she first climbed into the wagon: sitting on a heap of cushions and blankets beside the still, pale corpse of the Dowager Queen of Kanibar.

She'd willed herself to move after Maysa's chest stopped rising and falling, knowing she had to let the soldiers know, but she couldn't do it. She was locked in a trance, replaying everything Maysa had told her. Somehow, despite the oracle revealing so much in her final moments, Aurelia was still left with more questions than answers.

When Jack finally coaxed Aurelia out of the wagon, Diantha instructed a few of the soldiers—after they finished uttering a prayer for Maysa, of course—to fetch her own men from the palace. She had no intention of sending Maysa's body back to Kanibar on the back of a wagon, so she wanted to loan them a funerary carriage.

Aurelia and Jack stayed outside with Diantha as they waited for Dofelli soldiers to arrive with the carriage. Aurelia barely processed what Jack was saying when he told her he'd already sent word to Vrurith on her behalf. She thought she'd thanked him, but she couldn't be sure. She'd stopped thinking about Vrurith and Krotis since she climbed into the wagon.

When the carriage arrived, they watched and murmured prayers for Maysa's soul as she was carefully placed into a coffin inside the carriage. They didn't move a muscle as the Kanish soldiers climbed into the coachman's seat or took their positions on either side of the carriage. Until it rolled away into the distance, they remained still and silent.

"We can stay for the funeral," Jack murmured, rubbing Aurelia's back in comforting circles. "I'm sure the king would appreciate us attending. He knows how fond his grandmother was of you."

Aurelia released a shuddering exhale. "I think May would want me to continue on my quest rather than cry over her coffin. She didn't tell me what she did so I could waste time on mourning."

"I thought you might say that."

Diantha raised an eyebrow. "What now? I'll keep an eye out for any suspicious activity in my area, and if word spreads of Krotis's activities, I'll let you know. But as of now, there's not much I can do to help you."

"We have to go to Taundosa." Aurelia cleared her throat and tore her eyes away from the hill the carriage had traveled over before it disappeared. "Reyna needs to know about the curse, and...and I think we have to pay a visit to the Elotheon."

"The Elotheon?" Jack frowned. "What does Gianla's temple have to do with—oh." His face went slack. "Vanhylde."

Aurelia only nodded.

"Wherever it is you're going, and whatever it is you're doing," Diantha said, "I don't think I want to know. But I wouldn't be a very good host if I let you leave now. Spend the night here—Halvor needs the rest, and judging by how ghastly the two of you look, you could use a good night's sleep, too."

Aurelia and Jack grimaced when they observed one another, making the former sock her husband in the arm. He rubbed his arm as he apologized and grinned at her, but that only made the exhaustion on his face more apparent.

Until then, she hadn't realized how long it'd been since they rested. They'd flown for an entire day without stopping before they were attacked, and the short battle had only made them wearier. After losing Maysa, too...Aurelia needed a break more than she cared to admit.

Tonight, she would mourn for Maysa in her nightly prayers, and maybe—just maybe—the oracle would visit her in Vanhylde, the land of dreams.

XIX

The following morning, after saying goodbye to Diantha and thanking her for everything she'd done, Aurelia and Jack mounted Halvor once again, then set off for Taundosa. It was a short flight, so they were landing in the gardens at Reyna's palace in half an hour. They then interrupted a meeting between Reyna and one of her noblemen—which the Golden Queen didn't seem to mind—to inform her about the Hollow Dream.

Aurelia had prefaced by stating that she and Jack couldn't stay long, and she was glad she did: Reyna didn't seem to be in a very hospitable mood after learning that her Lord Hand and close friend might have his soul trapped in purgatory for all eternity. In fact, she'd left her study in a hurry before the couple did, and Aurelia could've sworn she heard Reyna's sobs echoing through the halls.

It wasn't a long journey from the palace to the Elotheon, so they made the trek on foot rather than taking Halvor. The temple for Gianla was located in Agotia, just beside Ardiham Castle—the Cristos family's ancestral home. It was the holiest place in Taundosa, and other than the library in Bozar, it was considered one of the most divine locations in all of Carthe. Aurelia was certain that it was blessed enough to serve as a portal to Vanhylde.

Only one priest was at the temple when they arrived, along with a few patrons. He recognized Aurelia from her previous visits, and when she asked to see the archives, he didn't hesitate to escort her and Jack to the room. The Elotheon was a tall, pillar-shaped building, with no corners and only one room per floor, and there were about seven stories. Aurelia wasn't surprised to find the archives on the very top floor, where patrons seldom visited.

The priest didn't bother asking why they wanted to see the archives. He'd only glanced at something across from the doorway—a faded, rust-colored handprint on the stone wall—and sighed before leaving them alone. As soon as she saw the handprint, she knew they'd come to the right place.

"In all honesty," she told Jack, strolling over to the wall, "I don't know what my body looks like when my soul visits Vanhylde. I might look dead. You can't panic, though. I'll be all right."

Jack gave her a look like she'd just slapped him. "What are you talking about?"

She gave him the same look. "What are *you* talking about?"

"I'm coming with you, you fool," he stated. She started to protest, but he only chuckled and talked over her. "For one, I didn't like the idea of you going in the first place, so if I have the opportunity to be your escort, I'm taking it. For another, I may never get the chance to visit Vanhylde again. It'd be the adventure of a lifetime."

Aurelia couldn't help but grin at that. "You've never been one to turn down an adventure, and I've never been one to stop you from embarking on one."

"So it's settled." Jack pulled his dagger from his boot and held it out, wiggling his eyebrows as that innocent, wicked grin she loved so much formed on his lips. "After you, Lily dear."

Rolling her eyes, she gave him a quick kiss, then accepted the dagger and cut her palm. She barely winced as she cupped her hand to keep the pool of blood from spilling onto the floor. Jack did the same, also without flinching, then mimicked her as she set her palm on the stone wall. The faded handprint sat right between their hands—an eerie reminder that many souls who visited Vanhylde never came back. She hoped whoever this handprint belonged to, they'd found their way home.

A breeze cascaded through the windowless room, lifting Aurelia's hair from her shoulders and tousling Jack's dark curls. His eyes widened, but she only nodded to let him know it was all right.

She'd memorized the words to open the portal by then, but she said them slowly, giving Jack enough time to repeat each sentence after her. Their free hands united while they spoke, and Aurelia felt Jack trembling while the wind picked up, enveloping them completely.

Exactly as it'd happened before, her eyes fell shut as she surrendered her soul to the magical breeze. She felt a lurch in her chest right before all sensation disappeared from her being. She couldn't feel Jack's hand in hers anymore, but she could hear soft whisperings echoing in her ears.

As soon as the breeze faded, she opened her eyes. Her hand was still pressed against a flat surface, but it wasn't the stone wall at the Elotheon. It was a plain, painted beige wall, and just above her hand was a portrait of her parents on their wedding day.

She stepped back, studying her parents' faces, then quickly turned to her right to find Jack. He was standing beside her, as he had been when they were in the Elotheon. He stared at his hand on the wall, then looked up at her with pure bewilderment gleaming in his oceanic eyes.

"Are we—?" he whispered, eyes widening.

"I think so. It looks like we're at home, but—"

Aurelia stopped when she heard a familiar melody from behind them. The song being played on the piano was one she knew well—*The March of the Pretender*. It'd been written by a supporter of Alora Cherrane, the last Queen of Akkinor before Aurelia herself, to protest the rebellion led by the first Brentwood king, Oleander the Great. Nobody had ever played that song, especially in the Folly, because it was meant for the woman who nearly led Akkinor to its downfall. Only one person had ever dared to play it.

Feeling like a fist was clenching her gut, she turned slowly, finally realizing the room they were standing in. It was a large, open room with little other than knickknacks and antiques on display. This was where Aurelia's mother, Cressida—and, eventually, Archie—kept the pianoforte. Both claimed it had the best acoustics in the palace, though Aurelia never understood that. She hadn't even stepped foot into the room in eight years.

There he was, sitting at the pianoforte with his head bowed, his mop of blond hair falling into his eyes while his fingers danced along the keys. Aurelia took a few steps toward him, Jack not far behind, but her brother didn't look up.

By the time the song ended, Aurelia and Jack were standing on the other side of the instrument, staring at Archie in utter silence. He paused for a moment, hands still resting on the keys, before finally looking up and brushing hair from his clear blue eyes. Aurelia sucked in a sharp breath, startled by how much he resembled Hyacinth. She often forgot that Hyacinth was Archie's daughter, but seeing him again, there was no doubting it.

"Hello, Li." The sound of her childhood nickname made every hair on Aurelia's flesh stand up. His eyes flicked over to Jack while she stared. "Hello, Mister Ashford. Or, shall I say, *brother*. We're family now, aren't we?"

Jack didn't answer, and for a moment, neither did Aurelia. When she finally found her voice, all she could say was, "Hi, Archie."

"Surprised to find me here, of all places?" He chuckled when she shook her head. "Of course not. This is the good end of the bargain here in Vanhylde: I can exist in my favorite place in the realm for eternity. The rest isn't so grand."

Jack raised an eyebrow. "How do you mean?"

Archie sighed. "There are three doors in this room. If I try to leave through any of them, I emerge through a different one, and I end up right back here. I can't open the windows to feel the sun on my skin. I can't summon a servant for a bottle of wine. I'm not entirely alone, though. Sometimes, I'll get a visitor. Usually you, sister, or Mother and Father. Others, too, on occasion."

"Your visitors are meant to test you," Aurelia said. She'd thought it, but alas—thoughts became speech in Vanhylde. "They're not really Mother and Father. Just images of them to see how far you've come." A ghost of a smile formed on his lips, almost like he was proud of her cleverness. "So? Do you continue to maintain your childish greed and ignorance, or have you chosen to approach things differently?"

His eyes flashed, startling her. He looked so...*alive*. "It depends."

"It depends." She shook her head, chuckling with no humor. "You have the opportunity of a lifetime to move on to Hanhalla, one that you maybe don't even deserve. Yet you can't put your pride aside enough to do it wholeheartedly."

He ignored her. "I know I told you to visit me, Li, but I wasn't sure you'd actually do it. I'm surprised you found your way here. Now, I presume to know why you've come, and it isn't because you wanted to see me."

"Not exactly." She rested her hands on the pianoforte, ignoring the scalding look he gave her. "We need to know the prophecy. It'd be wise to tell us instead of playing games with us, brother. Helping us might get you out of here."

"It's not that easy," he said, snorting. "But regardless of what it means for me, I'll tell you. I don't actually know the exact words, though. Nobody does. Only your oracle friend knew it word-for-word, and she didn't write the whole thing down when it came to her. She couldn't risk it falling into the wrong hands, like your friend Willem. What your enemies know may be dangerous, but not as dangerous as the parts they don't know. The rest of it...They'd try to prevent those bits from coming to fruition, and the oracle couldn't take that chance."

Jack folded his arms over his chest, unimpressed. "Care to elaborate?"

Archie released a frustrated exhale and set his hands on his lap. "Words hold power, especially when they come from the gods. The oracle didn't want that kind of power in anyone's hands. Even yours, Li. More often than not, the word of the divine isn't meant to be heard in full by mortal ears unless the mortal is a prophet."

"All right." Aurelia knew that much. Maysa had already told her that Willem—and now, Krotis—only knew pieces of the prophecy. "What can you tell us, then? I only know what you told me in my dream: *'Three cycles after the moon falls from the sky, the Four Pillars shall emerge from the shadows, and their return shall mark the end of the beginning.'*"

"We know the time has come," Jack added. "The moon goddess fell from the sky three years ago. Whatever this talk is about *the Four Pillars* and *the end of the beginning*, it's bound to happen soon."

He nodded. "That's right. That's only one of two full sentences I'm allowed to tell you, though. What you ought to be worried about is the part that speaks of one who breathes fire severing the realm."

Aurelia's breath caught. "Is that supposed to mean Halvor? Or me?"

Her brother snorted again. "Who else?"

"But—"

"That's why they're all so shaken. It doesn't mean what you or they think it does, though. It's a matter of the wording—the interpretation." He took a long, deep breath and brushed his fingertips over the keys. "*'The one who breathes fire will sever the realm at the edge of the world.'* That's the other complete line I can share. The one who breathes the four winds will play a part, too, as will the one who breathes ice, and the one who breathes the dust of stone."

"That sounds like the Elementals," Jack murmured. "Is that what the prophecy means by the Four Pillars? Will the Elementals return? I thought they were dead."

"That wouldn't add up," Aurelia told him. "If the one who breathes fire is me or Halvor, then we have to assume the others are humans or dragons across the realm, too." A quiet gasp escaped her as the realization struck. "Rieza is an air dragon. *The one who breathes the four winds.* The Pillars have to be dragons *and* their riders. The four elements are the foundation of magic—it was the Elementals who turned humans into mages, after all—so it makes sense that they'd be at the center of this."

Archie nodded. "Very good. Now, I can't say much about the others, because it's not my job to tell you what everything means in exact detail. But you also need to know that the one who breathes the dust of stone will change. That person lives, and you may know of them, but they aren't the same person who will complete the Four Pillars. The prophecy talks about that, too. Your friend Willem left that part out when he relayed the prophecy to Krotis."

"Stop calling him that," she snapped. He only rolled his eyes in response. "That must mean the one who breathes the dust of stone is in Krotis. If the Four Pillars are dragons..." She swallowed the lump in her throat. "That little emerald longbelly. It must belong to one of the Kroti leaders, and it must be an earth dragon. I-I think it belongs to the Selle family—Lady Shasta. Willem wrote to Lord Amarion about an object the latter possessed while referencing the Four Pillars."

Jack hung his head and sighed. "Gods..."

"That just leaves the water dragon. The one who breathes ice." She brought a hand to her stomach, nausea overwhelming her. "There's another one out there."

"Maybe." Archie shrugged. "I can't tell you where to find it, or if it's even alive yet. I've already told you enough as it is."

She clenched her jaw, resisting the urge to snap at him again for his cryptic messages. She knew he was only doing what the gods demanded of him, like Maysa. Even if he knew more than he let on—though it was entirely possible that he knew only as much as he was sharing—he was in no position to speak on that knowledge if the gods didn't allow it.

"This can't be right," Jack argued. "Aurelia would never *sever* the realm. Her destiny is to salvage it, not break it."

"Again," Archie said tiredly, "it's all a matter of interpretation. You'll see what I mean, eventually."

"The edge of the world has to refer to Krotis," Aurelia said thoughtfully. "In the old days, Krotis was often referred to as the edge of the world because it's too treacherous for humans to travel there. Sailors always knew to turn back when they reached the western side of Krotis. That's where most maps end." She shook her head and clenched her jaw. "It's no wonder Willem got Krotis involved. He knew they'd do everything in their power to stop me if they thought I'd destroy the realm by starting with them."

"Exactly." Her brother lightly pressed on the keys, playing a gentle melody, before exhaling and dropping his hands to his lap again. "If Krotis can stop you before you destroy them, then they've succeeded in saving the realm. That's their interpretation of the prophecy, but you really can't fault them for thinking that way. Willem only told them what he wanted them to know, and they believed the word of a man some of them trusted."

Aurelia swallowed the hot, thick lump in her throat. "I-If it's all a matter of interpretation, and you're saying I won't actually destroy the realm...What does it mean by *sever*?"

Archie grinned, but she couldn't tell if he was mocking or encouraging her. "That's for you to find out on your own. You know as well as I do—

even if it pains me to admit it—that you could never do anything, even unintentionally, to destroy the realm. Krotis chose to believe otherwise because they don't know you, and they don't care to. They trust the word of a friend more than the reputation of a stranger."

Rather than letting Aurelia or Jack reply, Archie stood from the bench and joined them on the other side of the piano. Aurelia resisted the urge to flinch when he reached out and placed a hand on her shoulder.

"If, gods forbid, I find myself in Saendah someday," he told her, "I'll find a way to make Willem pay for what he did. Nobody threatens my sister except for me."

Aurelia shrugged his hand away. "Not funny."

Archie guffawed. "I thought it was."

"And that's probably why you're here."

"Come *on*, Li. Play nice with your dear departed brother." He grinned again, folded his arms over his chest, and leaned his weight on one foot. "If you're looking for more, I'm afraid I've said enough as it is. Just remember that they'll keep doing everything in their power to break you, to make you falter so they can strike you in a gap in your armor. Keep your eyes open at all times."

She nodded and took a long, deep breath. "What now?"

"Go through there." He nodded his head toward the door behind her. "Someone else wants to speak with you. Our audience is finished, though. I can see in your eyes that you're itching to get away from me."

Actually, no, she thought. *Everything else aside, it's nice to hear your voice again.* When his grin widened, she cursed herself, having forgotten he could hear her thoughts.

"It's been a pleasure, sister." Archie bowed mockingly, making her roll her eyes, before he did the same to Jack. "It's been nice to see you, too, Jack. Safe travels back to the land of the living. Don't be shy about visiting me again, either."

Aurelia lost the battle when she finally smiled. "Goodbye, brother."

Jack only nodded his head in farewell, took Aurelia's hand, and let her guide him toward the door. She paused before she opened it and looked over her shoulder at Archie. Her brother merely settled at the piano again, stretched his fingers, and winked before *The March of the Pretender* flooded her eardrums once more.

XX

When Aurelia and Jack emerged from the other side of the door, she immediately recognized their surroundings. This was the same field she'd visited during her first trip to Vanhylde when she spoke with Halvor. Just as she thought it, she spotted the dragon's human form sitting by a nearby river, his toes wiggling in the silt.

At first, Jack didn't understand why she was so eager to rush toward the handsome, muscular man with eyes like gemstones and hair like molten gold. She reminded him that Halvor presented himself to her in Vanhylde as a human; and as soon as he realized who the man was, he relaxed like someone had taken a few tons of bricks from his back.

Halvor glanced up when they joined him by the riverside, smiling. "Welcome back, my friend. I didn't expect to see you here again so soon, but I was pleased to feel your presence when you arrived." He tipped his head to Jack. "Hello, Jack. It's nice to finally speak with you. My apologies for making you so sick."

"I-uh—" Jack stammered. He cleared his throat and awkwardly itched at the back of his head. "It's nice to talk to you, too. And it's not your fault. My body was built for riding, not flying."

"You should drink some ginger tea before you fly. That's what Anysa used to do when Katryna took her for rides. It always settled her stomach."

Jack only stared at him. "Uh...Will do. Thanks for the suggestion."

"My pleasure." Halvor's gaze flicked over to Aurelia again, and for a moment, she could've sworn she saw shame in his eyes. "I wanted to see you today because I feel I owe you an apology. I promised never to disobey any of your commands, and yesterday, I failed."

She frowned. "Whatever do you mean?"

"You told me to destroy only one ship. I didn't listen. I'm afraid I let Rieza get inside my head."

Aurelia waved a dismissive hand. "Honestly...After what they did to you, I don't blame you for lashing out. It was wrong of me to restrict you when they hurt you like they did. I may be your mistress, but if someone targets you like that, you should have a say in how they're handled." Her eyebrows furrowed when she replayed her own words. "Say—I don't like that word. *Mistress.* I wish there was a different way to describe our relationship. That sounds like I own you, and I don't."

"Dragons choose our riders. Ownership has nothing to do with it," Halvor confirmed, smiling. "It's all right, though. That terminology has been used for as long as I've been alive. Don't feel poorly about it."

"All right." She mirrored his smile as he dipped his finger into the water, chuckling at the way it rippled. "Is there another reason you wished to see us today?"

He grimaced. "I fear I didn't tell you quite enough about Rieza last time you were here. I truly didn't know if Diantha would ever claim her or take her to battle. Now that she has, and you've seen what she's capable of..." He sighed. "I don't wish to sound like a narcissist, but I'm still stronger than she is. She was dormant for too long. But, generally speaking, air dragons tend to be more powerful than the rest of us. I imagine she'll find her footing again in due time. Air dragons are also the most unpredictable. You cannot let it surprise you if she becomes disobedient to Diantha."

Jack furrowed his brows. "What makes them so volatile?"

"The four winds," Aurelia murmured.

Halvor nodded, beaming at her. "Exactly. Air dragons—and air mages, for that matter—possess the ability to summon the winds from all corners of the realm: north, south, east, and west. Fire, water, and earth are relatively the same regardless of where you go. Fire will always be hot, and it will always be destructive. Water will always boil or freeze. The earth will always be grounding. But the four winds are different. Northern winds are sharper, fiercer. Southern winds are calmer, smoother. You get the idea. That being said, Rieza is constantly being influenced by clashing forces. There's never any telling which wind she'll choose to follow, which path she'll want to take."

Aurelia raised an eyebrow. "Does Diantha know this?"

"If she's as educated on dragonkind as she claims to be, she'll have some idea. But she may not wish to accept that Rieza isn't entirely obedient to her, either."

"And what about the emerald longbelly?" Jack inquired. "The earth dragon. We think it belongs to Shasta Selle."

"Her name is Annera," Halvor said, looking a bit annoyed at Jack for calling the dragon an *it*. "Like I said, earth dragons tend to be quite grounded. But the earth can still tremble and break beneath our feet if we don't see the warning signs in time. She may become dangerous—especially because she's still so young and unfamiliar with the world. I don't think she'll purposely do anything destructive, though. It's not in the nature of emerald dragons to do such things. But if she does, it's because she's lost control."

A shudder wracked Aurelia's body. Of the three pillars they'd already uncovered, only one—Halvor, naturally—felt stable and trustworthy. He may have posed the greatest threat because of his size, power, and experience, but Rieza's unpredictability and Annera's immaturity made them enormous threats, too. Aurelia wanted to trust that Rieza and Diantha would help resolve the situation rather than make it worse, but she couldn't be sure. And Annera...Though small and inexperienced, the youth's lack of control made Aurelia worry about meeting her in battle.

There was, of course, another pillar they hadn't yet discovered. If anyone knew about it, it was Halvor, but Aurelia wasn't so sure she wanted to hear what he had to say.

"The fourth pillar. The water dragon." Jack brought it up before she could, and briefly explained to Halvor the concept of the Four Pillars as told by the prophecy. "Do you know anything about that one? Archie didn't give us much to go on."

Halvor sighed. "I'm not sure. It could be a youngling that's yet to hatch, or it could be one like me or Rieza that's been in hiding." He pressed his lips together, the wind blowing his hair into his face as something flashed across his sapphire eyes. "I may have an idea. Do you recall the Legend of the Icelord?"

Aurelia chuckled a little. "Of course. In the old days, when the first Isalders settled in Glacier Bay, the continent was inhabited only by the Mountain Clan—they still live there today, so the stories say, but only deep within the Ealair Mountain Range. They retreated there after a time to seek solace from an endless winter, as the mountains provided shelter. The legend says that a mage, the son of the water Elemental Glacia, cursed the continent with the endless winter after he was rejected by his neighbors. They feared him because of how much power he held as the son of an Elemental. The First Mortals called him the *Icelord*. It's believed that his curse is the reason Glacier Bay has never seen a day without snow."

"Is that all?" Halvor raised his brows, making Aurelia frown and shrug. "No, I suppose you wouldn't know. The rest of the story has been lost in time."

"What is it?"

He inhaled sharply, ignoring a bumblebee buzzing around his head. "The Icelord claimed a dragon as a young man. A water dragon, naturally. The First Mortals believed it was the dragon who enacted the curse on the Icelord's behalf. He faced the sky and roared, causing snow to fall from the heavens, and the snow did not cease. The inhabitants of Glacier Bay went hunting for the Icelord and his dragon, intending to kill them both. The Icelord hid the dragon somewhere nobody would ever find him, then gave himself up to his hunters, claiming the dragon had abandoned him. The mortals believed that killing him would stop the eternal winter, but it didn't. That's why they thought the dragon was responsible for the curse—because they hadn't managed to kill *him*, and the winter prevailed."

Aurelia wrapped her arms around herself, shivering. "What was the dragon's name?"

Halvor's eyes flashed. "Caathet."

Jack shuddered, too. "Did it just get colder here? I think it got colder."

"Shh," Aurelia hushed, nudging him in the side with her elbow.

"If the Icelord managed to hide Caathet, and he's been hibernating all these years," Halvor continued, grimacing, "he'd pose a significant threat. I imagine he isn't very pleased with humanity after being hunted and forced to hide for over a thousand years—particularly because they killed his only master."

"I wouldn't blame him," Aurelia admitted. "This is all very good to know, but I don't understand how the dragons come into play for the prophecy. How does the emergence of four dragons, one of each element, bring about the end of the beginning?"

Halvor gave her a pointed look. "It's not us. It's our riders. Your greatest power may lie with us, but dragons don't run the world. Humans do. We are your vessels, your representatives, but you are the ones the prophecy speaks of."

She smiled weakly. "Does all that just mean you're unsure about what *the end of the beginning* means?"

"I have no idea what it means." He offered her a small, sheepish smile, like he was ashamed he couldn't tell her what he didn't know. "You'll figure it out soon enough, though. You always do."

"He's right about that," Jack chimed in, making Aurelia grin and roll her eyes. "Is there anything else you can tell us, Halvor?"

"That depends. What more did Archie say about the prophecy?"

They filled him in, relaying everything else Archie had told them. He listened intently, neck craned a bit—reminding Aurelia of his dragon form—and nodded along while they spoke, absorbing every word.

"Hmm." Halvor pressed his lips together and watched as the breeze carried a dandelion through the air. "So, Shasta Selle isn't the one referenced in the prophecy. That could mean one of two things: either she will die, or Annera will abandon her."

Aurelia's fiddling hands in her lap froze. "Dragons can do that?"

"Yes." He looked amused, despite her terror at realizing he could abandon their bond if he so desired. "Not all riders care for their dragons like you do, Aurelia. I suppose that's part of the reason mortals turned on us all those years ago. We were being used as weapons, as tools to further humanity's greed and power. We weren't always cared for or appreciated by those we bonded with after they realized what we could do for them. I shall never abandon you or your family, and I can say the same about Rieza, but Annera...Even if I knew her, I couldn't say. She's too young."

"Let's pray her second rider doesn't live in Krotis," Jack grumbled, plucking blades of grass from the ground. "If they do, it'll be a lot harder to figure this out. They won't want to work with us to fulfill the prophecy." He stilled, eyes widening. "Is it possible the prophecy won't be fulfilled?"

Halvor shrugged. "I admit, I don't know that much about prophecies. That would've been a good question for your oracle friend. But in my experience, if the gods wish for something to happen, it will. Then again..." He sighed and closed his eyes. "The gods left us because humanity behaved in ways they couldn't predict. This prophecy could be just another test, a way of observing mortals and how far you've come. If it isn't fulfilled, I imagine the world will carry on exactly as it has for the last one-thousand years."

A fist clenched Aurelia's heart. She knew what that meant. Humanity would find more ways to turn on each other than to unite as one, and the most obvious way to do that was to divide the two already-uneasy groups that'd dominated the realm from the start: mages and mortals. Those who wanted magic and protected it, and those who wanted it gone. Perhaps there would be a second blight of the persecution. Perhaps some countries would be envious of others because of their magic and their creatures, and they'd attempt to steal it. There was no shortage of possibilities.

That was exactly what'd happened to send the gods away before, and even after magic had almost gone extinct, mortals found other reasons to squabble and destroy each other. It'd be an endless cycle until, hopefully, someone stepped up to break it like Aurelia had.

She didn't want to see the last eight years amount to nothing if the prophecy wasn't fulfilled. She'd find herself trapped in a world on fire, and she'd be powerless to stop it.

***

After leaving Halvor in Vanhylde and returning to the Elotheon, Aurelia and Jack headed back to the Palace of Taundosa to reunite with Halvor's physical form. They thought about stopping in to tell Reyna what they'd learned in Vanhylde, but Aurelia decided against it: for some reason, she was eager to get the hell out of Carthe.

They went to the gardens immediately, where Halvor was awaiting them. He'd been sleeping when they arrived, so she assumed a piece of his consciousness was still in Vanhylde. As soon as he felt her approaching, though, his eyes opened, and the knowing look he gave her made her shiver.

"This is so strange," Jack muttered, his hand on Halvor's snout. The dragon's eyes were still trained on Aurelia, though. "Are you sure he remembers Vanhylde?"

Halvor's eyes snapped over to Jack immediately, making the latter gasp and step away. Aurelia chuckled a little when Halvor chuffed at her husband. Jack only gulped, apologized as if he'd offended the dragon, and muttered something to Aurelia about how he'd never be able to look at Halvor the same way again.

Just as Jack was starting to climb onto Halvor's back, a voice rang out through the gardens, capturing their attention. A breathless messenger boy sprinted across the lawn and skidded to a stop in front of them, holding up a crumpled scroll with a yellow wax seal.

"F-Forgive me," he wheezed, "b-but this just arrived for you, Your Grace."

"Thank you." Aurelia accepted the scroll as the boy sat on a nearby bench to catch his breath. She frowned at the symbol stamped onto the wax: a peacock, symbolic of Vrurith. "That's odd. I wonder how Lord Reesa knew to send his reply here instead of Dofell or Akkinor."

Jack shrugged. "He has spies in Dofell, so we can't be surprised if he has spies in Taundosa, too. It's not hard to spot Halvor, and ravens fly faster than you think. I imagine he was expecting a message from you sooner than later, too. He's probably had the majority of this response prepared for weeks now."

Still frowning, Aurelia broke the seal and unraveled the scroll while Jack read over her shoulder.

Aurelia Brentwood, Queen of Akkinor:
I commend you for reaching out to me regarding the incident in Khaba yesterday morning. I cannot imagine why you and your beast attacked my fleet,

and I'm offended at the insinuation that it was my men who attacked first. That would go against everything Krotis stands for.

I believe a conversation is needed so we might discuss this matter in greater detail. That being said, I invite you to Vrurith at your earliest convenience. I will be expecting you from this point onward. I must ask that you come alone, though. I myself will be unavailable, but I shall send my two most trusted representatives in my stead. We'd like to see what you're like without men at your side to defend your name.

They will be waiting for you on the southeast coast of Vrurith, just north of the harbor. I hope the conversation goes smoothly, and I'm eager to hear about it from my representatives. I do wish we could meet in person, but frankly, I wouldn't trust you, even if my engagement diary was empty.

My people will behave. At this point in time, I don't want to know what your dragon would do to us if we harmed you. I'm not normally one to admit my fears, but I have chosen humility today. Good luck, Your Grace.

Sincerely,
Darius Reesa, Lord of Vrurith.

Jack sighed. "You're going, aren't you?"

"I have to."

"Aurelia—"

"If there's a chance I can say something that might get through to them, I have to take it," she reminded him, crumpling the letter into a ball. "Even if they aren't persuaded to see me and the prophecy differently, I might be able to get more information out of them. If they admit they had something to do with what happened to Arian, that could change everything. Reyna would have a foolproof reason for declaring war on Krotis, and we'd stand behind her as her ally. And if they admit to attacking us in Khaba, that's all the more reason for us to declare war, too."

Jack grimaced, uneasy, and shook his head. "You're awfully eager for war. I wouldn't expect—"

"Look what they've done, Jack," she interrupted. "They've tried to sentence Arian to a terrible fate, and for all we know, they might succeed. And they did it to get to me. If they manage to break me, and I make a wrong move, they'll see it as the prophecy coming to fruition, and they'll come after us. It seems like war is inevitable, but if there's a chance I can do something to break them, too..."

He held his ground. "I don't think it's a good idea for you to go alone. Even with Halvor at your side...They managed to restrain him once. If they do it again, you're trapped there."

"I'll make sure they don't get the opportunity."

He clenched his jaw, scowling, but pulled her into his arms anyway. "If you get yourself killed out there, I swear to every god in the realm, I'll find a way to bring you back just so I can kill you myself."

Aurelia's smile widened against his chest. "I love you, too."

XXI

The next day, after taking the evening to rest following their trip to Vanhylde, Aurelia and Jack said goodbye to one another in the gardens at Reyna's palace. Not long after, Aurelia and Halvor set out to meet the enemy.

Her heart rattled as she and Halvor descended toward the southeastern coast of Krotis. She couldn't stop replaying Jack's warning in her head: if the Kroti attempted to incapacitate Halvor like they had in Khaba, then her only hope was Rieza. She had to believe the vipertail would sense Halvor's pain like she had before, and she'd come to the rescue.

Either way, she had a feeling that Lord Reesa would be true to his word, even if the nobleman himself wasn't attending the meeting. If anything happened to Aurelia or Halvor, chaos would ensue around the realm. Striking down the Queen of Akkinor and her dragon for no just reason would turn the realm's leaders against Krotis. Akkinor, Taundosa, and Bozar would have no choice but to declare war, and Krotis wasn't strong enough to defeat them, even with Annera.

She knew Krotis wanted to get rid of her eventually, but as of now, they hadn't told the world about the prophecy or what they believed Aurelia was meant to do. They only believed it because they'd trusted Willem—even though his last mission had failed—but the rest of the realm wasn't so foolish.

All of that gave her some comfort, but not nearly enough.

Halvor flew to the southern tip of Krotis, then turned north to coast over the Vrurithian Harbor. Just a few miles north of the harbor, Aurelia spotted their destination: a large, empty space atop a sandy cliff, where approximately two dozen individuals cloaked in amber and bronze awaited them.

Before landing, Halvor dipped downward to fly directly over their heads, spooking them. Some of the soldiers shuffled around and backed away, but they didn't abandon their positions. Halvor flew toward the sea before turning again, then landed at the edge of the cliff to face the Vrurithians, shaking the earth beneath their feet when his body met the ground.

While Halvor bellowed at them, blocking their view of Aurelia with his head, she quickly removed her concealed dagger from her boot and slid it up the sleeve of her shirt. She didn't think the Kroti would attempt to harm her, but if they did, she wanted to be prepared without relying on Halvor completely.

Aurelia tried her best to study them as she dismounted. She counted twenty soldiers positioned in two groups of ten, all gathered behind two men standing a few feet ahead of them. The pair were dressed in fine clothing, unlike their armor-clad protectors. One of the men wore a tunic with a peacock stitched into the fabric, but the second had two sigils adorning his shirt: a peacock for Vrurith, and a gazelle for Bruila.

She wanted to be angry that Lord Reesa had sent so many men after instructing her to come alone, but a part of her had expected this. He wouldn't send two of his most trusted allies to meet a dragon without some sort of protection detail, even if Halvor could've taken down every single one of them in a matter of seconds.

When her feet were on the ground, Aurelia ran her hand along the length of Halvor's body, seeking comfort in his touch. He roared at the men, startling the soldiers, but the two leading the pack weren't fazed. They merely stood with their hands clasped behind their backs, faces stony and stoic as she approached.

Like all Kroti men—save the soldiers, who wore helmets—the two individuals wore heavy turbans to conceal their hair. One end of the fabric was draped over their right shoulders and hung over their chests, symbolizing their married status.

"Hello, gentlemen." Aurelia stopped a few feet away from the group, just far enough that they could still hear each other without getting too close. Behind her, Halvor growled, warning them to be on their best behavior. "I take it the two of you are Lord Reesa's representatives. With whom do I have the pleasure of speaking?"

"I am Syronno Quill, primary advisor to the Lord of Vrurith." The shorter of the two men, with only the peacock on his tunic, tipped his head in greeting. "This is His Lordship, Kaius Reesa, Lord of Bruila and second son of Lord Darius."

Aurelia frowned. "The last Lord of Bruila was the late Amarion Selle. Forgive me, but isn't his daughter the Lady of Bruila?"

Syronno's dark eyes narrowed. "Lord Kaius was recently married to Lady Shasta Selle."

"I wasn't under the impression that marrying a Lady of Krotis makes one her equal." Her lips curled into a smile as she turned her gaze to Kaius. "You're the Lord Consort, not the lord."

For a moment, he only stared at her, his green eyes twinkling with rage. He was handsome, she'd give him that, but something about the way he looked at her reminded her of Willem, and she didn't like that one bit.

"Now, we both know why we're here," Aurelia continued. "Your mages attacked me and my dragon in Khaba two days ago. Have you anything to say?"

Syronno only blinked at her. "That's where you're wrong, Your Grace. Our men reported that it was you and your dragon who struck first. Vrurith responded out of defense, as anyone would. So, you may take this opportunity to explain yourself, or you may return home and await a declaration of war."

That made Aurelia laugh. "We all know that's not what happened. Halvor has never attacked anyone for no reason, by my command or his own. The entire realm knows that. If you wish to sell the story, you'll have to do better than that."

"I wouldn't be so sure," Kaius said, settling his hand on the hilt of his sword. "The people of Khaba were spoken to thoroughly after you fled the scene. They all saw you strike first. Who do you suppose the realm will believe, Your Grace? The word of a queen with a restless dragon of old at her side, or hundreds of innocent civilians who feared they'd be burned next?"

Her breath caught in her throat. She knew that wasn't true—after all, that wasn't what had happened—which more than likely meant that the people of Khaba had been offered coin or some other form of bribery if they agreed to tell Vrurith's version of the story. That wouldn't end well for Aurelia if others turned to the Khabish to hear what the witnesses had to say about the attack.

"It's a clever tactic. I'll admit that much." Aurelia swallowed the lump in her throat. "It won't work, though. The truth will be revealed, as always—especially when word spreads about what your people did to Lord Arian Cristos. You see, he's something of a beloved figure. I don't suppose the continent will be happy with you when they find out what fate you condemned him to."

Kaius's eyes flashed. "Careful. That's a lofty accusation."

"It's not an accusation. My mages traced the origins of the curse back to you." She was bluffing a bit, but judging by the looks on their faces, they had no idea. "Now, everything that's happened as of late—Lord Cristos's curse, the attack in Khaba, and the little emerald dragon you sent to my doorstep—suggests you have some sort of vendetta against me. I'm aware of the prophecy shared with the Iron Council by the late King Willem of Kanibar. You must believe me when I say that no harm will come to the realm by my hand. I'd never do anything to threaten Krotis, either, unless you gave me a reason."

"And you think we'd take your word for it?" Kaius guffawed so hard that he had to adjust his amber turban to keep it steady. "My, my. Not very clever, are you? *The one who breathes fire will sever the realm at the edge of the world.* The gods have predicted that you and your beast will destroy our beautiful world, and you'll start here in Krotis. It's your word against the word of the gods."

"The word of the gods is always open to interpretation," she fired back. "They've never been entirely forthcoming in the past, have they? That's why we're here today: King Willem believed a prophecy meant something it didn't, and he—along with many of your citizens—ended up dead because of it."

She saw Syronno's gaze falter for a moment, his eyes dropping to the ground, and she knew she'd gotten through to him—even just a little bit. Kaius, on the other hand, didn't so much as bat an eye.

"There is no mistaking what the prophecy foretells," Kaius insisted, his jaw clenching. "Don't feel poorly for being so wrong, though. I imagine even *you* don't know what you'll do to us, but you will. An opportunity will present itself, and you won't be able to resist the temptation. Just know that we'll do everything in our power to stop you. Of course, you know by now that we possess a dragon, too."

Aurelia laughed. "That tiny thing? Oh, my. Desperation isn't a good color on you, my lord. Do you really believe she'd stand a chance against Halvor? Or the other dragon of old who intervened when your men attacked me?"

His face turned crimson as he gritted his teeth. "Syronno, please escort our men elsewhere. I'd like a private word with the queen."

The advisor shifted his weight, uneasy. "But your father—"

"Just do it!" he snapped.

Flinching, Syronno turned to face the soldiers and commanded them to follow him, all while Kaius and Aurelia maintained eye contact. She still managed to see Syronno look back at them, pale and clammy, before trailing behind the men while they marched toward a nearby hill.

"Don't want your men to hear about your weaknesses and misdoings, do you?" Aurelia taunted, smirking. "I don't blame you. They'd lose all respect for you. Your people want to take me to war because a dead, fool of a king told you I'm the enemy, when half of Carthe saw him exposed for the liar he was. I helped bring one of the Twelve back to the realm, and still, you see me as your greatest threat? As someone who would destroy the world?"

He shook his head and laughed bitterly. "That's what you don't seem to understand. We don't believe you'll destroy us on purpose, Your Grace. You'll do what you've always done—attempt to change things for the better—and it'll backfire on you. We don't care what your intentions are. Those don't matter. What matters is what the gods have predicted, and for once, they don't seem to have much faith in their champion."

Aurelia winced, unwillingly revealing that his words had stung her. He laughed again and said, "See? Even you know it's possible. Whatever you may do, it'll have dire consequences, and by the time you realize what you've done, it'll be too late."

"What do you propose, then?" she demanded. "You've done enough already to warrant combat—if not between Krotis and Akkinor, then between Krotis and Taundosa. Queen Reyna won't have mercy on the people who attacked her Lord Hand. I won't forget your lies and threats, either. So, what will it be? Will you continue to taunt me until I retaliate with force, just so you can use that as justification for destroying me? Or will you make the first move, ensuring I never have the chance to do whatever the prophecy suggests?"

Kaius squared his shoulders, defiant. "My father—and all of us in charge—are prepared to make an arrangement with you. Go home, keep your attention focused on your people and your people only, and stop meddling in affairs across the realm. We'll forget the Khaba incident ever happened, and we'll keep our distance from you. And maybe, if you keep your word, I'll consider lifting the curse on Lord Cristos."

Aurelia stilled, eyes widening. "It was you. You cast the curse."

"Guilty as charged." As he grinned, green magic sparkled on his fingertips, drawing her eyes. He chuckled when he saw her observing his power, her fear of magic nearly overpowering her anger at his confession. "Don't worry, Your Grace. My father made me promise to be on my best behavior. I won't hurt you."

She gritted her teeth. "Is that it, then?"

"Not quite." His grin morphed into something maniacal—something that made her afraid enough to step back from him. "Of course, it'd be hard for us to trust your word alone. That being said, the entire realm is aware of where your true power lies: the dragon. You may have a vast army and tremendous wealth, but neither of those things has the potential to destroy the world. Only he does. So, upon your return to Akkinor, you will slaughter the beast, and we will uphold our end of the bargain."

Aurelia was so shocked that all she could do was laugh. "My gods. You're the maddest person alive, aren't you? You or your father, who I assume offered up that suggestion. I'd never harm him, even if my life depended on it." She shook her head, still laughing, as Kaius sneered at her. "If the realm requires my service in the future, I won't sit on my throne and do nothing simply because you're threatened by something that may not come to pass. I certainly won't murder my dragon for the slim chance that you'll leave me alone, either."

"I suggest you reconsider."

"And I'd stop talking, if I were you," she shot back. As Halvor growled behind her—staying put, as instructed—she felt comforted by the length of the dagger against her forearm. "Halvor may respond to my commands, but he's not so tame as to ignore a threat. Say another word about it, and I can't assure you that he won't take matters into his own hands."

Kaius's eyes flashed with malice. "That wouldn't do much good to defend all the claims you've made today, now, would it?"

She ignored him. "I don't know what you think you'll achieve. You can try to strike me and Akkinor down, and you'll fail. That's not my opinion—it's a fact. Save us all the trouble by sparing Lord Cristos and pretending none of this ever happened. Maybe if you do, it'll be Pherena who visits the realm next."

That didn't seem to mean anything to him. "Immor would be more preferable."

She opened her mouth to reply, but stopped when she saw something she shouldn't have: a tattoo on his left wrist, made visible when the breeze briefly fluttered the cuff of his shirt, moving the fabric just enough to reveal the marking. The tattoo was a sword encased in a broken circle. By itself, the sword was symbolic of Immor, the god of war. When accompanied by the broken circle, though, the marking was symbolic of the Guild of Steel.

The Guild of Steel had once been secret groups of individuals that formed across the realm, though they hardly existed anymore. Immor had never been appointed as the Almighty of any kingdom because of what he represented: violence, carnage, and destruction. There were some people, however, who believed Immor should've been their kingdom's Almighty, as he was known for being one of the more powerful gods in the universe— if not the most powerful. They thought their kingdom would rise to a divine status if they allowed Immor's influence to guide them. The guilds were always brought down when they were discovered, but many people believed they still existed over time, lurking in the shadows.

Aurelia had a fairly good idea of what the tattoo meant: Kaius and other powerful people in Krotis were hoping to abandon Pherena as their Almighty in favor of Immor—likely inspired by Edea taking over Dofell from Myenar three years ago.

If Immor accepted Krotis as his representatives in Icareth, there was no telling what would happen—particularly now that one of the Twelve had already visited the realm. He could destroy Aurelia and Halvor with a twitch of his nose.

"I believe you have my answer." Aurelia took a few steps back, swallowing her fear. "I'm sure we'll meet again soon. Tell your father that I look forward to hearing what he has to say about our audience today."

For a fraction of a second, his eyes landed on his wrist, and his entire body tensed like he was being turned to stone.

As she turned to walk toward Halvor, anxiety making her heart hammer, she heard something unmistakable: the sound of a sword being pulled from its sheath.

Aurelia whipped around just as Halvor roared and surged forward, but unfortunately, Aurelia was too close to her assailant for Halvor to do much without hurting her, too.

Her dagger slid down her arm until the handle met her palm, and without a second thought, she plunged the weapon forward. At the same time, her instincts led her to raise her left arm, and she managed to grab Kaius's wrist while his sword was raised. She stumbled back a bit when his weight collided with her blade, and the rapid beating of her heart only increased when she looked down and saw his blood staining her hands.

Fighting the urge to tremble, she looked into his eyes as they widened, then down at his lips while they parted. She didn't know what'd come over her when she twisted the blade, making him grunt and gasp. While his body froze, she curled her fingers around the hilt of his sword, prying the weapon from his grip before letting it fall.

"I don't know what makes me pity your wife more," she seethed. "That she's become a widow so soon and so young, or that she married a man who didn't think twice about stabbing a queen in the back."

His eyes flashed over to Halvor before she pulled the blade from his gut, letting him fall to the ground in a heap. Only then, when she saw the anger in his eyes as he looked at the dragon, did she realize he hadn't been aiming for her—he'd been aiming for Halvor.

"He would've killed you, anyway," she said, standing over him as blood spurted from his lips. "What a great fool you are for thinking you could kill a dragon."

She turned to Halvor again, shaking now that the adrenaline had worn off, and intended to leave until the dragon nudged her in the abdomen with his snout. She frowned and asked him why he was acting so strangely, then followed his gaze back to Kaius. At the same time, Halvor pawed at the air with his left hand, as if trying to tell her something.

She understood. Though it sickened her to do it, she returned to Kaius's now-dead body, and she used his own sword to sever his left hand—about two inches below the tattoo on his wrist. Trying her hardest not to vomit, she tore off a piece of her blouse to wrap the hand in, then tucked it into her pocket. The Reesa family ring on his middle finger would be more than enough to identify him, and if not, any skilled mage could analyze his blood as coming from a Reesa.

Either way, she wasn't taking it just to prove to others that Kaius was associated with the Guild. She was taking it so Kaius's allies knew that she was onto them.

Shouting rattled her eardrums. Only then did she remember Kaius hadn't come alone. She hurried back to Halvor while he roared at the soldiers descending the hill, climbed onto his back, and instructed him to fly even before she found a stable position.

As they flew back to Taundosa with Kaius's still-warm hand bleeding into her pocket, Aurelia leaned over to the side and vomited into the Alkamura.

XXII

J ack knew what his wife expected of him when she left for Vrurith: to stay put at Reyna's palace until she came back, and to stay out of trouble.

That, of course, was easier said than done.

He hadn't stopped thinking about Vanhylde, that strange land between worlds, since it spit them back out in the Elotheon the day prior. He felt a pull, something calling him back there. He hadn't mentioned it to Aurelia—she had enough on her plate as it was—and though he couldn't explain it, he knew he had a purpose in purgatory.

He didn't give it nearly enough thought when he left the palace, asked a servant to tell Aurelia he'd gone to Agotia if she returned before he did, and borrowed one of Reyna's horses from the stables. Before he realized what he was doing, he was standing outside of the Elotheon, neck craned back as he studied the massive structure.

As he returned to the archives, heart pounding harder and harder with each step, he still couldn't figure out what was calling him back to Vanhylde. He thought about what Aurelia had said: that many people never returned to the land of the living after visiting Vanhylde because something compelled them to stay. But he knew that wouldn't happen to him. Only his wife and children would compel him to stay somewhere other than home. Or, at least, he hoped.

"You're an idiot." He shook his head as he muttered to himself, reopening the wound on his palm with his knife. "An idiot whose wife is going to absolutely murder you."

Aurelia would understand, though. Hopefully. Even if something hadn't been summoning him, he'd been itching to set off on his own—to do something daring and adventurous, like Jack Sherbourne once did. He'd agreed to share his every adventure with his family since he decided to return home with Aurelia all those years ago, and while there was nothing he loved more than that, he still yearned to be the man he once was.

This was just a little adventure. He'd go to Vanhylde, find out what was calling him, and return home before Aurelia even realized he was missing. What was the harm in that?

With a deep breath, Jack pressed his bleeding hand to the print he'd left behind earlier, muttered the same sentences Aurelia had taught him, and closed his eyes as his soul was transported to Vanhylde.

When the tunnel of wind ceased and he opened his eyes, he knew exactly where he was. The towering trees, the vibrant fields of wildflowers, the smell of fresh rainfall and smoldering firewood—it all mirrored his memories of his five years as Jack Sherbourne, when his only purpose in life was exploring the western continent.

"Well, well. Look who it is."

Jack froze, the sound of the voice nearly paralyzing him. It was distantly familiar, but until he turned and saw the person warming their hands by the fire, he didn't fully comprehend who the voice belonged to.

"Varn," he whispered.

His old friend—and the first friend he'd made in Carthe all those years ago—grinned from his seat on a fallen tree trunk. He looked almost exactly as Jack remembered him: tall but wiry, with long black hair tied in a braid and eyes like bronze. He had a thick white scar that cut diagonally across his face, from the side of his crooked nose to just below his ear. His brown breeches had been cut at the knees to help combat the heat, and the sleeves of his tattered blue tunic were rolled up to the elbows. He wore two different boots, and the layers of grime on his skin and beneath his fingernails were evident of the many seasons he'd spent living off the land.

"Have a seat." Varn gestured to a log beside him while picking at his nails with his knife. Jack obeyed, but he couldn't summon words as he studied the Kanish traveler he'd once loved like a brother. "I'm glad you found me. I appreciate the visit."

Jack swallowed the lump in his throat. "Why are you here?"

Varn grimaced. "I may have lived a decent life, for the most part, but I did some things I shouldn't have, long before you and I met. It's my own fault I'm here instead of Hanhalla, so I won't bore you with the details. You would've ended up here, too, if you hadn't met your wife when you did."

No kidding, Jack thought. "I felt something calling me here today. Was it you? Is there something you have to tell me?"

"Somewhat," Varn replied, chuckling a little. "You're here with me because of a story I once told you. The gods wish for you to remember it."

"What story?"

Varn's eyes twinkled against the firelight. "Do you remember the tale about my fifteenth name day?"

Jack thought for a moment, but came up empty. "No. I'm sorry."

"It's been a while." Varn waved a dismissive hand. "As I said, it was my fifteenth name day, and because my family was very poor, I wasn't expecting to receive a gift. But my parents surprised me with a family heirloom: a painting from the old days. The painting showed a hoard of magical creatures attempting to flee an attack by mortals during the persecution. It took place in Caedia, where mortals from across the realm banded together to destroy Carthe's magic." He shook his head. "Horrible image, really. My parents said our ancestor had painted it—he was there that day, trying to guide the creatures to safety. He was killed later on when he was caught trying to shelter some centaurs. It wasn't long after that the people of Carthe succeeded in stopping the persecution here, opting to let whatever magic remained prevail as it was meant to."

"That's a nice story, but—"

"Not finished, you big brute." Varn grinned as Jack glowered at him. "The painting was important because every single creature on the canvas had been led to safety by my ancestor. He sent them away, and nobody ever knew where they went. Many people in my family chose to believe that he transported them to a different world. A safer world."

Jack furrowed his brows. "I don't think you ever told me that last bit."

"No, I didn't. You wouldn't have believed me back then," he said pointedly, making Jack wince. "I ended up selling the painting a few years later. My parents were dead, I had no money for food, and I knew how much people would be willing to pay for ancient artwork. Only after I died did I realize the true importance of it. Those very same creatures are here, roaming the plains and fields of Vanhylde, awaiting the day they might return home."

A shiver traced Jack's spine. He'd assumed that most of Carthe's ancient creatures, like Akkinor's, had been hibernating, hiding in plain sight, or protected by people like Lady Swann. He hadn't really considered that a large number of them, like Halvor, had been here in Vanhylde.

"There was a rumor in my family," Varn continued, "which stated that, in the event the creatures returned to Icareth, their images would disappear from the painting. I don't know where the painting is, or if it even still exists, but I want to believe that's true."

"You want me to bring them home." Jack's statement was met with a massive, beaming grin from his old friend. "I don't know how to do that. Would they even follow me? Me, a mortal. I don't think I'm the right person for the job."

"You're the only person who's visited this place with the intention to help the realm, not yourself—other than your wife, of course," Varn told him. "They'll trust you. Won't you, friends?"

Jack opened his mouth to reply, but he didn't get the chance. Behind Varn, the trees swayed and fluttered for a moment, until a pair of women wearing leafy garments emerged from the shadows. At the same time, tiny spheres of golden light appeared on the branches—sprites—and giggling female voices echoed in Jack's ears, carried around the campsite by wind.

Not knowing what to do with himself, Jack stood and looked around, lips parting in shock. In the direction he'd come from, about six centaurs appeared, composed of both adults and youngsters. Two Cyclopes came up behind them, shaking the ground with every step. What he assumed were goblins, about a dozen of them, walked through the darkness in the foliage next. The humanoid creatures were said to have gone completely extinct after the persecution, and yet, here they were.

"My gods." Jack turned in a full circle, staring at the groups that'd amassed around him. "Is this...Is this real?"

Varn's eyes twinkled. "Vanhylde is more than the land of dreams, my friend."

Jack swallowed and shook his surprise away as best he could. "If this is real, and all of you are itching to return to Icareth...Why haven't you done so before? Or why haven't the gods come to free you?"

"The gods don't come here. Not ever," Varn said with a short laugh. "Vanhylde is a purgatory for them, too. They designed it that way as a means of establishing order among the divine. Think of it like a failsafe in the event that one of them betrays the others. If a god visits or is sent here by one of their own, their essence becomes tethered to this prison, and they can only be freed by another deity."

"It works the same way for us," a centaur added. "A human brought us here, and only a human can bring us home."

Jack frowned. What a tragedy—even now, centuries after the persecution, the fate of magical creatures still rested in the hands of humans. Not to mention, the gods themselves had created a plane of existence capable of holding *them* hostage, too.

"If you want to come back," he said slowly, "I will escort you. Are there more of you?"

"Of course." A wind nymph, whose transparent image manifested as a real woman when she sat on the log he'd claimed earlier, smiled as she flicked a lock of pale blonde hair over her shoulder. "They're on their way."

A shiver traced Jack's spine, from the nape of his neck to the top of his tailbone. He recalled what Aurelia had told him about a conversation between she, Reyna, and Arian prior to the ball at the palace: the Taundosans had asked if any of Akkinor's creatures would be willing to migrate to Carthe, to help repopulate the western continent with magic. Aurelia had left the choice up to the creatures, but now, there was no need for the migration. Carthe's ancient creatures were ready to go home.

Jack met Varn's eyes, still flabbergasted. "Was it you summoning me here, or them?"

"A little bit of both." Varn grinned as Jack chuckled at him. "Your wife may weep golden tears, but she isn't the only person with a destiny to fulfill. The gods have always had a plan for you, too."

Jack's heart leapt to his throat. "I see. Well..." He smiled a bit and looked around at the creatures again. "As soon as the rest of you arrive, we'll be on our way." They cheered and spoke over one another, thanking him and celebrating amongst themselves, as he looked to Varn again. "As for you...I'm sorry about what happened. I'm the reason you're dead."

Varn raised an eyebrow, amused. "Did you plunge a dagger into my gut?"

"Well, no, but—"

"I defended my friend, and I died without a single regret about it. Don't let it keep you up at night."

Jack tried to smile, but it was forced and unconvincing. He still felt like he was partially to blame for his friend's death: after a group of native Carthinians attacked him for invading their lands with his Akkinorian blood, Varn spoke up in his defense, and they killed him for it. That day still haunted him, even thirteen years later.

"Take that door." Varn stood and pointed at something to his right, and to Jack's surprise, there was a wooden door planted in the middle of a dirt path, where only darkness had been moments earlier. "It'll bring you back to where you came from. Hold Dae's hand while you walk, and the others will follow with linked hands. One of them must be touching you for all of them to pass through."

Jack nodded, heart hammering as more and more creatures—some that existed in Akkinor or Carthe, and some thought to be extinct—emerged from the shadows. Before he left, he shook Varn's hand before pulling his friend into an embrace, thanked him, and apologized once more for his death.

"It's all right. I'll find my way out of here, eventually." Varn smiled and clapped Jack on the back. "Good luck, Jack Sherbourne."

Grinning, Jack winked before walking toward the door, the tallest of the centaurs trailing just behind him. He took the creature's hand—assuming this was Dae—and opened the door with his free hand. Nothing awaited behind the door other than the eerie silence and darkness of the Violet Forest.

He took a long, deep breath and glanced up at Dae. "Watch your head." The centaur stifled laughter. "Will do."

Jack met Varn's gaze one last time, smiling when his friend nodded at him, and walked through the door into an abyss of nothingness. He didn't feel Dae's hand anymore as his body was encased by the now familiar tunnel of wind, and though he was certain he was moving, he couldn't feel his feet on the ground. The only thing he could feel was a pulling sensation in his chest, guiding him home again.

When he arrived in the archives of the Elotheon, Dae was right behind him. He took a few steps back toward the exit as Dae's other arm emerged from the stone wall. Holding Dae's hand was a smaller centaur, an adolescent, and holding *her* hand was a larger female centaur.

Before he knew it, the room was flooded with creatures of all kinds, and there wasn't nearly enough space for them. Jack urged them to follow him out of the archives and through the Elotheon, where priests and patrons alike either gasped, fainted, or fell to their knees in prayer as the group passed them by.

Feeling more empowered than he had in years, Jack escorted them out of the temple and onto the streets of Agotia. As soon as the people spotted the group, they stopped to gather around the Elotheon, hollering for others nearby to join them. In mere moments, the entire building was surrounded by curious, excited—and not at all frightened—Taundosans, all watching with mesmerized eyes as dozens of creatures of old stepped out of Taundosa's most sacred place.

While Jack stood there for a moment, surrounded by creatures on all sides, he heard a familiar roar approaching. He smiled when Halvor appeared within the clouds, a massive streak of blue and gold against the cloudless sky. They must've seen what was happening at the Elotheon, as they landed just behind the crowd of spectators, momentarily drawing the people's eyes away from Jack and his new friends.

Jack waited for Aurelia, eagerly anticipating the look on her face when she realized what he'd done. Beside him, Dae asked, "A dragon of old survives? *And* bears a rider? How is that possible?"

He only smiled. "Halvor used to live in Vanhylde, too. He was freed by his rider eight years ago."

"Who is it? His rider?"

Jack's smile morphed into a full-fledged grin. "My wife."

Just then, the sea of onlookers parted to make way for the woman in question. All eyes turned to her, as her very presence demanded attention.

When Jack could finally see her, a fleeting feeling of panic overcame him at the sight of blood staining her clothing and her hands. Only when he saw the look on her face—defiant, yet slightly worried—did he realize the blood wasn't hers.

Apparently, her audience with Vrurith had taken a nasty turn.

She stopped in front of him, eyes widening as she realized the people behind him weren't humans, but creatures. She surveyed each of them, one by one, as they did the same to her—and Halvor.

"What's all this?" she murmured.

Jack smiled. "I made some friends."

XXIII

To say Aurelia was shocked to hear the story of how Jack brought over a hundred creatures back to Icareth would be an understatement.

However, she wasn't surprised he'd gone back to Vanhylde. He wasn't the type to sit idly by while she embarked on her own mission, so a part of her had assumed he'd do something while she was gone. Going to Vanhylde was one thing, but to return with a hoard of ancient creatures at his side? She was certainly glad he'd followed his gut when he did.

Before they left Carthe, they returned to the Palace of Taundosa to let Reyna know what had happened: Jack had brought creatures back to Carthe from Vanhylde; Kaius Reesa was dead, and he'd admitted to cursing Arian; and Aurelia suspected the Iron Council of Krotis was hoping to make Immor their Almighty deity instead of Pherena.

It was Reyna who reminded Aurelia that her uncle's curse could only be broken if the caster died. Until then, she hadn't realized that killing Kaius Reesa would save Arian's life. That was all the more reason to get home as quickly as possible.

"I'll send word to the others, as I'm sure you will, too," Reyna assured her. "I think it's best if I stay here, though. Krotis will know by now that I'm aware of who cursed my Hand, so I want to be prepared for any ramifications. I have quite a few letters to send, too, now that Taundosa is swarming with magical creatures. I'll set out for Akkinor to retrieve Arian as soon as I can. I imagine he needs time to recover before he can sail, anyway."

Aurelia nodded as she, Jack, and Reyna stood on the front steps of the palace, looking out at the grounds as some of the creatures laughed, danced, and explored the surroundings they hadn't seen in over a thousand years. Most of them had split off from the group immediately, hoping to see the rest of the continent they'd missed so dearly, but a large number seemed content with staying in Taundosa.

"We'll have to get going," Aurelia said, giddiness nearly overwhelming her. "After I've checked on Arian, I'll spread the word of what happened today to my advisors and my nobility—then I'll send Kaius's hand back to Vrurith. I'll make sure the rest of the realm knows about Krotis's association with the Guild, too."

Reyna nodded, but she winced at the mention of the Guild. "Good luck. Let me know how it—who's that?"

Aurelia and Jack followed the queen's gaze toward the front of the palace grounds, where a woman was riding through the gates on the back of a wagon pulled by a mule. A loose scarf was draped over her graying brown hair, likely to combat the wind and sand, and she wore plain, simple clothing. Even from a distance, Aurelia noted fiercely blue eyes and fawny brown skin. The woman could've been from anywhere in the south with such features—but more likely Taundosa or Bozar.

"*Oh.*" Reyna's eyes widened, her lips parting in shock, as she brought a hand to her heart. "It can't be..."

"What?" Jack asked, frowning. "Who is it?"

Reyna's lips moved like she wanted to reply, but no sound emerged. Curious, Aurelia descended the steps as the woman stopped the wagon and stepped out. Jack trailed behind his wife, Reyna still stuck in place behind them, as the woman met them halfway across the grounds.

She looked like a normal common woman, but something about her—the knowing look in her eyes, the curling of her lips, and the expression on her face—made her look like a noblewoman. There was something familiar about her, too, but Aurelia couldn't place it for the life of her.

"You must be Queen Aurelia." The woman lowered into a perfect curtsy—uncommon for civilians—before rising again. Her eyes flashed as she studied Aurelia's face. "I've heard stories about you. It's nice to finally put a face to the name."

Aurelia raised an eyebrow. "And you are?"

"Anysa." It was Reyna who spoke next, having sneaked up behind Aurelia and Jack. The couple stepped aside to make room for her as she observed the woman from head to toe. "Gods be good."

Jack frowned. "Anysa. Isn't that—?"

"Arian's sister." Aurelia's eyes widened as Anysa smiled at her. *No wonder she looks so familiar,* she thought. "I-I thought you'd left Carthe. At least, that's what Arian believed after you ran away all those years ago. He thought you would've come home by now if you were still nearby."

Guilt shimmered in her eyes, but it was gone as quickly as it'd come. "I've been living in Khaba for over three decades now. It's been my home since the day I arrived. My life as Anysa Cristos had to end, though I regret putting my brother and sister through such pain."

"He looks for you. All the time." Aurelia gritted her teeth, suddenly enraged. "You broke his heart when you left. He needed you when Katryna died."

For a moment, her defiant expression faltered, and her eyes filled with grief. "I know. It was wrong of me to stay away, but I knew that if I came back, he'd do everything in his power to keep me at this side. I wouldn't be accepted by society with my fishmonger husband and our three children—two of whom were born out of wedlock. I would've caused more problems for him."

Reyna sighed. "I hate to admit it, but she's right. Such things are ruinous for nobility here in Taundosa. The people would've demanded that Arian step down as Lord Hand if they knew his family was tied to such dishonor."

Anysa didn't so much as blink. "Exactly."

Aurelia softened, but not by much. "Fine, then. So why have you come today, after all this time?"

"For you." She looked up and over her shoulder as Halvor flew in circles around the palace. Her eyes fluttered shut for a moment, a distant smile forming on her lips. "I'd heard eight years ago that the Queen of Akkinor released a dragon of old into the realm. I never heard the dragon's name, and I never saw him fly over Khaba. I think the gods were doing me a kindness by keeping me from seeing what I'd left behind. I didn't see him until two days ago during the attack in Khaba. As soon as I saw him...I knew it was Halvor. There wasn't a doubt in my mind."

Jack coughed awkwardly into his elbow. "I'm assuming you put it together, then?"

"Of course." She turned her gaze back to Aurelia, her eyes now shimmering with both sadness and admiration. "I'd heard rumors that my brother had grown close to Akkinor's queen. I know Halvor is only loyal to the women of my family, so I had to assume you're not exactly what you seem. I attempted summoning your soul, and when I succeeded, I knew for certain. We can only summon the souls of our blood relatives." She swallowed like her next words were hard to get out. "You're my niece, aren't you?"

Aurelia couldn't help but smile. "Guilty as charged."

Anysa's gaze lit up. "I suppose I didn't have to ask. You look exactly like my sister."

"I've been told."

"Mhm. Now, I've also heard rumors that my brother was recently cursed in Akkinor. I may not have been a good sister to him these last three decades, but I didn't get the chance to say goodbye to Katryna, and if he's going to leave us, too..." She sighed, her face crumpling with sadness. "I'd like to say goodbye to him. It's the least I can do."

"You want to come to Akkinor?" Jack asked. She nodded. "Hmm. Well, regardless of what happened, I think he'd be most pleased to have you there."

"I do, too." Aurelia smiled. "You're welcome to come home with us. Halvor's saddle isn't big enough for three of us when Jack comes along, so we'll have to squeeze. He takes some getting used to, but—"

Anysa interrupted her with a booming laugh. "Oh, I know. Katryna didn't take him to flight on her own, you know. That wouldn't have been fair."

Right, Aurelia thought. *Anysa knew Halvor before I did.*

As if on cue, Halvor landed on the grass behind them. Anysa turned as soon as she felt the ground shake, and without a second thought, she hiked up her skirts and rushed over to him. Aurelia watched, still a bit shocked, as Halvor lowered his head to nuzzle against Anysa while she set her hands on either side of his snout. If Aurelia didn't know any better, she'd think Halvor was mewling like a kitten when Anysa embraced him.

"This is good," Reyna whispered, her eyes welling with tears. "It's exactly what Arian needs."

There may have been some tension lingering between the siblings, but Aurelia knew her uncle better than she knew most people, and he'd throw that tension aside for a fresh start as soon as he held Anysa in his arms.

What a way to wake up from a curse.

***

Anysa appeared just as comfortable riding Halvor as Aurelia did, which probably didn't make Jack feel any better about his upset stomach. Anysa whooped and laughed almost the entire flight back to Akkinor, making Aurelia wonder if her aunt ever imagined she'd get the chance to do this after she left home at the tender age of thirteen.

When they landed in the gardens at the palace, Anysa seemed to forget all about Halvor as she marveled at her new surroundings. She soaked it all in, from the majesty of the gardens to the beautiful, enormous palace towering over her.

"What a wonder this land is," she murmured, inhaling the Akkinorian air. "I've seen so little of it, and yet, I understand why my brother and my father loved it here so much. I can see why it was so hard for Arian to leave it behind. It feels...*different* here."

Aurelia smiled, but for some reason, Anysa's words made her remember something she'd forgotten to do: search Arian's belongings in Taundosa in hopes of finding Shale. Now that Arian was awake—hopefully—he'd be able to help her find him, if that was still his desire, but she felt horrible for forgetting about it.

"Anysa," she said as they walked toward the palace, "do you recall your brother ever talking about a man named Shale?"

Anysa stopped. "You know Shale?"

"I know *of* him. Arian wished for me to find Shale in the event of his death."

Anysa sighed and offered a curt nod. "I know of him, too. Arian spoke about him often after he returned to Taundosa. I never wanted to hear it—I was an immature young girl who couldn't understand why he held so much love for foreigners. It took me a long time to realize there's room in his heart, and others', for more than one kingdom. I couldn't tell you where Shale is now, or if he's still alive, but right before I left, I heard Arian say something about Shale living in Laynoa. He was trying to become a painter."

"That's a good place to start. Perhaps Arian—"

"Aurelia!" A booming female voice interrupted the conversation, making Aurelia roll her eyes as soon as she recognized the aggravated tone. Lucyra appeared on the cobblestone path ahead, apparently having come from somewhere else in the gardens, and jogged toward them before skidding to a stop. "Good gods. What happened to you?"

Aurelia looked down at her bloody clothing—which Anysa hadn't bothered addressing—and said, "There was an incident with Krotis. I'll tell you more later."

Lucyra stilled, made a face, and brought a hand to her nose. "Why do you smell like a rotting corpse?"

"There's a hand in her pocket," Jack said simply.

"I beg your pardon?"

"Later," Aurelia promised, grimacing. "Lucyra, I'd like you to meet Anysa. Anysa, this is—"

"Lucyra?" Anysa's face lit up. "Gods be good! I haven't seen you since you were a wee babe!"

Halvor's caretaker looked at Aurelia, puzzled, before turning back to Anysa. "Erm, who are you?"

"This is Arian's sister," Aurelia intervened. Lucyra's eyes flashed as her jaw dropped. "She found us in Taundosa after she spotted Halvor. It's a long story, but she's come to see Arian. Speaking of—has he woken yet?"

Lucyra only stared at her. "Should he have?"

Aurelia's heart fell to her stomach as Jack sighed in disappointment. "My love," Jack murmured, "should we consider the possibility that Kaius was lying about cursing Arian?"

"No." She shook her head. "That's a big risk for him to take. Admitting to being the caster meant letting me know who needed to die to break the curse. I could've killed him to save Arian because of what he said."

Jack's eyes flashed with realization. "He would've known he'd die by striking at you or Halvor, too. He gave you multiple reasons to kill him. Do you suppose he *wanted* you to kill him? To do something that would warrant a declaration of war from Krotis?"

Her stomach lurched. "M-Maybe. I don't know."

"If he sacrificed himself to get the war started..."

Lucyra scowled at them. "I'd ask what the hell you're talking about, but you'll just tell me that I have to wait for my explanation until later."

"Clever woman," Jack told her, earning himself an elbow in the gut. *"Ouch*, Lu."

"While I appreciate the entertainment," Anysa intervened, "I'd very much like to see my brother."

Aurelia nodded. "Of course. Just keep in mind that he doesn't look so well. H-He's been unconscious for a few weeks now."

As the quartet strolled into the palace and made their way upstairs to Arian's bedroom, Aurelia tried her best to explain what had happened to him. Anysa recognized the Hollow Dream, and the mortified look on her face when she heard the curse's name made Aurelia want to vomit.

When they reached his room, Aurelia dismissed the medics tending to him, then lingered in the doorway with Jack and Lucyra while Anysa took a few steps forward. Much to her disappointment, Arian was exactly where Aurelia had left him: laying in the massive bed with his hands splayed over his stomach, still gray, clammy, and gaunt.

Anysa stood a few paces from his bed and brought a trembling hand to her mouth. Aurelia couldn't imagine what she was thinking or feeling. When she left Taundosa, Arian had been a strong, healthy man of less than thirty years; now, he was about sixty or so, frail and withered, his life hanging from a thread as fragments of his soul were lost to Vanhylde.

Anysa didn't waste time staring at him, though. After taking a minute to compose herself, she rushed toward him and climbed into bed beside him. Her hip was pressed against his, her legs dangling over the edge of the bed, and for a moment, her hands hovered over either side of his face. Then her shoulders began to shake as she took his face in her hands, pressed her forehead to his, and wept.

"We should go," Aurelia whispered. "She needs a private moment to—"

She gasped with such force that her words lodged in her throat, nearly choking her, when she saw Arian lift a weak arm to splay it over Anysa's back. Lucyra clutched both Aurelia and Jack with a vise-like grip on their arms while the couple held their breath, eyes wide and unblinking.

Anysa lifted her head just enough for Aurelia to see Arian's face. If not for Jack and Lucyra pressed up against her sides, she would've collapsed to her knees at the sight of his eyes.

Arian Cristos was awake.

"Sister." His voice was raspy and groggy, but it was still his, and Aurelia had never been so glad to hear it. "You're...You're here."

Anysa sniffled and brushed sweaty hair from his forehead. "I should've come to you a long time ago."

"I-It's all right." His hand tightened on her back as he cleared his throat. "You pulled me out of oblivion."

XXIV

I'd like a moment alone with Aurelia."

Anysa frowned. "But—"

"Do you hear those little footsteps?" Arian's eyes were closed, but he was smiling. "Those are Kitty's grandchildren. Go meet them."

Anysa looked over her shoulder at where Aurelia lingered in the doorway, entranced by the idea of meeting her late sister's children. Down the hall, Jack was keeping the children at bay, as they were eager to see their uncle again after one of Hyacinth's visions alerted her of the broken curse. Arian needed more time to recover before they bombarded him, so for now, their aunt would have to do.

After kissing him on the forehead, Anysa left Arian's bedside, and Aurelia quickly took her place. When Anysa closed the door behind her, Aurelia took her uncle's outstretched hands and squeezed them, fighting the urge to sob.

"You did it," he murmured. "I knew you would."

She chuckled through her tears. "I had to kill Kaius Reesa to do it, and I'm not sorry I did. I'm just glad to see your eyes again. How do you feel?"

"Tired, despite sleeping like a rock for the last several weeks," he joked. "I'm sore and a bit stiff, but the medics will take excellent care of me. After I've had a few days to regain my strength, I should be as good as new. Anysa told me about the Hollow Dream, but I don't feel disconnected to my soul. I suppose I fought harder than I realized while I was...away."

Aurelia's smile trembled on her lips. "You certainly did."

"Enough about me." Arian sat up straighter, ignoring her protests, and leaned forward a bit as his eyes began to twinkle. His face was still gray, and his body was still weak and clammy, but his eyes were shining as brightly as ever. "Tell me more about what's happened."

She told him everything, starting at the very beginning—the aftermath of his curse, when she went to Dofell for help and learned about Rieza. She told him about her conversations with Maysa and the oracle's sudden death, her meeting with the Haze family, her trips to Vanhylde, Lazelus Swann's letter, Annera, and the everything going on with Krotis. When she got to the part about her ill-fated meeting with Kaius Swann, she slowed down, ensuring she relayed every detail.

Arian took a moment to process when she finished. His face was a bit strained, like it was taking every fiber of his being to focus on understanding her words, but at the same time, his eyes danced like they often did when he was analyzing something.

"Kaius Reesa..." He shook his head. "He didn't curse me on his own command. Willem's letter was sent to Amarion Selle, and if memory serves, Kaius Reesa was a mage employed by the late lord. It was the Selles who sought to eliminate me, and the rest of them supported it when they realized distracting you would allow them to see their dreams realized. It's hard to say if the Selles know about the others' association with the Guild. Young Shasta may be an unwilling accomplice."

"Even so, she's done enough on her own to be a problem for us."

"Indeed." Arian managed a weak smile. "If the curse hadn't put me to sleep, and it'd affected me in some other way, I would've advised you against killing Kaius to save me. Make no mistake—I'm eternally grateful for what you did. But I wish there'd been another way. It shouldn't have been you, but I suppose you were the only person it could've been." He winced, then widened his smile as if he'd regained all his strength in a matter of seconds. "Forgive me. I'm still a bit loopy, you see." Aurelia chuckled. "If the person responsible had to be anyone, I'm glad it was Kaius Reesa. I've never met another man whose presence reminds me so strongly of a cockroach."

That made her laugh, but she quickly stopped and raised a brow. "You've met him?"

"Only once, and very briefly. Do you remember three years ago when I spotted Kanish spies in Dofell? I was traveling on business for Reyna. She needed me to collect something from a contact in Caedia. The contact was a mage and an apothecary known for creating special tonics, but his methods weren't very honorable—I won't go into details—so his business was somewhat clandestine. Kaius was there, too. We met in passing when he arrived to collect a tonic."

"What was it?"

"I don't know what he came for, but he was awfully casual about the whole thing. Me and others who purchased from this apothecary went to great lengths to keep our identities hidden. Kaius had no problem announcing himself—I think he believed he'd receive a free tonic if the apothecary knew he was a nobleman."

Aurelia frowned. "It doesn't make sense. Krotis is the most pious of every civilization in the realm, finding strength, unity, and peace in respecting the fundamental virtues of human life. When did the Council's perspectives change? When did they decide to stop acting like Kroti, and to start acting like Willem?"

"I wish I knew." He sighed. "Edea's return to the realm must've opened the door of communication between gods and humans. Perhaps Immor has been planting ideas in their heads for the last three years, all without them knowing it, and his voice in their subconscious led them to take drastic measures."

"That sounds plausible enough to me," she muttered. As he nodded, a moment of silence washed over them, and she seized the opportunity to discuss something else. "Uncle...I received the message you gave to Linden."

Shame washed over his face in an instant. "Oh."

Aurelia squeezed his hands and smiled when he averted his gaze. "You needn't feel poorly about what you and Father did, nor about keeping it from me. I understand. I only wish you'd told me everything sooner. This situation has made me realize how little I know about you."

"You know everything about me, Aurelia." His voice had softened to a near-whisper by then, and he finally met her gaze again. He managed a smile, but his eyes were still dim. "I was going to tell you about this eventually, but talking about the man I love—the only man I've ever loved, gods help me—means telling *that* part of the story, too. I could never seem to find the right moment to lay it all out. I hope you can forgive me."

"Of course I can. And when you're ready, I'd love to hear every story about Shale that you can remember. Maybe I'll even get to meet him someday."

Just like that, the light in his eyes burned brighter. "We'll see if that can be arranged. But there's another man you've yet to meet—properly, anyway. No lies." When she looked away, her cheeks warming, he gave her hands a slight tug until she met his eyes again. "I know why you haven't told him, or even Rayan, for that matter. We have the same mind, you and I. It's my place to tell Eric about my sister—about how she died, and about what she left behind."

She swallowed the hard lump in her throat. "It was selfish. I wasn't thinking about your preference. I was only thinking about what'd be easiest for me."

"That's all right. You're allowed to be selfish once in a while." He yawned and repositioned himself so he was laying down again, his head melting into the pillow behind him. "I'll have a chat with him after I've rested for a bit. Then you can tell Rayan—that's most certainly your job, not mine—and a three-and-thirty-year-old weight will finally be lifted."

Aurelia sniffled. "Thank you."

"For what, my dear?"

"Understanding me, supporting me, protecting me—everything, really."

"Oh, stop it." He waved his hand to dismiss her, but his eyes were misty. "You needn't thank me for loving you, Aurelia. Imagine if one of your children thanked you for that!"

A grin spread over her lips. He really was the father to her that Edmund and Eric couldn't be over the last few years, and she was the child he'd never have. She'd always known it, and she knew he did, too, but hearing it out loud filled her with an unexplainable joy.

"I'll leave you to rest." Aurelia leaned up to kiss his forehead. "You need it—especially because the children will be demanding to see you as soon as the sun rises tomorrow."

Arian grinned. "Good."

He was already asleep by the time she walked away. She lingered by the door before she left, watching his chest rise and fall with more power than it had while he was cursed, and thanked the gods for sparing him.

Her life wouldn't have been the same without him. That much had been inevitable since the day he named her as the Queen of Akkinor when she arrived on his doorstep eight years ago, disguised as a commoner and putting her faith in a complete stranger.

***

After leaving Arian, Aurelia went to her bedchamber to wash up and ready for bed. She was still covered in Kaius's blood, and though she'd given the hand to Rayan, she could still feel its weight in her pocket. She'd told Rayan to keep it in the infirmary for now and send a message to Vrurith after she filled him in, and with Jack's epiphany not long ago, she was even more curious to read Lord Reesa's response.

She and Jack had told Rayan everything while Anysa was visiting with Arian, and he'd kindly offered to send word of the day's events to their allies—especially now that Arian was awake. She prayed the ravens made it to their destinations, and that Krotis didn't intercept them.

She was pulling on her dressing robe when the door to her bedchamber swung open. She expected to see Jack, but instead, it was a frenzied Rayan.

"Rayan?" She frowned as he tried to catch his breath. "What's the matter?"

"I-I was just met by soldiers in the foyer. They looked like they'd just come from battle. There are riots happening across Kalenbrar—the people have taken up arms against each other."

Her heart sank to her knees. She should've known her hectic day wouldn't end with a good night's sleep.

"Why? What's going on?" She fled into her closet to change into real clothing, and while Rayan followed, he turned to face the main chamber of her room to avoid looking at her as she undressed.

"A group of wealthier folk were caught trying to force some of the poorer folk into the dreary part of the city—the part they've started referring to as *Amanbrar*. Their supporters started protesting and attacking our soldiers not long ago."

"All of this, because they think the poor are costing them business?" She shook her head as she laced up her boots. "This is ridiculous. What are they thinking?"

"I spoke to Lady Linderli this morning, too, coincidentally. Foreign tradesmen arrived in the Folly at dawn today, and they refused to do business with some of their usual merchants because the streets were crawling with beggars. They wanted nothing to do with any of it, so they left."

"I thought we offered higher wages to the less fortunate since this was last brought to our attention. There shouldn't be beggars anymore."

As she brushed by Rayan, he winced. "Apparently, it wasn't enough."

She pressed her lips together. "The poor have never turned to begging like this, and they're far richer than they were ten years ago. I can't imagine the wealthier Follians feeling so disturbed by their less fortunate neighbors, either. I suppose I haven't been paying enough attention to them—any of them."

He only sighed. "They may be getting higher wages, but the cost of living in the Folly has increased exponentially since so many of its inhabitants have grown wealthier over the years. We can't offer them more without bankrupting the Folly's civilian funding."

"We'll have to think of another solution, but for now, we have to contain the riots before they escalate. Sending our troops to apprehend everyone involved would only heighten the violence—past incidents have proven that much."

"You can't go to Kalenbrar," he said firmly, folding his arms over his chest. "Jack will say the same. It's too dangerous right now."

"Clearly, they haven't taken to obeying Odessa, and they don't seem to care about the increased number of soldiers prowling the city," she reminded him. "They need to hear from their queen, and soon. If the fighting escalates, they could take it out of the city."

"It's not a good idea."

"Have you any suggestions? Other than letting our soldiers loose on the capital city, of course." At his silence, she walked past him and opened the door. "I thought so. Let's go."

After finding Jack on their way to the foyer—who'd already heard about the riots, and had expected Aurelia to visit the scene—Aurelia told Lucyra and Anysa to stay inside with the children, ordered the palace's knights to secure the property, and met a troop of about fifty soldiers on the bailey with Cheol and Geon. Aurelia, Jack, and Rayan climbed into the carriage as the centaurs pulled them through the gates, the soldiers on horseback flanking either side of the vehicle.

"This is madness," Jack muttered. Now that they were outside of the palace, they could hear yelling and fighting in the near distance. "What's gotten into them?"

"Desperation," Aurelia replied, her heart sinking with guilt. "I thought I'd done everything in my power to better life in the Folly, to give everyone the same chance at prosperity, but apparently, I was wrong."

"The middle class became as wealthy as the upper, but the lower..." Rayan sighed. "At the very least, the middle class always had access to the ladder they needed to climb to get out of the hole of poverty. The lower class never had the ladder to begin with. The coin we've given them just isn't enough. It's like dangling the ladder in front of them, but never giving them the chance to climb."

Aurelia winced. He was right. The most impoverished people in Akkinor were trapped at the bottom for a reason: either they'd amassed tremendous debts, or they'd spent all of their coin to pay fines for past crimes. Most of them were good people who'd been dealt a bad hand at life. They were different from the lower middle class civilians, who normally struggled because of low-paying jobs or things they couldn't control, like deaths in their families. Increasing their wages had seemed like a good idea at the time, but it'd been a grievous mistake. Many of them had criminal pasts, which made employers turn them away, so the extra coin was always spent quickly. Others were so deeply in debt that they couldn't pay what they owed while also paying for daily necessities. Whatever extra coin they got, it disappeared almost as quickly as it arrived.

The trio was stunned into silence when they caught their first glimpse of Kalenbrar. For a moment, the sight reminded Aurelia of the night of the uprising, when Archie's mercenaries wreaked havoc on the kingdom. Homes and establishments had been set ablaze, animals ran about after escaping their pens or stables, and people were running around the streets, either searching for shelter or battling one another. The sounds of terrified screams and clanging swords echoed in Aurelia's eardrums, while the smell of smoke and burning flesh made her stomach churn.

Soldiers were trying to stop the madness, to no avail. Every time they tried to intervene, a commoner charged at them with a makeshift weapon in hand. Some soldiers were spit or cursed at, even if they were doing nothing more than trying to escort elders, women, and children away from the carnage.

"We have to stop this." Jack's eyes were wide with disbelief as he peered out the window. "If they see our faces, they'll stop and listen. They have to. Right?"

Rayan winced, and Aurelia didn't have to ask to know what he was thinking: without Halvor, it wasn't likely the people would stop long enough to listen to their queen. She didn't want to use Halvor to inspire fear or to intimidate her subjects, but if this went on any longer, she'd have to call him.

As soon as they stepped out of the carriage, the soldiers who'd accompanied them dispersed into the crowd, immediately going after the civilians bearing torches and weapons. Some of them followed Rayan toward a nearby well to help put the fires out and salvage what was left of the buildings. One stayed with Aurelia and Jack, blowing a horn to silence the carnage, but the civilians ignored it.

"*You!*" Jack grabbed a man running past them by the back of his shirt, forcing the scrawny civilian to drop his hammer. "What on earth is going on here? Who started this?"

"Bollocks if I know!" His eyes landed on Aurelia for a split second, but he didn't seem to recognize her. "The peasants went mad, they did! Had no choice but to round 'em up and try sending 'em away to Amanbrar. Didn't hold, though! They came back like they were out for blood. Had to defend ourselves!"

Jack released his shirt and gave him a little shove, but the man hardly noticed. He was already running back into the action, long before he'd even regained his balance.

Aurelia gazed around, heart pounding. Her men were seizing weapons left and right, and luckily, most of the civilians cooperated when they were unarmed. Others kept fighting, using their hands and bodies as weapons, and for a time, Aurelia wasn't sure they knew who they were supposed to be fighting.

Then she saw something that made her heart drop: a little boy standing in the middle of the violence, screaming for his mother. Aurelia was running before she realized what she was doing, the sound of Jack's hollering fading into silence.

In the blink of an eye, she'd swept the sobbing toddler into her arms, but she'd ended up in the center of the bloodshed. Jack fought his way through the crowd, shoving people out of the way with nothing but his body. When he reached them, Aurelia practically threw the child into his arms, just as someone grabbed her shirt from behind and yanked her down.

She knew Jack was nearby, but she also knew he'd get the child to safety first, like she wanted. She tried to get to her feet as she sent a plea toward Halvor, but was quickly pushed back down by boots and falling bodies. Her body ached from the impact, but just as she braced herself to be trampled, someone swung her up in their arms like she weighed no more than a ragdoll.

It was Cheol. He hurried out of the crowd, but before he could deliver her to safety, something struck him in the back and left him howling. Aurelia tumbled out of his arms while he collapsed, and just as she cried out for him and looked for him within the madness, Jack grabbed her by the underarms and dragged her away to a nearby alley.

"Are you all right?" He held her by the shoulders, a wild look in his eyes as he studied her face, and all she could do was nod. She must've said Cheol's name, because he quickly added, "I'll go get him! Stay here!"

"The boy!" she yelled. "Is he all right?"

"He's fine! Stay here!"

She wanted to follow him, to do something, but it wouldn't have made a difference. She was small enough to get lost in the crowd and trampled, as was proven only moments ago. It's not like anyone recognized her, anyway—or cared that she was there.

Just before she lost Jack in the crowd, a roar rattled the streets of Kalenbrar. A sigh of relief escaped her when Halvor appeared overhead, momentarily aligned with the moon as he coasted.

We have to stop this. It has to end before it gets any worse. She pushed the thoughts toward him, ignoring the way her people failed to react to him. They'd gotten too used to him—and his normally peaceful nature.

She watched, heart pounding, as Halvor hovered in the air to her immediate right, facing the majority of the fighting on the streets. She felt him eyeing her, as if he were asking her permission to do something. She gave it to him, not knowing what it was he planned to do, and hoped to every god she could think of that he made the right move; and that it stopped the fighting.

The roar that emitted from Halvor's throat not only sounded different—more guttural and primal than usual—but its impact was different, too. Rather than merely scaring the people out of their wits, the roar caused a chain reaction of events: the people and objects closest to Halvor burst into flames; fires broke out in pockets throughout the fighting; and the ground began to tremble, like the roar had been so ferocious that it disrupted the stability of the earth.

For the first time since the battle with Archie, Aurelia's people weren't screaming with joy and wonder at seeing Halvor. They were screaming in terror, running about like headless chickens, and dropping their weapons— and all intentions of fighting with one another—when they realized what he'd done.

Fire dragons have a power known as the combustion roar. Lucyra's voice echoed in Aurelia's head. *Only a few records mention it at all. It's said to be a rare ability only mastered by the most ancient of dragons.*

By then, Aurelia had scrambled to her feet, and she managed to find Jack and a handful of her knights in the chaos. They started fetching buckets of water from the well to put out the fires, trying their utmost to ignore the blazing, dying figures running around as they awaited their demise.

Rayan found them, too, during their efforts to stop the damage from spreading. He, Jack, and Aurelia exchanged identical looks, so she knew they were thinking the same thing: *This was a bad idea.*

XXV

urelia, Jack, and Rayan didn't get to sleep that night. Aurelia sent Halvor back to the palace, knowing his presence would only terrify the people even more after what he'd done, but the trio stayed behind with the soldiers.

By the time the fires were put out, the streets were still blanketed in thick layers of smoke and ash, but they were able to make sense of the damage. A few homes had been burnt to the ground, but they'd already been ablaze by the time Aurelia arrived. They counted only five incinerated bodies—a small number compared to the damage Halvor could've inflicted. Other than those five poor souls, the most Halvor had done was spook the civilians by igniting a few wagons, bales of hay, and wooden barrels.

Six of Aurelia's soldiers had been killed in the fighting, along with a few dozen civilians who hadn't been incinerated. Fortunately, Cheol was okay—he'd gotten hit on the back with a club so forcefully that it'd knocked him down, but he wasn't harmed. He was more ashamed at having dropped Aurelia than he was in pain at being struck.

The remaining soldiers, along with others who'd arrived—too late—to help contain the riots, rounded up everyone in the vicinity. After ensuring the vulnerable civilians were safe, the soldiers located anyone with blood and soot on their clothing or skin, and they were all presented before the queen on the smoldering streets to explain what had happened.

A part of her expected them all to say the same thing: the wealthy had attacked the poor first, or vice versa, and the other side had been forced to defend themselves. Instead, they stuck to the same story: a large group of the wealthier civilians had tried forcing the poorer folk to relocate to Amanbrar in the middle of the night, claiming they didn't belong in the

City of Light if they were going to continue clawing at the crown's coin, only to refuse to contribute to the Folly's economy.

The poorer civilians had fought back—some when they were taken from their beds in Kalenbrar, and some when they heard the commotion from Amanbrar and fled to investigate—and before they knew it, they were at each other's throats, not caring if they took down the soldiers posted nearby who were meant to keep the peace.

When it was Aurelia's turn to speak, she took a few steps forward to face the battered, beaten, angry crowd, keeping an eye on them as they tossed hateful looks at one another. Again, they didn't really seem to care about her presence.

"These tensions between you began several weeks ago, and I tried my utmost to deter them." She brought a hand to her abdomen as she spoke, still aching from nearly being trampled. "You were warned against fighting over such a petty squabble. I was forced to deploy more soldiers to Kalenbrar in hopes that you'd respect their authority and leave each other be. Lady Linderli, too, offered more coin and protection detail, and yet, you continued to bicker in the shadows. Fighting with your neighbors is one thing, but to try to force your neighbors out of their family homes and into squalor, just to raise arms against them when they resisted...There's no honor in that. You can't call yourselves Follians if you believe that was the best course of action."

She took a moment to catch her breath. "In truth, I don't fully understand what escalated this disagreement to such a horrid display of violence. You couldn't be stopped when your queen rode into your streets to offer assistance. You could only be stopped when something stronger than man intervened. That is no way to behave, especially for citizens of Akkinor's new capital city. What happened tonight can never happen again, and if it does, the consequences will be dire. Still, there's a price to be paid for what you put each other through tonight. Brothers and sisters, sons and daughters, husbands and wives—they died today at the hands of their neighbors, and they will have justice."

Rayan stepped forward. "Both sides of this battle will choose three people to hang. The rest of you will go free, without any sort of fine or punishment. You have one hour to choose—without further bloodshed—and if you don't, everyone here will spend a season in the dungeons."

Furious mutterings echoed throughout the streets, making Aurelia's throat feel thick. She didn't like it now, and she hadn't liked it an hour ago when she discussed it with Jack and Rayan, but it had to be done: there was always a consequence for such horror, and if she didn't do something to show them how stern she was about preventing future incidents, they wouldn't take her seriously. They'd already ignored warnings from both the crown and the Lady of the Folly, after all.

An hour later, after a few small brawls that were quickly broken up by the soldiers, six men were presented before Aurelia. Three were said to be included in the original group of wealthier folk who'd started tearing the poor out of their beds. The other three were said to be poorer folk who'd previously been forced into Amanbrar, only to gather as many fighters as they could before marching to Kalenbrar when they heard about the conflict.

Even though they were being spared, the remaining Follians stared at Aurelia with pure hatred in their eyes. It was the first time in weeks that both sides of the aisle seemed to agree on something. She didn't know which part they were angry at—Halvor, the executions, or the matter in general—but regardless, they weren't very pleased with her.

She didn't blame them. She knew she hadn't been the leader they deserved while matters abroad took priority, and her response to the conflict hadn't been the kind of attention they wanted or needed from her. She just hoped that in due time, they'd come to understand why she was so distant from them. They didn't have to like it—she didn't like it, either—but it was a necessary sacrifice for the good of the country.

An hour after that, the six men were brought to the gallows, where they gave their lives as retribution for what the city of Kalenbrar had done that night.

***

"...take it?"

"Probably as evidence to show anyone who bothers to listen to her."

"Half the realm will know soon enough. We must proceed with caution."

"We need a distraction, then. Do you think your son managed to—?"

A pause. "I'd assume so. They're both young and healthy, and Kaius was a Reesa, after all. His seed was strong."

Shasta brought a hand to her stomach, nausea overwhelming her, as she continued pressing her ear to the wooden door. On the other side, Lord Reesa and Lord Quagg were conversing in a private room. Not at all to her surprise, they'd started talking about her again.

The last few days had been the most chaotic of her life. The day after the incident in Khaba, she'd been married to Kaius Reesa. The day after that, Kaius met with Queen Aurelia in Vrurith, where she'd stabbed him and left him there to die. Shasta had been married for all of one day, and it pained her to dress head-to-toe in mourning black—not because she grieved the husband she hadn't particularly liked, but because she knew what her fate had become.

If Kaius hadn't succeeded in impregnating her on their wedding night—and even if he did, and the child was a girl—she'd be married off again, because one couldn't rule in Krotis unless they were married or widowed with a son, to ensure the line of succession. If Kaius had succeeded, and Shasta was carrying a son, she'd be overlooked as soon as the child was old enough to read and write. For all she knew, the lords would take her son away to be raised as they saw fit, because a child without a father needed strong men to guide him.

Lord Reesa's muffled voice caught her attention: "We can tell everyone she's with child, even if she isn't. Queen Aurelia knows Amarion was Willem's way into Krotis, so soon enough, she'll be paying closer attention to Bruila, especially with Annera. The only thing this gods-forsaken realm can agree on is protecting women who carry the future of our world—if they find out Queen Aurelia's target is a new widow with a babe in her womb, they'll turn on her."

Lord Quagg hesitated. "It's possible. That wouldn't do us much good if the queen has already spread word of Kaius's affiliation with the Guild, though. With Kaius as Lady Selle's late husband, the realm will only assume she's associated with the Guild, too. They'd come after her, pregnant or not. We'd have to act sooner rather than later, and we're vastly underprepared. The Guild isn't strong enough yet, and we can't prevent the realm from scorning us unless we have *him* on our side."

Shasta's lips parted in preparation for a gasp, but before she got the chance, a hand clamped over her mouth. She turned ever so slightly, eyes widening with fear, but relaxed when she saw Lord Swann at her side. He held a finger to his lips, dropped his hand from her mouth, and beckoned her to follow him.

Swallowing her nerves, Shasta trailed behind him as they walked through the halls of Sharith—an estate in the capital city of Malicia, where the Iron Council often gathered for a few days at a time to discuss important matters. He eventually guided her into an empty parlor, quietly closed the door when both were safely inside, and released a shuddering exhale.

"My lord—" she whispered.

"What were they talking about?"

She knew it wasn't wise to share her allies' private conversation with another after eavesdropping on them, but they'd already turned to plotting without the rest of the Council. If they could keep secrets, so could she.

She told him as much as she'd overheard: the noblemen hoped she was with child; Queen Aurelia had sawed off Kaius's hand after killing him, only to send it back to his father; Lord Reesa didn't seem to be exactly grieving the loss of his second son; and the two lords had traded nervous words about something called *the Guild*.

"Gods be good." Lazelus's dark eyes widened as he collapsed in an armchair. Shasta sat beside him in an identical seat, the worry in his eyes unsettling her. "If I'm being honest, I had a feeling your husband wouldn't make it home. He was known for being impulsive and having a short temper, so I can only imagine what he did to provoke the queen."

Shasta's lips parted. "You think he sealed his own fate?"

"Of course I do," he replied. "I think Lord Reesa played a hand in it, too. That's why he isn't drowning in black like you are." She smoothed her dark skirts, feeling embarrassed for some reason, as he continued. "Before she died, my grandmother told me she suspected the Reesa and Quagg families of being members of the Guild of Steel. It's a secret organization with factions across the realm, where members unite in hopes of finding a way to replace their kingdom's Almighty with Immor. I didn't believe her because she was old and senile, and in truth, I thought the Guild was only legend."

She gasped and brought a hand to her heart. "B-But—"

"I thought it was rubbish, but our fellow lords have been acting too strangely as of late. Even though our spies just found pieces of the prophecy King Willem shared with your father in Kanibar, it's not enough to warrant all of this, and I can't believe that One Forged in Gold attacked us unprovoked. It seems like our counterparts are using the prophecy to justify the Guild's plans. After all, the realm would protest at the idea of Krotis replacing Pherena with Immor for no just cause, but if we did so because it's our only hope at surviving our prophesized downfall..."

A shiver wracked Shasta's body. She didn't want to believe that. She'd never heard of such an organization before, and if it was becoming as relevant as Lord Swann seemed to imply, she should've. Lord Reesa and Lord Quagg may not have been the greatest men in the world, but she still couldn't see them doing all of this—not to mention sacrificing Kaius in the process—simply because they wished for a new Almighty.

"I don't know if Lord Keer is aware of this." Lord Swann chewed on his lower lip, contemplating. "My grandmother never said anything about his family being involved with the Guild. But if he's not involved, the other two will get inside his head, and he'll stand by them. They'll try to sway the two of us, too. Even if we resist...I think they'd succeed in their endeavors, anyway. They'd replace our virtuous Almighty with the god of war, and we'd be powerless to—"

"Stop." Shasta shook her head as she held an arm out in his direction to silence him. "T-This can't be true. Pherena has been the Almighty of Krotis since the kingdom was established. Our people won't accept Immor in her stead. The realm wouldn't stand for it, either, even if we claim to have made the choice in hopes of stopping Queen Aurelia from fulfilling the prophecy."

His eyes hardened. "You saw those few bits and pieces of the prophecy. It never directly states that Queen Aurelia will destroy the realm, but many—like our fellow lords—will disagree. They'll be too frightened to care about what Immor's role in Krotis might do. They'd see the god of war's intervention as our only hope."

"I refuse to believe this. Lord Reesa and Lord Quagg are too smart to—"

"—take such a risk?" Lord Swann scoffed. "They didn't join the Guild because they're smart. They joined the Guild because they're hungry for power."

"That's not true."

"Isn't it?" He shook his head, clearly annoyed by her refusal to believe him. "You'll have to make a choice sooner than later, my lady. Queen Aurelia knows by now that Annera belongs to you. Though Annera is still small, she poses the greatest threat to the queen. Aurelia will want to know if you're her friend or her enemy, and if you stand beside the Guild, you're her enemy."

Shasta shook her head again, hugging herself for comfort. "How could she possibly know that?"

In a flash, the aggravated look on his face morphed into one of utter shame. He bowed his head and clenched his jaw, averting his gaze from hers. She studied him for a moment, curious about his sudden change in demeanor, until she remembered something everyone—even Lord Swann—had chosen to ignore as of late: Runeia was allied with Akkinor.

Her breath caught in her throat. "You told her."

"I didn't tell her anything," he said quickly, finally meeting her eyes. "I only...pointed her in the right direction."

"You betrayed us." Shasta's voice was lower than a whisper as tears burned in her eyes, and her hands trembled in her lap. "Even before you knew about the Guild's plan and the ramifications of it, you provided crucial information to the enemy. You didn't just betray Krotis and the Council, either—you betrayed *me*."

Lord Swann's face was crimson with anguish. "Shasta, I—"

"You have no right to call me by my given name." She rose on shaking legs, refusing to meet his eyes again. "I almost thought we were becoming friends. Now, I see how blind I was—to everything."

She walked away, letting the door slam against the wall when she tore it open, and ignored his pleas for forgiveness as she marched away.

***

After finally returning to the palace around midday, Aurelia made a beeline for her bedchamber. She asked Jack and Rayan not to follow her as she rushed upstairs and into her room, then locked herself in the washroom.

She put her hands on either side of the empty basin, her head hanging low as her eyes fell shut, and tried to steady her breathing. She hadn't been breathing right since the moment she arrived in Kalenbrar. She kept seeing the night's events playing over and over in her head, making her wonder if there was anything she could've done differently to put an end to the riots.

She didn't realize she was crying until she heard a gentle *plop* against the porcelain basin. She opened her eyes and lifted a hand to wipe the tears from her cheeks, but stopped short when she glanced down at the white bowl. Her breath caught in her throat, making her so dizzy that after a moment, she had to remind herself to breathe.

There wasn't a golden teardrop sitting at the bottom of the basin. There wasn't a liquid gold smudge on her hand, either, when she finally touched her cheek. The tears falling from her eyes were as clear as rainwater.

Intermission

Hyacinth Brentwood, Princess of Akkinor, always loved to dream.

It was funny: she often spoke to her twin sister about dreams, and Halle never seemed to experience them the same way. *I don't remember my dreams,* she'd say. *I never know when I'm dreaming,* she'd claim.

That was strange to Hyacinth. She always knew when she was dreaming, and she always remembered them. To her, dreaming was like visiting a far-off land made just for her, like an adventure she got to embark on every night when she closed her eyes.

Her papa always talked about his grand adventures. Maybe he dreamed like she did, too.

Only a few of her dreams were bad ones. She didn't like thinking about those, but sometimes, she couldn't help it. She'd once dreamt of her dear mama, sobbing with shackles around her wrists, and when she'd tried to call out for her, her mama didn't answer. She'd dreamt of her beloved Uncle Arian, too, collapsing at a ball in her home. A part of her knew when she woke up from those dreams that she was seeing real events, not figments of her imagination, but she liked to tell herself they were just made-up. It was better that way.

Hyacinth was hoping for a good dream tonight. Her mama and papa were home from their adventure, her uncle was awake after sleeping for what felt like an eternity, and she'd been given a strange candy to try by her new aunt, Anysa. It'd been a good evening, so she was excited for an even better dream.

As soon as sleep pulled her away, she knew it was not a good dream. She could feel it in her stomach—the same feeling she got before something bad happened.

In the dream, she was walking through the halls of the palace, but nobody was there. She called out for someone, anyone, but nobody answered. Then the palace began to shake, making everything on the walls fall to the ground, and she released a terrified squeak before running for cover.

She knew where to go if something bad happened and she couldn't find someone to help her: Halvor. She ran to a nearby balcony that overlooked the gardens, hoping to find him there, but he wasn't in his sanctuary.

Maybe he's out front, she told herself, and started for the foyer. Still, she didn't find anyone else in the palace. She didn't want to cry, because her brother would make fun of her if she did, but she was frightened, and all she wanted was for her papa to hold her.

As she scurried down the grand staircase, she saw the front doors were open. Another massive tremor shook the palace, making her gasp and duck while using the railing for cover. She screamed when the chandelier fell from the ceiling and crashed to the ground, directly between the staircase and the doors.

Trust Halvor. It was her mama's voice that played in her head. *He'll bring you to safety.*

Taking a deep breath, a whimpering Hyacinth continued down the steps, avoiding the smoking chandelier as she raced for the doors. She ran down the steps and onto the bailey, shouting for Halvor to come rescue her. She knew he could see her down here, and if he heard her pleas, he'd come for her. He'd always come for her.

She felt hopeful when she heard a mighty roar, but she knew in her heart it wasn't Halvor. The roar sounded...*mean.* Halvor didn't sound mean. Not to her, anyway. This roar sounded like a stranger, like someone who'd come to hurt her.

Still whimpering and fighting the urge to sob, Hyacinth looked around for any sign of Halvor, her family, or her friends. The sky was smoky and dark, and there was nobody around as far as she could see, but there were fires burning in the distance. Then a big shadow came toward her from the sky, and a pretty green dragon soared over her head, bellowing so loudly that the ground beneath the princess's feet threatened to give way.

She ran back into the palace and hid in a corner, curled up in a ball, while covering her ears with her hands. *I want to go home,* she thought. *I want to wake up now.*

She did. As soon as she squeezed her eyes shut, they shot open again, and she found herself sitting upright in her bed. The palace wasn't shaking anymore, but she still wasn't sure she'd woken up. She had to see for herself that she wasn't alone.

Hyacinth crawled out of bed and tiptoed down the hallway toward her parents' room. All she wanted after that horrible dream was a hug from her papa, because he always made her feel safe.

She put her hand on the doorknob to open it, but she stopped when she heard voices inside. *They're here*, she thought. *I'm awake.* She still had every intention of going inside, but she couldn't do it when she realized her mama wasn't talking—she was weeping.

"...all right." Her papa's voice was muffled, but she still heard it. "It's going to be okay, lovely. Take a deep breath and try to sleep. We'll figure it out in the morning."

"What if we can't?" her mama said. "What if I've lost who I am for good? What then, Jack? What purpose do I have? What legacy will I leave behind?"

"Lily—"

"Don't call me that!"

"I'm sorry." Her papa's voice sounded odd, like it was broken. "I-I don't know how to help you, my love. I don't know what I can do to make this better."

Her mama only wept louder in response.

Backing away from the door with wide eyes, Hyacinth turned and ran for another safe place: Halle's room. She didn't bother knocking before slipping inside and quietly closing the door behind her. She crawled into bed beside her sister, burrowing under the covers, but Halle didn't so much as stir.

For what felt like hours, Hyacinth laid with the covers pulled over her head, replaying her dream—and the sound of her mama's weeping—over and over again. She wondered why the pretty green dragon had come to the Folly, only to be such a bully, and why Halvor wasn't there to save her.

As exhaustion coaxed her back to sleep, the last thought on her mind was the dragon. Just before she surrendered to the god of dreams once again, a name popped into her head:

Annera.

BOOK TWO: LEGENDS

*F*or the eyes of Balor Zhoqa, Third of His Name, Lord of Kazamir:
In the late hours of the night, riots broke out across the capital city of Kalenbrar here in the Folly. Her Grace, accompanied by the King Consort and the Lord Hand, attempted to deescalate the fighting. Halvor was crucial for this, though he released an odd power that contributed to the city's destruction. The people have sheltered themselves in fear of him. While they succeeded in the end, Kalenbrar has been left with significant damages, and Her Grace has confined herself to her bedchamber for reasons unknown.

The King Consort seems to think some sort of foul play was involved, likely a result of our difficult relationship with Krotis. He requests that you, along with Queen Reyna and Lord Zhaaran, keep an eye and an ear out for any information. We would not be surprised if Krotis played a hand in urging this conflict, by whatever means. They have already proven that they're willing to take drastic measures to weaken our queen, and destroying the new capital of Akkinor—while making it appear like a civil dispute—would not be beyond them.

Please keep us in your thoughts and prayers, and promptly respond to this message if you happen to learn anything of relevance. We will continue sending updates in the near future.

Sincerely,
Emilia Litten, advisor to Her Grace, Queen Aurelia of Akkinor.

Balor leaned back in his chair and clicked his tongue. Riots in Akkinor? And in the capital, no less? He certainly wasn't expecting this kind of news from his allies to the east, though a part of him knew it was bound to happen sooner or later. That country was far too peaceful now that they'd bridged the gap between mages and mortals. If the civilians hadn't found another reason to fight each other, they'd look elsewhere for a reason to get their hands dirty.

Of course, it was difficult to imagine such a response to Aurelia's beast. The people seemed to like him, for the most part, given what protection he offered. But sooner or later, there'd come a time—like this one—when Aurelia was forced to use him to intervene in domestic matters, and the people wouldn't like him so much after that. Balor wouldn't be surprised if they abandoned whatever they'd been fighting about to join forces against Aurelia and her beast, fearing what the pair would be capable of now that they'd proven their willingness to go after their own people.

It probably wasn't as bad as he made it out to be, though. Not when Aurelia was involved. That woman had the tendency to shock everyone— even herself, at times—with some sort of miraculous solution.

Balor took a sip of wine and smacked his lips together. "You may have tamed the beast, Your Grace, but what will you do if the time comes when you can no longer control him? When you may be forced to slay him?" He chuckled to himself. "No, no. You'd rather die than hurt him. The entire realm knows that."

Talk of Aurelia and her dragon made him wonder about the hoard of magical creatures that'd recently trickled into Bozar. According to his men, the creatures had been freed from purgatory by none other than Aurelia's oaf of a husband, Jack. Balor had no idea how the enormous fool managed it, and he'd never admit it aloud, but he was grateful for it.

He looked out the window and smiled when a water nymph emerged from the stream in the courtyard at his estate. She crawled out and sat on the lawn so casually that one might assume she'd been doing it for her entire existence. Not true. She'd arrived only the day prior, and she'd made herself at home immediately—likely because she'd lived here once before, centuries prior to Balor's birth.

He never imagined he'd see something like that, but then again, he never imagined he'd see a dragon of old flying overhead, either. Now, there were three of them. When he remembered who that massive purple dragon belonged to, he snorted into a laugh, wondering how a peasant-turned-queen had managed to hide her beast for so long.

Perhaps, one day, he'd thank Aurelia for everything she'd done for the realm. She deserved his gratitude. He couldn't give her the satisfaction just yet, though.

After a few moments, one of his men—whose name he couldn't recall— found him in his study, interrupting his afternoon of peace with heavy footsteps and obnoxiously loud breathing.

"Good day, my lord," the man said with a bow. "I thought you'd be interested to know that our scouts spotted a small fleet of Kroti ships sailing east."

Balor raised an eyebrow. "Really? Interesting. They move faster than I expected."

Just the day prior, he'd received a letter from Aurelia's Lord Hand about an incident between her and Vrurith. It'd started with an attack at Khaba, and it'd ended with Aurelia killing the second son of Darius Reesa, Lord of Vrurith. Apparently, Kaius Reesa had been the one to curse Arian Cristos, and the latter woke upon Aurelia's return to Akkinor. The Hand had also written that the little emerald dragon seen lurking around the realm belonged to Shasta Selle, the teenage Lady of Bruila.

More importantly, though, was what Aurelia had learned during her brief interaction with Kaius: he was a member of the Guild of Steel. Balor wasn't worried about that yet—the Guild had many factions across the realm, as it had for generations, and no faction had ever come close to bringing Immor to their kingdom. The fact that Kaius was a member, however, suggested that other leaders in Krotis were associated with the Guild, too.

Balor was telling himself that they'd never succeed. For one, Immor had to accept Krotis as his representatives on earth, and the kingdom wasn't exactly known for its warring spirit or exceptional power. For another, their current Almighty hadn't done anything to warrant being abandoned by her patrons, so she—and the other gods, for that matter—probably wouldn't take very well to the action.

Then again, Krotis had grown stronger recently, and if everything Balor had heard thus far was true, they were getting bolder and bolder by the day. It was entirely possible that the god of war would establish himself as Krotis's Almighty, simply because the thought of influencing a kingdom with a dragon was too grand an offer to pass up.

Balor snapped his fingers, causing a cupbearer in the corner of the room to rush over and fill his chalice with wine. The cupbearer quickly scurried back to the corner as Balor took a long sip, still eyeing the messenger.

"What did it look like?" he asked. "The fleet."

"No warships among them, my lord. The scouts identified three ships from each province of Krotis. I can't be certain, but if I had to guess, I'd assume they're sending emissaries to make negotiations with Akkinor."

"Maybe." Balor set his chalice down and stood, now eye-level with the messenger. "Send word to Jalhor Zhaaran if you haven't already. Might as well let Zoma and Xada know, too, though they won't care about Akkinor. We need to hold a meeting at the Nexus, anyway, after what Queen Aurelia has claimed about the Guild of Steel in Krotis."

"At once." The messenger tipped his head, but made no move to leave.

Balor raised an annoyed eyebrow. "Do you need something?"

"I have a question, my lord."

He sighed and gestured with his hand. "Get on with it, then."

The messenger cleared his throat. "I can't help but wonder, my lord, if your loyalty lies with Akkinor and Queen Aurelia, or with Carthe."

For a moment, Balor only stared at him, dumbfounded. "That's the most ridiculous question I've ever heard. What the hell is between your ears, boy? Sand? Mud? It can't possibly be a brain."

"That doesn't answer my question."

"Why, you—" Balor stopped himself, gritting his teeth, when he felt the urge to throttle the young man. The messenger kept looking at him expectantly, not at all frightened of the nobleman's wrath. For some reason, the man's inability to be intimidated made Balor soften. "My loyalty lies with both Akkinor and Carthe, but right now, my ally needs my help. Assisting her is my priority."

The messenger's dark eyes flashed. In the blink of an eye, he surged forward, and the next thing Balor knew, he was choking on air while a white-hot pain spread throughout his abdomen. He tried to speak, to no avail, and managed to look down at his gut. At the same time, the messenger twisted the knife in Balor's stomach before removing it, just to stab him a few inches upward.

"Wrong answer," the man hissed, his lips curling into a sneer.

Balor sputtered and groaned, but his limbs felt petrified, and he couldn't fight back if he tried. When the man finally removed the knife, Balor staggered backward and covered the wound with his hand. The sight of his own blood spilling onto the floor was one he'd seen many times before, but never this much.

The cupbearer in the corner screamed for help and fled the room, but the assailant didn't seem to care. He waited for Balor to collapse to the ground, then hovered over the nobleman with his foot pressing on the first stab wound. Balor would've grunted if he had any strength left, but now, he was numb.

"You never should've promised your sword to her all those years ago," the messenger stated. "It cost you your life, in the end."

Balor groaned, black spots clouding his vision, as the man looked up at the sound of commotion growing closer. Just as Balor's vision began to fade, and he lost all sensation throughout his body, he saw the man reach into his pocket. As he did so, the sleeve of his shirt lifted, revealing two tattoos on his left wrist: one of a lotus flower, symbolic of Krotis; and one of a sword encased in a broken circle, symbolic of the Guild.

Balor blinked, praying his men reached him in time to save him, as the man produced a small, clear vial from his pocket. He uncorked it, held it up to inspect it against the sunlight, and swallowed the contents in one gulp.

With his last breath, the Lord of Kazamir watched his killer collapse to the floor, convulsing and foaming at the mouth. They met eyes as their hearts stopped beating, and in a matter of seconds, both of their souls left the earthly realm at the exact same time.

XXVI

Aurelia spent the next five days isolated in her bedchamber, agonizing over where she could've possibly gone wrong.

Had it been the moment she plunged her dagger into Kaius Reesa's gut? Or the moment she let Halvor frighten her people into submission in Kalenbrar? Or a moment she couldn't recall—a moment when she hadn't realized she'd done something worthy of making the gods turn their backs on her? Even worse, had it been a combination of events?

The morning after she realized her golden tears were gone, she'd been practically catatonic. She refused to speak to anyone, even Jack, and couldn't bring herself to eat more than a few morsels. She stayed that way for the next three days, climbing out of bed only to check in the mirror that the tears staining her cheeks were still clear.

She'd started talking to Jack again these past two days, but when she did, she found herself snapping at him. She willed herself to be gracious and kind while he tried to help her, but no matter how hard she tried, the temper she'd managed to bury for the last eight years exploded from her lips.

The feeling was one Aurelia could only describe as grief. She mourned for the destiny that had forsaken her, and she didn't know who or what she was meant to be anymore. She'd always be the Queen of Akkinor, and her duty to her country would never change, but she felt less equipped to do the job when she knew the gods had lost faith in her.

What would the realm think of her now? She'd revealed her destiny to her allies three years ago, and since then, she'd never been shy about hiding it or denying the rumors as they spread. Anyone who believed in the 'legend' of The Ones Forged in Gold believed in her because of her golden tears. So what would happen when they found out her tears had become ordinary? That *she* had become ordinary?

On the fifth day, she returned to the main chamber of her suite from the washroom, but paused before climbing into bed again. Her beige pillowcase was stained and damp with tears. The sight made her stomach churn, but before she could plant her face directly onto the wetness again, a knock came at her door. She ignored it and climbed into bed, but the knocker entered without permission, anyway. She was opening her mouth to scold whoever it was when she looked up and saw her uncle closing the door behind him.

She knew Jack had sent him, because her husband knew as well as she did that if anyone could get through to her, it was Arian Cristos.

"Hello, my dear." He moved toward her slowly, as his body still hadn't fully recovered from being comatose for weeks, and carefully lowered himself onto the edge of her bed. "How are you?"

"I've been better." She winced at the sound of her voice—hoarse, dry, and utterly unfamiliar. The only thing that brought her solace was seeing the color in Arian's cheeks, the weight he'd started to regain, and the light beaming in his eyes. "And yourself?"

"Almost back to normal. I think." He offered her a small smile, but when she didn't return it—only turned her head to the side to stare off into space—he sighed. "I grew worried when I hadn't seen you in a few days, so Jack told me what happened. Everyone else thinks you're ill. He's hoping I may be able to help you find some peace of mind."

"I figured."

A ghost of a smile appeared on his face. "What are you thinking?"

Her swollen eyes fell shut. "I'm wondering what I did to lose favor with the gods, and what this means for my future. For all of our futures. Maysa said The Ones Forged in Gold are chosen before birth, and that another will take my place when I die. But I'm not dead, and I no longer weep golden tears. Does that mean the next person has assumed the role? And does it mean the gods were wrong when they chose me?"

Arian pondered that for a moment, brushing a lock of shaggy gray hair out of his face as he did so. Lucyra had been trimming his beard for him while he was asleep, but she didn't touch his hair, and so far, nobody else had given it a proper cut. He looked more disheveled than usual, but he didn't seem to mind it.

"I think you must heed what Maysa told you," he said after a moment of silence. "You can't assume your destiny was passed onto another if she told you that can only happen when you die." He raised an eyebrow. "Have you considered what happened with Edea?"

"How do you mean?"

"The amulet. She was testing you, wasn't she? You had a perfect opportunity to use it—on more than one occasion, actually—but you didn't. You gave it back to her as you wanted to do from the start. Perhaps this is another test of your character."

She pressed her lips together as she recalled something else Maysa had told her. When the gods left humanity to their wits, it was because humans had done atrocious things the gods hadn't believed they were capable of. Instead of presenting themselves to unworthy humans, they disappeared and studied the people they'd created, observing how humanity used the power of free will. It would've made sense if the gods intervened in earthly matters to further test humanity, to observe how their creations responded to things that may not have happened naturally. If they were impressed, then maybe all of them would find themselves returning to Icareth.

"Test or not," Aurelia muttered, "I did something to deserve this. I've done a few things I'm not entirely proud of, but still, I felt they were justified. I just can't identify which action was the damning one."

"Don't waste your energy on that," he insisted, eyes twinkling with a fatherly sternness. "Maybe you did nothing at all to deserve this, and—like I said—the gods are merely testing you. We can't know anything for certain. All we can control is how you proceed."

She wiped the tears from her puffy cheeks. "How do you mean?"

Arian chuckled a little. "Everything you've done to better the world over the years...Would you have done so if you weren't Forged in Gold?"

"Of course."

"What did your golden tears offer you that you didn't have before?"

"A purpose."

"A purpose!" He shook his head and tsked her. "My brave, darling girl—you had a purpose long before you wept tears of gold. You did wonderful things, expecting nothing in return, ages before the battle with your brother. Golden tears or not, your character has never changed, and you've always had a purpose in this world."

She fought the urge to sob when her chest tightened. "Have you ever stopped to consider that every good thing I've ever done was a result of my destiny, not my character? It's like Maysa said—I was chosen before I was born. This 'free will' everyone speaks of...Did it ever exist for me? Or did the gods mold me into their pawn from the second I was born, leaving me with no choice but to fulfill that destiny?"

For a moment, Arian's eyebrows lifted in surprise, and his face blanched with defeat. She could see in his eyes that he had no answer for her.

"It doesn't matter," he decided. "Remember what I said: what's important is where you go from here. You can stop trying to better things around the world because you feel it's no longer your responsibility, your purpose. Or, you can proceed as you always have, doing what you can to transform the realm into the magnificent place it once was. And if not the realm, then perhaps consider all the good you've done for those who know and love you—your husband, your children, Rayan, myself. Small victories are still victories, you know." He reached over to squeeze her hand. "I'll let you think on that."

Aurelia wasn't looking at him, but she felt the bed wobble when he stood, and she heard the door close behind him. When he was gone, she looked at the spot where he'd been sitting, and she replayed what he'd said until her head started to spin.

She knew he was right, but that didn't do anything to lessen her anguish. If the gods had chosen her to be Forged in Gold before her birth, then she could only assume that every good deed she'd ever done had been a subconscious response to that—ways for her to unlock her destiny and her golden tears, so she'd then feel empowered to do even better for the realm.

Were her efforts to better the world really a result of her own hopes, of her own moral code? Or were they forced upon her by the gods so she could become what they needed her to be? And now that her destiny was gone, would everything that made her a good, just, kind leader fade away? Would she even care about salvaging the realm anymore? *Was* she going to sever it?

Knowing she'd never get the answers to her questions, Aurelia turned her face into the pillow as tears swam in her eyes, and spent yet another night alone in her bedchamber while the world moved on around her.

***

After six days of grieving her destiny, Aurelia finally made it out of her bedchamber. She'd been woken that morning by her children's laughter echoing in the halls, and she knew that even if the gods had given up on her, others hadn't—her children, Jack, the Akkinorians. She refused to let them down.

Perhaps, she thought, her odd new relationship with the realm would repair itself in due time. For now, though, trying her utmost to improve things for her children's sake was reason enough for her to keep going.

She rang for her lady's maids, who arrived swiftly—albeit in surprise—to help her bathe and dress. They changed her bedsheets for the first time in almost a week, failing to hide their pitiful expressions when they saw the tears burned into the fabric.

When she asked about what had happened in her absence, they didn't have much to say. She was worried the people of the Folly had turned on her after what Halvor had done, and how she'd responded to the civil dispute, but her lady's maids insisted there hadn't been whispers of displeasure or anger since that night.

"I know this isn't what you want to hear," Geena told her as she braided the queen's hair, "but often times, when a leader rules with such mercy, the people take advantage of their kindness, and start thinking they can get away with anything—laws and consequences be damned. Sometimes, a leader has no choice but to remind their people to fear them."

Aurelia frowned. "I don't want them to fear me."

"It's difficult for some to be obedient if they aren't afraid," Daisy added as she fluffed the pillows. "Many are empowered when they're shown kindness by the one who leads them, and others view kindness as an opportunity to test the boundaries of leniency."

Aurelia thought on that for a moment. "Do you think I was wrong to do what I did in Kalenbrar?"

The women exchanged looks, visibly surprised that she'd asked them such a vulnerable question. She didn't normally speak about politics with her lady's maids, and they weren't accustomed to being asked such questions by anyone.

"If you're asking my opinion," Jana said as she tidied up, "I think the matter in Kalenbrar would've escalated, bleeding into surrounding areas until, perhaps, it made its way to the palace gates. You would've had to intervene sooner or later, and bringing Halvor to the scene was the best way to deescalate the fighting quickly. The people battled our soldiers as much as they battled each other, but they couldn't do a thing to Halvor. I fear the situation would've worsened if you hadn't summoned him. And the executions..." She sighed. "There has to be accountability for such actions. You could've punished the lot of them in many different ways, but instead, you found a way to spare as many people as you could, though I doubt half of them deserved your mercy."

That made her feel a little bit better, but not enough to soothe her conscience completely. She'd felt that she had no choice but to intervene and respond the way she did, but she couldn't shake the feeling that she'd betrayed her people by unleashing Halvor on them—even if he'd only warned them, for the most part.

Jack was waiting in the hallway for her when she left their bedchamber, having heard the bellpull when she summoned her lady's maids. He looked like he wanted to say something, but he only stared at her, as if he were frightened of saying the wrong thing. Instead of talking, Aurelia sighed and surged toward him, the feel of his arms around her giving her the strength she'd been lacking recently.

After a moment of silence, she murmured against his chest, "Where are the children?"

"The elder four are attending their lessons. The twins have gone for a stroll around the grounds with Irina."

"I should like to see them soon."

"I'll call for them in a bit."

His body had tensed ever so slightly, so she knew there was something he wanted to tell her. She pulled away enough to look up at his face, where she was met with a taut, somewhat anxious expression.

Aurelia could only exhale. "What is it?"

Jack hesitated. "Have you eaten yet? It's a bit late for breakfast, but I can have the cooks—"

"Jack."

That made him wince. "Fiora found Rayan and I while we were taking a ride through the Folly this morning. She and the other wind nymphs spotted Kroti ships approaching Akkinor. If their estimations are accurate, we should have some visitors within the next hour or so."

A fist clenched around Aurelia's stomach. "How many?"

"Three ships from each province—fifteen in total."

"Even Runeia?"

Jack nodded, grimacing.

"I can't say I'm surprised. Even if he'd hoped to respect our alliance, Lord Swann is vastly outnumbered, and he won't choose me over Krotis." Aurelia gnawed on her lower lip, her chest tightening with worry. "You know why they're coming, don't you?"

"To make negotiations?"

She shook her head. "They'll be declaring war now that I've killed one of their own. There's no escaping what's to come, if there was ever such a chance."

"Rayan wrote to every reigning leader in the realm about Kaius Reesa's association with the Guild, and what that might mean for the entirety of Krotis." Jack rubbed her back in comforting circles as he spoke, and Aurelia wasn't sure he realized he was doing it. "We've only heard back from Reyna about it. I believe the rest of the realm wishes to remain neutral for now. They won't risk their men and their resources to stop the Guild unless there's definitive proof of Krotis's intentions. Kaius Reesa being a member of the Guild doesn't necessarily mean—"

"I know," she interrupted, her tone sharper than intended. "It's just a theory, but it's one to be taken seriously. Do you recall the story of the last time Immor visited Icareth?" He shook his head, lips pursed with curiosity, as she sighed. "It was two years before the persecution officially began. There were tensions in Quapebet at the time, brought on by the emperor's decision to have only mages and magical creatures serving in his army. The people tried to rebel, fearing the mages and the creatures would use their abilities to dominate the mortals. A group of mortals summoned Immor to the realm, offering sacrifices so he'd be swayed into defending them."

Recognition flickered in Jack's eyes. "Right. They only wanted Immor's help in restoring the balance of power across the empire, in ensuring the magical advantage wasn't used to control and demean the mortal population. Immor fulfilled their desires, but not in the way they'd expected."

Aurelia nodded. "He extended his influence to the mortals, and their desire for equality became a need for vengeance. They took up arms against the mages and magical creatures, with Immor's strength and power guiding them, and by the time they emerged victorious, almost all of Quapebet's magic was gone. It wasn't long after that Akkinor, and other countries, sought to exterminate magic, too."

"A god who can turn peaceful people into merciless killers..." Jack clenched his jaw, and for a moment, fear flickered over his face. "Imagine what he'd do to those who are already out for blood."

She shivered. "The realm may wish to remain neutral for now, but soon enough, they'll see the threat in Krotis for what it is."

"And what if we're wrong? What if it was just Kaius who's associated with the Guild, and we're accusing the whole of Krotis for no reason?"

"We're not wrong." Aurelia sank into his chest again. "If we were, we would've received a few angry letters from Lord Reesa by now. I imagine he's still furious about what I did to Kaius, of course, but he's controlling his reaction to avoid confirming any association with the Guild."

Jack's chest rumbled with laughter. "That's what the hand was for. He knows that you know about Kaius, just as he knows what conclusions you'd draw from it. One wrong move, and he'd practically be announcing to the realm that he—if not the whole of the Council—plans to replace Pherena with Immor."

Aurelia sighed. "There's only one thing left to do now."

"What's that?"

"Prepare for war."

XXVII

When the Kroti ships docked in Seaport, Aurelia expected at least three or four dozen men to arrive on her doorstep: an emissary from each province, and soldiers to protect them. Instead, only one man came to see her.

Four of Aurelia's knights escorted him to the throne room, where he knelt in front of Aurelia's throne. Jack and Rayan stood on either side of her, and two dozen soldiers flanked the perimeter of the room. Some of the soldiers were armed with bows and arrows in the event that the emissary revealed himself as a mage; if he attempted to use his power against Aurelia, he'd be shot down in the blink of an eye.

The man bowed his head as he knelt, refusing to speak until Aurelia did so first: "Why have you come alone?"

He finally met her eyes. "We thought it best, so you do not feel threatened in your own home today."

"I presume to know why you're here, so your very presence—even you alone—is a threat." She narrowed her eyes. "Who are you?"

"Firadus Treel, Your Grace. I'm the Elder of Krotis."

Only then did she realize he wasn't dressed like a highborn. His clothing was simple: a white robe held together around the waist by a golden rope, with a white turban wrapped around his head. A large golden pin bearing the symbol of Pherena—a hand holding a lit torch—connected the two ends of the rope, directly over his midriff.

"And why did *you* come, of all people?" Jack inquired, arms folded over his chest.

Firadus adjusted the spectacles on the bridge of his nose. "This is a matter of the divine. Prophecy or not, it has been proven that the gods favor Her Grace. The Iron Council believed our message would be more persuasive if it came from one with a particularly close relationship to the gods."

It has been proven that the gods favor Her Grace. Aurelia hoped he didn't notice the way she recoiled when he said it.

It was ironic: Krotis acknowledged that the gods favored Aurelia—even if that was no longer true—and yet, they still had no problem painting her as the villain of their story, as an enemy of the realm.

Aurelia cleared her throat. "You've come to tell me that Krotis has declared war on Akkinor, haven't you? That could've been achieved by sending a raven."

"Indeed, Your Grace." He grimaced. "The Iron Council has decreed that the murder of Kaius Reesa is enough to warrant a declaration of war. It is considered the highest form of indecency for a foreigner to kill a man on his native soil. That, and...Not only did you kill him, but you stripped him of his opportunity to reach the heavens. It is the belief of all Kroti that a soul cannot enter the heavens if a piece of their physical form has been removed from the whole. The Council wishes for you to know that."

Jack snorted. "He wouldn't have made it there, anyway."

Firadus ignored him. "Additionally, the Council has a message for you. The same message has already been delivered to every other leader in the realm. I was instructed to give it to you by hand, Your Grace. May I approach?"

A few knights stepped forward, warning him, but Aurelia waved them off. The Elder had been searched for anything that could harm Aurelia when he arrived, so the only weapon he had was his body. He couldn't do much while he was surrounded—not to mention, he was at least seventy years of age, and Aurelia could've fended him off without breaking a sweat.

As Firadus climbed the few short steps to the podium, Rayan took a step forward to accept the scroll in the Elder's hands. Firadus hesitated, looking like he wanted to retreat, as his nervous eyes landed on Aurelia. She saw something in his gaze that, much to her chagrin, made her trust him. She told Rayan to stand down, then held out her hand and urged Firadus to approach.

He set the scroll on her palm gently, but rather than pulling away, he curled his fingers around hers. Jack and Rayan surged forward again, but she held out her free hand to stop them. Her eyes searched the Elder's curiously, and she wasn't at all surprised to find a combination of urgency, dread, and fear burning in his gaze.

She knew that look. It was the same look she'd seen in Linden's eyes, even from across the battlefield, when he told her it was all right to let

Archie kill him. It was the same look she'd seen in the eyes of everyone who'd seen their death approaching—everyone who knew they were living their final moments.

She understood what was happening, just as she understood there was nothing she could do to help him.

Firadus released her after a few seconds, turned on wobbly legs, and descended the steps. He didn't turn around at first, but rather bowed his head and hesitated for a moment. When he finally turned, he looked older and weaker, like that short journey had drained him of life.

Jack and Rayan peered over her shoulder as she unraveled the scroll. The message wasn't addressed to anyone, but when she glanced down at the bottom of the parchment, she saw it'd been signed by the Iron Council. That alone made her queasy, but as soon as she began reading, she had to swallow her nausea.

The story told once before cannot exist in perpetuity, for a few guiding words cannot assure that all which was promised will come to fruition.

There shall come a time when all appears to be well across the earthly realm, though the reason for such peace will soon lose its sanctity.

Three cycles after the moon falls from the sky, the Four Pillars shall emerge from the shadows, and their return shall mark the end of the beginning.

The one who breathes fire will sever the realm at the edge of the world. The one who breathes the four winds will bring catastrophe but not destruction. The one who breathes the dust of stone will heal what survives. The one who breathes ice will rediscover what was lost.

One will bring about the end of existence as it is currently known. Two will be lost where time no longer turns. Three will hear the voices of the divine. Four will find strength in unity. Five will become a phoenix risen from the ashes.

Aurelia held her breath as she reread the first two sentences. Together, those lines meant only one thing to her: the prophecy that'd initiated the conflict between her and Willem, which spoke of a hero of western blood salvaging the realm, hadn't been entirely forthcoming. It must've meant that such salvation would only last for a short time, just to be broken when the one who brought it on—Aurelia—lost her sanctity, her divinity. Now that she no longer wept golden tears, that piece of the prophecy had been confirmed.

She didn't know what to make of the rest of it, but that first part chilled her to her bones.

Rayan cleared his throat. "The other leaders of the realm have this, too?"

Firadus nodded. "Yes, my lord."

"This isn't the full prophecy." Aurelia's voice cracked when she spoke, but she smoothed it out as quickly as she could. "The oracle who wrote this told me as much. Crucial pieces are missing, yet your lords thought it wise to share it with the realm, anyway."

His eyes flashed with uneasiness. "The Iron Council does not have reason to believe this prophecy is incomplete."

"Where did they find it?" Jack demanded.

"He won't tell us that." Rayan raised a curious eyebrow at the Elder. "Will you?"

Firadus's gaze met Aurelia's. Once more, she knew the look in his eyes: it was the look of a man who had nothing more to lose.

"The words were buried in an empty tomb containing nothing but the ashen remains of a fallen king."

Aurelia sighed. "Willem would've demanded that Maysa write the prophecy down for him—his tiny brain couldn't remember it. She must've found it after he died, then buried it with whatever remained of his body in the Kanish crypts. I imagine grave robbery isn't beyond what measures the Council was willing to take to retrieve the prophecy, even if it isn't complete."

Firadus gave no response to that. "There's one other message I was instructed to deliver to Your Grace."

"What is it?"

"Well..." He fiddled with his hands over his midriff, beads of sweat trickling down the sides of his face. "Lord Reesa says there is always an exchange of goods during times of war: an eye for an eye." He cleared his throat. "That's all."

A chill traced Aurelia's spine. *An eye for an eye.* But whose eye were they coming for this time?

"Thank you for your time," Rayan said to Firadus. "Our men will escort you to your carriage."

Firadus nodded, bowed, and shot one last, nervous look in Aurelia's direction. Neither she, nor Jack or Rayan, spoke until the Elder left the throne room. As soon as the doors closed behind him, an even heavier weight settled in Aurelia's gut, and she found herself pitying the poor old man almost as much as she pitied herself.

"I assume we'll be receiving a plethora of ravens in the days to come," Jack muttered, running a hand through his hair. "The other leaders won't be pleased with this. With the missing pieces, it doesn't sound so good for us."

"For *me*." Aurelia sighed. "Akkinor has nothing to do with this. It's just me."

No answer. After a few seconds of silence, Rayan said, "I wonder what the rest of Krotis will have to say about today's audience. It's not like the Elder will have anything to report back, since we didn't give him much in return."

Aurelia sighed. "They won't hear about any of it."

"How do you mean?"

"He's the Elder of Krotis. The one individual with the closest possible relationship to Pherena," she reminded him. "Didn't you see the look in his eyes? The fear? He must know about the Council's affiliation with the Guild. He has a sworn duty to serve Pherena above all others, and he won't betray the promise he made to her—and to Krotis—by supporting his leaders while they abandon her in favor of Immor. The people will need their Elder's support in accepting Immor as their Almighty, and he'll never give it to them. He has a responsibility to resist what the Council plans to do, but they won't give him the chance. I'm surprised they haven't gotten rid of him yet." She sighed again. "This was the last task they gave him. He was a dead man from the second he left this room."

***

Even though she wasn't particularly pleased with him at the moment, Lazelus was glad to see Shasta looking so well. Somehow, her husband's death—after only a day of marriage—seemed to have empowered her. It was like his loss had reminded her of what was at stake, and she, with her dragon, had become the most powerful ruler in Krotis.

The others would've disagreed, of course, but they knew it was true in their hearts. She was the key to winning this fight, and Krotis didn't stand a chance without her.

Since her wedding, she'd traded her usual, plain scarf for the type of hair covering that was deemed more suitable for a married woman of her status. A silver, diamond-encrusted hair comb sat atop her head, and silver strings adorned with diamonds and sapphires flowed down her face, back, chest, and arms as they hung from the hairpiece. Her dark hair had been pinned back in a tight bun at the nape of her neck, but it was covered by a sheer, tulle-like fabric that'd been draped over her head. The fabric came from the back of her gown, so any non-Kroti natives might've assumed it was meant to be a cape. As Lazelus knew, that fabric had been sewn into the dress specifically so a woman could cover her hair with it.

It was customary in Krotis for all men and women to conceal their hair, as hair was considered to be the most beautiful aspect of one's being—so beautiful that only one's immediate family was worthy enough to see it in its entirety. Lazelus would have loved to see what Shasta's hair really looked like, but he never would.

The Iron Council was meeting in the symposium at Sharith, as they had been nearly every day for the last few weeks. Lazelus yearned to return to Runeia, where he would no longer have to hide his distrust of his counterparts, but he knew none of them would be going home for a very long time.

When Shasta walked into the symposium—the last of the five to arrive—Lazelus nearly forgot about their last conversation, when he'd inadvertently told her that he'd sent Queen Aurelia the letter from King Willem to Amarion Selle. After he'd let it slip, a part of him hoped she'd forgive him, and that she'd understand why he did it; particularly after learning that their fellow noblemen were associated with the Guild of Steel.

Of course, she *hadn't* understood, and she'd turned to ignoring him every single time they were in the same room.

For a while there, he thought the two of them were becoming friends. Now, though, all hopes of friendship had fizzled away. It was his own fault for trying to do the right thing.

"Thank you for joining us so promptly, *Lady Selle*." Lord Reesa sneered when he said her name, as he always did, but she ignored him. She sat in her chair between Lazelus and Lord Keer, refusing to meet the former's eyes. "Now, as we're all aware, Lord Zhoqa of Kazamir is dead. His death has bought us at least eight weeks' time—if we're lucky, Queen Aurelia will refrain from inciting a battle here in Krotis while her Bozari allies are distracted by his succession. The alternative is that she proceeds, anyway, which wouldn't be in her best interest. Bozar's soldiers are perhaps the most lethal of all in the realm, and without their help, Queen Aurelia will lose more manpower than she can afford."

"She has more than enough to distract her in the meantime, anyway," Lord Quagg added. "We've ordered every Kroti businessman who trades or purchases goods in Akkinor to refrain from doing so. They managed to sway some of their associates in Caedia to do the same. They've gone to Akkinor's capital and refused to make any deals or transactions with their usual buyers, insisting they feel threatened by the plethora of beggars surrounding the shops. Many have reported growing tensions between the wealthy and the poor in the Folly since this began. The queen's new capital city has already begun to fail, and hopefully, she'll be scorned by her people if she ignores them in favor of fighting us."

"She will soon face the consequences of what she did to my dear Kaius, too," Lord Reesa muttered, feigning grief as he bowed his head and sighed. "That should be enough to occupy her for the time being."

Shasta cleared her throat. "Forgive me, but why do we need time? With Bozar and Akkinor both distracted—and Taundosa, for that matter—wouldn't this be the opportune time for us to strike?"

"We have powerful magic and strong soldiers," Lord Keer responded, "but Queen Aurelia has a dragon. So does Queen Diantha, but with Dofell still rising from the ashes, we have to assume she'll remain uninvolved in the war for the sake of her kingdom. Even so, one dragon on his own poses a significant threat to us. We need Annera to grow larger and stronger before we strike. The more time we can give her, the better."

Lazelus frowned as he thought about Shasta's little emerald dragon. The last time he'd seen her, she'd been living in the bottom of a well. Since then, she'd outgrown the well, and the elder lords had her moved elsewhere: the old fighting pit on the border of Bruila and Vrurith. The pit was completely concealed by a dome made of stone, as it had been for centuries.

The fighting pit was never supposed to exist—it went against everything the Almighty stood for—but it'd been created in secret long ago, and used to force animals and magical creatures to fight each other to the death. Nobody dared to venture there nowadays, and because it was dug several feet into the ground, it seemed like the perfect place for a fast-growing dragon who loved the warmth of the earth.

"For now, we can only hope that Queen Aurelia is smart enough to keep her distance," Lord Reesa continued. "Though we're officially at war, there's no way her people will cooperate with the efforts right now. If she can't control things in her own capital, then she's in no position to be leading her men to war. She'll be grieving for a while, anyway, giving us plenty of time to strike while she's at her most vulnerable."

Lazelus raised an eyebrow. "Who is she grieving?"

Lord Reesa's nostrils flared as his eyes hardened, but he kept his composure. "Lord Zhoqa, of course. They're allies."

"They didn't get along splendidly, from what my grandmother told me. Are you sure you aren't thinking of someone else?"

"Who are you to question your elder lord, boy?" Lord Quagg snapped.

"Never mind that. You've risen another important matter, anyway," Lord Reesa said, looking directly at Lazelus. "It's been brought to my attention that you, Lord Swann, may have delivered crucial information to the enemy. Is that true?"

Lazelus's lips parted. Dumbfounded, he flicked his gaze over to Shasta, who only stared straight ahead with her hands folded on the table before her.

"I-um—"

"We have reason to believe that you informed Queen Aurelia of what King Willem wrote to the late Lord Selle, and thus, about Annera belonging to Lady Selle." Lord Keer—the one elder lord Lazelus had hoped would see things clearly—narrowed his eyes, making Lazelus's stomach churn. "If this is true, then you have betrayed us by revealing our greatest strength. You have placed a target directly on Lady Selle's back, too."

"Judging by the way your hands are trembling, I'd say you're guilty," Lord Quagg added, snorting. "I can't say I'm surprised. Your grandmother all but betrayed us three years ago, too. She raised her heir with the same misguided loyalties."

By the time Lazelus found his voice, he could hardly get the words out. "Y-You must be mistaken. I would never—"

"You're lying, but that's all right. We don't need you to confess to know what you did." Lord Reesa rang a bell sitting on the table by his chalice, and a few moments later, a familiar face entered the symposium: Lazelus's cousin, Essino. "You remember your cousin, don't you? The son of your father's only surviving brother—other than the one who left us for Akkinor, of course. Unfortunately, your uncle can no longer walk after his spine was injured last season, so we've chosen Essino instead."

Lazelus's throat felt thick. "Chosen him for what?"

Lord Quagg blinked at him. "He's your replacement."

Lazelus's trembling hands stilled on the table, his eyes widening to the size of saucers. He looked around at the other faces in the room, and it soon became clear that all of them had planned this together—even Shasta.

"T-That's impossible," Lazelus whispered. "Such a thing has never happened before in the history of Krotis."

"Well..." Lord Reesa smirked like this was the greatest moment of his life. "You never did have an official coronation ceremony. Lady Selle's coronation was made official when she married my son, but *you* are still unmarried—as such, we cannot proceed with your coronation. The Council has decided to spare you from an arranged marriage by renouncing you as Lord of Runeia."

Lazelus looked back at his cousin, who was a year younger than him, but already married and with a child on the way. When Essino moved to cross his arms over his chest, grinning a horrid, proud grin, his sleeve shifted enough for Lazelus to see the tattoo on his wrist: the symbol of the Guild of Steel.

"You can't do this," Lazelus insisted, turning his pleading gaze to the others as he rose from his seat. "A liege lord of Krotis, officially crowned or not, cannot be succeeded unless he's dead. That's the law."

"That brings us to our last order of business." Lord Reesa's grin only widened. "Your execution is scheduled for tomorrow evening. Young Annera hasn't yet grown familiar with the taste of human flesh, but she needs to, if she's going to be of any use to us in the future. Tomorrow, we shall see what she's capable of. We might even find that she's more than ready to go to war, her size be damned."

Lazelus fell to his knees, pleading and crying in earnest as terror overwhelmed every fiber of his being. Before he knew it, soldiers were hefting him by the underarms and dragging him out of the symposium while he thrashed and howled.

The last thing he saw before the doors closed was Essino claiming his seat, and Shasta looking back at him with guilt and horror clouding her eyes.

XXVIII

urelia wasn't sure how her people would take the news about the war with Krotis. They'd been summoned to battle three times now in less than a decade, and though they'd recovered from the first two, no amount of reparations could ever truly supplement the lives lost.

To her surprise, when word spread of the call to arms three days after the Kroti fleet left Seaport, she heard nothing but good responses. Apparently, with so many mages and magical creatures on their side, the Akkinorians were eager to show off their strengths—and to defend their queen's honor after it was sullied by the enemy. Aurelia hadn't shared the prophecy with the masses, but the other leaders across the realm hadn't bothered keeping the information to themselves, so the words quickly spread like wildfire across Akkinor.

The Akkinorians didn't take kindly to the accusations being thrown at their queen, for they refused to believe she was capable of destroying the realm—even if certain parts of the prophecy seemed to suggest as much, and even given what'd happened in the capital. The rumors about the Guild were more than enough to make them eager for combat, too. No Akkinorian wanted to live in a world where the god of war influenced an entire civilization, particularly when that civilization had it out for Akkinor.

Even the people of Kalenbrar cooperated with the war preparations. Aurelia's men reported displeased whisperings from the capital about what she'd done to deescalate the fighting, but every whisper had come from the wealthy folk who wished she would've seen things as they did. Everyone else was grateful she'd intervened when she did—and just as grateful that she hadn't used Halvor to execute the six individuals, which only would've replaced her people's awe and pride with an even greater fear of him.

On the fourth day after Krotis's departure, Aurelia met Rayan in his study to discuss the precautionary measures they'd taken throughout the Folly. The palace grounds were on lockdown for the time being, meaning nobody could enter or leave without Aurelia's permission. She'd even tripled patrol across the entire kingdom, worried Krotis had left spies behind.

"I was unable to convince the Assembly to extend the lockdown to the entire kingdom," Rayan informed her. He'd given up his seat at his desk and was now sitting across from her, despite her protests. "Lady Linderli wasn't fond of the idea, either. The Follians would lose business if buyers and tradesmen were unable to reach the heart of the kingdom from Seaport, and as you know, the people have had enough concerns about losing business lately."

Aurelia grimaced. "That's all right. Have our patrolmen reported anything suspicious?"

"Not yet. Erastus Swann was kind enough to send a dozen of his men to the Folly yesterday—he believes they'd have better luck identifying any potential Kroti infiltrators. They're under orders to report directly to me if they find anyone."

"That's good," she murmured. "We have no reason to distrust any of them. They renounced their Kroti citizenship long ago, and they're well aware of the penalty for committing treason. We're fortunate to have them on our side."

Lady Swann's youngest son, Erastus, had married Dahlia Crowland, the future Lady of Myra, about eight years ago. He'd brought some of his men to Akkinor with him, and not long after he officially became an Akkinorian citizen when he was wed, his soldiers followed suit. Akkinor may have been at war with their kin and their home, but Aurelia trusted Erastus enough—and his men, by default—to know he'd never betray her.

"Indeed." Rayan cleared his throat and ran a hand through his auburn hair. "Anysa is leaving tomorrow, by the way. We have a ship departing for Khaba at dawn, and she's requested passage back home. She's going to try turning the people of Khaba back in our favor."

Aurelia forced a wry smile. "It's a valiant effort, but I'm afraid it won't do much good. They were paid to lie for Vrurith, and they won't be swayed to change their story unless I provide them with even more coin. As much as I'd like to pay them to tell the truth, that coin is better spent on our people."

"Then we must hope that Anysa's relationship with her neighbors is strong enough to remind them of their honor," he replied. That made her smile grow, but even so, she was wary. "I assume she'll be in touch when she returns. Arian wishes to go home with her, to have Reyna collect him in Khaba, but Bodren has advised against it. He's not strong enough to make the voyage yet."

Aurelia sighed. "He's a dutiful Hand—he only wishes to resume his services to Reyna as quickly as possible. But I think he's secretly glad to be stuck here for a little while longer. It's not often that he gets to visit for such an extended stay."

"He'll be heading home by the end of the season, anyway. It won't be much longer." Rayan paused for a moment, eyeing an unraveled scroll on his desk just a few inches from Aurelia's folded hands. "I was going to summon you before you found me today. We received word from Quapebet earlier this morning."

She raised an eyebrow, fidgeting with eagerness. "What have they said?"

Rayan's sour expression betrayed him, making Aurelia's heart sink. "As you know, our alliance with Quapebet is strictly economic. Though we didn't request their swords when we informed them of Krotis's association with the Guild, we had hoped they'd stand beside us—if not as allies, then as fellow lovers of peace who don't wish to see Immor granted more power in the realm. Unfortunately, the emperor refuses to believe that Kaius Reesa's affiliation with the Guild extends to the whole of the Council. The only way he'd involve Quapebet is if we establish a military and political alliance between our two countries."

"Let me guess: he won't consider such an alliance unless I promise one of my daughters to the son he doesn't yet have."

"That's right. His new wife is with child, and he's convinced the babe is a son, but how could anyone know that for sure? Even if he does have a son, you've made it clear that you have no interest in arranging marriages for your children. I don't understand why he keeps coming back to this."

"It's because he knows Halvor is loyal mainly to the women of my family. While Holly or Halyna will never claim Halvor as riders, they're still bonded to him. The emperor would be overjoyed if he had a granddaughter, and she was bonded with a dragon of old." She stifled laughter, shaking her head. "That's the only reason he'd ever be happy to have a girl in his family."

Wanting to read the emperor's message for herself, Aurelia snatched the scroll and scanned the writing. She couldn't help but roll her eyes when she saw that he'd mentioned Holly by name. He was already planning nuptials, even before he held a son in his arms. Aurelia would give anything to see the look on his face if his new wife gave birth to a daughter.

As they discussed how to respond to the emperor, the sound of boots squeaking against tiles echoed from the hallway. In the blink of an eye, the door to Rayan's study flung open, revealing a flustered Jack. Edom was perched on his shoulder, hanging on for dear life with its wiry fingers clutching Jack's shirt.

"Jack? What is it?" Aurelia inquired, rising from her seat.

"We've just gotten a raven from Orestes. It was addressed to the palace, so I opened it—I assumed it was just Lord Zhaaran's response to what we learned about the Guild." His eyes were wide, very wide, and didn't blink even once while he spoke. "He didn't say a word about the Guild. He wrote that Lord Zhoqa is dead, and has been for over a week now. Bozar has been so frenzied over it that he forgot to send word sooner."

Aurelia reached a hand out for the desk to steady herself. "What?"

"That can't be right," Rayan stated, frowning.

"It's true," Jack insisted. "A servant left Lord Zhoqa's chambers in a frenzy, hollering about an assassination. When the soldiers arrived, they found His Lordship dead on the ground, stabbed to death. His murderer was lying dead beside him, having killed himself with poison. This was just after Lord Zhoqa received a letter from Akkinor informing him about what happened in Kalenbrar."

Aurelia brought her other hand to her pounding heart. Tears welled in her eyes, but she refused to let them fall for fear of seeing clear droplets rather than gold, yet again. She wasn't sure why she felt so grief-stricken, either. Balor might've been her ally, but he was a foul man most of the time, and not always easy to be around. He was one of her least favorite acquaintances, and yet, she mourned for him.

"Why-Why did we write to him about Kalenbrar?" she asked, voice hoarse.

"The Assembly thought it prudent to inform our allies in case Krotis played a hand in instigating the civil dispute," Rayan told her. "We haven't found any evidence to confirm that theory thus far, but we hoped our allies might hear something through the grapevine. They'd already been informed of everything else—the attack in Khaba, Kaius Reesa's death, and the Guild—so Lord Zhoqa knew all of that well before he died."

"His killer was Kroti." It was Edom's voice that hissed through the air next. "If Bozar did not wish to fight before—"

"—Krotis has given them the perfect excuse," Aurelia finished, sighing. "Reyna will fight not only because she's our ally, but because Krotis targeted her Lord Hand. Kazamir and Orestes would've sent us a few troops because of our alliances, but now that Krotis killed one of Bozar's liege lords...The entire kingdom will join us. I'm just not fully understanding why Krotis cares so much about creating such a long list of adversaries."

"Bozar won't be joining us just yet." Jack grimaced as he held up the letter. "His successor hasn't been chosen, according to Lord Zhaaran. He has two sons who were born only hours apart, but to different mothers. Apparently, this isn't out of the norm in Bozar, given the popularity of polygamy, and succession depends on the day of birth alone—the brother born later that day has as much of a right to ascend the throne as the other. The two brothers have to fight to the death, and the victor will become the next Lord of Kazamir."

"So, until then, our alliance is temporarily frozen," Aurelia summarized, disappointment settling in her chest. "We can't strategize with Kazamir if they don't have an established leader. We still have Orestes, of course, but..."

"But Bozar's attention will be focused on Kazamir until the victor is announced." Rayan kneaded his temples with his fingers, his face flushed with anxiety. "At least we know for certain that all Four Lords will declare war on Krotis. It's odd, though, isn't it? Krotis has made enemies in not one, not two, but *three* kingdoms across the realm, just like Kanibar did three years ago. They could've avoided facing even more Bozari on the battlefield, yet they seem eager to gain as many enemies as possible. If their goal is to weaken you, why risk war with Bozar and Taundosa, too?"

"They went after Taundosa because they needed Arian to weaken me. It was a risk they had to take," she deduced. "As for Bozar...I don't know. There has to be something we're missing."

Edom's golden glow brightened. "Idea."

Jack snorted. "Are you going to share it?"

The sprite ignored him. "This is a holy time for Bozar. There is a protocol they must follow. They cannot involve themselves in war until this period has ended."

"What does *that* mean?" Rayan asked.

In as much detail as it could provide, the sprite explained what would happen in Bozar moving forward. Apparently, it was quite common for a nobleman to have more than one successor, resulting in a fight to the death for the position. When this happened, the entire kingdom would be placed on lockdown—meaning they wouldn't accept outside correspondences, engage in any event beyond their borders, and temporarily halt all trade and transport—for the next eight weeks. Lord Zhaaran hadn't mentioned that in his letter, likely because he assumed Aurelia, and the rest of the realm's leaders, already knew.

The two successors were always given four weeks to prepare for the fight. A fifth week was dedicated to leisure, so the successors could enjoy everything life had to offer before they potentially died in combat. On the day of the fight, everyone in Bozar ceased working out of respect for the event. When the successor emerged victorious, they spent the next week in celebration, and the last two weeks establishing themselves in their new position.

Aurelia chewed on her lower lip. "Will the same practice apply during wartime? One would think they'd excuse some of their protocol, given what caused this."

"No. Tradition is tradition," Edom insisted. "Cannot be broken."

The queen sighed. "Naturally."

***

"I wonder if he's *there.*"

Jack looked down at Aurelia as they strolled. "Vanhylde?"

She nodded.

"I would assume so," he muttered. "I imagine he'll be waiting for us when we visit again."

"*If* we visit again." Aurelia sighed. "As insufferable as he could be, I fear I'm going to miss him, oddly enough."

Jack forced a wobbly smile. "Me, too."

Aurelia glanced out the window to her right as they passed it by. It was late at night, and while most of the Folly had gone to sleep, she and Jack hadn't felt the slightest bit of exhaustion. The news of Balor's death had rattled them. Their ally had been murdered just to keep Bozar from fighting at Aurelia's side for at least the next eight weeks.

That could only mean that Krotis had something planned between now and then, and despite the call to arms, Aurelia's forces weren't prepared. How could she get a blissful night's sleep while she was both mourning for her ally, and panicking over when her enemy would strike?

Jack and Rayan had told her that it'd be wise for Akkinor to strike first, but she couldn't convince herself to agree with them. The gods had already lost faith in her, and until she was certain about what the right move was, she didn't want to do anything that might put her in an even worse position. If she made the first move, and thousands of innocent Kroti citizens died because of it...That wasn't how she wanted to win this fight.

As Aurelia and Jack walked by the rear doors of the palace, a sudden crash and bang flooded their eardrums, making them flinch and come to a halt.

"That came from the gardens," Jack said with a frown. "Do you think Halvor leveled another fountain?"

Aurelia's heart hammered. "He left to hunt twenty minutes ago. I saw him fly east toward Omara—he wouldn't have made it back so soon. He's always out hunting for at least an hour or two."

"Maybe a tree came down, then. Let's go have a look."

As soon as they opened the doors, Aurelia knew something was wrong. Nowadays, particularly after the call to arms, she had six soldiers posted at the rear entrance at all times of the day. Right now, nobody was there.

Jack immediately hollered into the palace, and in just a few seconds, four soldiers had joined the couple. Jack instructed them to stay close, then took Aurelia's shaking hand and squeezed while they took a few cautious steps into the gardens.

They hadn't made it more than a few feet from the doors when they came across three bodies. Two of the soldiers were already dead, but one was propped up against the side of a marble fountain, gasping and shuddering while pressing a bloody hand to his neck.

"Trent." Aurelia knelt down at his side, eyes welling with tears as his desperate gaze met hers. "W-What happened?"

Rayan manifested at the fountain, likely having heard the commotion. "What's going on? Trent?"

Trent wheezed for air, blood spurting from between his fingers. "S-Sh-Shed. L-Lu-Lu—"

Aurelia's heart dropped to her knees. She set a hand on the side of his face, quickly thanking him for his sacrifice, before hiking up her skirts and running toward Halvor's sanctuary. Jack, Rayan, and three of the summoned soldiers followed her, but one stayed behind with Trent.

As they ran for the back of the gardens, they passed another two bodies belonging to Aurelia's nightguards. Like Trent and the other two, they'd received wounds to the neck. As painful as it was to see what'd become of them, Aurelia didn't stop moving.

The small wooden shed, not far from Halvor's sanctuary, had been erected recently to store some of the equipment Lucyra used while caring for Halvor: giant pliers to pluck foreign objects from his feet, a wheelbarrow to collect the remains of his meals, and so on. Lucyra spent so much time in the gardens that she'd left some of her own belongings in the shed, too. Aurelia couldn't count how many times she'd found her cousin in the shed, curled up on a pile of pillows and blankets, reading against the light of a lantern.

The last of the six soldiers was lying dead on the ground a few feet from the shed, his eyes still open and wide with terror. There was another body in front of the shed's door, lying face down and wearing Akkinorian bronze armor. That was seven soldiers instead of six—one more than expected.

When she spotted a trail of blood leading to the side of the shed, Aurelia swallowed the bile that'd risen up in her throat as she followed it. A cross between a moan and a gasp escaped her when she turned the corner to find Lucyra sitting with her back against the side of the shed, her face gray and clammy, and her entire body covered in blood.

"Lu." Aurelia collapsed at Lucyra's side, her hands hovering over the enormous crimson stain on her cousin's chest. She could barely see through the darkness and her tears, but even so, she knew she'd never forget what was in front of her. "Lu-Lucyra—"

"Open your eyes, Lu." Aurelia hadn't realized that Jack was kneeling on Lucyra's other side until he spoke. Tears swam in his eyes, and the look on his face reminded Aurelia of the way she'd felt when she saw Linden die. "C-Come on now, you stubborn ass. Enough of this. Wake up."

Rayan, from his crouching position beside Jack, whispered, "I don't—"

Just then, Lucyra's dark eyes snapped open, a shuddering gasp escaping her. "Yes!" Jack hollered, gently holding her face in his hands. "Stay awake, Lu. Help is coming. We're going to get you out of here, all right? Just stay awake for me."

Lucyra's misty, wide-eyed gaze found Aurelia. "H-Hen..."

"Shh." Aurelia bit back tears as she clasped her cousin's hand between both of hers. "Don't strain yourself. You need to keep your strength so—"

"*Henry.*"

When she finally managed to get the word out, Lucyra closed her eyes, a single tear sliding down her cheek. Her shuddering chest rose and fell one last time as a final breath fled her lips. In a matter of seconds, her hand in Aurelia's went limp, and her head slumped to the side. It all happened so quickly that for a few moments, Aurelia hadn't comprehended Lucyra's last word.

"No." Jack gave her cheek a gentle tap with his palm, eyes wide and frenzied, before shaking her shoulders with more force than necessary. "Wake up, Lu. I won't tell you again. Open your damn eyes, you stubborn—"

"Jack," Aurelia croaked, choking on a sob, "she's gone."

"She's not gone. She's *not*, Lily. She can't be."

Rayan set a hand on Jack's shoulder, which Jack angrily shrugged off. Jack released a roar of frustration, climbed to his feet, and put his fist through the side of the shed. Aurelia winced, sniffling as she brushed a lock of hair from Lucyra's pretty face, and prepared to utter a small prayer for her cousin's soul—but stopped abruptly when she finally processed the last word Lucyra had spoken.

"Henry." She blinked through her tears as she looked between Jack and Rayan. "Why would she say his name?"

Rayan stared at Lucyra as he pondered. Then his eyes widened as he bent down to collect something at her side: a wooden figurine shaped like a dragon.

"This is Henry's. I gave it to him on his last name day," Rayan murmured.

Aurelia's stomach dropped, terror turning her blood to ice. "W-What was that last message Firadus gave us from Lord Reesa?"

The anger in Jack's eyes morphed into pure horror. "An eye for an eye."

XXIX

urelia, Jack, and Rayan were rushing toward the palace in the blink of an eye. They had to be sure Henry was where they'd left him earlier in the evening—asleep in his bed. Aurelia almost didn't want them to check for themselves, terrified of what they might find.

They didn't make it halfway across the gardens before they were stopped. A hoard of fairies appeared out of nowhere, fluttering around the trio's heads in an effort to stop them. Jack barked at the fairies to go away while Rayan waved his hands around his head, trying to shoo the creatures. Aurelia couldn't hear what the fairies were saying—their voices were soft and high-pitched, sometimes indecipherable, and it was impossible to understand them when eight of them spoke at the same time—but at the very least, she knew they were trying to get her attention.

"What is it?" she demanded. "Calm down and talk to me, for gods' sakes!"

The fairies immediately joined together, creating a large sphere of pink light now that they were flying close to one another, then zipped to the right toward a large strip of trees, bushes, and flowerbeds along the side of the garden wall. While Aurelia followed them immediately, Jack and Rayan paused only to tell their soldiers to check on the royal children, and to stay posted in the children's bedchambers until further notice—and, of course, to make sure Henry was still in his bed.

Aurelia didn't understand why the fairies were guiding her to the wall until their light briefly illuminated a face in the bushes, partially camouflaged by leaves and twigs. It was a woman—a tree nymph—hiding in the foliage. Only her face was visible, and it looked like she'd done something to increase what was camouflaging her: branches, twigs, leaves, and flowers were creeping out of her body, snaking around her entire being so well that nobody would've known she was there unless they were kneeling directly in front of her face.

"Willow." Aurelia crouched down, careful not to trample the nymph, as the woman sniffled. Her face had been marred by bloody scratches, and tears streamed down her cheeks. "Are you all right? What happened?"

Squeezing her eyes shut and inhaling sharply, Willow kept silent, but the branches and leaves protruding from her body began to retract. As soon as the camouflage was gone, a gasp escaped Aurelia's lips. A sleeping Henry was curled up in Willow's arms, and by the look of him, he was unharmed.

Aurelia cried out in relief. She took Henry from Willow, cradling her son as he began to stir, and squeezed him against her while Jack and Rayan helped Willow to her feet. She held him for a moment longer before handing him to Jack, who'd started reaching for their son as soon as Willow was standing.

"Take him inside," Aurelia croaked, running a hand through Henry's auburn hair. "I'll fill you in later." She turned back to Willow when Jack left with their son. The nymph was tiredly leaning against the side of a tree while wincing as she touched the scratches on her cheek. "What happened?"

"I-I was sleeping in my tree when I heard Lucyra. She was scolding the prince for sneaking out," Willow murmured, eyes misty. "I tried to go back to sleep, and that's when I heard the commotion. One of our soldiers attacked the others, using both magic and a sword. He'd already spotted Lucyra with Henry, and he demanded she give him the prince. She told Henry to run into the foliage and hide while she battled the soldier, and that's when I found the prince. I was trying to find a spot for us to hide when the soldier came after us. H-He wrestled me to the ground and clawed at me like an animal, but I'd told Henry to run, so he'd gotten away by then. The poor thing was too frightened to cry out or scream."

Aurelia's heart lurched. She'd have to talk to her son about what he'd endured tonight, but she couldn't stomach the idea of forcing him to relive such a traumatic experience.

"L-Lucyra saved me from the soldier," Willow continued. "She was badly hurt, but she regained just enough strength to strike him. I ran and grabbed Henry, and I hid us in the foliage. If she hadn't saved me, I wouldn't have had time to hide Henry. I managed to sing him to sleep somehow, by the grace of the gods, so he wouldn't hear what the soldier was doing to Lucyra. I-I heard a crash, so I knew one or both of them had fallen. I-I know I should've gone for help, but I was so frightened, and Henry—"

253

"It's all right." Aurelia brought the weeping nymph into her arms, trying as hard as she could to keep from crying, too. "You did very well, Willow. I don't know if Henry would still be here if you hadn't intervened. Thank you for protecting him."

"I tried to call for you when I heard you in the gardens. I couldn't speak. I tried and tried, but I was so afraid, and I didn't want Henry—"

"It's okay." Aurelia tried her best to calm Willow, and luckily, another tree nymph arrived to help. "Juniper is here now. She'll look after you while I check on Henry. Is there anything you need?"

Willow shook her head, shaking like a leaf as she sobbed. Aurelia wanted to stay, to offer her some sort of comfort, but she couldn't—not while her cousin and six of her soldiers were dead, her son had almost gotten kidnapped (or worse), and she still didn't know who was responsible.

That's when it hit her. She whirled around to face Rayan, who was still crying—albeit silently—after what'd happened to Lucyra. She'd almost forgotten how much Rayan fancied her cousin; after all, he was professional and a gentleman, and he rarely let his romantic feelings be known.

"The dead soldier at the shed," she whispered. "He was found closest to Lu."

Rayan was already running to the shed. She dashed after him, nearly slamming into his back when they both skidded to a stop in front of the structure. Rayan didn't hesitate to flip the soldier's body over, and even in the darkness, Aurelia saw that his head was barely attached to his body. She knew what that meant: Lucyra had attempted decapitating him before she succumbed to her wounds, but she'd been too weak to cut all the way through.

"Wait." Aurelia studied his face under the light of the moon before meeting Rayan's eyes. "Does Trent have a twin brother?"

"Not to my knowledge." He scowled as he leaned in closer to inspect the corpse. "He doesn't just look like Trent—this *is* Trent. He has the same scar under his left eye."

"But Trent was over there, by the fountain," Aurelia reminded him. "He'd never do something like this, anyway. None of my soldiers would—*oh.*"

When it struck her, she felt like someone had swung a club at her gut. She hollered at a nearby soldier—who was collecting the body of a dead comrade—and ordered him to fetch Lord Chilton, a mage and one of her advisors, from his bedchamber. While they waited for him, they stripped the soldier of his armor until he was wearing nothing but his underthings.

"Look." Aurelia lifted his wrist and squinted through the darkness. "That's the symbol of the Guild."

Rayan's lips pursed. "One of our own men was a member of the Guild?"

"I don't think he's one of ours."

"But—"

Lord Chilton scurried over, wide awake despite wearing his nightclothes and slippers. He muttered something about the incident, but Aurelia hardly heard him—she was talking over him before he could finish his sentence.

"I believe there's a glamour spell on this man's face," Aurelia told him. "Can you remove it?"

"If it's there, I can do it."

She and Rayan stepped back while Lord Chilton's glowing hands hovered over the soldier's face. She explained to Rayan what she'd learned after her time with Willem: if one wanted to glamour their entire being, they had to apply the spell to every area of concern, and it tended to be a long, painful process. It wasn't as simple as casting a spell over one's face and expecting it to work on their entire body. Willem had needed his mage to work separately on his face, hands, gut, and so on. She'd learned through her own research that a mage could glamour themselves without the assistance of others, though it was an even more strenuous ordeal.

"His armor and his gloves hid his wrist," Aurelia continued. "He didn't bother glamouring the rest of him because he didn't think we'd get the chance to inspect his body."

Rayan frowned. "Wouldn't the others have seen him and recognized him as Trent? That would've been problematic for him, given that the real Trent was on duty tonight."

"Look." She pointed to a discarded bronze helmet a few feet away. "He was wearing his helmet, for the most part. They wouldn't have seen his face unless he lost the helmet, and it doesn't look like he did so until the others were dead."

"Done." Lord Chilton stood and stepped back, sweat peppering his brow. "This man doesn't look a thing like Trent to me, Your Grace."

A chill traced Aurelia's spine. "That's it, then," she murmured. "He must've departed one of the Kroti ships when Firadus visited us. Do you know where Trent was stationed that day, Rayan?" Her Hand shook his head. "I'll bet he was patrolling Seaport, and this man just so happened to see him in passing. I don't know how he managed to fool the other guards, but..."

"He had a mission to complete. You'd be surprised at how successful someone can be if failure means death." Rayan scowled at the corpse, looking like he wished the man would come back to life just so he could kill him himself. "He must've been following Henry since he arrived, waiting for an opportune moment. It'd be difficult to flee with Henry from the gardens, so I imagine—"

"He didn't intend to flee with Henry. He intended to kill my boy on Lord Reesa's behalf." Aurelia's words stuck in her throat like tar. "An eye for an eye. A son for a son."

***

"Did anything like this ever happen to you as a child?"

"Not that I can recall." Aurelia tore her eyes from her children to meet Rayan's curious gaze. "If I was ever targeted to get at my father, I was either too young to remember it, or I didn't understand what was happening enough to be affected by it."

Rayan offered her a hopeful smile. "Sisi will remember what happened to her because she's Sisi, but Henry...He'll forget about last night. He's only five."

"I hope so." She sighed as she watched Jack play with their children in the nursery. "I suppose it's time to talk with him."

She and Rayan walked into the nursery, and while it saddened her to send her children away instead of playing with them, she'd make it up to them later on. The governesses whisked the children away, leaving a confused Henry alone with his parents and Rayan.

"Am I in trouble?" the prince asked.

"Far from it," Aurelia assured him as she and Rayan sat on the floor. She pulled him onto her lap and held one of his hands between hers. "I have some questions about what happened last night, my love."

Henry bowed his head. "It was bad to go to the gardens alone. I'm sorry."

"It's all right," Jack said, reaching over to run his fingers through Henry's hair. "While we're on the subject, though, you know better than to leave the palace on your own, especially in the middle of the night. Why did you go to the gardens?"

"I couldn't sleep. I wanted to play with Lulu."

"You managed to sneak out without anyone seeing you."

Henry sniffled. "I was very quiet."

Aurelia fought the urge to smile. "You climbed through a window, didn't you? Like Halle and Sisi did the other day."

He didn't answer her, but she knew she was right. Just a few weeks earlier, she'd caught her elder two daughters, having sneaked away from the governesses, climbing through a window on the first floor—just out of curiosity, to see if they could manage it. Henry had been watching, begging to be included, but the girls told him he was too small to climb up. Apparently, he wasn't.

"You went to the gardens to play with Lucyra, and she told you to go back inside. Is that right?" Rayan asked.

Henry nodded. "She was very upset, but she was smiling, too. I do that a lot—go see her when I'm not meant to."

"She was worried about you, even if she was honored by your visit," Aurelia murmured, choosing to ignore that last part for now. "Do you remember what happened after she told you to go inside?"

He leaned against Aurelia's chest for comfort. "I heard lots of yelling. Lulu said we were going to play hide-and-seek, and it was my turn to hide, so I went into the trees. Willow found me and said she would help me hide. Then the bad man found us, and I heard Lulu yelling, and then Willow fell down, and I ran away."

Aurelia's heart ached—both because of what her son had experienced, and because she was asking him to relive it.

"Did you hear Lucyra say anything else?" Jack questioned.

Henry shook his head. "No. Willow brought me to the bushes and said I had to be very quiet. She sang to me, but she was quiet, too. I like it when she sings to me. Lulu sings better, but not anymore. Sisi says Lulu is gone."

She met eyes with Jack and Rayan. They hadn't yet told the children the news about Lucyra, but apparently, they didn't have to. Aurelia hoped Hyacinth hadn't seen Lucyra's death for herself, and that she only knew Lucyra was gone. A part of her knew that was only wishful thinking, though. Hyacinth always saw more than what she was willing to share.

"You must have been terribly frightened," Rayan said, giving the prince a wooden ship to play with. "You were very brave, Henry."

Henry sniffled again. "Thanks."

"Before we find your brother and sisters, I've hidden something for you in the toy chest." Aurelia smiled and brushed hair from her son's forehead. "How about you go look for it?"

Henry sprung up from her lap and dashed over to the other side of the nursery, tearing through the chest with everything he had. As soon as he was out of earshot, Aurelia turned to Jack and Rayan again, lowering her voice.

"We still don't know exactly what Lord Reesa wanted his soldier to do with Henry." Talking about it made her feel sick, but she pushed the nausea aside. "It's possible he would've done what Willem did with Hyacinth: use Henry as a bargaining chip to force my hand. I don't want to believe that Krotis has lost sight of its values so much that they'd stoop to murdering a five-year-old boy, but Firadus's message..."

"We have to assume Lord Reesa gave the order to have Henry killed," Jack insisted, his eyes igniting with rage. "Since he appears to have such a strong association with the Guild, I doubt Pherena's values mean anything to him anymore. Ordering the murder of a little boy is certainly what Immor would do during wartime."

"We all know what this means," Rayan said lowly. "We may not have Bozar fighting alongside us in the near future, but we have Taundosa, at the very least. Reyna won't hesitate to send her men to battle after what Krotis did to Arian, especially now that she knows about the Guild. But what about Diantha?"

Aurelia winced. "I think she'd come to our aid if absolutely necessary, like she did in Khaba. But I don't believe she'd take up arms against Krotis. We can send word, anyway, but it's likely a lost cause. She has no sworn obligation to fight beside us, and while Dofell has come a long way, the kingdom hasn't fully recovered yet. It would hinder Dofell's progress if she sent what few soldiers she has to war."

"Quapebet refused to join the fight, too, but we haven't heard back from Glacier Bay yet," Rayan added. "There's hope for them still."

"I doubt they'll help us. The Isalders care for nobody but themselves."

Jack sighed. "So it's just us and Taundosa for now—and possibly Diantha, but she'd only know that we need her help in battle—*Rieza's* help—if something happens to Halvor."

"I found it!" Henry rushed back to his parents and Rayan, proudly holding up his new toy—a stuffed bear with a blue bow around its neck. "Is this the one?"

Aurelia forced a smile. "That's it. I thought he would be nice for you to snuggle with while you sleep. He'll protect you."

Jack lifted Henry onto his shoulders as the group left the nursery to find the rest of their family. The children were sitting on the floor in the morning room, the governesses taking tea by the window, while Arian sat on the couch and told them a story. Anysa was gone by now, but she'd left the children with a treat: a story she'd written down in a journal for Arian to share with them in her absence.

Henry rushed over to join his siblings, clutching the bear to his chest, and skillfully ignored Halyna when she asked if she could have the toy. Halle, ever the dutiful eldest sibling, sat herself between them, hushing her little sister when Halyna began whining in protest. The twins crawled around the floor, ignoring their siblings and their great-uncle's story, and entertained themselves by playing with the rug. Hyacinth looked over her shoulder at them every so often, like she was worried they'd start eating the rug's shaggy fabric.

Arian smiled at the adults in the doorway, but he didn't stop reading from Anysa's storybook. His smile wasn't the same as it usually was, though. It seemed like everyone who lived in the palace had lost their glow since Lucyra's passing.

With all the chaos, it'd been difficult for Aurelia to be present today. Only now, as she reflected on everything she'd seen and heard in passing, did she realize the toll Lucyra's loss had taken on the palace. Rayan's three children—Alexandria, Nereida, and Brooks—hadn't gone for their morning stroll like they usually did, claiming it'd be too painful to walk through the gardens without being scolded by Lucyra for distracting her while she worked. It was always in good fun, of course, and she'd dropped her stern facade as soon as she knew she'd succeeded in making them sweat.

The cook had been late preparing breakfast that morning. Lucyra always visited the kitchens before sunrise to fetch Halvor's morning treat—a whole, raw chicken—and apparently, the cook had been waiting for her like usual, only to be told by a scullery maid that Lucyra was dead. He'd sat at a table in the kitchens and wept for hours, leaving the scullery maids to take over for him.

Handmaidens, footmen, and soldiers alike had been comforting each other in the halls all day, sniffling and weeping. They'd talked about how much they'd miss Lucyra's snarky quips and clever jokes. They'd even shared their regrets about how they hadn't told her how much they enjoyed having her around while she was alive.

There were so many things Aurelia wished she could've told her cousin, too, but how was she to know they'd only get three years together when the young, healthy woman should've had several decades more to live?

"I have a few letters to write," Aurelia said softly, turning away from Arian and the children. She took Rayan's hand and squeezed. "Take the rest of the day to grieve, my friend. I-I know how much you cared for her."

Rayan's glassy eyes were bloodshot, as they had been since last night. "Thank you."

"The Assembly is overseeing the memorial," Jack said hoarsely. "I'll join them to make sure everything is planned as Lu would've wanted it."

A sharp pang pierced Aurelia's heart. "Remind them that she—"

"—wished to be placed in a wooden casket atop the highest hill in the kingdom, where Halvor can ignite her remains for all to see." He chuckled a little, but the sound was choked and painful, like he was being stabbed in the gut. "She liked to make a spectacle."

Aurelia forced a smile, took Jack's hand as well as Rayan's, and squeezed both of them before walking away. As the trio set out in different directions, Halvor shrieked from somewhere on the grounds, mourning for Lucyra as much as the humans did.

***

Thinking about Lucyra's premature death made Aurelia reflect on all of the things she wished she'd told her cousin when she had the chance. Rather than saying all of it to Lucyra's remains, Aurelia wrote it down in a letter, intending to leave the parchment inside of the casket before Halvor set it ablaze.

It was funny: if things had happened differently, it was entirely possible that Lucyra would've been Halvor's mistress instead of Aurelia. Lucyra's grandmother, Veryna, had been the younger sister of Aurelia's grandfather, Lord Dyron Cristos of Agotia. For some reason, she'd never been able to bond with Halvor—he'd rejected her over and over again, and nobody knew why. He'd refused her so greatly that the locket containing him had seared her flesh whenever she wore it. Even Dyron and Veryna's grandmother didn't understand why Halvor disliked Veryna.

When Dyron wore the locket, however, all was well. He, Veryna, and their grandmother—according to Arian's tales—had even released Halvor together once in the Ngora Valley. Halvor had wanted nothing to do with Veryna, but he'd adored Dyron. It was odd: he was loyal to the women of the Cristos family, yet he'd chosen Dyron over Veryna.

Arian liked to say it was because Halvor knew what was to come in the future: Dyron's granddaughter would become Forged in Gold, with a destiny to restore the realm to its former glory. The gods prevented him from bonding with Veryna so he'd end up with Aurelia.

Aurelia wondered what would've become of her if Halvor hadn't rejected Veryna Cristos all those years ago. She wondered what would've become of Lucyra, too. With that in mind, she wrote an apology to Lucyra—despite her cousin insisting she didn't resent Aurelia, as it was nobody's fault Halvor had rejected Veryna. Even so, a part of Aurelia felt guilty that she had been born to inherit the realm's greatest power, while Lucyra, her mother, and her grandmother were snubbed from their birthright.

Of course, thinking about things she wished she'd done differently brought her back to when she'd failed Arian when she last visited

Taundosa. She'd tried asking Arian about Shale after he woke, but he hadn't seemed willing to go into detail about it. Instead of pushing him, she'd used her connections to help locate Shale. She'd been given his full name and his address the day Firadus arrived in Akkinor, but she hadn't had time to do anything with it.

Regardless of Arian's reasons for not wanting to talk about everything, Aurelia knew she had to do something about it. Arian clearly still cared for Shale, given the request he'd made to Linden and Aurelia, and it didn't feel right that he'd only planned on reaching out to his former lover again posthumously. Even if they'd both moved on, Aurelia was certain Arian would want to see Shale again—after all, this could've been the last chance they got.

She crafted a brief letter for Shale, explaining what had happened to Arian and what her uncle wished for her to do in the event of his death. Though Arian was alive and well now, she told him that she was certain Arian would be pleased to see him again, if he felt the same way. Hopefully, Shale would write back confirming his interest, and in a few weeks, the former lovers would be reunited in the Folly.

Perhaps it wasn't wise to meddle in Arian's affairs. Perhaps he didn't wish to see Shale again in life, and he'd only wished to do his old love the courtesy of being informed of his death. Either way, contacting Shale was the one thing Arian had asked Aurelia to do for him if he died; she couldn't imagine he'd be displeased if they were reunited.

After writing and sealing the letter, she set it atop the letter meant for Lucyra, then stretched her fingers and cracked her knuckles as she prepared to craft one last message.

At first, the only thing she could think to write was six words on the envelope: *For the one who succeeds me.*

The rest was writing itself before she knew what she was doing. She tried not to cry as her quill danced along the parchment, wondering if she had any right to craft this message now that her destiny had forsaken her. Still, she minded Maysa's voice in the back of her head, knowing she still had a responsibility to the realm, even if the gods no longer demanded it of her.

The letter wouldn't be sent until after Aurelia was gone, so she'd hide it away in a drawer, leaving instructions for her family to deliver the message on her behalf when Halle took her place as Queen of Akkinor.

She signed the letter, folded it, and sealed it inside of the envelope. She held the envelope in her hands for a moment, staring at the six words, and prayed to the gods that she was right about the identity of the woman she'd seen in her vision—the teenage girl with white hair and silver eyes.

XXX

Three days after Lucyra's death, her memorial took place exactly as she'd wished for it. Her casket had been placed atop the highest hill in the Folly, while mourners gathered on the valley below it. There weren't many people other than those who lived in the palace—and a few Follians who'd sold goods to Lucyra over the years—but Aurelia knew Lucyra would've wanted her memorial to be intimate, anyway.

After Aurelia said a few words, and a priest led a prayer for Lucyra's soul, Halvor shot up from the ground on the other side of the hill. He circled the hill a few times, then ignited the casket with a powerful stream of fire. He hovered in the air as the casket smoldered, releasing a grief-stricken shriek, before returning to the palace. By the time the fire extinguished itself, nothing remained but the nails used to build the coffin.

The hill had been nameless, so Aurelia decided to change that. Now, it would be known as *Lucyra's Knoll*—a geographical landmark that sat between Kalenbrar and the northernmost part of the Folly. As soon as the smoldering remains were no longer a danger to her people, Aurelia would order her best stonemasons to craft a headstone and place it atop the hill in Lucyra's honor.

By the time the mourners left, only Aurelia, Jack, Rayan, and Arian remained with a handful of soldiers. They were preparing to leave when Jack asked for a few moments alone. Aurelia obliged, but she hadn't expected him to start climbing the steep hill. Arian and Rayan, exhausted by their grief, returned to the carriage while Aurelia followed her husband, using the thick shoeprints he'd left in the grass and dirt to gain traction while she climbed.

She was breathless when she reached the top to find Jack kneeling by the smoldering remains. It was terribly hot, even for her, but he didn't seem to mind it. Neither did Edom, as the creature was perched on Jack's shoulder, dabbing at its eyes with a leaf from its garments. Aurelia knelt beside them, her heart aching as she stared at the blackened grass where Lucyra's casket had been.

"I know I didn't know her as long as you knew Linden," Jack said hoarsely, "but...but I think I finally understand how you felt when you lost him. How you still feel."

The fist around her heart only clenched tighter. "I-I'm glad you two grew as close as you did. I used to pity you—not because you deserved it, but because I've always felt so sorry for anyone who's never known such powerful friendship. Linden was the brightest light in my life for five-and-twenty years, and it always pained me that you'd never had a friend like that."

He nodded in understanding, his eyes glassy and bloodshot. "Do you remember the first thing she said to me? After she'd healed me in Dofell, and I thanked her for it."

Aurelia snorted into a laugh as she quoted her cousin: "'Arian says you're one of the greatest swordsmen he's ever seen. I highly doubt that, since I spent half the day saving your incompetent ass from meeting the gods.'"

"I knew then she'd become a good friend. Not many people are willing to talk that way to a stranger, let alone a stranger who outranks them." He was smiling, but it wasn't a joyous expression in the slightest. "She felt like a sister to me, like someone I'd known my entire life. She once told me that she never wished for a brother, but if she ever did, she'd want him to be exactly like me."

Aurelia's lower lip trembled. She was glad he wasn't looking at her so he wouldn't see how hard she was trying to keep her emotions in check. He would've understood if she cried, of course, but that wouldn't have done much to help him—and in this moment, she had to prioritize his grief over her own. After all, she knew exactly what it was like to lose a best friend.

"You'll meet again, some day," Edom said to Jack. "I know it."

Jack sniffled. "I know it, too."

Aurelia set a comforting hand over his on his thigh. "I'll give you a few moments, but we should be heading home shortly. I-I want to set sail for Krotis soon. Bozar or not, after what Krotis did to Lucyra—and what they intended to do to Henry—I can no longer sit idly by and wait for them to make the first move. They won't expect us to strike first without the full force of our alliances backing us, so it'd be wise of us to attack when they least expect it."

He nodded in understanding. "If you delayed this any longer, I think Lu's spirit would torment you for it. She was the vengeful sort, wasn't she?"

"Indeed she was," Aurelia agreed, smiling. "Do you remember when she put a garden snake down the back of your shirt after you cheated while the two of you were sparring?"

"How could I forget?" The pair laughed, but it died down quickly, and Jack's face became somber again. "Gods. I'm going to miss that insufferable woman."

Aurelia pressed a soft kiss to his cheek. "So am I."

***

Less than a week after Lucyra's death, Aurelia watched from one of the palace balconies as her soldiers—mages and mortals from across Akkinor—marched for Seaport. Those who'd traveled a great distance hadn't been in the Folly for a full day before they set out for the ships. As soon as the troops from the other side of Akkinor arrived, the time to set sail for Krotis had come.

Aurelia wanted nothing more than to stay at home for the next few weeks, grieving her cousin, holding her children close, and keeping an eye on things on her own soil. But after what Krotis had done in the last week alone, they'd given her no choice. She had no intention of sitting on her throne for the next few weeks, waiting for Bozar to confirm that the entire kingdom would fight by her side, while that meant giving Krotis plenty of opportunities to strike.

Reyna had agreed to send her troops to meet Aurelia's at the border of Taundosa and Krotis—more specifically, the province of Runeia. There was a harbor on the southern coast of Taundosa where Aurelia's fleet would dock, as it was less than a day's journey by foot from the harbor to Runeia. She'd thought about bringing the fighting directly to Vrurith, as the Reesa family seemed to be orchestrating this mess, but that wouldn't have been wise: for one, Krotis would've seen Reyna's troops marching across their kingdom; and for another, she wanted Runeia—and Lord Swann—to remember that they'd betrayed their ally when they found themselves fighting Akkinor on their own land.

Even if this wasn't what Aurelia had planned for, she was confident in her success. Shasta Selle's dragon was too small and inexperienced to stand a chance against Halvor, particularly if Diantha and Rieza decided to join the fight. Krotis may have had stronger mages than Akkinor did, too, but Akkinorians were better fighters, and even half of Aurelia's army was larger than all five Kroti armies combined.

"I don't know what we've been so worried about." Jack's voice rang out, pulling Aurelia from her thoughts, as he joined her on the balcony. His eyes were trained on the sea of bronze marching past the palace toward Seaport. "We're stronger than Krotis in every way that matters."

She sighed. "They have far more mages than we do, and their magic is more powerful. That alone poses a significant threat."

"Still, though. We have more men—stronger men—and an ancient dragon capable of leveling their entire kingdom."

"That's why all of this started," she reminded him. "They believe that's exactly what Halvor will do, and that it'll set the stage for the realm's destruction. I know we can defeat them, Jack. It's just a matter of containing what we inflict upon them, so the prophecy doesn't come to fruition."

He furrowed his eyebrows. "Most prophecies, if not all, come to fruition. It's the word of the gods, after all. If it's meant to happen, it will happen. We can't control any of it."

Aurelia winced. "I suppose it's less about *what* happens, and more about *how* it happens. It's like what Archie said about the matter of interpretation." She peeled her eyes from the troops and raised an eyebrow at him. "Are you ready to go?"

Jack squared his shoulders. "Always."

They'd already said goodbye to their children, and it'd been unexpectedly reassuring. When Hyacinth hugged them, she'd said, "You're going to tell us a great story when you get back." Though neither Aurelia nor Jack knew what she meant, it seemed like Hyacinth had seen their success and their safe return.

"Before we go," Jack continued, "something's been bugging me. I understand why Krotis has made so many enemies, but even so, both of their reasons are foolish ones. Why take such risks when they know the combined forces of Akkinor, Taundosa, and Bozar could destroy them?"

"My allies would've fought alongside us no matter what, as per our contracts. But while Willem wanted to fight all of us so he'd be seen as the hero who succeeded against unbeatable odds, I think Krotis merely hopes to eliminate their competition. Their end goals are the same, but their motives are different."

"How do you mean?"

She toyed with the ends of her braided hair, an uneasiness settling in her gut. "Krotis is the smallest kingdom in Carthe. It's never once been seen as a powerhouse in the realm—its Almighty is too passive. With Pherena guiding them, they've never been taken seriously, and they've never been seen as a threat." She exhaled, shaking her head. "Willem wanted to conquer the continent. Maybe Krotis wishes to do the same, and they don't stand a chance without Immor. If they manage to appoint him as their Almighty, he'll eliminate their greatest threats, and he'll give them the power they need to conquer Carthe. Taundosa and Bozar are the strongest forces in the west, as they have been for centuries. If I wanted to conquer Carthe, I'd start with them."

"It all comes down to power, doesn't it? Every time."

"Every time." She tried to smile, but she could feel her lips trembling as she did so. "Willem got inside their heads. They've now set out to do what he couldn't. I just can't believe that all five leaders of Krotis have come to the same conclusion."

"Maybe they haven't," he offered. "We have to assume that Lazelus Swann sent Willem's letter to you. And Shasta Selle..."

"She's young enough that the other lords can dominate her if she isn't clever. And if she's anything like me, she'd trust her father's word no matter what. Her father seemed to be supportive of this—he was the one who started everything, wasn't he? With Willem's letter."

Jack grimaced. "So, you don't think you could talk some sense into her if you were given the chance?"

"No." Aurelia sighed and clenched her jaw. "I want to try, but I don't think she'll be willing to listen."

***

"You lied to me."

Lord Reesa laughed as he poured himself a tall glass of gin. "Pray tell."

"You said we would force him to abdicate, and then we'd exile him." Shasta folded her arms over her chest, disrupting the strings of diamonds cascading over her body. "You never said a word about executing him, nor about using Annera to do it. I never would've—"

"What? You never would've told us that one of our own betrayed us?" he demanded. Her face burned as she turned her gaze to the tiled floor, silent. "To exile is to banish an individual from their homeland. The realm is our homeland, first and foremost, and the only way to banish one from our world is to execute them. Krotis has spent centuries showing mercy and leniency to traitors, and we cannot afford to be seen as weak during a time like this. Lazelus Swann's fate was inevitable."

She shook her head. "I had a right to know."

266

"Yes, you did," he agreed, surprising her, "and it was our mistake for failing to inform you."

"You should have asked my permission before using Annera as an executioner, too."

Lord Reesa's eyes hardened as he sipped from his goblet. "You would not have agreed to it."

"No, I wouldn't have," she admitted, lifting her chin. "There are countless methods of execution. Why choose Annera?"

"I've already told you. Annera has had no combat training, and frankly, we're unable to provide it. Nobody alive knows how to train a young dragon for combat. At the very least, we had to ensure she's capable of taking human lives. We needed to get a feel for her abilities, too. Now we know exactly the kind of damage she can inflict on our enemies. She'll be hungry for human flesh now that she's had a taste of it, and soon enough, she won't be able to fight the urge to wreak havoc upon those we send her way."

Shasta shivered. "That's barbaric."

Lord Reesa only grinned, and the maniacal expression frightened her enough to make her take a step backward. It was just the two of them in Sharith's symposium, and while she didn't particularly care for the other lords, she'd never yearned for their presences more than she did now. Darius Reesa may have been traditional enough to refrain from raising a hand against a woman, but as many knew, his words were as dangerous as his fists.

When Shasta told the elder nobles that Lord Swann had betrayed them, they'd promised her that he would be justly tried and punished. But she'd wanted him reprimanded and stripped of his throne, not murdered by her dragon. She felt terribly for what'd happened, but at the same time, she knew there was a price to be paid for treason.

Other than flying, Shasta hadn't seen any of Annera's abilities until the day of Lazelus's execution, when the Council brought him to the old fighting pit. It was a horrid sight: a soldier had placed a string of raw meat around Lazelus's shoulders, then pushed the poor young man—blindfolded, and with his hands bound behind his back—into the pit while the others watched from the entryway. Shasta hadn't wanted to watch what her dragon was going to do to someone she'd once considered a friend, but curiosity compelled her to keep her eyes trained on the scene.

At first, Annera only circled him, sniffing at the air and making a low, growling sound in the back of her throat. Lazelus hadn't stopped trembling and begging for mercy since they arrived at the fighting pit, and when Annera released her first growl, his knees buckled, causing him to land face-first on the dirt. He'd managed to lift himself up to his knees just in time for Annera to roar in his face. The roar made the entire pit—and the surrounding woodlands, according to soldiers standing guard—tremor, even causing a few stone slabs to break off from the dome.

To everyone's surprise, Annera had gotten close to Lazelus, drool dripping from her jaws, only to snatch the string of meat and carry it away. The lords were disappointed by her behavior and demanded that Shasta command her to kill Lazelus. Shasta couldn't bring herself to do it.

But the soul bond between dragon and rider (even if Shasta hadn't actually ridden Annera yet) was stronger than Shasta thought. Annera had stopped eating and lifted her head from the meat, like a hound sensing danger approaching. She'd met Shasta's gaze, and in that moment, Shasta knew that Annera was aware of what she was meant to do. Though Shasta disapproved of it, she feared the other lords enough to oblige—even deep in her soul, where they couldn't reach her.

Something had compelled Shasta to step even farther back from the entryway, prompting the others to follow suit. As soon as she was completely out of harm's way, Annera faced a trembling Lazelus and bellowed. Shasta expected flames to spew from the dragon's mouth, but instead, something else happened: tiny fragments of stone and dust crept up Annera's throat and flew through the air at the speed of light, immediately tearing Lazelus's flesh to shreds. It was almost like an enormous glass window had shattered in front of him, the shards mercilessly ripping through his body until he collapsed in a bloody, meaty heap.

The one who breathes the dust of stone. It was right there in the prophecy. When Shasta thought about the rest of the prophecy, paired with the stories the Vrurithian sailors had told about Queen Diantha's dragon in Khaba, she realized dragons had elemental specialties, just like mages. Shasta herself was an earth mage, and naturally, Annera was an earth dragon. It was no wonder Annera liked to be as close to the earth as possible.

"What happened to Lazelus Swann was...unexpected, but interesting, to be certain." Lord Reesa's voice pulled Shasta away from her thoughts, the image of Lord Swann's mangled remains fading away. "As gruesome as it was, he didn't appear to suffer for very long."

Shasta cleared her throat. "Maybe so, but—"

"My lord. My lady." One of Lord Reesa's advisors, who'd entered the symposium so quietly that neither noble had heard him, bowed and grimaced. "I have troubling news. One of our scouts in Khaba has reported an Akkinorian fleet approaching the continent. It appears to be about a day away."

"What?" Lord Reesa's lips parted, shocked, as Shasta gasped and clutched her heart. "That's impossible. That woman has to be the maddest person alive to come after us now after—"

"Forgive me for interrupting, my liege, but that's not all. We have yet to receive a report from Rhello Teek. He was meant to send word from Akkinor when his mission was complete. It's been some time since then. We must assume he failed, and is now dead."

"Or he succeeded, and he was caught. No," the nobleman muttered to himself, shaking his head. "If he succeeded, the queen would be too overwhelmed by grief to lead her men to war. Unless, of course, she isn't with them. Did our scout happen to spot the dragon?"

"No, my liege."

"There's still hope in Teek's success, then. I should hope he managed it—an eye for an eye." Lord Reesa's lips curled into a grin. "Or, shall I say, a hand for a hand."

"What are you talking about?" Shasta said.

The two men looked at her, then at each other, as if they'd forgotten she was there. "It's nothing for you to be concerned with," Lord Reesa replied. "You might as well go fetch Annera, Lady Selle. It would appear the time has come to officially reveal her as ours. I'll inform the others while you're gone."

Her heart hammered. "This is it, then? We're going to war?"

"You will command Annera from a safe distance. You have no combat training, and we cannot risk losing Annera's rider during her first battle. But yes—we're going to war. Tomorrow or the day after, if our scout's estimation is correct." He made an impatient gesture with his hand. "Go on, then."

Shasta glowered, unable to hide her displeasure, but did as she was told. As she walked to Sharith's exit so she could fetch Annera from the fighting pit, she wondered what more her fellow lords weren't telling her— and why they were keeping it from her. If they won this battle, and she proved herself as a worthy ally by commanding Annera as they desired, maybe they'd be convinced to include her in the future. After all, the five of them were equals; if they didn't start treating her as such, she'd have to remind them somehow.

XXXI

When Aurelia's fleet arrived in Taundosa, the first thing she saw was a sea of gold gathered at the border of the harbor. Reyna wasn't there to lead her troops, but she'd sent more than enough soldiers to frighten Krotis out of their wits.

Rayan had stayed at home to rule in Aurelia's absence, leaving her, Jack, and their war generals to command the troops. None of Akkinor's nobility had joined the fight, either. They hadn't told her why, so she'd come to her own conclusion: they'd rather sit at home on their thrones while servants shined their shoes and filled their cups, instead of being caught in the crossfire when two dragons were pitted against each other.

As much as she disapproved of their cowardice, she understood. She understood why all of her soldiers, and even Reyna's, were trembling in their boots, too. To fight beside a dragon was one thing, but to fight against one was something else entirely.

The skies were clear, so Annera hadn't come to spy on or threaten them before the battle, assuming the Kroti knew by now that Akkinor was on its way. Halvor wasn't there, either. Aurelia had a plan for him, and part of that plan relied on the Kroti believing Aurelia hadn't joined the fight— because everyone knew she wouldn't march to battle without her dragon.

She'd thought about it extensively on the two-week-long voyage to Carthe. Jack had proposed that she try to speak with Shasta Sella, that maybe, just maybe, the Lady of Bruila could've been swayed into pulling Annera from battle. Aurelia didn't believe Shasta would listen to her, but at the same time, she knew what it was like to be at the mercy of powerful men. If not because of her father's friendship with Willem, then Shasta's efforts to destroy Aurelia were because her fellow lords demanded it of her. Aurelia hoped that Shasta could be convinced to see things clearly and objectively, but that was only possible if someone who'd been in Shasta's shoes once before was able to reach her ear.

Aurelia also knew that women in Krotis were never trained for combat—even noblewomen. The Council needed Shasta nearby to command Annera, but they'd never let her get close to the battlefield or ride on Annera's back. They'd hide her someplace where she was close to Annera, yet not so close that her life was at risk. If Aurelia could find her and speak with her while the others believed she was missing, she stood a chance at swaying Shasta in the other direction.

If not, Halvor would pick her up, and the two of them would join the fighting as they always did.

Once all of Aurelia's troops were on land, they met with Reyna's soldiers and began marching toward the border of Taundosa and Runeia. Jack and Lord Chilton—Aurelia's advisor, a mage, and a seasoned war veteran—led the troops. Aurelia marched alongside her soldiers, blending right in as she walked shoulder-to-shoulder with the men and women who'd answered her call to arms.

The woman to her left said to her, "Do you hear that, Your Grace?"

Aurelia frowned. "Our footsteps?"

"No." The woman grinned. "Hissing."

Aurelia strained herself to hear it, and after a few moments, she did. It was, indeed, hissing. She knew that sound—Edom often made it when the creature was cross with her. As she observed her surroundings, she saw tiny balls of golden light floating around her troops, staying close to the ground.

At the same time, while they marched through a heavily wooded area, she spotted faces partially camouflaged by the foliage and the shadows. The faces weren't quite human, but close enough to be mistaken for human. *Centaurs,* she thought. And when she took a closer look, she saw additional humanoid faces behind the centaurs—likely perched on their backs—brandishing axes. These faces were rather horrid, unpleasant to glimpse at by no fault of their own, with extremely long noses, beady eyes, and razor-sharp teeth. Goblins.

The creatures were letting the troops pass through peacefully, and when Aurelia looked over her shoulder after passing them by, she saw a few of them—only goblins and sprites—slip into the ranks, hiding within the sea of humans. She knew that Jack, wherever he was while leagues ahead of her, had seen them, too. She could practically see the smile on his face, and she had to resist the urge to roll her eyes when she pictured him gloating.

These were some of the creatures he'd freed from Vanhylde. She had to assume that a portion of them had gone to Krotis if the kingdom was their ancestral home, but the ones who'd stayed in Taundosa were eager to fight for the man who'd freed them.

The centaurs and half of the goblins hadn't left the woods, so she knew they'd make a grand entrance. Even so, they didn't stand much of a chance against Runeia's gryphons, and Aurelia was sure Krotis would deploy the creatures as soon as they could.

When they crossed the border into Runeia, they immediately heard commotion from the east. The Kroti clearly knew to expect them, and while they'd come to Runeia like Aurelia hoped, it seemed like they'd chosen a less-than-agreeable location for the battlefield. They were luring Aurelia's troops toward the coast instead of inland, using Krotis's unique geography to their advantage.

As the foliage thinned, the Kroti troops came into view, though they were still a ways away. Aurelia couldn't tell if it was the distance or their formation that made their army look so large, but either way, their numbers seemed to mirror hers. There was no sign of Annera, though, or Shasta.

As opposed to other parts of Krotis that were elevated, like Vrurith, the eastern coast of Runeia sat at sea-level. The troops were gathered on the beach, the sunlight twinkling against the ocean behind them. As Aurelia and her army inched closer, she saw that some of Krotis's troops were positioned on a sandbar several yards behind the others. Those soldiers would wait for the opportune moment to join the fighting, and it'd be difficult for Aurelia's forces to get to them, especially when the tide came in. The Kroti were probably skilled at wading through water in armor, given their place of birth, but Aurelia's forces were not.

Aurelia was forced to stop when she nearly collided with the person in front of her. Everyone had stilled by then, and while there was still a decent-sized gap between the warring parties, they were close enough that Aurelia could see four of Krotis's five leaders standing at the frontlines.

"Surprised to see us?" When Jack's voice rang out, as loud as if he were standing at Aurelia's side, she knew Lord Chilton had cast an amplifier spell on her husband's voice. "You shouldn't be. You sent an assassin after my five-year-old son three weeks ago. You had to know we'd retaliate against such an unforgivable act."

"Ha!" Aurelia didn't recognize the voice that cackled in response, but something in her gut told her it was Lord Reesa. "It was your wife who came after my son first. There's a debt to be paid when such atrocities are committed. It was meant to be a peaceful audience, and yet, your wife sealed your son's fate when she did the same to mine."

"It was your insufferable spawn's fault for thinking he could kill a dragon," Jack shot back. The fire in his voice made Aurelia shiver. "I suppose it's an understandable delusion, given his loyalties. He must have hoped that Immor would favor him—and Krotis—if he managed to kill the unkillable. But the Guild of Steel hasn't been successful thus far, has it? And why on earth would Krotis, of all places, think they could conquer Carthe? Hmm?"

"Enough of this!" another Kroti man shouted. Aurelia assumed it was one of the other lords, but she didn't know which one. "You kill one of our own on his native land, abuse his body as he lay dying, and have the audacity to battle us on our own soil without a proper warning. What if we hadn't seen you coming? Would you have laid siege to our kingdom, slaughtering innocents? You've proven nothing but your willingness to let Krotis fall—and the entire realm, for that matter."

He wasn't entirely wrong. The realization made Aurelia's stomach churn.

"You know exactly why we're here, and it isn't to destroy Krotis," Lord Chilton retorted. "You have painted our queen as a villain on your quest for power, and you have committed unspeakable horrors against three kingdoms. Not to mention, many of you are allied with the same people you've either killed, threatened, or incapacitated. Good, honorable people are dead because you've jumped to conclusions on an incomplete prophecy. Admit your wrongdoings, beg forgiveness for what you've done, and lay down your swords here and now if you wish to avoid bloodshed."

Lord Reesa cackled. "What fools you are! If we were going to surrender, we would only kneel before your queen. She is the Akkinorian equivalent of the Iron Council, and we will not kneel to the meager subordinates she's sent in her place. But alas—she has chosen to stay home and grieve what we had every right to take from her. What kind of commander sends their soldiers to war while they cower in their palace?"

Aurelia gritted her teeth. She wanted nothing more than to push through the soldiers in front of her to prove him wrong, but it would've been pointless. They'd never surrender, anyway, and she'd lose all hope of talking to Shasta.

"You're even more dense than we thought," Jack snarled. "You accuse a champion of the gods of seeking to destroy the realm, yet you've shown us all that you're the true threat to our world. If and when you do what we know you will, the realm will turn on you, and you'll be the masters of your own destruction."

Just then, a shriek echoed in the near distance, making the troops nervously shift their weight and mutter to one another. Aurelia's heart pounded as she looked for the source, and the organ practically fell to her knees when Annera flew over her head, demanding attention with her vibrant green scales. She was much bigger than she had been when she visited Akkinor: before, she'd been the size of a small writing desk, and now, she appeared to be about the length of three massive centaurs put together. She was certainly large enough to bear a rider now, but she was still much smaller than Halvor.

Annera landed on the ground between the warring parties, and as soon as she roared at Aurelia's troops, an enormous cloud of sand blew in their direction. It reminded Aurelia of the sandstorm that'd struck the Ngora Valley when she and Jack had stopped at the desert inn eight years ago. They hadn't been outside during the event, of course, but they'd seen the thick cloud of brown dust through their bedroom window. Even Halvor would've been undetectable during such a storm.

Aurelia and those around her quickly turned around, shielding their faces and grimacing as sharp granules pierced their exposed flesh. Before the sandstorm came to an end, the Kroti released ferocious battle cries, and Aurelia's troops had no choice but to run through the sand to meet them.

***

By the time the dust settled, the scenic Runeian beach had become a chaotic bloodbath.

The telltale shrieking of gryphons echoed from the sky as Annera stayed put to protect the noblemen. Aurelia pulled two of her soldiers out of the way when she saw a shadow falling from the sky, and in seconds, an enormous boulder landed on the ground where they'd been standing. She released a strangled cry when one of those soldiers was snatched up in a gryphon's claws.

The world seemed to turn in slow motion as she watched the man struggle while airborne. Another gryphon flew at him, tearing off his armor and chunks of flesh with its talons, before the one carrying him dropped him. Aurelia stumbled backward, falling onto her bottom, when the soldier landed a few feet in front of her, his eyes open and his neck broken from the impact.

The air was still slightly cloudy, and with the chaos unfolding around her, Aurelia couldn't locate Shasta's hiding spot. She accepted defeat, reaching out for Halvor through the bond between their souls, and drew her sword to combat a Mekyan soldier who'd set his sights on her.

She managed to stab the soldier in the gut through an exposed patch of skin his armor didn't cover, and when he fell to his knees, she slit his throat to make sure the job was done. She tried to move forward toward the ocean to find Jack, but she—along with a few dozen of her soldiers—were halted by five gryphons blocking their path on the ground.

Luckily, the sprites were on Aurelia's side.

She would've missed it if she blinked. Small golden spheres darted around the gryphons, moving so quickly that the gryphons had no hope of capturing them. She couldn't see what the tiny creatures were doing, but the gryphons howled in pain as blood spurted from mystery wounds on their necks, feet, and wings. Aurelia pictured Edom's razor-sharp teeth and claws, knowing what sprites were capable of, but still, it was hard to imagine such little things inflicting such carnage.

Some of the gryphons flew away, and the others were injured enough for the soldiers to finish them off. Unfortunately, Aurelia and the soldiers were quickly met by another wave of Kroti, all armed with magic.

One of Aurelia's soldiers—a male mage from Holos—erected a shield composed of nothing but pure power. The shield deflected the Kroti mages' strikes, but that only encouraged the gryphons to attack from above and behind. When Aurelia felt claws on her arms, she yelped as her feet skidded against the ground, but she refused to meet the same fate as the soldier from earlier. She clutched the hilt of her sword with both hands and jerked her weapon upward between her neck and her shoulder, piercing the gryphon through the neck just as her feet lifted about a foot off the ground. She collapsed onto the sand, the gryphon dead behind her, and climbed to her feet just in time to hear a mighty roar.

Relief coursed through her veins when Halvor's telltale sapphire scales appeared overhead. He circled the beach, bellowing, but Annera made no move to meet him. After incinerating a group of gryphons that attempted to attack him in the sky, Halvor landed on the beach by the edge of the woodlands, shrieking at anyone who dared to get close to him.

Aurelia started for him, but another roar—more juvenile than Halvor's—echoed throughout the beach, followed by another sandstorm. Aurelia turned away so her back would take the brunt of it, gritting her teeth as sand somehow made its way into her nostrils and her mouth while whipping against her face.

She could hardly see Halvor anymore, but even if she could, it'd be close to impossible to get to him from here. He was too far away, and the fighting surrounding her was too thick. As the sand settled and she caught a glimpse of him, she saw him shaking his head, irritated by the sand, and scouring the beach for her. He bellowed again, a sound of frustration, and started prowling toward the water.

He couldn't see her.

Aurelia reached out for him, trying her hardest to focus on their connection while defending herself, but he only roared in response. He couldn't find her in the carnage, and even if he could, it'd be hard for him to come to her without trampling their own soldiers.

Jack. She pushed the thought toward Halvor while fending off a Runeian. *Can you see him? Is he all right?*

Halvor prowled forward, and for a moment, Aurelia lost sight of his head when he lowered his neck and shrieked. She finished off the Runeian, and by the time she pulled her sword from his body, she saw that Halvor had lowered his wings. *What on earth is he doing?* she thought. *Why would he—*

Her thoughts were silenced when she saw a glittering sheet of bronze and a head of black curls settling on Halvor's back. If the hair wasn't enough to identify the soldier who'd managed to mount a dragon, then the way he comfortably settled on Halvor's saddle—as seamlessly as Aurelia would've done—certainly was.

Halvor hadn't just made sure Jack was okay. He'd given Jack permission to ride him—*without* Aurelia. Even Arian, a Cristos, had never been able to ride Halvor on his own.

Her amazement was cut short when Halvor lifted into the sky, soaring out to sea before circling back around. Aurelia wanted to laugh when she saw Jack gripping Halvor's spikes, but she didn't get the chance. She was knocked onto her back by a Kroti soldier, her legs flying over her head in the process, and her sword fell several feet to her left.

Just before the soldier could finish her off, his hands glowing with white magic, a blade cut through his legs, severing him in two at the knees. He howled as he collapsed, blood pooling around him, but he was silenced when his head was cut from his body. Aurelia's wide eyes settled on her savior: a goblin, who only nodded his head before running off.

Swallowing her fear, she reclaimed her sword and jumped to her feet. The Kroti soldiers who'd been on the sandbar had now joined the fighting, too, likely encouraged by Halvor's arrival. The noblemen were gathered a ways away from the conflict—the cowards were merely watching the battle unfold while Annera stood guard over them.

Aurelia tried scanning her surroundings for Shasta, but again, she couldn't see enough to spot a young woman, much less one in hiding. She assumed Shasta was in the surrounding woodlands somewhere, but she'd have soldiers with her, and Aurelia didn't want to risk being pitted against a group of vengeful men while wandering in an unfamiliar forest.

At the very least, it seemed like Annera was being held back. It would've been a deeply foolish thing to send her after Halvor, or even her human enemies. She may have been a dragon, but she was still small, and emerald longbellies weren't exactly known for being vicious opponents. One sword to her neck would've ended her, and Krotis certainly couldn't risk that. For now, her only purpose was protecting the noblemen, and reminding Aurelia's forces that their leader wasn't the only one with a dragon anymore.

A shriek caught Aurelia's attention—she recognized the sound as one of terror. Her blood turned to ice when she turned her gaze to the sky, where a cyclone had formed in midair. On the sandbar, a group of Kroti mages had gathered, protected by gryphons, and their hands were held up toward Halvor, glowing with white magic.

Aurelia's heart plummeted. The air mages' cyclone had swallowed Halvor and Jack, encasing them completely in an impenetrable wind tunnel. Halvor didn't breathe fire, likely because he knew the cyclone would deflect the flames and send them hurtling at Jack. She could see Halvor's silhouette as he fought, his wings flapping faster than she'd ever seen them, but the most he managed to do was stick his snout through the cyclone before he was dragged back in.

Then, without warning, the cyclone disappeared completely. Aurelia didn't get the chance to see the mages back down—she was too distracted by her own screams as Halvor, his wings curled up and tucked against his body, plummeted about two-hundred feet toward the ocean like a massive blue cannonball.

With Jack still on his back, Halvor crashed into the water, disappearing into the Alkamura.

XXXII

nemies were summoned by the sound of Aurelia's screams.

As soldiers stalked toward her, recognition flashing in their eyes, her own soldiers formed a perimeter around her. Now, the Kroti would know for certain that the Queen of Akkinor was, indeed, on the battlefield—and that she'd seen both her husband and her dragon plummet into the sea.

She hiccupped into a sob, unable to fully comprehend what was happening as others came to her aid, too. Two centaurs positioned themselves on either side of her, nearly crushing her, and crossed their swords in front of her, making it clear to the enemy that she was not to be trifled with.

She wanted to fall to her knees, to give up right then and there after what she'd just seen, as the image replayed in her head. It must've been the mages' plan: the force of the wind tunnel overcame Halvor so greatly that when it disappeared, the sudden lack of force stalled him, and he hadn't recovered in time to steady himself. The weight of his own body pulled him down, and Jack along with him.

Just then, while the centaurs' weight was the only thing keeping her upright, a familiar roar echoed in her ears. She cried out as Halvor shot into the air like a magnificent sapphire arrow, soaking wet but alive, and roared again with such rage that even Aurelia found herself fearing him.

In his fury, he set a group of Kroti soldiers ablaze, catching a few Akkinorians and Taundosans in the crossfire. Another stream of flames hit the woodlands, igniting a large portion of the trees and causing most of them to collapse. He circled the area, momentarily flying behind Aurelia, and when he passed overhead, she caught a glimpse of his back.

Jack wasn't there.

Dread seeped down her throat like bile. Even if Jack had made it out of the water, she wouldn't have been able to see him—the fighting was still too thick, and he blended in with the other Akkinorian soldiers.

Desperate, she tapped one of the centaurs on his back. "Take me to the shore!"

"What?" He stared at her, dumbfounded. "Your Grace—"

"*Now!*"

Obeying, the centaur wrapped one arm around her waist before settling her on his back. He pushed through the crowd while his comrade followed, the two of them slaying any enemies in their path as they galloped. Aurelia shrieked for him to stop when she saw a sopping mop of black hair on the sandbar. A sigh of relief escaped her as Jack, on his hands and knees, expelled seawater from his lungs and retched onto the sand.

He's alive, she told herself. *He's okay. He's okay.*

"We'll go help him," the centaur told her, removing her from his back. He yelled something at a nearby group of goblins, who immediately scurried over. "Protect the queen, lads!"

The goblins nodded, but they fled as soon as the centaurs did, more eager to shed blood than to mind Aurelia. That was fine—Halvor had seen her by then, and he landed a few yards away from her, squashing a handful of Kroti and two gryphons beneath his feet as he did so.

She ran for him, breathless and aching, and found herself climbing onto his back before she knew it. She ran her hand over his scales, ensuring he was all right while finding comfort in his touch, as he lifted into the sky. She looked down and allowed herself a small smile when she saw the Kroti lords staring at her. Clearly, they hadn't truly believed she was here.

Halvor circled the beach as Aurelia scanned the scene for a good place to strike. She spotted the centaurs guiding Jack from the sandbar, just as the tide began to conceal it, and fending off opponents while Jack limped between them. Aurelia wanted to pick him up, but there wasn't a good place for Halvor to land, so she had to trust the centaurs would bring him somewhere safe.

A roar rattled Aurelia's eardrums, but it hadn't come from Halvor. It hadn't come from Annera, either, who merely snarled from her stance in front of the lords. No, it'd come from the sky across the beach— from Rieza, who burst through the clouds like a violet beacon, releasing a gust of wind so powerful that about ten Kroti soldiers wading through the water were blown backward, falling deep into the sea.

When Rieza dipped and curved, Aurelia saw a head of black hair on her back. Diantha hadn't just sent Rieza—she'd come to help, too.

After Halvor ignited a group of gryphons who'd set their sights on his sister, Aurelia sent a command toward his soul. He hovered for a moment, giving her time to flatten herself against his body as much as she could. She'd shared this plan with him before they left Akkinor, explaining it as she would've to human Halvor. If she knew her dragon at all, he'd execute it exactly as she'd outlined it.

In a flash, he bolted upward, straighter than an arrow as he soared toward the sun. A ball of fire emitted from his throat, making Aurelia grimace as they flew through it. She felt the heat, but no pain. When he turned toward the beach again, the fire in the air now nothing but smoke, Aurelia just barely heard an ear-piercing whistle. It was Lord Chilton, who'd also been made aware of the plan before their departure so he could do his part, responding to her signal.

The Akkinorian and Taundosan armies began running through the woods toward the border of Runeia and Taundosa. A few gryphons followed them, and what looked like a handful of Kroti, but for the most part, the enemy stayed behind—likely assuming Aurelia had given her men the signal to retreat so she could surrender.

While watching her confused enemies shout for her troops to come back, to stop running away like cowards, Aurelia uttered one word: "Now."

Halvor released the greatest roar she'd ever heard, and in the blink of an eye, pockets of flames burst from the ground on the beach, incinerating anyone who was unlucky enough to have fire sprout from beneath them. It was like flaming geysers were popping up across the once-scenic beach, as unpredictable as they were catastrophic.

Aurelia had gotten so distracted by observing the effects of Halvor's combustion roar that she hadn't bothered glancing at the Council. Only when Rieza shrieked in pain, the sound like nails against slate, did she look at them. Her eyes found Rieza first, struggling in the air with her tail pointed down at the ocean, and her belly facing inland. Glowing golden lassos were wrapped around her body, leaving her wings and limbs alone, but growing tighter and tighter around her neck, belly, and chest.

The lassos were produced by the four lords as they stood behind Annera. The longbelly, too, looked distressed: she was shaking her head and snorting like something was buzzing around her face, pawing at the ground, and whimpering. Compared to Rieza's wails of pain, though, Annera sounded like a child throwing a tantrum.

Do you know what to do? Aurelia pushed the thought toward Halvor, as she herself was unsure of what they could do to help Rieza—other than killing the lords, which wouldn't be in her best interest. The only thing worse than going to war with Krotis's rulers was facing the consequences of leaving the kingdom without leadership, without the family names that'd ruled the kingdom for centuries. That'd only create another mess for her to clean up.

Halvor bellowed and set out for Rieza, but once he was close to her, he took a sharp turn, now facing the lords. Releasing another mighty roar, he terrified two of them—Lord Keer and Lord Swann, based on the sigils engraved on their breastplates—enough that they dropped their arms. Two of the four lassos disappeared, giving Rieza just enough strength to break free of the others.

In doing so, Rieza craned her body backward, and Diantha fell into the sea.

***

Shasta woke with a gasp, coughing and choking on ash, and managed to pull herself from her stomach onto her hands and knees. She dry heaved onto the blackened ground below, trembling, then wheezed until one lone breath of fresh air filled her lungs.

The ringing in her ears only worsened when she stood. She brought a hand to her right ear when she felt it throbbing, then resisted the urge to vomit when she saw a pool of crimson dripping down her fingers. She took a step forward, unsure of where she was while everything was smoking and burning around her, but nearly tripped and fell to the ground again. She'd stepped on something that felt hard at first, but when she put her full weight on it, her foot went right through it.

She turned to the side and vomited when she saw what she'd stepped on: a human torso, so charred that the flesh and muscle had melted away, and the bones had become as fragile as paper. It was the ribcage she'd felt originally, snapped beneath a one-hundred-pound woman's foot.

This wasn't the only body nearby. She counted four other blackened remains in the vicinity. One man had survived, though his armor had melted, and his entire body was covered in nauseating burns—burns that penetrated his flesh so deeply, she could see his bones. Even his hair was gone, leaving nothing but raw flesh atop his head.

Shasta finally mustered the courage to look at her own body. The breastplate she'd been given was still intact, though the fabric of her gown on her arms and legs had mostly turned to ash. She had a few burns on her arms and on the backs of her legs, but she couldn't feel the pain. Not yet, anyway.

As she stood in the center of the woodlands, fires surrounding her while the battle raged on the beach behind her, she vaguely recalled what had happened. She'd seen Queen Aurelia's dragon burst out of the ocean, enraged, and turn to incinerating anything in his path. When he turned to the woodlands, jaw opening and a massive orange glow forming deep in his throat, the five men tasked with protecting Shasta had erected magical shields to protect them against the flames.

Unfortunately, the shields weren't strong enough to deflect dragonfire.

Before she hit the ground and lost consciousness, she'd just barely felt a weight striking her from behind. She assumed it was a soldier's last attempt to help her by shoving her to the ground, using his body to protect her. He'd barely pushed her down in time, but he'd taken the brunt of the flames for her.

She wondered which body was his. Had she defiled his corpse by trampling his charred ribcage? Or was he the man moaning with his back against a fallen tree, wailing about how he could see his organs beneath layers of melting flesh and blackened bones? Or was he one of the other bodies lying nearby, unidentifiable not only in name, but in every possible way?

Shasta wanted to run, to get the hell out of the woods before flaming trees collapsed on top of her, but she couldn't leave Annera. She summoned every ounce of courage she could and navigated through the blazing forest until she found a semi-stable position that allowed her to observe the battle. She could still hear cracking trees and roaring fires behind her as Halvor's flames swallowed the woodlands, but at this point, she could only pray to Pherena that her safe spot would hold up.

She found Annera by the shore, protecting the four lords. She knew they'd be cross with her, but in this moment, she didn't care: she wanted Annera—and herself—as far from this atrocity as possible.

Shasta hadn't been given the chance to master the connection between dragon and rider. A priest in Bruila, who'd once studied ancient dragonkind as a hobby in his youth, had assured her that a dragon could understand their rider's commands through nothing but thoughts and feelings—a result of their souls being bonded as one. Annera had proved that was true when she executed Lazelus Swann, but now, as Shasta begged Annera to fly home, the dragon didn't seem to be getting the message.

Shasta coughed when her throat began to tickle, and only then did she realize how much smoke was building up in the forest. She couldn't run to the beach without everyone seeing her, and she was too far from civilization to make it to safety on foot. She had to try, though. At this point, while smoke filled her lungs and clouded her vision, she knew she had to go with or without her dragon.

She ran for the west, inland toward the heart of Runeia, hacking and wheezing with every step. She didn't know this forest, but even if she did, it wouldn't have mattered—everything looked the same when it was ablaze.

She ran until her legs gave out. When she collapsed on the ground, just barely managing to save her fall with her hands, she coughed and gasped, inhaling both dirt and sand. She tried and failed to pick herself up again, and when her cheek hit the ground, she knew she could go no further.

At the very least, the flames hadn't reached this part of the forest yet. The fire would spread, as it always did in the woodlands, but hopefully, someone—or something—would find her before she was swallowed by the flames.

As her eyes fell shut and her mind slipped away, the last thing she heard was Annera's shriek—of pain, terror, or anger, Shasta didn't know.

When Shasta woke again, not knowing how much time had passed since she'd collapsed, it wasn't because someone had found her. It was because the earth was trembling beneath her feet, the lurching and shaking so powerful that she could feel it in her bones.

She passed out again before she could find out what had happened.

***

Rieza flew away from the noblemen as soon as she broke free from the lassos. Aurelia and Halvor followed her, and as they did so, Aurelia looked down at the foamy circle in the ocean where Diantha had landed. She expelled a long sigh of relief when Diantha's head bobbed up to the surface.

Fortunately, Diantha hadn't worn armor—likely because she thought it was too uncomfortable and bulky to wear while on dragonback. She'd be aching from the fall, but she could swim to safety, and that was all that mattered.

The sight made Aurelia wonder how Jack had managed to get back to shore. He was dressed head-to-toe in Akkinorian bronze armor, the heaviest there was. Then she saw vibrant, iridescent fins, fan-shaped and looking like they were made of a fleshy tulle, splashing in the waves. *Mermaids*, she thought. For whatever reason, they must've saved him—and maybe they'd help Diantha, too, if she needed it.

Half of the Kroti had run away by then, terrified by the thought of facing two enormous dragons while their own was so small—and being held back from helping them so she could protect their leaders. The other half, though, didn't seem to care that Aurelia's troops had retreated. They turned their attention to the dragons now, doing everything in their power to bring Halvor and Rieza down.

Some shot arrows at them, which deflected off the dragons' body armor like the weapons were made of rubber. Others used their magic, attempting to mimic what the noblemen had done to Rieza. The two dragons avoided the attacks, dodging left and right, but neither fired back just yet.

The dragons flew inland, intending to turn around over the forest and circle the beach again. For just a moment as they flew side-by-side, the world seemed to still when Rieza's golden eyes met Aurelia's blue ones. Aurelia sucked in a breath, knowing how dangerous it was to look into the eyes of a dragon that wasn't one's own, and for a fraction of a second, she saw the volatility in Rieza's gaze that Halvor had warned her about.

This was not a dragon who sought permission. This was a dragon who expected her rider to obey *her*.

Rieza darted forward, shrieking as she coasted over the beach and then over the ocean. Halvor followed, and both made a sharp, abrupt turn to face land again. Aurelia's heart hammered when Rieza opened her jaw—everything feeling slower than it really was—and roared, sending a powerful shockwave hurtling toward the beach.

Without thinking, Aurelia gave Halvor a command: *Show them how we defend the realm.*

In an instant, Halvor released an enormous fiery sphere. The sphere collided with Rieza's shockwave, meshing the two together. What looked like a wall of flames fell over the beach, and anyone who didn't move quickly enough—to jump into the water, or to be carried away by fleeing gryphons—was incinerated on impact.

Aurelia hardly noticed when Rieza dipped toward the ocean. When she finally looked, she saw Rieza's talons grazing the water. If the scene around her hadn't been so catastrophic, Aurelia would've chuckled at the sight of Diantha dangling from Rieza's talons.

She didn't understand why Rieza had recovered Diantha now instead of earlier—why Rieza seemed more concerned than before. Then she spotted Rieza and Diantha flying away, with Halvor following suit almost immediately. What came next answered her question, but it mortified her, too.

A sharp shriek echoed in Aurelia's ears. Through the smoke and the flames, she saw Annera's silhouette lift off into the air as the young dragon continued to wail. Annera flew straight up into the sky, screeching in terror, before her wings and limbs curled up against her body. She rolled around in the air like she'd completely lost control of herself, and before Aurelia knew it, the longbelly was hurling herself onto the beach.

Aurelia looked over her shoulder as Halvor followed Rieza northeast toward the Taundosan border. When Annera collided with the ground, a shockwave that rivaled the size of Rieza's emitted from her body, spreading throughout the land and sea. The waves grew angry, rising several feet into the air, and the ground tremored like tens of thousands of centaurs were galloping over the earth. Trees swayed, bodies rolled, and sea stacks in the near distance crumbled into the water.

The earth didn't stop shaking. Halvor had left the beach behind before Aurelia could see what'd become of Annera—and the lords, too—but even as they flew away, the earth continued to rattle and groan.

By the time they reached the border, Aurelia saw something that shook her to her core. A fissure had formed in the earth, almost directly along the border, revealing dirt, roots, and stones several feet deep. The land on Krotis's side of the border seemed to be pulling outward toward the sea, as ocean water from the coast—the very edge of Runeia and Taundosa—filled the gap between the two kingdoms.

Centaurs were helping Aurelia's soldiers cross the gap as it filled, the water level growing higher and higher by the minute. The chunk of land that'd broken off seemed to extend for miles, as far as Aurelia could see from the sky, and it was being sucked out faster and faster by the second.

The one who breathes fire will sever the realm at the edge of the world.

XXXIII

Aurelia and Halvor inspected the scene as their soldiers ran further into Taundosa. The fissure was only getting bigger, with Krotis only floating farther away. In the distance, though, Aurelia heard Annera's juvenile—yet pained—shriek, and she knew the longbelly had survived the crash.

But then again, she'd caused it.

Rieza's shockwave might've contributed to the damage, but it couldn't be seen. There was no sheen, shimmer, or glow; only vibrations and pressure, the combination of the four winds. But fire was impossible to miss, and when Halvor joined Rieza in sending one final message to Krotis, his power was the only one Annera, and the people, had seen.

She knew that prophecies were never black-and-white. They never spoke about exactly what would happen. It was like Archie had said: it was all a matter of interpretation. Halvor hadn't been the one to sever Krotis from the continent of Carthe, but he'd been the one to spook Annera into doing it—the indirect cause.

Aurelia and Halvor landed in southern Taundosa to join their troops. The Taundosan civilians had disappeared from the streets and into their homes, even going as far as to close their shutters and seal their doors, when they saw the bloodied, burned, and moaning soldiers trudging through the streets. The Taundosan soldiers didn't bother waiting to hear from Aurelia before turning to reconvene at Reyna's palace. Aurelia's soldiers merely followed Lord Chilton's orders as he directed them toward the harbor.

Aurelia rushed up to her advisor, wiping soot and sweat from her brow. "Where's Jack?"

"He's already on the dock."

"Is he all right?"

"He's fine. After what just happened, though, we both thought it best to get our men the hell off of this continent."

Aurelia grimaced. "Reyna—"

"Her soldiers will tell her what happened, and I'll write to her from the ship. We need to leave, Your Grace. Though I imagine Krotis will be distracted for quite a while, word will spread quickly, and people will start forming their own conclusions." His expression was riddled with pity, which she didn't understand until he spoke again: "Krotis spread the prophecy as far and wide as they could. Do you really want to be here when Carthe realizes Krotis is no longer attached to the continent? That it's been severed?"

She shivered. "No, but Halvor didn't—"

"It doesn't matter. Respectfully, my queen. They weren't there to see how it happened. They'll only know that it *did* happen, and they'll put the pieces together for themselves."

When she saw the darkness in his eyes, she swallowed and said, "Did you see it?"

"Of course. I stayed close until I knew you were retreating," he replied. "I saw what I saw—the emerald dragon fell and caused the earth to tremor until the kingdom fractured. Most of our men saw it, too. But all of us, Akkinorians and Taundosans alike, are biased in your favor. Our word won't be believed by the masses."

She understood that much. Just as she gave Halvor the command to fly home, Rieza appeared in the sky. Nobody so much as glanced at her. Aurelia wasn't sure if the people were ignoring her because they were afraid after seeing her in battle, or because they simply had no energy left to exert on awe or fear.

When Diantha climbed down from Rieza's back, Aurelia rushed to meet her. "Are you hurt?"

Diantha shook her head. "No. It wasn't pleasant when I hit the water, but the fall could've been worse. It was quite thrilling, actually."

Aurelia sighed. "Gods..."

"We flew the length of Krotis when we saw the crack forming," she continued, wiping soot from her face. "There's a spot at the border of Mekya and the Ngora Valley that seems to be intact. For whatever reason, the quake didn't disrupt it. I suppose it looks like something of a bridge now—a land bridge connecting Krotis to the desert. I don't know if it will hold up, because the kingdom is still moving toward the sea, but it's there for now. If it breaks, Krotis will officially become an island."

Aurelia's stomach churned. "You know what this means. Part of the prophecy has been fulfilled, and I'm to blame for it."

"It was the two of us together who frightened the longbelly, but she's the one who caused the quake."

"It doesn't matter." She then echoed what Lord Chilton had told her, making Diantha's face fall. "I have to leave, but...did you see anything else in Krotis? What's the damage?"

Diantha grimaced. "I didn't go back to the beach, if that's what you're asking. I don't know what became of the noblemen or the soldiers who were still there when everything happened. I did see a few hundred armor-clad men running through the trees, though. And there doesn't seem to be significant damage to the parts of the kingdom I flew over. It's like the tremors spared the kingdom, only striking the border and what sat around it."

"This was always meant to happen," Aurelia murmured, her chest feeling tight. "The gods intended for Krotis to separate from the continent, but they wanted the kingdom spared. I wonder why. It doesn't reflect well on us."

"For now, anyway." Diantha made a face as she pulled red seaweed from a knot in her hair. "We may gain more support if we can find the rest of the prophecy."

Emphasis on if, Aurelia thought. "You know they'll be declaring war on Dofell now, too, don't you?"

There was a glimmer in Diantha's eyes. "If they're still alive to do it."

***

"I hate this."

Aurelia glowered. "Stop toying with it."

Jack mirrored her expression as he stared at the thick bandage wrapped around his hand, from his knuckles to his forearm. Surprisingly, a sprained wrist was the only injury he'd sustained when he fell from Halvor's back. One would think he'd be grateful that his injury was so minor after what'd happened, but he couldn't stand having his hand constricted.

"I've been thinking about those mermaids." He sat on the edge of their bed beside her, ignoring the way the ship lurched as he did so. "I didn't bring them back from Vanhylde. I wonder why they saved me."

"They probably heard about what you did from others, and they wanted to repay you somehow."

"Maybe. I didn't see them rescuing any drowning Kroti."

She smiled a little, but it quickly faded when she remembered what'd happened a few short weeks ago during the battle in Runeia. She'd been right about how Jack pulled himself out of the water—mermaids had brought him to the sandbar—but she couldn't appreciate how Jack's selfless action in Vanhylde had earned him such favor with the creatures. Not now, anyway, after she'd inadvertently caused Krotis to detach from Carthe.

It'd been a horrible sight. From the initial carnage, to the damage Halvor had inflicted after the cyclone, to what the three dragons had done together toward the end...Aurelia hadn't seen what became of whoever remained on the beach when she and Halvor fled, but she could picture it well enough, and she didn't like what her imagination came up with.

"At least we won." Jack seemed to know what she was thinking as he set a comforting hand on her lower back. "We lost good men, and it got hairy there for a moment, but we won."

"Did we? It was ghastly," she retorted. "They were right, you know, before the battle started. What if they hadn't seen us coming? We didn't think about that. We just expected they'd meet us in battle. We didn't stop to consider what we might've done if their troops weren't at the ready—if we'd been forced to infiltrate Krotis."

"We knew they'd see us. It wasn't an expectation—it was a fact. They'd have to be the biggest morons in the realm to ignore a fleet of Akkinorian warships approaching, and Taundosan troops rallying at their border. But even if they didn't meet us...It's not like we would've laid siege to Krotis, my love. We wouldn't have murdered innocents like others do during wartime. We would've gone for the Council in their homes or in their capital, and we would've given them the chance to surrender, just as we did on the battlefield."

"Still..."

Jack's eyes hardened. "They killed Lucyra. They tried to kill our son. We had to respond, even if our plan wasn't perfect."

"They're going to turn the entire realm against us, you know. If they haven't already."

"No." He shook his head, smiling a little, as he cupped her cheek and buried his fingers in her hair. "If the Council survived, they'll realize the disadvantage they're at, and they'll stop this madness. They aren't as strong as they think they are, and soon enough, the realm will know what their true intentions are."

"If they appoint Immor as their Almighty before—"

"They haven't done it yet. There has to be a reason for that. We have nothing to fear while Pherena prevails, and we have time to ensure the realm sees things as they are—not as Krotis wants them to."

Aurelia sighed. "This is only the beginning of the war. I can feel it."

Jack leaned forward and kissed her temple. "We'll continue to win every battle that comes our way. I know we will."

She wanted to believe him, but while her tears remained clear, she had a sinking feeling that their success in this latest conflict was simply a stroke of luck.

Their ship docked in Akkinor about an hour later, with Cheol and Geon waiting for them on the streets of Seaport with a carriage to take them home. When Aurelia asked the centaurs if they'd received word about what had happened in Krotis, they assured her they hadn't.

That made her feel better, but not by much. It only meant that her soldiers—and anyone in Carthe—hadn't written to their acquaintances in Akkinor since the battle ended. Everyone was probably too shaken up to talk about it just yet, even in writing. That would change in a day or so when the troops settled in and told their neighbors their war stories.

Of course, after returning to the palace and reuniting with Rayan, Aurelia and Jack quickly learned that word *had* spread about the incident— just privately between politicians. Jalhor hadn't sent word (and he wouldn't, not until the eight-week succession period in Bozar was over), but Reyna had, and so had Quapebet. The letters had arrived at the palace long before Aurelia and Jack did, so Rayan—and the Assembly— had been made aware of what happened in Krotis while the Akkinorian troops were sailing home.

At least the general public hasn't heard yet, Aurelia thought.

She didn't bother taking time to settle back in. She'd done quite enough waiting and recovering aboard the ship, and there would always be something that demanded her attention—whether it be whispers of retaliation by Krotis, squabbling in the capital, or something else far more trivial.

After bathing and eating a quick luncheon, Aurelia and Jack spent some time with their children, but only Hyacinth was curious about their time away. *You have a story to tell us*, she'd said. Neither Aurelia nor Jack had responded; mainly because the entire battle had been a story for the ages, but not one part of it was suitable for children's ears.

Now, Aurelia was back in her study again, waiting for Rayan to meet her here while she thought about what'd happened. Diantha said the damage to the kingdom hadn't been catastrophic after the tremors, but still, innocent lives had been affected by the quake. That, and all of Krotis was being forced into finding a new way to exist now that they were so distant from the continent. Life would be harder for the average citizen now, and even if two other dragons had contributed to the unwanted change, only

Halvor and Aurelia would be blamed for the hardships—because only a wall of fire had been seen inflicting the damage.

She wished she could forget the things she'd seen: the flaming geysers popping up out of the sand, swallowing men in a blazing inferno; Jack and Diantha falling after both dragons were incapacitated; the soldiers who'd been thrown into the ocean, left to drown when their armor weighed them down; and even poor Annera as she plummeted toward the earth like a child falling from a tree.

"Aurelia." Rayan slipped into her study, snapping her out of her daze, and offered her a small, tired smile as he sat on the other side of her desk. "Are you sure you wouldn't rather be resting with Jack? You just fought in battle, after all."

"I'd almost forgotten," she replied, rolling her eyes. That made him laugh. "No, I'm all right. It doesn't feel right to rest after what happened, particularly when I have no idea if or when Krotis plans to retaliate. I want to stay on my toes."

"Understandable." He plucked a letter from her desk—one with a broken golden seal stamped with the image of a phoenix. "As I mentioned when I greeted you earlier, Reyna's soldiers informed her of everything that happened in Runeia. She wrote that she felt the tremors in Taundosa, but surprisingly, there was very little damage. She seems to think the gods protected the people of Carthe from being affected by the earthquake."

Aurelia nodded. "I've been thinking the same. They prophesized this, after all, so perhaps it's always been part of their plan to have Krotis detach from the continent. What I can't understand is why."

Rayan's eyes shone with something she couldn't decipher. "Read the letter."

She obeyed. For the most part, Reyna had only written about what her soldiers had reported back after the battle, and how Krotis had stopped floating out to sea at a certain point. Her men could clearly see the coast of Runeia from the coast of Taundosa: it was too far away to swim there, but close enough that it was a somewhat short trip by boat.

Then she got to the interesting part.

The obstacles at sea, which once prevented us from traveling to the western coast of Carthe, are gone. The sea stacks and hazardous rocks appear to have broken apart and collapsed into the ocean. There is now a clearer, safer path from southern to western Carthe, which has never existed before; even during the old days.

You said something during the Battle for Dofell when we demolished a portion of the walls: 'Carthe is a place of liberty, not confinement.' I believe the gods agree with you. This land is known for being a place of freedom and adventure, yet so many obstacles—the walls, the southern coast, the valley—make it more inaccessible than anywhere else in the realm. We took the first step toward restoring some of our liberty when we opened Dofell up to the world again. Perhaps what happened in Krotis was merely the gods' way of freeing Carthe, too, in a way we never expected.

Or, perhaps, the gods wish to keep Krotis as far from the rest of us as possible. Perhaps Immor is actively battling Pherena for control, and the others are doing everything in their power to stop him. They know what horrors he could inflict if he were to influence the people of Krotis, and making it harder for Krotis to reach us may be their attempt to save us.

In truth, I don't know what any of this means, or what it may lead to in the near future. All I know is that I shall stand by you while we face the realm— always.

Aurelia sighed when she finished reading. "Both of her theories are entirely plausible. I suppose we won't know anything for certain unless one of the gods themselves tells us, and none of them have made an effort to return since Edea visited Dofell."

"Indeed." Rayan's lips curled into a grimace. "If they intended for this to protect Carthe from Immor...They must believe he'll become Krotis's Almighty in due time. How does that work?"

"Heavens if I know," she admitted. "I don't exactly know how it worked with Edea replacing Myenar in Dofell, either. We shall have to speak with someone closer to the gods. Perhaps Elder Marvion will have some insight." She set the letter aside and plucked an opened scroll from her desk, stamped with the seal of the Kaplo family of Quapebet. "And what's this?"

He exhaled and ran a hand through his hair. "The Imperial Princess has gone missing. She disappeared about two weeks ago. The Emperor requests that we write to him with any information if we happen to hear something regarding her whereabouts."

Aurelia froze. "The emperor's daughter has disappeared? From the most fortified country in the realm? How can that be?"

Fleeing Quapebet without permission was close to impossible. Everyone knew that. Even mercenaries and pillagers departed the continent with permission from some high-ranking nobleman. Nothing was as simple as smuggling oneself aboard a ship or buying passage across the sea. Without proper documentation signed by a reigning highborn, even a fisherman couldn't take a tiny boat several yards out to sea to catch a meal.

Princess Zemira was Emperor Timman's only heir, even if she'd never see the throne; but heir or not, a royal disappearing from Quapebet was unheard of. The fact that she was the future of the country—for now, anyway—only made the situation more dire. More than half of the country would be scouring the world for her, and now wasn't exactly a good time for even more chaos.

"The Emperor doesn't say anything about how this happened," Aurelia muttered as she scanned the scroll. "I wonder if she fled on her own somehow, or if she was kidnapped. If someone took her, the crown won't admit it—they won't want to appear weak. The palace in Xinidal is more like a fortress, and a formidable one, at that. If someone managed to get in and out with the princess in tow, then Quapebet's strongest defense has become an easy foe to best."

"We'll have to keep our eyes and ears sharp," Rayan advised. "If she happens to come to Akkinor, alone or with a captor, our involvement may do more than save her life—it may earn us favor with Quapebet, without having to betroth one of your daughters to the son the Emperor doesn't yet have. They could be swayed to fight for us to repay our kindness."

Her heart swelled with hope, but she knew it wouldn't be that simple. Nothing was—not anymore.

XXXIV

Shasta woke up in her bedchamber—not in Bruila, but Sharith—and tried to move, but a soothing voice urged her to stay still. Her head felt foggy and her body numb, and for the life of her, she couldn't remember what'd happened before she fell asleep.

Then she cracked an eye open and saw her body laying atop her bedspread, her dress rolled up to her thighs. Leaves smelling of something earthy and potent were wrapped around her legs like bandages. She could feel the damp, sticky leaves on her arms and her chest, too. Then another smell, like burnt hair, wafted into her nostrils, and she instantly remembered where she'd been before this: trapped in a blazing forest on the coast of Runeia, having survived being burned to death after Queen Aurelia's dragon incinerated half of Krotis's forces.

"Shh." A male voice spoke again, but when she tried to turn to the left to face him, her head pounded in protest. "Proceed slowly, my lady. No sharp movements."

She opened her mouth to speak, but no sound came out. The room was dark, and it only darkened more when the man's head appeared above her, blocking whatever light had managed to peek through the closed curtains. She just barely registered the man as Izaius, a healer who lived in Sharith, when she saw the many moles spotting his face.

"You may find it difficult to speak for a few hours. It's a side effect of the tonic I've been giving you to numb the pain from your injuries." He set a cool, damp cloth on her fiery forehead before sinking into a chair beside her. "You're going to be just fine, my lady. You've been asleep for about a week now, but I've been looking after you and treating your injuries to the best of my ability. You may have some scarring from the burns, but you'll regain full control of your body within the next day or so.

It was certainly lucky that our soldiers found you when they did, or you might not be here today."

"How...?" Her throat felt like sandpaper when she spoke, and her voice didn't sound anything like her own.

Izaius sighed. "You have missed a great deal, Lady Shasta. I will tell you more when you've rested a bit longer. Just know that your dragon is all right, and you will be, too."

That wasn't good enough for her. "Coun...Council."

The healer cleared his throat. "I regret to inform you that Lord Keer has died. The new Lord Swann was gravely injured, but he's expected to survive. Lords Quagg and Reesa sustained minor injuries, but they are well. Gryphons managed to snatch them up before it happened, but the other two—Keer and Swann—weren't as fortunate. They were recovered...after."

It ached her to utter even one syllable, but she had to: "'It?'"

"My lady..." He sighed. "From what I've been told by our surviving soldiers, the two enemy dragons inflicted catastrophic damage. Our Annera responded bravely, but the combined power of the three beasts caused a massive tremor in the earth. Krotis now sits a few miles away from mainland Carthe. By some miracle, a chunk of land managed to stay intact. Now, other than traveling by sea, our only route to the mainland is a land bridge connecting Mekya to the desert."

Her hand twitched when she tried lifting it to touch him. He seemed to sense what she was doing, as he quickly sandwiched her hand between his. She was grateful for the comfort, but what she really wanted was for him to continue. None of this was making any sense to her; she didn't know if it was because of shock or whatever tonic he'd been feeding her.

"The damage to our borders was significant, but it would appear the rest of the kingdom has been spared." Izaius paused for a moment when she squeezed his hand unintentionally. "We lost a handful of structures, and some of our civilians in the process, but we were fortunate, all things considered. The Almighty protected us from further carnage, without a doubt. He is the only reason Krotis hasn't become a graveyard."

He? Shasta tried to say it aloud, but her voice wouldn't work. *What do you mean* he?

"As for other news..." Izaius readjusted the cloth on her head when she moved enough to disrupt it. "This battle was lost to us, of course, but we now have reason to declare war on Dofell. The surviving lords hope to incapacitate the queen and her dragon, at which point they can seize Dofell—the kingdom isn't strong enough to defend itself without the beast. Then, Krotis will demand Kanibar's assistance in the fight to come. If they refuse, they will be treated as equally guilty to our enemies. If they agree, our combined power will then force Taundosa's hand, and then Bozar's. The Almighty will assure our success here in Carthe, and the Dragon of Akkinor will be at our mercy. She will be stopped before she can inflict further damage."

That made Shasta's breath catch. As jumbled as her thoughts were, she knew what the prophecy said: *The one who breathes fire will sever the realm at the edge of the world.* Shasta and her allies had prepared for the realm's destruction at Queen Aurelia's hand, but clearly, the prophecy had been referring to Krotis splitting off from the continent. Even Shasta, in her groggy state, knew that much. If that piece of the puzzle had already happened, what more could the queen do? What more was there for Krotis to protect the realm from?

None of this made sense to her. Her allies—and her father, for that matter—had told her that their only concern was stopping Queen Aurelia from destroying the realm because, as prophesized, she was meant to start with Krotis. They'd risked conflicts and broken promises with their neighbors in Carthe in their efforts to prevent this; but now, according to Izaius, Shasta's allies planned on forcing the continent to bow to them, all to stop Queen Aurelia from doing something she'd already done. Where was the logic in that?

Her face must've revealed more than she realized, because Izaius quickly said, "The prophecy hasn't been completed yet, my lady. Remember the last bit: *One will bring about the end of existence as it is currently known.* Given what's happened, we have to believe the *one* is Queen Aurelia. One piece of the prophecy may have been fulfilled already, albeit not in the way we'd expected, but the rest has yet to come to fruition. She will destroy everything in due time if we don't stop her, and we don't stand a chance unless we succeed in uniting Carthe under our thumb."

"How?" she managed to croak.

He hesitated for a moment. "Rest now, my lady. Our liege lords will explain everything soon enough."

***

"The Crowlands have written." Jack grimaced as he handed Aurelia an opened letter while she lounged on a couch in the morning room. He sat beside her as she scanned the letter, careful not to crush Edom as the sprite sprawled on the cushions. "Some Myrans have threatened Erastus Swann and the other Kroti. It's been handled, but Lord Crowland has placed his daughter, Erastus, their children, and the other Kroti in protective custody. They're staying with a relative in Sadia for now."

Aurelia sighed. "I had a feeling this was coming. Despite Erastus's loyalty and support, he's Kroti, and some of our people will be distrustful of him no matter what."

"There's something else, too," he added. She glowered at him—she did, after all, have the letter in her hands—but let him tell her, anyway. "Erastus recently received a letter from his uncle in Runeia. His uncle's son has replaced Lazelus Swann as Lord of Runeia. Apparently, Lazelus was executed not long before the battle. I imagine he was caught for sending Willem's letter to us."

A pit formed in Aurelia's stomach. "I'd wondered if Runeia had been secretly respecting our alliance. It seemed likely after we received Willem's letter, but I couldn't be certain. I suppose the alliance is officially dismantled now that Lazelus has been executed for helping us. But why would Erastus's uncle tell him that when he knows Erastus is loyal to Akkinor?"

Jack shrugged. "Probably to boast about it. I've heard he's lame, so in the absence of his own rise to power, he's living vicariously through his son's achievements. I'd probably do the same thing if I had a bigger ego."

That made her crack a smile—one of the first smiles she'd managed since returning to Akkinor four days ago. There still hadn't been any word from Krotis other than this letter to Erastus, nor from anyone else. The only person other than Reyna who'd written was Anysa, who'd only told Arian of her safe return to Khaba. She hadn't said anything about her efforts to convince her neighbors to tell the truth about Vrurith's attack, though.

After a few moments passed, the visitor Aurelia had been expecting that morning arrived: Marvion, the Elder of Akkinor.

"Your Grace. Your Royal Highness." Marvion managed a shaky bow when he entered the room, then sat in an armchair across from the couch while a servant brought refreshments. "You wished to see me?"

"Yes." Aurelia smoothed her skirts as Edom perched on her shoulder, playing with a lock of her hair. "As you know by now, we have good reason to believe that the Guild of Steel is active among Krotis's nobility, and they plan to replace Pherena with Immor. We were hoping you could tell us a little bit more about that—specifically, how the process works. We didn't think to learn about it when Edea replaced Myenar in Dofell."

The Elder blew his nose into a handkerchief. "It varies, my queen, like all things in life. There are two ways of looking at it. Firstly, imagine a rose bush in a garden that has begun to wither and die because of infected roots, putting the other flora in the garden at risk of death, too. If one extracts the bush and replaces it with another, the garden has been saved. Secondly, imagine the rose bush is healthy and blooming, yet it is extracted incorrectly for no reason. This could infect the soil with disease and bacteria, risking the other flora that feed from the same earth—all because someone had grown tired of a rose bush in their garden, and wished to see a blueberry bush in its place."

Aurelia nodded in understanding, prompting him to continue: "Myenar was the infected rose bush, and Dofell was the garden. Replacing him with Edea saved the kingdom. He was the one to infect it and let the wound fester, and she was the one who healed it. Edea herself made it clear to you that replacing Myenar was a decision favored by the gods—even if Myenar alone was opposed to it."

"Because the replacement brought salvation to Dofell, and if Myenar had prevailed as its Almighty, the kingdom only would've suffered more," Jack concluded. "Dofell chose Myenar as their Almighty centuries ago. He accepted their plea to have him guide and influence them, and he promised to dedicate his existence to looking after them. That's the case for every Almighty in every kingdom. Breaking that promise gave the people of Dofell every right to appoint a new patron—not because they'd grown tired of Myenar, but because he'd left them to rot."

"The gods may not like it when humanity defies or insults them in any way, but it's less about what is said or done, and more about the motivation behind the action," Marvion said. "They show forgiveness and mercy when something is done in the name of bettering the realm. That's what we believe within the priesthood, and we've been given no reason to think otherwise."

"So that's why replacing Myenar didn't require a ritual or a coronation, so to speak, because—Myenar himself excluded—the decision was unanimous," Aurelia summarized. "But in Krotis, they don't want Immor to replace Pherena because the latter has betrayed the kingdom. It's not about saving the garden, even if that's what they like to tell the world. They've merely grown tired of the roses."

The Elder offered her a weak smile. "Indeed. To replace one's Almighty for no just cause isn't simple. In this case, Pherena must willingly step down from her role, or Immor must take it from her. The other gods, I imagine, will try to prevent this."

"Can they succeed?" Jack pressed. "I'd assume so. Minor deities excluded, it'd be eleven to one. Immor alone can't overpower the eleven other deities who created the realm."

Marvion grimaced a bit. "As I'm sure you know, gods grow stronger the more they're worshipped. Immor is already considered to be the strongest of the deities. Every civilization in the realm, at every point in time, has experienced war in some form—and we've all prayed to the god of war for victory, each and every time. The seas may dry up, prosperity may become a distant dream, and virtue may disappear forever, but war will always prevail in one way or another. He may not be able to defeat the rest of the Twelve, but he can certainly weaken Pherena; and the moment he does, Krotis will be free for the taking. No other deity could step in to become Krotis's Almighty instead, either."

"Why?" Aurelia knew the answer as soon as she asked the question. She sighed and bowed her head. "I see. A god doesn't choose a kingdom—the kingdom chooses the god. If enough Kroti start worshipping Immor and pleading with him to become their patron, he'll accept. The other gods can't insert themselves in Krotis if the people don't wish for their influence."

"Precisely."

"So, what now?" Jack asked, furrowing his brows. Edom was perched on his lap now, nibbling at the scone in his hand with its razor-like teeth. "It's a trickier process, I know that, but what can we expect in the days to come?"

"I don't know. Not for certain," Marvion admitted, shame shimmering in his eyes. "If Krotis requests Immor's influence—not just the Council, either, but the vast majority of the population—Immor will accept, either after Pherena willingly abdicates, or after he forces her hand. She's the goddess of virtues, after all. I can't imagine she'd put up much of a fight. But like I said, even if the others attempt to stop him from succeeding her, the power of the people will work in his favor, eventually."

Aurelia winced. "I suppose it won't be hard to convince Krotis to accept Immor after what happened in Runeia. They'll be led to believe that having Immor as their Almighty will be their salvation—their defense against me, Rieza, and even the others. They know they've become an enemy to many, and they'd choose Immor's protection over everything."

Jack shook his head and shifted, making Edom hiss when he moved the scone out of reach. Jack paused for only a moment to glare at the sprite as it wrapped its wiry limbs around his hand, intent on finishing every last bite.

"Krotis respects their values perhaps more than any of us," he pointed out. "Maybe not the nobility, not anymore, but the average person certainly does. They've been the most pious civilization in the realm since the old days. I can't imagine they'd be so quick to abandon Pherena simply because their leaders have made them afraid."

"Fear is the greatest weapon known to man, even if it cannot be wielded in one's hand." Marvion looked ten years older when he scrubbed a hand down his face. "A child may tell you there's a monster under their bed. The monster isn't real, but the fear of it certainly is. How easy is it to prove to a child that they're afraid of something that doesn't exist?"

"Close to impossible," Aurelia muttered, recalling a season-long battle with Halle in which the then-four-year-old princess had been utterly convinced there was a humanoid, spider-like monster watching her sleep. It'd been a figment of her imagination, of course, but no matter what Aurelia and Jack told her, she refused to believe it wasn't really there. "The Kroti trust their leaders, and their leaders are telling them to fear me and my allies."

"All because of an incomplete, ambiguous prophecy." Jack scoffed and wiped the crumbs from his fingers onto his trousers when Edom finished snacking. "I wonder if Willem knew about the Guild in Krotis."

"I wouldn't think so, Your Highness." Marvion stood as his eyes flicked over to the clock behind the couch. "Vyena is the goddess of blessings, not power, or war, or even prosperity. While you and I might understand that true power comes from favor from the gods, Willem Trevas doesn't strike me as the type of man who appreciated blessings. If he had thought it was possible to replace Vyena with Immor, he would've done it before Krotis had the chance."

Aurelia offered him a wobbly smile. "Thank the gods he wasn't smart enough to think about the Guild."

"Indeed." Marvion mirrored her smile, but it was equally unconvincing. "I must take my leave now, Your Grace. Thank you for having me today. I hope my insight was helpful."

"It was," she assured him, rising to take his hands. "Thank you very much."

"It's been my sincere pleasure, my queen."

He bowed, said goodbye to Jack and Edom, and disappeared through the door. When he was gone, his refreshments sitting untouched on a tray beside the chair he'd claimed, Aurelia sunk onto the couch again and released a long, tired exhale.

"What are you thinking?" Jack murmured, twisting a lock of her hair around his finger.

Aurelia closed her eyes. "The world is going to fall apart, all because I told Halvor to brandish his power."

"That's not true. We were at war, my love, and the two of you weren't the only ones responsible for what happened."

"Maybe so, but that's not how it looked."

"Well, yes, but—"

"We may have Halvor, and even Rieza now, but if Krotis succeeds, Immor can destroy both of them without so much as twitching," she reminded him. He winced, and that only made her sigh again. "If only we knew what the prophecy really means—what the gods have truly foreseen. We need more guidance."

"Why?" Edom asked. "You have always done so well on your own."

She felt her eyes burning with tears, but she wouldn't let them fall. She couldn't bear to see—or for Jack and Edom to see—the translucent liquid leak down her cheeks instead of glittering gold.

The only thing she could think to say was this: "I don't know that I have."

XXXV

"Mama?"

Aurelia looked up from the document she'd been reading. Hyacinth was standing in the doorway of Aurelia's study, rubbing her tired eyes. She and her siblings had been put to bed a few hours ago, but clearly, something was on the princess's mind. Aurelia wasn't surprised—Hyacinth had been acting strangely since Marvion's visit earlier that day.

"Sisi. What are you doing up?" Aurelia scooted her chair backward and opened her arms, prompting her daughter to scurry over and climb onto her lap. "Did Henry sneak into your room again?"

"No." Hyacinth yawned and toyed with the edges of the document on the desk. "I wanted to hear your story."

"What story?"

"About where you and Papa went the other day."

Aurelia chewed on the inside of her cheek. "Sisi—"

"I wanted to hear it, and then I did. I know why you didn't want to tell me, Mama. It's not done yet."

Something unsettling gurgled in her gut. "How do you mean?"

"The story. It's not over yet."

"W-What are you talking about?"

Hyacinth swiveled on Aurelia's lap so she was facing her mother, her legs dangling on either side of Aurelia's hips while her back pressed up against the edge of the desk. All traces of sleepiness had disappeared from her wide, pale eyes, now replaced by intrigue.

"The story of the Four Pillars, Mama."

Aurelia sucked in a sharp breath. "Hyacinth—"

"Can you read it to me?"

"I-I..."

Aurelia tried to think of something to say, but words failed her. She knew Hyacinth was talking about the prophecy, but how could she share such information with her eight-year-old daughter? Then again, Hyacinth knew things that most people didn't, even those who'd been alive for most of the century. There was nothing in the prophecy so terrible that it was inappropriate for a little girl to hear, either.

Aurelia sighed. "All right. Don't go telling your brothers and sisters about it, though. Do you understand?"

Hyacinth nodded, an eager smile playing on her lips. "I understand."

Internally cursing herself for being so easily persuaded by her child, Aurelia reached into her desk drawer to produce the prophecy Firadus had given her. It felt strange to read it aloud to her daughter like it was a fairytale, but she carried on, anyhow—until Hyacinth interrupted her when she started the second sentence.

"No." Hyacinth shook her head. "You missed a part."

Aurelia frowned. "No, I didn't."

"Yes, you did."

"I *didn't*, Sisi."

"You *did*, Mama."

For a second, Aurelia wanted to laugh. She was reminded of many conversations she'd had with Archie, Hyacinth's biological father, that played out exactly like this.

Hyacinth pointed to the end of the first line. "'The end of the masquerader will indeed restore the voice of the divine, but it will also create a prison of amber.' That's supposed to come next."

Aurelia stared at her, her lips parted in bewilderment. Hyacinth certainly didn't always talk like an eight-year-old should, but this was different. Even her tone...She sounded like a grown woman, a scholar.

An oracle.

A jolt of both anxiety and excitement bubbled up in Aurelia's chest. Careful not to disrupt Hyacinth on her lap, she reached over for a quill and an inkwell, then asked Hyacinth to repeat the sentence. She scrawled it in just after the first line of the prophecy, and after she read the following sentence, Hyacinth told her something else was missing, too.

As Aurelia continued to read, Hyacinth continued to fill in missing pieces, sharing the sentences so effortlessly that one might assume they were burned into her brain. Aurelia knew what was happening, even if a part of her wanted to brush it off as an absurd thought: Hyacinth didn't just have foresight, a sign of early magic in young children—she had prophetic abilities.

Aurelia understood the ways of the *odirasen*, the art of prophesizing. An oracle, like those Forged in Gold, was chosen before birth, meant to share messages from the gods with those in Icareth. If an oracle died before their messages could be shared or before the prophecies came to fruition, another took their place, destined to fulfill the same purpose. A prophecy didn't die with an oracle; it merely found another vessel.

Aurelia didn't want to believe that her eight-year-old child had been chosen to replace Maysa, but what else was she supposed to think? She'd known for some time now that the prophecy Maysa told Willem—and, subsequently, the prophecy he'd shared with Krotis—was incomplete, yet here Hyacinth was, adding sentences left and right.

When they finished adjusting the message, Aurelia read it aloud from the start, the ball of nerves and adrenaline in her gut threatening to burst as she compared the original, fading writing to her bold, fresh ink:

The story told once before cannot exist in perpetuity, for a few guiding words cannot assure that all which was promised will come to fruition. **The end of the masquerader will indeed restore the voice of the divine, but it will also create a prison of amber.**

There shall come a time when all appears to be well across the earthly realm, though the reason for such peace will soon lose its sanctity. **The curse of the masquerader will prevail within the shadows of false security, and its effects will threaten both friend and foe.**

Three cycles after the moon falls from the sky, the Four Pillars shall emerge from the shadows, and their return shall mark the end of the beginning. **The end of the road shall be a doorway to the unknown, opened by one and closed by five.**

The one who breathes fire will sever the realm at the edge of the world. The one who breathes the four winds will bring catastrophe but not destruction. The one who breathes the dust of stone will heal what survives. The one who breathes ice will rediscover what was lost.

The soul of green will be lost and found again, but they will not emerge as they once were. The song of war will play for the ears of many, and the song of righteousness will play for the ears of few. A chain of gold will silence the drums of death beneath a sunless sky.

The just will be welcomed by the stars, and the progeny will sit amongst the clouds. The stallion will halt the stampede, and the swords will shatter at the feet of five.

One will bring about the end of existence as it is currently known. Two will be lost where time no longer turns. Three will hear the voices of the divine. Four will find strength in unity. Five will become a phoenix risen from the ashes.

"No." Hyacinth, perched on the very edge of Aurelia's knees, shook her head and pointed at the word *war* in the fifth paragraph. "It's supposed to be a big W, Mama."

Aurelia made the change and swallowed the lump in her throat. "How does it look now?"

"Perfect." Hyacinth leaned back, slumping against her mother's chest. "It's very mysterious."

Aurelia couldn't help but chuckle. "Yes, it is. Do you know why?"

"No."

"It's telling the story of something that hasn't happened yet, just like you said earlier. Perhaps some of it has, but not all of it. It's meant to give us an idea of what will happen, but we can't know everything for sure."

Hyacinth pondered that for a moment. "It's like we have to use our imaginations."

"Exactly." Aurelia chewed on her lower lip. "Do you...Do you have any ideas about it?"

Her daughter yawned. "No, Mama. I'm sleepy now."

Aurelia kissed her cheek. "All right."

She folded the prophecy and slipped it into her pocket, then carefully rose from her desk to carry Hyacinth upstairs to her bedchamber. By the time they arrived, Hyacinth was snoring, like helping her mother finish the prophecy had absolutely drained her. Aurelia tucked her back into bed, kissed her on the forehead, and made a beeline for her bedroom.

Jack was still awake, telling Edom a story about his travels while the two ate biscuits in bed. He tried to hide the treats when Aurelia walked in—he was ashamed of his late-night snacking habit, despite Aurelia never saying a word about it—which, naturally, made the sprite cackle at him.

"We were just, erm—" Jack started.

"Sisi finished the prophecy," Aurelia blurted.

His eyes widened to the size of saucers. "What?"

She explained what'd happened as quickly as she could, then took the prophecy from her pocket and handed it to him. Edom perched on his shoulder to read it, too, its enormous eyes shimmering with intrigue. She sat next to them on her side of the bed, watching as they read. By the time Jack finished, he seemed more frustrated by it than he'd been when it was incomplete.

"It's awfully long," he drawled.

Aurelia glowered at him. "Prophecies can be as short as a sentence or two, or as long as a story. You should know this."

"I'm no oracle, Aurelia—though, apparently, our daughter is."

She flinched. "You know what this means. We have to let her keep her powers. I know it may cause some problems for us in the future, but we can find a way around it all."

"I know." Jack mirrored her smile and scanned the parchment again. "Are we entirely certain it's correct? We can't know for sure if these are the same sentences Maysa knew."

"It is correct," Edom insisted. "Look at the words. They match."

"Edom's right," Aurelia murmured. "The language, the tone of voice, the content...Everything Sisi added mirrors the rest of it. And...I find it odd that Sisi came to me with this just hours after I told you I wished we knew the full prophecy. It's like the gods knew it was time for us to hear it, and they gave her a sign to share it with us."

And maybe, she thought to herself, *this means they haven't completely given up on me, too.*

Jack still looked suspicious, but he didn't question it further. "Do you have any theories?"

"The masquerader has to be Willem. He glamoured himself physically and emotionally, and he pretended to be a hero to gain favor and power," she replied, pointing to the parchment. "The end of him brought Edea to the realm, but it also led Krotis—whose symbolic color is amber—to entrap me, and others, within their scheme. And the line about the masquerader's curse...It has to be referring to how I thought I was free of him after his death, only to have his ghost come back to haunt me with all of this conflict. At least it seems to suggest that this supposed curse will have consequences for Krotis, too."

He nodded. "'The soul of green...'"

"Annera," Edom suggested. "Emerald longbelly."

"And Shasta Selle—maybe." Jack's eyes seemed to glow with excitement now that everything was piecing itself together. "Archie and Halvor both said Annera will have a new rider. As for the bit about *the song of War*...Why is it capitalized?"

"I don't know," she admitted. "Sisi told me to capitalize it."

"Gods above." Jack's lips parted as he straightened up and stared at her, nearly squishing Edom against the headboard. "Did she think it was a name?"

Aurelia's eyes widened. "It means Immor. The god of war."

"Has to be," Edom chimed in.

Jack nodded in agreement as he turned his gaze back to the parchment. "I don't know about the rest of it, though. *The just, the progeny, the stallion...*"

"From what I can gather, there will be five important players in whatever's to come," Aurelia deduced. "There are only Four Pillars,

306

though. If four of the five are me, Diantha, Shasta—or Annera's next rider—and whomever claims the water dragon...That leaves someone unaccounted for. Someone we haven't given any thought to."

Jack only sighed. "They'll reveal themselves, eventually. It could be the Council, too, but I doubt it."

Aurelia's eyes flickered over to the prophecy in Jack's hands. She'd thought everything would make more sense when she had the full story, but now, she was left with even more questions.

***

Jiluan Zhoqa, who'd killed his brother in hand-to-hand combat for their father's throne in Kazamir, hadn't wasted any time writing to Aurelia.

He wrote on the day the eight-week period came to an end, and the raven arrived just a day after that. It was brought to Aurelia directly by a messenger while she ate breakfast with Jack, Rayan, and the children. She normally didn't take messages at the dining table, but as soon as she realized who it was from, she was too eager to wait.

She asked the governesses to take the children outside to finish breakfast, and they never turned down an opportunity for a picnic, so they didn't protest. Rayan's children, plus Thea and Mycah, on the other hand, were a bit bothered to be sent away. She'd make it up to them later.

As soon as the young ears had gone, she unraveled the scroll and read it aloud:

For Her Grace, the Dragon of Akkinor:

I hope this message finds you well. Now that the matter of my father's succession has been dealt with, and I've taken my rightful place as Lord of Kazamir, we must address several urgent concerns. Before I proceed, I'd like to start by saying that Kazamir's alliance with Akkinor will not be affected by the change in leadership. Rest assured that I have every intention of maintaining the promises my father made to you.

Naturally, the entirety of Bozar plans to join you in the fight against Krotis after they had my father so needlessly murdered. Though it may be some time before we see battle again, given what your dragon inflicted in Krotis several weeks ago, I imagine this is not the end of Krotis's efforts to change the way of things across the realm. I stood by my father's side many years ago when he dismantled a branch of the Guild of Steel here in Kazamir, so I am familiar with the risks. I will not take the chance of letting the Guild succeed in Krotis, rumor or not. My father would've said the same.

However, as Lord Zhaaran will surely relay to you, we Four Lords have some hesitations. The prophecy speaks of Four Pillars, and as you explained, these pillars are dragons and their riders. We have turned to uncovering the identity of the fourth pillar: the water dragon and its rider. The pillars appear to be at the forefront of the prophecy, and we believe it will be difficult to proceed if we remain unaware of this missing piece.

As of now, we have no plans to retaliate against Krotis, as their current state of disarray gives us an opportunity to dissect the prophecy in greater detail. Hopefully, the answers we uncover will put an end to Krotis's schemes before things can go any further. It is our hope that our findings will turn the people of Krotis in our favor, shedding light on the Council's corruption. But if you or Queen Reyna have cause to initiate another battle, or if Krotis happens to respond to any of us in the near future, please know that all of Bozar will be fighting at your side.

Knowledge is the greatest power in the realm. Without it, we are but flesh and bone existing in a world we are unworthy of.

Sincerely,

Jiluan Zhoqa, Lord of Kazamir.

Jack raised an eyebrow. "He seems a bit more...*together* than his father was. He sounds quite rational and articulate."

"I believe the word you're looking for is *professional*." Rayan snorted and shook his head. "I wonder what the other brother was like."

Aurelia cracked a smile. "At least we know for certain that the entirety of Bozar is prepared for what's to come. But this business with the water dragon...It's like searching for a needle in a haystack. We know Halvor's theory about Caathet, but it's just that—a theory. Even if Caathet is the dragon in question, nobody knows where to find him or who his rider might be."

"The prophecy doesn't appear to hint at anything, either." Rayan sighed. "As for other news...I sent spies to Krotis not long after you returned from battle. Despite our allies keeping us informed on anything their scouts might find, I thought it best to send reinforcements. One was killed by Vrurith under suspicion of being a spy—another witnessed the execution. The same witness claims that Lord Keer is dead, and the other nobles were gravely injured in battle. Lords Quagg and Reesa seem to have recovered, though."

Aurelia nodded in approval. She hadn't told Rayan to send spies to Carthe, but she was glad he did. She knew there were likely many Kroti spies lingering across Akkinor, hiding in plain sight, and she had to return to favor—especially after what she'd helped inflict in Krotis.

"Anything else?" Jack pressed, swallowing a mouthful of eggs. "Did they happen to overhear anything about the Guild, the Council's plans, the dragon—?"

"Annera hasn't been spotted since the battle. Our spies believe Krotis is keeping her hidden so she can recover," Rayan replied. "Nothing about the Council's plans, but apparently, secret meetings have been occurring across the kingdom. Our spies haven't managed to acquire invitations to these meetings thus far, and they claim it's impossible to sneak past security. After one of our spies was executed, I imagine Krotis is taking extra precautions to avoid the very thing we need."

Aurelia grimaced. "Naturally."

***

"My gods." Darius Reesa's eyes nearly bugged out of his head when he ducked into the old fighting pit to visit his dragon, Annera. "You've certainly grown, haven't you?"

The emerald beast chuffed at him. Her tense demeanor suggested it was unwise for him to approach her, but he did so anyhow, knowing she wouldn't hurt him after she'd protected him in battle. She knew what her duty was, even for a young thing—though she didn't look so young anymore. She'd grown exponentially since the battle several weeks ago, and while she was still smaller than the other two dragons, she was now about half the size of that reckless violet one.

She stepped back when he held out a hand to touch her snout, making the chains around her ankles and her neck rattle like clanging swords. He dropped his hand, smiling a bit, and searched those soulless reptilian eyes for any sign that she understood him—and what he needed her to do. He didn't find evidence of that last bit, but something deep in his gut told him that she understood him. After all, dragons were said to be as intelligent as humans.

We'll see, he thought.

"You'll be free of those soon enough," Darius promised, gesturing toward the chains. "It's for your own good, you see. If the wrong person were to spot you out and about, they might try to kill you. You understand that, don't you?"

The beast only stared at him.

"Now, there's something I've been thinking about." He paused when the chuckling voices of his soldiers outside interrupted his thoughts, making him scowl. "Queen Aurelia was rescued by her dragon when she broke her oath to King Willem three years ago. He felt her calling for him from across the sea. I have to believe the connection between every dragon and their rider is that strong. Your mistress is too weak to contribute to what needs to be done—both mentally and physically—on the battlefield. You shall have to carry out the mission without her. Can I trust you to heed her directions from afar?"

Annera continued staring at him. He sighed, aggravated, and tried his hardest to keep his composure. She was as difficult as any adolescent—and being bonded to yet another adolescent probably didn't help her temperament. But he'd raised children before, and he knew that the best way to get a response out of them was to frighten them.

"The only reason your mistress lives and reigns is because of you," Darius told her. "She is without a husband, and even if my son managed to impregnate her before his death, the trauma her body sustained after the battle would have killed the child. She has no heir, and the law demands that each reigning noble has a spouse. So, Annera, if you cannot serve us as we need you to, she will not survive, and you will be left without a rider."

A low growl rose up in Annera's throat, frightening him just enough that he took a step back. But he knew in his heart that she wouldn't hurt him, even if he had her mistress killed; she was too timid to incite violence without being given the command to do so.

"I do hope you understand," he continued. "You will do for us what we noblemen cannot while other matters take precedent. It won't be long now before we're unstoppable, but we need you to remove the obstacle in our path. Both you and your mistress will be generously rewarded if you succeed. The Almighty Immor will ensure it." Annera bowed her head, like a surrender, and the motion made Darius grin from ear to ear. "Good. Now, I shall leave you to rest before your next adventure. Goodbye, Annera."

The dragon released a loud whine when he turned his back on her, but he didn't bother addressing her again—he had a battle to plan.

XXXVI

Aurelia toyed with Jack's dark, sweaty hair as he laid his head on her chest, watching as his finger carved a path down her stomach. He splayed his hand flat over her stomach, running his palm over to her side and down to her thigh, and tilted his head just enough to press a kiss to her ribs.

"I wish every day could be like this," he murmured.

"So do I."

He picked his head up to rest his chin on her belly so he could meet her gaze. "I wonder what Lily Linden and Jack Sherbourne would be doing right now."

That made her laugh. "Exactly what we're doing—only on a blanket in the Ngora Valley, and probably without an enormous brood of children to mind."

"One or two children, though. Right?"

"Of course. I couldn't survive with my sanity if it was just the two of us forever."

Jack grinned that wicked grin she loved so much. "I do love it when you say such romantic things to me, Lily dear."

"I know." She hooked one of her bare legs around his backside, holding him closer to her, as he hugged her around the middle and rested his head on her chest again. "I'm not as skilled at romance as you are. You're a romantic without having to try."

"Oh?" That made him lift his head again, and she rolled her eyes when she saw that the grin hadn't faded from his lips. "Like when I do this?"

He snaked his hand between her thighs, making her shiver and squirm. She pushed him away—it was already nearing time to get ready for the day, and they'd had enough fun this morning as it was—as they laughed, now lying beside one another on their sides.

She matched his grin. "No, but I do like that."

"I know you do." He paused, looking like he was deep in thought, as he tucked his hands under his head, just like she was doing. "Like when I tell you that every part of me burns like dragonfire when you're on top of me? Or below me, for that matter?"

"Not quite."

"Hmm." His grin only deepened, making her giggle. After a few seconds, though, the silliness faded as he brushed hair from her face. "I see. It's when I tell you that looking into your eyes reminds me to seek the beauty in our darkened world, and the sound of your voice is like a melody made just for me. Or maybe it's when I tell you that I still struggle for air in your presence, even after all these years, because I cannot think about something as trivial as breathing when my every thought is consumed by you."

Aurelia's eyes burned as he splayed his hand over her cheek. "Jack..."

He leaned over to silence her with a kiss. "I know. I'm too good for you."

She laughed, but a few tears escaped the corners of her eyes. He brushed them away instinctively and kissed her again, and for the first time in weeks, she didn't care that the liquid on his fingers was clear instead of gold.

"I love you," she whispered, grazing his cheek with the side of her finger. "Meeting you was the greatest thing to ever happen to me."

Jack smiled as he kissed the tip of her nose. "There's that look in your eyes again."

"What look?"

"The one that saved me from a lifetime of solitude all those years ago." Before she could reply, he lifted his head higher and furrowed his eyebrows. "I think I hear little footsteps in the hall. We'd better—"

Just then, the door flew open, and the couple barely had time to cover themselves with their bedsheets before their four elder children came barreling in. The governesses hollered after them and skidded into the room as the children climbed onto their parents' bed, but when the women realized what the queen and her husband had been doing only moments prior, they ducked out of the room and called for the children from there.

The children had been promised a day with their parents, and excitement had overtaken them. By the time Aurelia and Jack got dressed, the children were still waiting for them in the hallway with the governesses, having refused to move an inch without their parents.

Aurelia and Jack took the children—the twins now with them—to the gardens for breakfast. They gathered under Linden's tree on a massive white blanket, surrounded by food, toys, and flowers the children had plucked on their short stroll to the tree. Aurelia didn't hesitate to take off her shoes and bury her toes in the grass before she took a single bite of breakfast, and her children quickly mimicked her while Jack merely chuckled at them.

"Mother," Halle began, "can we hear a story?"

"Of course." Aurelia brushed off the twinge of sadness she felt at being called *Mother*. Halle had taken to calling her parents *Mother* and *Father* rather than *Mama* and *Papa* in recent weeks, and neither of them particularly liked it. "What kind of story?"

"A love story!"

Jack nearly choked on his tea. "Mother of Buen. You're too young to be thinking about love stories, little miss."

Halle sniffed. "Please?"

"All right." Aurelia smiled and finished the strawberry she'd been nibbling on. "Many years ago, there lived a prince who'd spent years searching for a wife. One day, he attended the wedding of an old lord and his much younger, lovelier bride. The prince took one look at the bride and fell madly in love with her. Unfortunately for the old lord, he died before he could dance with his new wife for the first time. The prince was heartbroken to know that the bride would have to trade pretty colors for mourning black, and that she had been forced to marry an old man she didn't love. He asked her to marry him that very same night, and she said yes."

Henry blinked at her. "Is it a true story?"

"Mhm." Hyacinth nodded as she scarfed down a large bite of potatoes, holding out her arm to keep little Harlen from snatching a fistful off her plate. "It's about Mama's parents."

"How do you know?" he demanded.

"I just know."

"She's right," Aurelia mused, smiling. "As for your other Grandmama and Grandpapa...I think your father can share that story for you."

Jack grunted. "It's nowhere near as exciting."

"What about *your* love story, Mother?" Halle asked, her oceanic eyes a perfect replica of Jack's. "How did you and Father fall in love?"

"Well..." Aurelia tried to ignore the way Jack was looking at her, but her cheeks burned as soon as she felt his eyes on her. "I was traveling alone one day, and I shouldn't have been. It was dangerous. Two scary men found me and tried to, erm, take my coin." *Tied me to a tree and tried to rape me.* "All of a sudden, a great bear of a man appeared in the near distance, and he shot an arrow at the tree behind me, just above my head, to scare them. He commanded the two men to let me go, and they did." *They didn't, but we killed them together.* "After that, we became inseparable, and we continued on our adventures together."

"Who was the bear?" Halyna whispered, overcome by intrigue.

While Aurelia and Jack laughed, Hyacinth replied, "It's Papa, Lena. *Obviously.*"

Jack reached over to brush hair from Aurelia's eyes. "It was the best decision I ever made, stopping to help a strange woman in the forest. For a while, though, I didn't realize how lucky I was."

Henry gulped from a chalice of orange juice. "Why, Papa?"

"Your mother was often cross with me."

"Why?"

"I was a bit of a pest back then, I'm afraid. I still am, but she's gotten used to me."

"For the most part." Aurelia cracked a smile and tilted her face into his touch when he cupped her cheek. "And now, I have six more little pests to save me from anything that should come my way."

"We aren't pests!" Henry protested. "We're *children!*"

"Are you?" Jack teased. "I hadn't noticed!"

Henry climbed on top of Jack, knocking him down and onto his back, and soon enough, his sisters were inspired to follow suit. Jack managed to wrap his arms around all four of them, tickling, kissing, and squeezing them until they were red with laughter. Aurelia watched from the sidelines with the twins on her lap, the sound of her children's laughter filling her with a kind of peace she hadn't known in seasons.

Not long after, the servants came to clear breakfast away. As soon as the plates and cups were gone, the family splayed out on the blanket to watch the clouds floating through the clear sky while their food settled. They were all connected somehow: Harlen and Holly crawling over their parents' legs, Halyna laying on top of Jack while holding Henry's hand, Halle pressing the top of her head against Aurelia's, and Hyacinth resting her head on Aurelia's stomach while her feet sat on Henry's chest. Nobody complained, cried, or fought—they just existed together, marveling at the cloud formations as morning turned to afternoon before their eyes.

For the entire day, Aurelia forgot about the war, the Guild, the prophecy. She forgot about the paperwork on her desks, the soldiers she was meant to knight tomorrow, the bickering noblemen waiting for her to settle yet another petty dispute. She forgot about the missing Quenosi princess, the nymphs sleeping in the trees, the golden tears she no longer wept. She forgot about everything, good and bad—and for a moment there, she even forgot that she was a queen.

Today, she was just a normal wife and mother, without a worry on her mind other than the fact that her firstborn had stopped calling her *Mama*.

***

About a week after that perfect day with her family, Aurelia left her study after dinnertime to find Thea and Mycah. They'd asked her permission to spend a few weeks in Sadia, as Thea had been courting a nobleman's son in West Droweg after meeting him at Aurelia's ball. She wished to spend time with him—with her brother as a chaperone, of course. Aurelia was thrilled to tell them the invitation had been accepted by the Earl of West Droweg, who was beyond pleased that his son may have found a bride favored by the queen.

On her way to find the siblings, Aurelia skidded to a stop when she approached the foyer. She quickly hid herself behind a pillar, her heart racing, as Rayan escorted Eric Haze through the front doors and into the palace. Eric took off his hat, crinkled it in his hands, and muttered something she couldn't hear as he followed Rayan into another hallway.

Nobody had told her that Eric was coming to visit tonight. Rayan knew by now that he could invite anyone he so desired to visit him at the palace. It was his home, too, after all—he didn't need Aurelia's permission to have his father visit him. It still felt strange to have Eric in the palace, but if she steered clear of him, she wouldn't have to continue lying to his face.

Only Rayan's.

It got harder every day to lie to him about their relationship, but she couldn't bring herself to tell him the truth. She didn't want to complicate things for him. Not yet.

After finding Thea and Mycah and telling them the good news, Aurelia set out for her study again, but she stopped when she found herself outside of a parlor. The door was cracked open, and Arian's voice flooded her eardrums. She peeked through the crack, and to her surprise, she found her uncle sitting in an armchair across from Eric. Rayan was nowhere to be found.

"...low opinion of me," Eric was saying. His back was facing the door, but even so, Aurelia could see him fiddling with the hat on his lap. "Katryna forbade me to tell you anything, but I should have told you the truth about why I had to leave. You see, I came to Carthe because I thought my family had died. My wife, our two children, my parents. I'd lost everything, and I needed to go somewhere to clear my head. Just before I left Taundosa, I learned that my wife and children had survived. Katryna urged me to go back to them. It was a difficult choice—I didn't want to leave her, but I missed my family. She made the decision for me."

"As she often did for so many of us," Arian murmured. "She was stubborn as a mule, and she rarely took no for an answer. I can't blame you for doing what you did."

He must've sensed Aurelia eavesdropping, because his gaze flicked over to the door. They met eyes, and for a fraction of a second, it felt like he was asking her permission for something.

She knew. She gave him a slight nod, her heart hammering, and watched as his entire body appeared to deflate.

"I'm glad your visit to Rayan brought us together today, even if it wasn't planned," Arian continued. "There's something I have to tell you, old friend."

Eric's hands shook as he lifted a teacup to his lips. "What is it?"

Arian hesitated. His face crumpled, but in the blink of an eye, it was smooth again. Aurelia's heart yearned for him—she wished she could be there, telling her father alongside him, but she couldn't do it. She wasn't strong enough to see his eyes when he found out Katryna was dead. That, and...she wasn't quite ready to face him as her father just yet.

"About three-and-thirty years ago," Arian croaked, "Katryna's soul left the earthly realm following complications from childbirth."

The teacup fell from Eric's grasp and onto the floor, staining the rug with tea but not shattering. Aurelia winced at the loud thump, and she had to bite her cheeks to keep from crying when she saw the way Eric trembled like he was suffering from hypothermia.

"Katryna...is dead?"

"Yes."

"B-But—"

"I never understood why she didn't tell you about the babe until I met Rayan," Arian murmured, his dark eyes welling with tears. "She knew you had a family to return to. Instead of forcing you to choose between families, she chose for you. I-I think she knew you would've stayed with her if you'd known she was pregnant." Eric made no reply, but his shoulders were slumped now, and his head was slightly bowed like his neck couldn't support its weight. "She didn't want you to make an impossible choice. She loved you too much to ask that of you. I know that now."

That broke the dam. Eric fell forward, his head in his hands, as sobs flowed freely. Aurelia squeezed her eyes shut in hopes that she'd forget what she saw, but it was too late. The memory would be burned in her brain forever: the sight of his body collapsing with grief, and the sound of his heartbroken wailing.

"I-I wrote," Eric blubbered, the poor old man shaking like a leaf. "I wrote twice a season for twenty years. She never responded, so I gave up. I thought she-she'd moved on. And all this time, she was-she was *gone?*" Arian couldn't so much as nod. "And she died...in childbirth?"

"Yes."

The reminder seemed to calm him enough to realize what that meant. "W-What happened to our child? Where are they? Are they all right? Did they live?"

"Katryna gave birth to a daughter before the gods took her. I'm afraid I can't say much about her, because it's her choice to find you and tell you exactly who she is. When she does find you, though, you'll see Kitty's eyes again as I have. I hope it brings you the same peace it's brought me." Arian's words made Aurelia feel like someone had punched her in the gut and knocked her onto the ground, sucking the air out of her lungs. Eric only hiccupped into another sob. "What I will tell you is this: she's a happy, healthy, extravagant woman with a beautiful family of her own. She's kind, clever, handy with a bow, and particularly adept at getting herself into trouble."

Eric managed a guttural chuckle. "She's...She's like her mother, then."

"Very much so. But she's wise and rational, and fiercely protective over those she loves. She can have quite the temper sometimes, but she always finds her peace of mind. She gets all of that from you."

"And she...she knows about me?"

"She does."

"Does she despise me?"

Arian paused, making Aurelia's heart lurch. "No. She will come to you when she's ready, and she will welcome you with open arms. I'm sure of it."

Aurelia knew that was a message for her, too: *Let's not wait much longer. For his sake and for yours.*

Eric accepted a handkerchief from Arian to wipe his eyes. "I-I can hardly fathom it. All this time, I thought Kitty was alive. I've always felt her presence near me, like I can hold her hand if my imagination is strong enough, but I've told myself it's simply because I miss her. I never thought it could be her spirit walking beside me."

"I'm surprised her spirit hasn't attempted to scare all of us out of our wits."

That made Eric chuckle. "She was quite devious, wasn't she?"

"Always."

He paused for a moment. "When she left us...Was it painful?"

Arian hesitated again, too. "I don't believe so. She lost too much blood, but she didn't appear to be in any pain. She was strong throughout the entire ordeal. I can't say the same about myself. I don't recognize the man I was in those moments, but Kitty was never anything but herself. Brave until the end."

"She was afraid of very little in this world, including looking death in the eye."

Arian's smile shook on his lips. "The last thing she said was that she was not afraid."

Eric burst into tears all over again, shoulders wracking with every sob. "Oh, my love..."

Aurelia peeled herself away from the door and pressed her back up against the wall, but when sickness stirred in her gut, she hunched over with her hands on her knees, counting her breaths to keep from vomiting. A servant rushed over to offer aid, but she waved them off with her hand, unable to speak.

It was one thing to hear her birth father learn about the daughter he didn't know he had. It was something else entirely to hear an old man learn that the woman he'd loved for most of his life had been dead for three decades after bringing their child into the world.

Aurelia didn't know how long she was out there with her back against the wall, but she eventually sunk onto the floor with her knees drawn to her chest, like a child frightened of a monster under their bed. Her legs felt too weak to support her weight, and with the way her heart was pounding, she feared it would give out if she tried to move even an inch.

Then she heard footsteps approaching the parlor door, and a sudden strength willed her to stand. She wiped her cheeks and smoothed her skirts just in time for the door to open. She started walking as if she'd been strolling the halls and just passing by, but it was hard to keep her emotions in check when she saw Eric's tear-stained cheeks and puffy eyes staring back at her.

"Y-Your Grace." He managed a weak, wobbling bow when she greeted him with a forced smile. "F-Forgive the state of me. I have just..."

He trailed off as his gaze lowered to her chest. His eyebrows furrowed and his lips parted a bit while he stared. Behind him, Arian only sighed and bowed his head. Aurelia didn't understand the look of defeat in her uncle's eyes until she realized what Eric was staring at: her locket.

Katryna's locket.

His gaze shot up to hers in an instant, making her breath catch. He studied her face for a moment, then looked at the locket again, and then back to her face. His eyes widened more and more as the seconds passed, and when the realization struck him fully, he took a step backward, nearly bumping into Arian.

"Y-You—" he started.

That was all he managed to say before deafening bells rang out, chiming six times. The Folly was under attack.

XXXVII

The chaos began as soon as the first round of bells silenced.

Explosions echoed across the Folly, sending tremors throughout the earth that rattled the ground, shook the buildings, and sent decor toppling over or shattering onto the floor. Bursts of light from both fires and magic illuminated the night sky, visible from every window in every corridor of the palace. Screeching gryphons, battle cries, and terrified screams could be heard in the near distance, inching closer and closer to the grounds.

For some reason, during the initial chaos, Aurelia was reminded of Elder Firadus's visit to Akkinor, and something he'd said before he left: *So you do not feel threatened in your own home today.* He hadn't needed to add *today,* but he did.

It made sense to her now. He'd been trying to warn her.

Aurelia didn't need to tell Halvor what to do when everything began. The instant the first round of bells chimed, she felt a tug in her chest, and she could've sworn her brain was showing her images of Halvor lifting off into the sky to circle the palace grounds. He knew what he was meant to do until she came for him: guard the palace and his family from the intruders.

At that same time, Aurelia had instinctively pushed herself against Arian and Eric, backing them into a wall and shielding them with her own body. Both of them tried to push her away to protect her instead, but she held her ground, refusing to let them overpower her.

After this first wave of tremors subsided, she turned and shoved them back into the parlor. She commanded them to stay put until she assessed the incident, not wanting them to be out in the halls—and potentially lost—if something were to happen to threaten the palace.

Arian protested, and as she ignored him, she briefly met Eric's gaze. Her heart ached when she recognized the look in his light eyes: despite what was happening, he cared more about the realization he'd just come to. Unfortunately, now wasn't the time to explain how his queen was also his daughter.

"Get to the crypt!" The moment she left them in the parlor, Aurelia heard herself yelling before she realized what she was saying. She directed the words at the frenzied servants bustling around the halls, running and covering their heads. "Find everyone you can, and wait there!"

Some of them listened to her and started yelling about the crypt, but others were too panicked to understand her—or even realize it was Aurelia and not someone else giving the order.

"Aurelia!"

She turned as another tremor shook the palace, making the chandelier in the foyer sway and rattle. Jack was rushing toward her with Edom perched on his shoulder, the sprite hanging onto Jack's tunic for dear life.

"What on earth is happening?" she said, taking his hands when he slowed to a stop in front of her. "Why didn't—"

"—we see them approaching?" He shook his head and gritted his teeth. "I was having a whisky with Lord Chilton and Lord Baylor when we heard the bells. We tried to look around using the telescope, and while we saw plenty of soldiers and gryphons throughout the kingdom, we didn't see a single ship at sea. Lord Chilton thinks they must've cast some sort of invisibility spell, or perhaps—"

He stopped when another explosion in the distance made the ground shake. In the blink of an eye, he'd engulfed Aurelia in his arms and practically dragged her over to a nearby pillar, where he squished her between his body and the pillar while covering her head with his arms. She sunk into his chest, wrapping her arms around his middle, and buried her cheek in his tunic, trembling, as the tremor subsided.

"Are you all right?" he murmured, pulling back and cupping her face. She managed a nod, though words seemed to fail her, as he quickly resumed what he'd been saying before. "He thinks they used an invisibility spell, or perhaps a reflection spell—something to hide the fleet."

She wanted to tease him for showing off his newfound knowledge of magic, but there'd be time enough for that later.

"What else did you see?" she asked.

"It's Krotis, obviously. Even in the darkness, their amber banners and capes are impossible to miss. No sighting of Annera yet, though—just gryphons and men. They're laying siege to nearby villages and towns, but their formations are dividing. I suspect half of them will try to infiltrate the palace, and the other half will go after Kalenbrar."

She nodded and swallowed the thick lump in her throat. "The children—"

"The governesses and ten of our soldiers are with them. I moved them into a windowless room for now—I don't wish for them to see what's happening. We may have to move them to the crypt if the carnage comes any closer to the palace, though."

"How bad is it?" She winced when everything in the foyer, including she and Jack, were bathed in an eerie orange glow flooding through the windows. "What are they doing?"

"Flaming stones have leveled buildings and destroyed roads, so I assume they have catapults on their ships," he replied, grimacing. "The gryphons are dropping debris from the sky and snatching people from the streets. Kroti mages and mortals alike are—"

"There you are!" Rayan appeared at the end of the hall and rushed over to them, navigating between panicked servants. "I've sent my children to the crypt with Thea and Mycah, but my father—"

"He's all right. He's with Arian," Aurelia assured him. "We'll move them when we find a safer place, but for now, Arian's magic will protect them."

He sighed in relief. "Good. I've already sent our men out to fight, and half of the Assembly has gone with them. I imagine most of our civilians will form a militia to join the fight, too. I instructed Lady Litten to write to our nobles for support, but only Myra would arrive within the next few hours, and we have no way of knowing how long this will last. It could be over by the time reinforcements arrive."

"There are more Kroti than we could've expected," Jack added, shaking his head. "It looks like they didn't bring the full force of their military to the beach in Runeia."

Aurelia hadn't considered that before, but now that he said it, it made sense. She hadn't brought her entire military to Runeia, and Reyna hadn't sent every fighter under her banners, either. With Krotis being so small, they'd assumed they could win the battle with less than half of their forces. They'd won, of course, but they'd won under the impression that Krotis's entire military was there that day. Nobody had realized how large the Kroti army actually was.

"If I were attacking a kingdom in hopes of weakening its leader," Aurelia started, wincing at the explosions and the screaming in the distance, "I'd do two things: strike the leader in their place of refuge, and leave them with only ashes and rubble to rule over."

"We have to evacuate as many civilians as we can," Rayan concluded.

She nodded. "I-I have a feeling Annera will be coming sooner or later. They'd never be stupid enough to attack Akkinor without her while Halvor is here. She can level the Folly exactly as she leveled the beach in Runeia. They'd be expecting us to bring the civilians into our gates for safety, just to pit dragon against dragon here on the grounds, thus eliminating everyone inside. We have to get them out of the Folly, and we have to get everyone here out of the palace, too."

Jack squared his shoulders and raised an eyebrow. "What do you need us to do?"

Aurelia took a long, deep breath and took only a moment to think. She'd trained for this since she was a young girl—trained to be queen, and the Commander of the Royal Army. Her father had prepared her for this day, but only time would tell if his words of wisdom had been enough.

As much as it pained her to send Jack into the carnage, he was needed outside of the grounds. The people recognized him and trusted him. They'd follow him out of the Folly and toward Oleander's Valley, where they could seek shelter in the arena. If the arena happened to be threatened, the border of Myra was only a stone's throw from the valley, and they could seek refuge there. Hopefully, by that point, Myran soldiers would be there to help guide them and join the defense.

Edom would go with Jack, too. The sprite was instructed to gather as many other sprites and fairies as it could, as their glows would illuminate paths to safety for the civilians amidst the darkness, smoke, and dust clouds from collapsing debris. After giving the sprites and fairies their task, Edom would then try to gather the other creatures in the Folly, giving them the choice to evacuate with the humans, or join the fight alongside Aurelia's troops.

Rayan and the Assembly members still in the palace, on the other hand, would evacuate the grounds, directing everyone toward the valley and Myra, too. The crypt was a safe place for now, but if anything happened to the palace, it was possible they'd get stuck there. The last thing Aurelia wanted was for a ceiling to cave in or walls to crumble, blocking all exits and even collapsing on top of the crypt, trapping or killing everyone inside: her friends, her lady's maids, her messengers and cooks and priests—and worst of all, her children.

"What about the children?" Jack pressed, as if he could read her thoughts. "We can't expose them by bringing them outside. It's too dangerous. If any enemies follow us and happen to recognize them—"

"They're going to Omara," she interrupted, making his eyes bug. "Arian will take them to your family on dragonback. Halvor will allow it if our girls are there."

Jack shook his head. "Halvor is needed here."

"He needs to protect the children first," she insisted. She could see in his eyes and Rayan's that they understood, but at the same time, they all knew Halvor was Aurelia's greatest defense—and the Folly's. "Sieges have been overcome in the Folly many times before *without* the assistance of a dragon. It won't be a long flight, either. He'll see them to safety at Witton Castle, and he'll come right back here to help us. We'll be all right in the meantime."

Jack shook his head. "Aurelia..."

"The children need him more than I do." She set a hand on his arm, squeezed, and forced a smile. "It'll be fine."

"Arian can't take all six of them by himself," Rayan reminded her. "The governesses won't fit on Halvor's back with seven others, even children, and they're too terrified of Halvor to consider making the flight, anyway."

She raised an eyebrow. "What are you saying?"

Rayan inhaled sharply. "I think my father should go with them."

"If he's willing to, he can go. If not, I'll send a soldier with them." Aurelia turned to Jack. "Fetch the children, and bring them to the back doors. I'll meet you there, and I'll have Halvor retreat to the gardens. Tell the governesses to meet the others in the crypt, where they'll follow Rayan to safety. Leave two soldiers with you and the children for now, but send the others to fight."

Jack nodded and rushed off, Edom still clinging to his shoulder. Aurelia took Rayan's hand and hurried over to the parlor where she'd left Arian and Eric. Both men rushed over to the door as soon as it opened, though Eric seemed less concerned about the attack, and more curious about studying Aurelia.

"Krotis is laying siege to the Folly. We need to get everyone out," she said quickly, ignoring the way Eric stared at her. "I-I have something to ask the two of you, though. Halvor will take the children to Witton Castle in Omara as a precautionary measure, but they can't go alone."

Arian nodded without a second thought. "Halvor and I will get them to the Ashfords quickly and safely."

"Y-You want me to go, too?" Eric's eyes widened as he realized what she meant. "B-But—"

"You may not know him, but he knows you." Arian set a comforting hand on his old friend's trembling shoulder. Aurelia winced at his words, hoping Rayan didn't think anything of them, as she realized Arian must've told Eric all about Halvor's relationship to the Cristos family after she left them tonight. "You'll be just fine."

Rayan gave his father an encouraging smile. "You've always been enamored with Halvor, Father. Now's your chance to know what it's like to fly with him."

Eric didn't answer as he turned his gaze to Aurelia. "You're trusting me to escort your children to safety?"

She smiled. "I am."

Again, he didn't answer. Then he lifted a shaking hand to her face, ignoring the way the walls trembled around them, and pressed his cool palm to her cheek. She froze instinctively, but after a second went by, she found herself leaning her face into his touch. She wanted to close her eyes, to stay there for a few moments longer while she and her father recognized their relationship for the first time, but she couldn't.

Eric managed two hoarse words: "All right."

"Thank you." She cleared her throat, blinking the burning tears from her eyes, as he dropped his hand. "We need to leave soon."

Rayan embraced his father, murmuring words for good luck, and the two held the hug for just a moment. Eric pulled back, held his son's face in his hands, and briefly looked back and forth between Rayan and Aurelia. A beaming smile formed on his lips as he compared his children, making a fist clench around Aurelia's heart.

Rayan left to assist with the evacuations, and Arian and Eric followed Aurelia through the halls toward the back door. Nearly everyone had fled the halls by then, following the instruction to gather in the crypt. The only people at the rear of the palace were Jack, the children, and two knights awaiting Aurelia's arrival.

The sight of her children broke her heart. They'd been bundled up in cloaks and hats to help disguise their identities, and the elder three were wearing packs on their backs—likely crammed with whatever necessities all six siblings couldn't leave the premises without. Jack held the twins in either arm while their carrier dangled off his shoulder, but the other four were sitting on the floor, huddled together at his feet while they whimpered at the sounds of war.

They scampered to their feet and rushed toward Aurelia when they saw her. She squished all four of them in her arms, holding them close, and inhaled the scent of infancy that still lingered on their heads.

She pulled away, sniffling, and looked at each of them. "I know you're frightened. I am, too. But some very bad people have come to hurt our home, and your papa and I can't stop them unless we know you're safe. You're going to stay with Grandmama and Grandpapa until the bad people have been stopped. Arian and Mister Haze will take you there on Halvor, and they'll stay with you."

"But—" Halle started, pouting her lower lip.

"No buts, little miss," Aurelia murmured, ignoring the aching in her heart. "I need you all to look out for each other. No quarreling. Your brothers and sisters are the greatest gift you'll ever know—protect each other, and remind each other to be brave. Papa and I will see you soon." She kissed each of them on the forehead, one by one. "I love you very much."

She squeezed them once more, then stood up to kiss the twins on their cheeks. The aching in her heart only worsened when both Harlen and Holly reached for her, wanting to snuggle with their mother.

The soldiers opened the doors for them, and instantly, the sounds of battle grew louder, and the smell of smoke, burning flesh, and magic wafted through Aurelia's nostrils. Bursts of light illuminated the darkness, revealing Halvor's massive silhouette prowling toward them.

Arian scooped up Halyna while Henry asked Eric—who happily obliged—to carry him. Aurelia took her elder daughters' hands in either of hers, inhaled sharply, and led her family toward Halvor while the sky changed colors around them, and while screaming and clanging swords flooded their eardrums.

While Jack said goodbye to the children, Aurelia approached Halvor and set her hands on either side of his snout. She touched her forehead to his scales, heart hammering, and managed a small smile when he chuffed against her.

"Bring them to safety," she whispered, running her hand along his scales. "Bring them to safety, and don't come back until you're absolutely certain they'll be okay."

He chuffed again, and she translated the response well enough: *It is my honor.*

Jack fitted Arian with a leather child carrier made specifically for the twins, so one was secured against Arian's chest, and the other against his back. When the carrier was fitted, Arian climbed onto Halvor's back with surprising ease. It was often hard for Aurelia to remember that he'd flown on Halvor numerous times before with Katryna and Anysa, but even now, over thirty years later, he did it as seamlessly as he must've back then.

Muscle memory, she thought.

Aurelia carried Holly while she climbed Halvor, kissed her daughter on the cheek, and put the babe on Arian's front. After taking Harlen from Jack, she put him on Arian's back and gave him a small peck, too. Halle came up next, sitting in front of Arian—close enough that he could wrap his arms around her, but not so close that she squished Holly.

Henry was next, seated behind Arian, and followed by Hyacinth. Hyacinth immediately reached around Henry to hold onto the carrier with both hands, holding Henry in place. The next to climb up was a trembling Eric, who moved slowly and cautiously while heeding each of Aurelia's instructions. He was pale and sweating by the time he was seated behind Hyacinth, though the awe in his eyes overpowered the fear on his face.

Lastly was mischievous Halyna, who sat perched on Eric's lap. Aurelia knew Halvor would keep himself as steady and level as possible, but still— things happened, and Aurelia was terrified by the thought of sending her children away to safety, only to have them fall from Halvor's back.

"Uncle," she said, balancing herself on the joints connecting Halvor's wings to his body, "is there a spell you can cast to keep everyone in place?"

"Hmm." He thought on that for a moment, wincing at the sounds of horror echoing in the distance. "There's something we mages like to refer to as the *sticky spell*—it makes one's skin like an adhesive. Some use it during battle to ensure they never drop their weapon. I don't know how long it lasts, though."

Aurelia nodded. "It'll last long enough. I know it will."

Arian closed his eyes, his palms glowing with blue light as they rested on Halle's middle. Halle giggled at the warmth of the magic while Arian's lips moved. Aurelia heard no sound, but she knew the spell was working when she saw the blue light spread from Halle and Arian to the others.

"I can't move!" Henry howled. He wiggled his bottom against the saddle and tried to lift himself up, to no avail. "I'm stuck!"

"I am, too," Hyacinth added.

"So am I," Eric chimed in. He still looked a bit green, but having Halyna in his arms—relying on him completely—seemed to steady him. "I don't think we'll be going anywhere."

"Everything will be just fine." Aurelia reached out to grasp Hyacinth's hand when her daughter reached down, but she was too far away, and their fingertips barely grazed each other's. "We'll send for you when everything is right here again. I love you all very much—be on your best behavior, look out for each other, and listen to Arian and Mister Haze."

Halle smiled. "We'll be okay, Mama."

Mama. Aurelia could've cried right then and there.

Aurelia climbed onto the ground again and met Halvor's eyes. He chuffed at her as if to wish her good luck, then turned to face the other end of the gardens. Aurelia stood back with Jack, clutching his hand with a vise-like grip, watching as Halvor stalked toward the wall. Her heart lurched when he lifted off into the sky after getting a running start, and somehow, the sound of her children's delighted squeals overpowered the sound of carnage from the kingdom.

They watched until Halvor was out of sight, took just a minute to pray for a safe arrival, and fled the gardens to meet their foes in battle.

XXXVIII

*Y*ou're trusting me to escort your children to safety?
I am.
All right.

The interaction had been a short one, but it was all Rayan could think about as he rushed to the crypt, summoning soldiers to accompany him whenever he passed them by. He wanted to keep his thoughts focused on the task at hand, but even as he walked into the resting place of Akkinor's greatest leaders, his mind revisited the conversation between his father and his queen.

While Rayan had been the one to suggest Eric accompany Arian and the children on dragonback, he hadn't thought Aurelia would agree with him. Eric was an aging, senile man who'd never even touched Halvor before. He may have been a soldier once, but he was just an older man with a poor memory and weak muscles nowadays—Rayan could see how any parent would decide against having Eric mind six young children on dragonback.

But she hadn't even hesitated. Her reply had been instant, and nothing about her demeanor suggested she was worried about it. It almost felt like she'd trusted Eric instinctively. Perhaps it was because Eric was Rayan's father, and she trusted Rayan like that; either way, it felt odd to him.

The dozens upon dozens of people in the crypt, who'd either been pacing or sitting on the floor, stilled and turned to face Rayan as soon as he and the soldiers arrived. They were talking over one another, a mile a minute, begging to know what was happening. Rayan's children were sitting on the ground beside Thea and Mycah, staring up at him with a kind of terror that filled him with guilt. After all, he was meant to protect them and rid them of fear, yet there was nothing he could do now other than see them out of their home while he stayed behind.

"Her Grace and the King Consort believe the palace will be targeted by the enemy," Rayan announced. "His Royal Highness is escorting the

Follians out of the kingdom and to Robert's Arena. I'll be taking you there, too. The crypt would be safe for a time, but not if the palace is breached. It's best if we leave now."

Murmurs echoed throughout the crypt. "What if they find us in the arena?" Irina, a governess, asked him. "What if they see us fleeing and follow us?"

"Then our soldiers—and anyone else who wishes to fight—will hold them off while the rest of you continue on to Myra," he replied. "We've sent word to the other kingdoms. Myra's response time will be the quickest, so we expect their reinforcements to arrive swiftly. They have men posted along their borders, anyway, so they will come to your aid when they see you."

"And what if the enemy follows us into Myra?" a footman cried out. "What if we're overwhelmed there, too?"

Rayan hesitated, but only briefly. "Her Grace and Halvor won't let that happen. She will contain the fighting here in the Folly to protect our neighbors." He gestured toward the soldier nearest to him. "Oscar here will lead you. I'll be at the rear. The others will weave themselves between groups of you as you go—if you cannot see a soldier in your vicinity, you must find one and stay close to him. Always ensure you can see a man in bronze walking in front of you, behind you, or beside you."

"It'd be wise to arm yourselves with whatever you can find," Oscar added. "Some of you have already acquired weapons. There may be stray weapons to claim on our trek, but if not, anything will do—a plank of wood, a hammer. It's best to be prepared." He turned to face the doorway as the other soldiers moved out of his path. "Follow me. We need to move quickly."

More murmurs followed, but they died out soon enough as the first few people began to move, shaking like leaves. After so many people followed Oscar, another soldier slipped into the crowd beside them, and so on until nearly everyone was gone. By the end, only Rayan remained with his children and the Bolas siblings.

"We're at the end," he said, failing when he attempted a lighthearted tone. "I want you all to listen to me very closely. If anything should happen, I've given one of our soldiers—Kent, the one with the missing finger on his left hand—the order to escort the five of you to safety separately. Everyone else would be headed for Myra, but Kent would take you to the monastery. It's farther away, but if we're caught fleeing to Myra, we'll draw the enemy's attention to us. The enemy wouldn't bother with six of you fleeing in the opposite direction."

Brooks furrowed his eyebrows. "But—"

"That's only if we're caught," Rayan continued, his throat feeling thick. "I-I don't want any of you nearby if that should happen. Kent will find you, you'll ensure everyone is together, and you'll set out for the monastery. Even if you don't make it there, getting to Omara is what's most important. No enemy of the kingdom can cross the border into Omara, remember? Ancient magic protects the borders."

"Yes." Thea nodded and squared her shoulders, shifting the bow and sheath slung over her shoulders. "We understand."

"Good." Forcing a smile, he set his palm against Nereida's cheek, making her tilt her face into his touch. "Let's catch up before we're left behind."

As he dropped his hand, the five of them moved toward the exit, increasing their pace to meet up with the others. Before he followed them, though, he recalled the way he'd comforted his daughter, and it made him think of Aurelia and his father again.

Eric had done the same thing to Aurelia. Rayan never would've expected his father to even consider touching the queen, let alone actually do it. After all, nobody in their right mind would try to touch the queen without her permission—except for Ginny, who'd given Aurelia a hug like it was second nature.

Ginny. Eric caressed her face like that, too, when he was trying to comfort her or show how much he adored her. As he thought about it, Rayan remembered moments from his youth when Eric would hold his hand to Rayan's cheek, too. Sometimes, it was in place of an *I'm sorry* or an *I love you, son.* Other times, it was Eric's way of comforting Rayan, or showing Rayan that he was proud of him, or even just his way of saying hello to his son.

Rayan felt his knees buckle, and quickly reached out for the stone wall to steady himself. Another memory struck him—a memory of his confrontation with Aurelia, when she admitted she wasn't a true Brentwood, but rather the daughter of Arian's late sister and her Akkinorian lover. Not to mention, Eric had gotten tongue-tied when he saw Aurelia for the first time, and he had something of a history with Arian and Taundosa.

Then the crypts rattled, dust rained down on his shoulders, and cracks formed in the ceiling. Rayan darted for the stairs to follow his children out of the palace, but with every step he took, his heart grew heavier, and his brain formed connections he felt like a fool for missing.

I'm not your uncle, he'd told Henry more than once.

But that wasn't true, was it?

***

After suiting up in armor and acquiring their weapons, Aurelia and Jack—and Edom, of course—met their troops on the bailey. Most of their soldiers had already gone, but these men were the ones meant to guard the palace. A few more were staying behind in the event that the palace was breached, but now that everyone was being evacuated, there was nobody left inside to protect.

Aurelia turned to Jack as the soldiers opened the gates. "This is madness."

"Our entire existence is madness." He grimaced and looked down at her while squeezing her hand. "Are you going to be all right?"

"Of course. I've faced worse trials than this one." She raised an eyebrow. "Are *you* going to be all right?"

"I've faced worse than this, too. I think."

"Of course." She tried to smile, but the scene awaiting them behind the gates—even if it was still a ways away—made it impossible. She leaned up on her toes to kiss him, more forcefully and passionately than usual, and for a moment, she thought she might cry. "Be safe, Jack. I love you, today and every day."

"I love you, too. Today and every day." He pecked her one last time before taking the helmet tucked between his arm and his side, and slipping it over his head. "If you can't find me out in the carnage, follow the sound of my heart beating for you. It's the loudest sound I hear at any given moment, so I imagine you'll be able to hear it, too."

A gurgling laugh escaped her. "I will. I'll see you soon, my love."

He winked at her, took his horse's reins from a nearby soldier waiting for him, and mounted the massive stallion. The sea of soldiers parted for him as he headed for the gates, and while half of them followed as he shouted to rile them up, the other half lingered to wait for Aurelia.

Lord Chilton removed his helmet as he approached her. "I know that some of our employees here at the palace are mages, so I took the liberty of asking if they'd be willing to fight beside us. Most of them agreed, so I had them fitted for armor. They'll be at the rear of our formation. The Follian coven will have responded already, so we'll meet them out there."

She nodded. "Thank you."

"Of course, Your Grace. I'll stay at the back with the mages, and—"

"I have a favor to ask," she blurted.

He raised an eyebrow. "Anything."

Aurelia cleared her throat. "Do you...Do you remember the portrait Ansyl used to keep in his study? Thea has it in her bedchamber now. It's of—"

"Their late sister. Your friend from Carthe." He raised a brow. "What about it?"

When she told him what she had in mind, she thought he'd look at her like she'd gone mad. Instead, his eyes glimmered with intrigue, and he assured her that he could do what she desired—but it'd be a painful process.

As the soldiers watched and waited, Lord Chilton brought his hands to her face as his palms began to glow with white magic. Almost instantly, she gritted her teeth and resisted the urge to cry out. It was like someone had taken a dagger straight from the forge and used it to carve patterns across her face, only to take a needle and thread to her flesh while her skin still bled and burned. But as soon as he lowered his hands—after only a few minutes, though it felt like hours—the pain began to disappear.

Aurelia swallowed. "How-How do I look?"

He offered her a small smile. "Not like *you*."

She tried to laugh, but it got stuck in her throat and ended up sounding more like a groan. He winced at the sound, then wished her well, put on his helmet, and rejoined the troops.

She'd come up with the idea while she and Jack were changing. She'd spotted a portrait of her late grandmother, and she'd wondered if she'd be as easily recognizable if her hair was less recognizable, perhaps a pale blonde like Charlotte's had been. That made her think about how nobody had known about the assassin who'd killed Lucyra, because he'd made himself unrecognizable as a Kroti.

Aurelia wasn't fond of wearing a helmet in battle—it obstructed her senses—but she knew she'd be easily spotted without one. Most of them knew what she looked like just because of her hair, as it was the only part of her that they could see clearly while she was on dragonback. She knew they were here for her, to weaken her and potentially destroy her, and making it harder for them to find her would be another line of defense while Halvor was away.

She hadn't told Jack or Rayan about her plan, either. They would've known exactly what she looked like while under the glamour spell, so if they happened to go looking for her, they'd risk drawing attention to her. She needed as few people as possible flocking to her and making it known that she was someone important—if not, both Annera and the Kroti would be on her like flies to sugar.

She could've chosen anyone's likeness, but Kaia was one of few people who'd made Aurelia feel strong and empowered when she had nothing;

even the mere memory of Kaia brought Aurelia strength. She knew Kaia would get a good laugh out of it if she knew Aurelia was using her likeness as a disguise, too.

Aurelia mounted her steed, and as soon as she did so, Cheol and Geon rode up on either side of her. The soldiers silenced and parted for her as she and the centaurs rode to the front of the gates, both awe and disbelief etched onto their faces as they observed Lord Chilton's handiwork.

She turned to face the troops when she stopped at the gates. "Our first priority, other than ending this carnage, is directing the fighting away from the civilian population!" she called out. "Though the others will hopefully evacuate the kingdom, we mustn't let our enemies destroy what generations of Follians have built together. We will try to lead them toward the forest between the Folly and Seaport, where the collateral damage will be less severe. And don't forget that many of Krotis's soldiers are mages, too—strike to kill, not to maim or injure. They can still kill you with magic if they take a sword to the leg."

"What of the dragon?" a soldier yelled.

"Halvor will be joining us shortly," she replied, "and as for Krotis's dragon...She has not made an appearance yet, but I believe that will change. If you happen to come across her, do not engage! She is unpredictable. Leave her to Halvor and I."

One soldier released a battle cry, prompting others to do the same, and Aurelia didn't get the chance to finish speaking. She winced as they rushed past her in flashes of bronze, then quickly turned her horse around as she, Cheol, and Geon galloped toward the heart of the fighting.

The journey was shorter than she'd expected. The closest civilian territory, the village of Mistcairn, hadn't been touched yet; but just beyond a small patch of foliage north of Mistcairn, the small village of Fayside was practically in ruins. They were inching closer to the capital now, and judging by the damage to Fayside, Aurelia had to believe Kalenbrar had taken the brunt of it. After all, what better place to lay siege to than the brand-new capital city?

Of course, the fighting in Fayside was still happening, but despite the damage, there weren't many enemies here. Kroti mages were using their powers to destroy the homes, establishments, and structures, while others were attacking any civilians who hadn't yet managed to flee. Aurelia and her soldiers arrived just in time to see a Kroti man dragging a woman out from an alleyway while she thrashed and screamed beneath him. Aurelia put an end to him by shooting him through the eye.

Aurelia dismounted her horse, knowing she'd draw attention to herself as the only Akkinorian soldier on horseback, and took shelter behind a well while she nocked and shot arrows. Cheol and Geon lingered nearby to keep an eye on her, but without making it obvious that they were staying close to her.

The Kroti didn't stop coming. At one point, while Aurelia ducked to dodge flying debris, she thought the threats to Fayside had been defeated, and the rest of Krotis's troops were still focused on Kalenbrar. Then a hoard of soldiers wearing amber capes and leather armor charged the village from the north, gryphons flying above them, and Aurelia's forces were quickly—and vastly—outnumbered.

When she ran out of arrows, she slung her bow over her shoulder and drew her sword. She prayed that Jack had managed to find a safe route while evacuating the Follians, and that their soldiers were distracting the Kroti well enough to clear Jack's path. She was starting to doubt it when she realized just how many people lived in the Folly, and just how many villages, towns, and cities Jack would have to visit. At a certain point, he'd have to leave some civilizations behind to save who he'd already gathered, and it'd eat him alive to do it.

The ground shook beneath her feet, but this time, it wasn't from explosions or boulders from the catapults and gryphons. Cyclopes stormed onto the scene, trampling the destroyed buildings and debris under their massive feet. They grabbed Kroti soldiers by their necks and squeezed, killing them instantly when their necks snapped at an unnatural angle.

Unfortunately, the gryphons seemed to view the Cyclopes as easy targets, as they swooped down and brought their talons to the Cyclopes' only eye. Soldiers tried to intervene by shooting the gryphons, and one Cyclops managed to tear a gryphon in half before it injured him, but others weren't so lucky. Aurelia saw three of them get their eye scratched out. Cyclopes—while ferocious in battle and frightening to look at—were actually quite gentle and sensitive creatures, so it didn't surprise her when they began to wail like babes and curl up into balls on the ground.

Distracted by the Cyclopes, Aurelia was blown backward by what she assumed was an air mage's power. Before she could jump to her feet, a Kroti climbed on top of her and straddled her, trying to force his dagger onto her neck.

She grabbed his wrists to stop him while the dagger kissed her skin, and somehow, she managed to flip them over using her body weight so she was on top of him. She gritted her teeth as she tried to turn the dagger in his direction, all while digging her knee into his groin and making him howl.

"Where are they?" she seethed. "Shasta Selle and her dragon. Where are they?"

He spat in her face. She used her rage to her advantage and turned the dagger, making it slip out of his grasp. After collecting it, she plunged it into his throat twice for good measure. She took it with her and left him there to drown in his own blood, pausing only to wipe his saliva from her face as she moved on to her next target.

More and more Kroti were flooding into Fayside, but Akkinorians were coming in behind them now. There were more Akkinorians than Aurelia expected—including knights of the Royal Army, Follian soldiers who now served Odessa Linderli, and even a civilian militia. She had to assume her forces had successfully pushed the enemy out of the capital, but they were headed in the wrong direction: south toward the palace rather than west toward the forest.

After using her sword to behead a Mekyan soldier, Aurelia yelled the word *Seaport* at her nearby allies. Some of them listened and started inching westward, taunting the Kroti into following them, but others were too distracted to hear her.

Once more, Aurelia was blown off her feet and sent sailing several feet backward when a massive boulder struck the ground not far from where she'd been standing. She landed atop a heap of bodies, which thankfully—and nauseatingly—broke her fall. She still struggled to breathe for a moment, especially with the dust from the debris floating through the air, and her ears were ringing so badly that she couldn't tell the ringing apart from the clanging of swords.

"Your Grace." A female voice tickled her ear, but when she looked around, nobody was there. "I know it's you. You still have your scent."

For a fleeting moment, Aurelia heard Jack's voice in her head: *Wind nymphs can smell something from a mile away, naturally. Noses like bloodhounds, those sneaky creatures.*

"Fiora?" Aurelia glanced around for the friend she couldn't see.

"I wanted to tell you that me and the other wind nymphs dismantled the catapults on the ships. It was difficult, with whatever spell they cast to conceal the ships, but the mermaids helped. They saw the ships from below and tried to tip them over by pushing from one side. That distracted the mages enough to break their spell, and we were able to see the ships and collapse the catapults."

Aurelia's head was spinning. "M-Mermaids? In Akkinor?"

"They followed the Kroti from Carthe when they overheard their plans." Fiora's voice was muffled by approaching combat. "Get up, Your Grace. They're still coming. We'll try to handle the gryphons."

"Push them toward Seaport!"

"Will do."

Aurelia groaned as she rose to her feet, and she just barely had time to lift her sword before a Kroti spotted her and struck at her. They danced around each other for a bit, swinging their swords and hopping over corpses and debris, but Aurelia's body still felt weak after her fall. That, and she was distracted by the sight of gryphons overhead battling fierce gusts of wind forcing them westward, screeching when they weren't strong enough to fight the current.

Aurelia cried out when the Kroti's sword nicked the side of her neck. It surprised her enough that she fell backward, and the Kroti didn't hesitate to raise his sword in preparation to plunge it into her chest. She rolled out of the way just in time, but she'd lost her sword.

What she wouldn't have given for Arian's sticky spell right about now.

She managed to climb to her feet when he slashed at her again, hitting nothing but air as she fumbled for an abandoned sword nearby. They circled one another for a second, the Kroti hissing profanities at her, but before either of them could strike first, Cheol came up behind him and snapped his neck.

She sighed in relief. "Thank you, Cheol."

He bowed his head. "I shall always be here to—"

Then the tip of a sword poked through his throat, silencing him, and a mortified scream escaped Aurelia's mouth. As he fell to the ground in a heap, choking and gurgling, Aurelia defended an attack by his killer. She had to crouch down when he swung at her neck, giving her the chance to swipe at his legs with her sword. His armor saved him from having his legs cut off, but the impact sent him to his knees. While he struggled for a minute, she grabbed a large rock from the ground and bashed it into his head until he collapsed.

As soon as he was dead, she fell at Cheol's side, holding his face on her lap while his eyes dimmed. He was already gone, her wonderful friend, though his eyes were still looking up at her. She brushed hair from his face while her tears fell onto his cheeks, and despite the battle raging around her, she wanted nothing more than to hold him to her chest and mourn.

Then she saw something reflecting in his eyes: the silhouette of a flighted creature with reptilian limbs and a tail, its body blocking the moon.

Gasping, Aurelia looked up at the sky in hopes of spotting Halvor, but she knew in her soul it wasn't him; she hadn't felt him approaching. Instead, it was Annera, her vibrant green scales glowing against the moonlight, as she circled overhead and roared. After making her presence known, she stopped circling Fayside and started south toward the palace.

Aurelia followed her.

XXXIX

Aurelia reached the forest dividing Fayside from Mistcairn, panting after running so quickly and for so long, before skidding to a stop. Her heart shattered when she saw that the village—the village she and Linden used to treat like a second home—had been destroyed.

No soldiers had made it here yet, but Annera had. Whatever the earth dragon had done, she'd managed to level the structures. There were small sinkholes scattered about, swallowing up merchants' stands and small homes, and a dust cloud partially obstructed her view. The fires that had been left burning in the hearths before the village was evacuated were growing hotter and larger by the second. The collapsing walls and roofs hadn't extinguished the fires—the wood had only given them more strength, more to consume and destroy.

The fires spread more and more as the wind from Annera's flapping wings sent sparks flying in every direction. The sparks clung to whatever they could and erupted in full-fledged fires, the smoke mixing with the dust and making it difficult to see the palace in the near distance.

Hurry. Aurelia pushed the thought toward Halvor, wherever he was. *I need you.*

She tore her eyes away from Annera and Mistcairn to look over her shoulder. She could still see flashes of magic and the glowing of flames from Fayside and beyond, and she could still hear the screaming and clanging of swords. Fortunately, the shadows of gryphons in the sky seemed to be inching westward, and the sounds were getting more muffled. She had to believe her soldiers had begun to succeed in leading the enemy away.

Annera shrieked, making Aurelia wince and turn back to Mistcairn. Annera landed on the ground and roared, making the earth tremble beneath Aurelia's feet. Aurelia clung to a tree for support and watched with wide, horrified eyes as whatever structures still standing in Mistcairn crumbled to the ground.

She watched as Annera prowled, and she didn't see a rider on the dragon's back. Perhaps Shasta Selle was aboard one of the Kroti ships—or perhaps she hadn't come at all, and she was giving Annera commands from across the sea.

Aurelia knelt on the ground, still hiding behind the tree, and thought about Shasta. She was only seventeen years old, surrounded by men, and navigating a power she barely understood. Despite everything, Aurelia didn't want to believe that she agreed with the Council's plans to replace Pherena with Immor. Shasta had been tossed into the role of Lady of Bruila as an adolescent during wartime—if she protested what her counterparts planned to do, they wouldn't listen to her.

Aurelia knew what it was to be a young woman with a unique power and a role to fulfill. She had been raised to be more combative, but Shasta had been raised in a place that demanded mercy and forgiveness, even if most of Krotis had since lost sight of that. Aurelia had to believe that Shasta didn't want her dead—only weakened enough that she didn't interfere with Krotis's plans.

Aurelia didn't know how far away Halvor was. She didn't know how much longer Annera would wait before she turned her attention to the palace. The dragon had come here for a reason: destroying the queen's palace, the heart of Akkinor, would be a severe blow that would take years, if not decades, for Aurelia to recover from. How could Aurelia worry about who Krotis wanted their Almighty to be—and what they had planned for Carthe—when her home had been reduced to nothing? When one of her six kingdoms would need every bit of her attention, coin, and care as they recovered?

Annera lifted into the sky again, pulling Aurelia from her thoughts, and coasted in front of the palace. Without realizing what she was doing, Aurelia darted out of the woods and toward her home, unwilling to watch it crumble. She ran through the rubble and debris, dodging obstacles left and right, and nearly tripped and fell into a sinkhole before catching herself.

She steadied her feet again and kept moving forward, slower this time. She was painfully aware that the dragon was now facing her rather than the palace, but for a moment, she stopped thinking about it. All she could think about was the fact that Mistcairn was gone, flattened, unrecognizable. She couldn't even identify the roads where she and Linden used to stop to pluck hyacinths from decorative pots, or the shops the pair would frequent while disguised as common children, or the bakery whose elderly owner always stopped them to offer lessons on how to make the perfect pastries.

It was all gone now. Every bit of it.

She climbed on top of a large chunk of sandstone that might've been the wall of a library or a seamstress's shop this morning, but now, it was unidentifiable rubble. Only then, as she got a closer look at Annera, did she realize how large the longbelly had become—almost a third of Halvor's size.

"I know you know who I am!" Aurelia shouted. "I know you can sense it! You're here for me, aren't you? You've come to warn me, to tell me I need to stand down before your friends unleash Immor's wrath on my home!" She spread her arms out to either side. "Halvor isn't here! You have me right where you want me!"

Annera shrieked, making Aurelia wince as her heart rattled. "What will it be, then?" Aurelia demanded. "Are you going to kill me while I stand here defenseless and alone? Is that what Shasta told you to do?"

Another shriek rang out as Annera lowered to the ground, landing just a few yards away from Aurelia. The dragon chuffed, but somehow, it didn't feel aggressive. Sensing an opportunity, Aurelia hopped down from the debris and took a few slow, cautious steps forward. Something in her gut told her that she needed to change tactics. Annera reminded her of a child scolded over an accident—a child who needed a gentle touch and perhaps a hug, not another scolding or a punishment.

Before she could say or do anything, though, she heard shouting from behind. Annera retreated backward, growling, as Aurelia turned to find the source of the commotion. A perfect blend of relief and concern bubbled up in her gut when she spotted her soldiers approaching Mistcairn, with Jack leading the pack.

They were coming for her, but she knew their presence would only spook Annera, and there was no telling what the dragon would do then. It was a risk Aurelia couldn't take, especially with her husband nearby. The last thing she wanted was to see him hurt or killed because she'd let him get too close to Annera.

She turned her body halfway so she could still see Annera from the corner of her eye. She held out her hands, signaling Jack and the others to halt. He yelled something indecipherable, to which she only shook her head, her hands still outstretched. To her surprise and relief, he stopped, and the soldiers followed his lead.

Aurelia swiveled back to face Annera, trembling when the longbelly chuffed again and sent a hot gust of air directly at Aurelia's face. She was closer to Annera than she should've been, but she knew that while she had Annera distracted, her people and her home were safe from death by dragon.

"I know you're frightened." She softened her tone as she inched closer to Annera, who didn't back away or growl at her as she approached. "I would be, too. You're so very young, and yet, your leaders expect so much of you. They see you as their weapon, not their treasure. A-And as hard as you may try to be free to explore the world as you wish, you can't fight what they demand of you. They have you in chains, and you can't escape unless you do what they want."

As she got closer, Aurelia saw raw red marks around Annera's ankles and her throat. A sharp pang pierced her heart; she'd been referencing metaphorical chains, but apparently, Annera had been chained up physically, too.

"I won't hurt you." Aurelia's voice was low, practically a whisper, as she held out a trembling hand. Annera's head was slightly cocked to the side, her gaze averted, but she was almost close enough for Aurelia to touch her. "I can see you've been hurt enough. I-If you can understand me, and if you truly don't wish to be the vessel for such carnage, I urge you to fly back home. You're stronger than you think you are. Those people may frighten you and try to control you, but you can overpower them. You don't have to obey them. Neither does Shasta."

Aurelia was a mere inch away from Annera's scales, but when she said Shasta's name, something seemed to click in the dragon's brain as she relaxed and mewled. And then, to Aurelia's bewilderment, Annera did something completely unexpected: she lowered her body to the ground, tucked her wings against her middle, and locked eyes with Aurelia.

Ancient lore claimed it was often a death sentence to look into a dragon's eyes—unless, of course, one was the dragon's rider, or if they'd established trust with the dragon. Yet here Annera was, slowly blinking at Aurelia and mewling like a kitten, and doing absolutely nothing to suggest she was a threat.

Swallowing, Aurelia reached out to stroke Annera's cool, slippery scales. A sigh of relief escaped her when Annera allowed it and continued to mewl. Then another shock came when Annera curled her neck to nudge Aurelia's knees with her snout—a motion that made Aurelia gasp in alarm as she stumbled forward against the dragon's body. Annera didn't so much as flinch when Aurelia fell against her. She just kept on mewling, then leaned her body against Aurelia's.

Taking a long, deep breath, Aurelia lifted a leg and carefully planted her foot on the stable joint at Annera's knee. She could hardly fathom what she was doing as she climbed onto the dragon's back, staring down at green scales rather than blue ones for the first time in her life.

As Annera shifted beneath her, she recalled the prophecy and what Archie had told her about Annera claiming a new rider. Perhaps this was what it meant: somehow, Annera had been swayed into abandoning Shasta Selle, only to choose Aurelia to take her place. Aurelia told herself it wasn't possible, since she was already bonded to another dragon, and nobody in the realm's recorded history had ever bonded with more than one.

For a split second, Aurelia forgot where she was and what was happening. She forgot about the state of Mistcairn, the Kroti soldiers demolishing her kingdom and murdering her people, Jack and the others watching her from afar—all of it.

It was just Aurelia and Annera, rider and dragon.

A strangled cry escaped her throat when Annera began to run, then lifted off into the sky. Annera felt a bit unsteady, like she wasn't accustomed to flying with a human on her back, so Aurelia knew she hadn't taken Shasta to flight before. She'd chosen Aurelia as her partner for her maiden voyage.

They flew around the palace grounds, parting clouds and soaring through the smoky haze, and Aurelia couldn't help but laugh at the sheer absurdity of it all. She was on top of the world now, and Krotis didn't stand a chance.

Suddenly, Annera lurched backward as if something was tugging her, and an anguished, furious shriek tore from her throat. Aurelia's heart pounded violently as she clung to Annera's spikes for stability while the dragon thrashed. She tried to speak soothing words and rub Annera's scales for comfort, but it didn't do much good.

Then, as time seemed to slow, Annera turned her neck just enough to meet Aurelia's eyes again. The queen gasped when she recognized the look in Annera's gaze: it was the same look Halvor got when he felt Aurelia's commands reach his soul—a look of obedience, even if he didn't agree with what he was being told to do.

Annera took a sharp turn, making Aurelia yelp, before soaring up toward the sky, where the full moon shone like a beacon. Though she didn't realize she'd spoken, Aurelia heard herself begging Annera to slow down, to stop, to find her serenity. In response, Annera coasted vertically while facing the moon, her body adjacent to the palace while her tail pointed down at the ground, and her wings extended fully to either side.

She bellowed, and in doing so, released a burst of power that emitted from her chest and spread toward everything around her, worsening the fractures in the earth and rattling every stone, brick, and pebble below. The force of her power blew Aurelia backward, and the queen watched in vain as her fingers slid from Annera's spikes.

Aurelia fell through the air, her eyes widening as she watched Annera fly away toward Seaport. For just a moment while she fell, she felt a calmness wash over her, as if the winds had fashioned a blanket to wrap her in. Maybe it was Fiora and the other wind nymphs, having come to save her.

Then her body was flung against something impossibly hard when she hit the ground, and a sickening crack echoed in her eardrums.

She couldn't move, and her ears were ringing so loudly that she couldn't hear her own thoughts anymore—only the sound of Jack's blood-curdling screams, which grew quieter and quieter as the seconds passed. The initial burst of pain was gone in an instant, replaced by a cold, dark numbness.

The last thing she saw before her leaking eyes fell shut was Halvor approaching from behind the palace. The last thing she heard was the painful shriek that tore from his throat, as if his heart had been ripped out of his chest.

Then, there was nothing.

***

Aurelia opened her eyes to find herself staring at her own reflection in a clear, gurgling brook. She blinked a few times and looked away from the brook, puzzled by the sight of lush trees, chirping birds, and vibrant butterflies in every direction.

"Aurelia."

Frowning, she pulled herself to her feet and turned to follow the direction of the voice. Halvor's human form was standing behind her, his sapphire eyes shimmering with sadness. He held out a hand for her, and she accepted it without a second thought.

"I'm so sorry," he murmured, holding her hand between both of his. He was trembling, and the guilt in his eyes shone brighter than his grief. "I-I wasn't fast enough. I'm so sorry, Aurelia."

She blinked at him. "Am I back in Vanhylde?"

"You are."

She sighed. She didn't remember what happened before this, but she knew she hadn't been trying to visit the land between worlds. Despite her confusion, she felt a strange sense of peace, and it didn't ache her heart to realize why she was here.

"I'm dead."

Halvor's face crumpled. "Yes."

"Oh."

"You are not staying here, my friend. This is only temporary." He squeezed her hand as he offered her a small smile. "There's a reason you're here, and it isn't because of me. I only wished to say goodbye, and to apologize for failing you."

"Failing me?" Aurelia cocked her head to the side as the memories came flooding back to her. "Oh, Halvor. You did nothing but what I asked of you. Are my children safe? And my uncle and my father?"

"They are."

"Then you haven't failed me. You never could."

Tears streamed down his cheeks. "I'm going to miss you."

"I'm going to miss you, too. Will we meet again?"

"You may visit me here whenever you wish, and one day, I shall find you in Hanhalla. I promise."

Aurelia nodded. "All right."

Halvor pointed toward the woodlands across from them. "Go through the trees. Eternal salvation awaits you."

She nodded again, leaned forward to kiss his cheek, and let go of his hand. She followed his instructions and disappeared into the foliage, reminded of the first time she'd visited Vanhylde and followed the same steps to find Linden. However, when the darkness faded, she wasn't in the palace gardens. She was standing in the middle of an upstairs hallway in the palace, staring out a window at the bailey.

The sound of children's laughter caught her attention from behind. Curious, she followed the sound down the hallway, where she found herself outside of a familiar door. Smiling at the thought of seeing her children one last time, she opened the door to the nursery, but her six little loves weren't there. Instead, a young girl and a toddler boy were playing on the floor with wooden ships.

She stood in the doorway and watched, but neither of them acknowledged her presence. As she struggled to identify them, the boy played too roughly with his ship, snapping it in two. He began to cry, and the girl quickly rushed over to a toy bin in the corner of the room, only to return with a painted wooden soldier.

"Shh. It's all right." She rubbed the boy's back and held out the soldier. "Here. Play with my knight instead."

The boy sniffled and accepted the toy. "Thanks, Li."

Li.

A presence appeared at Aurelia's side. "Adorable little hellions, weren't we?"

She smiled at the sound of Archie's voice. "We were."

"I kept that toy for years, you know. Even after...everything."

"I know. I found it when I cleared out your bedchamber. I...I never thought anything of it. I didn't remember this."

"It's all right."

Aurelia sighed and lowered her head as she thought about her family again, and how soon enough, they'd be clearing away her things, too. Her children, Jack, Arian, Rayan...It was finally occurring to her that she'd never see them again—that she'd left them.

She was certain her loved ones would exist in Hanhalla, even if they weren't real. Perhaps she'd know at first that they were only entities created by the gods to give her a lovely afterlife, but eventually, she'd forget, and it would feel like she was home again.

Now, though, she already missed them. She missed the way the ocean raged in Jack's eyes, and the way his grin always appeared both wicked and innocent. She missed the way his arms felt like home when he held her, the way his lips were a perfect fit for hers, and the way he filled her soul with a fire that burned brighter and hotter than even Halvor was capable of emitting. She missed his jokes, his laugh, his smile. She missed the incredible father he was, how he never failed to make a friend wherever he went, and that indescribable look in his eyes whenever she was near him.

And her children...She missed Halle's hugs, the way she scolded her siblings like it was her duty, and even—surprisingly—the way she'd started calling Aurelia *Mother*. She missed Hyacinth's prophetic stories, her attitude, and the beautiful melodies she played on the pianoforte. She missed Henry's disobedience, his unruly auburn hair, and the way he liked to pick fights for the fun of it. She missed Halyna's wildness, her need to snuggle anyone who looked even remotely comforting, and her free spirit that was so much like her father's. She missed Harlen's explorative gaze, the way he latched to her and never wanted to let go, and the way he tried to catch butterflies in his chubby fingers. She missed Holly's infectious laugh, the way she always pulled on Jack's hair but nobody else's, and the way she smiled in her sleep.

"They're going to be all right, you know." Aurelia looked up and over at Archie for the first time when he spoke again. He looked the same as he did when she last visited Vanhylde, but something was different—something she couldn't quite put her finger on. "Your family. They'll be all right."

"Will they?"

"It'll be hard, but they'll get through it. I promise."

Aurelia nodded and sniffled through tears. "What now?"

He raised an eyebrow as his lips curled into a smile. "Are you ready to go home?"

"To Hanhalla?" she asked. He nodded, making her furrow her brows. "We're *both* going? You've earned your place there?"

Archie's smile widened into a grin, but it wasn't the mischievous, calculating grin she remembered from his life. It was a peaceful, empowering expression that, during his life, would've looked foreign on his face—but now, it looked like it was meant to be there all along.

"Not long after your last visit, I realized what I had to do to move on: I had to wait for you." His eyes became glassy as he held out a hand. "Do you forgive me?"

Aurelia hesitated for only a moment, and as she lifted her hand to set it over his, the tears in her eyes finally broke free. A few droplets splashed on the back of her hand, and to her surprise, they weren't clear—they were gold.

"Ah, yes." Archie kept smiling as she stared at her hand in shock. "Losing that power was never about the gods giving up on you, sister. It was your own guilt, however deeply in your subconscious it was buried. You've forgiven yourself for anything you might've done, but once more, I have to ask: do you forgive me, too?"

Inhaling sharply, she set her hand over his and squeezed. "Yes."

Tears leaked down his cheeks, but he made no effort to wipe them away. "Thank you, Aurelia."

He clutched her hand firmly, as if he were afraid of losing her, and turned them away from the nursery. Her lips parted when they faced the direction she'd come from: the window was gone, and so was the end of the hallway. Instead, a glowing pool of white light awaited them, spreading so far in every direction that she could no longer see the palace around them.

As brother and sister walked toward it, the silhouettes of two individuals—one large, stout man and one dainty, graceful woman—appeared within the light, inching closer and closer.

Just as she stepped foot into the light, Aurelia heard her own young voice echoing in her head, giggling with joy as she called for her mama and papa to bring her home.

XL

As Jack watched civilian after civilian slip through the many entrances of Robert's Arena, he wondered about the others. He'd gotten as far north as Kalenbrar before he was forced to turn around and head south with everyone he'd managed to rescue.

To his surprise, Kalenbrar hadn't been reduced to rubble when he arrived. There was some demolition here and there, but it wasn't nearly as bad as he'd expected. The smaller towns and cities surrounding the capital had taken most of the damage. According to a Linderli soldier he'd spoken to, it was Lady Odessa's command that saved most of Kalenbrar: she'd been hosting the Folly's coven of mages for a dinner that night, and as soon as they heard the warning bells, they'd fortified the city using magical shields. The only reason a few Kroti had managed to infiltrate Kalenbrar was because there were small areas left undefended—there weren't enough mages to cover the entire perimeter.

It was no wonder the Kroti had taken to destroying the smaller, more defenseless civilizations. They'd wanted the capital, and they hadn't been able to breach it like intended, so they took their anger out on everything surrounding Kalenbrar instead.

"Your Highness." A soldier rode up beside Jack. "I've just come from Fayside. We've managed to redirect most of the conflict toward the forest between Seaport and the Folly, as Her Grace commanded, but the enemy still pushes eastward. I believe some of them are approaching the palace—I saw fires and heard a bit of commotion in Mistcairn. We need more men over there."

Jack nodded. "I'll take some of my soldiers with me, but we need others to stay here in case Krotis arrives. Myra's reinforcements should be arriving shortly, too." He raised an eyebrow. "Have you seen Aurelia?"

"She was with us in Fayside, but I lost sight of her."

"What about the dragons?"

"No sign of Halvor yet, but the green one flew overhead not long ago. She was headed for the palace."

Jack's heart lurched. "Halvor will be here soon. She'll flee as soon as she sees him."

He didn't believe it—not after what Annera had done in Krotis—and judging by the way the soldier was looking at him, he didn't believe it, either.

Jack spotted Rayan several yards away, guiding more civilians into entrances along a different side of the arena. He recognized Thea and Mycah, his valet, and the governesses, so he knew Rayan had succeeded in evacuating the palace.

Some soldiers were joining the civilians inside the arena, but others had formed a perimeter around the property. Those standing guard weren't alone, either. Centaurs, Cyclopes, and even nymphs were armed to the teeth and facing every direction, prepared to defend the Folly with their lives. Sprites and fairies buzzed around, too, illuminating paths for the civilians and keeping an eye out for anyone approaching in the distance.

Jack rode over to Rayan. "I'm going to help the others, but I'd like you to stay here. Our people need a leader they recognize to guide them out of here if Krotis approaches. You know the route to Myra."

Rayan nodded. "Of course. Have you seen—"

"No."

"What about—"

"No." Jack grimaced. "Aurelia was last seen in Fayside, so I'll go there first. It shouldn't be much longer before Halvor arrives. I imagine Aurelia will want him guarding the palace—if he goes elsewhere, Annera will have an opening to strike the estate."

"Aurelia won't save the palace at the expense of civilian lives."

"No, she won't," he agreed. "That's why she's pushing Krotis toward Seaport. I'll take some men and help steer the fighting away from civilization to make things easier for them." He reached out, forcing a smile, and set a hand on Rayan's shoulder. "Good luck."

Rayan nodded. "The same to you."

After giving his friend one last, encouraging smile—and making note of Rayan's strange, distant demeanor—Jack hollered at the surrounding troops, calling for soldiers to follow him back into the fighting. When a few dozen of them fell into line behind him, he was startled to see a handful of civilians, armed with weapons or miscellaneous objects, fill in the spots around the perimeter to help stand guard. Elderly men, adolescent boys, young women...So many different people, all risking their lives to defend their neighbors rather than seeking shelter inside the arena.

As Jack led his troops out of Oleander's Valley, he wondered about the parts of the Folly he hadn't seen. Krotis had docked off the coast of Seaport and infiltrated the kingdom from the west, so it was only rational to think Seaport had been left in ruins. If any civilians were still there, and alive, they didn't have anywhere to go: fleeing to sea would've pitted them against whatever Kroti soldiers remained on their ships, and fleeing east would've taken them directly into the heart of the fighting.

Perhaps the northern parts of the Folly—everything beyond Kalenbrar—hadn't been touched, since there were fewer civilizations there. If the Kroti wanted to focus on the capital and the palace, they wouldn't waste time on the north. Even so, Jack hoped the civilians in those areas had managed to get out and head for Sadia.

He'd been trying to forget what he'd seen while evacuating the civilians. He hardly recognized establishments he'd frequented dozens of times before, roads he'd traveled on time after time, and landmarks he'd always stopped to admire. Between Krotis's magic, catapults, and gryphons, everything had been either destroyed completely, or damaged enough that it was beyond recognition.

Bodies and limbs poked out from beneath the rubble, and people had turned to taking shelter against heaps of corpses the Kroti mages had flung aside and piled up. Jack had mostly been fending off the enemy while his men ushered the civilians out, but he'd pulled some people from the carnage and rubble, too. It made him wish he'd stuck to fighting.

At one point, while clearing the village of Mossmill, Jack pulled a young woman out from the ruins of her home. She'd been yelling something, but he could hardly hear her. The Kroti mages had created a shockwave a moment earlier, and it'd created a ripple effect: from the mages' position at the other end of the village, every weakened structure had begun to collapse, spreading like wildfire toward the woman's house. Jack soon realized the woman was begging him to retrieve her two children from the ruins, and as he watched buildings collapse onto the road they were standing on, he'd been left with no choice but to force her onto his horse and ride away before they were crushed.

There'd been a lot of that: telling someone who'd survived a nightmare that their family couldn't be saved, or meeting eyes with someone trapped under debris as they realized they were being left behind, or simply riding away while voices screamed for help. Jack could still see and hear all of it, burned into his brain forever.

As they inched closer to Fayside, it sounded like the battle had, indeed, started moving west toward Seaport. Jack was starting to lead the men in that direction when he heard a roar he recognized as belonging to a dragon, but he knew it wasn't Halvor. Even worse was that the sound had come from the palace.

He redirected half of the men toward the palace while the others continued to Fayside, knowing full well that if they ran into Annera without Halvor or Aurelia nearby, they'd be in a world of trouble. But Jack wasn't about to let anything, dragon or man, destroy his home if he could help it.

As he galloped through the trees, the wind blowing a combination of ash, dust, debris, and the smell of death directly onto his face, a cold pit began to brew in his gut. Bile rose up in his throat when they reached the border of Mistcairn, and not because he hardly recognized the village anymore. It was because he'd spotted Annera standing in the rubble, her back to the palace, and Aurelia was directly in front of her—alone. It had to be her, because who else would do something so rash?

While the men hollered to encourage one another, Jack shouted Aurelia's name. He saw the dragon retreat a bit when Aurelia turned to face him. She didn't look like herself, even from a distance, but he could feel her energy from here. As soon as she saw him, she held out her hand, telling him to stay put.

"What the hell are you doing?" he yelled. "Get away from her!"

He knew she couldn't hear him. She only stared at him for a moment, her hand still outstretched. Whatever she was doing, she didn't want him near—and as much as it pained him to stay back, he trusted her gut more than he trusted his own.

"Stand down," he told the soldiers. "She doesn't want us to approach."

Jack watched, heart hammering, as Aurelia turned back to Annera. He wondered what she was saying as she inched closer to the dragon. Then, after a few moments, something remarkable happened: Annera lowered herself to the ground and nudged Aurelia with her snout, inviting Aurelia to ride her.

"Gods be good," one of the soldiers remarked. "That's not...She can't...How...?"

They knew what this was as much as Jack did: a second dragon had claimed Aurelia as her rider—the first time in history a human had managed to form two separate bonds with the realm's most magnificent, dangerous creatures.

Jack laughed when Annera lifted into the sky with Aurelia on her back. They soared for a bit, as if they'd been doing it forever. Their presences demanded attention, distracting Jack from everything else around him.

Jack only hoped Halvor wasn't jealous when he finally made it back.

Then Annera froze while facing the palace, her limbs and wings outstretched like her appendages were being pulled in each direction. Jack opened his mouth to yell for Aurelia at the same time Annera roared, releasing a shockwave that shook the earth beneath Jack's feet. He and his men were all either thrown from their horses or knocked to the ground while it trembled, and by the time Jack steadied himself, Annera was already flying toward Seaport.

Aurelia wasn't with her.

Jack's heart collapsed to his knees when he spotted his wife in the rubble. She was lying flat against a large slab of stone, and she wasn't moving. He was jumping onto his horse and galloping toward her before he knew what he was doing, breathless not from the fall or the ride, but from the realization that Aurelia had just fallen over a hundred feet from a dragon's back, directly onto stone.

Halvor appeared behind the palace, shrieking, and landed in front of Aurelia before Jack was halfway there. A combination of sounds—weak screeches, moans, and whimpers—escaped Halvor's throat. Jack's entire body felt like it'd begun to fail him as Halvor extended his wings around Aurelia, hiding her from view.

As his heart broke in his chest, Jack urged his horse forward, and when he was close enough, he jumped off without slowing the steed down. He landed on one knee, ignoring the pain that spread throughout his leg, and managed to catch himself and stumble to his feet as he ran. Halvor sensed him approaching and opened his wings, moaning in pain and heartache.

Jack skidded to a stop and fell to his knees when he saw Aurelia laying a few feet from Halvor's snout. She didn't look like herself—she looked like the portrait of Kaia in Thea's room. She was lying flat against a tilted chunk of debris, and there was a dark crimson stain on the stone behind her head.

Feeling like he was worlds away, he crawled the rest of the way to her on his hands and knees. He brought his shaking hands to her face when he was kneeling beside her, and though he knew she was gone, he touched his ear to her chest, anyhow. Whatever remained of his heart shattered into dust when he was met with nothing but a hollow silence.

He told himself that as long as it wasn't her face lying lifeless against the stone, it wasn't her. It didn't matter that Halvor was here mourning, or that she wore her wedding ring and her golden locket, or that he knew in his soul that it was her. If he couldn't see her face, she wasn't gone.

Across the way, soldiers had removed their helmets and taken a knee. One of them approached Jack, hesitating only when Halvor released another grief-stricken shriek. Jack barely acknowledged the soldier as he sunk beside him. He only looked at him and reached out to grasp his wrist when the soldier brought his hands to Aurelia's face.

"I'm a mage, Your Highness," the soldier said softly. "Let me help."

Jack nodded, shaking, as the man's palms began to glow with white magic. After a minute, her features—fawny brown skin, straight dark hair, bold brows, and eyes that he assumed were green beneath her closed lids—began to shift before they morphed into the woman Jack loved. To make things even worse, there were golden pools at the corners of her eyes.

When he saw her, he no longer had reason to hope he'd been wrong. There she was, the woman he loved, lying there with a fatal wound to the back of her head.

"Aur-Aurelia." He barely heard himself as he held her face between his hands, his tears landing on her cheeks. "C-Come on, lovely. You're all right. You're okay. Come on, now."

Not knowing what else to do, Jack lifted her into his arms and held her close, shaking with silent sobs when she fell limply against him. Her arms dangled by her sides, her fingers brushing the dirt, and he had to hold the back of her head against his shoulder to keep it from falling. He rocked back and forth as he held her, choking on sobs when he couldn't feel her heart beating against his.

"Gods." His voice sounded echoed, muffled, far away in a different land. "Please come back. *Gods*—don't go. Don't leave me. *Please*, Lily. Please come back. I'll go instead—just please, don't leave."

With the side of her face pressed against his shoulder, he touched his cheek to her temple. He pulled away just enough to kiss her cheek, over and over again as he wept, willing her to open her eyes. His hand on the back of her head tightened, and he forced himself to ignore the feel of her blood seeping onto his skin.

After a time, he couldn't hear his own sobs anymore. He was still rocking with his wife in his arms, begging her to come back, as her body grew stiffer and colder.

Then he felt a hand on his shoulder, pulling him back to reality. He didn't bother acknowledging the person until they knelt across from him, and he just barely recognized Rayan's auburn hair. Somehow, Rayan managed to coax Jack into setting her down against the stone again. Jack stopped weeping for a moment when he saw the blood staining his hands, then turned to the side and vomited. He was on his hands and knees, and after expelling everything in his stomach, he dry heaved onto the ground until he couldn't breathe.

From the corner of his eye, he saw Rayan brush hair from Aurelia's face and bend over to kiss her forehead. He touched his forehead to hers and murmured, "Goodbye, sister."

Jack managed to return to her side, clutching her hand between both of his, and buried his face into her stomach while he wept. Rayan said nothing as he held her other hand, unable to do anything other than stare at her face.

Then a quiet buzzing made Jack's ears prick, and he lifted his head enough to see Edom standing on Aurelia's chest. The sprite slowly lowered itself and curled up on her chest in the fetal position, as if it intended to sleep there.

"Stop it. Go away." Jack didn't realize what he was saying—or how cruelly he was saying it—but he couldn't stop himself. "Now isn't the time..."

He trailed off, heart sinking even more, when Edom's golden glow began to fade, and its breathing became shallow. In just a minute, the sprite's glow had dimmed completely, and it was no longer moving.

"E-Edom?" Jack tried to nudge the creature with his fingertip, and the sprite didn't respond. It moved where he nudged it, but its body was limp, and its chest was no longer rising and falling. "Edom..."

Rayan sniffled. "It's gone."

Jack vaguely recalled something Varn had once told him about sprites. The creatures tended to bond with humans like dragons did. But unlike dragons, a sprite's lifeforce often became tethered to its human's: if its human died, so did the sprite.

Edom hadn't even mourned for her. It couldn't—it had to leave with her, to avoid living even a moment without her.

In this moment, Jack wanted to do the very same.

***

Soon enough, everyone who'd fought to defend the Folly had gathered in the remains of Mistcairn, and the civilians were starting to return from the arena. Jack didn't know how much time had passed since he found his wife in the ruins, but it must've been longer than he thought, because the Kroti had left.

Though Rayan had to repeat himself a few times for Jack to comprehend it, he managed to explain what'd happened. Fiora, a wind nymph, had found Rayan and told him about Aurelia when she saw Jack with the queen's body. As Rayan rushed to meet them, he ran into soldiers returning from the battle, who said the Kroti had fled onto their ships as soon as they saw Annera flying toward Carthe.

They'd done what they came for, and they'd fled like cowards as soon as Annera gave the cue to leave.

Jack didn't move from his kneeling position beside Aurelia, and neither did Halvor. He was aware of the hundreds of people gathering around, falling to their knees, weeping, and praying for their queen. He didn't bother addressing them. All he could do was stare at her lifeless face, wondering why the gods had punished him by giving him a mere eight years with the love of his life before they took her.

Not only took her—they'd let her die alone. Completely, utterly alone. Jack had been a distance away. Rayan hadn't even been in the village. Halvor had only found her when it was too late; if he *had* been there, she'd probably still be alive. That was no fault of his, but it didn't change the fact that she'd taken her last breaths alone.

Someone should've been there with her. But they'd all been off fighting their own battles, fulfilling their own duties, following her orders. She'd set off on her own, likely hoping that her defenseless presence would distract Annera enough to save the palace; and whether she'd known that her efforts would become a sacrifice or not, she hadn't had anyone at her side to support her.

Jack would never forgive himself for that. He hadn't been there to hold her as she took her last breath, but he'd stay here with her now, even if he had to be pulled away when the time came to prepare her for burial.

After a time, Lord Baylor appeared at Jack's side. He said something, but Jack couldn't hear it over the sound of blood pounding in his ears—a combination of grief, rage, and the primal need to plunge his sword through the hearts of the five nobles on the Iron Council.

"...move her," Lord Baylor said.

Jack snapped out of his daze. "What?"

The advisor cleared his throat, and for a moment, it looked like he was struggling to speak. He was staring at Aurelia while his lips moved, but no sound emerged. His eyes were bloodshot, though he managed to keep his tears from falling. Only then did Jack remember that Lord Baylor had been a constant figure in Aurelia's life since she was a little girl—longer than anyone else alive.

"We should move her," Lord Baylor said softly. "She doesn't belong here in the carnage, Your Grace."

Jack stilled as a scowl corrupted his face. "I beg your pardon?"

The advisor's eyebrows furrowed. "I only—"

"You only *what?* Hmm?" Jack snapped. "She's been gone for less than half a day, and you've already given her title to me?"

"Jack." Rayan manifested on Lord Baylor's other side, making the advisor scamper away like a wounded animal. "I-It's only protocol. I know it's hard, but the people still need a leader. Halle is Queen of Akkinor now, but you're King Regent until she comes of age. That became true the moment Aurelia..."

His face crumpled as he trailed off, unable to finish his sentence. *The moment Aurelia died.* It didn't feel real, even saying it aloud, nor did it feel right to start moving forward so quickly when her body was barely cold.

Jack shook his head. "No. My eight-year-old daughter isn't the queen. My wife is the queen."

Rayan's chin trembled. "Jack..."

Jack jumped to his feet, shouting things even he didn't understand, and without realizing what he was doing, he started shoving Rayan's chest, unable to resist the urge to attack whatever was closest to him. Rayan let him do it, but when Jack faltered, Rayan grabbed him by the arms and pulled him into an embrace. Jack's knees gave way, and he collapsed onto the ground again, bringing Rayan down with him as he wept.

Again, he barely heard his own voice when he spoke: "I want my wife." He sounded like a child, and he felt as helpless as one, too. "I want my wife back."

Rayan's shoulders shook against him. "I know."

Then the sun began to rise behind the palace, forcing Jack to accept an impossible reality: starting today, he'd never live another day with his wife. He'd never hear her voice or her laugh again. He'd never see her smile or the way she threw her head back when she laughed. He'd never feel her arms around him or wake up to her tracing patterns on his face. He'd never hide from servants under their bed with her, or race around the palace while she scampered after him on bare feet.

Now, all he had left were his memories.

XLI

Lord Reesa had visited Shasta in her bedchamber—nursing burns on his arms and a cut to the forehead, but nothing else—while she recovered. Her burns were healing nicely, and though there was nothing to be done about the horrid scarring for now, she'd use her magic to erase them as soon as she was completely healed.

According to her counterpart, her injuries weren't the worst among the Council. Lord Keer had perished, so his son and successor—kept away from the battle to preserve the line of succession—was in the best shape of the group. Lord Quagg had sustained a few minor injuries, but Lord Swann was confined to a wheelchair while wounds to his legs, hips, and back continued to heal.

He'd told her that Annera was being kept in the fighting pit for her protection, and the Council was actively planning a retaliation attempt against Akkinor. They'd found and apprehended a few Akkinorians serving as spies in Krotis, too, and now, all of those men were dead.

"What's our goal?" she'd asked him.

"We must give Queen Aurelia a foolproof reason to keep her distance," Lord Reesa had replied. "Something far greater than cursing her uncle or temporarily getting Bozar out of the way. While our soldiers wreak havoc on the queen's kingdom, she and her dragon will follow them in an effort to save their people. Annera will strike the palace while they're distracted. We expect that the queen will attempt to evacuate the civilians from the Folly and offer them refuge in the palace. If her home is destroyed, though, then neither she nor her people will have anywhere to go. That should distract her for a very long time."

Shasta had frantically shaken her head. "You're sending Annera to die. She's not strong enough to face Halvor, and he'll go after her the moment—"

"Which do you think Queen Aurelia would choose: using Halvor to defend her commonfolk, or her home? Human lives, or material possessions?"

She'd pressed her lips together and bowed her head. He was right.

Shasta didn't like the idea of laying siege to an Akkinorian kingdom and leveling the queen's palace—and killing everyone inside—but as Lord Reesa had so delicately reminded her, these things were necessary during wartime.

Now, after what'd felt like an eternity of being bedridden, Shasta had been given the go-ahead by Izaius to return to her duties. She thought she'd help the others orchestrate the retaliation effort, but to her surprise, everything was already set in motion. But they hadn't waited for her permission to deploy Annera or her troops before they did it.

That was weeks ago.

"We planned everything precisely," Lord Quagg explained, pouring a bit of gin into his tea. "Our soldiers are under orders to attack Akkinor within the hour. They set sail earlier than necessary, leaving them plenty of time to incite the battle on this day, at this time, even if their voyage was delayed. We wouldn't have been so meticulous if not for Annera. We need you, Lady Selle, to command her from afar."

Shasta nodded. Lord Reesa had already told her this.

"We have to believe your bond with her is just as strong from a distance, given what we know about Queen Aurelia and her dragon," the new Lord Keer told her. "Even if it isn't, Annera will inflict prolific damage across the Folly. That's all we need."

I haven't felt her in weeks, Shasta thought. She'd never say it aloud, though. She'd communicated with Annera through the bond between their souls since the battle, and while she knew in her gut that Annera received the messages, *she* hadn't received any signs from her dragon. She told herself it was because Annera had gotten spooked in Runeia, and she wasn't yet ready to return to business as usual.

However, the lords' theory proved true when, as they sat in the symposium waiting for a sign, Shasta felt a pull in her chest, and she could almost feel sea spray and wind against her skin. She couldn't explain it, but she knew it was Annera's way of letting her know that she was approaching the Akkinorian coast.

There you are, she thought.

"Have her stay back for a bit," Lord Reesa ordered when she shared the news. "Let our men cause a distraction in the kingdom. The queen will take her beast to stop them, and that's Annera's opportunity to strike the palace unchallenged."

Shasta didn't believe any of that, but she did as she was told and relayed the message.

After a while, a sense of relief, courage, and excitement washed over her. She could feel that Annera was growing empowered. Again, she couldn't explain how she knew it, but her soul—*their* soul—told her that Annera's giddiness was a result of Halvor's unexplained absence.

"Send her to the palace before he comes back!" Lord Quagg had partially risen out of his seat, his dark eyes glowing with hunger and eagerness, after Shasta shared her understanding of the signs Annera was sending her. "Crumble the entire estate! Tell her to stay until it sinks into the earth, then get out of there. Our men will retreat to the ships when they see her leave, as they've been instructed."

She relayed the message once more, but a minute later, she felt something else burning in her soul—akin to the feeling of seeing someone in passing and recognizing their face, but being unable to place them in her memories. It wasn't just recognition of someone Annera might've known or seen before, either. It was recognition of someone who reminded Annera of Shasta, who understood the dragon nearly as well as her rider did; if not more so.

"She's there." Shasta's voice was softer than a whisper. "The queen. She's with Annera at the palace. Alone."

"*Alone?*" Lord Swann cackled. "Tell the beast to kill her, then! Dismantle the threat at its root while we can!"

"Are you *mad?*" Lord Keer demanded. "Halvor wouldn't hesitate to fly here and destroy whatever he left behind after Runeia, and we don't have the power we need to stop him yet. Krotis would be nothing but a blackened island cluttered with bones and soot!"

As the lords bickered, Shasta closed her eyes and attempted to understand what Annera was sharing. She felt Annera's fear and anger at first, like Queen Aurelia was taunting her; then she felt something she could only describe as understanding. It was like Annera had found some sort of solace, some brief reprieve Shasta couldn't comprehend.

"Do it, girl!" Lord Quagg had snapped at her. "Do *something!*"

"Don't kill her, you fool," Lord Keer growled. "You'll damn us all!"

"The dragon won't slaughter our kingdom. The realm wouldn't stand for it," Lord Reesa retorted. "We have nothing to lose. End her while we can. Any consequences we face will be less severe than what the queen will do to the realm if she survives."

As the lords continued to shout over one another, arguing while giving her different orders, Shasta felt pain through the bond—both mental and physical. Then, for a fraction of a second, that feeling of solace returned, flooding her soul with peace.

Then, there was nothing.

She'd felt empty—as if her soul had been carved out of her being, leaving her hollow and numb. She reached out for Annera, but her efforts were in vain. It was like the rope tethering her soul to Annera's had snapped.

"Well?" Lord Reesa demanded. "What's happening?"

"I-I don't know," Shasta whispered. "I can't tell."

"What do you mean *you can't tell?* Has your mind gone lame?"

She'd brushed off the insult to focus on Annera. *Come on, my friend.* She pushed the thought toward the dragon, reaching aimlessly into oblivion, while she kept her eyes squeezed shut. *I need you to find me again. Please.*

Shasta knew what would happen to her if Annera failed. If their bond was fractured, the Council would have no use for Shasta anymore. She might've been crowned when she married Kaius Reesa, but she had no husband anymore, and no heirs to succeed her—giving the Council plenty of excuses to dispose of her, to force her to abdicate and potentially even execute her.

Please. She tried in vain one last time, fighting the urge to sob. *Please find me again. They'll kill me if you don't. They might kill you, too. I'm not ready to die. Please, Annera. I need you.*

In the blink of an eye, pressure built up in her chest, threatening to swallow her whole. A gasp escaped her when she felt that rope tether itself back to Annera's soul—a soul that, for whatever reason, ached with guilt and confusion. Those feelings only worsened as the minutes passed, and soon enough, the guilt overpowered Shasta so greatly that it brought her to tears.

Then she'd snapped her eyes open to face the noblemen, and as soon as she did, she knew exactly why Annera felt so guilty.

"She's leaving," she announced, swallowing. "Annera."

"Well?" Lord Reesa barked. "What happened? Did she do it? Does the palace still stand?"

"I don't know. Our connection went...silent, I suppose." It was true, but not entirely. "We'll have to wait and see."

They hadn't liked that, but she insisted there was nothing she could do while Annera controlled her end of the bond, choosing what she shared with Shasta. Shasta didn't think that was true, though. She'd had enough of sharing her soul for one day, so she'd merely...stopped listening.

A day later, Annera returned to Krotis, leagues ahead of the troops while they voyaged across the Alkamura. Shasta felt a tugging in her chest the moment Annera was in her sights: a horrible, guilt-laden feeling, like a child who'd accidentally destroyed a priceless family heirloom.

Queen Aurelia was dead. Shasta couldn't explain how she knew it, but she did—just as she knew Annera had been the one to kill the queen without intending to. But she couldn't tell the Council without proof; they'd be furious if she gave them false hope.

Annera returned to the safety of the fighting pit, and the Council refused to let Shasta visit her. They claimed both dragon and rider needed their rest, and as long as Annera was unharmed—which she was—everything was going to be just fine.

Another day went by before a raven from Akkinor arrived, promising vengeance now that Krotis's dragon had killed their queen. The Council celebrated Queen Aurelia's death, even going as far as to bring the jubilations to the streets with the commonfolk.

Shasta didn't feel like celebrating. It was her dragon who'd killed the Queen of Akkinor, even if it'd been accidental, though the Council—and the whole of Krotis—seemed to believe she'd given the order. She didn't bother telling them otherwise: they'd think less of her if they knew what really happened.

The Council was so pleased that they'd sworn to every god in the realm that Shasta's rule wouldn't be contested. They wouldn't force her to marry again to keep her crown; instead, they'd give her the choice to marry whomever she pleased, so long as she provided an heir for Bruila before her thirtieth name day.

Shasta had feared an early death for longer than she wished to admit, and at the hands of the men she was meant to rule beside, no less. Now that she'd done something to earn their favor—no matter the cost, the lies, or the guilt—she knew she'd secured her place, and the Selle line would go on.

And now that she knew she'd be all right, she completely forgot about that moment of disconnect between her and Annera—that moment of abandonment, and whatever it meant for them.

**

Smoky gray wasn't a good color for the Folly. Neither was mourning black.

It'd been hours before Rayan was able to convince Jack to let their knights bring Aurelia's body into the palace. By that point, nobody gave a second thought to the state of the Folly. Homes had been demolished, businesses had been destroyed, and food and fresh water were scarce—and the Queen of Akkinor was dead. Nobody gave a damn about the Folly's condition now that every single person in the kingdom was in mourning.

Rayan hardly had the chance to grieve his queen, let alone his sister— the sister he'd only found out about a few hours ago. There was so much to digest, so many feelings threatening to burst out of him, but he had no choice but to ignore everything. After all, he was the Lord Hand, and it was his duty to rule in the queen's absence.

He'd managed to coax Jack into letting a few Assembly members bring him inside the palace, but he'd given the advisors firm instructions to keep mum and calm. Jack was in a broken state Rayan had never seen from him before, and without Aurelia, there was nobody around to keep him steady. They'd have to proceed with caution until Jack found himself again; if he ever did.

When both Jack and Aurelia were gone, Rayan turned to Halvor, who hadn't moved from his position on the ground where Aurelia's body had been. Rayan knew Halvor wasn't obedient to him, but he asked the dragon to fetch Eric, Arian, and the children from Omara, anyhow. Halvor released a low, grief-stricken rumble from deep in his throat, then lifted off into the sky to do as he was asked. Rayan was too heartbroken to take pride in commanding a dragon, though.

The Follians still needed a place to sleep. Rayan knew Jack wouldn't want the palace flooded with civilians, so instead, he called for everyone— excluding those who lived in the palace, of course—to follow him to Kalenbrar. The capital had been spared from heavy damage, and if there weren't enough places to stay in the city for everyone without a home, Lady Linderli would have to open the gates of Briarwood to her people.

The time for reparations and permanent arrangements would come later. For now, Akkinor was in mourning.

When he'd returned to the palace, Rayan first checked on his children and the Bolas siblings, and after ensuring they were all right, he went to find Jack. A servant directed him to Aurelia's study, but when he arrived, he couldn't bring himself to enter. The sound of Jack's sobs tore him apart. His friend needed time to grieve on his own, particularly before the children returned.

The children. How was Jack going to tell them? How was he going to tell Arian, too, for that matter? Rayan wished he could do it for Jack, to take that burden from him, but he knew he couldn't. Jack, despite how shattered he was, would want to do it himself.

Instead of talking to Jack, Rayan had gone to the infirmary, where he knew Aurelia's body would be resting in a private room. He walked past the many injured soldiers, trying his hardest to ignore the way they cried for their queen and their fallen friends. He found himself outside of the only private room with light peeking through from beneath the door, and opened it without knocking.

Three medics, a priest, and two advisors stood gathered around a table, the room illuminated by a few dim candles. They'd stopped crying and sniffling when they heard the door open. He must've asked them to leave, because they nodded and slipped past him, murmuring sympathetic words.

A sharp pain pierced his chest when he saw her on the table. Her hands were folded over her abdomen, and Edom's body was still curled up on her chest, just above her hands. Her skin was whiter than a sheet, and some of her curly golden hair was stained crimson. She looked surprisingly peaceful, and Rayan couldn't help but smile when he saw the traces of gold flaked around the corners of her eyes.

He'd hoped she knew her golden tears had come back before she died. It would've made her so very happy.

Sniffling, he'd approached the table and set his hands over hers, wincing at how cold and stiff she was. For some reason, he recalled the day she'd asked him to be her Lord Hand, when she'd hugged him for the first time. Even then, he'd felt the hug was different. It didn't feel like being hugged by one's queen, but rather like being embraced by one's family. He hadn't put that together back then.

"I-I know why you didn't tell me." He cleared his throat when his voice cracked. "You were scared of my reaction. Scared of asking me to keep another secret. Scared of changing everything I've ever known about my life." Tears burned in his eyes and slid down his cheeks, but he kept going. "I understand, and I forgive you. I just hate that we missed out on three years of living as brother and sister—though, in truth, a part of me has always felt like your family."

He could've sworn he heard her voice reply, *You never felt like my family. You were* my family.

Then he'd lost it. First he'd sobbed, and then he'd turned to destruction: flipping a table topped with embalming materials, throwing whatever he could grab onto the floor, and putting his fist through the wall. He'd calmed and softened when he looked at her again, that peaceful face laying there cold and lifeless, and he'd started to weep silent tears as he sunk to the floor.

Somehow, he'd found his way out of the room, and he'd been surrounded by people begging for answers and direction, neither of which he could offer. Everything else was a blur after that. He wound up in his bedchamber eventually, and though he didn't sleep, he felt like Arian must have while cursed with the Hollow Dream: unable to move or speak, trapped in his own head, and utterly alone.

Later in the day, someone slipped into his bedchamber and sat on the edge of his bed. He knew it was his father, just as he knew that somewhere in the palace, Jack was telling the children that Aurelia was dead. The thought made him want to vomit.

"Do you know?" Eric had croaked. Rayan closed his eyes and managed a nod. "I-I only found out right before the bells. There's so much—"

"You can tell me everything later."

Eric hesitated. "Son, I...I'm sorry for your loss. I know you cared for her very much."

Rayan's heart lurched. "If I had known who she was to me..."

"I've been thinking the same. But dwelling on the past doesn't close wounds, my boy—it only deepens them. I-I did not know her well, but I admired and respected my queen, and I mourn for her. I mourn for my daughter even more, and for the years as a family we shall never have."

Not knowing what else to do, Rayan sat up in bed and pulled his father into his arms. He'd hugged him tighter than he ever had, burying his face in Eric's shoulder, and fought the urge to break down and sob. Eric held him back, trembling while he tried to maintain his composure.

"The king will need us, now more than ever," Eric whispered. "Even without her, we still have a family to support. Those poor children..."

Neither of them had realized the depth of what he'd said—*those poor children*—until a few days later, when the time came to hold Aurelia's memorial. Rayan worried that mourners from across the country wouldn't be able to attend, what with the distance, but nearly everyone had made it: they'd ridden nonstop since the Assembly sent out ravens on the day of Aurelia's death. The only people who hadn't come were their allies abroad, but they'd come eventually.

The memorial was held at Robert's Arena to fit all the attendees in one place—after all, there were thousands of them. Some civilians managed to find seating within the arena, but most were gathered outside, surrounding the premises.

In the center of the arena sat a large stone table, and atop the table was Aurelia's embalmed body. Edom's tiny body was resting just beside her, too. She'd been scrubbed clean of blood, her hair had been brushed, and her cheeks and lips had been painted to mask the blueness of her complexion.

She was wearing her favorite gown: a massive, royal blue dress with floral patterns and dragons stitched along the fabric in gold thread. Her hands were folded over her chest, though the billowing sleeves hung low over the sides of the table. Her new crown, one she'd designed herself, sat atop her head, though it'd be saved for Halle after the memorial.

She wasn't wearing shoes, so her bare feet poked out from the hem of her skirt. Jack had insisted upon it: "She didn't like wearing shoes in life," he'd said, "and she wouldn't want to be buried with them, either."

Rayan, his children, Eric, and Arian stood with the royal family along one side of the table, several feet away. The governesses stood behind the children, and behind them, those closest to Aurelia—Thea and Mycah, her parents' siblings, and the Ashfords—were huddled together. The Assembly stood on the other side of the table behind Elder Marvion, who'd lead the mourners in prayer.

Halvor was there, too. He coasted overhead, visible to all thanks to the lack of a roof at the amphitheater, and released ear-piercing, anguished cries from the sky.

Marvion started the ceremony, able to be heard by all after Lord Chilton cast an amplifier spell on his voice. He spoke of the queen's life, her loss, her legacy. He talked about the destiny she'd been given by the gods, and how she'd dedicated her life to serving them. He spoke of her duties not only to Akkinor, but to her family, to the realm, and to everyone who came to her for help.

Rayan couldn't bear to look at anyone except for Marvion. He refused to glance over at the children while they stared at their mother's body, knowing that only two of them fully understood what had happened. He didn't wish to see the look on Jack's face, either. He had to be strong for them, and he couldn't do that if he saw the pain on their faces.

"Her Grace was more than our queen." Marvion's voice cracked a bit, but he smoothed it out. "She was a loving wife and mother, a devoted daughter, a sister, a niece—and more than anything, she was a friend to all. We may ask the gods why they took such a wonderful soul from the realm so soon, when she had so much life left to live and so much peace, wisdom, and love to spread. But we cannot be angry at them, despite our confusion and our pain. The gods have called her home so she may share her light with the heavens, and so her memory may inspire us to restore wonder and peace to our world. Let her death not be in vain, for with her loss, we shall pave a new path forward—a new age for humanity's existence. We shall pray for..."

Marvion fell silent when Jack took a few steps forward. There wasn't a sound to be heard as he approached the table, then held out a shaking hand to set it over Aurelia's. He was still and silent for a moment, and then he bent over to kiss her forehead. As soon as his lips touched her skin, his entire body faltered and gave way, forcing him against the table for support. His arms spread over her as his face fell onto her chest, and his shoulders wracked mercilessly while he sobbed.

It was the only sound to be heard for miles.

He cried incoherent words as he clutched her, breaking whatever was left of the mourners' hearts. Others started to cry, too, but Rayan couldn't tell where the sounds were coming from—probably because they were all around, the grief taking mercy on no one.

"Papa?"

Only at the sound of Halyna's little voice did Rayan remember the children. He turned to face them, nearly losing his composure when he saw the four of them—Harlen and Holly having stayed at the palace with Irina—watching Jack with wide, terrified eyes. Halle was crying silently, and Hyacinth only stared like she couldn't comprehend what she was seeing. Henry and Halyna, holding hands, looked more frightened and confused than sad, as they probably didn't understand what was happening; even while staring at their mother's body.

He snapped his gaze over to the governesses, hoping they'd meet his eyes and understand that they needed to take the children away. But they didn't react to the children at all. They were both covering their mouths, weeping without making a sound, while their shoulders shook and their eyes squeezed shut.

Then someone else moved to crouch in front of the children: Eric. He murmured something Rayan couldn't hear, then lifted Halyna into his arms. Henry took his free hand while Halle and Hyacinth held onto his coat, and without another word, he guided them toward the exit. Nobody said a thing about it, tried to stop them, or offered to help. They couldn't—everyone was frozen in place, paralyzed by the heart-wrenching scene unfolding before their eyes.

The memorial came to an end not long after when it was clear that Jack wouldn't budge. Everyone slowly trickled out until only Jack and Rayan remained in the arena, neither having moved an inch.

XLII

For a while, Diantha saw nothing but blackness. She'd closed her eyes the moment her knees touched the cushion in front of the altar, and they remained that way for what felt like hours as her lips moved in a silent prayer. She was the only soul in the Temple of Edea tonight, needing absolute solitude as she mourned.

She thought she'd cry as soon as she clasped her hands and began to pray, but she didn't. Her tear ducts were empty. She'd done more than enough crying in the week that'd passed since she received word of Aurelia's death. She may not have particularly liked Akkinor's queen when they first met, but she'd become fond of Aurelia over the years, especially since coming clean about Rieza. She'd miss having another dragonrider to soar through the skies with.

She prayed for Aurelia's safe journey to the heavens first, and then she prayed for forgiveness. She and Rieza should have been there when Krotis attacked the Folly. If they had been, then maybe Aurelia would be alive. But at the same time, she knew it wasn't right to think that way. There was no way she could've known Krotis would lay siege to the Folly, and even if Halvor had gotten incapacitated so badly that Rieza felt his pain, they wouldn't have made it to Akkinor in time.

Of course, Rieza *had* felt Halvor's pain, though it was emotional rather than physical. Diantha didn't understand why Rieza had started moaning and moping around until she received the raven from Akkinor. Then she found herself moping right alongside her dragon.

As thoughts of forgiveness faded, she found herself enraged. The gods had chosen Aurelia to fulfill a purpose in the realm, yet they'd allowed others to corrupt that purpose. That, and her destiny hadn't been enough to save her. Why put such a weight on her shoulders if they couldn't let her live long enough to do what they'd demanded of her?

Diantha felt herself beginning to tremble with fury, but she was tugged from her thoughts when her vision transformed from a steady black to a bright, reddish hue, like someone was holding up a candle directly in front of her closed eyes. Frowning, she opened her eyes, and a sigh escaped her when she looked out the circular window behind the altar.

Flashes of white light burst against the sky in the distance, and even from inside the temple, she could hear hollering voices. Her eyes flicked over to the massive clock on the wall to her left. *Right on time,* she thought.

Since the battle in Runeia, Diantha—plus Reyna of Taundosa and the Four Lords of Bozar—had taken a page out of King Willem's book. It'd been an incredibly clever move when he erected magical shields around the borders of Kanibar, preventing any non-natives from entering without an invitation. Now that Krotis had proven to be a rash and dangerous enemy, Diantha and her friends had done the same. It wasn't great for business, since the economies of nearly every Carthinian kingdom relied on tourism and trade, but it was better to lose a bit of coin than to lose everything.

Dofell didn't have mages skilled enough to cast protective shields around the entire kingdom, but both Reyna and Lord Jalhor Zhaaran had sent aid. The mages replaced one another four times a day so they could rest and replenish, ensuring the kingdom's borders were never left undefended. This was the last switch of the day, so the mages who'd just taken their places would be there until tomorrow morning.

Diantha rose from the cushion and approached the window. She could just barely see the mages atop the watchtowers, where they stood with their arms outstretched, palms facing what lay beyond the borders. They were stronger than anyone gave them credit for; Diantha wasn't so sure she could stand there for hours at a time, refusing to let herself so much as sneeze so she didn't break her concentration.

The Queen of Dofell sighed. *Only the ungoverned territories of Carthe are free now,* she thought. *The rest of us are trapped within our own borders like pigs in pens.*

Somewhere nearby, Rieza bellowed, likely in preparation to devour whatever livestock she'd managed to find. Diantha knew it was paining Rieza to stay within Dofell's borders rather than exploring the continent to feed and stretch her wings, but for now, this was their only option. She didn't want to think about what Krotis would do to Rieza if they set their sights on her. Until Vrurith attacked Aurelia in Khaba, Diantha hadn't been convinced that any human attempt at defeating a dragon—mage or mortal—would be successful.

"Krotis." Diantha couldn't help but snort as she watched the sky shimmer. "Of all the enemies we could've faced..."

"Even sheep can become threatening if their shepherd treats them like lions."

Diantha gasped and brought a hand to her racing heart. She just barely looked over her shoulder, where she saw a shadowy figure standing behind her. She knew this woman was probably just another patron who'd come to pay her respects to Edea, so she didn't let the visitor disturb her.

"I think you might be right," the queen muttered, still watching the mages in the distance. "But what happens when there are five shepherds, all raising the flock like lions? What chance is there for the rest of the livestock?"

"Humans are no shepherds, and in this world, there is only one shepherd per flock."

"I can't say I agree with you."

"That is because you have yet to understand what I mean."

"I know what you mean," Diantha snapped, jutting her chin over her shoulder. "Every civilization has one Almighty. I understand that. I disagree with what you said about humans not being shepherds. If that were untrue, we leaders of the realm wouldn't be able to sway our people with nothing but a few clever words."

The woman chuckled. "You are the sheep who lead the others on the shepherd's command. Nothing more."

"I beg your—"

Diantha swiveled around to face the patron, only for her words to die on her lips when she saw the woman—really saw her—for the first time: her long white hair, eyes like molten silver, and silver gown. Both her gown and her hair were partially hidden by her dark cloak, like she'd hoped to avoid drawing attention to herself when she entered the temple. Now that the two of them were alone, though, and she had Diantha's attention, she didn't hesitate to remove the hood.

Diantha froze. When Edea only stared at her, smiling a bit, Diantha snapped out of her daze and fell to her knees. She flattened her upper body against the floor, her arms outstretched in front of her, and fumbled over words even she couldn't understand.

There she was, making a fool out of herself in front of the Almighty of her kingdom. It was just her luck.

"Rise." Edea's voice cut through the air, and somehow, Diantha mustered the strength to stand again. She refused to meet the moon goddess's eyes when they were face-to-face, though. "I know you have questions, so I shall do my best to answer them now. I have not returned since my last visit because I have not been needed here. However, I have been hoping to speak with you for some time now—I would have come sooner, but I did not wish to draw attention to myself. This is the first time you have been entirely alone in quite a while."

Diantha swallowed the lump in her throat. She knew what Edea meant by that: *This is the first time you've bothered coming to the temple to pray to me in weeks.*

"The others do not know that I have left Hanhalla. There is quite a bit of chaos unfolding in my domain at present, and we are not meant to leave during such trying times." Edea sunk into a pew, her skirts swirling around her. "I would not have left unless the matter was urgent. We have exhausted ourselves while attempting to keep Immor from seizing Krotis from Pherena, but our efforts have been in vain. They are only moments away from success, and we cannot stop it once it's begun. The laws of the universe prevent us from intervening when something like this happens."

Diantha cleared her throat. "All due respect, but the Twelve wrote the laws of the universe. Can't you rewrite them?"

"It doesn't work that way. What's done is done," Edea said with a small, sad smile. "When a kingdom chooses an Almighty, and the deity accepts the request, they form a bond—much like your bond with your dragon. The rest of us cannot break that bond without inciting a chain reaction of catastrophic events. We can, however, offer our strength and guidance to our own patrons in an effort to dismantle the threat."

"So, you can't prevent Immor from replacing Pherena, but you can help us put an end to all of this after the fact." Diantha resisted the urge to snort in the goddess's face. "I don't understand what this means for us."

"The people of Krotis must be shown another way when their current path fails them. You may consume rotting fruit because you are hungry, but after it pains you, you learn to never touch it again, and to find something else to ease your hunger."

Diantha raised an eyebrow. "Does this mean that you and the others will help us defeat them?"

"Help is a petition, not a privilege."

"What on earth does *that* mean?"

Edea laughed, a sound that reminded Diantha of Dofell's nighttime cicadas. "You are a clever woman, Diantha Pharos. You can find that answer for yourself." She rose from the pews and smiled. "I must go before my absence is noticed. Goodbye."

Diantha was so distracted by Edea's riddle that she hardly noticed when the goddess began gliding toward the exit. She snapped out of her daze when the doors shut, and only then did she realize she'd let her Almighty walk away without so much as a *goodbye* or a *thank you*.

She rushed toward the doors and flung them open, but when she stepped outside, Edea was nowhere to be found.

***

There's...There's something I have to tell you.
What is it, Papa?
Your mother...
Jack squeezed his eyes shut. He couldn't stop replaying that moment in his head—the moment he'd told his children that their mother was gone, and they'd never see her again.

A part of him expected them to return and already know. Perhaps Hyacinth had seen it in a vision—but she hadn't seen it, for whatever reason, and Jack was grateful for it. She'd been scarred enough in her eight years without seeing the moment her mother was killed.

An advisor had directed the group to Aurelia's study, where Jack had hunkered down since returning to the palace, as soon as Halvor brought them back. Arian had figured it out by then after seeing the way everyone in the palace sobbed and mourned. Jack saw it in his eyes, the heartache and the pain, as soon as Arian walked into the study. Though Jack wanted Arian's support, he knew he had to tell his children on his own. Arian knew this, too. He'd left the study with Eric and the twins, and the pair found their answers elsewhere.

He'd barely been able to say it. He'd sat the four children on the couch and crouched down across from them, trying to think of a way to phrase it while he looked into their curious, expectant eyes. He saw more of Aurelia in them now than he ever did before, and that only made it harder.

"There was a very bad accident this morning," he'd managed. "Your mama...She was very brave. S-She tried to help during the accident, but it became too much for her. She...She..."

Halle had furrowed her brows. "Where is she, Papa?"

"Is she ill?" Henry had asked.

It'd taken everything Jack had to keep from bawling. "I-I'm so sorry, my little loves. The gods came, and they brought Mama back to the heavens. They need her there with them now."

"That's not true," Hyacinth insisted, anger stirring in her eyes. "They need her here with us. She has to be here to make things better. They wouldn't take her. They *wouldn't.*"

"Sisi—" he'd started.

"They said they needed her. They *said* it, Papa."

"I know they did, sweetheart," he whispered, tears welling in his eyes. "But sometimes, the gods change their minds. They have other plans. A-And this time, they needed Mama to go home with them."

Halyna had only frowned. "Is she...sleeping?"

"In a way," Jack replied, wiping his eyes. "B-But I need you all to understand that she is no longer with us. Do you...Do you understand?"

Halle's chin trembled. "Mama's gone?"

"Yes."

"Forever?"

"Not forever. We'll see her again, someday, when we meet her in the heavens."

"But for a long time?"

Jack wanted to give up and run away right then and there. "Yes. She's gone for a long time." He wiped his eyes again and held out his arms. "Come here. All of you."

The younger two rushed into his embrace, but the elder two hesitated, as only they fully comprehended what he was saying. When they eventually joined their siblings, they fell against Jack's chest as if they could no longer support their own weight. He held them all close and stayed quiet for a moment, internally asking the gods what he'd done to deserve such torture.

"We'll be all right. We're still a family, even if Mama isn't here with us," he'd whispered. "We have to be strong for each other. I-I love you all very much, and so did your mama. Being your mother was her favorite thing in the world. A-And she'll always be with you, watching over you from the heavens."

Hyacinth shook as she wept. "I want my mama."

The gods must've given him strength, because Jack had no idea how he managed to continue on without falling apart in his children's arms.

He'd told them about Edom that day, too, and he wished he hadn't. They'd wept even harder after realizing they'd never see their mama or their favorite friend ever again, and it'd crushed him. He hadn't realized how much he'd miss Edom until he acknowledged the sprite's passing out loud.

Jack knew he'd let them down days later at the memorial. He'd let them see him break. He'd let the entire country see him break. But it couldn't be helped—it was the last time he'd see his wife before her body was entombed in the crypt below the palace. He'd only meant to kiss her goodbye, but he'd lost control of himself, and he'd shattered where he stood.

Now, a day after the memorial, he still hadn't managed to pull himself out of bed to face his children, to be their pillar of strength, to comfort them when they needed him most. He didn't even remember how he got back to the palace after leaving the arena, let alone to Aurelia's study. He'd been sleeping there since her death, as he couldn't face the thought of sleeping in their bed without her.

Today, though, he knew he had to find his strength again. He had to find the man Aurelia had fallen in love with—for his sake, his children's, and Akkinor's. He was, after all, the King Regent now, and the people needed their leader. Even if his eight-year-old daughter was technically now the Queen of Akkinor, all of her responsibilities fell to him until she came of age in eight years.

He'd never once imagined himself in this position, yet it was his new reality, forced upon him by five shameful leaders who were too threatened by his wife's good heart to let her live.

He spent the entire morning thinking about what he could possibly do to ease this pain, to find it within him to move on. The answer came to him out of the blue, and he took it as a sign from the gods before he took the time to fully consider it.

He got up, still wearing the clothing he'd worn to the memorial, and found Rayan in his study. The Hand tried to speak as he stood from his desk, but Jack didn't give him the chance.

"I'm going to Vanhylde."

Rayan's eyes bugged out of his skull. "What?"

"I need to see her."

He shook his head rapidly. "No. That's a fool's gambit, Jack. You know the one true danger of visiting Vanhylde: you might find something you don't wish to live without, and it'll keep you there forever, tethering your soul to purgatory. If she's there, and you see her, you won't come back."

"I'll come back for my children. Always," Jack insisted, narrowing his eyes. "I-I just need to see her, to say a proper goodbye. I need to hear her voice one last time. And...And she'll know what we have to do next. How we have to respond to Krotis. We still need her, Rayan."

His eyes were hard, but his face was twisted with pain. "Jack..."

"I'm going whether you like it or not. Tell Arian where I've gone after I'm out of the Folly, so he doesn't try to intervene."

Rayan offered him a reluctant nod. "All right. Be careful, and...and tell her goodbye for me, and that I love her very much."

A fist clenched around what remained of Jack's heart. "I will."

After leaving Rayan, Jack rushed out to the stables to collect his horse, Valor. He set out for the monastery in Omara on his own, not giving a damn about bringing protection detail or even a sword. The only threat he'd face on the road was the religious radicals who'd already tried to kill him once, but even *they* were in mourning. Anyone who shed blood during the mourning period disgraced the gods—all of them, regardless of which one a person chose to worship more than the others.

At the monastery, he ordered a priest to take him into an empty room, not bothering to explain what he was doing there. It didn't matter that he wasn't in the same room Aurelia had been in when she first visited Vanhylde; so long as he was in a holy building, he could find his way there.

He cut his palm and pressed it to the wall while muttering the words Aurelia had engrained in his mind. He felt the whooshing, the emptiness, as soon as the last syllable escaped his lips. Everything went black for a moment, but when he felt a tugging sensation in his chest, he willed his eyes to open, and he came face-to-face with a tropical tree his hand was pressed against.

Jack took a few steps backward, immediately recognizing the environment as Carthe, and wondered why on earth Aurelia's slice of Vanhylde resembled Carthe and not Akkinor. Then he heard a gentle, melodic voice—familiar, but at the same time, foreign—behind him. He turned slowly, heart pounding in his chest, and found his wife there waiting for him, perched on the edge of a marble water fountain.

"Lily," he breathed.

XLIII

Not quite," Aurelia said with a laugh.

Jack frowned as he took a few steps toward her, every muscle in his body trembling against his bones. Only then did he realize this woman *wasn't* his wife: her skin was a bit darker, her hair was straight and brunette, and she wore a looser, simpler gown than Aurelia would have—a garment more popular in Taundosa than it was in Akkinor.

"Katryna," he murmured.

She grinned. "There you go."

He slowly lowered himself onto the edge of the fountain beside her, unable to take his eyes off of her. She was the spitting image of Aurelia; other than her complexion and her hair, of course. They had the same eye shape, the same nose, the same beaming smile. Even her body language reminded him of Aurelia: poised and graceful, but also a bit excitable, like she was ready to spring into action at any given moment.

"As nice as it is to meet you," he said, "I was hoping to see my wife."

Katryna's grin faded into a small, sad smile. "She's very sorry she didn't come herself. She said that as much as you try to argue it, you wouldn't be able to leave if she came to see you. That, or you'd return time and time again, and your life would revolve around Vanhylde. She thought it best that she stays away so you can learn to live without her."

"My life will never revolve around Vanhylde. It revolves around her, as it has since the day we met."

"Oh, you sweet man." Her smile widened, but her eyes welled with tears. "She told me I'd adore you. I struggled to believe it, because no mother wants to believe any man is good enough for her daughter, but I daresay I'm impressed by you already."

He looked down at his hands in his lap, trying to think of something to say or do that wouldn't show her just how disappointed he was.

"Don't bother trying to hide your displeasure. I can hear your thoughts, remember?" The tone in Katryna's voice felt mocking, but at the same time, like she didn't intend to poke fun at him. It was wildly confusing. "I'm sorry about this. Really, I am. But she said—"

"I know what she said."

Katryna grinned. "You have fire. It's no wonder Halvor has taken to you."

"I'm not here to talk about Halvor. I'm here—"

"—to see your wife, who's currently playing a round of knucklebones with Linden in Hanhalla. So, the way I see it, we have two options: either you leave and let your disappointment fester until it consumes you, or you take advantage of what you've been given, and hopefully, it brings you some solace. What will it be, Jack Ashford?"

There was no doubting this was Aurelia's mother. It was strange, he thought, how two people could be so alike without ever having met one another.

"It's definitely strange, but it's nice," Katryna said, making him curse. She laughed. "You still haven't answered me."

Jack only sighed. "I came here to say a proper goodbye, and to see if there's anything she might know that could help us. The war hasn't ended just because we lost her."

"Very true. She gave me a few messages to pass along, but saying goodbye wasn't one of them. She'll be with you until you meet her in Hanhalla." She paused for a moment. "Don't feel guilty that you weren't there when she took her last breath. She wouldn't have wanted you to feel the life leave her body. She said that's the worst curse anyone could place upon someone they love. Ask Arian, and he'll agree."

His eyes stung. "I know, but—"

"I haven't finished. She asked me to tell you to ignore how things ended, just for a moment, so you can focus on something she wishes she'd gotten the chance to tell you in life: since her parents died and she became queen, she was alive, but she didn't feel like she was living. But when she met you that day in the Violet Forest, you breathed air into her lungs, and you gave her a purpose beyond the crown. The last eight years were the best ones because of you—because you brought her back to life."

Jack's chin wobbled as the dam in his eyes shattered. "She brought me back to life, too. Everything I've become is because of her."

Katryna tried to smile, but it was forced and unconvincing. "She knows. She adores you for the man, husband, father, soldier, and leader you are. You're the man she spent the better portion of her life dreaming about. She asked me specifically to tell you this, too: 'You are my love and my life, today and every day.'"

"Today and every day." He averted his gaze and squeezed his eyes shut, trying his utmost to refrain from sobbing. "I don't know how I'm meant to move on without her."

"That's what your children are for. They'll guide you forward in every way." Real joy sparkled in her smile now. "Halle is officially the youngest monarch ever to be crowned in the realm. She's the youngest Cristos to ever claim Halvor, too. It's mad, but it's wondrous, too, don't you think? Of course, you'll be ruling in her stead for the time being. Aurelia knows this isn't what you wanted, and she's sorry to leave you with such a responsibility, but she knows you'll be grand."

Jack grimaced. Even with the *Regent* in his title, he was still considered the King of Akkinor now, and would be for the next eight years. He never once expected such a thing when he met a beautiful woman with golden hair in the Violet Forest eight years ago, but here he was.

He cleared his throat. "And the war?"

"There isn't much she can tell you. The gods forbid it," Katryna shared, flicking a lock of hair over her shoulder. "She said that when all of this is over, regardless of the outcome, she wants you to look at the stars. You'll know what she means, but you must be patient." She chuckled. "She also told me that patience isn't one of your strong suits. We have that in common, you and I."

Jack cracked a smile. "Despite this visit being the opposite of what I expected, I'm glad to have met you. When Arian hears about this..."

Her joyous expression faded into an indescribable look of pain. "He wanted to see me when he was here, cursed by the Hollow Dream. I stayed away—as did our loved ones—so he wouldn't feel inclined to stop fighting to return home. I knew Aurelia would save him, and I didn't want to give him a reason to fight it. I won't be here if he tries to visit, either. He'd be inclined to stay, and I can't do that to him. B-But if you're willing to pass on a few messages on my behalf, I'd be eternally in your debt."

"It would be my honor."

Her face brightened, but only for a moment. "Firstly, I'd like you to tell my sister that I forgive her for leaving, and I'm pleased she's found such happiness in life, even if it's not the life we envisioned for her. Tell her I'm sorry for not being a better sister to her, and I love her very much. She's become more like me than I ever expected, and it brings me such joy. Our parents are very proud of her, too, for forging her own path in the world. She has the true spirit of the dragon. And my brother..."

Katryna's face crumpled as she dipped a finger into the fountain. "He was one of my dearest friends, and I never told him how much he meant to me. I know a version of him in Hanhalla, but even so, I yearn for the real Arian every day. Tell him I'm sorry for the pain I caused him when I left. I broke him, and despite how strong he appears, he's never been the same. I've always felt such guilt for stripping him—and the world—of the man he once was. I fear you wouldn't recognize him if you knew him back then."

"Really?"

"Really. He was even more spectacular than he is now, that darling man." She wiped her eyes and smiled a little. "Tell him I'm proud of him, and so are our parents. He has become the most beloved figure in the realm, and he's done so all on his own. I continue to idolize him from Hanhalla, and the thing I miss most about being alive is hugging my brother. Tell him that. And tell him how much I love him. Please."

Jack's heart ached for her, so much so that he could barely summon the strength to nod. He wondered how Aurelia had looked and sounded when she'd been the one asking Katryna to relay her messages. If she'd been anything like Katryna was now, then it'd probably hurt her more to send the messages than it did for Jack to hear them.

"And Eric..." Katryna cleared her throat and looked down at her fingers in her lap. It looked like she was going to cry again, and then her lips curled into a wide, beaming smile. "Tell him that I'm sorry for withholding the truth from him. I wanted to make things easier for him, but he had every right to know, and every right to make the decision for himself. Tell him I've been walking at his side all these years, laughing at his silly jokes and scolding him for losing his temper. He's always had a nasty one, like our daughter. I've been keeping his hyacinths alive, too—they'd have died ten times over by now if not for me. I'm that voice in the back of his head reminding him to water them. And tell him..."

She trailed off, her voice cracking, before clearing her throat and trying again: "Tell him that I have loved him since I was one-and-twenty years old. I loved him in Icareth, and I love him in Hanhalla, more and more every day as I watch the wonderful man he continues to become. I shall be here waiting for him when his time comes, and I'll have so many stories to share with him. And tell him—" She interrupted herself with a snort that turned into a cackle. "Tell him the card is under the wardrobe in his bedchamber. It fell under there ages ago. Might as well tell him it means I've still won, too. He'll know what I mean."

Jack laughed a little. "All right. I'll tell everyone as much as I can remember."

That made her laugh, too. "Fair enough."

"Is there...Is there anything else before I go?"

"I think I've about covered it."

Nodding, Jack stood from the fountain, prompting Katryna to do the same. He reached out, intending to take her hand and kiss her knuckles as a token of respect, but instead, she wrapped her arms around him and pulled him into an embrace. She was much stronger than she looked, but Jack had a hard time focusing on the strength of her grip—her hug felt exactly like Aurelia's, and it was the only thing plaguing his thoughts.

He knew she wasn't Aurelia, but for just a moment, he could pretend that this was the last time he'd be holding his wife in his arms.

"She loves you so much that it frightens me, for I have never known someone who loves another so fiercely, so completely." Katryna squeezed him tighter as he bit back tears, his hands trembling on her back. "It takes a great man to earn that kind of love from such a remarkable woman. Don't forget it."

Jack barely managed a nod. When they separated, he took a few steps backward, too overwhelmed by the embrace to stay close to her without feeling the urge to hug her again, to stay there forever while he pretended she was Aurelia. She pointed toward a door across the way—one he recognized as being the rear entrance to Ardiham Castle in Taundosa—and told him to walk through it to return home. At the same time, she climbed up on the fountain again, and she started walking along the marble with her arms outstretched for balance. The way her arms fluttered in the air reminded him of Halvor, especially when paired with her blue and gold gown.

"It was lovely to meet you," she said, not bothering to look at him while she observed her path. "Until we meet again."

He forced a smile. "Goodbye, Katryna."

As he turned to walk toward the door, she yelled, "Wait! I forgot something!"

"What is it?" he asked, turning back to face her.

Her lips curled into a mischievous grin. "Lucyra says hello. She's pleased by the great fuss you made over her death—she always hoped someone would love her enough to mourn her like that. And she says that if she catches you cheating while playing a game or sparring with anyone in the future, she'll demand that the gods smite you."

That made him guffaw. "Does she really think the gods would listen to the commands of a dead woman? That they'd be pleased to be commanded by a mortal? I see death hasn't made her any less...*her.*"

"You'd be surprised at what the gods are willing to do for the souls in their domain." Humor had disappeared from her face and her smile, replaced by something Jack could only describe as genuine solace. "Goodbye for now, Jack Ashford."

***

It'd been some time since Arian learned that his beloved niece was gone, and yet, it felt like it'd happened just this morning.

He remembered every detail, from the moment he saw what Krotis had done to the Folly while he was flying on Halvor's back, to the moment he escorted Aurelia's children through a palace overwhelmed by sobbing employees, to the moment he saw the shattered look on Jack's face.

A part of him had known from the moment Halvor picked him and the others up in Omara. He could feel the dragon's anguish—a radiating combination of pain and fury. It was the exact same feeling Arian had when he felt Katryna's hand go limp in his after she gave birth to Aurelia.

His fears were proven when he saw Jack. There was no doubting it then. A man like Jack Ashford didn't look like his entire world had collapsed unless he'd been torn from the one he loved. Only Aurelia had that effect on him—on everyone, really.

He'd left the children with Jack in Aurelia's study, and as soon as he turned to Eric to say, *I think something terrible happened,* they were ambushed by Anna, Aurelia's lady-in-waiting. She'd been crying so hard that he could barely understand her. When she calmed down enough to speak coherently, she said exactly what Arian had feared: *The queen is dead.*

He didn't want to believe it. He knew it, but he refused to believe it. Reality didn't sink in completely until he saw her body for himself. For a moment, he could only see Katryna as he stared at her. He was reliving his sister's loss while simultaneously coming to the realization that he'd broken the last promise he'd made to her.

You-You have to look after her, Katryna had said. *You have to protect her. Give her all the years of life that...that have escaped me. Please, Arian.*

I will, Kitty. I promise. On my life, I swear it to you.

Aurelia was supposed to live a long life. Arian wasn't supposed to outlive her. He wasn't supposed to watch as she was entombed in the crypt beside her parents, just as Katryna had been when his sister was only ten years younger than Aurelia was now. He'd promised Edmund and Cressida that he'd look out for her, too, if anything happened to them. He'd broken more than one promise, and he knew that whatever remained of the man he once was would crumble into dust because of it.

Aurelia was dead. His niece was dead. It didn't feel real, yet reminders were all around him, threatening to swallow him whole and spit him out as a fractured, unrecognizable version of himself.

At first, he'd been so shocked and paralyzed by grief that he hadn't been able to cry. Then, on the eve of Aurelia's memorial, he returned to his bedchamber to find two intruders sleeping in his bed: Halle and Hyacinth. He'd retreated into the hallway, where he broke down by himself for hours. He only snapped out of it and managed to dry his tears when sunlight poked through the windows and flooded the hallway. The girls would be waking up soon, and he didn't wish for them to see him like this.

He had to be strong for them, for Jack, for Eric and Rayan and everyone else who'd loved Aurelia as much as he did. But as hard as he tried, he still couldn't fight it when he wept through every night, unable to control his emotions. Sleep and peace had become distant friends who'd left him when Aurelia did.

Now, the day after the memorial, Arian stared at a bottle of scotch in his bedchamber, fighting the urge to swallow the contents and numb the pain. Instead of falling victim to the drink, he left in search of Jack, knowing that offering comfort to the one who needed it most would bring himself a bit of solace, too.

A servant told him the king had left the premises, his destination unknown. Arian changed course toward the nursery, hoping to distract himself by spending time with the children, but he was soon stopped by Anna, who claimed he had a visitor in the morning room.

He assumed it was Anysa, or even Reyna, having come to pay their respects and offer him comfort. But it couldn't be either of them—the voyage from Carthe was too long for them to have arrived by now.

He opened the door to the parlor, puzzled, and nearly lost his footing when he saw an older man with dark skin and short-cropped gray hair sitting at Hyacinth's pianoforte. He recognized the man not by his appearance, but by the song he was humming—the same Taundosan tune Arian had taught him many years ago, when they were just boys growing up in the Palace of Akkinor.

He could barely get the man's name out: "Sh-Shale?"

The man he loved stopped humming and looked up from the pianoforte, a grin beaming on his lips. Arian felt his knees buckle, but he maintained his composure as he took a few steps forward. The two looked each other up and down, studying one another. It'd been so many years since they last stood in the same room, and so much had changed—and yet, to Arian, Shale was still the young man he'd fallen in love with.

"My muse." The sound of Shale's voice made Arian dizzy. "Hello."

Arian choked on a nervous chuckle. "Hello."

He frowned. "You got old."

"So did you."

He stroked his beard and raised an amused eyebrow. "I always knew you'd get gray and saggy, like me, but I never painted you any differently. The muse I picture when I bring my brush to canvas is still the same young man who used to shove me against a tree and kiss me in a way that would've made our mothers faint. Do you remember those days?"

Arian's heart pounded. "How could I forget?"

"Old age. Poor memory. You know how it is." Shale kept on grinning as he trailed his finger along the piano's keys. "Her Grace wrote to me several weeks ago. She told me you'd nearly perished, and it was your last wish that she let me know if you were to die. Though you survived, she thought you'd like to see me again. I suppose I should've written to you before I came, but I couldn't wait. I needed to see for myself if the eyes I've been painting are the same eyes—"

Arian didn't give him the chance to finish. He surged forward and pulled Shale into his arms, nearly crushing the poor man's ribcage. Shale chuckled at first as his arms fell around Arian, but in a matter of seconds, both had gone silent.

"I never thought I'd hold you again," Arian whispered.

Shale squeezed him tighter as Arian's eyes fell shut. "Neither did I. The queen, rest her soul, fulfilled my only wish in life without even knowing it."

Arian's chin trembled. He opened his glassy eyes and looked through the window across from him, where the sun was shining down on the palace grounds. He squinted through the sunlight and to the heavens, and he mouthed a silent *thank you* to Aurelia. Once again, she'd given him more than he ever could've hoped for.

He only wished she was here to see it.

XLIV

"H mm." Shasta smiled as she ran her fingers over her smooth legs. Now that her burns had healed completely, she'd used her magic to erase the scarring entirely. "Remarkable handiwork, Shasta."

"Indeed."

She gasped, dropped the hem of her skirt, and fumbled out of her chair before rushing toward the corner of the room. She hadn't heard anyone enter her bedchamber, but just a few feet behind where she'd been sitting, an enormous man stood in the center of the room, watching her like a lion watched its prey.

She tried to place him in her memories, but she couldn't. He was the largest man she'd ever seen, standing as tall as her canopy bed, with biceps the size of watermelons. With his warm bronze skin and dark eyes, he looked Kroti enough, but everything else about him suggested he was a foreigner. No Kroti man had his long, dark hair cascading over his shoulders rather than wrapped in a turban. No Kroti man walked around wearing nothing but a knee-length battle skirt, a pauldron, and scabbards holding numerous weapons, either.

She'd never seen a man so exposed before—even her husband, as short lived as their marriage had been. On the one night they'd spent together, both she and Kaius had kept their clothing on, leaving nothing exposed except for the parts they needed to do the job. This man wore nothing to cover his arms, torso, or lower legs, and though Kaius was dead, she couldn't help but feel like she was being disloyal to him by looking at this stranger; a result of being raised with Pherena's values in mind.

She tore her eyes away from him. "W-Who are you? Why are you here?"

"You don't recognize me?" He tsked her, making her blush and press herself deeper into the corner. "It's all right. You needn't fear me, Shasta. I haven't come to hurt you." He held out a hand, beckoning her. "Come."

Shasta hesitated. "I-I—"

"If I wanted to hurt you, I would have done so already."

"That's what many strange men say to earn a woman's trust before they defile her."

His dark eyes hardened, making her gasp. "I won't hurt you, but I won't stand for such accusations, either. Watch yourself."

She wished Annera was here. She wished the other nobles were here, too—they may not have made her feel safe most of the time, but at the very least, she knew they'd protect her against whoever this terrifying man was.

"Come here."

When he spoke again, his voice was more commanding, as if he couldn't take no for an answer. She found herself scampering forward before she realized what she was doing, though she trembled every step of the way. When he was within arm's reach, he closed the gap between them and brought a hand to her cheek. His massive hand was longer than her face was, and as she stilled at the warm feel of his flesh against hers, he did something that made her gasp: he removed her headpiece and her veil with a flick of his fingers, letting her long, silky black hair spring free while the garments fell to the ground.

It was the first time in her life she'd ever stood in a man's presence with her hair on display.

He smiled. "There. Much better."

His voice was softer and gentler than it had been moments before, but it still made her shiver with fear.

"I-I—" she stammered.

"You mustn't start speaking unless you know what you wish to say. It's bad form." He twirled a lock of her hair around his finger, paralyzing her. "You asked me why I'm here. It's because of you, Shasta Selle. You are the last piece of the puzzle."

"I-I don't understand."

The man's smile only widened. "I suppose this is no fault of yours. The others have kept you in the dark. If you refused them, they would be trapped, so they have tried to find other means of earning your favor. You have never needed to worry about them killing you or replacing you, you know. Carthe wouldn't stand for the Selle line to come to an end after your family has ruled for so many centuries. The others have made false threats to make you submit—they never had any intention of removing you from the equation."

Shasta cleared her throat. "If I refused them how?"

"Plans have been brewing for some time now within the Iron Council. Your father died unaware of it, and the one who perished in battle didn't learn about it until recently. The others knew it would be easier to sway you than your father—they didn't fully commit to their plans until after he was gone, despite him unknowingly leading them in the right direction. But they knew you would be difficult to persuade, too. Instead of telling you the truth, they have attempted to plant ideas in your head, hoping you might come to the same conclusion they did on your own. Unfortunately, you haven't."

She took a small step backward when his eyes hardened again. "F-Forgive me, but I don't know what you're talking about."

He sighed irritably. "The people of Krotis have begun to see things as your fellow rulers do—partly because of what your enemy did to this land, and partly because they shall always heed the word of their Elder. The new Elder of Krotis is involved in the plans as much as your counterparts are. But I cannot take my place until the majority of the people and all leaders of the land have accepted me."

"W-What do you—"

He took her chin a bit too roughly, making her gasp in alarm. "You have answered to a deity who demands submission and weakness for far too long. A deity who insists that you conceal your beauty, for it is a distraction from what she values. A deity who stood back and watched as your kingdom was ostracized from the realm rather than giving you the strength you needed to defeat the enemy. One threat has been dismantled, but the tools it left behind will continue to aid in your destruction unless you seek power elsewhere. Without me, you will die."

Shasta's lower lip wobbled. As she looked into his eyes, finally feeling the power radiating from his very being, she realized who he was. At the same time, guilt flooded her veins as she recalled the last conversation she had with Lazelus Swann before she betrayed him to the Council.

He'd been right about his theory, and she'd shut him down. The Council had, indeed, been associated with the Guild of Steel—and apparently, while keeping it hidden from Shasta, they'd come so far that Immor himself had been summoned to the realm, all to convince Shasta to accept him as Krotis's Almighty.

Queen Aurelia was dead. Shasta had assumed that meant everything the prophecy foretold had happened in one way or another. Now, she realized they'd been wrong about Aurelia bringing about the end of

384

existence. Someone else would be responsible for it, likely in an effort to retaliate against the queen's death; and after making so many enemies in their attempts to stop Aurelia, Krotis's only hope was the strongest god in the realm putting an end to the threats.

Shasta was too terrified by what the future held to feel awestruck at standing in a deity's presence. Had he visited her for any other reason, she would've celebrated, but now didn't feel like the time to acknowledge the wonder of it all.

"Akkinor has more friends than Krotis does," Immor continued, dropping his hand to his side. "The realm has already begun to turn on you after receiving word of the queen's death—you, specifically, for it was your dragon that killed her. Without me, they will come for you. They'll call for your head, and your dragon's, and Krotis won't be strong enough to stop them. Pherena would rather submit than fight back, letting her kingdom fall even more than it already has. I would protect you, and I would ensure the realm never raises a sword against Krotis again."

She felt like a little girl when she squeaked, "How?"

He grinned. "If every inch of Carthe was decorated in amber flags, do you really think the rest of the realm would dare to rise against you?"

Shasta's eyes widened. "Y-You would help Krotis conquer the continent?"

"I would."

"And that's...that's the only way to keep us safe? The only way for me to keep my life?"

"It is." Immor held out his hand and raised a dark, bushy eyebrow. "What say you, Shasta of Bruila?"

She hesitated only briefly before reaching out and clasping his hand. As soon as they shook, a sudden darkness fell over Krotis and blanketed her bedchamber in shadows. The eeriness made her shiver, but the feel of Immor's powerful grip in hers made her feel like a goddess.

Immor only grinned at her. "Well done."

***

When Jack returned home after leaving Vanhylde, he felt stronger somehow, like his conversation with Katryna had given him the closure he needed—despite his disappointment at being unable to see his wife one last time.

He didn't understand why he felt so empowered until he met Eric, Rayan, and Arian in the morning room—plus Shale, Arian's long lost lover, who'd come to visit after receiving a letter from Aurelia. They seemed relieved that he hadn't seen Aurelia in Vanhylde, likely because they feared what might've become of him if he had, but when he told them about Katryna, it was like the entire realm had flipped upside-down.

As he relayed her messages to the best of his ability, he watched as a whirlwind of emotions passed over them. They wept as much as they laughed, but by the end of it, both Arian and Eric were smiling with tears of joy shimmering in their eyes.

That's when Jack understood why he felt so much better: he'd been responsible for bringing closure to Arian and Eric after they'd spent over thirty years wishing she could reply to them, wishing they could hear her say she forgave them, loved them, missed them. Jack himself may not have gotten exactly what he wanted out of his trip, but he'd given a wonderful gift to Arian and Eric.

Aurelia's voice in the back of his head told him that it was more fulfilling to bring peace to others than to find peace for oneself. He never believed her when she said that in life, but now that she was gone, he knew she'd been right all along.

She always was.

When Jack finished his recollection of his trip, Arian turned to Eric. "What did she mean about a card?"

Eric thought for a moment, his face contorted with confusion. Jack's eyes flicked over to Rayan, who watched his father with a worried crease between his brows. It ached Jack's heart to see Eric struggling like that; after everything he'd just heard, it must've felt horrible to lose track of his memories.

Then his face lit up, and the tears lingering in his eyes seemed to dry. "Do you remember how fond we were of card games?"

Arian nodded. "I do. I once heard you quarreling from the other side of the grounds after she marked her cards. She was a horrible cheat, my sister."

It runs in the family, Jack thought, reminiscing on the many times Aurelia had cheated her way to victory during their silly games.

"She was," Eric mused, smiling. "Not long before I left, we were playing a card game, and she stole one of mine when I wasn't looking. She somehow managed to slip it into my pocket, and after she won, she tried to convince me I'd put it there when I scolded her for cheating." He stifled laughter. "We had a good laugh about it after. I put the card back in the deck when we finished playing, but she told me to keep it. She said, 'The next time you're cross with me, I want you to look at this card. Let it be a reminder not only that I won this game, but that I only rile you so badly because you love me so much, too. We feel emotions more strongly, whether it be anger, joy, or sadness, when they're inflicted by someone we love.'"

Arian's smile wobbled. "Our father used to say that."

"I know," Eric murmured. "I did as she asked, and whenever she drove me mad, I looked at the card, and I found my peace of mind when I remembered how deeply I loved her. I brought it home with me—not because she still riled me from afar, but because it continued to be a reminder of what the two of us shared. I lost it ages ago, and the guilt nearly consumed me. Now, I know exactly where it is." He chuckled a bit. "That was the only card in the deck with a dragon painted on both sides. The only one."

Rayan cracked a smile. "Figures."

"I would have loved the chance to meet her," Shale said, squeezing Arian's hand. "She sounds like a spitfire."

Jack snorted. "That's putting it lightly."

Arian boomed with laughter. "Now you know where Aurelia got it from."

Jack grinned, as did the others, and for the first time since Aurelia's death, he didn't feel the urge to topple over and weep when she was spoken about in the past tense.

Just as Arian began telling a story about Katryna, the door to the morning room opened, and the soldier who'd entered barely had the chance to open his mouth before someone slipped past him: Elder Marvion, who looked like he'd suffered through a journey across the Ngora Valley to make it here. He was panting, red-faced, and sweating so much that his short gray hair clung to his face and neck in clumps.

"Marvion." Jack frowned as he and the others stood to greet the priest. "What's happened? Are you all right?"

The Elder gasped for air, but waved Rayan off when the Hand offered him a chalice of water. He hunched over, catching his breath, then lifted his head up to meet Jack's eyes. He didn't need to speak for Jack to know what had happened.

"We felt a great disturbance at the monastery," he managed, still wheezing. "The drums of war have begun to play in Icareth."

Shale furrowed his brows. "Well, given what's happened, that—"

"'*The song of War will play for the ears of many.*'" Rayan's eyes snapped over to Jack's. "Isn't that what the prophecy said?"

Heart hammering, Jack glanced over at Marvion. "Are you sure?"

"Without a doubt. He walks among us now. I can feel it. We all can."

"What's going on?" Eric asked, looking between Jack, Rayan, and Arian. "Who are you talking about?"

"Immor," Jack replied, running a nervous hand through his hair. "The Guild of Steel has succeeded in Krotis. Immor has replaced Pherena, and he has presented himself to the Kroti."

Eric and Shale collapsed onto the sofa again, startled beyond words. Arian started pressing Marvion for more information, but Jack didn't bother listening. He only locked eyes with Rayan again, and the two of them had a silent conversation, debating their next move without panicking the others.

They hadn't discussed their retaliation against Krotis. Everyone was still in mourning, for one, and for another, how could they ask their people to rally for war, yet again, when an entire kingdoms' worth of soldiers were without homes? They knew it would be some time before they could seek vengeance for what Krotis had done, but now that Immor had officially taken his place in Krotis...

It wasn't as if Halvor would be of any use to them. Even if Immor hadn't taken over in Krotis, Halle was Halvor's mistress now, and only she and her sisters could command him. Jack certainly wasn't going to ask his eight-year-old daughter to command a dragon during wartime, even from the safety of the palace—what good would that do? Halvor might've known what his role was, but even then, there were always moments of doubt.

Now with Immor added to the mix, Halvor was like any other human soldier. Immor could destroy the dragon with a snap of his fingers. The same was true for Rieza, leaving the allies at a horrible disadvantage.

"If Aurelia's theory was right," Rayan said slowly, "then Krotis hopes to conquer Carthe. I don't know how they'll justify their actions now that Aurelia is gone, and their largest, supposed threat has been dismantled—but I suppose they don't care about justifying their actions anymore, or using the prophecy to do it. They made it far enough to see the Guild's hopes come to life, and that's what they wanted all along. They'll forget about the prophecy to focus only on conquering the continent."

"If they succeed, our allies will be dead," Jack added, making Arian wince. "We couldn't go to Carthe and try to give the kingdoms back to their rightful leaders. Akkinor isn't strong enough to manage that alone, especially with Immor as the patron of the entire continent, and both Quapebet and Glacier Bay have made it clear they want nothing to do with this. They'll be even less inclined to get involved out of fear of Immor."

"We have no way of knowing how this will unfold, either." Arian's face had turned a sickly shade of gray, and Jack didn't blame him. He was probably realizing that he might never return home again. "Immor's power hasn't been seen in the realm since before the persecution. His plan is a mystery to us."

"Even a god cannot snap his fingers and change the way of things like that," Marvion said pointedly. "He can't kill the other Carthinian leaders or force the people into submission. He can share his strength and his skill with Krotis while they take their neighbors to war, and he can intervene when absolutely necessary—like if the Kroti face a threat they can't defeat on their own."

"The dragons," Rayan offered.

"Yes. Although, he can't harm Halvor or Rieza unless the dragons are within his sights and posing an active threat to the people he's sworn to protect. He may be one of the Twelve, but even they have their own rules to follow, and he's already upset the others enough as it is. He won't do more than what I've outlined unless he wishes for a divine war."

Jack nodded in understanding. "So, the Kroti will march to the other kingdoms and lay siege as they would in any other war. They'll be stronger than any civilization currently in existence, so they'll win each battle, and they'll seize each kingdom. It'll take time, though."

"Where would they start?" Rayan said. "Krotis's only direct path to Carthe is through the valley. They could sail to Taundosa, I suppose, but—"

"No." Jack shook his head. "The greatest threat to them—in Carthe, at least—is Rieza. They'll want to take her out before they look elsewhere. They're going to Dofell first. I'm sure they know that if Rieza is in distress, Halvor will try to aid her, too. And without a rider to command him...I don't know if Halvor would stay here."

Arian frowned. "Halle is here. She's his mistress now. He wouldn't abandon her."

Jack only sighed. "Halvor is already distressed after losing Aurelia. It may make him more unpredictable than usual. If he tries to aid his sister, and Immor has the chance to destroy both of them at once..."

He trailed off, and before he had the chance to speak again, the door to the morning room opened once more. Yet again, the same soldier wasn't given the chance to utter a single syllable before someone pushed him aside and hurried into the room.

It was Anysa. Her hair was tousled by the wind, and she smelled like she'd been sleeping in a fisherman's boat for the last fortnight. The look in her eyes was one Jack knew well: grief.

"I just heard about the queen," she said breathlessly, embracing Arian when he rushed to greet her. "I'm so sorry, brother."

He gave her a squeeze before releasing her. "What are you doing here?"

She flicked a lock of dark, graying hair over her shoulder. "I bought passage on a mercantile vessel destined for Akkinor not long after I returned home. I tried to sway my neighbors to tell the truth about what happened, but they're too frightened of Vrurith—and too easily persuaded by coin—to oblige. I was going to send a raven, and then I heard about Krotis splitting off from the continent. I knew things would be difficult for Aurelia, given what happened, so I thought I'd come to offer support in any way I can. Then we were unable to dock at Seaport, so we had to dock in Sadia instead, and I took a carriage to the Folly. The coachman told me everything as we rode through the rubble."

She hugged Arian again, murmuring things Jack couldn't hear, and as the siblings took a moment to themselves, Jack came to a marvelous—albeit somewhat terrifying—realization.

"Anysa," he said, making the siblings separate, "can you command Halvor?"

She frowned. "Not like Katryna or Aurelia could, but I suppose he'd listen to me, to a certain degree."

"No." Arian shook his head. "We're not sending my sister to war with Halvor."

"Of course not," Jack said quickly. "She can command him from here. Right?"

Anysa shrugged. "Maybe."

"Immor just now took his place in Krotis, right? Within the last few days?" Rayan directed the question at Marvion, who nodded. Rayan then raised his eyebrows at Jack. "How long would it take Krotis to reach Dofell?"

"A few weeks at most."

"If they've already set out, they're a few days ahead of us. We'll need time to prepare our soldiers for war, though. It could take weeks before we're ready to set sail for Carthe, and by that time, Dofell might already be lost."

Jack pondered that for a moment, but it was Shale who spoke next: "You've all forgotten about something."

"What is it?" Jack demanded.

Shale shrugged. "Piracy."

"Piracy," Jack repeated. "What do you mean?"

"Pirates will do just about anything for coin. They'd fight on behalf of their worst enemy if it meant filling their pockets with gold."

"You think Espos would fight with us?" Rayan winced. "I don't know. Immor might persuade them to stay on their island."

"Pirates fight for three things, my Lord Hand: riches, glory, and the thrill of it. You may be able to summon only half of Akkinor's military in time to reach Dofell, but Espos is a stop on your voyage to Carthe, and they have plenty of fighting men to spare. They'd make up for your lost numbers. Give them a good reason to fight, and they'll do it."

Marvion sighed. "It's a good plan, but we're forgetting something else: Krotis has a god on their side. We don't. Regardless of how many soldiers we bring to Carthe, we will lose against Immor."

"No, we won't." Jack's lips curled into a grin as he remembered—for some unexplained reason—a conversation he'd recently had with an old friend. "We have to send out the call to arms at once, Rayan. I have an idea."

XLV

Diantha -
    I won't bother with formalities for the sake of urgency. We're on our way to you, as we have good reason to believe that Krotis and Immor will seek to conquer Dofell first. I've sent similar messages to Taundosa and Bozar, too, but as of now, I can't say for certain that they'll rush to your aid instead of focusing on reinforcing their own kingdoms.

We've given a great deal of thought to the timing of it all, plus other factors, and if our estimations are correct, we should arrive within a day or so of the enemy. Please trust that we have a plan, but if we don't make it in time, you need to protect yourself. Get your family out of Dofell as soon as possible. King Harryn still owes you a favor after what Willem tried to do to Dofell, so I imagine he'd be willing to offer refuge to your family. If Krotis seeks to conquer Kanibar next, have your family brought to a tavern called The Drunken Stag in Caedia. I have a friend there, Alec, who will smuggle them out of Carthe and aboard a ship destined for Akkinor. Tell him Jack Sherbourne sent them, and he'll help.

I know this will strike you as a bit mad, but you __must__ send Rieza away from Dofell. She's the greatest threat to Krotis there is, and Immor won't hesitate to eliminate her at first sight.

We're doing everything in our power to make it to you before Krotis does. In the meantime, be safe, and follow your family to Caedia if Krotis arrives before we do.

    Your friend,
    Jack Ashford.

Diantha read the message for the hundredth time since it arrived about three weeks ago. She hadn't sent a response out of fear of interception, and Jack hadn't sent a follow-up message. She'd waited for an update or even his arrival every single day since this message came, feeling more like a sitting duck than she ever had before.

She trusted him and whatever plan he had in mind. He was, after all, a tremendous soldier, a wise leader, and the widower of someone she'd trusted. He had Arian Cristos on his side, too. Though there were still so many things she feared about the fight to come, she had to trust him; it was the only thing keeping her from losing her mind.

She'd heeded his warning about her family as soon as the raven arrived. If her calculations were correct, then her husband, their children, and a dozen soldiers had already arrived in Kanibar, where King Harryn had promised to shelter them. If things took a turn for the worst here in Dofell, Diantha would set out to join them; and if she didn't make it in time, she'd send word to have them smuggled out of Carthe as soon as she could.

She never once had to think about smuggling her family out of the continent three years ago. They were a normal Dofelli family back then. She didn't think she'd ever yearn for those days after she was crowned, and now, she'd do anything to get back to them.

Rieza was gone, too. Diantha had sent her back to the cave on the Dofelli coast, and she was commanded to flee to Akkinor—and Halvor— if the enemy drew near. She'd be all right if only Kroti soldiers found her, but gods forbid Immor did, too...

A loud, echoing thumping sound in the distance drew her attention from her thoughts. Jack's letter slipped from her grasp as she rushed toward one of her bedchamber windows. She couldn't see anything from here, so she fled her room and set out for a different corridor in the palace. Her two Hands, Aesin and Erinya, hollered after her when she passed them by, but her heart was hammering too loudly for her to hear what they were saying.

She tore open a set of doors leading to a balcony and clung to the railing as she observed the hills in the distance—the hills along the border of Dofell and the Ngora Valley. Bile rose up in her throat when she saw exactly what she'd been fearing since the Elder of Dofell told her about a great disturbance: a large man with long, dark hair, weapons strapped to every inch of his body, standing atop the hill.

Immor.

He stood there by himself for a moment, but soon enough, a sea of soldiers appeared behind him. Even from a distance, she saw they wore mismatched armor: some leather, and some gold and bronze, likely stolen from the corpses or captured soldiers from Akkinor and Taundosa. Amber banners whipped in the wind above their heads, but the banners didn't bear the symbolic lotus flower of Krotis. Instead, the symbol of the Guild of Steel had been sewn into the fabric.

Behind her, she just barely processed Aesin and Erinya telling her that their troops were taking their positions after evacuating the civilians. There was nowhere for the civilians to go in such a short time, especially with the shields around the kingdom, so they'd been brought to the palace crypt for the time being. Erinya said she'd ordered the mages to cast a protection spell around the palace, so only those with Dofelli blood could enter or leave.

"The shields will hold." The confidence in Aesin's voice fractured with every syllable. "They'll buy us some time while Krotis attempts to disarm them. And even if the enemy breaches the borders, the shields around the palace will be yet another obstacle for them to overcome. They won't exert their energy on the palace if we give them a good fight to start."

As soon as he finished speaking, bursts of light in various colors struck the magical shields around Dofell's borders. Diantha winced when the shields rippled with flashes of light, thumping along to the rhythm of Krotis's drums like a heartbeat. Diantha's mages were stronger than anyone gave them credit for, though, and they managed to keep the shields intact.

Then Immor took a few steps forward, and the queen's heart sank to her knees. He held up one hand while the other sat comfortably on the hilt of the sword strapped to his waist. Diantha turned away, unable to watch as screams echoed throughout the kingdom. Even with her back facing the scene, she saw flashes of light illuminating the interior of the palace. Panicked ramblings from Erinya and Aesin confirmed what she knew had happened: Immor had disarmed the shields.

"We have to get out there." The words stuck in Diantha's throat like tar. "We can't wait any longer. I-I'll meet you outside once I've dressed."

They nodded, fear and worry etched onto their faces, and scurried away. As they left, Diantha's eyes snapped over to a suit of Akkinorian bronze armor—a gift from Aurelia—on display in the hallway. With one word from the queen, the armor began to march toward her, with nothing inside of it other than the essence of the palace's secret magic.

She suited up, silently thanking the many hours she'd spent watching her soldiers do the same so she could prepare for a day like today. She didn't like the feeling of being trapped in metal, but without Rieza, it was her greatest defense.

Fighting the urge to shake in her boots, Diantha rushed into the artifacts room, where she took down a glass display case that'd been hanging on the wall. Wincing, she smashed the case on the floor. She was careful not to cut herself when she collected the object in the case: a massive iron sword wielded by her ancestor, Ophelos Phyre III.

She took a moment to prepare herself as she stood alone in the room, then fled like she was being chased by a pack of ravenous hounds when she heard the drums getting louder—and closer.

In moments, Diantha found herself standing beside Aesin and Erinya on the other side of the palace walls. Their soldiers had fallen into formation by then, leaving the trio in the center of an aisle formed by two sets of troops. As soon as the queen arrived, everyone began marching south to meet the enemy, hoping to keep the fighting as far from the palace—and the civilians—as possible.

They watched as the Kroti descended the hill and approached, shrieking battle cries. Immor hadn't moved from atop the hill as the Kroti rushed past him. As Diantha watched the scene unfold, her sword trembling in her grasp, she realized none of the Kroti were actually holding or playing drums. The sound was coming from Immor himself, letting the whole of Dofell know who he was and what he was there to do.

Just then, the sound of ear-piercing horns overpowered the drums. Diantha's heart hammered as she jerked her head to the side, and she couldn't help but laugh when the drums, shrieking Kroti, and horns were silenced by yet another set of battle cries.

Alongside soldiers wearing various types of armor, four different banners appeared from eastern Dofell: a dragon for Akkinor, a sun for Taundosa, an eternal flame for Bozar, and a red fish for Espos.

A gurgling laugh escaped Diantha's throat. If Jack Ashford was anything, he was a man of his word.

***

Jack had fought beside Taundosans, Bozari, and Dofelli before, but never once had he ever imagined himself marching alongside the pirates of Espos—on their way to combat a god, nonetheless.

As the troops marched into Dofell, Jack looked at the men around him—the men with gold caps on their teeth, grime permanently embedded in their flesh, and not an ounce of armor on their bodies. One might've thought they were overly confident to decline armor while marching to face the god of war, and maybe they were; but nobody could deny their combat skills, either.

The Esposi weren't trained like soldiers were, but if anything, that made them more ruthless. They didn't follow procedure. They didn't plan for battle. Everything they did was impulsive, instinctive, driven by bloodthirst and promised rewards. That, and the fact that Espos was the only civilization in the world where firearms were legal, made them a force to be reckoned with.

In perfect truth, Jack hadn't expected them to join the fight. Jack's ship, plus one other vessel from Akkinor's fleet, had docked in Espos two days prior to arriving in Carthe. Captain Lukos, the leader of Espos, thought Jack had come because the pirates were causing issues for Akkinorian ships. After Jack had told him everything, the old man—who hadn't slowed down or gotten less intimidating with age—had only this to say:

"While I'm honored ye thought of us, we got no dog in this fight. I canna send my boys to die at a god's hands because Carthe is at war. *Again.*"

Jack had only smiled and pointed at the other docked ship. "See that ship there? The *Golden Siren?* Climb aboard, and you'll find nothing but a handful of crewmates, and enough jewels, gold, and Akkinorian bronze to sink Espos. I couldn't help but notice upon my arrival that half of your fleet seems to be decommissioned. Looks like you've taken quite a bit of damage as of late. The riches I'd offer you could repair your entire fleet and build another one. There'd be enough leftover for you to build a palace, too—after you've done what I ask, of course."

Lukos had raised an eyebrow. "I got no desire for a palace."

"It doesn't have to be a palace. I was just making a point."

The captain had guffawed. "So ye were. I canna say yer offer dinna excite me, Yer Highness. Ye musta cleared out yer whole bank to twist me arm. I'll accept, but if ye die before I get me coin, yer people's ships won't be safe in me waters no more."

Jack had taken Lukos's hand and shook. "We have a deal, Captain."

And that was that. The Assembly hadn't liked the idea of sacrificing so much of Akkinor's wealth, but Jack knew it had to be done. Besides, Akkinor was blessed by the god of prosperity: despite small pockets of poverty, Akkinor was the wealthiest civilization in the realm thanks to Buen's influence, and he'd help them recover.

After Lukos gathered his available fighting men, the pirates joined Jack on his ship or boarded their own. They'd dock in Orestes in Bozar, meet up with their allies, and make the journey to Dofell on foot from there. The *Golden Siren* would follow them, returning to Espos with the riches only after—and if—the war was won.

Thankfully, a pirate leader called Sherv had given Jack an alternative strategy. It would take too long to reach Dofell from Orestes, and according to ravens from Taundosa and Bozar, the allies' troops were already closing in on Dofell. That would've placed Akkinor leagues behind the others.

There was nowhere to safely dock on the northeastern coast of Dofell, and even if there was, the kingdom sat too high above sea level for the troops to make it there without climbing a vast distance. Sherv told Jack about a spot on the eastern coast of the Violet Forest, just an hour's walk from Dofell: there was no harbor, but if the soldiers took rowboats to the coastline, they'd find a small sandbar that led to a series of steps carved into the rocky cliffs. Apparently, the pirates had carved those steps long ago for the purpose of sneaking into this side of Carthe to pillage.

The Akkinorians had followed Sherv's instructions, and when they'd crossed the border into Dofell, they kept moving south until they met up with their allies. Reyna, plus all four Bozari lords, didn't hesitate to join Jack and a few members of the Assembly at the head of the formations. Then, together, the troops from the four civilizations started eastbound, following the sound of battle drums in the distance.

An eerie chill washed over Jack, like his veins had been pumped full of ice water, as they approached the battlefield. It was a distantly familiar, yet strangely foreign sensation, and one he could only attribute to his proximity to the god of war.

Diantha's troops were gathered a few miles from the palace on a flat stretch of land Jack recognized from his last visit to Dofell. There were towns and villages in the near distance, but the valley itself was empty other than patches of decorative flora. Diantha's two Hands had told Jack that this area was meant to be a wildlife reservation to encourage more fauna to return to Dofell, so the land was protected in every way.

Not anymore, thanks to Krotis.

Jack saw the deity as soon as the allies' troops rode onto the valley. Immor was standing atop a hill in all his divine glory, watching from a distance. Even from afar, Jack could smell the arrogance radiating off of Immor like the smell of decay on a corpse. It was suffocating, and it forced everyone to remember exactly who he was.

The Kroti were rushing down the hill to meet Diantha's forces when Jack and the allies arrived. The Kroti stopped for a few moments, visibly startled by Dofell's unexpected reinforcements, but they were moving again in the blink of an eye. Clearly, they had no intention of engaging in conversation or negotiations like before.

There was no time for hesitation. No time for the leaders to meet up and wish each other well before the fighting began. No time to discuss strategy or to take a moment to breathe before diving headfirst into battle.

Jack's forces merged with Diantha's as they raced forward to meet Krotis, focused on nothing but the fight.

He'd only had one conversation with his allies while riding to Dofell, for fear of facing Immor had rendered them mute for most of it. All they'd managed to do was say good luck, and to remind each other of the deaths they were avenging today.

But as the Kroti charged them, Jack forgot about vengeance, conquest, and victory. None of that mattered anymore—not when the Kroti moved with a speed, agility, and strength they hadn't shown before. Even the Esposi and the Bozari, the greatest fighters amongst the allies, were struck down the moment the warring parties united.

Jack had fought in countless battles before. He'd been a militiaman in Bozar once, long before he met Aurelia, and just for the hell of it, during a civil dispute that allowed him to witness mages in combat for the first time. He'd fought for Aurelia's throne eight years ago, where he'd become one of the first people alive to see a dragon in battle. He'd seen gryphons in combat for the first time during the Battle for Dofell, and other creatures during the Battle of Runeia. He'd fought beside and against mortals, mages, and creatures of all kinds—but in all his years, he'd never once experienced anything of this caliber.

He stood back at first to get a feel for the enemy's strengths, observing while a group of knights protected him from all sides. He was glad for the knights' Akkinorian bronze armor, helmets, and shields—if not for the indestructible material, they'd all be dead already.

Every arrow and spear sent sailing through the air by the Kroti met their mark. They weren't aiming to maim or injure—they were aiming for the heart, the neck, the arteries. They never once dropped their weapons or stumbled, even when an opponent shoved or struck them with full force. When they swung their swords, they always hit *something*, even if their blades bounced off of an opponent's armor like rubber. In close combat, they plunged their daggers without hesitation, always precisely hitting the gaps in their victims' armor.

The mages were stronger, too. They were no longer using their power over the elements, the strongest abilities for all mages; instead, they'd turned to shooting spheres of pure power at their enemies. The balls of light hit their targets every time, resulting in the victims having holes blown through their chests, or—at the very least—being sent sailing through the air until they sustained critical injuries when their bodies finally hit the ground.

Jack's forces were dropping like flies, left and right. They fought valiantly, and with every bit of strength they could, but it wasn't enough.

Jack knew the smart thing to do: keep a safe distance away from the thick of the fighting like the other leaders were doing, avoid drawing attention to himself, and stay close to those sworn to defend him. He had six children and a country he needed to survive for, even if the odds seemed stacked against him—but if he was wise about it, he stood a chance at fleeing when his forces exhausted themselves against an undefeatable enemy.

He would've done exactly that, if not for Aurelia's voice in his head: *I'll see you soon, my love.* It was the last thing she'd ever said to him. Neither of them had even considered that one or the other wouldn't survive the siege on the Folly; but now, Aurelia was gone, and this might be Jack's last chance to avenge her.

A flash of gold to his right caught his attention. He craned his neck to the side, frowning, as a dozen Goldmen—in a circular formation—started running away in the direction they'd come from. Their shields were positioned over their heads, like they were creating a roof over the empty space in the middle of their circle. Jack knew what that meant: they'd realized they were going to lose, and they were escorting Reyna to safety.

He didn't blame her for letting her men take her away. If Krotis succeeded, Reyna would die anyway when they made their way to Taundosa, but at least she'd get an extra few days at home before everything was taken from her.

He'd lost sight of Diantha and the Four Lords. He wasn't sure if Diantha was still here, or if she'd fled to meet up with her family, but he was certain the Lords of Bozar remained. They, too, had a loved one to avenge today.

The thirst for vengeance made Jack bring a hand to his breastplate. The armor created a barrier between his palm and Aurelia's locket pressed against his chest, but he imagined he could still feel it. Lord Baylor, an advisor, had given the locket to Jack before Aurelia was buried, as her postmortem instructions requested that it be passed on to Halle someday. Jack wasn't quite ready to part with it yet.

And if his theory about stopping Immor was correct, he'd need it.

XLVI

Without fully comprehending what he was doing, Jack drew his sword and urged his horse forward, leaving his protection detail behind as he rode through the carnage to reach the hill. He swung his sword to incapacitate any Kroti in his path, and fortunately, most of them were too distracted by finding the most violent, creative ways to kill their enemies to see him approaching.

Suddenly, the horse let out a horrible shriek as he fell forward, his front legs collapsing. Jack was thrown from the steed's back, but luckily, he managed to curl his body to the side as he fell. Rather than his head and neck hitting the ground, his shoulder and hip took the brunt of the impact. Pain flared through his body, his bones rattling against the armor.

The horse was dead, having been shot by an arrow Jack hadn't seen coming. As he took just a second to recover, he realized the arrow wasn't Kroti. It wasn't crafted with vulture feathers like the Kroti used, but rather goose feathers—and of all the warring parties on the battlefield today, only Akkinorians used goose feather arrows.

Jack climbed to his feet, heart racing, as he looked around for the shooter. That's when he saw one of his own men tossing his bow aside and drawing his sword. Jack deflected the attack when they met, his shoulder screaming in protest, and managed to hit the soldier on the back of the head with the butt of his sword when the man stumbled. The soldier's helmet went flying, revealing his identity.

"Gordy?" Jack's sword faltered in his grip while the young soldier, an eighteen-year-old Follian who worked at the palace, struggled to recover. "What are you doing?"

That's when Gordy met his eyes, and a gasp caught in Jack's throat. His eyes weren't the kind, friendly hazel ones Jack remembered, but rather emotionless, hollow, and orange like flickering flames.

Gordy let out a cry and charged Jack again. Jack managed to deflect him, then slammed the flat of his sword against the back of Gordy's knees. When the soldier fell, Jack hit him in the back of the head with the butt of his sword once more. Gordy collapsed in a heap, unconscious but still breathing.

As Jack combatted another enemy—a man wearing the sigil of Kazamir, whose telltale Bozari blue eyes had also turned orange—he tried to catch a glimpse of his surroundings. He didn't get a good look until the Bozari soldier was defeated, and when he did, his stomach dropped to his knees.

The allies' forces weren't just fighting the Kroti anymore. They were fighting *each other.*

"*Rolan!*" Shouting from the left caught Jack's attention. Two Esposi pirates were sparring, and though their faces were identical, one had orange eyes while the other had brown. "What are ye doing? It's me, brother! It's Dolan! Stop—"

Dolan didn't get the chance to finish. Rolan swung his sword, and his twin brother's head fell to the ground, rolling several feet down a bloody hill of mud until it smacked against Jack's boot. Jack met eyes with Rolan, and the pirate screamed before charging him, forcing Jack to kick the head out of the way.

Just as the pair came in contact, the pirate's head whipped backward, and a bloody hole formed in the center of his forehead. Wide-eyed, Jack turned to the side, where Sherv was standing several yards away. Sherv's pistol smoked in his grip, still aimed at the spot where Rolan had been only seconds earlier.

Just as Jack offered Sherv a grateful smile, the tip of a sword poked through the pirate's throat, and he fell forward onto the ground with the weapon still lodged in his flesh.

Roaring in frustration, Jack ran toward Sherv's now-defenseless Kroti killer. He managed to get the soldier onto his knees and cut his throat before the Kroti had the chance to reach for another weapon. Blood sprayed over Jack's face, and while his helmet protected his forehead and his nose, it didn't stop the blood from getting into his eyes and mouth. He blinked through the veil of crimson, knowing better than to remove his helmet to wipe it away, and spit out a mouthful of the Kroti's blood before turning back toward Immor.

He knew exactly what was happening when he saw the Council flanking either side of Immor. The palms of the four noblemen were glowing with orange magic, and even from a distance, they appeared to be deep in concentration. That could only mean one thing: with Immor's blessings, their magic had become strong enough for them to cast a spell on not just a handful of enemies, but on half of the allies' forces. It'd weaken them too much to target everyone at once, but as Jack could see, controlling even a portion of the allies' troops was getting the job done well enough.

Aurelia had told him about an old story once, in which a mage scorned by his family had cast a spell over them to make them turn on each other. Rather than killing them himself for the suffering they'd caused him, he stood back and watched while they tore each other to shreds. Apparently, Immor and the Council were familiar with the story, too.

Going into this, Jack and the allies had known that Krotis would be stronger than them—but they'd also known that they had greater numbers. That didn't apply anymore. By the look of it, there was now an equal number of opponents on both sides.

At least the Kroti hadn't deployed their gryphons. Then again, they didn't need them when they had Immor.

As Jack incapacitated yet another of his own men who'd been turned against him, a roar echoed throughout the battlefield, and Annera soared over the hill. When she roared again, the ground trembled, causing Jack and a few others to take to their knees for stability. He looked up at the hill while the ground slowly steadied, overcome by rage at the sight of his wife's killer, and his fury only intensified when the last noble on the Council took her place at Immor's side: Shasta Selle.

Jack knew he'd probably fail in his endeavor to defeat Immor. He knew that when he told Rayan and Arian the plan back in Akkinor, when he was sailing across the Alkamura on his voyage to Carthe, and when he first stepped onto the battlefield here in Dofell. But somehow, he could now make peace with the thought of failure. He may not have stood much of a chance against Immor, but if he was clever like his wife, he wouldn't go down alone.

He'd take Shasta Selle with him. After all, it was her commanding of Annera that had caused Aurelia's death. He knew it was—what else could it have been?

Panting and ignoring the aching in his hip, Jack ran toward the hill. He barely acknowledged the men and women he slashed out of his path, and he'd stopped noticing the orange eyes of both friends and acquaintances. Only one person, a Dofelli, dared to follow him to the base of the hill, and the poor man lost his head before he could raise his sword.

Jack craned his neck back to look at the figures atop the hill. They were staring down at him. All of them—everyone except for Shasta, whose eyes were trained on Annera as the dragon plucked Jack's soldiers from the ground and swallowed them whole.

They wouldn't kill him right away. He knew they wouldn't. They would've struck him down already if they weren't curious to see what he had planned. Even the four noblemen had ceased casting their spell over the allies, clearly more intrigued by Jack's suicide mission than by focusing on a war they'd already won.

Behind him, Jack heard the screams of those who were waking up from the spell as they realized what they'd done to loved ones and allies alike.

When he reached the top of the hill, breathless, Immor and the noblemen only stared at him, amusement etched onto their faces. He weighed his sword in his hands as his eyes snapped over to Shasta, who didn't seem to realize he was there.

"The new King of Akkinor." Lord Reesa grinned like a madman. "I imagine your country must be very pleased by this turn of events. They've been wanting for a king since..."

"Finish your sentence. Go on." Jack gritted his teeth. "Say her name. *Say it.*"

"Since the day your *Aurelia* took the throne," he spat, still grinning.

"Oh, enough." The sound of Immor's voice—low, dark, and emotionless—made Jack freeze before he could lash out. "There's no need to instigate him, Arthur Ashford. You will do nothing but make a fool out of yourself when he riles you enough that your sword swings on its own. I would claim your life as a trophy without moving an inch."

"Do it, then," Jack seethed. "Go on. Get rid of me."

Immor guffawed, the sound rough like stone against stone. "I'd like to have some fun with you first. Tell us—why have you come when you know your life is forfeit?" Jack's gaze unintentionally snapped over to Shasta, making Immor laugh again. "Oh, I see. You hope to kill the person responsible for your wife's death. You are a great fool, indeed, but a brave one. If you were any other soldier, I might spare you out of respect for your courage."

Jack spat on the ground at Immor's feet. "I'd rather let vultures eat me alive a thousand times over than owe my life to you."

The god's eyes flashed with a danger that made Jack's heart stop, but to his surprise, Immor didn't smite him on the spot. Instead, he only laughed again.

"Fine, then. Go on and try what you have come here to do," Immor urged, grinning from ear to ear. "See what becomes of you, but do keep your children in mind. It's better to have them know that you died a brave man who challenged a god than a stupid one who got himself eaten by a dragon."

"I'll worry about *her* later." From the corner of Jack's eye, he saw Shasta turn her head ever-so-slightly in his direction, acknowledging his presence before she turned back to Annera. Jack reached beneath his breastplate for Aurelia's necklace, flashing the cylindrical gold tube at his enemies. "Do you know what this is?"

Lord Keer snorted and rolled his eyes. "A woman's trinket?"

Immor's eyes, on the other hand, flashed with recognition. "You allowed a man to defile your wife's corpse so he could collect that for you? That's terribly poor conduct."

Jack ignored him. "I imagine you know what it was made for, too."

The god of war narrowed his dark eyes. "You dare to question the knowledge of an immortal? Of one of your Creators?"

Jack refused to so much as blink. "You're no Creator of mine."

As they all laughed at him, he began murmuring the words Aurelia had engrained in his brain many years ago. Just after the war with Archie, she'd researched exactly how her ancestor had used the locket to send Halvor to the land between worlds. She already knew how to free Halvor, of course, but it'd taken quite a bit of digging for her to learn how he'd gotten there in the first place.

Neither Immor nor the noblemen seemed threatened by Jack's mumblings. He knew Immor understood the ancient tongue he was speaking, even if Jack himself didn't know what the words meant. Immor's lack of a reaction worried him, but Jack knew he had to try, even if he failed.

On the day Anysa had arrived in Akkinor before Jack left for Carthe, he was reminded of the conversation he'd had with Varn in Vanhylde, and he knew there was only one way to even attempt incapacitating a deity:

The gods don't come here. Not ever, his old friend had said. *Vanhylde is a purgatory for them, too. They designed it that way as a means of establishing order among the divine. Think of it like a failsafe in the event that one of them betrays the others. If a god visits or is sent here by one of their own, their essence becomes tethered to this prison, and they can only be freed by another deity.*

When he finished, smoke spewed from the ends of the cylinder and pooled at Immor's feet, but that was the extent of it. The smoke didn't envelope his being and carry his essence into the locket—into Vanhylde. It lingered around the god's ankles for a moment, and then it was carried away by the wind as if nothing had happened.

Jack's heart sank, but the feeling of defeat was quickly replaced by dread and terror. His only plan had failed, and here he was, standing just a few feet away from the worst enemy he could've made.

Immor only laughed. "Bravery is often admirable, Arthur Ashford, but today, it has betrayed you."

***

Diantha had never felt more like a coward.

She wasn't a fighter, but she also refused to be the kind of leader who ran and hid while her men gave their lives for her. She'd managed to keep a safe distance away from the worst of it at first; then, when she saw her own men turning against each other—and the other troops, too—she realized her cause was a lost one, and it didn't matter if she fought. They were all going to die, anyway.

She'd lost sight of nearly everyone she knew by then. She had a handful of soldiers protecting her, but she'd started with a much larger number than she had now. Still, she fought to stay, even after spotting both Reyna and Lord Zhaaran fleeing.

What finally stopped her was Aesin. Her Lord Hand had been trying to encourage her to find Erinya and flee, and he'd been shot through the throat with an arrow mid-sentence. She heard herself scream, but she hadn't been given the chance to give him a second look. Her remaining soldiers started pulling her away as soon as Aesin fell.

They practically dragged her to the edge of the valley, where they hid her behind a tree while they scoped an escape route. She observed the battle from a short distance away, her tears mixing with the blood on her cheeks, while soldier after soldier, ally after ally, collapsed in mangled heaps.

She'd thought what happened in Runeia was a living nightmare. What was happening here today...It was beyond her comprehension, a level of carnage and destruction she hadn't even read about in books.

"We may have a clear path," one of the soldiers said to her, wiping sweat from his brow. "If we—"

"I'm not going without Erinya," she blurted.

They exchanged worried looks. "Your Majesty—" another started.

She shook her head frantically. "No! No. I've already lost Aesin. I'm not leaving unless we find her and bring her with us, or..." She swallowed the thick lump in her throat. "Or until I know for certain that she's dead."

The first soldier nodded begrudgingly and said, "Two of us will search for her. The rest will stay here to protect you, my queen."

405

He grabbed another soldier, both pale and trembling, and darted toward the fighting. Diantha watched them go, but she lost them almost instantly when something distracted her—Annera landing on the ground nearby. Fragments of stone emitted from her throat as she roared, and any soldiers in her path had their flesh torn to shreds.

"My gods." One of the soldiers practically choked on his words. "That's mad."

Diantha winced as Annera trampled the bodies she'd torn up. "That dragon will kill everyone unless—"

"No." He shook his head and pointed at something to their right. "Look."

Diantha's breath caught in her throat when she followed his eyes. He wasn't looking at Annera, but rather at the hilltop the Kroti had come from. Immor was still standing there, flanked on either side by the leaders of Krotis. But they weren't alone—a large man with dark hair, wearing Akkinorian bronze armor, was facing them with his sword drawn.

Jack.

She bowed her head as her eyes fell shut. She'd grown fond of Jack, despite not being particularly close to him, and now, she'd have to watch him die at the hands of the god of war.

"What on earth—?" Another soldier took a step forward, staring at Jack in utter bewilderment.

Diantha's lips parted in confusion when smoke seemed to emit from Jack's body, only to pool at Immor's feet. The smoke disappeared quickly, so whatever Jack had meant to do, he'd failed. After a moment, Immor reached out toward Jack's chest, and Diantha's heart leapt while she prepared for the worst. Rather than killing Jack, though, Immor tore something from Jack's neck. He held it up for a moment, letting the light from the fires on the battlefield reflect on the golden object, then tossed it aside.

A golden object Jack had been wearing around his neck...It could only be Aurelia's locket, which the late queen claimed had been used to house Halvor in a land between worlds—Vanhylde. Diantha had been studying up on Vanhylde, hoping to find a way to speak with Rieza there, and she'd learned that it was a purgatory for the divine, too. Jack must've known the same. What he didn't seem to know, however, was that only a god could imprison another god in Vanhylde.

There was something else Diantha was sure he didn't know—something Diantha herself wasn't supposed to know, either. Rumors had been spreading about this lately, but Diantha had confirmed it for herself through her connection to Rieza.

Aurelia, a mortal, had been able to open and close the locket for Halvor because she was born a mage. She may not have had active powers, but she still had her mother's magical blood in her veins, giving her a connection to magic that was just strong enough to cast certain spells. Perhaps the gods' golden blood had helped to make that possible for her, too. But Jack hadn't been born a mage, and he hadn't been chosen by the gods. It was no wonder his efforts failed.

Just as Diantha's heart began to sink all over again, Edea's voice echoed in her head: *Help is a petition, not a privilege.* Diantha knew what that meant: help was something one needed to ask for, not something one should expect. But what was she supposed to do with this?

Aurelia would've known what to do. Diantha never longed for the queen more than she did now. She needed a bit of Aurelia's cleverness right about now, and so did Jack.

Then, as if Aurelia's spirit had heard her thoughts, a memory popped into her head from the night Aurelia and Jack had stayed in Dofell after the attack in Khaba. They'd been chatting at the dinner table, discussing the different kinds of tales popular in their kingdoms, because both queens were fond of stories.

"On the theme of gods visiting the realm," Aurelia had said, winking at Diantha, "there's an Akkinorian folktale from the old days that tells of a young woman named Cherith. Pirates had murdered her family and stolen their fortune. They left her alone and penniless, but for some reason, they let her live. She spent two weeks in the woodlands, but she had no survival skills, and she knew she'd die there. One night, she drew the symbol of Buen—a horn of plenty—into the dirt, as she had nothing else to aid in her prayers. She had nothing to offer him other than herself, either, so she cut her palm and let the blood fill the shape.

"She prayed to him for wealth, promising that she and her descendants would always be more loyal to Buen than any other god if he helped her," Aurelia had continued. "To her surprise, Buen visited her in the forest, having heard her prayers from the heavens and taking pity on her, for she had done no wrong in life. He cast a blessing over her, and the next day, she stumbled upon a buried chest of coin in the forest. Before Buen left, he told her that he would always ensure her prosperity, so long as she kept her promise. Many scholars and priests have debated whether it was Cherith who inspired Akkinor to claim Buen as our Almighty, though nobody knows for sure."

"All because she'd bled into a drawing in the dirt." Diantha had shaken her head and chuckled. "If only it were that easy today."

As Diantha returned to reality, she had a mad, wonderful thought: perhaps it *was* that easy. After all, it was easy enough for a human to visit a different plane of existence—maybe the gods just liked to toy with humanity, to make them think divinity was more complicated than it really was.

Diantha snapped a twig from the tree and fell to her knees. She started carving a moon into the dirt, but looked up when her instincts told her something was wrong. Her stomach churned when she saw Jack on his knees, his arms bound behind his back with magic, while a glowing, orange rope tightened around his neck, the other end tethered to Immor's hands.

"Help me," Diantha snapped at her soldiers, tearing her eyes away from Jack. "We have to move quickly. Draw the symbols of the gods here in the dirt—anyone but Immor."

They did as they were told, but stopped short when Diantha took her dagger from its sheath. Grimacing at the sharp pain, she held her hand over the moon she'd drawn, watching as blood poured from the deep incision and filled the grooves.

"Do it," she ordered, eyeing each of them. She looked up at Jack again, her heart pounding harder when, even from a distance, she saw him turning purple. "Hurry, now!"

Not knowing what else to do, she bowed her head and began to pray. The soldiers mimicked her when they finished, praying to whichever god whose sigil they'd drawn and bled into.

It was mad. Foolish. Desperate. It was all kinds of insanity, and based on a silly story Diantha had heard from a woman who loved folktales more than real stories. There was no way drawing a symbol in the dirt and filling it with blood could serve as a proper offering to the gods, let alone a plea for assistance. There was just no way. But still, she had to try.

Yet another memory—the voice of Arian Cristos, this time—played in her head: *It's my personal belief that the gods left not only because we broke what they made for us, but also because we stopped trusting them to answer our calls. No self-respecting deity would wait around to offer their assistance if humans stopped believing they'd come.*

Diantha's eyes snapped open. At the exact same time, five glowing white spheres descended from the sky like falling stars, directly over the hill. Diantha's breath hitched when the spheres collided with the ground, sending a wave of power cascading over the entire valley. The light atop the hill morphed into human-like shapes, and when the glowing faded, three women and two men stood on either side of Jack. The magical restraints binding him disappeared, and he fell over onto the ground, writhing in pain.

The disturbance was enough to stop the fighting. A few soldiers finished off their opponents before turning their attention to the hill, and when they realized what had happened, they dropped their weapons and sank to their knees—even the Kroti.

"Mother of..." One of Diantha's soldiers trailed off, eyes wide and glassy. "Is that...?"

Diantha smiled. "Yes."

It worked, she thought to herself. *I can't believe it worked.*

She recognized Edea standing at Jack's left. Beside her was a man with a long white beard, wearing gray robes and a tall hat. Buen, god of prosperity and Almighty of Akkinor. On his other side was a woman with coarse black curls, wearing a golden dress that looked like it was made out of pure sunlight. Gianla, goddess of the sun and Almighty of Taundosa. To Jack's immediate right was a woman with flowing brown hair, wearing a bright turquoise gown. Alkamura, goddess of the seas and Almighty of Espos. Standing on her right was a man wearing blue robes, with dark hair and a short-cropped beard. Dhylo, god of knowledge and Almighty of Bozar.

The Council took a few steps backward while Immor's face blanched. Even so, the god of war continued to stand tall and strong, like the arrival of his fellow deities didn't affect him in the slightest. Diantha let out a laugh when Alkamura stepped toward Immor, frightening him enough that he moved away from her.

Immor and Alkamura were considered to be the most powerful of the twelve gods of Creation, and for good reason: they both represented the two most dangerous, volatile aspects of life on earth.

Annera bellowed from the battlefield, clearly rattled, and Shasta took an instinctive step forward. Alkamura's head snapped over to the young noblewoman, making Shasta freeze, then turned around to face Annera. The goddess held out a hand, and Annera's anxious shrieking silenced. The dragon merely situated herself on the ground, laying her head on her front paws, and didn't utter another sound.

At the same time, another bellow echoed throughout the valley, closely followed by another. Diantha laughed when a flash of deep violet flew overhead from the east, and a flash of sapphire flew in from the west. Rieza and Halvor circled the valley for a moment, shrieking, before they landed on either side of the battlefield and roared at the troops. Wherever they'd been lying in wait, they'd been together, waiting for a moment like this one.

A ragged shout tore through the air, directing Diantha's attention back to the hilltop. Immor had surged forward, enraged, with his glowing hands directed at a still-recovering Jack. Both Edea and Alkamura stepped between them, protecting Jack with their bodies. Buen slammed the butt of his staff against the ground, making the hill tremble so greatly that everyone in front of him—Immor and the Council—fell to the ground.

Dhylo crouched down to pick something up. Immor started for it, hollering something indecipherable as thunder boomed throughout Dofell. The sky had darkened significantly by now, and if it weren't for the moon shining so brightly over the kingdom, it might've been bathed completely in blackness.

Glowing tethers shot out from the ground and wrapped around Immor's wrists and neck, like he'd done to Jack earlier. He struggled against the magical shackles, roaring in fury, to no avail.

Edea cast a glance over her shoulder, making Diantha gasp when the goddess's eyes met hers. They held each other's gaze for a moment, a silent understanding passing between them. She couldn't explain it, but she knew the look—and the message Edea was sending her—confirmed what Arian had said.

Trust us, Edea seemed to be telling her. *Trust us to help when it is asked for, and we shall come. This era of silence has come to an end.*

XLVII

J ack thought he was done for as soon as Immor's rope wrapped around his neck. The pain was instant, blinding, and unlike anything he'd ever felt. He'd been choked like this before—once by a tribesman in the Violet Forest, and once during a horrible sexual endeavor in Caedia that'd left him running across the province without his trousers. He didn't particularly enjoy being unable to fill his lungs with air, but the pain had been manageable enough; this pain, however, was something else entirely.

It was like he could feel his very life force being sucked out of him—like his soul was slipping away. The god of war wasn't just killing him; he was torturing him, physically and mentally.

As dark spots clouded his vision and suffocation overcame him, he saw a bright burst of light. Relief followed, and he soon found himself sprawled out on the ground, coughing and gasping for air while inhaling specks of dirt. He willed himself to move, but his body hadn't recovered yet.

He thought Immor had released him, only to let him recover before torturing him again and again like any sadistic deity might, but that wasn't it. Someone had intervened, and he soon felt a dainty hand on his shoulder. It didn't feel like being touched by another person, but rather like a wave of prickly, warm magic had settled on his shoulder.

While gasping and convulsing, Jack managed to blink through his hazy vision and glance up to his left. He still couldn't see the person touching him, but he saw the man standing beside them: a man who looked nearly identical to the sculptures and paintings across Akkinor of their Almighty deity, Buen.

Buen met Jack's eyes when he felt him looking at him, winked, and turned his dark eyes back to Immor.

His ears were ringing, so he couldn't hear exactly what was being said until Immor released a roar of frustration. Not long after, more animalistic roars echoed in Jack's eardrums. Even as he gasped and sputtered, he managed a choked laugh. He'd recognize the sound of Halvor's bellowing anywhere.

Before leaving Akkinor, he'd told Anysa to have Halvor stay a safe distance away from the battle, but still close enough that he could reach Dofell if necessary. He wasn't sure if Halvor would obey Anysa, but he had to try, anyway. He didn't want Halvor there until Marvion, who'd agreed to return to the palace and stay there until the battle ended, felt that Immor had been weakened. The Elder's connection to the divine would let him know if Jack's plan had succeeded, if Immor was gone, and he'd relay the message to Anysa so she could tell Halvor when to go.

Jack had also told her to ensure Halvor didn't inflict too much damage in battle. He didn't want to give the realm another reason to fear Halvor after what'd happened in Runeia. Halvor would defend the allies' soldiers and keep Annera at bay, but he couldn't let his thirst for vengeance convince him to decimate the Kroti. Aurelia wouldn't want him to stoop to that level, either.

Apparently, Jack's hopes hadn't been misplaced, and Halvor had even collected Rieza on his way to the battle after receiving Anysa's command. But Halvor wouldn't get the chance to prove his obedience to Anysa any further, and Rieza wouldn't get the chance to do something unpredictable—not while five gods were here to mind them.

"...clever thinking." A voice to Jack's right made him lift his head enough to see who he thought was Dhylo. Immor lunged for him, but a hiss from Alkamura made him surge backward again. He'd been aiming for Aurelia's locket in Dhylo's hand. The god of knowledge ignored Immor and met Jack's gaze. "Your wife would be very proud of you."

Jack only bowed his head in response.

"What shame you have brought to us." Alkamura's voice, like the sound of crashing waves, rang out in Jack's ears as she spoke to Immor. "We exhausted ourselves in our attempts to sway you against committing such selfish acts—and against Pherena, no less. The purest and kindest of us all. We may have been unable to stop those who called for you, but we couldn't stop those who called for *us*, either. You should have known."

Immor growled at her. "Only my humans have proven to be wise and strong enough to enlist the assistance of the divine. The others are too pompous, believing they are capable enough on their own—weakening us, sullying our names, and picking and choosing when we're valuable to them. You praise them for their arrogance and their idiocy, yet you condemn the only ones who trust in our power."

Gianla, the radiant sun goddess, laughed. "It is not arrogance or idiocy. It is autonomy. We have allowed them to forge their own path in this world, to find their own power with what we have given them. To ask the divine to interfere when their liberty is at stake—their very existences, the ones we worked so tirelessly to create for them—is an act of humility and courage we cannot ignore. But to ask the divine to interfere so we can destroy the sanctity of our world...*That* is what weakens us and sullies our name. We built this world, Immor. We cannot aid in its destruction."

When magical binds shot out from the ground and trapped Immor in place, he roared and struggled, but the others paid him no heed. Alkamura took a step forward and crouched down in front of him until they were nearly nose-to-nose, her sparkling brown hair—as if it was imbedded with tiny droplets of water—cascading around her back and shoulders like a blanket.

She murmured something Jack couldn't hear, and as she spoke, a thick cloud of smoke began to form around him. Immor kept roaring and struggling, all while the Kroti watched in terror and disbelief behind him, until the smoke enveloped him completely. Alkamura blew a breath of air in his direction, and the smoke disappeared into the winds, revealing nothing but a broken sword laying on the grass where Immor had been standing.

"I have been waiting centuries for this day." Buen chuckled to himself, then extended a hand toward Jack. Jack blinked at him, awestruck, before accepting the deity's hand. It again felt warm and tingly, yet oddly comforting. Jack managed a strangled *thank you*, to which Buen only nodded. "It has been our sincere pleasure to aid you today, Arthur."

"He prefers *Jack*," Dhylo said.

Buen frowned. "My apologies. I should have known."

"It's all right," Jack said hoarsely. "You aren't the god of knowledge."

To his surprise, the deities laughed. What a thing—not only had he been saved by the gods, who'd also put an end to Immor and Krotis's plans for conquest, but he'd also succeeded in making them *laugh*.

It'd be a wonderful story to tell the children.

A whimpering sound caught their attention. Only then did everyone focus on the Council, who knelt on the ground behind where Immor had been, bowing their heads and trembling like wet dogs.

"Ah, yes. What to do with you." Alkamura chuckled and tossed a length of hair over her shoulder. "I say we smite them."

"No," Edea intervened, shooting her a look. "We came to preserve life, not to destroy it."

Buen stroked his beard. "I hear Vanhylde is nice this time of year—albeit not for our fallen brother, though."

"It will not be pleasant for them, either," Dhylo added. "Even so, we cannot imprison living humans in Vanhylde. That's the law of the universe. It must be a choice for them to exist there, whether their reality is pleasant or not."

"Don't kill us!" Lord Reesa, for all his narcissism, had turned to begging like a fool. Jack would've been lying if he said he didn't enjoy it. "P-Please. Let us live."

"*Silence!*" Alkamura snapped, making him gasp and shudder. "You have no right to speak."

"They must be left to the realm," Dhylo decided. "If the other humans wish to imprison them or execute them, it makes no difference to us, so long as they are punished for their crimes against the realm. But we cannot leave Krotis without proper leadership, either. Not when they are already without an Almighty. Pherena may be forgiving, but she will not return to the people who cast her aside."

"Only some cast her aside." A small, trembling voice interrupted the deities, and all eyes landed on Shasta Selle. Her head was still bowed, and despite how defenseless she looked, Jack was still filled with rage at the sight of her. "Our people were influenced by fear—as was I. I-I believe their values have not changed; they listened to the voices they trusted, but they will find their way back to her. I know they will. They will ask for her forgiveness if given the chance."

"Perhaps." Edea narrowed her eyes. "And what about the five of you? There's no place for you in Krotis anymore. You sullied your kingdom's good name with your greed, and you led the entire realm to live in fear. That cannot be forgiven."

"Firadus. He was the Elder of Krotis before they had him killed," Jack said, jerking his chin out toward the Council. "He was loyal to Pherena until the end—at least, that's what Aurelia believed. Perhaps he might know of members of each reigning family who can be trusted to succeed the traitors. If not members of the current reigning families, then others, too."

"We shall speak with him in Hanhalla, and if he cannot be of service, we shall find another option ourselves," the goddess of the moon decided. The others nodded and murmured in agreement as she raised her eyebrows at Jack. "You came here for another reason—not just to put an end to Immor's schemes. If you wish to proceed, we will not stand in your way."

Jack's heart pounded. He felt all five of the deities staring at him, and while he'd expected some sort of judgment, they appeared rather understanding. He drew in a sharp breath as he collected his sword from the ground, then positioned himself directly in front of Shasta Selle.

"I saw it happen with my own eyes." His voice was hoarse and gruff, nearly unfamiliar to him. "Annera had accepted her. Chosen her. Then something appeared to make Annera conflicted, and the next thing I know, my wife is dead, and the dragon is flying back to you. Whatever you said or did, it's the reason my wife is gone. I don't care if it was direct or indirect, intentional or unintentional. All I know is that Aurelia would still be here if it weren't for you, and we don't allow Queenslayers to walk free in my country."

Shasta didn't move an inch. "I pleaded with Annera to come back to me. I knew I'd be killed if she didn't. I-I don't know exactly what happened that day, but I think Annera must have found herself torn between loyalties, and the stress caused her to lose control. S-She's too young to know how to separate her emotions from her physical responses. Whatever it was, though, I didn't order the death of a queen. I wouldn't. I'm sorry she's gone, but it's not because of me."

Jack lifted his sword. "I'm not sure I believe you."

Shasta finally looked up at him when the flat of his blade touched her throat. He faltered a bit when they met eyes. This was the first time he'd seen her up close, and until now, he hadn't realized how young she was. He'd known she was only seventeen years of age, of course, but he hadn't pictured her as an adolescent, for whatever reason. Now, while looking into her bloodshot eyes, he saw nothing but a terrified child looking back at him.

Spare her. It was Aurelia's voice in his head that kept his sword still. *She's only a girl, Jack. A frightened girl who has been manipulated by the greedy men in her life. Whatever happened, she didn't intend for it. She was only trying to survive.*

Jack's eyes burned with tears. A strangled cry escaped him as he raised his sword, and Shasta turned her head to the side as she trembled, preparing for the blow that would sever her head from her neck.

The blow never came. Jack stuck his sword in the ground beside her, making her gasp and whimper as her wide eyes flicked over to it. Tears streamed down her cheeks as she looked from the sword to Jack, her lips parted in shock.

"I'll show you the mercy you didn't offer my wife," he croaked, stepping back, "because that's what she would've done, if roles were reversed. But if you or your dragon ever come near my family again, I can promise it won't end well for either of you."

Then he walked away, not caring to hear her response, and left the Council at the mercy of the five deities.

***

"They fought valiantly until the end."

Diantha sniffled but didn't look up at the woman standing beside her. She knew it was Edea, just as she knew the goddess wouldn't be displeased with her for neglecting to respond—not while Diantha watched her soldiers carry Aesin and Erinya's bodies away from the heaps of corpses on the battlefield.

"Your family is safe. They will begin the journey back to Dofell as soon as you call for them," Edea continued, her voice soft and gentle. "And do not fret about this land. As soon as the remains have been buried, I will return the valley to the sanctuary you intended for it to be. All will be right again."

Diantha closed her eyes and sighed. "I've lost both of my Hands. Dofell, Taundosa, Bozar, Akkinor, and even Espos have lost close to half of our militaries. Aurelia Brentwood is dead. Krotis is not only sitting apart from the continent, but it's also without leadership, too. How can everything be right again when so much destruction has been inflicted?"

"You will find others who will serve you well until the end of your days. The kingdoms will recover, and they will emerge stronger. Aurelia Brentwood may be dead, but her legacy is not. And Krotis..." Diantha wasn't looking at Edea, but she heard the smile in the goddess's voice. "We have that taken care of."

"What about Immor? Won't the universe implode on itself if one of the Twelve no longer rules from the heavens?"

Edea sighed. "Not exactly. Immor's distance from the realm will drastically weaken his power. We deities are strengthened by prayer, and none will reach his essence while he remains trapped in Vanhylde. When we are certain he has calmed down, we will hold a trial, just as we always do when a deity puts the realm at risk—just as you do here in Icareth. If we find that he continues to pose a threat, he will be replaced as one of the Twelve, and the god of war will become a minor deity. His power will be significantly diminished, and as you know, a minor deity cannot be the Almighty of a kingdom."

Diantha furrowed her eyebrows, not understanding. "The Twelve are the deities responsible for the realm's creation. How is it possible to just...*replace* one of you?"

When she finally looked at Edea, she saw a small, sad smile on the goddess's lips. The disheartened expression was one Diantha knew well: it was the same way Aurelia had looked whenever she'd spoken of her late brother. Grief, but conflicted—as if she didn't know if it was right to feel that pain.

"We swore an oath when we created this world," Edea murmured, her silver eyes sparkling. "It is not for you to know. All you must know is that Immor broke that oath when he decided to aid Krotis—effectively attempting to strip myself, Gianla, Dhylo, and Vyena of our domains here in Carthe, and our humans of the opportunity to thrive under our guidance. The entire realm would have suffered the consequences of his actions, and if humanity had taken too long to ask for our help, significant damage would have already been done by the time we arrived. We may be immortals, but we cannot turn back time or undo catastrophic damage. We can try to prevent it, and we can intervene when our assistance is requested, but things are more complicated than humans like to believe."

Diantha knew that well enough. Immor himself may not have directly inflicted such damage to the realm, but he would've given Krotis—and everyone conquered in the kingdom's name—the power to do it. The gods weren't known for interfering in human squabbling; they'd made that clear when they hadn't come to stop the persecution centuries ago. Stopping one of their own was one thing, but stopping humanity was something else entirely.

Diantha mirrored Edea's bleak smile. "That doesn't exactly answer my question."

"No, it doesn't," the goddess replied, chuckling. "Answer this for me: do you really believe the god of prosperity helped create the realm? Or the goddess of beauty, or the goddess of blessings? Our world is more than capable of existing without any of them, and the Twelve gods of Creation are meant to represent elements of life the world cannot survive without."

Diantha's lips parted. "The Twelve as I know them today aren't the same deities who created the realm?"

"Indeed. Some of us began as minor deities. When a few of the original Creators broke the oath we'd all sworn, they switched places with minor deities who had proven to be more capable and honorable. Stories of the Twelve have been rewritten time and time again so humanity remains unaware that such turmoil can exist within the immortal plane."

A shiver traced the queen's spine. "Why are you telling me this, then?"

A real, genuine smile formed on Edea's lips. "You are destined for so much more than you realize, Diantha Pharos. Many years from now, you will find yourself seated upon a second throne—a throne that keeps your feet planted here in Icareth, and that allows your eyes to bear witness to the divine."

"What does *that* mean?"

"You will understand when the five of you finally find one another." Edea chuckled again and tossed a length of white hair over her shoulder. "I have said enough as it is. I must join the others to handle matters in Krotis, but do not forget what I told you all those weeks ago: help is a petition. If you require assistance, you need only ask, and I will come. If you ask for what you do not need, I will not." She tipped her head in farewell. "Goodbye."

Diantha readied to speak again, but she didn't get the chance. As Edea took a few slow strides away, her back facing Diantha, her body was encased in a glowing white light that brightened and expanded with every step. Soon enough, her entire being was illuminated, the light so blinding that Diantha had to look away and shield her eyes. By the time the light faded, a moon-like sphere was rising into the sky, and Edea was gone.

Diantha sighed. She had a feeling this was the last she'd be seeing or hearing of her Almighty for a very, very long time.

XLVIII

S hasta didn't know what had terrified her more: preparing herself to be executed by the husband of the woman her dragon had killed, only for him to spare her at the last moment; or being left entirely at the mercy of five deities, forced to wait for them to decide her fate like a pig for slaughter.

At least she wasn't alone in the second one. The rest of the Council was in the same boat. It was the first time since taking the Bruilan throne that Shasta felt equal to them, and somehow, that frightened her even more.

"You and your men will be transported back to Krotis immediately." The god of knowledge had burned the words into the Council's brains while they trembled atop the hill in Dofell. "The five of you will await our decision in Sharith, and you will be confined to your living spaces with no outside interaction. A temporary ward will be placed over Krotis's borders to prevent any of your people from leaving the kingdom until our decision has been made."

None of the nobles had responded. It was the first time Shasta had ever seen her male counterparts scared into silence, and she would've relished the realization if she hadn't been terrified right alongside them.

One moment, she'd been staring at a sleeping Annera on the battlefield, and the next, she'd been encased in a veil of light that completely obstructed her vision. After a moment or so, the light faded to reveal her bedchamber in Sharith. She immediately ran for the door, only to find it locked from the other side, then tried the windows. They, too, wouldn't budge.

A tray of food and drink appeared on her desk shortly after, so at the very least, the gods were ensuring the Council was kept alive and healthy. That, however, still wasn't enough to stop Shasta from bursting into tears every time she remembered what had happened, and how she could've prevented all of this if she hadn't been so blind to the truth—and blinded by the need to preserve her own life, for that matter.

She'd thought Krotis would win the battle with Immor on their side. There hadn't been a doubt in her mind until Jack Ashford met them on the hilltop, only for the five gods to arrive moments later. The arrival of the divine was the very last thing she and the others had expected. The gods hadn't hesitated to send Immor away, effectively ending Krotis's plans—and the Council's reign.

Selfishly, she'd accepted Immor out of fear for her life, and she'd known it was wrong the moment the battle began—especially since he'd told her that her life had never really been in any danger, and she'd chosen to ignore that. He'd given Krotis so much power that it hadn't been a fair fight. Watching Krotis's enemies drop like flies had opened her eyes to the horror of what she'd agreed to, and the only way she'd managed to distract herself from taking accountability was by watching Annera. Her dragon brought her strength and comfort, and focusing on commanding Annera took her mind away from what she'd allowed Immor to do.

Now, all of that was over, and Immor was gone. She and the four noblemen would be stripped of everything, and they'd be entirely at the mercy of whomever replaced them.

Five sunrises after the battle—with Shasta's cheeks perpetually puffy, and her eyes swollen and red—a note appeared alongside her breakfast tray. The writing appeared on the parchment before her eyes as she picked it up: *You are hereby summoned to trial in the symposium at the ninth hour.* That was only minutes away.

Shasta didn't get the chance to prepare herself or even to see if her door would open. She took one step toward the door, and the next thing she knew, another veil of white light enveloped her being. When the light faded, she found herself seated at the round table in the symposium, strapped to her chair by glowing, magical ropes. The four noblemen sat around her, also confined to their chairs, growling and hollering about being treated like animals.

"Summon the beast!" Lord Reesa barked at Shasta, making her wince. "Get us out of here!"

Shasta only stared at him. "No."

"No?" His wild eyes widened with disbelief. "You dare—"

Before he could continue, the door opened, and an elderly woman wearing rags and covered in filth walked into the symposium. She looked no different from the impoverished beggars Shasta had often seen lining the streets of Bruila. With every step she took, though, her appearance began to change. The grime disappeared from her skin, her long white hair was combed and tied back in a braid, her posture straightened, and her rags were replaced by clean, silky white robes—the same sort of robes worn by priests.

"Who the hell are you?" Lord Reesa demanded. Despite what'd happened, he was still trying to assert his dominance—now out of fear rather than hunger for power. "What business have you in Krotis?"

The woman smiled. "My name is Larodha. I don't expect you to recognize me after all this time. I was a priestess here in Krotis two decades ago until the Council imprisoned me. It was ruled that an unmarried woman could not hold positions of power in this kingdom, despite all priests and priestesses across the realm being sworn to a life of celibacy. My defiance earned me a life in the dungeon."

Shasta stiffened. She'd known it was against the law for an unmarried noblewoman to hold power, but she'd been unaware that the rule applied to others, too. Her father had been Lord of Bruila when this law was passed, yet he'd never once pressured Shasta to marry and obey the law. How could he have been so lenient with his daughter, only to imprison a servant of the gods forever for the same reason?

Lord Keer struggled against his restraints. "The gods were meant to decide our fates, yet they sent a disgraced priestess in their place. Hmph!"

Larodha's dark eyes flicked over to him, but her face was expressionless. "The gods have not left. They are here, watching and listening, as they have been since you arrived. You cannot see them because they have deemed you unworthy of witnessing their majesty." Shasta shivered. The goddess of the seas could've been breathing down her neck, and she'd have no idea. "Our merciful gods have freed me and tasked me with serving as the new Elder of Krotis. My loyalty has always been to Pherena, and fortunately for Krotis, Lady Selle was right—our people have already begun begging for her forgiveness. She is willing to resume her role as the Almighty of Krotis, but she will not do so unless the five of you are removed from power."

Lord Quagg gulped. "What does that mean?"

She smiled. "The gods have spoken with Elder Firadus in Hanhalla. His insight has provided the answer to our predicament. The new members of the Council have already been brought here by the gods, and they are prepared to take their places in Krotis."

Shasta kept mum as the noblemen snapped at Larodha, having already forgotten they were being monitored by the gods in this very room. When Larodha turned to face the entrance, the door opened again, and five individuals entered the symposium.

Shasta could hardly believe her eyes. The five newcomers weren't at all what she'd expected, and they already wore the symbols of their respective domains stitched onto the fabric of their tunics or gowns. Two were practically children: the girl, wearing the sea lion of the Quaggs of Osanad, was no older than twelve; and the boy, wearing the otter of the Keers of Mekya, was about fifteen. A woman wearing the peacock of the Reesas of Vrurith was approximately twenty or so. A man, about thirty years old, wore the dragonfly of Runeia stitched onto one sleeve, and a crow—its allegiance unknown to Shasta—on the other.

Shasta didn't recognize the young man who wore her family's sigil—a gazelle—on his tunic. She knew they were related somehow, but as far as she'd been aware, there hadn't been any surviving men capable of leadership in her family. If there was, the Council would've turned to him instead of Shasta after her father died.

"Allow me to introduce the new reigning nobles of Krotis," Larodha said with a smile. "And by the way, it has also been decreed that your distasteful laws against women in power will be dismantled, too."

Lord Reesa practically roared with displeasure. "If you think my daughter is going to succeed me—"

"Oh, *enough.*" The woman wearing the peacock scowled at him. "Your time to speak has come to an end, Father."

He roared again, his speech indecipherable, but with a wave of his daughter's hand, his lips sealed together, and her magic rendered him silent.

Shasta knew Lord Reesa had a daughter, Devora. He'd sent her away at the age of three to ward with Lady Odeya Swann in Runeia, and he hadn't spoken of her since. It'd been twenty years since then, and most people had forgotten he had a daughter, as he'd intended. She was his youngest child and his greatest shame, according to whispers Shasta had overheard.

"Aviva." Lord Quagg's voice became frighteningly dark when he addressed the young girl wearing his sigil. Shasta recognized the name—it belonged to his only daughter, the third of his four children. "You have no business here. Your brothers—"

"—are dead," Larodha intervened. Aviva lowered her head and sniffled, and her father only stared at the priestess, agape. "The elder two gave their lives to fight the battle you started—even your heir. The youngest died of scarlet fever three nights ago. Had you been home with your family rather than attempting to conquer the continent, you would have known." Lord Quagg's face turned purple as she flicked her gaze over to Lord Keer. "This is your nephew, Markus. The son of your older sister. You and your brother, the late Lord Keer, banished your sister to Kanibar when she gave birth to prevent her and her son from succeeding your father."

Shasta's lips parted as Lord Keer bowed his head in shame. The former Lord Keer had been the most reasonable of the noblemen on the Iron Council—she couldn't imagine him doing such a thing to his sister. It seemed the Council's quest for power had begun long before Shasta's father received the letter from King Willem, even if the Guild hadn't had anything to do with it.

"You." Lord Swann interrupted Larodha when she began to speak again, his eyes burning holes through his successor's skull. "A traitor means to take my place? I won't stand for it! I won't—"

"You haven't another choice," his replacement interrupted.

Larodha smiled. "Lord Erastus Swann and his family were delivered here by the gods from Akkinor. It took only moments for them to decide to give Runeia the leadership it deserves—the leadership it saw under his mother, Lady Odeya. They sacrificed a great power in Akkinor to be here."

Shasta knew that name. Erastus Swann was the youngest child of Lady Odeya, and eight years ago, he'd married the future Lady of Myra in Akkinor. Shasta couldn't imagine how the decision to leave Myra in favor of Runeia had been such a quick one, but at the same time, people were easily persuaded when the voice of the divine echoed in their heads.

"Then, of course, there's Bruila." Larodha glanced at the strange man before meeting Shasta's eyes. "Do you recognize this man, Lady Selle?"

Shasta only shook her head.

"This is your father's bastard son, Shiko, born before your parents were married." The Elder's smile grew when Shasta gasped, clearly taking pleasure in Shasta's bewilderment. "He may not be a legitimate heir, but Pherena favors him. He became a great scholar while living as the adopted son of two academics in Bozar, so he will do wonderful things for Bruila. If not for his existence, the Selle line would end with you."

Shasta met her half-brother's eyes. To her surprise, he looked at her pitifully, without an ounce of hatred. There were so many things she wanted to say to him, to explain, to apologize for—and yet, she knew she'd never get the chance.

"Each of these five souls has been deemed worthy of ruling Krotis not only by Firadus, but by Pherena and the Twelve, as well," Larodha continued, beaming at the successors. "They have never strayed in their loyalty to Pherena, despite some of them having lived under other banners. It will take time and guidance, but they will become the rulers Krotis deserves, and they will repair what you have broken."

"What you mean to say," Lord Keer croaked, "is that you will reign while they find their footing. Krotis might as well bend the knee to you and call you queen."

"I am no queen. I am the voice of the gods in Icareth, and they have tasked me with guiding the future of Krotis on the path to greatness," she snapped, making him shrink into his seat. At the same time, the magical binds disappeared, and Shasta exhaled in relief when she could finally move in her chair. "Now, the gods have left the Council to determine your fates. Don't bother making your cases or pleading for mercy. We are all well aware of what you've done and why you did it. All that's left to do is pass the sentence."

"Even before I knew I'd find myself here, I imagined a dozen different ways to punish you." Erastus glared at Shasta and the others as he clasped his hands behind his back. "The Almighty Pherena demands that we be merciful, but mercy and forgiveness go hand-in-hand, and we believe you are unworthy of our forgiveness."

"*Aviva.*" Lord Quagg was trying his hardest to sway his daughter into seeing things his way, but she didn't budge. "This isn't you, girl. You won't sentence your father to death."

Aviva sniffed. "My father has told me every day of my life that I'm a waste of air."

"*You insolent—*"

"Enough," Devora interrupted. Lord Reesa glowered at his daughter, but she ignored him effortlessly. "We spoke of it briefly earlier today, and we have made a decision. The five of you will be stripped of everything you are, and you will be abandoned in the Ngora Valley. Pherena's mercy demands that we leave you with a few tools you'll need to survive: a dagger, a bag of bronze, a loaf of bread, and a canteen of water. What becomes of you after we leave you in the desert doesn't matter to us. But if you ever attempt to return to Krotis, you won't make it a foot into the kingdom. We will erect shields for the sole purpose of keeping you out."

Shasta's heart pounded violently in her chest. Maybe she'd survive on her own in a place like Kanibar or even Taundosa, but the Ngora Valley? It was nearly impossible to find one's bearings in the middle of the desert. And even if she managed to survive the horrors of the desert, what would she do after reaching another territory, with little to her name other than coin and a dagger?

As vomit rose up in her throat, she remembered something she cursed herself for forgetting: Annera.

Annera. She pushed the thought out toward her dragon, wherever the creature was. *If you can hear me, I need you. Please come. I won't make it without you. Please.*

"There is, of course, the matter of the dragon." It was Shiko who spoke next, turning Shasta's blood to ice as he looked at her, like he could read her thoughts. "We know she'll do everything in her power to protect you. For that reason, we have decided to offer you a choice, *sister.* You can forfeit your life to break the bond and spare her, or you can subject her to a life of imprisonment until you meet your death and break the bond that way. What will it be?"

A pulling sensation in her chest made Shasta rise to her feet. Nobody seemed off put by her sudden motion—after all, what could she do? The gods were against them, after all.

"I-I..." Shasta trailed off, unsure of what to say, as the pulling sensation intensified, threatening to swallow her whole. "Y-You can't execute me. Pherena would frown upon you. I knew nothing of what my fellow nobles had planned until Immor himself forced me to oblige. To take the life of one motivated by fear is to work against what the Almighty stands for."

"You may not have known about the Guild, but it was you who helped us eliminate Queen Aurelia," Lord Quagg sneered at her. "Everything you and your father told us about her gave us the opportunity to carry out our plans. We wouldn't be here if you hadn't been involved."

"S-She left me." Shasta didn't care about what the Council thought of her previous lie anymore—they couldn't do anything to her now, and she'd say whatever she needed to if it meant convincing their successors to change their minds. "On the night Queen Aurelia died, my connection to Annera was broken. O-Our bond doesn't seem to be as strong as others. I don't need to die, and Annera doesn't need to be imprisoned. She left me before—I'm sure she can do it again."

Larodha only stared at her. "Oh, yes. She felt safer with another rider than she did with you, but alas, it was only temporary—a result of her fear and confusion over what you'd asked of her in the moment. You pleaded for her help, didn't you? She could've stayed bonded to the Queen of Akkinor, but instead, she answered your call and came back for you, unable to ignore the need to protect the one who raised her from the egg. In exchange for her loyalty, you asked her to contribute to an event that could've destroyed the realm. If that wasn't enough to make her abandon you forever, nothing ever will be."

Shasta's heart sank to her knees. She wanted to cry, but not because of the ultimatum she'd been given. It was because she now knew for certain that she'd let Annera down. She didn't deserve Annera's loyalty after how horribly she'd treated her, and everyone knew it.

A shriek echoed throughout Sharith, making everyone freeze, as the pulling in Shasta's chest grew stronger. Even if Annera had been incapacitated somehow since the battle ended, Shasta's plea for help was clearly enough to make the dragon fight back to protect her rider. It was no wonder the Council—the new one—wanted Shasta gone so badly. As long as Shasta lived, Annera would do anything she asked, even if it meant eliminating Krotis's new leadership.

"Do what they say, girl," Lord Reesa advised, his face red with frustration. "It's the least you can do. You caused all of this the moment you presented us with the eggshell."

"I didn't cause anything." Shasta forced a wobbly smile. "You should have accepted me as Lady of Bruila before I had a dragon."

In the blink of an eye, she turned toward a window behind her and ran. The others hollered after her as she shielded her face with her arms and crashed through the window, biting through the pain from the shards of glass embedded in her skin. She knew it was a fool's gambit, but she trusted Annera—and she was right to. She was falling for only a moment before she slammed onto something hard and slippery. Annera roared as she tried to steady them while Shasta struggled to stay latched onto the dragon's spikes. Shasta gritted her teeth, ignoring the sharp pain from the glass and the fall, and hoisted herself onto Annera's back.

As Annera shrieked and flew away, Shasta couldn't help but laugh. Everyone in the realm had underestimated her for far too long—they'd never expect her to do something so daring. But she knew Annera would always come for her, just as she knew she wouldn't die for the actions of greedy men. Everything she'd done had been to preserve her own life, and she wouldn't let it all go to waste. Clearly, Annera had forgiven her; that was all she needed to forgive herself for the hand she'd played in this mess, and to know that she was doing what was right for both of them.

Another laugh gurgled up in her throat when she realized something phenomenal: this was her first time riding her dragon. The Council had forbidden it before, claiming it was too risky, and losing Shasta meant losing Annera, too. She'd listened to them like a fool, and she'd missed out on weeks of pure wonder because of it.

Not anymore.

She didn't know where Annera was taking them. Maybe the pair would find a nice, quiet, uninhabited island somewhere in the middle of the Alkamura, and they'd find a way to survive together. Maybe someone in the realm would welcome them, and they'd start anew with people who understood what they'd done, giving them a second chance. She had no idea what was in store for them, but she knew they'd be all right as long as they were together.

She was so distracted by feeling the wind whipping against her face and watching the people of Krotis down below—smaller than ants—that she hadn't noticed an approaching threat. They were soaring toward the coast of Runeia, blissfully unaware of anything or anyone bold enough to challenge a dragon, when a magnificent force hit Annera's stomach, making her howl in pain.

Shasta didn't see what had struck Annera or where it'd come from. She heard herself screaming as Annera shrieked and rolled through the air, her body becoming rigid and tense while she lost control. Shasta's stomach rose up to her throat as they descended, the force of the impact making it impossible for Annera to steady herself.

The last thing Shasta saw was a rocky line of cliffs inching closer and closer to her, Annera desperately attempting to recover from her injury. Rider and dragon were separated before they collided with the rocks, sent flying in opposite directions, both crying out for one another in one last display of loyalty and affection.

Both were swallowed up by the raging seas, but only one was ever seen again. The other, a young woman just shy of eighteen years, was lost forever.

XLIX

Rayan hadn't been able to breathe properly since the moment Jack and the troops left Akkinor. Every breath he took felt heavy, constricted, like an invisible weight was pressing down on his lungs. He knew he'd be cursed with this affliction until the end of his days if Jack didn't come home—if Immor and Krotis succeeded in conquering Carthe.

It was a strange and unusual form of torture. He was a knight at heart, yet he was also the Lord Hand of Akkinor, first and foremost. He felt like he should've been fighting beside his brothers and sisters in arms, but that much was impossible; he was needed in Akkinor to rule in Jack's absence, and if something happened to Jack, the responsibility of King Regent would fall to Rayan. It'd be up to him to govern the country until Halle came of age, and the idea of such responsibility frightened him more than the idea of facing the god of war in battle.

At least he'd been keeping busy. He'd received one last correspondence from a spy he'd sent to Krotis—now presumed dead—confirming that Krotis had instigated the conflict in Kalenbrar. Sharing that news with the public had eased the tension between the rich and the poor, but they refused to do away with Amanbrar. That was a problem for a later date, though. For now, Rayan was helping the poor earn more coin by hiring them for various reparations around the Folly. He could only hope that soon enough, the distribution of wealth across the capital was balanced, and all traces of Amanbrar would vanish as quickly as it'd been built.

He'd also received a raven from an advisor who'd left for Carthe after Jack succeeded in convincing Espos to lend their swords. Nobody could celebrate the news, though. It'd taken a horrifying amount of coin to convince Captain Lukos, and though the coin was meant to return to Akkinor if they lost the war, nobody trusted that it would happen. Lukos would probably follow the ship across the sea and loot it before it got back to Akkinor, and the economy would crumble more than it already was during wartime.

Then—faster than he'd expected—Rayan received yet another raven, this time written in Jack's hand. Jack had only written two sentences, but it was more than enough to lift the weight constricting Rayan's lungs: *It worked, but only after some divine intervention. We're on our way home now.*

Halvor had been the first to return. He'd left for Carthe weeks after the fleet did, given his quick travel time, and returned weeks before the others, too. He looked unharmed, and he went right back to his normal routine like nothing had happened. Rayan took that as a good sign.

Now, just about three weeks after receiving Jack's message, Rayan's men alerted him of an impending arrival approaching Sadia from the west. The fleet was too far away for the flags to be seen, but everyone knew it was Jack and the troops. They were forced to dock in Sadia while the harbor at Seaport was still under repair following Krotis's attack, so they'd be arriving in the Folly within a day or so.

Rayan rushed to tell his father, Arian, and Shale the news in the morning room, where they'd been taking tea. He'd have to tell Anysa, too. She was off somewhere with the children right now, but she'd made it clear when Jack left that she'd be returning to Khaba as soon as the battle ended—regardless of the outcome. Both Jack and Arian had tried convincing her to move her family to Akkinor, claiming her connection to Halvor would be a great help while his new mistress was still so young, but she'd refused.

Arian—and Shale along with him—would leave for Taundosa with Anysa, but Eric had accepted both Rayan and Jack's invitation to live in the palace. Rayan had recalled his father discussing how difficult it was becoming for him to live alone, and, well...It didn't feel right to keep Eric separated from his grandchildren after he'd just learned about them.

"I wonder what stories we'll hear about how such an...*unexpected* victory came to be," Eric commented after Rayan shared the news. He moved a chess piece on the board, prompting Arian to respond immediately by capturing Eric's pawn. "Drat."

Arian smiled. "After so many years of playing with my sister, I would've thought you'd be better at this." Eric only muttered something under his breath as Arian raised an eyebrow at Rayan. "Is our fleet intact?"

"It appears to be, but it's still too far away to know for sure," Rayan replied. "I've sent word to Taundosa, Bozar, and Dofell. I imagine Diantha will want to proceed with a formal alliance now, and the others...Jack would've told me if they sustained any significant damages or losses, but they'll be struggling for a bit either way, so I hope to discuss our arrangements as soon as they've taken the time to recover. I can only imagine how many soldiers they've had to bury, and how many families they've had to compensate for the losses."

Arian grimaced. "Things may be difficult for a while, but not as difficult as they'd be if Krotis had succeeded. We wouldn't have any allies to speak with at all." Rayan nodded in understanding as Arian captured yet another one of Eric's pieces. "Good grief, old friend! You're slacking!"

"I admit, I'm distracted," Eric said lowly, running a hand through his thinning hair. "Even with all that's happening right now, I find myself yearning for one last visit to Taundosa. Perhaps I might accompany you home and stay for a while."

"You're more than welcome to your old lodgings at Ardiham Castle. We'd be pleased to have you."

Shale nodded. "I'd like another Akkinorian nearby, too, while I settle into my new home."

Eric looked hesitant. "I'll have to think about it. I'm not sure if I wish to leave the children."

Rayan sat on the couch beside his father. "I remember you taking long business trips after we reunited when you left Carthe. I've been wondering lately if you went back to Carthe during those trips."

"No, no," Eric said quickly. "Until Aurelia made the deal with the pirates eight years ago, Akkinor couldn't reach Carthe from the south. I had to dock in Caedia and make the difficult journey across the continent to find my way to Taundosa. It wasn't something I would've done again without good reason. It's different now, of course, but I couldn't take such a risk back then when I had a family relying on me." He chuckled a bit. "I hadn't even planned to stay when I first arrived, you know."

"Really?" Rayan blinked at him. "I'd assumed you'd wanted to start over in the most miraculous place in the realm—the City of Gold—from the start."

Eric shook his head, smiling. "No. I only wanted to use the voyage to and from Carthe as a chance to grieve, far away from the place I associated with my family and our tragedy, before I began anew in Akkinor. But when I caught my first glimpse of the western continent, I saw a land I'd never seen before—a land whose air I hadn't yet breathed, whose waters I hadn't yet tasted—and I knew I had to stay, even for just a little while, to leave the past behind for a second chance. A real second chance. I didn't know where I was going. I thought I'd explore the continent for a while. Then I started overhearing stories about the City of Gold, and I knew I had to see it for myself."

Rayan mirrored his father's smile. After learning about Eric's time in Carthe, his relationship with Katryna Cristos, and everything else that'd contributed to his time away from his family, Rayan had buried his resentment toward his father. Losing Aurelia and Lucyra, too, had made him realize that life was too short to hold grudges; especially when his father's memory was slipping away.

The only thing Eric seemed to remember in perfect detail was Katryna. When she came up in conversation, he was a lively young man again, able to tell stories like he was reading from a book.

Still, Rayan had to ask the question that'd been pestering him: "Did you love Mother?"

Eric stiffened, but he was still smiling. "Yes. I wouldn't have married her if I didn't love her. I wasn't expecting to meet someone and fall in love again in Taundosa, son. It was the last thing on my mind, but it just...happened. I told your mother everything when I came back, and that I'd understand if she wanted to leave me. I couldn't ask her to stay with me when my heart belonged to another. But she was a wonderful woman, your mother, and though we'd stopped loving one another as husband and wife should, we maintained a strong relationship until the end. I never loved her any less than I did before. Only...differently."

Only when Rayan blinked did he realize he had tears in his eyes. He'd always admired his mother for how strong she was and how much she'd done for her family, but he admired her even more now. It took a special type of woman to stay married to a man who'd fallen in love with someone else for the sake of her family; but at the same time, it took a special type of man to walk away from the woman he loved and return to his family, all without knowing if they'd moved on from him.

A few minutes later, a messenger arrived with a scroll for Rayan. It was stamped with an amber seal in the shape of a lotus flower, symbolic of Krotis.

"What does it say?" Shale demanded the moment Rayan began to read.

Rayan fought the urge to sigh. Shale was rather bold and opinionated—he didn't seem to care when he spoke casually to those who outranked him—and despite how tiring he could be, he reminded Rayan a bit of Aurelia. That was a good thing; Arian would need a bit of Aurelia's fire to help him heal from her loss, so Rayan was glad Shale had accepted Arian's invitation to move to Taundosa with him.

"It says..." Rayan quickly scanned the short message, then let out a long sigh. "The gods themselves helped select the new leaders of Krotis. Erastus Swann and Dahlia Crowland are now taking charge of Runeia—they wish to revoke their Akkinorian citizenship, and to have Liliana Crowland serve as Lord Silas's heir in Dahlia's place. I received a raven from His Lordship two days ago requesting an audience, so I assume that's what he wishes to discuss. The former nobles on the Iron Council have been exiled to the Ngora Valley, too, though there's no way to know for certain if they'll survive out there. But Shasta Selle...She's dead."

The Lord Hand of Taundosa exhaled. "How?"

"She tried to escape with Annera," Rayan murmured, rereading the message, "but they were struck down by a group of civilian mages in Runeia. Apparently, the civilians had decided that everything turned to chaos the moment Annera came into play, and they blamed both she and Shasta for what'd happened. They crashed on the coastline, and Shasta's body hasn't been found. Annera was spotted fleeing out to sea, but that's the last anyone's seen of her."

Shale made a face. "So, that means—?"

"There's a rogue dragon somewhere out there." A distant look filled Arian's dark eyes. "'The soul of green will be lost and found again, but they will not emerge as they once were.' It's right there in the prophecy, and the line was never about Annera's brief kinship with Aurelia. Shasta Selle is dead, but eventually, Annera will bond with a new rider."

A shiver traced Rayan's spine. "The prophecy doesn't end here."

***

Jack and his troops emerged as the heroes of the realm when they returned to Akkinor. People had fallen at their feet and wept while they marched to the Folly from Sadia, having heard bits and pieces about what'd happened in Dofell from both acquaintances in Carthe, and soldiers who'd written while sailing home.

Everyone knew that the gods had come to aid Akkinor and their allies against what had seemed like an unstoppable enemy, but their praise wasn't directed only at those who'd fought in Dofell—it was directed at Aurelia, too. After all, she'd been the one to bring Edea back to the realm three years ago. The people believed she'd opened the doorway between Icareth and Hanhalla, inadvertently mending the broken bond between humanity and the divine.

Akkinor still didn't look like it had before Aurelia's death, but even so, Jack was happy to be home. He knew the reparations would take longer than usual, given the amount of coin he'd given to Espos in exchange for their swords, but this was the best possible outcome. Even if Krotis had succeeded, and he'd managed to survive, he'd have no allies to turn to for trade and commerce.

Jack took a few days to recover when he returned to the palace. He wanted to be with his children after he'd looked death in the eye, and despite how much he and Rayan had to do, it could all wait. They'd just defeated the god of war and his army of divinely-powered soldiers, after all—everyone who'd survived deserved the chance to relax and celebrate with their families.

On the fifth day after returning home, Jack said goodbye to Arian, Shale, and Anysa with Rayan, Eric, and the children. It was difficult to see Arian go after his extended stay in Akkinor, but he was needed in Taundosa at Reyna's side, and he'd been gone long enough as it was.

Arian gave Jack one long, firm hug before boarding the ship. "Send word if you need anything at all. I'll always come if you need it."

Jack squeezed Aurelia's uncle—his uncle now, too—in his arms. "I will. The same to you."

Arian pulled back and set his hands on Jack's shoulders, but with the height difference between them, he practically had to lean up on his toes. Still, it wasn't a silly sight—not when Arian's very being commanded respect and authority, even while facing a 'king.'

"Let us know when you figure out the prophecy," Arian said, eyes twinkling with curiosity. "I'll keep looking at it, but I think you'll have better luck. You and Rayan make quite the team—plus, you have Sisi, the Oracle of Akkinor."

Jack laughed and looked over his shoulder, where Hyacinth was saying goodbye to Shale and Anysa with her siblings. Hyacinth met his eyes immediately, smiled, and turned back to the others with a knowing look in her gaze.

The Brentwood and Haze families waved goodbye to their Carthinian family from the dock in Sadia as the ship sailed away. Jack hoped they'd be visiting again in the near future; he knew that he wouldn't be going back to Carthe any time soon.

He used to yearn for Carthe. He never regretted his decision to follow Aurelia home, not once, but he still missed the western continent. It'd given him his spirit back. It'd given him Aurelia, too, and their family, and the most incredible life he could've imagined. He'd missed how every day was a different adventure, unpredictable and thrilling in the best and worst ways; but not so much anymore. After everything that'd happened—Carthe's many battles, losing Aurelia, and nearly getting murdered by a god—he wanted nothing more than to stay at home forever, where he belonged.

Jack Sherbourne was gone now, his time in Carthe having finally come to an end. In his place was Jack Ashford, King Regent of Akkinor: husband of the greatest monarch to ever reign, and father of the youngest monarch to ever be crowned in the realm.

When they returned to the palace, Jack found himself thinking about what Arian had said about the prophecy. Rayan had told him upon his return that Shasta Selle was dead, and Annera was now a rogue dragon—confirming what the prophecy stated about *the soul of green* being lost and found again, but different than it was before. Other than that, Aurelia had figured out a few pieces of the prophecy, but some lines were still left unknown.

He sat on the couch with Rayan in the morning room while Eric—who'd opted to stay in Akkinor to spend time with his grandchildren—played on the floor with the children. Rayan didn't seem surprised when Jack reached into the pocket of his trousers and produced the piece of parchment Aurelia had scrawled the prophecy onto. Rather, Rayan shifted excitedly in his seat, eyes gleaming with intrigue.

"I've been thinking about it for days," Rayan admitted. "There's just no way the prophecy has been fulfilled entirely. If it has, we're missing something."

Jack nodded. "'*The story told once before cannot exist in perpetuity, for a few guiding words cannot assure that all which was promised will come to fruition.*' That's about the prophecy from our battle with Kanibar—how the salvation it promised was only temporary. '*The end of the masquerader will indeed restore the voice of the divine, but it will also create a prison of amber.*' This part tells about how Willem's defeat brought Edea to the realm, but it also caused Krotis to try to control the world."

"'*There shall come a time when all appears to be well across the earthly realm, though the reason for such peace will soon lose its sanctity,*'" Rayan read, grimacing. "That's about Aurelia losing her golden tears after defeating Willem and fulfilling the last prophecy. '*The curse of the masquerader will prevail within the shadows of false security, and its effects will threaten both friend and foe.*' We know this part, too. Willem was still trying to control things from beyond the grave, and his efforts put everyone at risk."

"'*Three cycles after the moon falls from the sky, the Four Pillars shall emerge from the shadows, and their return shall mark the end of the beginning. The end of the road shall be a doorway to the unknown, opened by one and closed by five.*'" Jack made a face. "We know the Four Pillars are dragons and their riders, and all of this is happening now, three years after Edea's return. But we still don't know what it means by '*the end of the beginning.*' I don't understand this *doorway* business, either."

"And the rest..." Rayan squinted to get a better look at Aurelia's messy, blotchy writing. "'The one who breathes fire will sever the realm at the edge of the world. The one who breathes the four winds will bring catastrophe but not destruction. The one who breathes the dust of stone will heal what survives. The one who breathes ice will rediscover what was lost.' Aurelia and Halvor were seen as responsible for separating Krotis from Carthe. Diantha and Rieza contributed, but it was Halvor everyone saw when it happened. Annera and Shasta didn't do anything to heal what survived, so we have to assume that's referring to something Annera and her second rider will do. As for the last bit...The rider and the water dragon remain unidentified. Bozar hasn't had any luck in their endeavors to find them."

Jack grimaced. Time was ticking—some day in the near future, an individual would claim a dragon that nobody had seen or heard of yet. Jack only hoped they'd keep their distance from Akkinor, because he wasn't so sure he could handle another battle between dragons right now.

"We know the bit about the soul of green, too," Jack continued. "'The song of War will play for the ears of many, and the song of righteousness will play for the ears of few. A chain of gold will silence the drums of death beneath a sunless sky.' That's about Immor's influence over the Kroti, and how they turned their enemies in their favor during the battle, leaving only a few of us who could still recall right from wrong. Aurelia's locket is the chain of gold, too. It led to Immor's banishment to Vanhylde in Dofell at nightfall."

Rayan nodded and pointed to the next paragraph. "'The just will be welcomed by the stars, and the progeny will sit amongst the clouds. The stallion will halt the stampede, and the swords will shatter at the feet of five.' I don't know what to make of the first part. I think the stallion means you, though. The Ashford family is symbolized by the horse, and it was your actions that instigated the end of the battle. As for the last line...Maybe it's referring to how five deities ended the fight, or even how there are five nobles sitting on the Council, and disposing of them put an end to the entire scheme."

"I don't know," Jack muttered, pointing at the last paragraph. "Look. The very last line talks about five individuals once more, but it doesn't seem to fit with the gods or the Council. 'One will bring about the end of existence as it is currently known. Two will be lost where time no longer turns. Three will hear the voices of the divine. Four will find strength in unity. Five will become a phoenix risen from the ashes.'"

Rayan thought on that for a moment. "Aurelia changed the way of things forever when she released Halvor and forged her alliances. Maybe she's the 'one.' She and Shasta died, and their souls were sent to planes of existence where time doesn't turn. That's the 'two.' I'm not sure about the rest, though."

"Whatever it means, it's not over," Jack mumbled, staring at the smudged ink. He looked up at Hyacinth, who was too distracted by laughing at Eric's shenanigans to notice him. "Perhaps..."

Rayan raised an eyebrow. "Perhaps we can ask Sisi?"

Jack sighed. "Maybe later. Until we find out more—like who Annera bonds with next, and this business with the water dragon and its rider—we're at a standstill. Oracles don't share more than absolutely necessary, and she's a child, after all. She may not be able to tell us what we need to know. For now, we'll focus on our recovery, and we'll let Sisi be a child for as long as she can. She deserves that much after all she's been through."

They locked eyes, and Jack knew they were thinking the same thing: until they knew for certain what it meant, the prophecy would continue to haunt them. Jack just hoped it wouldn't damn them, but heal them.

L

*T*hree cycles after the moon falls from the sky, the Four Pillars shall emerge from the shadows, and their return shall mark the end of the beginning.

That one line from the prophecy—the one that'd started all of this when Archie shared it with Aurelia—played on a loop in Jack's head as he sat at his wife's desk. He hadn't stopped thinking about the prophecy in the three days that'd passed since he and Rayan tried to make sense of it, and for whatever reason, this particular line demanded his attention.

The end of the beginning... In all honesty, he couldn't blame Krotis for their interpretation of the prophecy, however misguided their motives were. The prophecy *did* seem to suggest that the realm was in danger. The realm had only existed for less than two millennia—a short time compared to how long the gods had been around—so perhaps, the prophecy referred to an apocalypse of sorts, in which the gods would be forced to start the realm from scratch.

Jack took a swig from a glass of whisky as he stared off into space, deep in thought. He knew Aurelia hadn't come to any conclusions about this line before her death, but he wondered if she would've picked up on something if she was here to see what'd happened since.

For some reason, thinking about Aurelia brought him back to her memorial—specifically, to something Elder Marvion had said right before Jack's breakdown: *Let her death not be in vain, for with her loss, we shall pave a new path forward—a new age for humanity's existence.*

Shifting in his seat with unexpected giddiness, Jack made a note of his thoughts on the back of the parchment where Aurelia had written the prophecy. Maybe this wasn't foretelling an apocalyptic event at all, but rather something much grander: a Golden Age.

Perhaps *the beginning* referred to Aurelia's efforts to transform the realm into the world the gods intended for it to be—after all, she'd been the one to incite every realm-altering event that'd happened, however intentionally, since the war with Archie. She'd been given a responsibility by the gods, and she'd started bringing their hopes to life. Maybe this transformative period, the beginning of the realm's salvation, was nearing its end, which would only come when the Four Pillars revealed themselves.

Still giddy, Jack turned his attention to the rest of the prophecy, hoping this high would help him decipher the ambiguous lines. He didn't get the chance, though. The handle of the study door shook and wobbled, like someone was struggling to turn it, and a moment later, the eldest four Brentwood children tumbled inside.

Jack smiled at them. "What are you doing here, my little loves? I thought you were in the library with Irina and Hannah."

"Irina brought us here on her way to the infirmary," Halle replied.

"Why? Is she all right?"

She nodded. "She's all right, but Hannah has an upset tummy, so Irina took her to get medicine."

"I see." Jack folded the prophecy into a square and tucked it into his pocket while he stood. "I suppose I can take a break for a little while. What shall we do?"

"Hannah wanted to take us to Lulu's hill to plant flowers," Henry shared, admiring Aurelia's treasures on her bookshelves. "Can we do that?"

Jack chuckled. "I thought you didn't care for flowers."

"I didn't, but Lulu and Mama and Edom did, so I like them now."

A pang pierced Jack's heart. "All right. Let's plant some flowers."

As they left the study, he scooped up Halyna and set her on his shoulders, holding one of her legs for stability while Henry clutched his other hand. Halle and Hyacinth walked on either side of him, talking a mile a minute about the books they'd found in the library, and how many of those books had been vandalized by their mother's notes in the margins.

The story made Jack smile. In the many weeks that'd passed since Aurelia's death, he'd wondered how much their children would remember about her. He told himself now that it didn't matter if their memories faded over time, because there were pieces of Aurelia everywhere: the notes she'd left in her favorite books, the carvings she'd made in her favorite trees, the flowers she'd planted in the gardens. The children would have plenty of ways to know and remember their mother as they grew.

Jack asked a servant to ready a carriage to take them to Lucyra's Knoll, then brought the children outside to the gardener's shed. The children decided they wanted to plant seeds and bulbs instead of replanting young buds, so they could return to the hill whenever they pleased to watch the flowers grow.

They chose a great variety: daffodils, lilacs, peonies, tulips—plus lilies and hyacinths, of course. When they'd picked their seeds and bulbs, the children politely thanked the gardener for lending his materials, then practically raced Jack through the halls on their way to the carriage.

It pained Jack to see Geon pulling the carriage alongside another centaur, Deorn, instead of his brother, Cheol, who'd died during the attack on the Folly after saving Aurelia's life. Jack often pretended to scold Cheol for flirting with Aurelia, but it'd all been in good fun, and he'd miss that. He'd miss seeing Edom floating around the carriage in a golden, glowing sphere, too.

At least the repairs were going well. The palace had sustained minor damages, most of which had been repaired by the time Jack returned from Carthe. The rest of the Folly was still struggling, but they were on the road to recovery, slowly but surely. Mistcairn had to be rebuilt from scratch, but Arian—knowing how much the village meant to Aurelia—had sent coin from his personal inventory to make it even better than it'd been before.

There were so many faces—Aurelia, Lucyra, Cheol, Edom—he missed each and every day, but he was grateful for how well Akkinor was recovering. He was grateful for how well his allies were doing, too, given the circumstances. Taundosa and Bozar hadn't been directly impacted by the war, but they'd had their fair share of problems because of Krotis, too; now, they seemed to be settling back in. Edea had kept her promise to Diantha by repairing the battlefield, too, and the kingdom was starting to flourish again.

Krotis, of course, wasn't in the best shape. They were keeping their distance from Akkinor for now—except for Runeia, since Jack had approved of Erastus Swann and Dahlia Crowland revoking their Akkinorian citizenship to rule in Krotis. Most of the new members of the Iron Council were young and inexperienced, being guided by the Elder Larodha on the gods' command, and it wouldn't be easy to find their footing after the war. Their population was fiercely low, the kingdom was no longer attached to the continent, and they'd used up all of their money and resources on the war. They wouldn't be interacting with anyone for quite a while.

When they arrived at Lucyra's Knoll, Halvor appeared overhead, circling the hill while parting the clouds as he bellowed in greeting. The children raced out of the carriage and waved at him from the ground, delighted that he joined them. Jack followed them outside, leaving his sword behind in the carriage, and held up the gardening materials in either hand.

"Race you to the top?" he teased.

The children screamed and ran as fast as their tiny legs would carry them. Jack gave them a head start, watching with glassy eyes as he recalled the many races he'd won or lost to their mother. She'd be pleased to know he was keeping their silly habits alive through their children.

Halle and Hyacinth made it to the top effortlessly, with Henry lagging behind, but poor Halyna couldn't keep up. Jack let her climb onto his back as he joined them atop the hill, making the others protest and accuse him of helping Halyna cheat her way up.

Jack shuddered. If Lucyra heard he'd contributed to cheating while he stood atop her final resting place, she'd find a way to smite him all the way from Hanhalla.

He tried his best to direct the children as they gardened, but they didn't exactly follow his instructions. Halle and Hyacinth planted the seeds and bulbs as he did, while Henry and Halyna merely threw seeds onto the grass like they were feeding birds. The sides of the hill were rather plain other than a few dandelions, so if the seeds actually managed to take root wherever the wind carried them, it wouldn't be long before the entire hill was blooming with different types of vibrant flowers.

Jack hardly noticed when the sun began to set—he was too distracted by their mission. Only after Henry complained of hunger did Jack look up and realize the sky had darkened. It was probably well past dinnertime by then, and everyone at home was likely wondering what was keeping them.

"All right," Jack said, wiping his dirty hands on his trousers. "We've done enough for today. We can come back tomorrow if we'd like. The four of you need to be fed and bathed before bedtime, and—"

"Wait!" Hyacinth rushed toward him and grasped fistfuls of his tunic in her tiny hands. "This is the perfect place to watch. We can't leave yet."

He furrowed his eyebrows. "Watch what, Sisi?"

"The stars," Halle replied. "She's been talking about them for days."

"I don't understand. We can see the stars at home. They're always the same no matter where you go."

Hyacinth shook her head. "Not tonight. Watch."

She sat down on the grass and patted the ground beside her. Jack stared at her for a moment, not understanding, before following suit. The other children did the same, with Halyna on Jack's lap and Henry sitting cross-legged between his elder sisters. Halvor was gone now, leaving the skies clear, but it still wasn't dark enough to clearly make out the stars.

Jack was opening his mouth to suggest they return home when Hyacinth ordered everyone to lay down. He obliged—now out of curiosity more than anything—and watched, a bit impatiently, as the stars slowly began to twinkle brighter against the darkening sky. He still didn't understand what Hyacinth was talking about until she sprung to her feet and pointed.

"Look!" she exclaimed, bouncing on the balls of her feet. "It's Mama!"

Jack frowned. "What are you—"

He trailed off, voice catching in this throat, when he spotted exactly what she meant. To the left of the moon, nestled between two familiar constellations—one shaped like a caribou and known as *the Prancer*, and another shaped like a quill and known as *the Storyteller*—was a collection of stars that appeared to form the shape of a female archer. Though it was hard to make out without squinting, Jack could just barely see a woman's long hair, a bow, and what appeared to be wings—dragon's wings.

Jack froze, his lips parting in shock. "That's..."

"It's new," Halle insisted, eyes wide with wonder. "I've never seen it before."

"It's the prophecy, Papa," Hyacinth said, grinning from ear to ear. "*'The just will be welcomed by the stars.'*"

Jack tore his eyes away from the stars to look at her, unable to form words. The knowing, ancient look in her gaze made him shiver. Only then did he recall something Katryna had said when he met her in Vanhylde— a message she'd relayed on Aurelia's behalf: *She said that when all of this is over, regardless of the outcome, she wants you to look at the stars. You'll know what she means.*

Here it was, the answer to both the prophetic riddle and Katryna's ambiguous message. There was a new constellation in the midnight sky, and everything about it seemed to suggest it was symbolic of Aurelia Brentwood, the late Queen of Akkinor.

"Sisi," Jack croaked, his chest tight, "what does this mean?"

His daughter only shrugged. "She's immortal now."

Another shiver traced his spine. *Does she mean Aurelia has been immortalized?* he thought to himself. Either way, her words made the hairs on the back of his neck stand up. She was right—she had to be.

Aurelia had often told him stories from the old days, in which those who'd earned favor with the gods had their memories immortalized in a way that could be observed by everyone across the realm. *The Storyteller*, for example, symbolized an ancient Carthinian writer named Nadesh, who'd led Kanibar to appoint Vyena as their Almighty after he'd written stories about the goddess's incredible gifts. *The Prancer*, on the other hand, symbolized an ancient Isalder man who'd saved his village from starvation after sacrificing a family of caribous in the name of Hzarl, god of the hunt.

"There hasn't been a new constellation in centuries," Aurelia had told him. "After the persecution, the gods made certain that no humans would ever be immortalized again—it was punishment for what we did to mages and magical creatures. We just aren't worthy of such an honor, try as we might to earn the gods' favor back. The stars we see today are the same stars our descendants will see five hundred years from now."

It was one of the few times since he'd met her that Aurelia had been wrong about something. Jack wished she was here so he could tease her for finally being proven wrong, but if she was, there probably wouldn't be a constellation of her likeness illuminating the sky.

She'd hear him from the heavens, though. He pushed a thought toward her—one he'd never share with anyone but himself—to let her know that he was prouder of her than he could ever put into words, and that he was thoroughly enjoying how wrong she'd been about the gods and their constellations.

No human had earned this eternal honor since before the persecution a thousand years ago. No human had been deemed worthy of their legacy shining for all to see since the realm was a much different place. No human had done half of what Aurelia had in life—not to mention what she'd accomplished after her death—since the gods walked among them.

Aurelia had changed that, just like she'd changed everything.

***

Later that evening, Jack yawned as he slipped into Aurelia's study, intending to return the prophecy to her desk before settling in for the night. This would be the first night he'd sleep in his own bed since she died, and while it pained him to do it, he knew he had to keep moving forward.

He sat down at the desk and opened a drawer, and immediately, a nauseating lump formed in his throat. The drawer had been turned into a makeshift bed for a tiny creature—Edom. The sprite had enjoyed napping in there while Aurelia worked. Jack had no intention of emptying it out of respect for Edom; he missed the pesky little creature, and he didn't wish to forget the impact it'd left on him and his family.

Sighing, he opened another drawer, where he found nothing but stacks of half-written, discarded correspondences Aurelia hadn't wished to send, for whatever reason. He slipped the prophecy in with the other letters, but before he closed the drawer, he spotted one that caught his attention. It was the only message that'd been placed into an envelope and sealed with

Aurelia's sigil, but that wasn't what stuck out to him. It was his wife's handwriting on the envelope that read, *To the one who succeeds me.*

Believing the letter was meant for Halle, Jack cracked open the seal and removed the folded parchment inside. As soon as he began to read, he quickly realized it wasn't meant for Halle at all. It was meant for the next soul in the realm who had become Forged in Gold now that Aurelia was gone.

He knew he'd have to send the letter on Aurelia's behalf eventually, but the person's location hadn't been included in the message, and Aurelia had only written the recipient's name at the very end.

Jack sat back in the chair, frowning. "Who the hell is Tora Styrmodr?"

Epilogue

Zemira splashed water on her face and set a damp hand on the back of her neck, relishing the feel of the coolness on her sweaty skin. When she brought her hands back to the stream for another splash, she hesitated, frowning at the sight of her reflection staring back at her.

She hadn't seen her own face in weeks. Not since she shaved her head with a knife while using a sleek metal pitcher for a mirror, for what felt like the hundredth time since the first. The cuts she'd sustained on her scalp while doing so had all healed by now, and tufts of dark hair were already starting to grow back.

Even if she still had her beautiful, springy curls, she still wouldn't look like the woman she'd been before. Her face was a bit gaunter than it used to be, her eyes were a bit jaundiced, and the eyebrows she'd once plucked to perfection were wildly bushy.

Sighing, Zemira tore her eyes away from her unfamiliar reflection. She brought her hands—permanently embedded with blood and dirt under her fingernails—to her tunic and started to remove it, but froze when she heard guttural laughter nearby. As desperately as she wanted to wash up, she couldn't risk being seen naked by her crew. Even taking off her shirt, revealing the layers of fabric she'd been using to bind her breasts, would've damned her for good.

She collected her sheath and halter from the ground beside her, ensuring both her sword and her pistol were secure, and did what she'd come out to the stream to do: fill two buckets with drinking water. She grunted when she lifted the heavy buckets and started walking back toward the clearing, where the crew of the *Beacon* was waiting for her.

"About damn time." Edgar snatched one of the buckets from her before setting it down, dunked his hands inside, and slurped water as it leaked from between his fingers. "Ahh. Tastes good."

The others quickly followed his lead, but some of them had the decency to fill their empty flasks instead of using their bare hands. As soon as they finished hydrating, they didn't hesitate to march over to the wooden crates piled up behind their encampment. Zemira mimicked them, shoving men aside as they fought over bottles of stolen liquor to fill their flasks.

The crates of liquor weren't the only goods they'd managed to steal from a little tavern in the middle of the Violet Forest. There were also a few bags of miscellaneous goods, and whatever coin the innkeepers and patrons had in their possession had already been divided up amongst the crew. Zemira, being the most recent pirate to join the crew, had emerged with a measly ten pieces of bronze, while the others had walked away with a mix of bronze and silver.

It's not like she could do much with the coin, anyway. When the crew returned to Espos, they'd spend every bit of it on harlots, like they always did. She supposed she could spend it on liquor, or perhaps a new pair of boots, but she hoped to save what she'd fought for. If she was lucky, then one day, she'd amass a fortune large enough to buy her way to the top.

A captain doesn't always lose his place because of mutiny, or even because he went down with his ship. The words of a pirate Zemira had befriended before his death, Rule, echoed in her head. *Sometimes, he can be bought out. Fill his pockets with enough gold to sink him, and he'll walk away from his ship like he never knew her at all.*

Realistically, she knew she'd probably never command her own ship. Even if she did, there would be too much attention on her at any given time, and she risked revealing herself as a woman. There were no female pirates, let alone female pirate captains—she'd face mutiny and death the instant she was found out.

Still, she couldn't help but dream.

"Oi." Erv, a middle-aged pirate with one white eye and three fingers on his left hand, shoved an empty bucket against Zemira's chest. "See any mangoes out there?"

"I don't know."

She winced at the sound of her voice. She hardly spoke nowadays to avoid saying the wrong thing, so her voice always sounded raspy and deep when she did speak. That, and she'd smoked countless pipes of tobacco since sailing to Espos from the east, with the sole intention of making her voice sound more masculine. It'd certainly done the trick.

Erv gritted his teeth at her. "Go look. I like mangoes."

Zemira sighed irritably. "Fine."

"Good lad. Use that wee nose of yers to sniff out any droppings, too. Could be a deer nearby. Ye can help the cooks make us a nice venison dinner, *novice.*"

The others laughed, making her face grow hot, as she snatched the bucket and stormed off toward the stream again. That was another thing she despised about being a newer crewmate: the others forced her to do all the hard work, and it gave them a good laugh to send her into exile with the cooks while they drank and gambled elsewhere on the ship.

They'd made it clear she had to earn her place aboard the *Beacon.* She'd robbed and killed more people than she could count on her hands while they pillaged around the world, yet none of it had been enough to impress them. Perhaps, if the *Beacon* had been in Carthe two seasons ago to join the fight against Immor, she would've had the chance to do something memorable—not just for her crew to witness, but for the crews of a dozen Esposi ships to see, too.

As luck would have it, Zemira spotted a cluster of mangoes on the ground while she scoured the clearing, apparently having been knocked out of a tree. The sight of them made her think about every possible way she could kill Erv, if ever given the chance.

While she bent down to collect them, a large cloud blocked the sun, bathing the clearing in darkness. She didn't think much of it until she heard her crew shouting. She stood and looked over her shoulder, frowning, but as soon as she did so, the ground rumbled, and the trees began to sway. She yelped and dove to the side, just in time for a tree to fall down—exactly where she'd been standing seconds earlier.

Zemira coughed when dirt filled her lungs, then pushed herself up on her knees as she flipped from her stomach to her back. Her heart hammered when the rumbling ceased, only to be replaced by a low growling sound.

Erv had spoken of deer, but he seemed to have forgotten that more ravenous beasts tended to frequent these woods.

It wasn't a panther or even a bear that'd found her in the clearing. No, it was a beast much more terrifying: a dragon of old with emerald scales and hungry, golden reptilian eyes. She and her crew had heard through whispers that a Kroti noble had possessed a dragon like this, but it'd been believed by all that the creature had perished alongside its rider after the war. Apparently, that was only wishful thinking.

She didn't dare move as the dragon chuffed at her, pawing at the ground. Zemira had grown up surrounded by tigers and lions—she knew what that meant. The beast wanted her to run so it could chase her, so it could hunt her down and feast on her like the prey she was.

She wouldn't give it the satisfaction.

"Don't come any closer." Her voice wobbled when she spoke. "I-I'm going to back away slowly, and you're going to let me. There are plenty of other creatures for you to devour in this forest. Dragons aren't meant to eat humans. I-It's bad form."

She didn't understand a lick of what she was saying, but the more she talked, the more the dragon seemed to be distracted. She managed to get to her feet, but as she started walking backward toward her crew, the dragon inched closer. She froze, her breath catching in her throat, as the frenzied hollering of the pirates drew nearer. They'd flee as soon as they got close enough to the dragon, but not before watching it eat Zemira. They couldn't retreat back to the ship without such a magnificent story to tell the rest of Espos.

"M-My name is Zori." Her voice cracked as she took another step backward. "This is your land, not mine. I'll go back to my ship peacefully, and I'll leave you be. Can you let me do that?"

The dragon, who'd been bearing its teeth at her while drool puddled at its feet, cocked its head to the side as if to say, *That isn't your name.* Zemira gulped, and she found herself unable to move another step when the dragon prowled right up to her, its jaws only inches from her face.

Then, to her immense surprise, the creature did something unexpected: it lowered its head and neck to the ground, its body following suit, as if it were bowing in submission.

Not knowing what else to do, Zemira reached out a shaking hand toward the dragon's head. A choked gasp escaped her when her palm came in contact with the dragon's cool, slippery scales. Once more, she was startled when the dragon didn't eat her hand, but instead began to mewl.

Zemira relaxed just enough to stop trembling. "You're a timid thing, aren't you?"

Rustling from behind Zemira made the dragon jerk backward and growl. Zemira knew it was her crew by the way they gasped and shouted, but she didn't bother looking at them. She only held out her hands toward the dragon, hoping to keep the creature calm and avoid being eaten because her idiot crewmates had spooked it.

"Tough go, lad," Erv said from behind her. "We'll tell everyone on the island what happened to ye. Don't worry—ye won't ever be forgotten. The foolish boy who got 'imself eaten by a wee dragon!"

The others snickered, apparently too entertained—or too drunk—to remember to be afraid, but they were scared into silence when the dragon roared at them. Zemira's heart pounded when the dragon nudged her out of the way with its snout, positioning itself so Zemira was protected behind its wing. Zemira couldn't help but laugh when she saw the men fall onto their bottoms and scurry away into the foliage, yelling like frightened babes.

As she laughed, the dragon looked over its shoulder at her, blinking slowly as if to assure her, *You're all right now.*

It was the first time Zemira Kaplo, former Imperial Princess of Quapebet, had felt any sort of power since she traded a life at a royal court for a life of piracy.

THE GOLDEN ONE TRILOGY IS NOW COMPLETE! GET ALL THREE BOOKS ON AMAZON!

NOELLE EDWARDS

COMING SOON!

THE REALM'S TRANSFORMATION CONTINUES
WITH AN ALL-NEW ENSEMBLE CAST OF
CHARACTERS IN

THE DESTINY DUOLOGY

KEEP READING FOR A SNEAK PEEK!

No, no." Margrete tsked her daughter as she peered over the adolescent's shoulder. "See how the cotton puckers? You're using too much force while pulling your stitches. You must use a softer hand."

"I'm sorry, Mother." Tora Styrmodr, Vasirella of Glacier Bay— or *Princess,* in the common tongue—nodded in understanding. "I'll do better next time."

"It's all right. Start again."

Tora obeyed and removed the fabric from the tambour frame. She replaced it with a clean, white length of fabric and glanced over at her mother's embroidery. The Vasira's handiwork was much neater and prettier than her daughter's had been. They'd both been stitching a snow-capped mountain, the sigil of Glacier Bay.

As she brought her needle to the fabric again, Tora stopped when voices and footsteps echoed in the hallway outside of the Vasira's personal parlor. Tora's father, the Vasir—or King—of Glacier Bay, didn't so much as glance into the parlor when he passed it by. Her twin brother, Tomas, on the other hand, paused just long enough to wave and smile at her. She returned his greeting and held up her embroidery, mouthing the words *save me.* Tomas only chuckled, but he wiped the amusement from his face and nodded along when Viggo began spouting something to his son about diplomacy.

They were gone as quickly as they'd come, but Tora could still hear their voices as they walked off. She couldn't help but sigh—there her brother was, being trained for leadership by their father, while Tora was forced to spend her days perfecting her needlework with their mother as the Vasir pretended she didn't exist.

"Mother," she said, "why is it that I can't learn what Tomas does? I know he'll be the Vasir someday, but I'll be married to a lord. I should have an understanding of politics if I'm to be a noble lady. That seems more valuable than needlework."

Margrete laughed, making Tora's cheeks burn. "Being married to a nobleman doesn't mean you'll get an opinion on his duties. Being the Vasirella doesn't mean you're entitled to the same knowledge as your brother, either." She scowled at her daughter. "Look at you! Cheeks redder than a cardinal. You know better. Flushing like that does nothing for our complexion. You'll scare off any potential suitors if your face is always scarlet."

Tora's cheeks only burned hotter as she willed the blush to fade. Isalder women took immense pride in their porcelain skin—a near-perfect match for their white or pale blonde hair, and their gray or light blue eyes. Margrete always said an Isalder woman looked like a harlot who'd spent too much time beneath the sun, luring men into her bed, when her cheeks were red. Unfortunately for Tora, her face was perpetually pink in one way or another.

Margrete sighed when she saw the forlorn expression on Tora's face. "Now, now. Don't look so glum. Curiosity is a good quality, but you know your place. I don't understand why you care so much about what your brother is learning."

"I just..." Tora sighed when her words failed her. "I suppose I'm just looking for something more."

To her surprise, her mother's eyes filled with sadness. "I was a young woman like you once. I wanted more, too. But the realm and the gods have other plans for us. You know this." She moved over on the couch and patted the cushion beside her. "Come here."

Tora set her embroidery aside and moved from her armchair to the couch. Once more, she was surprised when Margrete took her hands in her lap and squeezed. Her mother wasn't often affectionate—at least, not with Tora—and it felt foreign to be held by her, even just the slightest bit.

"The Almighty Hzarl is a provider, first and foremost," the Vasira explained. "He represents true masculinity: a man who provides food, shelter, and protection for his family. He asks that the men who pray to his name lead by his example. But men are not alone in this world, and the Great Hunter has a plan for us women, too. We turn the fruits of male labor into delicacies to fill our bellies and clothing to keep us warm. We tend to the fires so our husbands, fathers, and brothers can know comfort after long days and nights of providing for us. We offer our wombs to our husbands so we, too, can provide. Our sons aid their fathers on the hunt, and our daughters help us care for them while they rest and age."

Tora frowned. "But—"

"No buts. You know what the Almighty demands," Margrete snapped. She softened when Tora winced, then smiled sadly and brushed hair from her daughter's face. "You're a pretty girl, Tora. The epitome of Isalder beauty. Powerful men from across the country will slaughter one another for your hand, for the chance to come home to and be looked after by the loveliest woman in Glacier Bay. *That* is your purpose. *That* is what you must learn. Your beauty is your power, and it will grant you all the responsibilities the Almighty demands of you. Nothing else matters."

Tora translated her mother's poor attempt at comfort well enough: *All you'll ever be in this world is pretty, so get used to it.*

She forced herself to nod. "I understand."

"Good." The Vasira recollected her embroidery, prompting Tora to do the same. She eyed her daughter for a moment, then pointed at the fabric. "Easy on the stitches."

"Yes, Mother."

They worked in silence for a few moments—Margrete humming to herself, and Tora fighting the urge to cry or holler in frustration at what her mother had said—until Tora caught a glimpse of her mother's needlework. The scenic mountain was done, sewn in various shades of gray and blue, but Margrete was stitching words in an arch shape above the mountain. That wasn't part of the original design.

"What is that writing?" Tora questioned.

"It's a prayer for the Icelord." Her mother smiled. "Do you know why Mount Lundheim is the sigil of Glacier Bay?"

It was a trick question, and they both knew it. The story was passed down from Vasir to heir, and few others knew of it. Tora knew her brother had shared the story with Margrete when their father told it to him years earlier, as Tomas had been punished for it when Margrete told Viggo. Tomas had told Tora, too—just to spite their parents after his punishment.

"No, Mother," she replied.

"Your father will be cross with the pair of us if he finds out I've told you," Margrete warned. Tora nodded in understanding as her mother exhaled. "You know the Legend of the Icelord. That's no secret to anyone. An ancient figure, said to have cursed this land with an endless winter, possessed a dragon called Caathet. When the people turned on them, he hid Caathet where nobody would ever find him. As the story goes—the story we aren't supposed to know—he cast a spell to put Caathet to sleep in the middle of the Ealair Mountain Range, north of our country. Mount Lundheim formed around Caathet's sleeping body, protecting and camouflaging him from the outside world."

"Mother—"

"Don't interrupt," the Vasira scolded. Tora hung her head and muttered an apology. "If the legend is to be believed, then Lundheim isn't simply the largest mountain in Ealair. It's Caathet, too. Your father, and all Vasirs who came before him, believe the two are indistinguishable now. Caathet has become one with the mountain, and even if a brave soul was daring enough to awaken him, they couldn't free him from Lundheim. And so long as Caathet lives beneath the mountain, our land will forever be one of ice and snow. It's an eternal curse punishing us for the way the ancient people rejected and attempted to destroy divine power."

Tora parted her lips, pretending to be awestruck. "Do you believe the story?"

"No," Margrete admitted, shrugging. "I don't believe a dragon sleeps beneath Mount Lundheim. It's an absurd idea, frankly. If Caathet really existed, I think the ancient man killed him as an act of mercy while the ancient people pursued them. He must have thought it was better for Caathet to die at his hands rather than at the hands of those who hated him. And I believe our eternal winter is, indeed, a curse—placed upon us by the ancient figure after what the people did to him, and never to be broken. He was forced to slay a creature who shared his soul, and he will never let us forget the pain it caused him."

Tora swallowed. She didn't know what to believe—her mother's cynicism, or Tomas and their father's more wondrous perspective—but either way, the story unsettled her now. It hadn't sounded so dreary when it'd been told to her by Tomas.

"If Caathet really is there," she said slowly, "do you think it'd be impossible for him to wake? For someone to free him?"

Margrete laughed. "I meant what I said before: curiosity is a good thing. But all good things have their limits, child. Be mindful of the answers you seek. Asking too many questions, particularly about a topic like this, could get you into trouble." She gestured toward Tora's half-finished, sloppy embroidery. "Get back to your needlework. Might as well start over again, too. Your stitches are too loose this time."

Tora sighed. "Yes, Mother."

She replaced the fabric once more, then looked at her mother's embroidery as the Vasira began to hum again. She didn't know what to make of the story, and while she knew her questions would never be answered, she knew she wouldn't stop thinking about it, either.

After all, with such a bleak future ahead of her, wondering about the impossible would be the only thing that brought excitement to her life. It didn't matter if she knew the truth about Caathet and Mount Lundheim or not; all that mattered was that she kept wondering and imagining, to keep the dying spark in her heart alive before she was forced into a life she didn't want.

Even as she told herself that her wonderings were good enough, she couldn't help but feel connected to the story—like there was something more she had to uncover, something that was just waiting for her to find it.

But it wouldn't be an ancient dragon sleeping beneath a mountain. No, not for her. She knew that—she wasn't worthy of it, even if the story was true, and even if it was possible to awaken Caathet from his thousand-year slumber.

Acknowledgements

Fun fact: Forged in Blood is actually the first draft of Forged in Ashes! I have to start off by thanking my trusty beta readers, whose feedback on that first draft made me realize that this story better serves as the grand finale of Aurelia's tale—hence, the new, epic, heartbreaking ending of Forged in Blood. I wouldn't have known how to say goodbye to Aurelia's trilogy if I hadn't been told to save Forged in Ashes draft one for another book!

I would also like to thank everyone else who contributed to making Forged in Blood a reality, namely my insanely talented cover artist, Katarina, and my interior illustrator, Aubrey. Your work helped transform all three of my books into pieces of art that I'm incredibly proud of. Thank you for being a part of this!

Forged in Blood is my first published book as an author with a Street Team. Thank you endlessly to my team of 25+ amazing women for supporting me so directly, helping me with difficult decisions, and loving my work as much as I do. You've given me even more to love about being an author, especially while closing out this trilogy, and I'm forever grateful that each of you signed on to be a part of this journey.

To my editor who prefers to remain anonymous: you've been my rock from start to finish with this trilogy. You don't just edit the kinks—you offer much-needed suggestions, force me to look at my work through a different lens when it's necessary, and hype me up when I need it most. Your honesty, dedication, kindness, and support made it possible for me to publish not one, not two, but three books in a little over a year. I couldn't have done this without you; and while it's bittersweet that our editing journey ends here, I'm so grateful for everything you've done for me, everything you've taught me, and everything in between. You're a superhero if there ever was one, and as proud as I am to call you my editor, I'm even prouder to call you a friend. Thank you.

To my friends and family: thank you so much for your eternal love and support. I wouldn't have made it to this point without each of you cheering me on every step of the way.

To my partner: thank you for being my rock when I need steadying, my anchor when I feel lost, and my boat when I feel like I'm drowning. You came into my life before I published Forged in Gold, and you've never been anything less than my biggest fan ever since, despite not being a reader whatsoever. I think the universe knew that I needed to wait until we met before sharing my writing with the world, because you have offered me that last bit of confidence I needed.

To my dad: you found yourself in the same position Jack found himself in at the end of this book. Not only did you become a single dad in the blink of an eye, but you also lost your partner who, like Aurelia, was larger than life. It's because of you that I can portray the grief one feels after losing a partner, but it's also because of you that I can portray the strength, resilience, and courage one needs to get through that while caring for others at the same time.

To my mom: Aurelia's death mirrors your loss in many ways, but mainly through the fact that she, like you, was the center of everyone's world. She touched the lives of everyone who knew her, just as you did. And as I've learned over the years, incredible loss and incredible tragedy also leads to incredible new beginnings.

Last but certainly not least, thank you to my readers who have followed me along on this journey and supported me every step of the way. I appreciate you more than you'll ever know.

About the Author

Noelle is a pseudonym for a writer, beta reader, and editor from Boston who found her passion for writing early on and pursued it wholeheartedly. Although she is a young writer, she has been honing her craft for more than a decade, having written her first story in middle school!

While Noelle enjoys genres like romance, historical fiction, and science fiction, fantasy has always been her favorite. She fell in love with the genre at an early age after reading C.S. Lewis's *Narnia* series and William Goldman's *The Princess Bride*. Since then, her love of fantasy has only grown!

Much of Noelle's early career reflects her lifelong love of children, having worked as a nanny, infant/toddler daycare teacher, and substitute elementary teacher. However, since graduating with her BA in English Literature, she has immersed herself in the exciting realm of freelancing. When away from her writing desk, Noelle can often be found curled up with a novel or avidly working on expanding the world of her creation.

Noelle currently resides with her father, younger sister, and her feisty kitty, Nugget. *Forged in Gold* is her debut fantasy novel and marks the first of an exciting, heart-stopping series. She writes in honor of her beloved mother, who passed away from cancer in 2015.

Glossary

AGOTIA (Ah-goh-sha): Taundosan district bordering the Ngora Valley; governed by the Cristos family.

Ardiham Castle: Ancestral home of the Cristos family.

AKKINOR (Ack-inn-or): The largest populated continent of the east; the most powerful country in the realm; ruled by the Brentwood family; composed of six kingdoms:

Holos (Holl-os): Region in southeast Akkinor; ruled by the Tarre family.

Laynoa (Lay-noh-ah): Region in northeast Akkinor; ruled by the Stone family.

Myra (Meer-ah): Region in southwest Akkinor; ruled by the Crowland family; borders Quapebet.

Omara (Oh-mar-ah): Centermost Akkinorian territory; ruled by the Ashford family; the last kingdom seized by the Akkinorian monarchy.

Sadia (Sah-dee-uh): Mountainous northern region of Akkinor; ruled by the Normindi family.

Seaport: Small coastal town on the west coast of Akkinor; borders the Folly; ungoverned; the only international port in Akkinor.

The Folly: Home to the palace and the royal family; ruled by the Linderli family.

Kalenbrar: Akkinor's capital city; translates to "City of Light."

Amanbrar: Civilian-made, impoverished district of Kalenbrar; translates to "City of Decay."

Mistcairn: A village in the Folly.

ALISTAIR ASHFORD: Former Lord of Omara; father of Arthur, Bryan, Cecelia, and Daniella; husband of Isobel; formerly exiled to Quapebet.

ANDREN NORMINDI: Lord of Sadia; elder brother of the late Queen Cressida.

ALKAMURA OCEAN: Also known as the Alka; massive ocean that lies between Carthe and Akkinor; corrupted by the Esposi following Oleander's Rebellion; formerly forbidden territory for Akkinorians.

ALKAMURA: Goddess of the seas; Almighty of Espos.

ALMIGHTY: The primary deity worshipped by individual cultures/civilizations.

ALORA CHERRANE: The last ruler of the Cherrane Dynasty in Akkinor; the last female monarch until Aurelia Brentwood.

ANSYL BOLAS: Native of Kanibar; elder brother of Kaia, Mycah, and Thea; former Kanish soldier; Hand of the Queen to Aurelia Brentwood.

ARCHIBALD BRENTWOOD (deceased): Former Prince of Akkinor; son of King Edmund II and Queen Cressida; younger brother and usurper of Queen Aurelia.

ARIAN CRISTOS: Lord of Agotia; Lord Hand to Queen Reyna; biological uncle of Aurelia Brentwood; water mage.

ARTHUR "JACK" ASHFORD: King Consort of Akkinor; husband of Queen Aurelia; father of Halle, Hyacinth, Henry, and Halyna; former heir to Lordship of Omara; alias: Jack Sherbourne.

AURELIA BRENTWOOD: Queen of Akkinor; adopted daughter of King Edmund II and Queen Cressida Brentwood; biological daughter of Katryna Cristos and Eric Haze; wife of Jack Ashford; mother of Halle, Hyacinth, Henry, and Halyna; mistress of the dragon Halvor; alias: Lily Linden.

BALOR ZHOQA II (Bay-lor Zoh-kah): Lord of Kazamir, Bozar; ally of Queen Aurelia.

BRYAN ASHFORD: Lord of Omara; younger brother of Jack Ashford.

BUEN (Bu-wen): God of prosperity; Almighty of Akkinor.

CARTHE: The largest populated continent in the west; a safe haven for mages and magical creatures; home to numerous civilizations:

> *Bozar* (Boh-zar): Kingdom east of the Ngora Valley; borders Taundosa and Khaba; ruled by four noble families: Zhaaran of Orestes, Zhoqa of Kazamir, Zoma of Iseppa, and Xada of Tucana.
>
> *Caedia* (Cay-dee-ah): Northernmost territory of Carthe; ungoverned port province frequented by travelers and merchants; borders the Violet Forest.
>
> *Dofell* (Doh-fell): Kingdom north of Taundosa and the Ngora Valley, south of the Violet Forest, and east of Kanibar; ruled by the Phyre family; formerly known as *the Great City*; the most impoverished kingdom in Carthe.
>
> *Kanibar* (Can-nih-bar): Kingdom north of the Ngora Valley; borders Dofell, Taundosa, and the Violet Forest; ruled by the Trevas family.
>
> *Khaba* (Cah-bah): Southernmost territory of Carthe; ungoverned port province; borders Bozar.

Krotis (Kroh-tis): Kingdom south of the Ngora Valley; borders Taundosa; governed by five noble families: Selle of Bruila, Keer of Mekya, Quagg of Osanad, Swann of Runeia, and Reesa of Vrurith.

Ngora Valley (Nih-gor-ah Valley): Vast desert that separates northern and southern Carthe; only accessible through Dofell and Taundosa.

Taundosa (Tawn-doh-sah): Kingdom east of the Ngora Valley and south of Dofell; the wealthiest Carthinian kingdom; ruled by the Caltheos family; known as *the City of Gold*.

> *Eight Kingdoms of Taundosa:* Agotia, Brorane, Cidour, Emerdes, Morvis, Thania, Trostall, and Vortea.

Violet Forest: Massive deciduous forest that lies between Caedia and the Carthinian kingdoms; home of nomadic native tribes; mostly frequented by travelers.

CERULEAN SEA: Body of water between Holos and Quapebet.

CHANGLING: A five-day celebration held in the Folly at the beginning/end of each season; attended by all highborn Akkinorians and citizens of the Folly; includes performances by jousters, theater actors, bards, jesters, etc.

CICELY POOLE (deceased): Close friend and lady-in-waiting to Queen Aurelia.

CRESSIDA BRENTWOOD (deceased): Former Queen Consort of Akkinor; wife of King Edmund II; mother of Queen Aurelia and Prince Archie.

CRYSTAL SEA: Body of water located between northwestern Akkinor and northeastern Carthe.

DHYLO (Die-loh): God of knowledge; Almighty of Bozar.

DIANTHA PHAROS: Queen of Dofell; Rieza's mistress; lowborn successor of King Elrin III.

EDEA (Ee-dee-ah): Goddess of the moon.

EDOM: A sprite befriended by Queen Aurelia.

EDMUND BRENTWOOD II (deceased): Former King of Akkinor; husband of Queen Cressida; father of Queen Aurelia and Prince Archie.

ERIC HAZE: Biological father of Aurelia Brentwood and Rayan Haze; native of Holos; former Cristos family soldier.

ESPOS: Island south of Carthe inhabited mainly by pirates.

GIANLA (Gee-ahn-lah): Goddess of the sun; Almighty of Taundosa.

GLACIER BAY: Northernmost continent; home of the Isalders; ruled by the Styrmodr family.

GLACIER SEA: Northernmost body of water; Isalder territory.

GOLDMEN: An esteemed organization of soldiers loyal to the Taundosan monarchy.

HALLE BRENTWOOD: Eldest child of Aurelia Brentwood and Jack Ashford; Crown Princess of Akkinor.

HALVOR: (Hal-vohr): (1) God of protection; (2) Dragon of old loyal to Aurelia Brentwood and the Cristos family.

HALYNA BRENTWOOD: Third child of Aurelia Brentwood and Jack Ashford.

HARLEN BRENTWOOD: Youngest child of Aurelia Brentwood and Jack Ashford; Holly's twin brother.

HENRY BRENTWOOD: Third child of Aurelia Brentwood and Jack Ashford.

HOLLY BRENTWOOD: Youngest child of Aurelia Brentwood and Jack Ashford; Harlen's twin sister.

HYACINTH BRENTWOOD: Second child and adopted daughter of Aurelia Brentwood and Jack Ashford; biological daughter of Archie Brentwood.

HZARL (His-arl): God of the hunt; Almighty of Glacier Bay.

IMMOR (Ee-mor): God of war.

INESIS (In-ness-iss): God of life and death; Almighty of Quapebet.

ISOBEL ASHFORD: Former Lady of Omara; mother of Arthur, Bryan, Cecelia, and Daniella; wife of Alistair; formerly exiled to Quapebet.

JALHOR ZHAARAN (Jall-or Zar-ran): Lord of Orestes in Bozar; air mage; ally of Queen Aurelia.

KAIA BOLAS (deceased): Native Kanish merchant; younger sister of Ansyl and elder sister of Thea and Mycah.

KATRYNA CRISTOS (deceased): Biological mother of Aurelia Brentwood; sister of Arian Cristos; native of Taundosa; fire mage.

LINDEN ELLIOT (deceased): Former Hand of the Queen and best friend of Aurelia Brentwood; murdered by Archie Brentwood.

LUKOS: Pirate captain of Espos.

LUNAR STAFF/STAFF OF EDEA: Ancient staff once wielded by the moon goddess; currently a small fragment of the original staff containing a piece of fallen moonrock.

MAGES: Humans with the ability to conjure magic from the gods.

MAGICAL PERSECUTION: The annihilation of mages and magical creatures during the old days that saw the extinction of numerous races and forced surviving mages into hiding.

MAROONER'S CHAIN: Archipelago off the western coast of Akkinor; mainly uninhabitable; serves as labor towns for low-ranking Akkinorians and criminals.

MAYSA: Kanish oracle; mother of King Willem.

MYENAR (My-enn-arr): God of judgement; Almighty of Dofell.

ODEYA SWANN: Lady of Runeia in Krotis; ally of Queen Aurelia.

OLEANDER BRENTWOOD: Usurper of Alora Cherrane during the old days; the first Brentwood king of Akkinor.

PHERENA (Ferr-ee-nah): Goddess of virtues; Almighty of Krotis.

QUAPEBET (Kwah-peh-bet): Continent south of Akkinor; ruled by the Kaplo family; shares the Cerulean Sea with Akkinor; connected to Myra by the neutral city of Vilgh-Azhor.

RAYAN HAZE: Akkinorian knight; Holosi-born; son of Eric Haze; biological half-brother of Aurelia Brentwood.

REYNA CALTHEOS: Queen of Taundosa.

SILAS CROWLAND: Lord of Myra.

SPRITES: Tiny, mischievous magical creatures known for being tricksters and liars; found predominantly in Kanibar; fast-traveling and easily concealed; mainly used by humans as spies.

THE ASSEMBLY: An esteemed group of Akkinorian nobles serving as advisors to the monarch.

THE ELEMENTALS: The first four mages to walk among mankind, created directly by the hands of the gods to introduce magic to humanity:

Ceruleus (Cerr-oo-lee-us): Elemental of air

Glacia (Glah-see-uh): Elemental of water

Igneus (Igg-nee-us): Elemental of fire

Terra (Ter-rah): Elemental of earth

THE ONES FORGED IN GOLD: Humans said to be chosen by the gods to restore peace and harmony to the realm during times of peril; known to weep golden tears.

THE TWELVE: The global religion worshipped by all cultures of the realm; follows the twelve deities responsible for the Creation: Alkamura, Buen, Dhylo, Edea, Gianla, Hzarl, Immor, Inesis, Myenar, Pherena, Vyena, Xienia.

TULLWEINE (Tull-whey-inn): An island off the western coast of Quapebet; nicknamed "The Grin" because of small bodies of water within the island that form the shape of a smiling face.

VILGH-AZHOR (Vilg-Ah-zor): A neutral trading zone on the border of southern Akkinor and northern Quapebet; named for the Myran town of Vilgh and the Quenosi town of Azhor.

VYENA (Vee-enn-ah): Goddess of blessings; Almighty of Kanibar.

WILLEM TREVAS: King of Kanibar.

XIENIA (Zee-nee-ah): Goddess of love and beauty.